THE ANGEL SERIES COLLECTION

BOOKS 1-3

JO WILDE

CONTENTS

DREAM ANGEL

DAUNTLESS ANGEL

DARK ANGEL

DREAM ANGEL

THE ANGEL SERIES BOOK 1

HEADS UP!

Louisiana is renowned for its unique way of expressing themselves. In this chilling romance, I have captured Louisiana's rich culture and its unique lingo. I purposely misspelled words to convey its one-of-a-kind dialect. Please keep in mind that the characters may or may not use perfect grammar. It is part of their unique way of life and sets them apart from the rest. I am a southerner through in and throughout. I have lived in Texas and on the border of Louisiana for most of my life. I love the south and our strange and different language. I especially love the diversity of many cultures blending together, making the south an exciting adventure and an intriguing way of life. Thank you for downloading my book. Enjoy!

Words to Know

ta = to
da = the
'em = them
mofo = motherfuc....
y'at = you at
y'all = you all
magick = magic
gul= girl
gurrrlfriend = girlfriend
her' = here
fer = for
git = get
chile = child (pronounced without the 'd')

JOURNEY

*I*t began in midsummer. The smell of honeysuckle wafted through the air. I'd been hanging out with my two BFFs, Laurie and Becky. We had gone to the movies to watch a crappy film, an alien sci-fi. The only good thing about it was the lead actor, a cute boy. The three of us had a blast eating popcorn and laughing over the lame lines. Romances sucked.

Later, we went to grab a bite at Big Boy's Bar-B-Que, messy but the best in Sweetwater, Texas.

We were sitting at a booth eating our sandwiches when Logan Hunter sauntered into the small diner. He carried the impressive title of the all-star linebacker for the last two years at Sweetwater High. He was a senior, a grade higher than I was. Logan had the cutest smile of any boy I'd ever met, and I, Stephanie Ray, had the biggest crush ever.

The door jangled, and I happened to look up. Fretfully, I twirled in my seat, about to have a cow. I jabbed Beck, who sat next to me, in the ribs. "Don't look up!"

She snapped her blonde head up and asked, "Why?"

Of course, she did what I asked her not to do... *she looked!*

"He's here? Logan?" I whispered frantically.

Laurie had just come back from the restroom, sliding into her seat. "What's wrong?" Her blue eyes bounced between Beck and me.

I leaned over the table, *"Logan,"* I whispered, shooting a hard stare at her to not repeat his name out loud.

She laughed, swatting her hand at me. *"Pfff, pleaseeee!* Stevie, chill out, for Christ's sake. I invited him to your birthday party tomorrow night."

Beck started jumping in her seat, ecstatic. "No, you didn't."

Laurie poked back, "Oh-yes-I-did." She threw a fry at Beck, laughing.

I hunkered down in my seat. The gratitude for sitting next to the wall fluttered through me, easier to hide.

"Y'all need to get over yourselves." Laurie's voice carried through the restaurant.

"Shush! He'll hear you!" I fretted, watching my life go down the crapper in only a matter of seconds. Logan stopping by our table and I'd spill food on myself or choke on my drink. I mean, the possibilities of me screwing this up were endless.

Laurie, parting words of wisdom. "I don't know why you hide from him. He likes you, and you like him," she laughed. "Besides, you owe it to all us girls."

I snorted. "Owe you what?"

She rolled her eyes. "We can all live vicariously through you and your hot make-out sessions."

"I'm not going to share such with y'all," I whispered at Laurie, appalled, mortified, but laughing inwardly.

Beck jabbed me with her elbow. "That's because a boy has never kissed you."

Laurie fell out of her seat, roaring with laughter, and Beck laid her head in my lap, giggling.

My lovely friends knew I'd never have the guts to speak to a boy I liked. I think they were hoping on my eighteenth birthday, Logan Hunter would do the honors. They were throwing me a party tomorrow night. That was why my girls invited Sweetwater High's all-star football player, and, well... I think the fact that I liked him had a significant impact on their decision-making too.

Logan was different than any of the boys at school. There was intelligence behind his soulful browns. A kiss from him would be any girl's dream. Bumping it up to the next level as a couple, I wasn't ready. Oh, I was crushing big time on the all-star football player. I mean! Look at him. A handsome, compact boy who walked with a spring in his step, his shoulders, a yard wide and tall like a towering spruce, and his soft blond curls reminded me of golden honey. I exhaled starry-eyed, ogling Logan standing at the food counter. "He's a he-man." I let out a long sigh, and then I suddenly become mortified, covering my mouth, eyes wide. "Tell me I didn't say that out loud?" Beck cackled, and Laurie followed.

$\sim$

Then my small window of happiness came to a screeching halt like a plane nose-diving into the Atlantic Ocean. Sara, my mother, decided it was time to pack our bags and vamoose to the next dive town. Another town, another school, another miserable life. I didn't know why I thought Sweetwater would've been any different. Sara never stayed anywhere long. Since Dad's death, we'd been living out of a suitcase.

I was eight years old when a hit-and-run driver had taken Dad's life, and just like that, our world changed forever. To this day, his cold case sat, collecting dust on a shelf. The police had never found the driver. For ten years, the thought of Dad's killer running amok grated against me worse than a spit-bath. I refused to let it go until the authorities caught the killer, and he was sitting behind bars, rotting.

At the time, I had no idea how much of an impact Sara's machination would affect my life until it was too late. Secrets kill. I would remember her words like it was yesterday.

"Mom, this isn't fair," I snapped. I suspected Sara's bipolar might be flaring up again. "I don't want to move to Louisiana!"

"Get over it." Her tone bulldozed me down.

"What about my birthday party this evening? My friends, Laurie and Becky, went through a lot of trouble. You haven't even bothered buying me a cake."

She cut her eyes at me. "Don't get an attitude with me, young lady!" Then she inhaled a calm breath, though the ice on her tongue never melted. "I'm sure there's a Wal-Mart somewhere between here and Louisiana. I'll get you a cake then." Sara turned back to her packing as if she were preparing for some tropical vacation. Bright-colored swimwear spread across the bed, along with shoes and other light dress wear.

As I stared at the luggage, a scowl crept across my face. That tattered suitcase had seen more towns than most people had seen in a lifetime. My stomach knotted every time I laid eyes on it too. It represented everything I hated... *starting over.* "What's wrong with this town? I like Sweetwater. You have that great job at Fashion Boutique. It doesn't make sense to move again. Can't we stay in one place for more than a minute?"

"I. Hate. Texas!"

I couldn't wrap my head around it, but this move appeared different than the other times. We were always rushing out of town for some cryptic reason. Either Sara got caught with her married boss, or we were getting evicted. Apart from the usual get-out-of-town-before-I-get-arrested list of reasons, this time seemed eerily aberrant. It was as if some compelling force had Sara by the hair like a breechcloth Neanderthal dragging her off to the land of yonder. "Can't we leave in the morning?" I tried to reason. "We'll both have a good night's sleep, and I can go to my birthday party."

Lines etched deep across Sara's forehead like petrified wood as she turned to me. "I've made my mind up. We're leaving today before nightfall."

"Mom, moving's wacko."

Sara quickly pinned her combative eyes at me. "Are you saying I'm crazy?"

I stepped back out of range of her reach. I liked my teeth. "That's not what I meant," I backpedaled. "I'm sorry."

"I've about had it with you!" Sara often struggled with her adult role. From her miniskirts to her mimicking a spoiled teenager, the lines often blurred. And as a result, I was forced to be the designated adult. "Mom, I'm doing well here. The school is great. My grades are dope. Can't you reconsider?"

"You'll make new friends. You're young. You'll adapt. We're moving, and that's final!"

"Do you care at all how I feel?" I bit my lip from saying what I wanted to say: selfish, self-absorbed, self-serving, self-centered—something like that.

"Don't be ridiculous."

"Every time we move, it eats at me."

"Stop acting like a drama queen."

I pointed to the suitcase. "Normal people don't behave irrationally, moving from town to town, living in a suitcase… never knowing where their next meal is coming from." Most of the time, I kept my mouth shut. This time was different. Sara needed to hear how her actions affected me. "No, Mom, only you prefer living like a gypsy."

"As opposed to your stuffy self, I'm adventurous." Sara picked up a mirror, checking her cherry-red lipstick. Then she tossed the mirror on the bed and attempted to reel the voice of reason into her insanity. "Try to look at this as a going-away birthday," she forced a smile as fake as her hot pink fingernails.

"I hope you're not planning another excursion, camping in the city? Or should I say homeless?"

"I don't know what you're talkin' about." Whenever Sara spun lies, her southern accent seemed more conspicuous.

"If Dad were alive, we wouldn't be bouncing from town to town, chasing rainbows and unicorns either." I was fighting dirty. Watching Sara flinch over the mention of Dad gave me a spike of triumph. Memory lane for Sara was like sticking your hand over an open fire. The mention of Dad's name bothered her as bad as a head full of lice. I think she'd placed Dad's memories in a shoebox and stuffed them away in a dank basement to avoid the stab. She even went as far as forbidding me to speak his name. I reckoned Sara struggled with Dad's death. Even so, at times, I didn't mind twisting the proverbial knife.

"Well, your daddy's not here. He's dead!" her words were cold and unfeeling. "You can call your friends when we get on the road. Go pack! I want to be on the road by sundown."

"I can't do this again. This is your life. Not mine. I won't go!"

"You don't have a choice!" Sara shouted, hands to her side, flexing her white-knuckled fists. Then she paused, taking a deep breath, dousing an extra coat of honey on her lies. "Sweetie, you're going to love this town. I promise no more moving. This is the last time."

"What's so special about this waterhole? Is it even on the map?"

"I heard the town is real good, friendly folks, and cheap living too."

I stood there eyeballing her, suspicion swirling in my mind. "What's the real reason, Mom?"

She dropped her clothes and flopped down on the edge of the bed. She reminded me of someone giving confession. Shoulders slumped, eyes fixed to the floor. "Don't get mad," she sighed. "We ain't got any rent money."

"What did you do, Mom?" The air in my lungs suddenly collapsed.

"I used it on a psychic. Legend Red is famous."

"Don't you know psychics are cons?"

"Not Red," Sara's brown eyes gleamed as if she were defending her lover. "He's real."

"Mom, he's no more a psychic than Miss Cleo on television," I argued. "Remember her? She got canned for fraud. He ain't no different!"

"Red foresaw us in this little town living on easy street." She scrunched her shoulders together like a child.

"Homelessness isn't easy street."

"Don't get sassy!" She leaped onto her feet, fists drawn, ready to Donnybrook me.

"Fine! I'm leaving." I stormed out of Sara's bedroom headed for the front door. I could hear Sara's bellow.

"Stevie Ray! Don't you walk…"

I couldn't listen to her nonsense any longer. Flying by the seat of your pants half-cocked to these dead-end towns might be Sara's idea of living. I sure didn't share the same aspirations.

Since Dad's death, dealing with Sara's bipolar hadn't been a cakewalk. Merely a child myself, I was ill-equipped to handle her manic episodes. I still struggled and dreaded every waking day.

Until I was old enough to work a secular job, I did odd jobs for the neighbors, from babysitting to dog walking. The cash came in handy for school lunches. I would've qualified for the free lunch program, but Sara felt it'd give folks the wrong impression. I reckoned she didn't realize they already knew we were poor. My faded, worn clothes were a dead giveaway.

By the time I reached seventeen, I had worked just about every hamburger joint stretching as far as Montana to the Florida Keys. During the school year, I worked after school and full-time in the summer. It helped with the bills, but it hindered my social life. Between school, work, and then riding out the waves of Sara's roller-coaster episodes, I had little time for friends. It sucked too.

As reality spun its bitter web, I discovered far worse things. No child should have to live in a cardboard box in the middle of winter.

Attending school in the same dirty clothes day after day taught me the cruelties of life at a very early age. After a few bloody noses, I began to fight back. I got where I could hold my own.

Despite my chaotic life, what kept me hopeful were my studies. I was smart, and my scores reflected it too. I understood that if I ever wanted to get out of poverty, education was my meal ticket.

Looking back, I thought eighteen would be the magic number. Free from bondage, no longer burdened to worry over Sara. The problem that stuck like oatmeal was my consciousness. Sara's incompetency kept me bound to this lifestyle I hated. If something happened to her, I'd never forgive myself. Despite everything, I loved her. She was the only family I had.

Knowing I was doing the right thing helped me get through the rough patches. When my dad was alive, he'd often say, "A family sticks together regardless." If Dad were still living, he'd be proud of my endeavors. For that reason, I stayed.

Yet at night, whenever things were quiet, I'd lie in bed, wincing from an endless pain deep inside me, and with each new town, the agony magnified.

SERIOUSLY

$\mathcal{W}$e rolled into Tangi right before dawn. Judging by the old buildings that lined the street, I knew this place was nothing more than a whistleblower. The morning air was sultry, and the mosquitoes were swarming in clusters. I already hated the place. I began ticking off all the diseases those bloodsuckers carried, such as Zika, Malaria, and the West Nile virus. A scowl tainted my face. I suspected that the pests outnumbered the locals.

Listening to Sara's constant babble the whole way here made me want to barf. The way she told it, it was as if we were moving to the land of OZ. I think she meant the land of bugs. The first hotel we found, Sara pulled into its parking lot. We were nearly out of gas, and nothing was open. It was either this or sleeping in the car. Sara cleared her throat. "We can stay here tonight. It ain't that bad." She made a weak attempt at a smile.

I scowled in my side-view window, hiding my sullen face. "Whatever," I mumbled darkly.

I couldn't say much about the place other than it was rundown and on the outskirts of town. The neon light shined brightly above our heads, barely hanging on its hinges. One blub sizzled, blinking off and on, as another had shattered, glass pooled around the post.

The sign read, "Welcome to Claude's Inn." Though the place wasn't much to look at, anything with a bed sounded good to me. After riding scrunched up in an old 1975 Volkswagen all night, I would've slept on rocks.

Sara climbed out of the car and darted inside the manager's office and paid for a room. I noticed iron bars divided the entrance. Alarm crept down my spine. "Crap! This must be where all the druggies hung out," I choked out a bitter laugh. "Just perfect!" I slid down in my seat, arms folded across my chest.

Soon Sara returned with a key dangling from her hand. We pulled up to our room, number ninety-three. Sara killed the engine, and we piled out of the car. I paused, stretching my stiff limbs, and yawned. It felt good to stand erect. Stopping for a quick piss was a luxury with Sara. The last time we braked was in Waskom, Texas.

Like always, Sara ordered me to bring in our items, and like a good little slave, I obeyed. After dragging in the last suitcase, I'd no sooner dropped it on the floor than I collapsed on the bed. Though the bed was slightly lumpy, it didn't matter. Eh! I'd slept on worse.

My mind started to drift. I thought about back home in Texas, Beck, Laurie, and even Logan. I swilled the aching brick in my throat. I missed home something fierce, the rumble of tumbleweeds, the flat plains, and horny toads. I blew out a sharp breath. Though missing my birthday felt like sharp teeth sinking into my skin, it was no comparison to leaving my friends behind. For the first time... *I belonged.*

Sara didn't understand. I reckoned she had her own idealism, her own vision. The woman never worried about how others saw her. A free spirit, doing as she pleased, not a care in the world. I was different. Fitting in meant everything to me. A roof over my head and a stable home were important to me. Staying in one place for more than a few weeks would be a dream come true.

Texas was lost to me forever. I had to put it behind me and move on. Just like I'd left my birthday back in Texas, in the same sense, I abandoned my friends back there too. I decided no more friends and no more crying over the birthdays of yesteryear. I just wanted to stop thinking. Soon, sleep devoured my thoughts, and all forgotten.

∾

Sunlight warmed my face as I opened my eyes. Sara's perfume drifted in the room as I jolted to a start as my memory came rushing in like a tsunami. A frown seized my face. Remembering that Texas had long passed my rear-view mirror gave me no inspiration to get out of bed. I flopped on my back with an ireful huff and spotted Sara's empty bed.

A couple of wet towels were in a heap on the floor in the corner. Sara's suitcase looked as if a thief had pilfered through it. Clothes scattered about on the bed and the floor, and Sara was nowhere in sight. I reckoned she might be job hunting.

Kicking out from under the covers, I hauled myself out of bed and padded to the door, swinging it wide open. "Geez!" I jumped back, squinting from the bright sunlight. I whistled. "Damn!" I checked the clock. "Only eight in the morning, and it was already sweltering hot," I grumbled as I wiped my sweat-beaded nose with the back of my hand. I stood there, taking in the surroundings. The only creatures stirring were the annoying bobwhites chirping in the brush of trees. A pungent smell wafted in the air. "Yuck!" I scrunched up my nose. "I hate fish!"

I stretched my eyes as far as I could see. I drew in a disparaging breath. I instantly disliked it here—such a contrast to Sweetwater. Here, I saw nothing but junkyards of rusted cars, an old fish-bait gas station at the corner of the parking lot.

What did Sara see in this Podunk town? No point in asking. She wouldn't tell the truth. Might as well accept my fate. We never stayed anywhere for long was the one consistency in my life. Another dirty town on the horizon, merely a tap of the heels away.

I stared outside at the long stretch of moss-green hills and towering pines swaying to a light breeze. My stomach lurched. Soon summer would be over, and my last year of school would be at hand. I dreaded it. Only a couple of weeks away from the main event, a new school, new faces, new fights, and the vicious cycle of fitting in once again. Fitting in was like the flip of a coin. In some schools, I managed to stay under the radar, and in others, I fought. Sweetwater High was badass! I'd made a place for myself there with Laurie and Becky, the best friends ever! It had been a nice change to have the camaraderie of friends rather than being the target of everyone's cruel jokes.

I exhaled a weary sigh and shut the door harder than intended. I preferred shoving my foot through it. Sara denying me a birthday party was one thing but moving me to the freaking sticks had me furious. I padded back to my bed and slipped under the covers, burrowing myself. I wanted to hide for the rest of my life under this stupid blanket.

~

The sky had grayed by the time Sara burst through the door. Her flushed face beamed with liquored-up mirth. The second she shut the door, I could smell the cheer on her breath. She stumbled over to my bed and pounced on the edge. I was playing possum. I'd seen headlights pulling up and her getting out of the car.

Sara leaned over my bunched-up body, shaking my shoulder and pulling my cover off my head. "Guess what?" She announced, too perky. Slowly my eyes drifted open as her soused grin came into focus.

"What?" I was still in a snit. "You found a pot of gold at the end of the rainbow?" My sarcasm felt liberating, even if it might spark a hard slap across the face.

"Why not show some support here?"

I faked a smile. "Yes, Mother Dear, I am quite happy we moved to the faraway land of bugs-gone-wild." I snatched the blanket from her grasp and covered my head, putting my back to Sara and stewing in icy silence.

Not getting the hint, she yanked the cover back down. "I got a job," she giggled into my ear. "I'm working at the Mudbug Café just around the corner, downtown. It doesn't pay much, but I'll make it up in tips." I sensed Sara's euphoria aiming at my back. She was trying to appease me, which made this whole move worse. I felt I'd earned the privilege to have at least one day to lie in bed and brood without Sara rubbing her bliss in my face.

I tossed the blanket to the side and rolled over facing her. I propped myself up on my elbow. "That's gonna be hard, getting to your job."

"Why do you say that?" Sara fiddled with a broken nail.

"The tires are low. If they go flat, you'll have to walk. Did you stop and have someone take a look?"

Sara smirked, "Nope! I didn't have to."

"Why?" Oh lord, did she wreak the car?

"The tires are ripped to shreds." She spoke with a devil-may-care tone as she tugged off her red bottom heels. "I drove the car anyway."

My eyes nearly went cross-eyed, gawking at her feet. Suddenly my concern switched to shock as I bolted to a sitting position. "Where did you get those shoes?" I gaped. "Those are no Wal-Mart shoes! Especially since, oh, I don't know since we're penniless."

Sara snatched the shoes up and tucked them in her suitcase. "Don't worry about it. We have other things to trouble ourselves over." It was crystal clear that Sara was lying. Apart from her southern accent kicking up, a twitch in her left eyebrow gave her away.

"Trouble ourselves," I scoffed. "You're ruining the only set of wheels we have." I eyeballed her with little patience. "You do know driving the car will damage the wheels?"

"How much more damage can the tires possibly take? The tires are already ruined."

"Mom, I'm not referring to the rubber. The wheel is the metal barrel that receives the tire."

"Oh!" She acted as if I'd spoken a foreign language. "Then you can walk. I have a ride." She swatted her hand in the air, dismissing the problem like every other hiccup we'd ever encountered. "Oh, all right. If you must, take the car to the gas station up at the corner. See if they can patch up the tires." With that said, Sara disappeared into the bathroom, closing the door behind her. A minute later, I heard the shower. I turned my back to the bathroom door, fuming. I wondered where Sara expected me to get the coins. The tires were beyond repair. We needed new tires.

Moving past the car troubles, I suspected Sara had a date tonight. The tight dress laid out flat on her bed with the killer heels gave it away. I had to give her credit. We hadn't been here twenty-four hours, and she'd already snagged a man. That had to be a record even for Sara. Of course, she never had a problem in that department. Finding a boyfriend was like plucking an apple from a tree. There was always an orchard of apple trees where Sara was concerned.

I stayed out of my mother's affairs. Keeping in mind all of her short-lived romances, any person of the male persuasion should take out a life insurance policy before hooking up with her. Boyfriends of Sara's either disappeared or turned up dead. Creepy, if you asked me.

GANG BANGERS

*T*he following morning started as a typical blistering day. West Texas was hot, but this place had Texas beat by a long shot. Then there were the insects. Folks talked about Texas mosquitoes. Well, they ain't been to Louisiana. These suckers here were gang bangers.

Sara left early for work. The missing uniform that once hung over the chair gave me a good indication she'd left for work. I didn't hear the car's engine roar over the hum of bugsville this morning. I presumed she hitched a ride with her new beau since our car was inoperable. I, the insignificant child, had to walk.

I didn't want to leave my security blanket, but I had to face my pathetic life. I felt like I'd joined the dead. Still, I huffed out an infuriating sigh, I had to find a job.

I dragged my feet to the shower and then dressed for the day. I picked out something light, a white cotton top and a pair of navy blue cocktail shorts, and to go with the ensemble, I snatched up a pair of strappy wedges out of Sara's luggage. Most of her shoes were spiked. Since I was flat-footed, I figured strappy wedges would be a better choice.

The main drag was literally around the block. The town was exactly what I'd expected, *run down and empty*. I never got why Sara preferred the dreary, small towns, only a short stick from a ghost town, precisely like this one. I liked the hustle and bustle of city life. Bus lines to travel, art museums to visit, and people to meet. A wave of sadness brushed over me. I knew my hopes of having a real-life might be a dream jammed in a pipe. Still, I hung on tight to my hope.

Just as Sara said, the gas station was right around the corner. I passed it by heading to the main circle. The sign read Claude's Stop and Go in bold colors. "Huh!" The same name as the hotel. My eyes brushed over the station as I snarled my nose. The gas stop was like everything else in this town… *rickety and dirty.*

I nodded in passing at a clump of grizzly dark skin men huddled around a card table under a large oak off to the side of the gas station. I got the impression that the pit stop didn't get much business other than selling fish bait, drinking soda pop, and a challenging game of dominoes.

Once I reached the downtown circle, I lingered a moment peering in the different store windows, dithering. A little pep talk was in order before I entered the land of rejection. I noted a post office on the south side of the circle, a beauty shop next to it and a couple of craft shops and a diner. Not a lot of activity. Tangi reminded me of one of those ghost towns where the only signs of life were the dust flying. My hope of snagging a job looked bleak.

Walking down the sidewalk, I accidentally bumped into an elderly woman heading in the opposite direction. Without uttering a word, I caught the ireful glint she'd flashed. My face blushed as I ducked my chin, picking up my pace. I quickly summed up that friendly locals in small towns were a myth.

One glance at the old woman's glare, and I was inclined to believe that Sara and I had become the towns' gossip. I reckoned this whistle-stop didn't see many newcomers like us. We sorta stuck out. Miniskirt-wearing, Sara, and plain-Jane me.

It didn't take long to cover the small cluster of stores. I think I filled out maybe two applications. Most folks just turned me away. Despite my spiel, convincing these fine hicks of my skills only got me shooed out the door. I reckoned southern hospitality had gone fishin'. Unable to look at another bitter-tasting rejection, I decided to take a break. I sighed, feeling thirsty and crabby.

I knocked the agitated dust off my feet and pressed my way down the sidewalk, wondering where to head next. When my eyes landed on a sign a couple of doors down that read, Mudbug Café, I froze. Crap! That was Sara's new job. I wanted to avoid Sara at all costs. With my luck, she'd put me on dish duty. I might be a lot of things, but one thing I wasn't was free!

I glanced across the street and spotted a bookstore. My hope heightened. Quickly, I made a beeline across the street. I didn't bother looking for cars. The traffic was nonexistent. I spotted a few busted-up whoop-de-dos on threadbare tires. My car should fit in nicely here. That was a big if. Saving money for new tires was an impossible feat. Which meant we were stuck here in the middle of bugsville until otherwise.

When I made it across the street, I stopped, checking out the window's display. The sign read, *Otherworldly*. I read out loud. "Astrology, Magic Spells, and Baubles." How odd, finding a store like this in the middle of nowhere.

I pushed past the door. A bell jingled, announcing my entrance. A rush of incense swirled up my nose, a woodsy smell but a little heavy with the smoke. I coughed, waving at the gray cloud.

I ventured down aisle after aisle, thrumming over the various books. The smell of new books sent waves of excitement through me. I loved curling up in bed on a rainy day with a good book. Gosh, I couldn't remember the last time I'd bought a new book. My eyes widened with wonder over the vast selection. I noted titles on witchcraft, voodoo, astrology, and new age. There were odd trinkets of all sorts, charms, and other strange emblems. One mysterious item spiked my curiosity, a doll made of simple burlap, ill-matched buttons for eyes, and a black patch in the shape of a heart sown to its chest with zigzag stitches. What possible use would such an ugly doll be for? Usually, I avoided this kind of shop like the bubonic plague. Chills spread over my arms. Strange how the lure of eerie sparked such a deep interest in me, and yet, it frightened me more.

Regretting my egress, I tore myself away from the little corner and headed on my way. I needed a job more than reading books. Just to make myself feel a little better for wasting time, I asked for an application and promised to drop it off first thing in the morning. The clerk informed me that they weren't hiring, but she'd be glad to keep my application on file. Great! Another rejection. I kindly thanked the lady and headed on my way.

With a ragged sigh, I headed off in the direction of the local newspaper, Tangi News Journal, the last of the great white buffalo, and my last hope. Like most newspapers, I expected they'd have an opening. I was aiming for an inside job. With no transportation, delivering papers was off the table. I pushed past the doubled glass doors as the smell of ink hit my face. My lips pressed into a flat line. This was it. It was do-or-die. Fingers crossed.

~

"That went swell!" I mumbled to myself as I left the Journal. Oh, I got the job all right! Just a minor complication. *No transportation!* I kicked an empty can, heading back to the hotel. I wanted to kick Sara for forcing me to come here! No, I didn't want to do that either. I wanted to go home back to Texas, back to my old job at the Dairy Queen and my friends. One thing f'sure, I wasn't in Oz clicking my ruby heels. I slouched my shoulders. I thought about hitchhiking back a million and one times. Between Becky and Laurie, I'd have a place to stay. Their families liked me. I could get a job, save money and by next year, attend college. Become an attorney like Dad. I could get student loans. Hopefully, a scholarship. It was doable.

Then I thought about Sara, and all my dreams burst like a balloon. I couldn't leave. I had to stay. Anger swooped in as I kicked a rock this time.

My head had been so far up in the dark clouds that I was right up on the gas station when I finally lifted my gaze. The men had gone, and the station appeared empty. I made my way to one of the chairs under a tree, flopping down and making myself at home. Beads of sweat had collected across my forehead. I'd used the back of my hand to wipe the sweat away. I was a mess. My feet were throbbing as I slipped the shoes off. With open blisters on my heels, the wedges no longer seemed so cute. In a tizzy, I hurled the shoes into an oil puddle. I stared at them for a minute, knowing Sara would blow a cap for ruining her shoes. "Eh!" I shrugged. I didn't care.

The heat was smothering, like a sauna. My throat was as parched as the dry soil under my feet. I didn't want to drink the water at the hotel. It was murky and smelled like fish. I dove into my pockets for my change. I hadn't eaten since lunch yesterday, though my thirst over-rode my hunger. An ice-cold Coke would settle my nerves.

I withdrew my hand from my pocket and looked at the contents, only seventy-five cents. "Crap!" Could my day get any worse? I slammed the coins onto the ground. They bounced with a ding, landing in a pool of oil, along with the shoes. I'd reached my limit. I laid my face into my palms, letting the tears rip.

Unaware how long I'd been sitting there when someone tapped my shoulder, I sat up, startled. I blinked back the blur of tears as my eyes encountered the evil-eyed woman who'd bumped into me earlier. What did she want? I stared back at her in silence.

"How ya are, chile?" The elderly lady whistled through what I assumed were dentures. "Eww wee! You sure do look mighty thirsty." She handed me a bottle of Coke. Droplets glided down the glass bottle. A good indication it was cold. My eyes rounded.

"Thank you, but I can't pay you back," I sniffled. "All I have is a few coins." I pointed to the quarters in the oil puddle.

The elderly woman waved her hand. "No worry, poupée," she smiled.

I wiped the tears from my cheeks with the back of my hand. "Thanks." I hid my gaze under my lashes.

The older woman sat down next to me and unsnapped her faded black purse. She drew out a white-bleached handkerchief. She reached out and handed it to me without a word. My mouth dropped open, unsure if I should take it or decline. My eyes dropped to the monogram initials, F.N. It must be vintage. Only old folks carried cloth handkerchiefs. I wrinkled my nose, hesitating. "Thanks," I mumbled, accepting her offer. I patted the streaks of tears and wiped my nose delicately. I crumbled the cloth in my fist, unsure of proper etiquette. Did I hand it back to her or return it after I washed it? Getting worked up over a stupid handkerchief, I did what any respectable teenager would do. I tucked it under my leg—outta sight, outta mind, or at least, outta mine. I silently took a drink, feeling uneasy.

I snuck a sideways glance at the elderly lady. Apart from her weird cadence, it was kind of her to buy me a cold drink, but I wasn't in the mood for company. I wanted to excuse myself, but I didn't want to be impolite. I decided to chill and play it cool. I shyly smiled up at her through my lashes and took another sip of my drink.

"Where y'at? Ya and ya mama stay at Claude's hotel?" she smiled warmly.

Her voice carried a twang, making it difficult for me to understand. I just nodded, answering, "Yes, ma'am." I quickly took a sip of my Coke.

"Ya been job huntin'?"

I scoffed, "Yes, ma'am! Been trying." I rolled the cold bottle between my palms. The moisture made me think of a refreshing dive in the swimming pool.

"Did ya get hired anywhere?"

"Yes." I took a third sip.

"That's good!" She flashed her white dentures.

I detected a little French in her timbre. "Not really," I cringed. "I can't take the job."

"What ya say?" Her white brows knitted.

"The job requires transportation. I don't have the money to fix our car." This time, I swigged my drink down in a rush. My lips pinched.

"Bless your heart, chile."

I shrugged, not making a reply.

A bright smile stretched across the elderly woman's golden skin. "I think I can help ya. I have customers I gotta look after, but later I'll be home. Come by after ya rested. Have ya eaten anything today?"

My face flushed, too embarrassed to say. I had to admit that my stomach was starting to gnaw at my insides.

"Ya gotta keep your strength up." She unsnapped her box-shaped purse. Its black leather was faded, and the edges were well worn. A good indication she wasn't flushed with cash. When she pulled out a ten-dollar bill and handed it to me, my eyes widened with surprise.

"I can't take this!" I gasped, lifting my gaze back at her. "Thank you, but I can't pay the money back." Taking an old woman's coins was beyond freeloading. It was downright deplorable.

"If ya insist on makin' it up to me, I have a small garden ya can help me with." Her pale blues glistened against her deep caramel skin.

"Uh…" I wrinkled my nose. "I don't know how to garden."

"No worry, honeychile. It's like beans and cornbread," she laughed as her barrel-shaped body jiggled.

"Do you live around here?" Why was I entertaining the thought? I knew I wasn't going.

"See down the road? Saint Anne Street," she pointed down the road.

22

Blocking the glare from the sun's blear, I cuffed my hand over my brows. "Oh, I see," I nodded, catching sight of the green street sign.

"My little house is right down there. It's the fourth house on the left. Right next ta the vacant house at the end of the street."

"Okay, thanks! What time?" I made myself smile. It wasn't that I didn't appreciate the woman's generosity. I was taken aback by her genuine interest in me—a rare act in my life.

She patted me on the back as she gathered to her feet. "Come by my house this evenin' at six."

"Okay," I smiled.

"By the way, I'm Florence Noel. All my friends call me Ms. Noel. Ya can call me that too!" Her smile reached her faint blue eyes.

"I'm Stephanie…" She stopped me in midsentence.

"I know who ya is." She flashed a mysterious smile. "There ain't much I miss in these parts. I'll see ya at six, Stevie. If I were ya, I'd change 'em shoes." Her gaze dropped to my feet. "Those buggers are da worst for walkin'."

"Yes, ma'am, indeed."

"Oh, I almost forgot! I'll call down at the newspaper and speak ta Frank, my cousin. I'll see ya this evening." A suspicious smile crept across her face.

"Oh, okay." I didn't know what to say. I watched as Ms. Noel moseyed along toward downtown. She fit the description of anyone's grandmother. A plump body, clothed in a loose-fitting blue dress, buttoned up in the front and white nursing shoes, hose rolled up to her knees. She seemed nice enough. I drew in a restless breath. I sure hope this ain't anything like Hansel and Gretel where the sweet old woman turned into a wicked witch and tried to eat me.

THUNDERSTRUCK

*S*traight up six o'clock, I was on Ms. Noel's front porch, knocking. Finding her house wasn't hard, the fourth house next to the vacant house on the left. The house was small and appeared to need some repair. White paint chipped, and the porch sagged a touch. Black shutters that could use a coat of paint like the rest of the house. Judging by the home's condition, I'd bet she'd lived here a good many years.

As I waited for her to answer the door, I questioned why she bothered calling her cousin, Frank? It wouldn't help the fact that I didn't have transportation.

All of a sudden, the screen squeaked, and there stood Ms. Noel, smiling. "Ah, you're on time!" Her bright voice was as pleasant as I remembered from earlier today. She stepped outside onto the porch, shutting the door behind her. "Follow me, babee." She waddled down the steps, waving for me to follow.

I followed her as she led me toward the back of the house. A faint breeze brushed my heated face as the cicadas amidst the pine trees buzzed in harmony. Oddly enough, I enjoyed their hum. Every evening about this time, the bugs would break out into a chorus.

We entered through the side gate, making our way to the back of the house. I noticed a patch of tilted soil that looked like the makings of a garden. I also spotted an old tin-shed in the far back of the yard. A sudden thought gave me chills. An old shed, no neighbors, and a stranger made me think of Hansel and Gretel. Shoving the ridiculous paranoia in my back pocket, I slapped a smile on my face as I combed the yard for an escape just in case.

She pulled a key from her apron pocket and unlocked the shed. The door squeaked open as I stood back. I hated dark, creepy places where bugs lurked. Ms. Noel disappeared inside the shed while I waited outside, peeking through the dimness at a faint shadow of junk collecting cobwebs. Only seconds later, I heard a click, and light showered the inside, revealing what I'd suspected-a lotta beat-up junk, like an old refrigerator with its door half off its hinges, a moth-eaten mattress, gardening tools, and other stuff that were in desperate need of hauling off.

With my feet planted to the grass, I waited outside. The shed was already leaning like the Tower of Pisa. The slightest breeze could cause it to collapse. I held my breath, fretting over Ms. Noel. Geez! Why did she have to go in there? I tapped my foot, chewing my nails, waiting for her return.

Moments later, Ms. Noel emerged from the shed, rolling a bike. I gaped in surprise. She stopped in front of me, grinning. "This is yours. It just needs a little cleaning and a tire fixed." She handed the bike to me. "When you leave here, go ta the gas station at the corner. My brother, Claude, will patch up the flat tire and check the other one too. It'll be as good as new then," she promised, wiping her hands on her apron.

"You're giving me this bike?"

"It ain't doin' me no good rustin' away in that old shed. I used ta ride it until I broke my hip. It's been sittin' collectin' dirt since." She waved at the bike. "Go on! Take it. You wouldn't want ta miss your first day of work, would you?"

I stood there with a blank face, stumped over what to say. "Uh, thanks!"

"Don't mention it, chile. I made you a couple of sandwiches for dinner and tomorrow too. Let me get those for you."

"Ms. Noel, you're too kind," I smiled, pleasantly surprised. This stranger didn't know me from Adam, and yet, she was more than generous. Not even my mother would've been this kind.

"It's no problem. C'mon." Ms. Noel waddled off to the gate. I trailed behind her with the bike. Ms. Noel disappeared into the house as I waited by the bike.

Moments later, I heard the plank board squeaking, and Ms. Noel reappearing at the door with a brown sack in her hand and a mason jar full of ice cubes and sweet tea. She opened the screen with a broad smile. "Here you go." I met her at the top of the steps as she handed me a brown sack and a mason jar with a lid screwed onto it. "When you get off tomorrow, come by, and I'll have a bowl of gumbo and cornbread fixed for you."

"You don't have to do this." I placed the sack and jar in the bike's basket.

"Stop your worry! I got you, babee."

"Thank you," I replied.

"If you lookin' for a place to settle, the house next door is for rent. It's a cute little place. From what I hear, the landlord ain't askin' much."

"I'll tell Mom. I'm sure she'll be interested," I paused. "Thanks for everything," I genuinely smiled. For the first time since we'd arrived, I felt a slight spark of happiness.

"Don't mention it, but you best git on down ta da station, so Claude can fix that tire," she urged. Ms. Noel reminded me of what a grand-mother would be like. I never had much experience with family. Apart from my mom and dad, that was all the family I knew. Sara and Dad were orphans. And now that Dad was dead, it was just Sara and me.

Precisely as Ms. Noel had promised, Claude fixed the bike. He checked the breaks, oiled, and tightened the chain, getting it in top shape. After he had finished, he let me take the bike to the back and hose it off.

The bike had some mileage. The red paint had faded, and rust had taken its place, but I didn't care. To me, it was a priceless treasure. Now I had transportation and a job.

The first day on the job wasn't so bad. I had to get up before daybreak. Heck, I was up before the roosters. Five in the morning was ridiculous, but I was happy to have a job. I went in early to sort out my newspapers. Everything seemed to fall in place. The route was in the downtown area, a perfect location for me. I'd get my route done and have plenty of time to make it to school on time. For now, it was convenient, and the cash would keep me afloat until the next move. For all I knew, Sara could decide to leave tomorrow.

Then I thought about the vacant house next to Ms. Noel. It sounded great, but we couldn't afford it. We were rubbing pennies together after Sara blew our money on that stupid fortuneteller. We were barely getting by paying for the cheap hotel. I suspected by the end of the week we'd be living in the streets.

After I'd finished my last paper, I was excited to relax and goof off the rest of the day. Then my stomach started to protest. I'd eaten the extra sandwich last night that Ms. Noel had made for today. Texas had its signature hamburgers, but this sandwich beat the burgers hands-down. Crusty French bread, crispy shredded lettuce, sliced tomatoes, Creole mayonnaise paired with sausage. The sandwiches were so tasty that I couldn't stop eating them until I'd finished the last bite, leaving me lunch-less today.

With the wind running through my hair as I glided down the steep hill, I tossed the idea back and forth whether I should visit Sara at the diner. I decided to go for it. She'd promised to feed me if I stopped by. It was about one in the afternoon. I figured folks would be clearing out, and I wouldn't be imposing too much. My mouth began watering thinking about an ice-cold chocolate shake and crispy fries, the universal food for champions, in my opinion. I put the pedal to the metal, and off I went, soaring. A catchy tune was running through my head. Mindlessly, I hummed to it. One of Charlie Puth's songs, *The Way I am*. The crisp air felt invigorating, a nice change from the heat. I closed my eyes, letting the cool breeze rest across my flushed face.

Then something alerted me. My eyes flew open, and panic slammed into first gear. A black Corvette and I were about to collide in less than half a second. I suddenly recalled the film *Men in Black* and the splattered bug across the windshield. With no time to veer, I shut my eyes tight. I began confessing the hundred and one sins I'd committed in the last week as I embraced my imminent death.

Holding my breath, clenching my teeth, I braced myself, but nothing happened. I opened one eye. *Nothing!* The black car had vanished. Then I opened the other eye, staring at an empty road in front of me. Hastily, I twisted in my seat as my eyes latched onto the license plate. How the heck did the car miss me? I stared in shock.

Unmindful of where I was going, my bike's tire slammed into the curb, sending both the bike and me sailing. With a hard thud, I landed on my derriere. "Ow!" I winced from the sudden impact.

Thunderstruck, I rose on my elbows, spotting the expensive car speeding off into the glorious sunset. Soon it'd disappeared. Only the sound of its gears shifting echoed in my ears.

After the sound had vanished, I collapsed on my back, feeling the pain shooting down my spine. Then my eyes landed on my bike…

THE FORESHADOWER

*A*fter what felt like an eternity, I finally peeled myself off the pavement. My whole backside was rocking with agony. I picked my bike up, moaning as I bent over. As my eyes brushed over the bike, I eased a breath of relief. No damages. *I, on the other hand, wasn't so lucky.*

My body screamed in agony. The throb of my scraped-up elbows and the sharp pain shooting up my spine sent me spinning. I supposed his rich, pampered ass thought it was okay to flatten the peasant. He had to have seen me coming unless the tinted windows hindered his vision. Boy, I'd love to get my hands on the driver. Just swell! I had work early tomorrow morning too. Throwing papers was going to be a challenge, I flinched. Crap! My body hurt.

I didn't get to make it to the diner or make it over to Ms. Noel's for dinner that evening, either. When I got back to the hotel, I tried using my cell phone to call Sara. No such luck. Mommy dearest didn't pay the bill. She lied, obviously. Geez! I wanted to have a temper tantrum, but my body ached too much. So, I did the next best thing, climbed under the covers, and sobbed. I hated my life, and I hated this town even more.

It was dark, around ten, when Sara came bursting through the door three sheets to the wind. The noise jolted me from a deep sleep. I jerked up to a sitting position, eyes droopy from sleep. "What's wrong?" I rubbed my eyes, feeling a panic attack coming on.

"Don't get your feathers ruffled. Everything is just peachy," Sara cooed, furthering her boasting. "I rented a house just around the corner. Cute as a button and fully furnished." Sara sashayed around the room, happy as a pig in mud.

"Say what?" My brows puckered, confused.

"I said I rented a house. Tomorrow we'll be moving." She flashed the keys in my face.

I sat there a minute, mulling over her announcement. "How did you get the money? We ain't gotta pot to piss in!"

"I declare! Stop your grumbling. We're fixin' to move to a house. Get to packin'. We're outta here first thing in the morning."

I crossed my arms, fit to be tied. "Hold your horses, Mother! I can't move us. Apart from my aches and scrapes from a bike accident today, I'm working in the morning."

"Well then, start on it tonight. How much can it be? We only brought four suitcases."

Like water off a duck's back, nothing I said registered with Sara. I narrowed my eyes. "Why can't you pack your suitcases?"

"Well, smarty-pants." She rested her hands on her hips. "I have a date tonight, and I'm not sure if I'll be back in time."

"Fine! Shall I draw your bath too, your highness?"

"Watch your mouth!" Sara threatened. "I just might kick you out." Sara's dark eyes were on me like a lioness inching closer to its prey. Nothing was new about Sara's threats, though the peculiar glint in her eyes felt foreign. Everything seemed off. How the blazes did she manage to lease a house blew my mind. We didn't have any money. I wondered who she'd knocked in the head for this rental.

"Fine! I'll pack. All the same to you, I'm not losing my job. I'll move us after I finish my route." I held my gaze to hers, but I didn't go any further. By the seedy glare on Sara's face, she'd crossed to the dark side, and that was one side I didn't dare go.

"Have it your way, then."

"What's the address?" I asked.

"805 Saint Anne Street. It's literally down the road. It's the last house on a dead-end street."

"You're kidding?" My eyes followed Sara as she applied makeup to her already caked face. "How did you find the house?"

"A customer told me." Before she said another word, a car's headlights penetrated the curtains. Sara's gaze lifted to the lights and then at me. "That's my ride." She nearly sprinted to the door. "Gotta run! See you tomorrow at the house."

With nothing else said, she was out the door in a flash, and minutes later, the bright light dropped from the window. Loneliness soon spread over me. The sting of tears welled, but I refused to relent. The last thing I wanted to do was harp on my mom and her relentless absence.

I lay in bed, staring at the ceiling, chewing my lip, wishing I had a book to read. My mind drifted back to Sweetwater, and instantly, I stopped. Reminiscing over Texas wasn't going to help my state of mind. I had to bury it in my all-too-well-forgotten past. A cesspool of many faces and places locked away in the back of my brain, crammed so far down that it surely would never return.

Then I thought about my near accident with the mysterious black Corvette. I rewound that moment in my head like a bad rerun. I kept smashing into a brick wall. How the driver managed to dodge me blew my brain. He was right up in my grill, far too close to have veered. I practically was the deer in the headlights. I sighed, racked with unease. I reckoned that mystery might remain unsolved, though one I'd forever remained baffled.

After I finished my route, pushing past the misery of the scorching sun all morning, I did as Sara ordered. I managed to cram all our stuff into the Volkswagen. Luckily, the house was only a street over. I felt ridiculous, driving with a flat and my rusty bike duct-taped to the top. At least it matched. My car was as rusty as my bike. I reckoned the neighbors might go bug-eyed when they saw us moving in.

When I spotted the house, my breath caught in my throat. Sara had rented the same cute house that Ms. Noel had mentioned. I blinked, staring. I rechecked the scribbled address on the piece of paper that I'd written down. "Yep! This was it. 807 Saint Ann Street. I let out a whistle as I tossed the note in the back seat. How Sara managed to pony up the dough for this house had me scratching my head.

Then it hit me. Jesus! What if Sara was turning tricks? Maybe she lied about spending the rent money on that phony psychic. Then again, she had snared a new beau. He could've paid for it. Either way, I wasn't going to question a gift horse in the mouth.

I rolled up into the drive and cut the engine. I sat there taking in the quaint little house. A smile played across my face. Most places we stayed at were dumps, but this place was like a palace. Taking in the curbside view, it was a simple white frame house, an older mid-century, I think. On the front porch, a wooden swing hung with bright yellow pillows. Deep purple hydrangeas in full bloom caressed each side of the steps, welcoming onlookers.

My mind filled with eagerness as I rushed to go inside. When I reached the top step, it dawned on me that I'd forgotten to get the keys from Sara. Suddenly I felt panicky. It wasn't beneath Sara to play a nasty prank. Holding my breath, I spread my fingers over the doorknob. It was cool to the touch. I tightened my grip and twisted the knob, and to my delight, the door opened. I jumped for joy!

Quickly, I stepped inside, shutting the door behind me. I stalled for a minute as my eyes combed over the living space. A giddy feeling washed over me as I bit my bottom lip, gawking. The main room was small, simple, yet cozy. The house was fully furnished. The couch sat under the windowsill, leaving the fireplace open to the room. Wheatshade lamps sat tall on each end table placed on each side of the sofa, offering a soft glow. Two big stuffy chairs faced the sofa on the opposite side and an accent chair nestled by the window with a small table and lamb. Light colors of blue and yellow accented the space bringing in a warm toasty feeling.

I sprinted upstairs, determined to get first dibs on the bedrooms. There were two rooms, one with a bathroom and a guest bathroom down the hall. I immediately claimed the master bedroom. It was the brightest room in the house and a double bonus... *a bathroom*. I knew Sara would want the one with less light, better for sleeping late.

Just like the living room downstairs, the bedrooms were fully loaded. Unable to resist, I made a dive onto my full-size bed. I bounced and sank into it. A long breath escaped my lips. "Ah, a feathered mattress, soft with no lumps! It's perfect," I mumbled, bouncing once more on the bed. I soon discovered that the whole house had everything we possibly needed.

I couldn't remember the last time we'd been this lucky. I reckoned I should count my blessings while they lasted. A little sadness pricked my heart. I frowned, thinking about my friends back in Texas.

I managed to sweat a jar full by the time I'd finished unloading our stuff in the house. The only thing I'd left were three bags sitting in the foyer. I figured Sara could lug her belongings upstairs.

I, in the meantime, made myself at home by filling my bedroom up with my stuff. I figured if I stored my clothes away that Sara wouldn't make a big fuss. Then again, if I moved her suitcases to her room and set up her junk all nice and organized, she'd likely stay put. She hated lugging her bags.

The doorbell alerted me, ringing throughout the house. Our first guest! I skirted downstairs to the front door. I swung the door open, forgetting to check the peephole. I was surprised to see my new neighbor. "Hi there, Ms. Noel," I smiled.

"Hey, neighbor! I hope I'm not pesterin' ya." A crooked smile spread across her face.

"Nope, not at all. Come on in." I stepped aside. " I'll show you the place."

"Thank you! I won't stay long. I was makin' grocers and picked you up a few items is all."

I glanced down, spotting two large brown sacks by her feet, spilling over the brim with groceries and thick blankets.

Ms. Noel brushed past me as she stepped into the living room. "This looks like brand new furniture in 'ere!"

All I could focus on was the sacks. "Oh, my," I gaped, wordless. Then my brain booted up as I eagerly grabbed up the grocery bags and brought them inside, kicking the door shut with my foot.

"Honeychile, let's take them sacks to the kitchen?" Ms. Noel waddled straight back as if she knew the place.

"Oh-my-oh-my! Not one thing has changed in 'ere." Her eyes beamed. "This old house once belonged to my older sister."

"Where is she living now?"

"Oh my, Fannie moved on to the big house a while ago. I talk to her now and then when she has a minute." Her eyes twinkled as if her thoughts wafted back to fond memories. "Don't mind me none." Ms.

Noel grabbed one of the bags from my arms, setting it on top of the counter and started to empty its content. "It's just a few things I know you need."

"Ms. Noel, you don't have to go to all this trouble."

"Hush, chile!" She stopped unloading the sack and turned to me, "When's the last time you ate?"

"Uh…" My cheeks blushed.

"Chile, hard times make a monkey eat pepper. Now sit down at the table and let me fix ya a bowl of gumbo." I obeyed, taking a seat at the small, rounded table in the corner by the window. My eyes washed over the large flower print curtains. I smiled to myself. The print was a bold yellow with large red roses. Not so trendy, but I didn't care. The curtains were perfect for the kitchen. A bemused smile played across my face. Elbows on the table as I gazed out the window. For the first time in a long time, I felt happy. This place might work after all. And I especially liked my new neighbor.

Ms. Noel made her way to the table and set down a hot bowl of soup in front of me. Curls of steam floated to my face as I drank in the delicious aroma. "I'm known around her' for my Creole gumbo." Pride colored her face. "I make my roux with chicken fat and brown it until it's dark as chocolate. Then I throw in chicken and sausage with onions, celery, and pepper. That makes it good tastin'. Now eat up before it gets cold," she handed my spoon to me. "When ya get done with that, I gotta sweet potato pie for ya too." She padded off to the counter, pulling out a gallon of milk from one of the sacks and poured a large glass. She made her way back to the table and set it beside my bowl.

"Thank you, but you don't have to fuss over me." Guilt rode hard on my heart. It was apparent she didn't have the money to feed me, and she shouldn't be waiting on me. Still, I appreciated her kindness. "Ms. Noel, you're far too considerate." I didn't mention that this was my first and only meal today. Before Sara left this morning, she'd discovered my stash and stole the ten bucks I'd been saving to give back to Ms. Noel.

"It's nothin', chile," she faintly groaned, taking a seat at the table across from me. Quiet rested between us momentarily while I slurped up the tasty gumbo. "You likin' your new job?" Ms. Noel asked.

I shrugged. "Yes, ma'am! It won't conflict with school." I took another large bite and savored the flavor.

"How did ya and ya mama discover Tangi? It's not often we get newcomers."

"I wish I knew myself." I snorted out a sharp laugh. "Sara has a way of finding places off the grid." I gulped down half my milk as my mouth burned and my eyes watered from the hot spices.

"It's sure nice havin' ya for a neighbor. My sister will like hearing that ya moved into her old house." The warmth of her smile echoed in her voice.

"When is your sister, Fannie, getting out of jail?"

Ms. Noel burst into laughter, slapping her knee.

I merely stared, tongue-tied. What did I say?

"Chile, Fannie is no longer with us."

"I don't understand."

"Fannie died a few years ago."

"Wait! I thought you said you've recently spoken to her?" A flicker of apprehension jabbed my chest.

"I talk to the dead often." Her pale blue eyes crinkled. "My sister comes to me when she hears talk."

"Your sister is a g-g-ghost?"

"That's right. I have the gift," Ms. Noel admitted with pride. "Folks in these parts call me... *The Foreshadower.*"

"What does that exactly entail?"

"I see you had an accident yesterday." She nodded at my skinned-up elbows.

"Oh! Yeah, I sorta ran into the curb." Blushing, I quickly hid my elbows under the table, "I forgot to look where I was going."

"Was a fancy black car somehow involved?" Her blue eyes dug deep into me.

"Uh, yeah," I paused. "Hey, how did you know?"

"You nearly collided, but somehow the car dodged you."

"How do you know this?"

"Chile, you'll soon find out that life's never what it seems."

A prickling sensation glided up my spine. Ms. Noel had my undivided attention. "Do you know the driver?"

"No, not directly." Her lips curled into a smile. "Your encounter has a strong presence. He jarred Fannie's attention."

"Uh, your sister's ghost saw the black Corvette that nearly pancaked me?"

"Yes." Her face radiated as if this conversation was nothing more than watercooler gossip.

I couldn't believe my ears.

"Fannie has been watching over you."

"Watching over me. Why?" My stomach contracted into a tight ball.

"Fannie brought you to my attention. She thought you were a lost spirit." Ms. Noel's eyes filled with concern.

I leaned closer. My curiosity overrode my trippin'. "Did Fannie see the driver?"

"Not exactly. It's different for the afterlife. They receive the living in broken pieces, like slicing film."

"So, what did your sister see?"

"Fannie didn't pick up much other than his soul was dark."

"That can't be good." I blew out a sharp breath. "That whole occurrence was whacked."

Ms. Noel listened quietly.

"All at once, I was staring death in the headlights of a black Corvette. All I could do was freeze. The driver was too close to veer from my path. Yet somehow, he pulled a Houdini, disappearing and reappearing on the other side of me." I shuddered, thinking how close I came to death.

"That is some story," Ms. Noel whistled.

"Did your sister say anything else?"

"No, but I'll keep my ears open." Then a light caught Ms. Noel's face. "I almost forgot! I do need to warn you about something that has come to my attention."

"What?" Crap! Ghost and disappearing cars... what next?

"I don't mean to pry."

"It's okay," I laughed a little.

"The fella, ya mama's been keepin' company with is a low down scoundrel. Uh-hmm, *God don't like ugly*." Ms. Noel slapped her hand on her knee, emphasizing her words.

"I don't get involved with Mom's love life. Usually, the life expectancy of her relationships lasts no longer than a month." I didn't say why.

"Well, stay away from that rascal, chile." She patted my shoulder as she lugged herself to her feet. "Don't forget to put up the rest of the food. If ya need me, ya know where I live."

I walked her to the door and thanked her again for her generosity. I didn't know why she took a shine to me. I certainly wasn't going to complain. Considering Ms. Noel's age and the generous kindness she'd shown me, I owed her the same in return. I reckoned it was time for me to get started on that garden she mentioned and lend a hand with other tasks like mowing the lawn. She was good folk and mighty impressive if I did say so myself.

DREAMS AND DREAMY BOYS

On the first day of school, I was nervous as a long-tailed cat in a room full of rocking chairs. Starting a new school was only the icing on the cake. My dream seemed to have kicked off the day with a smashing splash. Despite how hard I tried, I couldn't shake off the edginess.

It started sweetly. I was at school, standing by my locker. A tall boy with a dimpled smile greeted me, offering to carry my books. I returned his smile, thinking he was cute. It was more of a sense than visualizing his features. There was a blur veiling his face. I noted a ring on his finger. The stones were quite remarkable in size, black diamonds out-lining an eye, nestled in yellow diamonds. How strange. Why would someone wear such an ugly ring?

As the dream continued, the faceless boy took my hand, leading me down the hall. Honeysuckle lingered in the air as our tennis shoes squeaked across the polished floor. The boy seemed familiar, like a close friend, as he struck up a conversation. I strained to listen to his muffled words like I was watching a silent film.

We came to a halt at a door. Nothing unusual, just an ordinary white door. The boy opened it and stepped back for me to enter. I stepped inside, thinking we were entering class as aimless chatter echoed. I smiled at the boy for holding the door open, but when I drew my eyes from his face, the noise ceased, and I gasped. The room's temperature dropped to a frost. I hugged my waist, shivering as fright seized my body.

When my eyes settled, I saw thirteen men veiled in black robes, gathered in a circle, chanting in a strange language. I must've stumbled into the wrong room. I looked back at the boy, but to my horror, he'd vanished. Panic quickly soared through me. As if someone nudged me, I carefully emerged from the shadows into the dim light. I paused, eyeing all thirteen robed men. How odd, I thought. I'd escaped their notice. The men's attention appeared focused on an obscured object in the center of the circle.

An urge rushed over me. I had to see what held their interest. I edged my way through the black robes. The closer I got to the core, the robed men pushed me back, devouring me. I pushed and shoved with all my might, I had to see, but my efforts were futile. My heart hammered against my chest as if death was beckoning me.

Then the robed men stepped aside, allowing me to pass. I swallowed down my panic and eased my way through the maze of blackness. Once I reached the center, my gaze lowered and horror struck. I began screaming, blood-curdling screams.

At that moment, my alarm exploded, shattering fragments of my dream into a million pieces. My eyes flew open as I bolted to a sitting position. Coated in sweat, I labored. I searched the room for a second, confused about my surroundings. My eyes rested on a thin stream of light filtering through a small gap in the curtain. The soft glow comforted me as my lungs filled with air, and my erratic pulse slowed. It'd been a couple of months since my last dream. This time, it had returned tenfold. Since the night of my father's death, my dreams had been haunting me. That was eight years ago.

I inhaled a frayed breath as I dragged myself out of bed and headed to shower. I had a big day ahead of me, delivering papers and tackling a new school. I dreaded it too. I had to keep reminding myself this was my last year. That little slice of hope kept me going forward.

After I dressed, I went downstairs to the kitchen. I had a feeling the day was going to be all sunshine and smiles until I heard the rumble of thunder. Quickly I padded over to the window and peered outside. My heart sank. "Crap! Crap! Crap! Damn! Damn! Damn," I ranted. "Great!" I huffed, still staring out the window. Dark gray clouds bruised the sky as far as I could see. I flopped down at the table, stewing over my day ahead. I was unprepared. No raincoat, no rubber boots. My reputation was doomed. I could hear the taunting and giggles throughout the entire school at the new chick that looked like a drowned rat. *Me!* I couldn't wait for this day to end. Just a fun-filled day of kicks and giggles. Suddenly lightning ripped the sky, and thunder roared.

~

An endeavor ended, and a new adventure began as I entered past the double doors of Tangi High. A brush of warm air and the aroma of burnt toast smothered my senses. Apart from the unsavory smell of toast, the heat melted the stiffness in my fingers. Though, it did little to comfort me. My first day was already a disaster. A swamp witch looked better than I did. Stares targeted my back as I made my way down the hall. Two boys whistled at me as I passed. The giggles confirmed their intent was a jab.

Ignoring the ding wads, I searched for a restroom. My hair looked like a mop, and my wet clothes clung to my body like a second skin. I finally spotted the girl's restroom on the left and ducked inside. I was towel drying my hair, standing at the sink when the swish of the door opened as two girls passed by me, chatting about some hot new boy. I heard one of the girls say that she was already in love. I laughed to myself, shaking my head. The two girls were in their zone. My presence had slipped past their notice.

I turned back to my reflection in the mirror. I sighed, grabbing a hairband from my book bag and wrung my hair up into a ponytail. I sighed, staring at my pathetic reflection. A mess didn't begin to describe my disheveled hair. "Oh, well." There was nothing I could do. I shrugged off my waterlogged hoodie and tied it around my waist. I should be dried out by the end of the day. Although I think a raincoat would be a good investment. Sara needed to fork over some money. She dragged me to this hole in the ground. The least she could do is provide a few necessities. It wouldn't hurt her to sell a pair of her Louboutins. I leaned against the sink. The two girls had already left, and I had a moment to myself. I thought about calling Beck and Laurie. I missed them and my life in Texas. Those two were loyal to a fault. Best friends ever! I knuckled a tear. Maybe I'd call them when I got a phone. I kept teetering on that idea. Hearing their voices might throw me into a spiral, making me hate this place more if that were possible. I let out a long sigh and donned my book bag and headed out.

I ventured down the hall, pushing through the throng of students. Loud twaddle jacketed the air. Several students huddled in clumps by the lockers. Most of the students here grew up in Tangi. Small towns like this one, new kids usually struggled to fit in. I'd seen it a hundred times when newbies become an outcast like a LEOPARD.

I stretched my neck, looking for the office. It had to be here somewhere. After fighting through the cluster of bodies, I turned the corner and spotted Registration on my left. I pushed open the heavy glass door and approached the counter. The scent of a vanilla candle drifted in the small office. It was pleasant. Maybe after I get paid, I might buy a candle for the house. But I could do without the swarming students crowding the small space. I eyeballed the woman behind the counter. She must be going through a mid-life crisis. The vibrant pink hair screamed for attention. Pink hair was cool on a teen, but a middle-aged woman, not so much. I leaned my elbows on the counter and spoke up. "Excuse me!"

The woman's head snapped up and smiled. "What you need, honey?" She rushed her words. I spotted her name tag pinned to her chest: Mrs. Suzie Brown.

"Yes, ma'am. I need to enroll. I have my transcript and ID." I pulled out my papers and handed them over to her.

"Mercy me! You're late." Mrs. Brown glared at me as if I'd committed a carnal sin.

"Yeah, sorry," I swallowed, feeling flushed. "My mom couldn't come. She started her new job at Mudbug Café. She's a waitress."

Without another utter, Mrs. Brown placed her specs on the bridge of her nose and examined the forms. Then cut her gaze back at me. "Have a seat!"

"Oh… Okay." I was taken aback. She abruptly turned, heading off to a computer placed in a corner on the far back counter. Dread washed over me as I watched her punch keys. Trouble was embarking. I felt it down to my toes.

I turned from the counter to have a seat when I smacked into a student. The girl's books went flying as I stood there, gaping at the books puddled around my feet. "Whoops!" I yelped. The chick must've been peeking over my shoulder for me to have slammed into her. Whata weirdo! I paused a moment, eyeing her. Then my brain kicked in, and I rushed to apologize. "Hmm, sorry, I didn't see you." I bent down with the girl to help gather the books.

"It's okay," she smiled, loading her arms full of books. "Hey, you're the new girl that the town's been talking about!" The girl's voice was far too chipper for the morning.

"The town's talking about me?" I handed her a book and stood up. I shoved my hands in my pockets. Something about this chick's vibe made me uneasy.

"I hope you're settling in nicely?"

I shrugged. "So far, so good." If I told her how I felt, she'd have the whole school throwing spit-wads at me. I could spot her type a hundred miles away–*the greeter girl*. Very bubbly, way too much neon green, a good thirty pounds overweight, and the smell of desperation to ignite the fuel that pushed her into the overly excitable girl.

She tossed that sugarcoated smile that I'd seen so many times at previous schools. "You should come and hang out with me. I can give you the scoop on all the juicy gossip. Little things like who's cool and who's not."

"Cool!" I forced a smile.

"What's your schedule? Maybe we have classes together."

I nodded toward the counter. "I'm just registering now."

"Wow! You're late."

"That's what I keep hearing."

"You're a rebel," she giggled.

I shrugged, not responding.

She reached over me and snatched up a flyer about the next pep rally. "Well, I hope we have a class together. If not, I'll catch you at lunch. I'll introduce you to the pack."

"Thanks," I answered. Uncertain if I wanted to be lumped into her clique of friends.

"By the way, I'm Sally Freeman."

"Stevie Ray," I replied.

Her nose wrinkled. "Isn't that a boy's name?"

"It's a nickname." I got that stupid question often. Dad gave me the nickname. I kept it as a reminder of him.

"Bless your heart! You must get picked on a lot having a boy's name." She tossed a tight smile. "Gotta go! Later!"

"Yeah, later," I answered dryly. I watched the girl disappear into the assemblage of students. I couldn't put my finger on it, but there was something peculiar about that girl.

"Miss Ray!" I flinched, bouncing to my feet. Mrs. Brown's high pitch voice set me on edge.

I stepped up to the counter, feeling my face pale. "Yes, ma'am." Showing respect might get me off with a slap on the wrist. I smiled brightly into the woman's lemon face.

"Young lady, your transcript shows you've been to five different schools in the last year. Can you explain this?"

"My mother has to move a lot for her job," I answered sweetly. I hate questions. Always questions. "I can call her if you like?" I flitted my lashes. Of course, I lied.

Mrs. Brown drew her specs to examined my transcript. Then she caught my gaze. "Your mother is a waitress?"

Uh-oh! Caught lying. "Humm, that's right. The insurance job laid her off." I shifted in my feet.

"Where is your mother now?"

I held my hands clasped behind my back and slightly widened my eyes just enough to appear innocent. I had this act perfect. "My mom couldn't come today. Conflicting schedule," I smiled, hoping she'd buy my bluff.

"Wait here, miss," she snapped, and before I could protest, she torpedoed down a short hall, leading to buntuck Egypt for all I knew. This wasn't fair. Why didn't she drag Sara down here and ask her all these questions? It was Sara's fault.

I bit my bottom lip, stretching my eyes in the direction Mrs. Brown had darted off to. Eighteen was legal. I could home school. Then I thought, no! I needed a scholarship to help pay for my college and a high GPA to get into better universities. With a reluctant sigh, I planted my feet, waiting to get hauled into the dungeon master's chamber... *the principal.*

After several internal meltdowns, my eyes homed in on the high heels echoing across the tile floor and growing louder by the second.

"Miss. Ray!" Mrs. Brown brusquely spoke, a bit winded. "Come with me, *please*." I loved the way she bit out that last word, *"please."* Nothing was pleasing about the walk of doom.

I followed her fast-paced steps down the same short hall. We stopped at the door that read, *Principal, Dr. Ed Van*. The hairs on my neck bristled. I knew this walk far too well. I'd set foot many times in the principal's office. Mrs. Brown opened the door and stepped aside, letting me enter. A strong whiff of a pipe perfumed the air, and memories of my dad fluttered through my mind. When I was a child, Dad would take me to his small office in town. I'd sit on the floor coloring while he smoked his pipe, working on his clients' cases. He was a well-loved and respected attorney in a small Oklahoma community called Eufaula. To this day, I associated the scent of a pipe with Dad.

Mrs. Brown cleared her throat, jarring my attention. "Dr. Van, this is Stephanie Ray. Her voice appeared fisted with unease.

"Come, Miss Ray. Have a seat." An older man spoke in a raspy voice sitting behind a large desk, pointing to a chair, directly in front of his desk.

I realized this was not your typical principal's office. The chairs were dark brown, real leather, and his desk reminded me of something you'd see in the Oval Office at the White House. Dark mahogany finished with tooled leather inserts on top and brass fittings embellished the edge. Such an elaborate style on a principal's salary. "Yes, sir." I settled in the chair on the left and placed my hands in my lap, hiding my jitters.

"Well, Miss Ray, it has come to my attention you have quite a list of attending schools. I forget the number. How many?"

Instantly, I didn't like this man. I answered, "Five."

"Can you tell me how you've managed to keep your GPA at 3.9?"

Did he doubt my credibility? "Sir, I don't understand the question."

"I think you're stalling, Miss Ray."

"Every grade I've made, I have earned." Ire was starting to tingle my spine.

"That's quite remarkable, or should I say impossible?" He leaned back in his chair as his smothering eyes churned with mistrust.

"My mother can address your questions concerning my school attendance." I blamed Sara for this. I wouldn't be sitting here under the heated snare of a principal if it hadn't been for her incessant need to town hop.

Dr. Van's was as ugly as Rumpelstiltskin, a deeply wrinkled face. It was evident that he'd been smoking for years.

"Your mother is not here," he countered. "I'm asking *you*."

"Sir, I gave you my answer."

"Considering your unstable home life, it raises doubt as to how you've obtained your scores."

"Have I warranted cause for this interrogation?" It was evident that he harbored some sort of ill will toward me.

"It depends," he answered, not entirely quenching my thirst for clarity.

I had to reel in my temper and play nice. I inhaled inwardly. "Dr. Van, if you're implying that I've falsified my scores, I'll be more than happy to take any test you wish to provide."

Dr. Van's eyes hardened as he ripped my transcript in two and dropped the remains in the trashcan. "Miss Ray, here at Tangi High, you will be required to prove your worth."

I gawked with disbelief. "That's my transcript!"

"Yes, it was." Dr. Van's voice spewed with loathing. "Now prove to me you are the superb student you claim." I flinched as he glared at me through his thick eyewear. "Yes, sir, I'll do my best." I tried to hide the disdain in my voice. I took pride in my work, and it chafed my butt when someone questioned the validity of my achievements.

"We shall see," he gritted through his stained teeth. "That will be all, Miss Ray." He dismissed me, leaning back in his chair. There was something strange about this principal. It was almost as if he had a hidden agenda behind his words. I shrugged it off. It wouldn't be long before Sara would be ready to move to the next town, and I'd soon forget my worries with him. In the meantime, I planned to steer clear of this madman.

Shaking off the dust from that demented interval, I glimpsed at the hall clock. Only three minutes to get to class before the tardy bell sounded off, so I ran. English was my first class in the morning. It wasn't my favorite, but at least I'd get it out of the way. West wing, first left, Mrs. Brown had instructed. I hooked several corners and finally stumbled upon the room, one-oh-two. I quickly pushed past the door and came to a quick halt. I half expected an empty chair next to the teacher, but I didn't anticipate *this*. My gaze landed on the greeter girl, Sally. She was sitting in the far back row, waving her hands in the air like a person sinking in quicksand. I raked my eyes over the classroom. Just my luck, only one vacant desk behind Sally.

I dragged my feet down the back row and forced a painful smile, catching her glint. "Hey," I mumbled as I flopped down in the chair. I glimpsed at the desk behind me. A black coat hung over the back of the chair. Dang! Someone had already snagged it. I had no other recourse other than sitting next to the greeter girl.

"I'm so glad we have English together." She twisted in her seat, facing me, rattling about this and that. I mostly nodded, tuning her out. I think she was babbling about the football team. It made me think about Logan, and my heart dropped. My first crush and I never got to kiss him. I pulled my book out and shoved my bag under the desk. Sally continued to ramble on about much to do with nothing. She was like background noise, only louder.

I think Sally had changed to her fifteenth topic when *he* swaggered in as if he owned the place. Even Sally had quieted to ogle the boy. It seemed that every eye in the room drew to him.

Sally leaned over and whispered while not taking her sight off the eye candy. I kept my eyes lowered behind my lashes. "He's the new menu," she revealed. "His name is Aidan Bane. I hear he's rich too! Of course, every girl in school hopes to land him! Rumors, yonno," she giggled.

"Thanks for the heads up," I shrugged. Gossip didn't bother me. Sara and I never stayed long enough anywhere for gossip to affect us. I reckoned there was a silver lining to our constant drifting.

Taking a quick peek, the new boy was a looker. Not someone you'd often see in these parts. Polished and well-groomed. The city type. The dude carried himself with that rock star quality that commanded others to sit up and take notice. Considering his towering height, he stood out with his raven curls. His dark and mysterious blue eyes appeared cold. One baleful glance could freeze the Sahara Desert. I summed him up as a snob, definitely not my type.

A girl had caught his full attention as he leaned closer, fully invested in their conversation. He flashed a cocky grin revealing straight white teeth. A nice contrast against his tawny skin. My neck bristled, watching the girl smile sweetly into his face. Why did I care? He was an empty soul. By the end of the day, the girl would be long forgotten and a notch on his belt. The boy was an easy read. The smell of wealth exuded off him. With his designer clothes, his cool swag, and charm, he had every girls' head turned, but not one name would caress his lips the following day. Yeah, I had his number-revered by every girl and envied by every boy. I reckoned that was life in the fast lane of a heartless rich boy.

When I caught tall-dark-and-arrogant etching his way down my aisle, I rushed to doodle on my book cover, my eyes glued to my book. Then I remembered the black hoodie hanging on the back of the seat behind me. "Jesus!" I mumbled to myself. I slid down in my chair, steadily drawing. *Don't look up! Don't look up.* I chanted internally.

In the next tick, a soft breeze grazed my left shoulder, followed by a quick thud and a male's soft groan as the desk protested under his weight with a sharp squeak. A woodsy scent drifted over my shoulder. I bore down on the ink, homing in on my drawing, determined to ignore his presence.

Unaware, a sudden tap on my shoulder alerted me. I ignored the boy, hoping he'd go away. But he persisted, giving a yank on my pony-tail. I squawked, swiftly grabbing my hair as I spun in my seat to confront him. I had full intentions to go ham-bone on the boy until our eyes collided. All at once, my mind drew and blank. I'd gotten caught in his blue-eyed snare like a fly trapped in a web.

An amused dimple toyed with me as he nodded over my shoulder, "Umm, interesting artwork."

"Huh," I merely uttered. I glanced back at my book and gasped. I'd drawn a stupid cupid. I rushed to flip my book over. "Thanks," I mumbled, feeling my face blister. I tried to tune him out by facing the chalkboard, but his faint laughter kept drifting over my shoulder.

I'd forgotten about Sally until I caught her odd stare pointed at me. Her dark eyes were sharp as glass. What on earth was she mulling around in her head? I cut my eyes at her with a look of warning. I was about to ask Sally what her problem was, but Ms. Jenkins entered the class. I'd never been so happy to see a teacher.

Lunch rolled around, and I headed for the cafeteria. I followed the long trail of students. Once I passed the double doors, the smell of food smacked me in the face, resuscitating my stomach back to life. I didn't eat dinner last night. I wanted to save my last coins for lunch today.

I got in line, grabbing a tray and flatware wrapped in a white paper napkin. Right away, my eyes went for the tamales. When I handed my coins to the cashier, I felt a finger tap me from behind. Startled, I twirled around, facing Sally. "Hey," I answered.

Sally smiled, ignoring my solemn face. "Come sit at my table. I'll introduce you to everyone." I opened my mouth to decline, but Sally had snatched my arm and started dragging me across the cafeteria. Giving in, I let Sally lead the way. We came to a stop at a table of three. That meant that Sally was the fourth one. I reckoned I was the fifth wheel. Been there done that, didn't care. Sally began the introductions, "Hey, y'all, this is my new friend in English. Everyone, meet Stevie Ray." I nodded, straining a smile. Sally started going around the table. First, she pointed to a brown-haired boy, a little on the skinny side but still cute. "Meet Sam Reynolds." She moved on across from him. "This is Jen Li." The girl smiled and waved her hand. Sally pointed to the last person sitting next to the boy, Sam, a bleached blonde with deadly fingernails and a scowl glued to her face, "And my dearest and BFF, Gina Peters." Sally bubbled with pride. Everyone smiled but the blonde. She rolled her eyes, giving attitude. "Whatever," she snarled.

Then the skinny boy, Sam, interjected. "Gina, will it hurt you to be nice? How often do we get someone new to this tired town?"

"One too many," she retorted, eyeballing me from my head to my toe.

I hesitated, debating whether I should sit somewhere else. I figured somewhere in the vicinity of the moon.

Jen came to my defense. "Just ignore Gina. She's in a good mood today. It's when she's chewing bullets is when you watch out," she smiled.

I laughed.

Sally spoke up. "Come on! Gina's teasing."

Sam got out of his seat and pulled the chair that separated him from the blonde. "Come sit next to me. I don't bite," he smiled, patting the chair. "I'm much purdier than anyone else here." With his Southern accent and dazzling smile, I gathered Sam was the peacemaker. He earned a few brownie points with me. The twinkle in his eyes reminded me of Logan. I sighed with longing. I accepted his offer and took the seat he held out. Everyone seemed friendly enough, excluding the sourpuss blonde. Maybe she'd soften since the others were open to me.

Jen was the first to start with the questions. "Where did you come from," she smiled warmly.

"West Texas, Sweetwater."

Jen laughed. "Is the water sweet?"

Everyone snickered.

I laughed. "Not really."

Sally asked. Her child-like voice leaped above everyone else's. "How do you like our little town?"

"So far, so good," I lied.

Sam leaned back, taking in a full view of me and chuckled. "You lyin', gul!" he teased. "Nobody likes this place."

I laughed. I seldom got called out. My eyes caught Sam's deep browns. "What can I say? You caught me," I shrugged, laughing.

The table burst into laughter, all but Gina. It seemed stewing was her perfume of the day. Then she started. "I heard your daddy was killed in a hit-and-run accident?" Her eyes were pointy like a witch's wart.

How did this chick know? Then it hit me like a bat to the head, *The Internet*. "Yes. That's right." I responded with no intonation, nor did I clarify.

The table became pin-dropping quiet.

"Did the police find the killer," Gina asked, not a lick of empathy in her voice. This girl was out for blood.

The last thing I wanted to do was spark a fight on the first day of school. Instead, I gave her a curt reply. "No."

"I bet your daddy looked like roadkill?" Gina barbed.

Before I could stop myself, I'd sprung to my feet. Everything else went black. Fists loaded, I lunged for the blonde's throat. Sam leaped in front of her, blocking me from ripping out that fake, bleach-blonde hair. "Watch it!" I stretched my arm over Sam, grabbing for Gina. "No one talks about my dad like that and lives."

"If you don't like it, leave," Gina bellowed, stepping back from my reach.

I looked up, and the whole cafeteria had swooped in around us. Amidst the crowd, I heard some of the jocks chanting, "Fight, fight, girl on girl!" Without warning, I went air born over someone's shoulder, feet dangling. I heard an older man's voice shout. "Get her outta her' now!" The deep voice sounded like my history teacher, Coach Matthew.

In my next breath, I'd blacked out.

When my eyes opened, the scent of rain swirled my senses. I was sitting propped against something hard. I lifted my gaze and saw the bruised clouds beyond the foliage of the tree. My brow perked. "Where am I?" I murmured to the chilled air, pushing through the cobwebs in my brain. Rubbing my eyes, I grumbled. "What happened?"

My hand grazed something underneath me. I looked down and noticed a dark coat underneath me. Someone had propped me against the large oak outside the cafeteria! "But who?" I looked around, noting that the rain had stopped. But the cold continued to linger. A shiver rolled through me.

A male clearing his throat pierced my mind, knocking me back to the present. I bolted to my feet too quickly and stumbled, falling into someone's arms.

"Oops! Steady does it," a velvety voice pierced the brisk air. When our eyes locked, my heart stopped. *The new boy!* Why was he here? I twisted from his embrace.

Not a word uttered, he scanned me with agitated eyes, dark and ominous like the sea before a storm. "How do you feel?" He drawled in a lazy tone.

"How did I get out here?"

"I'm Aidan Bane. And you are?"

"Stephanie Ray." A headache had reared its ugly head, and the throbbing was blinding. "I'm light-headed."

"It'll wear off in a while." He sounded like a doctor, remote, and clinical.

"Are you some kind of expert?" I snipped.

"Here, take my jacket." He ignored my question, holding out his jacket.

Our eyes locked for a heartbeat, and then I dropped my gaze and took his hoodie. "Thanks," I whispered irefully.

"You're welcome."

I fumbled with the large coat, trying to find the arm.

He drew back a sultry smile. "Here, let me help." He snatched the hoodie from my clumsy hands and laid it over my shoulders. All at once, a heady mix of spice and churned earth swallowed me.

Nothing was making sense. Why were we out here in the damp weather? "W-w-w-what happened?"

The boy shoved his hands in his pockets as he casually answered. "No worries, love!" For a minute, I let myself sink into his chiseled features.

Silence loomed between us as he leaned against the tree, his arms rested across his chest. The new boy's gaze slowly drifted over me as if we'd known each other intimately. I sensed it too. A familiarity lingered between us. Yet how could that be? I'd never laid eyes on him before today.

"Did you get to eat something," he asked. His voice still held no emotion.

I shook my head. "No."

"I can get you a burger."

Why does he care? "I'm fine. Thanks," I snapped. "You can go back inside. I don't need a babysitter." I shrugged his jacket off and handed it back to him, or I attempted.

"I can stay." He ignored my gesture.

Why is he stalling? "No. It's not necessary." I was short with him, still extending the jacket.

The boy paused for a minute, imprisoning my gaze. My heart kicked up a notch, staring into his intense eyes. He made me uncomfortable as I shifted my weight from foot to foot. His face remained unreadable, almost cold as he finally spoke. "As you wish." He pushed off from the tree, snatching his coat from my fingers, sauntering off like in the movies, tossing the hoodie over his right shoulder, disappearing inside the building.

He didn't bother giving me another glance. I didn't know why, but it tugged at my heart. Maybe I could've been more polite. Though when he wouldn't explain how I ended up under the tree, it grated me like sand in my shorts.

EERIE

*W*hen the last bell rang, I sucked in an audible breath. Finally, the day had ended. I wanted nothing more than to go home, get into my pajamas, crawl into my warm bed, and forget this day ever existed.

First, I needed to stop by the hardware store and see about reactivating my cell phone. I wasn't hopeful. Apart from having to go to a feed store to activate my phone gave me pause. I lived in gator county. At this point, I'd take whatever phone I could get, providing it was cheap.

Every penny had to be accounted for, which reminded me, I needed to get the landlord's number. Sara sucked at paying rent. I needed to make sure she didn't go half-cocked like last time, losing our money to a stupid psychic. They were all cons. Every last one!

I pushed through the metal doors at the school's main entrance and stepped out under the awning. I stopped. From zero to sixty, my heart sank to an all-time low. It was as if the heavens had rained down its wrath upon us miserable souls. Rain poured like a monsoon, and the temperature shifted into a frosty bite since lunch.

I shrugged on my dried-out hoodie, eyeballing my tied bike taking a beating. I could suck it up and go home or wait out the rain. I kept rocking on my heels, chewing my bottom lip. "Screw it!" In a fury, I shouldered my book bag, flipping the hoodie over my head, darting for my bike.

I was straddling my bike when I caught a dark shadow in the corner of my eye. I looked up, and a black Corvette was encroaching. Rain fell in my face and hindered my vision. Still, I knew that Corvette from anywhere. I eyed the sports car as it came to a slow halt beside me. A slew of worries rushed over me. Did the driver realize who I was? He should remember me. After all, he left me for the buzzards.

Slowly the tinted window slid down, revealing the mysterious driver, and when my eyes met his, my breath seized. It was the new boy... *Aidan Bane!*

"Jump in!" he shouted over the pounding rain, leaning halfway on the passenger's side. "I'll give you a ride."

I stood there, biting my bottom lip, indecisive. I did value my toes.

"C'mon!" Bane bellowed. "It's miserable."

"My bike, I can't leave it," I yelled back.

"No problem! I'll put it in the trunk." Before I could protest, he'd slid out of his car and reached my side before I batted my eyes. Geez, he moved fast.

"My bike won't fit," I argued, spitting out the water that gushed over my face.

A hint of humor hid behind his glint. "I got it!" He placed his hands on the handlebars. I hesitated, unsure if I should trust him, but my fingers were getting numb by the second. So, I folded. "Alright, I don't live far from here."

He tossed his hoodie to me, shouting, "Get in! It's warm." He reached over and opened the door. I nodded, awkwardly jumping inside. As soon as I settled in the seat, a blast of heat smothered my face. "Ah," I moaned. I held my fingers to the warm air, letting it work its magic. I wiggled my fingers, thinking this was heaven.

A few seconds later, Bane slipped into the driver's side, rain dripping off his dark curls. Once his door closed, the cab filled with that same woodsy aroma that seemed to follow him. I became aware of how tight we were inside the two-seater Corvette. His massive shoulders filled the small space. Pushed against his arm, I stiffened, unsure of what to do. Whenever I was in the proximity of a boy, I suddenly became a staggering fool, stumbling over my two left feet. It sucked being socially inept. Bane raked his fingers through his dark curls and tossed a pearly smile at me. I averted my eyes to the side window, biting my bottom lip. Talk about igniting a spark. I'd never felt this way with Logan. Of course, I'd never been up in his grill either. This was unfamiliar territory for me.

I slipped a glance at him, and a rush of chills came over me. The five o'clock shade lining his jaw made him appear older. I rolled my eyes to myself as I continued to peer out my side window. I was wasting my time ogling the boy. It was like looking at candy behind glass. What was the point? Rich boys and poor girls never meshed well together. Judging by the fancy car, a blind, deaf-mute could see the silver spoon in his mouth. No high school kid drove a brand-new Corvette working at McDonald's unless his daddy owned the franchise. Hands down, this guy's parents were loaded.

I was the poor girl on the wrong side of the bayou. Girls like me go unseen by the popular boys. So, why was he offering me a ride? Did he think I was one of those girls that hung on his tailored shirttail? I rolled my eyes. I bet this dude broke hearts for kicks.

"You look all nice and toasty." He measured me with a cool appraising glint.

"Thank you." I tossed him a sugarcane smile. "My address is…"

He cut me off. "I know your address, Princess." His Nordic blue eyes churned with amusement.

"No, you don't."

"Tangi's a small town. Everyone knows everyone."

"Yeah, but you're new too, right?"

"Your point?"

"I'm just saying it's strange that you know where I live when you don't even know my name."

"Like I said, the town is small." Humor radiated in his blues.

"Being a peeping Tom can be a hazardous hobby."

"Whoa, Princess! I don't sneak around. I'm always invited." There went the self-entitled prick's words of wisdom.

"I like your car." I smiled sweetly, changing the subject. "Not too many folks in these parts drive a brand-new Corvette."

"You don't say?" One dark brow perked.

"Yeah, actually, I do. A car just like this one nearly ended my life a few weeks ago. I was practically the bug splattered across the windshield."

"Sorry to hear about your misfortune."

"You should be!" I twisted in my seat, aiming green shards at his face.

"Come again?"

"You were the driver who left me stranded and injured!"

He barked a curt laugh. "I'd remember if I was in an accident."

Liar! I thought.

"Maybe you have selective amnesia!"

"My memory is excellent. Perhaps you have mistaken me for someone else."

"Deny all you want, but there ain't many Corvettes with a license tag reading, *Dropout!*" I crossed my arms, driving home a very incriminating fact. I planned to make an excellent attorney someday.

His blues shifted as if a light went off in his head. "Oh! That was you? The girl on the rusty bike," he snorted.

"Yes, that was me. Rusty-bike, girl." I could feel the angry fumes curdling inside me.

"Those are your words, not mine."

"Really? Did you not say…"

He interrupted. "Are you always so miserable? At lunch today, if I hadn't jumped in, you would've ripped that poor girl a new one. Why the anger?"

"Why the arrogance," I scoffed. "Oh! Just shut up!" I slammed back in my seat, my back to him, staring out the window. All at once, it hit me. I remembered why I wanted to fight Gina. How could I have forgotten?

Bane's brows pulled into an affronted frown. "I've been nothing but nice to you. Can't you return the favor?"

"Why? Because you left me on the side of the road for dead?"

"You didn't die," he chuckled.

My mouth morphed into an O. "Tell you what, you donkey rappin' poop eater, let's end this beautiful friendship right now." Why explain myself to a stranger who pegged me for a troublemaker. "Stop the car," I demanded. "I'd rather walk in a damn blizzard!"

"I thought we were having a lovely chat!"

"Oh, I love our little tête-à-tête so much that I want to kick rocks at your precious car." I went to open my door and stopped. We were sitting in my drive. I turned to him, wide-eyed, "How did we get to my house so fast?"

"I haven't a clue to what you mean, Princess." His blues had a sheen of mischief.

"It's only been a hot minute, and here we are. Did we fly?" I might've been rude, but the sardonic twitch to the corners of his lips fueled my mistrust.

"Perhaps you got your wings. You are an angel, after all."

"An angel? That's rich." I flung the door open and jumped out, murmuring, "Douche bag." I slammed the car door in his face. I was done. I sprinted for the porch, taking two steps at a time, and all the while, I sensed his eyes fixated on my rump. Whatta dipstick!

I rushed inside, closing the door behind me. I leaned on the door wiping the tears with the back of my hand. All I wanted was to go home, back to Texas. I felt like my heart was shattering. Then I realized I'd forgotten my bike. I fled out the door to catch him but stopped. I blinked, startled. There stood my bike on its kickstand directly in front of the door. My mouth hung open. "How did he get my bike out so fast? There was no pitter-patter of footfalls on the porch. Only a minute had passed. I spotted a folded piece of paper in the basket. A note? I flipped it open and read, *Looking forward to our next tête-à-tête, Aidan Bane.* The audacity of this guy blew my mind. He was wrong about me. I was not miserable. I was pissed off. *Big-freaking difference!*

A MESSAGE FROM THE DEAD

*I*t was cloudless Saturday, and I couldn't get enough of the
sweet scent of crepe myrtle. I'd taken an extra paper route.
Tangi Journal needed a fill-in for the day. The assigned delivery guy
couldn't run his route, something to do with a sick relative in the
hospital. I gladly took the offer. We needed the cash. Sara wasn't doing
well with tips. Not sure if I believed her, but what other choice did I
have? Strip-search the woman?

Since our move, I'd become more acquainted with Ms. Noel. I once
thought the bookstore, *Otherworldly*, was fascinating. Now that I had
the opportunity to spend time with my neighbor, the store paled in
comparison.

Ms. Noel had mounds of knowledge of magick, herbs, voodoo,
dead people, and everything else that belonged to the weird world of
extraordinaire. Even the word magic, Ms. Noel spelled it differently.
She said it divided the line between the phonies from the authentic
casters.

Ms. Noel certainly had the imagination better than any blockbuster
movie, and since I didn't have a television or a social life, I had plenty
of time on my hands to fill my brain with all her stories. I might not
share her beliefs, but all the same, she told some mighty interesting
tales. Whether the tales were true or not, it didn't matter to me. The
spiels were thrilling, holding my every breath. Often, I'd sit outside

with Ms. Noel on her porch, eating sweet potato pie, listening to the adventures from the past. I treasured our lazy afternoons.

According to Ms. Noel, her talents came from a long line of ancestors, centuries past. One relative, in particular, grabbed my attention the most was Marie Laveau, a direct decedent. Ms. Noel's bloodline was a mixture of African and French. Creole of color, she'd say. I thought it was cool to have such a rich history of kinfolk. I was almost envious. My bloodline was more on the line of a Heinz fifty-seven. I knew nothing about my folks' lineage. Sara claimed she and Dad didn't have family. I didn't question it. I think Ms. Noel had taken me under her wing like a grandchild. She once told me that she and her husband, now deceased, never had any children. Maybe my being around filled the loneliness for her. I know she filled mine.

Sara never paid a lot of mind to me growing up. I remembered many times wishing for a soccer mom or one that baked. Sara was cut from a completely other cloth.

Speaking of which, Sara hadn't been home for the last two weeks. Rumor had it that a co-worker from the diner had taken up her evenings, spilling over into the day. I hadn't had the pleasure of meeting the man. Not that I'd given it much thought. If he didn't end up dead, it was only a matter of time before Sara becomes bored and kicked him to the curve. Either way, the new beau was doomed.

Sara didn't have the best track record when it came to keeping boyfriends. They either disappeared mysteriously or ended up dead. Like I said, I stayed out of Sara's love life.

Suddenly my attention was jarred as I spotted Ms. Noel standing on her porch. I was on my bike, heading to the diner to grab a bite. I'd stopped off at the house for a quick shower and a fresh change of clothes.

"Hey, neighbor! Can ya stop by for a visit?" Ms. Noel bellowed sweetly.

"Sure!" I figured she might need to make groceries. A couple of times a week, I'd been running errands for her. I believed in returning a favor for a favor. Besides, if it hadn't been for Ms. Noel's kindness, I would've been suffering something awful. I slid off my bike, kicked the stand down, and jogged up the steps to Ms. Noel.

She greeted me with a bright smile and a hug. "I hope I ain't holdin' ya up none?"

"No, ma'am. Just heading to the diner is all."

"Oh, good! I have something special that I meant to share with ya." She opened her screen door, inviting me in.

"Ms. Noel, you've been generous enough," I protested.

"Nonsense, chile! Ain't ya been workin' my garden?"

A broad smile broke across my face. "Yeah, did you see how fat the tomatoes are getting?" Who would've thought that I had a green thumb?

"Yep! I saw 'em this mornin'. They sure is pretty," Ms. Noel smiled. "Now git in 'ere!" she ordered with gentle persuasion.

"Okay," I replied, stepping inside, happy to oblige. "I'm all yours."

"Follow me," she nodded as she headed toward the back.

I trailed after her toward the back of the house as my eyes washed over the interior. I suspected the house had weathered many years. A sofa with faded red roses and a rickety rocking chair placed next to the fireplace with a basket filled with knitting, it was my guess she'd been here most of her life. I didn't know what it felt like living in the same place for more than a month. Sara and I lived like gypsies.

"Right here, babee." Ms. Noel tossed over her shoulder and halted.

At first, I thought she might've been confused. She was eyeballing the plasterboard. Then Ms. Noel faced me. The expression on her face appeared strange. "Stevie, I think it's time. Don't be frightened. What I'm 'bout to show you, you might not understand, but I hope ya trust me to keep an open mind."

Her words hit me like a stone-cold brick in the face.

"Alright!" I swallowed hard.

"I got ya, babee! Ain't nothin' gonna happen ta ya."

I only nodded. Cliché as it may be, but my freaking knees were knocking.

All at once, Ms. Noel commenced chanting some kind of unfamiliar tune. Its cadence felt eerie and unnatural. Without warning, the white wall vanished, and a small, hidden room appeared. "What the...!" I stood gaping. I knew my neighbor worked with herbs and stuff, but this was far from what I'd imagined. I turned my gaze back to Ms. Noel and blurted out. "Are you a witch?"

Ms. Noel gave me a smile that sent my pulse racing. "Go on!" she insisted. "Have a seat, chile."

I hesitated, raking my eyes over the small room. I knew once I stepped across the threshold that I'd be embarking upon a world that I knew very little about, and I wasn't sure if I was ready to accept it's a paradox. Slowly, I eased my hand past the threshold to confirm I wasn't hallucinating. Eerily, the only thing my fingers touched was the crisp air. I gasped, swiftly drawing my hand to my chest. Regardless of how much I wanted this to be a figment of my overactive imagination, I couldn't deny the fact that it was real.

Curious as nine cats and just as terrified, I eased a foot over into the room. I wrinkled my nose, turning back to Ms. Noel. "I can't believe my own eyes."

Ms. Noel's body jiggled as she laughed softly. "Chile, the possibilities have never been in question." She placed her hand gently on my shoulder. "It's always been at ya reach. Just open those pretty green eyes of yours."

"Alright." Even though I was terrified, I took a leap of faith and settled down in one of the chairs at a small round table draped with a deep velvety purple cloth that glistened in the candlelight. Ms. Noel sat across from me.

I sat in silence for a moment, eyeing the shadows dancing from the candlelight, making the tight space appear eerie. There was a library of various books on casting spells. I right away spotted a deck of tarot cards laid in a neat stack and a crystal ball placed on the table. All the things one would need to consort with the spirit world, I reckoned. Reading books and listening to stories about ghosts and things beyond was one thing. Dabbling was a whole 'nother story.

"Babee, how ya are?" she smiled. "Ya lookin' a little feeble."

"This is sorta freaky." I pointed to the hundreds of symbols that papered the interior walls.

A sheen of purpose sparkled in my neighbor's eyes. "I grew up with magick, and you have nothing to fear."

I shook my head, unconvinced, "Why are you showing me this now?"

"Fannie has a message ta give ya."

"Your dead sister?" My heart lurched.

"Yes, she has a message from someone on the other side."

"The other side?" My breath lodged in my throat. "Like someone dead?"

"Yes, do ya have a family member who's passed?"

"No." I hated lying to her, but I panicked.

"Do ya trust me, chile?"

"Yes, but it's not you, I fear." A faint thread of hysteria was teetering on the edge of me.

"Ya have hesitance?"

"Uh, kind of," I shrugged.

"Babee, has ya mama ever talked ta ya?"

My brow arched, "About what?"

"About ya life, babee."

"What's there to tell?"

"Chile, it's about the death of ya father."

My chin dropped. "My dad?"

"Babee, the spirit world speaks ta me."

"A ghost told you about my father's murderer?" Surprise drained the blood from my face.

"Yes," Ms. Noel answered with confidence. "In the afterlife, messages are never given all at once. It's like a puzzle. You receive only bits and pieces at a time until you can see the whole picture."

"What do you know about my father?"

"Ya father's death was deliberate." Ms. Noel's words were uncanny.

"Yeah, I reckoned it was deliberate. The authorities suspect it's a drunk driver."

"The driver wasn't bug-juiced."

"You mean drunk?"

"Chile, the police don't always get it right."

Tears began to sting. "I was eight when he died," I whispered.

"I feel your pain, babee. All the more reason why you need to hear what Fannie has to say."

I looked away, needing a moment to gather my thoughts. The loss of my father was still raw. I'd been so lost without him for such a long time.

"Fannie is here. She's been askin' about ya." Ms. Noel gently nudged.

"Can you relay the message?"

"Possibly, but we just have to see. The afterlife tells the story as they wish. We can't control their time of giving."

The thought of speaking to the dead twisted my gut something fierce, but if Fannie could shed some light on my dad's murder case, then I owed it to him to find out what I can. "Okay, let's do this."

Ms. Noel placed a lit candle in the middle of the table as we clasped hands. My pulse shot up, but I couldn't quit now. I'd stepped over the threshold to the point of no return.

Ms. Noel began with a strange incantation similar to Spanish, yet different. I think she was chanting Latin. The air in the room began to thicken, and I began to feel like the room was swirling like a merry-go-round at warp speed. No matter what, I kept my eyes glued to Ms. Noel's face. I shut my eyes tight, daring not to breathe. Ms. Noel proceeded, calling out to her sister. "Fannie, we're here. Come ta the light and speak ta us."

The candle in the center of the table began to ignite. Its flame licked at the ceiling like it was agitated. Doubt laced with raw fear started to sink in my mind. Had I made the right decision?

With no warning, Ms. Noel's body went limp. She'd fainted as her head dropped to the table, making a loud thud. Fear shot through me as I called out to her, "Ms. Noel, are you okay?" I raked my eyes over her, hoping to see any sign of life.

Finally, I caught a slight rise and fall of her chest. "Whew!" I blew out. This was a bad idea. I needed to end this séance now. Using all my strength, I tugged on my hands, but my efforts were futile. Ms. Noel's ironclad grip was much stronger than I had anticipated. Crap! I was powerless.

With a sudden force, Ms. Noel's head shot up. The iris of her eyes had vanished, revealing on the whites of her eyes like a person possessed.

"Holy hell!" I gasped. This took freaky to a whole new level.

Then terror strangled any chance of escape and got crazier than schizoids off meds. Ms. Noel's head started thrashing like a seizure, veins jutting from her temples. I swore if her head swiveled and she started puking green stuff, I was cutting my hands off!

Then Ms. Noel calmed like still waters, and her eyes returned to normal. "Mercy me! Someone else is interfering with my sister." She dragged in a raddled breath. "Do you know anyone by the name..." she paused, squinting her eyes tight. "The name sounds like John. Only it's spelled differently."

I nearly fainted. "My dad, Jon!"

"Yes, J.O.N," she spelled out the word. "He wishes to speak!"

A soft gasp escaped my lips.

"Ya father is talkin' about a soda parlor and Bubble Gum Jubilee."

"Oh, my God," I shook my head. "That's my favorite ice cream!"

"Yes, he's talkin' about a boy. He keeps repeatin' a faceless boy.'"

I sat there, blank-faced. I'd never told anyone about my dreams.

"He's warnin' ya! Keep away from him."

"A faceless boy?" The hairs on my neck stiffened like a Brillo pad. How could anyone have known?

"Yes, the boy is wearin' a ring on his left hand, the fourth finger. He says it is a symbol, an eye."

Oh-my-God! It was as if she was reading my mind. "I've been having that dream since my father's death. I was eight years old."

"Ya father has something to tell you. A warning." Ms. Noel's eyes closed. "He's tellin' me that the faceless boy, the ring, and a powerful family, are spooling spells of dark magick over ya."

"Seriously?" A wave of foreboding came over me.

"Does the term genetically engineered mean anything ta ya?"

I blinked back my confusion. "No. It doesn't."

"Your father keeps repeating this."

I shook my head, freaked out. "No! I haven't a clue." As strange and foreign as it sounded, I sensed an inherent familiarity with the phrase. Yet, I had no idea what my dad was meaning.

"Your father's repeating something about ya blood. He says it's not of his."

"What is that supposed to mean?" My brows puckered into a frown.

"His words are broken," she paused. "He's concern about a secret society, a very old faction. They're not gonna let ya go until they have taken what is theirs. Some kind of gift ya possess."

"A gift? I don't have anything of value."

"He keeps sayin' beware of the faceless boy." "Ms. Noel, you're scaring me!"

"Ya father is speakin' about ya mama now. He says ya should ask her why she's runnin'."

"My mom isn't running. She's bipolar." I wanted to hear more about my dad and his death.

Just as quickly as the séance had begun, it was over just as fast. Ms.

Noel released her grip, and I drew my hands to my chest, rubbing the numbness.

"Lord, have mercy! That was one strong spirit," she smiled weakly, patting the beaded sweat from her forehead with a napkin. I fretted that she might've had a stroke.

"Let me get you some water." I spun on my heels, rushing to the kitchen. I'd returned with a cold glass of water and ice wrapped in a dishtowel. "Here! This might help." I handed the water and the iced towel to her. My eyes washed over her, wondering what else I could do.

"Thank ya, babee," Ms. Noel flashed a weak smile. She sat there and sipped on the water, holding the towel to her head.

"Would you be more comfortable on your bed or the sofa?" Guilt racked my mind as I felt this was my fault.

"I'm fine." She patted my hand. "Mercy me! That was a doozy."

"Ms. Noel, let me help you to your bed." I should've protested, refused, and walked away. Anything other than sitting here, letting my good friend go through torture.

"Babee, I'll be just fine. Don't fret none!"

My lungs were starting to open, and I was beginning to relax. Ms. Noel's color started to return to normal. I smiled, though my concern continued. "Do you want more water?" I started reaching for her glass, but she patted my hand.

"No, Babee, I need ta speak about a pressing matter."

"Not now. You need your rest. Do I need to get your heart medicine?" I was at my max. I felt a headache on the horizon. I think I'd had my fill of seances to do me a lifetime.

"Babee, I need ta say something. Your mama is hidin' something from you."

"I don't want to talk about my mother."

"I don't like tellin' ya this, but your father is worried. He kept saying your mama is keepin' a dark secret." She drew in a frail breath.

My lips flattened, tight with tension. The topic of Sara always sent me into orbit. No one could subdue her spirit. I gave up a long time ago, trying to figure my mother out. "Ms. Noel, I doubt Sara can barely hold a thought. She's bipolar."

"I git what ya sayin', but ya need to know what secret ya mama is keepin'."

I appreciated her concern, but I didn't have the strength to waste on Sara. "I know you mean well, but my mother is who she is, and I can't change her." I shrugged. "I just deal with her mental illness."

"I'm sorry for ya troubles, babee, but I think it's in ya best interest ta hear me out."

I suddenly pushed away from the table. "I know Sara harbors secrets. She's been like this since my father's death." I raked my fingers through my hair. "Asking her questions will get me nowhere. If she is holding some traumatizing secret, I'll never know what it is. Sara will go to her grave before she confides in me." I crossed my arms, feeling shaky.

"Stevie… "

I held my palm up, halting her next words. I hated myself for my abruptness, but I had enough on my plate. "I don't understand any of this stuff." I paused. "You've had your whole life to make sense of the paranormal. I've had five minutes. I'm not even sure I believe in ghosts and magick. How am I supposed to accept something I know nothing about?"

"Everything is new, but ya will come around." Ms. Noel's voice was kind and hopeful. Yet, I wasn't ready to accept the world of extraordinaire. "I love your stories, but I can't swallow all of this in one sitting. Heck! I'm not sure I believe in God. So if you don't mind, I'd like to excuse myself."

"Of course, babee. I know it will take a bit of time, but ya'll come around."

I hugged Ms. Noel at the door. I didn't want her to think I was angry with her. I started to push past the screen, but I hesitated. "I'm sorry that I can't believe your way." Tears began to well up, and I ducked out before I made a fool of myself.

BURIED SECRETS

I darted inside the diner, scurrying past customers, headed straight to the far back booth. I scooted into the seat with an irritated huff. I rested my head on the cool table and closed my eyes. My heart was beating erratically.

I was crazy believing an eighty-something-year-old woman's tall tales about a stupid ghost. Then how the hell did she know about the faceless boy and the ring? How did Ms. Noel know about my life? She seemed to have this sick sense. Yeah, I meant sick. I had a hard time swallowing her far-fetched beliefs. What did I know? I never fretted over my lost soul or bothered putting faith in a God that I'd never met.

Then I recalled Ms. Noel rambling about some vile family coming for me. I found that hard to believe. I was a girl pushing newspapers. What would be the point of kidnapping me? I didn't have a penny to my name.

Unexpectedly, I got a weird sensation that jolted me to a sitting position. My eyes landed on a man staring at me like I was a deer in the scope of his gun. He must be Sara's new boyfriend. I watched as he headed my way.

Crap!

"Bonjour, beautiful!" he flashed a lustful smile as he slid into the booth next to me. I slid over with my back to the wall. He was the last person I wanted to see. I'd already developed a distaste for the man.

Between pickled boy's dirty ink hair to his cigarette-liquored breath and the wicked glint in his anthracite eyes, the man made my skin crawl.

Ms. Noel mentioned that rumors were floating about Francis spending time in prison. He'd gotten busted for drugs. I usually didn't put a lot of stock into hearsay, but I believed this rumor.

"Don't you have a dish to wash?" I eyed his dirty apron. I reckoned dishwashing was the best job he could get. He appeared younger than Sara. My guess, maybe a good fifteen years difference. I watched in silence as he lit his cigarette. His dark eyes never wavered from me as if I was a rib-eye steak. "I'm on break." He blew out a stream of smoke. "Since I'm practically family, I thought I should meet the person my girlfriend often speaks about," he grinned. "I'm Francis."

"Thanks for the introduction. You can leave now." I didn't care if I was behaving rudely. I just wanted to be left alone.

"You look like you've seen a ghost," he laughed with a thick Cajun French accent, drawing on his cigarette.

"I'm fine," I answered curtly.

He snickered as he rattled off French. "Vous ferez mieux d'être gentile avec, moi" (You will like me or else we will have an issue, yes?)

I didn't have to understand French to understand his threat. But I was one step ahead. I'd taken French in school, a little private joke that I intended to keep to myself. "Why don't you just say it?"

"I could say the same to you," he countered with disdain in his seedy eyes.

"What do you want?" It was evident he was trying to intimidate me.

He rubbed his scruffy chin, pinning his eyes to mine. "You remind me of a kitten I once had. A feisty little thing." He drew in his cigarette; the cherry burned a bright red. Then he released a stream of smoke directly in my face.

I began coughing, swatting to clear the cloud of smoke. The jerk was taunting me. Showing how big of a man he wasn't. I detested him. "I came here to see my mom. Do you mind?" Neither one of us held any love for each other. The funny part was I knew far too well his future. Maybe I should warn him to get life insurance? Nah, why bother with this piece of trash. Let him meet his own doom.

"No, not at all." His eyes glistened like black obsidian. "First, I have one thing I want you to understand." He flashed his tobacco-stained teeth. "Your mom and I are together. Don't give her any shit. I'm here to stay." Not another word uttered, he stamped out his cigarette on the laminated tabletop and slid from the booth, carting a fat smirk across his face like he'd made some gangsters move. I watched in silence as he disappeared to the back. His message was clear. He purposely bypassed the ashtray on the table to convey a message. He didn't want me pissing on his parade. Maybe I should've told him to get insurance? Then my mind drifted to Ms. Noel. I felt horrible leaving her. I overreacted. Talking about Dad was a hard subject for me. His death came unexpectedly. He was my world, and then he was gone, and my life had been a mess ever since.

Even Sara changed into an unrecognizable person. About six months after Dad's death, she ended up arrested for shoplifting at Neiman Marcus. When they had apprehended her, she became Batesville crazy. They had to admit her into the mental ward at the local hospital. That was when the doctors diagnosed Sara with bipolar, extreme highs, and lows. Though, I'd never seen very many highs.

Despite what Ms. Noel thought, I had to disagree. Sara's instability and paranoia stemmed from her illness. Apart from dodging landlords, Sara had no reason to run.

I raked my eyes over the diner and spied Sara. She was finishing up an order. When she stuck her pad in her pocket, she noticed me. A slight tug at the corner of her lips tipped upward as she made her way toward me. The lunch crowd had thinned, and the diner had only a couple of tables taken. Good! I might have a chance to talk with her.

Sara hadn't been to the house since we moved in. I suspected she'd been staying with Francis. Oddly, she hadn't been home to get any of her clothes. Sara never went without her precious possessions. She cherished the expensive gifts men had given her. She was good at getting men to buy her designer clothes. Though not one of her wealthy boyfriends ever stood before a preacher with her. I didn't understand what Sara saw in Francis. He wasn't her type. The man probably didn't have a bucket to piss in. Good grief, he washed dishes for a living. She usually dated men with deep pockets. It was just weird. Moving here was weird. "Well, hello there, stranger!" Sara wore her Mommy-smile today.

"If you'd come home once and a while, I wouldn't be a stranger," I smiled back with a little attitude.

"You want something to eat?" Smacking on a piece of gum, she pulled out her pad from her pocket and drew the pin from her ear.

"Just a chocolate shake and fries, please."

Suddenly Sara's brows knitted, staring down at the table. "Did you make that mess?" She pointed to the crumpled cigarette butt lying on the table.

"It belongs to lover boy, Frank," I shrugged, keeping my irritation undetected.

Sara eyed me for a minute. I knew she didn't believe me. "Francis is his name," she huffed. "I'll bring your food to you shortly." She stuck her pad in her pocket. "Clean this mess up before my boss sees it." Sara darted off before I could protest. I moved down to another booth. By the time he returned, her mind would be elsewhere.

I rested my head on my hands, propping my elbows on the table. My mind drifted to a time when life was happy. When Dad was alive, I had the best life. We lived in a farm community outside of Eufaula, Oklahoma. Dad ran a one-man law firm there. He might've been an attorney working in a small town, but he was no small fry. The locals' loved and respected him.

We owned a small farm just outside the city limits. Country life was wonderful. My favorite thing in the whole world was gathering eggs. I sighed. It was funny how the most mundane things brought happiness. If I had a time machine, I'd go back to that moment and stop Dad from jogging that unseemly morning. He'd be alive, and the world would be a better place. I withdrew a painful sigh.

I heard Sara's heels clanking down the aisle. I never got how she wore heels waitressing. I sat up straight, shoulders back. I needed to have my questions in order. Pulling answers from Sara was like yanking a tooth from a charging rhino.

The plate of curly fries was sizzling as Sara set the pile in front of me. I eyeballed the chocolate shake. I couldn't wait for it as I snatched it up first. Sara settled into the seat across from me, sipping on her coffee. We shared a moment of quiet while I ate my salty fries.

To my surprise, Sara started the conversation first. "Did you have a nice chat with Fran?" She sipped her coffee.

"I guess." I wanted to avoid this subject altogether.

"I hope you'll give him a chance. He's pretty special to me."

"What do you see in this greasy man?" I dropped my fry back on the plate.

Sara's pointed her heated eyes at me. "What do you mean?"

"I don't get why you like him?"

"If you'd give him five minutes of your time and cut out your attitude, you might like him."

"Mom, he's a loser and closer to my age than yours."

"Age is only a number. Francis makes me happy."

"He's a creep!"

"Fran is different, that's all." I knew I was treading on ice here. Sara shot me one of her hostile glares.

"Whatever!" I folded my arms. What was the point? Sara was hell-bent on staying with the scumbag.

"If it weren't for the landlord, he'd be living with us." Sara pouted like a toddler at nap time. "I've never met the landlord, only his butler. He's probably some old, fat fart."

"Sorry to hear that," I slurped my shake.

Sara snorted, "I bet you are." She turned her back to me, stewing as if it was my fault.

"If you give me the landlord's information, I'll handle him." I was glad she mentioned him. I needed to check if she was paying rent.

"Oh! No, you don't! I ain't givin' you nothin'. The last time I gave you that information, you made me look like a fool!"

"That's because you didn't pay the rent!"

"What are you talkin' about? I gave that man his money."

I loved my mother, but I think she believed her lies. I didn't want to get into it, so I changed the subject. "Mom, have you heard any news about Dad's case?"

Sara's body went rigid. "What do you mean?"

"I mean, has the police called on any new leads about Dad?"

"Why bother? That's one mystery that will never get resolved

"We can't give up?"

Sara twisted in her seat, facing me and scoffed. "That ship sailed ten years ago." The coldness in her voice gave me chills.

"If it had been one of us, Dad would've never stopped looking until he had found the killer."

"Oh, stop making Jon into a saint."

"And you're better?" I replied with reckless ire.

"Watch your mouth. Fran's on the other side of those doors." Sara nodded toward the back. "He won't tolerate you sassin' me."

"I can't believe you're threatening me with your new beau." I leaned closer and whispered. "We both know that your boy is doomed." I sat back up, holding my eyes to Sara's startled gaze.

"You act like I'm jinxed!"

"Remember, Charles?" I threw at Sara, hoping to jar her memory.

"I don't know what you're talkin' about." She shifted in her seat.

I knew this wasn't going to be easy. Sara was a master at skirting around questions. I pushed further. "Then, let's talk about why you have to move every other month."

"Who's been in your ear lately?"

"You need to know that I'm contacting the Eufaula police."

"Oh! For Pete's sake! Move on. Jon is dead, and he ain't ever coming back."

"I'll move on when Dad's killer is locked behind bars!"

"I am sure that person is paying for his mishaps in one way or another." It was easy for Sara to dismiss Dad's death. I think she thought if we didn't talk about it, it'd go away.

"Dad deserves our loyalty."

"Your father is nothing more than bones. Get a life! I have." Her words were hard-bitten. And it sent me mad to the moon.

"How can you say that?" My voice broke. "Moving on isn't jumping from one abandoned town after another, living in cheap hotels and being homeless, eating out of garbage cans!"

A muscle flicked angrily along Sara's jawline. "I'm getting tired of your piss poor attitude!"

"Fine!" I hissed through my teeth. Before I could stop myself, I shoved all the dishes off the table, sending them crashing to the floor in a flurry. The clatter echoed throughout the whole diner.

When my gaze lifted, I noticed several pairs of marbled eyes watching, and I couldn't bear to look at Sara's face anymore. I slid from the booth, and in my fleeting moment, I lashed out at her. "All my life, you've cared more about your boyfriends and your liquor than being a mother to me," Anger coiled around my heart and squeezed. "I wonder at times if I'm even your daughter."

Sara's eyes ignited. "You have no idea, missy, what I've sacrificed. I am dearly paying for it now. So don't you throw your shit at me!"

I refused to stand there another minute. Without further ado, I darted out the diner, and in seconds, I was on my bike and down the street, putting distance between Sara and me.

THIRD ENCOUNTER

The first week of school, I'd survived. Gina had pretty much resigned to leaving me alone except for an occasional eye roll. I could deal with that. I'd become more acquainted with Sam and Jen. Sally, I tolerated.

English, my first class, when I entered the room, Sally jerked her head up and smiled far too brightly for the morning. I hated happy people in the morning before I had my coffee. With Sally, I needed at least ten cups to fight off her un-abating yammering. The girl never stopped.

I dropped my books on my desk and flopped down in my seat. I noticed the desk behind me was empty. Bane had taken absence for the last weeks. I wondered if I'd seen the last of him. Maybe his family decided to leave this dead town. I wish I could do the same.

Without wasting a minute, Sally swiveled in her seat, facing me. "Good morning!" she sang. In the presence of Sally, it should be a requirement to wear shades. My clothes might be worn, but her choice of style could hurt a blind man. The loud orange and overzealous smile were giving me a headache.

"Morning," I grumbled, slipping down into my seat, lowering my cap over my eyes. I reached into my bag and pulled out a book that I'd been reading. It was one of my favorites. Since we didn't have TV, I had two choices, study or recreational reading.

Sally eyeballed the book cover. "Is that an assigned book for class?"

I sighed as I flashed the book up, showing her the cover. "Nope," I answered, returning to my book.

"To Kill a Mockingbird? That doesn't sound very exciting." She leaned over, peeking at the page.

"It's a classic."

She shrugged. "I usually just look at the cheat notes."

I rolled my eyes, not surprised. "You've never heard of Harper Lee. Her book won the Pulitzer Prize."

"Oh," she shrugged. "Unless it has a cute boy in the story, I'm not interested."

"There's more to life than ogling boys." Sally reminded me of a mule with blinders.

"Do you have a boyfriend," she probed.

"Nope! Don't have time." I went back to reading.

"I make time. I'd rather have a boyfriend than reading some old book that's not even current."

A thin line between my brows deepened in surprise. I think Sally just threw some shade at me. I dropped my book and looked her in the eye. "My book isn't boring. The author happens to be a renowned writer. Dating is pointless." I returned back to my book.

"Why do you say that?"

"Why start something I can't finish?" I shrugged. I didn't care to expose my wounds to Sally. Jump-skipping town after town was a sore spot for me.

"Oh, yeah, I see your point." There was a pause. "What about the new boy, Aidan? I saw you riding in his car the other day."

Good grief! Gossip girl was on the prowl. "Yeah, it was raining, and I was riding my bike. He was just trying to be nice." I stuffed my book back in my bag. Class would be starting soon anyway. Not that it would keep Sally from talking.

"What's he like?" Sally kept prying.

"Apart from him behaving like a total douche, nothing special." Geez! She was like a dog with a newfound bone.

"Who cares about his snobby attitude when he's hot?"

"Then, you date 'em!" My implacable expression was more than a hint that I didn't give a rat's ass.

When I twisted in my seat, reaching for my homework, my gaze collided with two steel-blue eyes. *Bane!* When did he get here? I could've sworn his seat was vacant a moment ago. I swore things just kept getting weirder whenever Bane decided to show his face.

I kept my eyes glued to my notes on Macbeth. Shakespeare's shortest tragedy, about a Scottish general who received a prophecy from a trio of witches that he would become King of Scotland. It ended badly. I reckoned ambition was the seal of his fate.

Unexpectedly, I felt a sharp poke in my back. Geez! Can't I sit here in peace without anyone pestering me? I tipped my shoulder down just enough to see him from the corner of my eye. The last thing I wanted was to be stuck in eye contact with those brain-eating blues. "Why are you stabbing me?" The irritation in my voice was quite apparent.

"Sorry, Princess! I only wanted to know the assignment?" I could feel his amusement bristling my neck.

"If you attended class once in a while, you wouldn't have to ask."

"Nah, I'd rather ask you, so I can see your beautiful face blister," he flashed a pearly smile.

A few snickers erupted down the row from a couple of boys.

"Whatever!" I turned back, facing the front. A chuckle wafted over my shoulder. I ignored it just like I planned on ignoring the occupant.

As usual, the teacher walked in as the bell rang. Even Sally faced the front. It was nice hearing from the teacher for a change.

The clock struck noon, and I headed to the cafeteria. Short on cash today, I had just enough to buy a Coke. Eh, I'd been worse off. I ran my dollar through the machine and punched the button. I grabbed my drink and headed off for the usual table. I enjoyed my lunchtime with Sam and Jen. I mostly ignored Sally and her BFF, Gina.

A little guilt pricked my conscience. Sally nearly busted her gut, trying to win me over. It wasn't that I didn't like her. I did. It was just that Sally was far too intense. Listening to her constant dribble exhausted me. If she'd take a breath between subjects, I might ease up on her.

Then there was Sally's best friend, Gina. The two were inseparable. Gina was a problem for me. It was sort of hard to forget the roadkill remark. So, if I had to keep my distance from Sally to avoid blondzilla, I reckoned that was a tough price to pay.

As I made my way to the back, I spotted Jen's dark head. She was waving at me. I smiled as I pushed through students to where we sat every day.

"Hey, girl! I saved you a seat." Jen patted the spot beside her and smiled up at me.

"Cool!" I grinned back. I flopped down into my chair and twisted the cap on my drink.

"That's all you're eating," Jen asked, eyeing my drink.

"Girl, I can live on Coke."

We laughed.

"You want some of my fries?" She pushed them over to me.

I had to admit they smelled delicious and taunted my growling stomach. "Thanks!" I grabbed one and smiled.

Just then, my gaze caught Gina's snarl. An eye roll to myself was in order. I dropped my gaze from the sourpuss and skirted around her, stopping on Sam. You couldn't tell by looking at the boy that he played football. It amazed me how he kept from getting clobbered. With all the muscled-up jocks, Sam got swallowed up. He was tall enough but didn't have much meat on his bones. With those long legs of his, he could run like the wind. I liked hanging out with Sam. He was charming and funny. From his chestnut hair to the twinkle in his hazel eyes, he put a smile on my face every time.

"Hey, Chickadee!" Sam had given me that nickname on the second day of school. It was silly, but it made me laugh.

"Hey, Sam!" My lips grew into an unconscious smile.

"Why ain't you eatin'?" His glistening eyes darted from my face to my drink. I loved his rich Southern drawl. "Oh, I'm not hungry." I lied. It was too embarrassing.

Sally just walked up with a tray full of food and plopped down beside me, directly across from Gina and Sam. "I'm starving," she announced, a little out of breath.

Gina snarled her nose. "You should eat a salad. You're fat enough."

Sam broke in. "Gina, leave her alone." He cut a sharp look at her.

"I'm just saying." She wallowed her eyes. "Sally, if you gain four hundred pounds, don't come crying to me."

Suddenly, I caught a shadow of an outline from the side of my view. *Bane!* I heard a chair screeching across the floor. He'd dragged up a chair next to me and leaned over, placing a white bag on the table directly in front of me. He was so close, our lips nearly touched. "Hope you like burgers." Amusement danced in his eyes.

"Umm, thanks."

"You are quite welcome, Princess."

Sally spoke up, eyeing my sack. "No fair! Where's everybody else's?"

"My apologies, just for Stevie." Aidan winked at me, but strangely, when he bounced to his feet, he flashed Sam a hard scowl. By the glares shared between the two, I sensed there was some sort of discord be. By the glares shared between the two, it was obvious those two harbored some kind of discord. It struck me odd when Bane was a new student. Yet, I didn't like Gina and nearly ended in a hair-pulling brawl.

I watched as Bane weaved his way through the students, leaving the cafeteria. I couldn't help but admire his stature, tall and poised, moving fluidly. If I could bottle his catwalk in a packaged, it would blow up the market. I sighed softly to myself.

Then I remembered the bag. I snatched it up and opened it. Inside, just as he promised, a burger and fries and a peanut butter cookie. A smile stretched across my face as I grabbed the cookie first.

When I lifted my eyes, I caught Sam staring a hole through me. resentment lingered behind his glint. "So, you and Old Blue are friends?"

I shrugged. "Not really. Bane gave me a ride home the other day. It didn't end well." I took a huge bite of my cookie.

Then Gina decided to add her two cents. "I'm not surprised he noticed you. With those faded clothes of yours, you look like you live in a dumpster."

I laughed darkly, firing back. "I reckon it beats standing at the corner like you." I shot a mocking grin.

Gina leaped to her feet, nearly blowing fire from her nose.

I grinned at the blonde, unbothered, taking another bite of my delicious cookie.

Quickly, Sam snaked his arms around Gina's waist, easing her back down into her seat. He swore under his breath. "You don't have a right to get torqued when you throw the first jab." He pressed his palm against her chest. "Sit your ass down and shut up!"

Jen and I shared a glance. Our arched brows parroted each other.

"I don't care," Gina bellowed. "I don't want her sitting at our table."

Jen jumped in. "Gina, if you don't like the company, you can leave."

Sally's face was solemn as she played with her food, not uttering a word.

"Fine! I'll leave," she snorted. "Come on, Sam!" Gina pulled from the table and gathered her tray. Sam remained seated. Gina gawked at Sam, totally taken by surprise. "You're not coming?"

"Nope!" he flashed a bright smile. "I'm stayin' right her', sugar-pie." Gina looked like she was going to sprout horns. Jen and I shared a sideways glance and giggled. Watching Gina getting rejected was priceless.

Gina turned her angry eyes on me. "Oh, shut up, bitch!" I snickered. Slinging mad never bothered me.

Jen intervened, "Gina, just go."

"You were my friend before she moved here!" Gina bellowed and then cut her eyes back at me. "I'm going to go find that blued eyed boy, Aidan. Bet he'd sit with me." At that moment, my burger nearly lodged in my throat. Gina's declaration bothered me. The idea of that girl putting her paws on Bane ripped through me.

Jen laughed. "Girl, bye! The only person you're friends with is your mirror."

Other than a sharp huff, Gina snatched her tray and stomped off. Sally scooted her chair from the table and gathered to her feet, gathering her tray. "Sorry, y'all I gotta stick with my girls." And without another word, Sally left with her friend.

"Gul," Sam tapped my hand, "Don't pay Gina no mind. The principal
stripped her cheerleading status and gave the position to one of her rivals."

"That's terrible," I laughed.

Jen snickered. "I never liked Gina anyway."

Sam bit down on his sandwich, leaving half. He chewed while giving his advice. "Just ignore the gul. She'll move on to someone else when she doesn't get a rise out of you."

Jen asked. "Hey, Saturday night, we're hanging out. You should come."

"I don't know," I answered, biting my bottom lip, indecisive. Did I want a repeat of Sweetwater? "Whatcha got planned?"

Jen pitched in. "Let's shoot pool at Mother Blues!"

"Great idea," Sam smiled.

I shrugged, unsure. "Who's coming?"

Sam answered. "Since Gina uninvited herself, it should just be us."

"Don't worry about Gina," Jen reassured me. "Tomorrow, she might be hating on Sally."

We all laughed.

"That new guy," Jen giggled. "We should invite him too."

"Nah, leave Old Blue alone. He's trouble, gul."

"What have you heard?" He suddenly grabbed my attention.

"Nothing good." Sam went on to say. "I heard he's had a run-in with the law. He has a bad temper. Beat the crap out of some guy. He got sent to juvie."

That explained the dirty looks between Sam and Bane. "Wow! I'm not surprised."

"A bad boy!" Jen nudged my shoulder. "That might be fun."

"So, I guess we won't be inviting him Saturday," I teased.

"You guessed right," Sam chimed in. "We'll pick you up at eight."

"Cool! Sounds like a plan," I smiled.

The last bell echoed through the halls sending students rushing for the doors. School had ended, and another day had passed for me to cross off the calendar.

I pushed my way to my locker to unload the load to lighten my bike ride home. I popped the lock open and started stuffing my books away. I took a mental note that I needed to clean my locker out first chance. Once I finished, I shouldered my bag and whirled on my feet to leave when I collided into a firm chest. "Ouch!" irritation fluttered through me, and then my gaze hitched with two very vivid blue eyes. "Damn! Bane, watch where you're going." His name slipped from my tongue too easily.

He seemed unruffled as a faint smile unfolded. "That's what I am doing...*watching*."

I glowered, not liking his innuendo. "Don't be a perv."

He leaned in, lightly pressing his palms on each side of the locker, pinning me against the wall and leaving only a thin wafer of space between our bodies. "First, you accused me of being a peeping-Tom, and now I'm a perv." Amusement churned in his blue eyes.

"Cut it out, Bane!" I shoved his chest.

"Did you enjoy your burger?" he asked.

"Yes, thank you, but you can't treat me like I'm one of the notches on your belt." He pressed his right palm across his chest like he was about to recite a ballad. "Must you despise me so?"

"What do you want." An unwelcomed blush crept into my cheeks.

"I believe there is an apology in order. It seems I have forgotten my manners. I hope you may be gracious enough to forgive my impropriety?"

I paused for a minute, soaking up his sapphire eyes. A girl could fall into those deep pools easily. I internally kicked myself for my moment of weakness. "You're forgiven!" I tossed a harsh smile and started to slide out from under his arms.

Swiftly, Bane clasped his fingers around my wrist, halting me. "Wait!" His voice dipped into a dark place that sent chills over my body, not the good kind either. "I have to warn you." His sobered eyes studied me for a brief minute. "You need to stay away from Sam."

I jerked my arm free. "Give me one reason why?"

"I can't tell you." A muscle twitched from his jaw.

"Sam's been nothing but nice to me."

"He's not who you think!" Bane bit out. The boyish charm had vanished, and loathing took its place.

"What's the deal between you two? Are you lovers?" Bingo! Bane was gay. Bummer for me.

Bane slightly dropped his head to the nook of my neck. His breath tickled. His shoulders shook with silent laughter. "No. Sam and I are *not* lovers. I'm merely looking out for your welfare."

I giggled internally. Straight guys hated it when a girl questioned their sexuality. "I don't know," I teased. "I'm gettin' a gay vibe from you."

A challenging brow arched. "I get a vibe that I make you nervous."

"Whatever!" I suddenly didn't want to play this game any longer.

"Would you care for a ride home?" Just like that, his demeanor changed to a lighter note. "I noticed your broken bike." Bane liked baiting me.

"My broken bike is working just fine. No thanks to you."

His dark brow arched. "Are you still blaming me for your little accident?"

"Duh! You nearly turned me into a pancake." I folded my arms across my chest.

"You should be counting your lucky stars. If it had been anyone else, you'd be six feet under rather than standing here jaw-jacking at me."

"What's that supposed to mean?"

"How did you manage to avoid hitting me?"

"Princess, some things are best left to the imagination." Bane slipped his fingers under my shoulder strap.

Chills! More damn chills!

"C'mon." A smile rested on his full lips. "I'll take you home."

The dude was slick as oil.

"Get out of my way!" I demanded with futile effort.

"Now you're starting to hurt my feelings." His black brows dipped down. "Thanks, but no thanks."

"Now, Princess, where are your manners?"

"That's calling the kettle black. Do you mind?" I eyeballed his arm and then cut my eyes back at him.

His shoulders shook with amused laughter. "I thought you were enjoying our little interlude?"

"Not in this lifetime!" I tossed my hair across my shoulder, glaring at him. Bane lingered a moment, humor icing his blues, then he stepped back, giving me space. "Thank you." I left him where he stood, but it took everything in me not to look back.

A CHANGE OF PLANS

*S*aturday night arrived and stoked was the word. The gang had made plans to hang out and invited me to come along. After Sweetwater, I'd resigned myself to work and school only. I decided to toss that rule aside and have some downtime.

I was trying not to worry about finances. Rent and the electric bill were due. Sara claimed she wasn't making much in tips, and I had no choice but to take her word at face value. That meant I had to make sure things got paid. I was no stranger to pooling my money with Sara's coins to pay bills.

To pick up the slack, I took on an extra route on the weekends. It wasn't much money, but every penny counted. Despite my efforts, I wasn't sure that the additional coins would make much difference. Sara still hadn't forked over the landlord's info. I expected an eviction notice any day. But tonight, I was going to let my hair hang down and have some fun.

The plan tonight was pool at Mother Blues. Not exactly my thing, but I'd make an exception. I didn't care where we went. I was in such a good mood that if Gina decided to bless us with her beautiful presence, I wouldn't care. Like a duck to water, nothing was gonna penetrate my unruffled feathers tonight. Not even a spiteful blonde.

With a limited choice of clothes, it wasn't hard picking out my ensemble. I decided to wear a pair of holey jeans and a powdered blue tank top, nothing fancy. After dressing, I was left with the most signifi-cant task to tackle… *my hair*. I looked at my mess in the mirror, and my shoulders slumped. I hated my mop.

When I was younger, kids loved teasing me. It wasn't fun getting picked on for my rustic hair and cat eyes. They even picked on my freckles. Often to escape my world, I would daydream that I was a stolen princess, and one day a gallant prince would rescue me from the wicked stepmother. I laughed to myself, dreams of a child, silly and unrealistic.

I once thought my parents had adopted me. Neither Sara nor Dad had red hair and fair skin. Genetics was funny like that. I sighed, thinking of Dad. I pushed down my woes, grabbing up my brush and started working out the knots, one painful tangle after another.

I stood in the mirror, staring back at myself. My hair looked great! I checked my back and whistled. I didn't realize how long my hair had grown. It reached past my waist. Most of the time, I wore it up in a ponytail. I never had time to mess with the thick mop.

Next, I borrowed some of Sara's makeup. I didn't want to cake it on, just a little blush and lipstick. Just as I tugged on my cowboy boots, the doorbell sounded like a siren. I leaped to my feet and ran down-stairs, swinging the door wide open.

Sam had his hand on the doorbell aiming for round three. "Hey! You're early." I smiled, a little out of breath.

"Am I?" His brow arched. Then his eyes roved over me from my head to my scuffed-up boots, drawing back an approving grin. "Mais! You look good enough to eat!"

I blushed. Compliments were like striking oil. It rarely happened, especially from a boy. "Thanks!" I hid under my lashes, blushing. I found myself liking his dimples. Sam was adorable, dressed in Levis and a deep charcoal shirt, western wear, and a straw hat, accompanied by a bright smile that showcased his nut-brown eyes. I wasn't the biggest fan of Western hats, but I could change my mind seeing Sam in a hat. It brought out his dimples and the chestnut curls that peeked from underneath his hat. A good look for him. After a minute of sharing smiles, my gaze slipped past Sam to his truck, an old green Ford. "Where is everyone?" I cut my eyes back at him. "Are they meeting us at Mother Blues?"

Sam shuffled in his feet, hands stuffed in his pockets. "Everyone canceled," he shrugged. "It looks like it's just you and me tonight."

"Just the two of us, huh?" I chewed my bottom lip, rocking on my heels.

"Yep, it looks that way," he smiled timidly. I could tell he was nervous.

I doubted Sam wanted to spend an evening with me alone. He showed up only out of kindness. "Hey, we can do this another time when everyone can come," I shrugged. "I'm sure there's somewhere else you'd rather be."

"Heck, no! I wanna take you out. There's a carnival in town. It's not exactly the Mardi Gras in New Orleans, but there'll be rides and cool things to do. It'd be fun!" There was an eagerness in his eyes.

It sounded fun, and I wanted to go. Sam was easy to hang with too. He was a good buddy. "Alright, let me get my money." I started back into the house, but he tugged on my arm.

"Don't worry. I got you covered," Sam offered, smiling.

My eyes widened. "You're going to pay my way?" I didn't know how I felt about that.

"It's cool! Leave your money."

"Okay, let's go!" I shrugged shyly.

As far as my eyes could stretch, cars of every make and model lined the streets. Where did all these people come from? Tangi was nothing more than a hole in the ground, and I knew these folks didn't crawl out from that tiny hole. Yet here we were, walking a mile before reaching the entrance gate.

There was no surprise to find the festival packed. Tons of folks standing shoulder to shoulder bumping against one another, and a line at the ticket booth seemed endless.

Once we entered through the gate, passed the ticket booth, the park was buzzing with life, music blasting, screams roaring, and laughter wafted in the air. Countless colors of neon lights dotted the dark sky. Energy honeyed the air as my heart raced with fervor.

"Hey, I'm hungry," Sam shouted over the noise. "Let's hit the food court first. We need fuel to tackle the rides." His eyes glistened in the lights.

"Sounds good to me," I yelled back in his ear as a strong whiff of corny dogs and funnel cake lingered in the air, making my stomach rumble.

Sam reached down and grabbed my hand as we pushed our way through the crowd. I didn't think anything of it. Sam just didn't want us to end up separated. The crowd was thick as syrup.

We stopped at the lemonade stand, and Sam ordered four corny dogs and two large lemonades. I ate half of mine and handed him the rest. He polished it off in one bite.

After we ate, Sam and I made our way to the rides. No stone went unturned. Every ride that flipped us high in the air turned us upside down, dropped us to our near death. We rode, screaming and laughing all the way. *Fearless, we were.*

Sam even won a stuffed bear for me, tossing balls. His face glowed, handing the prize to me. I smiled up at him and squeezed the animal, bubbling with joy. I would treasure this moment forever.

As the park started winding down near closing time, we saved the best for last... *the Ferris wheel*. We gathered in line, and soon, our time came to board the ride. Sam politely allowed me to go first. The Carney locked the bar, keeping us fastened safely. With each passenger boarding, our cart etched its way to the open stars. Once we reached the top, my breath hitched. "Look! It's beautiful," I whispered, peering below. From the bird's eye view, it was breath-stealing. Beneath us, the neon lights blanketed its soft glow over the park. I thought it was interesting watching people, ant size, dallying back and forth. I lifted my eyes to the stars taking in their wonder as a light breeze tousled my hair. I smiled, drinking in its wonders.

I tapped my shoulder to his. "Thanks for tonight. It's been a blast!" I gazed back up at the stars, soaking up the glory.

Then the mood shifted as Sam slid his arm around my waist, drawing me closer against him. He inclined his head and planted a wet kiss dead center on my closed mouth. I froze, confused over what I should do. My first kiss and it reeked of corny dog and mint. Yuck!

When he pulled back, a prideful grin, brighter than the neon lights, lit his face. He was too proud of his conquest to notice that I wasn't a participant. Good grief! A mannequin would've given him more action. I sat there staring at him, blinking. To my horror, he dove in for sloppy seconds. Hastily, I pressed my hands against his chest. "Whoa! What are you doing?" My eyes were wide with shock.

"Haven't you ever been kissed before?"

"I wasn't expecting you to... " in midsentence, I stopped.

As if Sam had been possessed, his eyes glazed with lust, totally ignoring my protest. "Let's get this cart a-rockin'!"

A surge of panic coursed through me. We were too high for me to jump. Sam had me where he wanted me... *trapped*. This time I pressed my palms against his chest harder. "Whoa, cowboy, hold on!"

He snorted. "Chickadee, I know you like me." He started to go in for another kiss, pushier this time.

I shoved him back with more force, gritting my teeth. "Stop!" I shouted. My cries went unheard. Obviously, rejection was uncharted territory for Sam.

"Oh, I get it! You don't wanna hook up until I kick Gina to the curb."

"Say what?" My brows dipped into an affronted frown.

"Yeah, Gina and I are dating."

"Why wasn't I informed?" I should go ahead and dig my grave.

He shrugged. "I didn't see the point. Now that we're dating, I planned on breaking up with Gina."

Did I need to hit this dude in the head with a rock? "Wait! You're breaking up with Gina because of me?" My stomach lurched with the Ferris wheel. "You can't be serious?"

"I have to tell her, you goofball!" Sam reached over, ruffling my hair. "We can't show up at school arm in arm without telling Gina first. What kind of guy do you think I am?"

"Sam, you can't break up with Gina!"

"Don't worry, Chickadee! This will all blow over in a week or two."

"Maybe for you!" I bellowed. "Gina will make my life a living hell! She already hates me!"

"So what's the problem?" He squeezed me too tightly. I pushed his arms away. "She can't hate you no more than she already does."

I sat there speechless over Sam's flippant attitude.

"I tell you what," he smiled. "I'll do it now."

"Do what now!" Panic rose over me like blistering boils.

He slipped his phone from his pocket and started texting. "I'll break up with Gina right now."

Holy cow! I snatched his phone, holding it over the cart. "No, no, no! Do not break up with Gina in a text." I gripped the phone with my fingers. "Don't break up with her at all!" I couldn't believe Sam! I was just starting to like it here, and he had to ruin it.

"Hey, give me my phone back," he insisted. "I'm breaking up with Gina because I like you!"

"No, you aren't!" Crap! I was dead meat. "I'm a stranger that you hardly know." I forced a smile. "You're going to go to school Monday and pretend this conversation never happened." I slapped the phone into his palm.

"Have you been leading me one with your flirting?" Sparks of anger flashed in his brown eyes.

"I've never flirted with you."

"If you don't like me, then why did you come on a date with me?"

"This isn't a date." I clarified.

"I paid your way!"

"You offered!" I roared.

"That's what I'm sayin'! When a guy pays, it's a date."

"Look! I'll pay you back every penny. But this here ain't no date."

Sam's face twisted. "Sally told me what you said. You might as well come clean."

"What did Sally tell you?"

"She said you told her that you liked-liked me."

"Like as in boyfriend?" I blinked back in shock.

"Yep!"

"I never said any such thing!"

"Me thinkies you're lyin'."

Oh, now he was trying to be cute. "Well, try not to think too hard. You wouldn't want to lose that last brain cell."

"I tell you what I'm thinkin'." Sam's glint darkened. "You changed your mind about me when Old Blue walked into the picture."

"I've about had it with your accusations." I started ticking off finger by finger. "First, you think I've been flirting with you, which I haven't been.

Seconds ago, you called me a liar, which I'm not, and last but not least, you think I have the hots for the new guy, which is none of your pea-pickin' business!"

When my eyes lifted from Sam's sour face, I realized we'd come to a halt. The swish of the hydraulics was music to my ears. When the carney released the locks, I rocketed out of the cart, keeping my feet moving. I heard Sam calling out my name, but I ignored him. Tears streamed down my cheeks. I was taken aback by Sam's complete switch of personality. I didn't see this coming. Then I remembered Bane's warning. Damn, I hated to admit he was right. But even more so, I wished I'd listened.

STALKER

By the time my tears dried, I had lifted my eyes and realized I was lost. Panic rushed over me. The crowd had thinned, and the park had grown dim. The rides, the lights, the aimless yatter that once wafted in the air had waned. Dumping Sam might've not been such a wise decision. My impulsiveness cost me a ride home. In a slow twirl, I glided my eyes over my surroundings. I raked my fingers through my hair, whiffing out alarm. My options were nada. I had no money for a cab. That was if such a thing existed in this Podunk town. Francis was the only person I knew with a car. The last person I wanted to call. Yet what other choice did I have? Walk twenty miles in the dark? Being on foot didn't bother me so much. But the part about bugs, snakes, and gators sent me reeling.

"Maybe Sara will still be at work." I withdrew a shaky sigh as I felt for my back pocket, but I came to a screeching halt. Frantically, I patted down my other pockets. "No freaking way!" My problem just became DEFCON. My phone was missing!

I commenced backtracking to all the spots Sam and I had been. I craned my neck, looking for anything familiar. My breath eased as I spotted the lemonade stand where Sam and I first stopped. Maybe I left it there? A spurt of hope shot through me. I sprinted off in its direction.

When I reached the concession booth, my hope plummeted. A sign reading, *Closed,* hung in the window. I stepped up to the glass and knocked. There was no stir of anyone inside, but the lights were still burning. This time, I pounded the pane with force as if I was trying to wake the dead. Bam! Bam! Bam! The window rattled.

My heart leaped as I spotted a gray-haired woman. She slid the small glass pane door open only a few inches, announcing in a brusque tone. "We're closed, sugar." She quickly shut the glass and vanished to the back.

"Wait!" I leaped up to the window, shrieking through the pane, my palms and face planted against the glass. "I left my phone here

The older woman reappeared, sliding the window a little wider this time. "Did you say you lost your phone?"

"Yes!" I jumped with joy. "Do you have it?" I rattled out in a rush, choking back a cry.

"Let me check," she spoke a little gruffly.

"Yes, ma'am!" I watched as she disappeared to the back. I stuffed my hands in my pockets, easing out a long breath. I started to relax until an eerie breeze bristled my neck. I looked over my shoulder, spotting a tall man wearing shades standing alone by the tables, only a few feet from where I stood. As if he were waiting for me, he lingered, giving me a strong sense he wanted something. One word came to mind... *otherworldly*! What a weird assumption. The man appeared out of sorts. Wearing a black suit to a carnival seemed odd enough, but the shades screamed creepy. I stepped under the booth's awning in the lighting. I think after Sam's stunt and me forfeiting my ride, paranoia seemed to be hitting me. Though, alarm still lingered on my shoulders. I slipped a glance at the suit. Did I know this person? A sick familiarity jabbed my skull.

Nudged from my thoughts, the woman returned, opening the glass pane all the way and popped her head out, holding up a phone. "Is this yours, sugar?" A smile drew her face into wrinkles.

"Yes! Thank you, thank you!" I jumped with glee, taking my phone, cradling it against my chest.

"My husband found it and figured before the night ended, someone would claim it. You have a good night," she smiled and quickly closed the window, disappearing.

"Oh, thank God!" I went to swipe my phone, but my euphoria ceased. I'd forgotten to charge the dang thing. "Damn, double, damn!" I looked back at the lemonade stand. The outside and interior lights were off this time. I rushed to the window, pounding on the glass pane. Nothing. I knocked harder, holding my breath—still no sign of the woman. My options were running out. I had to find a person with a phone.

I peered down the line of concession stands. Not a stir of life. Then my eyes landed on that weird man in the suit. Like Aphrodite's marbled statue, he stood, immovable, though his interest seemed fixed on me. Fear iced my blood. I needed to find someone with a working phone.

I took off in the opposite direction of the dark suit, trotting down the line of stands, hoping to spot at least one person. My eyes combed every direction, praying for any signs of life. "Geez! The police have disappeared too," I mumbled as my panic deepened.

Chances of finding someone was diminishing by the second. The park was shutting down. The music, the rides, and even the aimless chatter had ceased. Only a faint stir carried through the air. The idea of being alone stabbed my gut as I glanced behind me. To my horror, the suit was on my tail. Holy crap! He was stalking me.

My mind raced as I picked up the pace, but I couldn't think. My pulse was beating in my ears. I was defenseless, alone, and easy prey. My eyes combed the boarded stands. I glimpsed over my shoulder again, and this time, the dark suit was gaining momentum on me.

Terror became conspicuous as I sprinted toward the stockyard, hoping to find someone tending the stock, a pig, a horse, even a dang dog. I didn't care! Anybody, but this weirdo tailing me!

When I reached the stockyard, a mixture of dirt and strong animal urine drifted in the gentle breeze. The cattle appeared disturbed, mooing and shuffling in their corrals, but no sign of their caretaker. My whole life flashed

before me. The stranger had corralled me into a dead end. Seeing the seedy grin on his face, I knew he'd trapped me.

I decided to face this creep. I dug my heels into the dirt, hands fisted, ready to fight as I turned to confront my stalker. Instead, I yapped, startled, jumping back! The last person I thought to see... *Bane!*

"Gracious! Are you that happy to see me?" he flashed a pompous smile.

"Don't flatter yourself." I cut my eyes over Bane's shoulder, seeing if I spotted my stalker. To my surprise, he'd vanished. A sense of relief washed over me as I breathed out a long sigh.

"Something bothering you, Princess?"

I slid my eyes back to him. "What?"

A thin line appeared between his brows. "You look like you've seen a ghost?" Bane glanced over his shoulder and then back at me, toting puzzled brows.

"Nope! I'm happy as a kitten." I clasped my hands together.

"You're shaking." His eyes roamed over me. "Did something happen?" his voice perfumed with suspicion.

"What are you doing here?" I deflected.

"I could ask you the same."

"I lost my phone at one of the stands." I pointed over my shoulder at the booth.

"Did you find it?"

"Yep." I bit my bottom lip, shuffling my feet.

"Are you on a date?" I asked.

"Are you?" His blue eyes drilled a hole through me. "You don't look well. Did the guy hurt you?"

"No! I'm fine!"

"I somehow doubt that," he mocked. "With your porcupine personality, I assume you scared the poor fella away."

"I don't scare everyone," I retorted.

"I have my doubts from past experiences," he flashed his pearly smile. It was nice against his tawny skin. He was easy on the eyes until he opened his mouth.

"Are you here to torture me?"

"I thought you might like a ride home. You look lost."

"I'm not lost," I answered too fast.

"I think you are." He cuffed his mouth to smother a laugh. "C'mon! I'll take you home." There was an unexpected gentle touch to his eyes.

"No, thanks! I'm good." I waved my palm, protesting. I pivoted on my heels heading in the opposite direction.

A short laugh caught my ears.

"That's a dead end up there." Amusement oozed from his voice. "You're going to have to come back this way. Shall I wait?"

I whirled around to confront him but stopped. He was snickering with his shoulders shaking and arms folded over his chest. Nice chest, though. I huffed, feeling defeated. "You'll take me straight home? No funny business?"

"Cross my heart." He crisscrossed his chest. "I give you my word." I didn't' have a lot of choices here. It was the stalker behind door number one or frosty, the smug man behind door number two.

"Fine!" I so hated weakness. I stomped past him, walking like it was black Friday.

Bane caught up with me and slid his jacket over my shoulders. I suddenly was enshrouded with his warm woodsy scent. I didn't realize that I'd been shivering. I caught his sparkling gaze and shyly smiled back. I was glad for the semi-darkness that hid my flushed cheeks.

This was the second time that Bane had come to my rescue. Whether he knew it or not, I think he saved my life tonight. Maybe he ain't so bad.

FIREFLIES

*CW*hen we reached the exit gate, I could see that Bane had parked his car only a few feet past the gate. That seemed odd. It was as if he'd planned this.

"I see you got special parking. Convenient, huh?"

"I'm special," he teased.

"Whatever!" I blew out an annoying laugh. Why did I bother asking?

I went to the passenger's side, but Bane had beaten me to the punch. He'd already had the door opened, arm extended. Surprise struck me as our eyes touched. "Can't a guy open the door for a lady?" He flashed a dimpled smile.

I rolled my eyes. "I think women are more liberated these days. You didn't get the memo?"

"Au contraire, mon ami," he smiled. "It is my long experience that I find a woman appreciates a man's endeavors."

I laughed. "Long experience and endeavors? Since you were an infant?" Bane wasn't much older than I was. Yet there was a mystery behind his glint that suggested something different. It was as if he held a private joke.

I studied him for a brief moment. "Where are you from?"

"I'm from all over." Half-truths churned in his eyes.

Clearly, he wasn't going to clarify. I just rolled my eyes and kept my thoughts to myself.

Once he entered the driver's side, the small cab quickly filled with his delicious woodsy scent, and once again, I was bathed in his signature aroma.

"Do you mind if we take a detour before I take you home?"

"You promised me straight home!" *Liar!*

"I did, but I have something special to show you." How could I refuse? His dimpled smile was serenely compelling.

"It's not like you have other plans?"

"How do you know I don't have plans?" I asked.

"Because you don't, and I have something far better to offer."

Silence lingered between us for a brief moment.

"Alright." And with that, I gave myself over to the dark side.

"That's my girl." A grin spread across his face as he started the engine. Soon we were off into the night under the glistening stars.

I had no clue where we were headed. What if Bane left me stranded in the middle of the sticks? What would I do then? I drew my knees to my chest and quickly glanced at Bane.

I cleared my throat. "Umm, can I ask you something?"

He slid his eyes at me and then back on the road. "I'm an open book, Princess."

"First, you can stop calling me that name."

His brow arched. "Why does it offend you?"

"The name has a significant meaning to me. It feels weird when you call me that."

"Let me guess, your father?"

"Just don't call me that, please." Anything reminding me of my father tugged on my heart. Some matters were just too personal.

"Fair enough," he paused. "What shall I call you?"

"Stevie, call me Stevie."

"Stevie, it is." He eased into a smile.

I sat back in my seat as the quiet fell between us. I watched the tree line flash by in my window. The towering pines were endless, and it seemed we were sinking deeper into the woods. The idea set my teeth on edge, and I suddenly had to ask. "I have a question."

"Yes," he replied.

"How did you manage to keep from running me over? I was partially the deer in the headlights. Avoiding me, you would've had to crash into a tree."

He grinned to himself as if he possessed a secret. A secret, I wanted to know. "What can I say? I have quick reflexes."

"I call you on your BS."

"Are all redheads fiery as you?" he amused. There was a suspicious line at the corner of his mouth.

"I don't know. I haven't met the entire clan yet." I snapped, still hugging my knees to my chest. "Why are you evading my question?"

"Some things are meant to remain concealed." A muscle quivered at his jaw.

"That's a crock of sh-"

Bane interrupted me. "Did you know when you get angry, the green in your eyes glitter?" He stared into my eyes. "It's almost worth goading you just to see the sparkle."

"I remember you called me miserable."

"Yes. I recall," Bane admitted.

"I don't see what's the big mystery's about?" In a huff, I turned straight in my seat. "There has to be a logical reason how you were able to dodge me." Suddenly, he laughed, shaking his head. "What's so funny?"

"Do you ever let anything go?"

"I merely want to know."

"Can't you be happy that you're alive and well?"

"I am only asking for the truth. I should be dead, but somehow, you defeated the law of gravity. Was it luck?"

"Luck had nothing to do with it." A smile found its way through the mask of secrets, yet he still did not explain.

I crossed my arms, feeling exasperated. What was the point in asking Bane? He had no intention of explaining. I crossed my arms and stared out my window as quiet chilled the air.

We turned off the main highway down a narrow dirt road, sinking farther into the dark forest. Bane pulled off to the side of the road and stopped. He unsnapped his seatbelt and leaned to my side. "Love, if I tell you, I'd have to kill you." A faint smile teased the corner of his mouth, but it didn't reach his eyes. "Shall we leave it at that?"

"I want to go home. *NOW!*" Fear ripped through me. I should've never gotten in the car with him.

"I'm not trying to scare you."

"I'm not afraid," I lied as I tightened his jacket around me.

"I was kidding. C'mon, where's your sense of humor?"

"I left it back at the park."

"First, you have to see this!" Bane turned the engine off, and the small light extinguished, emerging us in total darkness. A faint gasp escaped my lips.

Bane was on my side and gathering me into his arms, whisking me away. I giggled as he whirled me around in his arms. "I have a treat in store for you." He whispered against my ear.

"You're not throwing me into a bed of gators, are you?"

He burst into chuckles. "That sounds rather tempting, but not tonight."

"I can walk." I had one arm curled around his neck, and the other hand fisted his T-shirt. Strangely, I found myself liking this.

"If I release you, my lady, I fear my gallant reputation would fare terribly." His powerful well-muscled body moved with grace.

"Mr. Dropout, I think that ship sailed a long time ago."

"And when did you arrive at that conclusion?"

"Oh, about ten minutes ago, but who's counting?"

Pressed against his chest, I could feel the soft rumble of his laughter.

After a few short heartbeats, I began to relax, listening to the chorus of cicadas among the dense trees. Insects, lots of insects, but I wasn't too bothered.

My mind began to drift to Bane. I had to admit, there was an inherent strength to his face, and his laugh was infectious. I felt drawn to him, yet I had this nagging feeling that I might be stepping off a cliff.

With Bane, nothing made sense. I had a crush on Logan, but he didn't get my blood boiling like this guy, leaving me weak at the knees and wanting to stab him all at the same time. This boy had something special, different than anyone I'd ever met. For example, Sam. He wasn't even in the same ballpark as Bane.

Whatever this was between Bane and me, it felt exciting and frightening, like climbing Mt. Everest without the proper gear. Geez! I was in trouble. "Where are you taking me?" I asked.

"You'll see."

Dang, goosebumps!

"I've read enough books to know that's code for dumping the girl's body in the lake. In my case, the bayou. "

His smile had a spark of mischief. "Love, I can assure you that killing you is the furthest thing from my mind."

A delicious shudder heated my body. This boy affected me. Funny, though, he appeared older than a boy. Even his speech pattern seemed like it was from another time.

Finally, he eased me down on my feet, setting me onto a patch of pine needles. From what I could tell, it looked like we were in a small circle surrounded by pines. We stood close, our thighs touching. His breathing, a soft, steady flow, eased my nerves. Then it dawned on me that my phone was dead. A knot of panic struck. "Give me your cell phone," I blurted out.

"What?" He chuckled.

"I want to hold your phone, please." I held out my palm.

"Why do you want my phone?"

"For security. Mine's dead." I knew I sounded crazy, but the rise of uneasiness took the wheel. "Just hand it over," I rolled my eyes.

"Whatever the lady wishes." Bane sighed as he dug his fingers into his back pocket, pulling out his phone and placing it into my palm. "Feel better now?" I could hear the lightness in his velvety voice.

"Yes, much!" I smiled, fingers clenching his phone to my chest.

"Now that you're comfy, watch the tip of the trees." He snaked his hand around my waist and pulled me close to his side.

"All right," I smiled to myself, still holding tight to his phone.

He lifted two fingers to his mouth and whistled. The sound echoed off the tree limbs. Then something extraordinary happened. From the very tip of the tallest pine, a thin line of tiny soft lights ascended, drifting from the shadows. I watched breathlessly, unable to believe my eyes.

"Isn't it amazing," Bane whispered.

"What is it?" I returned my gaze to the tiny dots of light flickering in and out from the tree-tops.

"Fireflies," he whispered as if he was releasing magick into the air.

Bane reached out, lacing his fingers with mine. In silence, we watched, mesmerized by the small glow balls flickering through the trees. They were increasing by the dozens, slowly descending. It reminded me of millions of massive raindrops reflecting the sunlight.

One firefly landed on my arm. I giggled, looking up at Bane. Our eyes locked. "It's incredible!" An excited warmth flowed through me.

"In all my years, I've never seen anything like this."

"How did you find this place?"

A sense of contentment flourished in his voice. "I find solitude in the forest."

"I'm the opposite. Not a big fan of bugs and creatures that have larger teeth than mine."

Bane laughed.

I found myself smiling at his deep throaty laughter.

He leaned closer, declining his head to my ear. "I hope not all bugs are on your hit list."

"I can assure you that the fireflies are safe from extinction."

Before I braced myself, Bane gently drew me into his arms, resting his hands in the small of my back. I exhaled a faint gasp, suddenly lost in his glistening blues. My hands fell against his chest as his phone fell to the ground, yet he didn't seem to care. "Have you ever been kissed?"

Breathlessly, I whispered, locked into his gaze. "Does nonparticipating count?" Sam was the last person I wanted in my head at this moment.

He gave a throaty laugh, shoulders slightly bouncing. "No, I suppose not."

"Then I'd have to say, no."

His fingers clamped over my trembling chin. The sudden sadness in his eyes touched me. I wanted to reach out and caress his face, but I was too frightened. I froze, my mouth half opened, waiting for him to kiss me. The prolonged anticipation was almost unbearable. God, I wanted that kiss too.

Then without explanation, his mood quickly darkened, his hands dropped to his side. "You ready to head back?" His lips tightened as he stepped back. Our magical moment had vanished as a cold settled between us.

Did I offend him in some way? I blinked, stunned, as he turned his back to me, heading in the direction of the car.

Flustered by his Dr. Jekyll-and- Mr. Hyde personality, I reacted.

"Hold on just a damn minute!" I stomped up to him and grabbed his arm. Bane stopped, though he kept his back to me. "What just happened?"

"Nothing. We have to go." Shadows veiled his face, yet his voice felt like ice.

I'd reached my limit with boys-gone-douche-bag tonight. Boldly, I stepped in front of Bane. "What is wrong with you?" I studied his face, hoping to make sense of his sudden aloofness. "I thought you were going to... " I stopped as humiliation colored my face a bright scarlet.

"Oh!" His brow arched. "You thought I was going to kiss you?"

The spite behind his reply angered me, and I lashed out. "You're a jackass!" I boldly met his cold eyes. "I didn't ask you to bring me here!"

"My mistake. I should've never brought you here."

I hesitated, blinking with bafflement, and then huffing out an exasperated breath, I fled from his side, heading for the car.

The trip home was the most uncomfortable ride that I'd ever experienced. Not even one word was uttered between us. If I lived to be a hundred, I would never understand boys. I might be inexperienced, but there was no doubt that Bane had his mindset on kissing me. I saw it in his eyes. Then with no explanation, his whole demeanor changed, and he dismissed me like I was the hired help. How stupid of me to think he could be interested in someone like me. After all, I was the rusty bike girl.

When we reached my house, the second the car came to a halt, I leaped out. I twirled about-face, hurling his jacket at him. He caught it in midair and tossed it to the floorboard. When our eyes locked, anger stormed through me. I flipped him off with the one-finger salute and slammed the door to his precious car. Surely he understood that!

Spotting the lights in the window, I thought Sara might be home. The house was lit up like a Christmas tree. When I reached the door, it was unlocked. As I shut the door, I heard Aidan's car peeling out. I closed my eyes, leaning against the door listening to the revving engine fade.

I realized I was alone. Sara must've come home earlier. I suspected she needed her clothes. My mom never was one to stay home very much. I recalled spending a lot of nights alone while she entertained men.

I slid to the cold floor, drawing my knees to my chest. I let myself have a good old fashion cry. The gates opened, and a flood of tears came. I wanted to go back to Texas. I missed my friends, Laurie, and Becky. I buried my head into the folds of my arms. I stayed like that until I fell asleep.

CONFESSIONS FROM THE DEAD

The doorbell rang, stirring me awake. I peeled myself off the floor. I wiped the tears from my face with the back of my hand and slowly opened the door.

"I'm sorry to be knockin' on your door so early, but I had a premonition that ya might be in trouble. Ya is lookin' a bit pale, babee." Ms. Noel's face deepened with lines. "Oh no, ya been cryin'."

"I'll live." I puffed a short breath. "Come on in." I stepped aside. I caught sight of two grocery bags in her arms. "Ms. Noel!" A pain of guilt struck. "I hope you didn't..." She stopped me before I could finish.

"Oh hush, chile! It's not much, just a little gumbo and cornbread. Oh, and my sweet potato pie that you love," she smiled as she entered. I took the two sacks from her arms as we headed to the kitchen.

"What time is it?" My brain felt cloudy.

"It's mornin'."

"Morning?" I peeked out the window. "It's not daylight!"

"Oh," she waved her hand in the air like swatting flies. "I get up before those darn roosters." Ms. Noel smiled. "I figured ya is awake since ya lights were on."

· · ·

"Oh, I hadn't made it to bed, to be honest." I stretched. "I'll fix some coffee." I must've dozed off.

"Lord, have mercy! Why on earth have you not gone to bed?"

I shrugged. "I had a bad night and… " My voice cracked. I didn't want to talk about it.

"You'll be fine after you get some food and rest." Ms. Noel's face brightened with a broad smile. "Let me help fix the coffee."

"The least I can do is fix coffee." I smiled, reaching for the cabinet, getting the coffee down.

I felt blessed to have Ms. Noel. Though I missed my friends in Texas, my friendship with Ms. Noel had made life here bearable.

After we had settled down at the table with coffee and a large dish of homemade pie, Ms. Noel asked. "Chile, what's got ya out in a bunch?" Her pale blues dug into me.

"I had a misunderstanding with a couple of frenemies." I shrugged, staring at the curls of steam rising from my coffee.

"Was that the boy who brought you home?"

"Yes, ma'am. Bane drives the black Corvette."

"You know him from school?"

"Kinda. Bane's hard to figure out."

Ms. Noel leaned back in her chair and sighed. "Babee, ya gotta be careful who to trust."

I caught something there, a hidden meaning. "Do you know this boy?"

Ms. Noel reached over, sliced a piece of pie, and placed it into one of the small plates, then slid it over to me. She laid the knife down and answered. "Fannie's been talkin'."

I leaned inward. "Why do I get a sneaky feeling there's something you're not telling me?"

"Fannie says ya were goin' to meet a dark-haired, blue-eyed boy. She senses darkness lurking amidst him."

"What kind of darkness?"

Ms. Noel shook her head. "I can't be certain, but nothin' good comes from the dark."

I twisted my lips into a frown. "Fannie needn't worry. I won't be seeing him anymore." Somehow, no matter how much I wanted to believe myself, my heart had different plans in store.

"Babee, ya like this boy?"

I lifted my shoulder into a short shrug, hiding behind my lashes. "Maybe."

She reached across and patted my hand. "Don't worry. Ya feel better after ya get some sleep."

My brows puckered. "Can I ask you something?"

"Sure!"

"At the fair, there was an older man dressed in a black suit, wearing shades." I swallowed, trying to calm myself. "I think he was stalking me."

She gasped. "Why do ya think that?"

"I first spotted him standing alone, staring at me." Chills rushed over me as I recalled what happened. "But it was not until I started walking that I realized he was tailing me."

"Oh, my heavens! How did ya get rid of him?" Her brows knitted.

"The blue-eyed boy in the Corvette showed up. I think he saved my life." I shivered, realizing the danger I'd almost gotten myself in.

"My goodness, chile!" She clenched her chest.

"Do you know anyone fitting this man's description?"

"No, but I have a sneaky feelin' ya mama knows."

"My mom?"

"Your mama has a heavy dark spirit encircling her. She's keeping secrets."

"Sara is private. It's part of her bipolar."

Ms. Noel's brows pulled down into a frown. "Ya mama is holdin' a dark secret that will change your life forever."

Sara had a whitewashed grave full of ugly secrets. "Is there anything you can do? Like read my palm or look into your crystal ball? I want to know who this man is."

"Sometimes, we have ta catch when catch can!"

"What do you mean?"

"Chile, we need ta find out who this snake is while it's fresh." She drew in a deep breath. "Do ya have a white candle?"

"Hmm, wait! Sara has one in her bedroom. She won't even notice it's gone." I jumped from my chair and darted upstairs.

Soon I'd made it back with the candle in hand. I placed it on the table and grabbed the matches from the drawer next to the stove. I held the small box up and asked. "Shall I light the candle?"

"Yes, since this man is locked ta ya. The spell will be stronger. First, let's clear the table and dim the lights. Spirits gravitate ta the light much like bugs ta a light bulb."

"You know best." After I had cleared the table, I flipped off the light switch. All of a sudden, blackness doused us—only a soft stream of moonlight filtered through the window, giving a silver sheen to the kitchen. I took my seat and exhaled to ease my pounding heart.

"Are ya sure ya wanna do this?"

A deep sense of shame stirred within me. I needed to make amends. "I'm sorry for the way I behaved. I was frightened, but I'm stronger now."

"Chile, it's all forgiven." She took my hand and squeezed it. "This is different! The door we're knockin' on will come from a dark place. Make sure this is what ya want. There's no goin' back, babee."

I didn't even begin to understand the magick world. Though, I believed the only way to put this to rest was to find the answer. That meant I needed to find out who the man in black was, and why he was stalking me, and I couldn't feel any safer than having Ms. Noel's guidance. "I'm prepared." I nodded, giving her the go-ahead.

"Let's get started, then. Place the candle in the center of the table and light it."

I nodded and took out a match from the box. My fingers fumbled as it took a couple of tries striking the matchstick. Soon the candle came to life, licking the small wick and casting shadows on the walls.

"Now let's gather hands. Whatever happens, do not break contact."

"I won't let go. I promise." I knew this was risky. Dilly-dallying with the supernatural frightened me, but I had to see what this man's intentions were.

"I think we're ready," she nodded. "Close ya eyes and clear ya head. Picture this man in ya mind just like ya were back at the festival.

Lock ya mind on that image and freeze-frame it."

"Okay." I closed my eyes and eased out a slow breath.

After several minutes, Ms. Noel asked. "What are ya seein', babee?"

I began to tremble as the fearful image grew in my mind. "I see my stalker standing by the lemonade stand," I paused. "I keep getting this feeling he's not human."

"Open ya internal eyes. Look for clues," Ms. Noel nudged.

"I'll try." I sat back, breathing in and out, allowing the quiet to take over my mind. A few moments passed as the clutter cleared, and my focus became more apparent. With each breath, I kept sinking deeper and deeper into my mind. It was like a roller coaster traveling through an electric tunnel, spiraling down at torque speed. As if dropped from the sky, I was standing at the same lemonade stand that night at the fair. I could feel the dirt under my feet. The smell of corny dogs and cotton candy drifted in the air. A light breeze tousled my hair. It all came tumbling back, roaring laughter, girls screaming, music playing, and neon lights overlaying the grounds. Then my eyes landed on *him*. I stalled, staring at the man in black. Like a magnet pulling me, I edged closer. Now only a few feet from him, I paused, studying his features. The stranger turned to me. At first, he moved his lip, similar to my dream. I strained to hear him. I stepped closer as I came into earshot. Unexpectedly, his words vibrated inside my head. "Hello, angel, I'm coming for you." He reached up and removed his dark shades. I gasped, and the vision shattered.

I jolted back in my chair—fear bulleted through me. I lifted my eyes to Ms. Noel breathlessly. "I saw him... and his *eyes*!"

"What did ya see?" Ms. Noel mirrored my fear.

Ice slid down my spine as I felt eyes watching me. "He's an alien! I know that sounds weird."

Ms. Noel's eyes rounded. "Why do ya say that, Catin?"

"The stalker pulled his shades off." I shook my head in disbelief. "His eyes were yellow like a cat!"

"Lord, have mercy!" Ms. Noel's eyes darted to the candle and then back to my face. "Did the man say anything?"

"Yes! The stalker called me, angel." A tense silence swathed the kitchen. Then I just said it aloud, "He's coming for me!"

"Let's not jump to conclusions just yet," she paused. "Did this strange man say anything else?"

"No. That was it." Fear gnawed at my insides. "Do you think this man is the one my father tried to warn me about?"

"I can't be certain. I'll speak to Fannie. She may have heard something."

"Please talk to her! None of this makes any sense." I couldn't take another minute in the dark. I jumped from my chair and jerked on the chain from the ceiling. The small bulb suddenly shed its generous light over us.

I felt edgy. I needed to busy myself. I grabbed up the pie and wrapped it up in saran wrap. Then I snatched up the pot of coffee and poured Ms. Noel and myself another cup. I handed Ms. Noel her cup and seated myself back down at the table. "I appreciate your help," I said as I sipped my coffee.

"Don't fret none. We gonna get ta the bottom of this." Ms. Noel reassured.

I appreciated Ms. Noel's determination. Still, it didn't give me much comfort. Chills broke out over me, and I suddenly needed to check all the doors and windows.

MY LIFE SUCKS

*S*ince it was still before daylight and I was off work today, I dragged myself upstairs and climbed into my bed. My mind kept wondering about the man at the fair, and then I stopped on Bane. I didn't understand his one-eighty change in mood. I didn't have the strength to try. I forced myself to count sheep, and finally, I drifted off to sleep.

When my eyes popped open, my memories of the early morning with Ms. Noel crept back slowly into my consciousness. I rolled over and looked at the clock. "Dang!" Straight up noon, I flopped back, staring at the white ceiling. I tugged a pillow over my face hoping to clear my brain. Regardless, I couldn't get the MIB, the man in black, out of my head.

I blew out a sigh and thought of Dad. I leaned over and pulled out a picture that I'd kept hidden from Sara in my nightstand. It was the only one left. Sara had destroyed all the others. I sat up, drawing my knees to my chest as I cradled the picture. A sudden tear fell from my cheek. If my dad were alive, he'd tell me what to do.

I remembered the day we took this picture. Dad and I were posing in front of the local drugstore. The salesclerk took the picture for us. The store kept an old fashion soda fountain in the back. Dad ordered Black Walnut and Bubble Gum Jubilee for me. I got that flavor every time.

It wasn't long after this picture that Dad died. He was jogging on a back road near our farm in Oklahoma. The road was practically useless for travel unless you were a farmer driving a tractor. The passage had seen better days back when horse and buggy were the means of travel. Considering all the potholes and erosion after years passed, most traffic took the highway.

In the police report, it stated that Dad was jogging on the path when he was killed by a hit-and-run driver. I didn't doubt their findings. What I questioned was that the old road was too narrow for modern vehicles to pass through. I had looked at the police photos countless times. Despite everything, I kept drawing the same conclusion. It was an impossible task. I took one more glance at Dad's picture and quickly stashed it away in my hiding spot.

I decided to get dressed and get some sunshine. Since the only means of transportation was my bike, I wouldn't be going too far. It didn't matter. At least I'd be out of the house. I'd grab my journal. Maybe do some writing, dear diary stuff!

Before shoving off, I stopped at Ms. Noel's to let her know I was all right. No need to worry about her any more than I have. Shortly after, I was whizzing away on my bike, heading to wherever the wind carried me.

As I rolled through downtown, the small circle was dead. Not a living soul in sight. I whistled as my eyes combed the cluster of shops. I had forgotten that life closed on Sundays. The only place alive in this dive was Mudbug Café. Later I might drop by and grab a bite to eat. I reckoned I should let Sara know I was breathing.

I needed to talk to her about rent. I managed to put back most of my checks, keeping in mind that rent was right around the corner. Since I didn't have the landlord's contact number, my hands were tied. Knowing Sara's track record, neglecting bills, and the little fact that she hadn't been home in weeks made me more than a little wary.

I caught the glint of a merry-go-round just ahead on the other side of the Piggy Wiggly grocery store. Adventuring past the city limits soured my stomach. After last night with Sam, a stalker, and the silver spoon, Bane, sorta overloaded me. Sticking close to home was more my speed today.

I'd reached my designation and had my blanket spread out over the plush grass. There was a gentle breeze blowing, cooling the day down to almost perfect. I stretched out across the quilt, flat on my tummy, feet up, ankles crossed with my notebook, and a pen in hand.

The park was empty. I delighted in the idea of having it to myself. I opened to my last page where I'd left off over a week ago. I was behind with my daily logs.

I stared at the blank page, undecided on what to write. My mind drifted to Aidan Bane. He was beautiful, I'll give him that, but I got the feeling there was much more to him than a pretty face. Bane was a mystery and a vault full of secrets.

What should I write? I tapped the pen on my lips.

I almost had my first kiss, Saturday night by the most intriguing and hottest boy at school, and I wanted him to kiss me too. Instead, I went home mad as hell and very disappointed.

Sam was not what I thought, the sleaze bag. Sally is in the no friend zone. Now Gina has reason to kill me. Stupid me! I should've stayed home.

My life sucks!

I tossed the pen and diary down, blowing out a frustrated sigh. I dreaded tomorrow. I didn't have a clue how I was going to wiggle my way out of this love triangle with Sam and the infamous Gina. Why didn't I see Sam's conniving self? Sally was the ringleader. She was the first on my hit list. That was if I survived the wrath of blondezilla.

Then my mind drifted back to the fair and the man in black. The vision with Ms. Noel seemed incredibly real. Was my imagination playing tricks on me? If so, that was one convincing trick. I shivered over the what-ifs that could've happened last night and the what-ifs that plagued my future. If the vision carried any clout, I might better consider getting Mace. If a crazy man was stalking me, I needed protection.

Maybe we had needed protection for some time now. When we lived in South Dakota eight years ago, Sara had met someone that I thought she'd marry. Sara had gotten a job at a grocery market. Charles was her boss and owner of the store, Sack and Save.

He was a giant of a man and had a potbelly to match, but his heart was gold. Charles had taken a shine to Sara, and she latched onto him quickly too. I didn't think she loved him, but he seemed to have grounded her. I liked Charles.

We were starting to feel like a family again. It wasn't long before he'd become a big part of our lives. I loved every minute we spent with him.

He took a genuine interest in both Sara and me. He just was a great guy.

Then fate struck once again. The night started no different than the others. Sara had prepared dinner. We were waiting for Charles to arrive. Though dinner never came that evening, nor did Charles.

It was downhill from there. Sara sent me to bed early and hungry. As I lay in bed with my tummy growling, I listened to angry voices late into the night. I assumed Sara was arguing with Charles, but I had guessed wrong.

Before sunrise, with no explanation, and not much more than the shirts on our backs, we left Dakota, never to return. After that night, Sara never uttered Charles' name again. I was ten, but I recalled that night like it was yesterday.

It was not until five years later that I'd discovered the truth. I stumbled onto an old shoebox, knocking it off the shelf with all its contents spilling out. Sara had kept newspaper clippings of Charles' death. The headline read in bold letters that his body was found in a heap of blood on his front doorstep. The mysterious crime had the detectives scratching their heads. I sat in Sara's closet, sobbing. I loved Charles, and it broke my heart that his life ended so violently. It seemed good people in my life died, first, my father and then Charles. Who was next?

When my eyes fluttered open, it took me a moment to realize that I'd drifted off to sleep. The sky had taken on a beautiful golden hue, nearing sunset. It was getting late, and I wanted to catch Sara before her shift ended. I snatched up my belongings, shoving everything in my bag. I hopped on my bike and headed toward town.

I set my bike upright under the bright red neon sign that read, Mudbug Café. I'd made it just in time before the last bit of sun had dropped behind the horizon. The bell jingled as I pushed the door open. A quick breeze and the smell of fried catfish rushed through me as I headed for the back to the usual booth. Craning my head to see if

Sara was still on her shift, I caught a peek of her blonde head through the opening to the kitchen. She was smiling at Francis. My heart sunk. She had the face of a woman in love. A look I didn't recall ever seeing, not even a shared glimpse with my dad. That bothered me… *a lot.*

Sliding into a booth, I kept my eyes out for Francis. I hoped he'd stay in the kitchen and leave me alone. A little winded from the ride, I leaned back, relaxing my head against the cool vinyl. I still felt sluggish from lack of sleep.

A bit of time had passed when I heard Sara's heels tapping against the floor. I popped my head up and caught her smiling. I smiled back, happy to see she was in a good mood. "Well, well! The only time I ever see you is when you're hungry," she snorted snidely.

Okay, sorta in a good mood.

"Sorry! I'll start coming by more often." The last thing I wanted was to get her riled. I decided to roll with Sara's irritable mood and keep my mouth shut. "Can I please get a chocolate shake and fries?"

"You payin'?" She looked up from her pad, one irritated brow arched.

"I suppose," I replied respectfully.

She dropped her pad and pen on the table, bending too close to my face and whispered. "I heard you had a date Saturday night. Is that right?"

What was her problem? "I went out but not on a date."

"I heard you were with a boy having sex! You better not go and get yourself knocked up, expecting me to take care of you and your child!"

"You heard lies," I wailed.

"Don't screw things up for me!"

Her words felt like a stab to my heart, and my anger quickly escalated. I bounced out of my seat, getting in her face. "Then you haven't anything to worry about, *Sara*!" I hissed. "You've never troubled yourself before, why would you start now?" I spewed. "You're worried that I'm going to screw up your life! You have ruined mine!" I screamed, fist to my side, flexing.

Sara stepped back, eyes rounded, shoulders stiff with anger.

"Get out!" She threw her arm out, pointing to the door. "Go home, you ungrateful bitch!" Her words hit me like bullets to the chest.

"Fine!" I stalked passed Sara, colliding my shoulder into hers, making her almost lose footing.

All eyes were on me as I hurried to leave, but my breath lodged in my throat when I caught sight of a pair of blue eyes looking back at me. Dang! Of all people... *Aidan Bane!* Why did he have to come here? And he wasn't alone. I recognized the girl from school. She clung to him like gravy on fried chicken. She appeared wasted, fumbling on her feet.

Our eyes hitched, and a glimmer of sorrow flickered in his blues for a second. I looked away. My spat with Sara was humiliating. Though, Bane's pity was mortifying.

I darted out of the café, heading for my bike. I wanted to hide. After witnessing my fight with Sara, Bane must think I'm trailer trash. Apparently, because of a stupid rumor, the whole town thought I was.

Just when I reached for my bike, I felt fingers clasping my upper arm. I swung around, expecting Sara but surprised to see Bane.

"Are you alright?" His eyes brimmed with concern.

I raked my fingers through my hair as my heart hammered my chest. "I don't know." Embarrassment made my voice harsh. I stared at my feet, unable to look Bane in the eye.

"Let me take you somewhere." He began gently stroking my upper arm.

"What about your date?" I pointed to the plastered girl, who'd followed him out the door.

"Not my date." His lip twitched. "My cousin's. He dumped the girl on me after he liquored her up. I called my butler, Jeffery. He's coming to pick her up and take her home. We're waiting on him now." His blues were more vibrant under the amber of dusk.

"Really?"

"Cross my heart." His face lit up, smiling.

"She seems friendly, like a girlfriend." I eyed him suspiciously. Though, I wanted to believe him.

A dark swath of curls fell over his face. "Hmm, I'm not fond of the impaired."

I laughed. "That's good to know, but I'm not sure I should leave with you. I don't want to add this girl to my list of pissed-off females."

Bane touched his finger to his mouth. I suspected he was stifling a laugh. "I give you my word that I will defend your honor to the death." He tossed a glance over his shoulder and then back at me. "See!" He smiled. "Here's Jeffery now. I'll be right back! Don't move."

He hurried off to the girl's side. I watched as he held the door open, and she slid in the back seat. He closed the door as the black limo pulled out and headed down the street and disappeared.

I mumbled to myself. "Yep, he has a butler."

In seconds, Bane was standing by my side. "See, now it's just you and me."

"My mother wouldn't approve. I'm sure you overheard our argument." I pulled my hair back off my shoulders and shuffled my feet. The sting of her words was like a fresh wound, raw, and bleeding.

Bane's fingers curled under my chin, forcing me to gaze into his face. "You didn't deserve that." His eyes were gentle.

Then I remembered our last encounter, and a glower fell over my face. "Why the sudden change?" I rested my hands on my hips, staring him in the eye.

"Change?" His brow bounced upward as he dropped his hand.

"Yeah! At the firefly nest." I glared at him. "You did a one-eighty on me. Not my favorite moment."

"Oh, that." He rubbed his bristled chin. "It appears that my urgent need for apologies is exponentially growing." His smile deepened, flashing his perfect white teeth.

"You think?" I folded my arms, not falling for his schoolboy's charm.

"I'm sorry! Let me make it up to you."

"You're going to have to come up with an explanation." He was smooth, but he'd have to do better to convince me.

He inhaled a sharp breath. "It made me uneasy realizing your innocence."

"So, you thought insulting me would help?"

Placing his left hand over his chest, he spoke. "I fear my behavior is inexcusable. Can you please forgive me?" With those pleading blues, he could've been an ax murderer, and I would've opened my door and invited him in.

I blew out a sigh, teetering on whether or not I should give him a second chance. "Where can we go?" My eyes kept shifting to the café's entrance. I expected Sara to come charging out any minute.

"There's another restaurant just down the road." He leaned in next to my ear and whispered, "The food's much tastier." When he lifted his head, his blues were dancing with mischief.

"I have my bike." I grabbed the handlebars.

"I'll get your bike then."

Clearly, he liked taking charge.

"Alright." I was reluctant. If Sara had gotten pissed over a rumor, what would she do when she saw me climbing in Bane's car? She couldn't miss it. He'd parked in front of the café. Not a lotta folks around here drove a Corvette.

Once we were in the car, Bane reached over, grabbing my seatbelt. Unmindful, our eyes locked, and we both froze. I bit my bottom lip, not daring to breathe. Why didn't he finish buckling me already?

"Your eyes," he softly whispered. "Remind me of a meadow. They're such a scintillating green." A hushed smile toyed with the corners of his lips. Then he drew in a sharp breath and finished buckling my seatbelt. We were rolling down the street in the next breath. Or should I say his breath? I still was holding mine.

We pulled into a vacant lot of an establishment that looked condemned. A rusty sign hung reading, Beans, and Cornbread. It wasn't much more than a dilapidated shack. I didn't get it. Bane and this place just didn't match. I reckoned I was up for whatever.

After cutting off the engine, Bane slipped me a sideways glance. "You'll like this place. It's fun." He flashed his dimples, jumping out of the car.

"Oh, okay." I really didn't care. Any place other than Sara's presence would work for me.

In a flash, Bane had my door open, smiling down at me. "You'll love this place." He smiled, taking my hand.

We entered the joint, and it took me a moment for my eyes to adjust to the dimness. Candlelight flickered in the small diner. We were the only ones here other than a waitress and a cook in the back wearing a stained white apron.

The place was as rustic as its exterior. Bare wood, no paint, pictures of men with fish hung on the walls and other odd décor. You know, three men in a tub kind of stuff.

"Is a booth all right with you?"

"Sure," I shrugged.

He led the way, holding my hand. It was nice, and whether I wanted to admit it, I kind of liked Bane.

We settled in a booth, cozy with a candle sitting in the center of the table. It took me back to last night with Ms. Noel. I suddenly felt the urge to look over my shoulder.

It was no time before the waitress greeted us. "Hello, there, handsome," she greeted Bane. Apparently, they knew each other pretty well.

He stood up, hugging the woman. The waitress was older, in her mid-twenties, give or take a few. "Hey, beautiful! How's that husband of yours?"

"He's much better, thanks to you," she grinned.

"It was nothing. Glad to help." Bane's eyes glimmered as he settled back down into the booth.

"What will you and the lady be havin' today?" The waitress asked.

"Bring us two Cokes, and the lady hasn't decided yet on what to eat. We'll need a moment."

"No problem! I'll be right back with your drinks, Mr. Bane," she smiled, patting him on his shoulder. The waitress spun on her heels and disappeared to the back.

Bane grabbed my gaze. "Her husband had been laid off his job. I'm their landlord, or I should say my parents are. I manage it for my folks while they're out of the country. Anyway, I referred her husband to a local farmer I knew who was hiring. That's all." He quieted a minute, keeping his eyes on me. "How are you?"

I looked away. For a minute, I'd forgotten the big scene with Sara. "I'll live." I really didn't want to talk about it.

"Does your mother treat you like that often?"

"It's life, right?" I shrugged.

"Not necessarily. Your mother is an abomination."

"Did you bring me here to feel sorry for me?" His pity was the last thing I wanted.

"I'm sorry." His tone had a degree of empathy. "I don't mean to pry."

"It's okay. My mother is bipolar, and when she's off her meds, which is pretty much most of the time, she can be difficult." I averted my eyes.

"Oh, is that what they're calling it these days." Bane's voice held a note of sarcasm.

"Why do you say that?"

116

"I apologize." His tone softened. " Of course, you're right. Mental illness is nothing to joke about."

Why did I get the impression that he knew something I didn't? "Can we talk about something else?" I didn't want to spend the rest of the evening discussing Sara and her troubles, especially with Bane.

"Sure! Are you hungry?" He grinned back with no trace of his former animosity.

"Not really," I shrugged.

"Come on, eat something. I hate eating alone," Bane winked. "I'll order for you."

"What is so special about this place?" My eyes washed over the rustic diner.

"Apart from the company," he smiled. "The food is fantastic. Have you ever eaten mudbugs?"

"No, I haven't." My cheeks blushed.

"Unlike other restaurants, this place has the real deal." His lips stretched into a natural smile.

I was pretty sure the pun was intended. I didn't mind.

The waitress returned with our drinks, and Bane ordered a considerable helping of mudbugs with the works.

When the waitress left, we continued with our conversation. Bane went on to say. "Apart from its rough aesthetics, it's a cool place. Food's good, folks are friendly, and they have lots of beer."

"Beer?" My brow perked. "Are you twenty-one?" I had to admit, he looked closer to twenty-one than eighteen. His whole demeanor screamed adult. Maybe money matured a person?

"I'm special," he teased.

"Yeah, right," I laugh.

A sportive grin stretched his lips.

"Where are you from? I hear you're new too." I was curious about what brought him to this dump.

"Uh, I was born in Marseille, France. My family and I moved to the States when I was an infant, though I don't claim any particular place. I've traveled the world, Europe, the Middle East." He folded his hands, elbows on the table.

Beautiful hands, I noted, strong and manicured. I glimpsed down at mine, and all of a sudden, I ducked them under the table. Self-conscious of myself was not my intentions, but let's be real, why was

Bane spending time with me? I wasn't prime-choice here. Suddenly I had to ask. "What are you doing?"

"Pardon me?" His dark brows darted upward.

"What is going on here?"

His smile slightly dropped. "We're having a nice meal."

"No, I mean, why the nice guy now?"

"Do I have to have a reason?" Confusion was evident in his eyes.

"I guess not." I fiddled with my straw. "I just... I just don't get why you want to hang out with me. Last night, you lost your temper at me. I'd like to know why?"

He shrugged. "When I looked into that angelic face of yours, it gave me pause. You're so young and inexperienced."

"My face is angelic?" I murmured. Did I hear him correctly?

Bane paused, holding my gaze. His eyes were compelling, magnetic. "Yes, quite stunning."

I was glad of the semidarkness that hid my blushed cheeks. Then my blush turned into frustration. "I'll never understand you," I blurted out, leaning back in my seat. "One minute, you're giving me a compliment, and then the next, you're ready to bite my head off." I shook my head. "One wacko in my life is enough."

"I'm a tough nut to crack, moody, and a wacko?" His shoulders slightly shook as he laughed to himself.

"It's not funny," I snapped. "The way you acted was a dick move." I crossed my arms, feeling the sting of last night and the tears he forced upon me.

"I'm sorry. I don't mean to laugh, but your choice of words is amusing to me."

"Where do you get your vocabulary? Abominable!"

"Perhaps, you can get me up to speed?"

"I don't know. You're pretty far behind. You gotta stop hanging out with Jesus!"

We both laughed.

Soon our waitress returned with our order. She laid out a newspaper over the table and dumped a massive pile of bright red bugs with whiskers larger than my hands. I gawked at the critters as the waitress finished setting the table with a basket of cornbread, corn on the cob and boiled potatoes.

I must've had the look of doom plastered across my face. When my eyes lifted, Bane's brows knitted. "Hmm, what's wrong?"

"They're bugs!"

A sudden rush of humor eddied in his blues. "They're not bugs, silly! They're fish."

"I thought the name mudbug was a metaphor. I didn't know they were real."

Bane threw back his head and let out a wail of laughter. "C'mon, where's your sense of adventure?"

"I don't know." I tried to pick one up without squirming but quickly drew my hand back.

"Don't worry," He chuckled. "There's nothing to it. Here watch." First, he rolled up his sleeves and then picked a bug from the pile and held it up. "Now watch," he demonstrated, "Pinch the head between two fingers with one hand, like this." He held his fingers up, gripping the bug. "Now, hold the tail with your other hand." He gathered the tail as he instructed. "Give the head a twist until it comes off." He held the severed parts in his fingers, juice dripping down his elbows.

"Uh, that's messy." I laughed, handing him a napkin.

"It can be." He took my napkin. "Thank you!"

I inhaled, trying not to freak out. I forced my fingers to grasp one of the bugs. I fought down my gag reflex. Geez! I did as he showed me, twisting the bugs head off. "Okay, now what?" I held up the severed bug, the tail in my left, and the head in my right hand.

"Now place the open part of the head between your lips and suck out the juices. This part of the crawfish is a delicacy." He demonstrated how.

I sat there, gawking. "You're kidding!" I wrinkled my nose. "That's gross!"

"Give it a shot," he coaxed.

I swallowed as if I was washing down a ton of pills.

"Okay, but no promises that I'm gonna like this."

He shook his head, grinning.

I wrapped my lips around the head, squeezing my eyes closed and drained the juice from the beheaded bug. To my surprise, it was good, a little on the spicy side. My eyes lifted to Bane's face and replied. "Not bad!"

He smiled. Pride gleamed in his blues. "I never doubted you, Princess."

I smiled back. I caught that last word... *princess*. I found myself kind of liking it. His voice was soft-edged and sweet.

"What are you waiting for? Dig in."

We stayed until closing. I'd never talked so much in my life. We discussed nothing of great importance unless one considered football a vital topic. He claimed his allegiance as a devout fan of the Dallas Cowboys while I preferred a nest of wasp. Bane nearly turned blue from laughter over my lack of fandom.

When we arrived at my house, he killed the engine. An uncomfortable silence grew tight between us. It felt like Bane was struggling to tell me something.

I sat there wringing my hands, wondering if I should thank him for the night and say good-bye. I always had a problem with proper etiquette. Strangely, I wasn't ready to leave his side. I hated to admit it, but I had fun tonight. I sat there waiting for him to give me a cue.

We were so tight in the two-seater sports that his breath warmed my cheeks. He slightly shifted in his seat. The beginning of a smile tipped the corners of his mouth.

My breath stilled.

Our eyes locked.

I drew in a sharp breath, fretting if I might blow it like last time.

"I enjoyed tonight." Tenderness lingered in his voice. "It's quite pleasant talking to you."

I bit my bottom lip, smiling. "Thank you for tonight."

"It was my pleasure, truly."

He quieted a moment, holding my gaze. Then in the next breath, he moved in. Our lips were almost touching. My heart pounded my chest. The anticipation was too much. I wanted his kiss more than anything I'd ever wanted. Dang, just do it! I screamed in my head at him, and then.

"What the hell do you think you're doing in that damn car, young lady?" I closed my eyes, mortified. Bane quickly drew in a sharp breath, sitting erect in his seat, shoulders stiffened.

Sara stood beside the car on the driver's side, pounding her fist against the window with the look of a mad scientist.

Perfect timing!

Appalled, I darted out of the car, rushing toward the house. I couldn't believe she was doing this to me. I didn't make it very far before Sara snatched me up by the nape of my hair, jerking me backward and forcing me to face her. Her teeth gnashed while she held a clump of my hair wound tightly in her fist. I flinched from the pain, flailing my hands at Sara's grip, trying to loosen her hold. "I told you, *no boys!*"

"Don't do this here!" I flinched, tears streaming. I spied a dark silhouette in the moonlight approaching fast. It was Francis coming from the rear of the house. Was this some kind of intervention? *Stop Stevie from having a life!*

"I meant what I said!" Sara hissed through clenched teeth.

It all went down so fast. Bane stepped in between Sara and me. With gentle authority, his hand forced Sara back. "I'm sorry. Is there a problem?" Though his body was taut, his voice appeared calm.

A dark flash streaked past the corner of my eye. It was Francis. He shoved Sara to the ground and was now standing in Bane's face, hostile, ready to wrangle. Just the one-time encounter with Francis, I knew he was dangerous. I feared for Bane.

Bane had me pressed against the car. His massive body blocked Francis from reaching me. I watched breathless, fretting over the worst scenario that could happen. I shuttered over the inevitable.

"I think you should leave." Francis bared his blackened teeth. "This is a family matter."

"Family!" Bane scoffed. "Perhaps you should leave." Bane's eyes were cold, dead steel.

"Listen, punk!" Something silver flickered in the moonlight. Francis had a switchblade clenched against Bane's jugular, "I won't think twice feedin' you to the gators." He clenched his teeth; his dark eyes flashed with anger.

Holy cow! My heart lurched. A bloodbath was the last thing I wanted. I started to speak up, but in a lightning-fast motion, I found myself standing on the other side of the car, and Bane had Francis kissing the asphalt, arms spread apart, and Bane's knee buried in Francis's back. The knife had vanished.

Murmurs drifted in the crisp night air as Bane bent low into Francis' ear. I strained to listen but couldn't make out his words. Francis' face was a glowering mask of pain, drool dripping from his mouth.

Strangely, Sara's face was flushed with deep hue, arms reaching for Francis, but unable to move her feet as if she were glued to the asphalt.

In the next instant, Bane rose off Francis, and Sara rushed to her boyfriend's side. With Bane's broad back to me, he leaned in, saying something to my mother. I couldn't see his face, but by Sara's frightful expression, he must've gotten his point across. The way her hazel eyes bulged, I saw fear.

Then just like that, it was over. Francis and Sara staggered to their feet, racing for the old Cadillac parked behind the house. The shock of them ambushing me ripped through me. Why would my mother and her creepy boyfriend want to jump me? If I'd been here alone, no telling what they would've done. I watched, unable to move as my mother and Francis burned rubber, speeding away. Unaware that I'd been holding my breath, I fell back against the car. My left hand pressed flat to my chest as I raked in oxygen.

Bane's lips tight, in a fit of anger, stalked to my side, muttering under his breath angrily, "Fuck it! I've waited long enough!" He forcefully swept me into the folds of his arms, taking my mouth with savage intensity. Possessively, his hands splayed over my face, drawing me closer.

Our tongues collided, toiling with one another. My hands reached up, gripping Bane's dark curls as I rose to meet his forceful kisses. As smooth as butter, his hands moved to the center of my back and reeled me in tighter. I delighted in every inch of his lean body pressed against mine as a swirl of fire licked through me, stealing my breath.

Raising his mouth from mine, Bane captured my gaze. I stared back, my chest heaving. I touched my swollen mouth, lips burning in the aftermath of his fiery kiss.

"I've wanted to do that since the first time I laid eyes on you." The huskiness lingered in his deep drawl.

I tried to make sense of what just happened, my mother and Francis, the fight, the electrifying kiss. Wow! "Umm, I don't know what to say." My brain felt short-circuited.

"Are you hurt?" His eyes searched as his hands gently rested on my hips.

"Hmm, I don't know." I pulled away, needing air. "What did you say to my mom?"

"It doesn't matter." His eyes combed the neighborhood. He gently placed his hand on the small of my back and urged me toward the house. "Let me get you inside the house."

I nodded, fighting back the tears.

Once we were inside, I switched on a lamp and then turned to Bane. "Would you care for some coffee?" I was starting to feel shaky as I ran my fingers through my messy hair.

"I'm good. Thank you. How are you?"

I felt his soulful eyes digging a hole through me.

"I'm as well as expected." I rubbed the back of my neck. My head was throbbing.

"I should have a look." He stepped forward. "You're injured." Concern pursed his lips.

I stepped back. Palms help up. "No! I'm okay."

He stopped, dropping his hands to his sides. "I'm sorry you had to see that tonight. Your mom's boyfriend overstepped his bounds."

"Yeah, he's a creep." I picked up my shawl and threw it over my shoulders. A chill rushed over me.

"Does he bother you?"

"Nothing I can't handle." I clenched my jaw to kill the sob in my throat.

Bane blew out a frustrated sigh, raking his fingers through his black curls. "He's threatened you, hasn't he?" He stepped closer, placing his hand on my shoulder.

"It's nothing. Really!" I hid my eyes under my lashes.

"You're shaking!" He smoothed his fingers over my arms.

"I'm fine," I pushed his hand away. "I'll be better in the morning."

"Why do I find that hard to believe?" He gathered my chin in the cuff of his hand, forcing me to look at him. "I give you my word. Neither Sara nor her boyfriend will harm you again."

I believed him. I witnessed his dark side. No argument. Bane could've ended Francis' life in a snap. I drew in a sharp breath. I felt enthralled and terrified at the same time. "No. Don't. I'll handle my mother and Francis."

"Do you think your mother and that *borachio* had a right to attack you?" His dark brows set in a straight line.

"No, of course not." My voice cracked. "I just think you could've handled it differently."

"Life isn't that simple, Love." His vexation was evident. "I'm a straightforward man, and I deal accordingly."

"Sara and Francis is my problem. You needn't worry." I hugged my waist. "Look! I appreciate you sticking up for me, but I think you should go." My voice sounded harsh to my ears. If Bane turned on Sara and Francis at the drop of a hat, who'd say he wouldn't do the same to me. Bane stood there, his eyes drilling me, but I couldn't look him in the eye. I stood there in silence, staring at my feet.

"Very well," his jaw hardened. "I'll see myself out. Lock up." He threw the door open and was gone by the time I reached the window. He flew out of here faster than a bat outta hell. I stood, frozen, shaking my head with complete confusion. How did Bane consistently defeat the laws of gravity? Was he Superman, or was I going mad?

I fell into the chair by the window, trying to process what just happened. I swore Bane must have a damsel-in-distress obsession. Now that I thought about it, it started when Bane pulled me out of a fight with Gina, then that weirdo at the carnival stalking me, Sara's outburst at the diner and last but not least, the brawl with Francis on my front lawn. The common denominator of these events was Bane. How did he manage to be at the right place at the right time, every freaking time?

I tapped my finger to my lip, tracing over that whole fiasco tonight. Sara appeared paralyzed. I mysteriously ended up on the other side of the car in a quick blink. Bane had disarmed Francis, pinning him on the ground. It all happened so fast.

First thing after school tomorrow, I planned to talk to Ms. Noel.

LIES

The sun rose to a bright morning. Unfortunately, it didn't help my mood. I compared the Monday blues to an ass-kickin' and a wicked hangover. I wanted to hide under my covers and stay in bed all day. I glanced at the alarm clock as I blew out a deep sigh as the bright numbers stared at me. Dang! It was 5 in the morning.

The residuals from last night still clung to my skin like a bad rash. I wasn't looking forward to another altercation with Sara. Whenever she decided to show her face again, I reckoned I'd worry about that when I crossed that bridge. Hating to leave the comforts of my bed, I shoved off the covers and headed to shower.

After I finished my paper route, I headed to school just in time to stop for the restroom. I was washing my hands when the door squeaked open, and footfalls slowly crept in. At first, I didn't think much about it until I glanced up in the mirror. Gina and Sally were standing directly behind me. Either the blonde had a sour tummy, or she wanted to pick a bone. I reckoned it was the latter.

I tossed the paper towel in the wastebasket and took a deep breath and turned to face both girls. "Hey, Gina." I nodded to Sally. "What's up?" I held my voice calm.

Gina stepped forward. Her bright pink lips stretched tight. "We need to talk."

"Ladies, I'd love to chat with y'all, but I'm gonna be late for

English. Let's do this up after school, off-campus?" I figured if our conversation came to blows, we'd at least avoid getting suspended.

"I'd rather do this now!" Gina's voice was sharp as thorns.

I dropped my eyes to her manicured hands and drew back a quick breath. Those long pointy nails were gonna hurt like a *mother*.

I'd had my fair share of brawls. Not something I prided myself over. It was the perks of being the new kid. I sighed. "Go on! Get it off your chest, then." I kept my eye on the hostile blonde and the other eye on a quick getaway.

"I heard you went out with my boyfriend on Saturday night."

"Are we talking about the whole football team?"

Gina's eyes went black. "I. Am. Talkin'. About. Sam!"

"You are aware that several of us had plans to go out that night? Your boyfriend showed up at my door alone." I leaned against the sink, crossing my feet. I kept my hands braced against the sink, ready for action. "I didn't know he was dating you."

Then it came to me that Sally was the source of trouble between Gina and me. I shot a glare at her as she coiled in the corner, remaining quiet.

"Why should I believe you?" Her hands flew to her hips. "You've been after him from day one."

I rolled my eyes. "Gina, I'm not interested in your beau. Never have been."

"You're lying!" she hissed. "Sam said you were all over him."

"What?" The shock of her accusation hit me full force.

"Tell the truth, Steve!" Gina brayed. "You and Sam had sex in the back of his truck."

I knew now where Sara heard the rumor. Sam's big mouth. Anger flashed from my eyes. "My name is Stephanie, and Sam's a liar!"

Then Gina took it up a notch, stepping into my personal space. Her peppermint breath fanned my heated cheeks. "With your daddy issues, any attention will do, won't it?"

Now the blonde was crossing the line. Pushing off from the sink, fist to my side, white-knuckled, I stood toe to toe with Gina. "Keep my father outta your mouth!"

"What's the matter," she laughed snidely. "I thought you liked attention?"

"I don't know." I smiled mockingly. "I'm not caring much for this."

Her eyes washed over me as she drew back a scowl. "Sam saw you get into the car with Aidan Bane. Did you do him too?"

"Now you're reaching." I nearly popped her in the jaw.

Suddenly jarred from our pleasantries, the door squeaked, and footsteps echoed. We all three stopped, our heads snapped up in the direction of the door. I expected to see the principal, Dr. Van, baring his teeth.

But to my surprise, it was Bane swaggering in as his musical voice sang. "Hello, ladies," he smiled wide as he wedged himself between Gina and me. "I heard you out in the hallway. Thought I'd join the fun." He quickly roamed his eyes over me as if he was checking for injuries.

Gina stood with her arms folded, eyeing Bane suspiciously. Sally remained in the corner, shaking like a cornered rat.

I almost felt sorry for her.

Almost.

Gina squeezed herself between Bane and me, pointing her back in my face. Staring at her blonde head was not exactly my favorite pastime, so I stepped back, leaning against the sink, arms crossed. I darkly laughed to myself. Watching *Gina manipulate Bane* might be an amusing sideshow.

"Aidan, you know I like you." Gina batted her fake lashes as she gently placed her hand on his chest. "This girl went out with Sam behind my back!" Gina tossed a leer over her shoulder at me.

"What night are you referring to?" He braced one arm by the elbow against his chest, and the other arm raised, a finger tapping his lips like he was Sherlock Homes investigating a murder mystery.

"Stevie talked Sam into standing up Sally and me, and together they went to the carnival." Another round of bullets shot over her shoulder at me. "Your girl exchanged sex for cash. They did it in the back of Sam's truck." Gina pouted her lips. "Didn't she leave with you that night?"

This girl has spun her last web. I jumped up, snatching Gina's arm off Bane, spinning her about-face to confront my fist! But Bane jumped between us, taking my shoulders in his hands and gently but forcefully planting me flat against the wall.

"Gina's lying!" I shouted through gritted teeth.

His stormy eyes collided with mine. "Back off!"

"This is my affair! I got this." I tried pushing past him.

Dark snappy eyes darted at me. "Settle down! "

Then Bane cut his eyes back to Gina. "There's been a misunderstanding." He spoke with quiet emphasis. "Sam has misled both you and Stevie." Bane paused, darting his grave glint at Sally, the coward in the corner, and then back at Gina. "Sally set this entire charade in motion, pitting the two of you against one another. Perhaps you should grill your BFF instead of Miss. Ray." Bane's poise was perfect. He performed like a king delegating authority.

"Sally's not a backstabber," Gina argued.

I almost choked on her idiocy. I said, "Gina, your BFF set this whole fiasco up. I heard it straight from the sleaze bag's mouth himself, Sam."

Gina turned her fiery eyes on me. "I don't believe lying whores!"

"I think you do," I fired back, cutting my eyes at Sally.

Bane stepped up, gently pushing me back once more while he flashed me a layered black look. "Quiet," he warned.

Hands thrown in the air, I relented in exasperation, but not before, I cast him an eat-shit-and-die glare. With a sharp huff, I stood back on the wall, stewing.

Bane drew back his attention to Gina. "Pardon me for speaking so candidly, but were you not with one of the football players under the bleachers last Friday?"

"That's a lie!" Her accusing eyes aimed at me.

"Let's just say, extracurricular activities."

Gina, lost for words, was priceless.

Bane's attention shifted to Sally as she shivered from his disdain glare. "You should come clean and tell the truth for once in your miserable life."

Sally cringed, not saying a word.

I, on the other hand, found myself astounded by the direction this hoedown was going. Bane's radar was starting to come in handy.

Gina drew me from my moment of triumph as her acidulous eyes bounced between Bane and me. "What I do is none of your business," she spat as she snapped orders at Sally. "We're late for class." Gina shot a heated look at me as she and Sally scurried out the door.

I inhaled a relieved breath, though this quarrel wasn't over. But for now, I could relax. I waited quietly for Bane to say something first.

After his eyes had finished roving over me, he asked. "Are you hurt?"

"I'm fine," I shrugged.

"You didn't tell me you were with Sam." His brows drew together in an ireful expression.

My gaze flew up at him. "You didn't ask."

"I believe I did. You lied to me."

"I didn't lie." Then I rolled my eyes. "Okay, I skirted around the truth."

Bane's left brow rose a fraction. "Uh-hmm. Go on."

"By the time I ran into you, Sam had split. I didn't see the point in rehashing the night."

"Didn't I tell you to stay away from him?"

"You're not my mother," I bit back.

"Thank goodness I'm not!" A melancholy frown flitted across his features.

"Are you going to accuse me of sleeping with Sam too?"

"Do I need to?" His expression held a note of mistrust.

"Actually, asshat, you don't have to ask crap! Then I don't have to lie!"

Sudden anger lit Bane's eyes as he stepped closer, forcing my backside against the wall. He leaned in, his breath hot against my face. "Is there more to this story than you're telling?"

I began to shake as the fearful images built in my mind of his violent behavior with Francis. Bane was no one to test. Setting aside my resolve, I lashed out. "It's true, and guess what?"

"Pray, tell." His curt voice was flat, edgy with impatience.

"Sam is a much better lover than you'll ever be!" I sputtered. I wanted to hurt him, so I lied. That was what he got for believing a lie.

There was a flicker of pain behind his glint. "Then, there's truth to the rumors?"

The swell of despair was beyond tears. I'd gone too far. I needed to end this between Bane and me. "Believe whatever you like!"

"What I like is for you to start behaving like a young lady and stop these childish tizzies."

His blues blazed like a lit match. "Your eyes are on fire!" Sheer black fright swept through me.

"Never mind about me." His voice was cutting. "Do we have an understanding?"

"What?" My mind reeled with confusion.

"I said, are we clear!" Aidan repeated.

"I'm sorry! I don't respond well to threats."

All at once, things became blurry. It was like an out-of-body experience. A strange sensation percolated inside me, a deep burning down to my core, like a pressure cooker, surging to the surface.

The ground started to shake. From that point on, everything spun out of control. The stall doors slammed back and forth, ripping off its hinges. Pipes burst, water spewed, and windows exploded, spraying shards of glass everywhere.

When it stopped, disoriented, I was in the arms of Bane. Soaking wet and lying in the middle of the football field. I had no idea how we ended up in the middle of an empty field unscathed.

Immediately, I kicked and shoved at Bane. "Get off me!" I shrieked.

He rolled over on his back, propping himself up on his elbows. I quickly saw the shock in his eyes.

"What just happened?" I puffed out short breaths, shivering.

"The fuck if I know," Bane half-whispered.

I jumped to my feet, legs wobbly. "Stay away from me! I mean it," I bellowed, breathless, scared and pissed. I stalked off, heading straight for my bike. I needed out of here and away from Aidan Bane and his bag of crazy tricks.

AFTERMATH

I went straight to Ms. Noel's house. If by chance, Sara had decided to come home, I needed to calm down first. After that horrible altercation in the front yard last night, the tiff with Gina and now blowing up the girl's restroom, I was standing on the ledge of a fifty-foot drop, ready to dive.

I climbed two steps at a time, rushing to Ms. Noel's door. I knocked three times. The door crept open, and there stood Ms. Noel smiling as always. "My lord! You're dripping wet." She eyed me from head to toe.

"May I come in, please?" My voice trembled.

"Come on in her'." She stepped aside, opening the screen door.

Quickly I made my way past Ms. Noel as she shut the door.

I twirled on my heels as I rushed my words, unable to wait. "The girls' restroom exploded, Aidan Bane is a sociopath, and Francis carries a switchblade."

"Chile, come sit down by the fire and let me get ya some hot tea." She pointed to the rocking chair. I settled in the chair as Ms. Noel disappeared to the kitchen. I didn't realize until I sat by the fire that I was chilled down to the bone. My fingers and toes felt numb. I bent over, palms stretched out, letting the heat loosen my stiff fingers.

· · ·

Ms. Noel returned with a cup of hot tea. "Thank you," I whispered. I grasped the cup in both hands. Its warmth felt good to my fingers.

Ms. Noel sat on the couch as she let out a slight groan. "Now start from the beginning and tell me what's got ya so rattled."

"It started yesterday." I began telling her about the fight with Sara, Bane wrestling Francis to the ground, ending the story with the explosion at school.

"Mercy sakes! The good Lord giveth and take it away, Chile," she preached, "Ya been workin' overtime."

A short laugh escaped my lips. "That's what I'm saying." I shook my head. "Can you explain any of this wacko stuff to me?"

"This feller who brought ya home, he's the blue-eyed boy?"

"Yes, Aidan Bane."

"Have you met this young man's folks?"

"No. Bane mentioned his parents are out of the country a lot. Even if they were at home, I'm not the type of girl he'd want his parents to meet." I set my cup down on a small table next to the chair.

Mrs. Noel's gray brows collided. "Why do ya say that, babee?"

I shrugged, staring at the fire. "Rich folks like Bane prefer their kind."

"Money ain't got nothin' ta do with a person's worth. It's the heart that makes a person good."

"I reckon."

"Bane, where have I heard that name," Ms. Noel asked.

"He's new to town."

"I think he's the son of your landlord."

I perked. "Are you serious?"

"My nephew works for the Bane family. Jeffery's been workin' for them for years. They just moved ta town. They come from New Awlinz."

"New Orleans," I asked. Ms. Noel's accent at times was a little thick.

"Yes, babee, that's where they're from."

"Can you ask your nephew?"

"I don't mind askin' but doesn't ya mama has that information."

"Yes, but she won't tell me."

"Bless your heart, chile. Ya shouldn't have ta worry about such things."

"I don't have much choice." Talking about Sara wasn't a subject I wanted to harp on. So, I could change the subject. "Ms. Noel, I think there's something off about Bane. I mean, every time I'm around him, weird things happen."

"I haven't told ya this." The worry lines around Ms. Noel's eyes deepened. "I think that young man has the touch."

"The touch?"

"Special gifts, paranormal abilities."

"How can you tell?" I asked.

"It's part of my foreshadowing. The feller's magick is *dark*."

"That's a scary thought."

"Do ya think this young man is the faceless boy in your dreams?"

"I don't know." I shook my head. "I think he's someone not to cross." I exhaled a long sigh. "When he tackled Francis to the ground, he moved so fast that I missed the whole thing right before my eyes."

"Maybe you should avoid that boy for now. Let me talk to Fannie."

"What about the explosion? Are you getting any kind of a vibe on that?"

"That one has me puzzled, chile. I'll talk to Fannie about that too."

"I appreciate everything you've done for me." My eyes became misty as I rose to my feet and hugged my dear friend. "I gotta go home. If you need me to go to the store for you, let me know."

"Thank you, babee. I'm good. Don't need ta make any grocers today." Her eyes sparkled. "Don't you worry none, we'll figure this out."

I smiled back and sighed. Ms. Noel always seemed to rest my worries. If anything good comes from moving to this little town, it was my friendship with Ms. Noel. I really loved her.

When I'd gotten home, the lights were out, and the house was drafty. I threw my keys down on the table by the door and sighed with relief. Tonight, I didn't mind the empty house. I needed some time alone to decompress. My brain felt muddled with all these eerie events that left me swooning with questions.

My body craved sleep. I dragged myself upstairs, shoulders slumped, one step at a time to the comforts of my soft, warm bed. First, I needed a shower and dry clothes.

. . .

Hours later, I awakened to the doorbell. It jarred me out of a dream, the same dream that I'd been having since Dad's death. I shivered, trying to knock off the eerie effect. I quickly scrambled to my feet and headed downstairs.

Ms. Noel must have some news to share. I swung the door open and paused with surprise. Jen was standing on my porch and smiling, tons of books in her arms.

"I bring cheer," she teased.

I laughed. "Just what the doctor ordered."

Jen laughed back.

"You want some pie," I asked, happy to have a visitor.

"Sure! Did you make it?" She entered as I closed the door behind her.

"Oh, heck no, my neighbor baked it. She's nice like that," I replied as we headed toward the kitchen. I poured two mugs of coffee as Jen and I settled at the table with our cups and a slice of sweet potato pie. I even had whipped cream to top it off.

Jen jumped right in on the current events of the day. My ears were burning as much as my stomach churned. "You missed out on all the excitement today."

As casually as I could manage, I asked, "What happened?"

"There was a huge eruption in the girls' restroom."

"That was my fault. I got into it with Gina and Sally." I knew I had to come clean, at least about the argument. I knew the trio, Gina, Sally, and Sam, were going to be talking smack.

"Oh yeah! I know about that. Good for you to stand up to those busy body bitches." Jen's eyes rounded, excitement danced.

"It was like shaving hair off my chest. Gina and Sally are real tools."

"Yeah, I thought everyone called it off? Sally didn't give me reasons why. She left a message on my phone."

"That dirty little rat! Sally lied to you too." My lips thinned with irritation.

"Oh lord, what has she done now?"

"Sally and Sam both set me up. Saturday evening, Sam came knocking at my door alone. He lied, saying everyone canceled."

"You're kidding!" Jen gaped.

"I wish I were." I scoffed. "As it goes, Sam and I went to the fair together. I honestly thought it was platonic, just two friends hanging out. Then on the last ride, Sam made a move on me and then confessed that he was dating Gina."

"You didn't know!" Jen's eyes widened in shock.

"No! I thought they were just friends." I said. "Anyway, Sam and I got into an argument, and I ditched him at the fair."

"Good for you!" Jen smiled and reached over, high-fiving me.

"It gets worse. Sam's saying that I had sex with him. A total lie, and now Gina is coming for me."

"Whatta loser!" Jen whistled.

"Yep! That's what I say." Apprehension over this whole fiasco had me tied in knots.

"Don't let those three amigos get you down. They are their own brand of poison."

"I wish I'd stayed home." I stabbed my pie.

"Something else happened that literally will blow your mind." I could see the excitement in Jen's eyes, but it put me on edge. What possible good could come from this nightmare? "What happened?"

"The girls' restroom went up in smoke." Jen's arms stretched out. "A gas leak ignited, and the whole restroom went boom. It was sick!"

"Did anyone get hurt?" Fear plagued my mind.

"No! Not one person got injured. The weird part is that no one even heard an explosion."

"You're kiddin'? Not one, huh?"

"Isn't that the wildest thing you've ever heard?"

"Yeah, the wildest," I replied, turning over in my mind how Bane and I landed in the football stadium unharmed. "So, they think it was a gas leak?" I snatched up my cup and got up from the table for more coffee. My heart was pounding in my ears. I poured another cup and turned to Jen. "You want another?"

"No, I'm good. Thanks!" She pushed her cup aside. "I can't believe you haven't watched the news. It's been blowing up on every channel."

I settled back down into my seat. "I don't have a television."

"Dang! That's gotta blow!"

"I guess," I shrugged. "I'm used to it." Jesus! It was on the news! I bet it'll be in the newspaper too. "I'm relieved no one got hurt."

"Hey, something good did come out of this." Jen tossed an elfish grin.

"What?" I thought my heart was going to implode.

"No school for the rest of the week!"

"We have a whole week?" That was music to my ears—no fights for at least a week.

"You should come hang out. Maybe catch a movie?"

"There's a movie theater here?"

"No, but there's a theater a few towns over. I got a car!" Jen held up her keys, dangling them.

"Sounds cool!"

"Hey, I almost forgot!" She nearly came out of her seat.

"Oh no, what?"

"Someone has a crush on you big time." A glint of humor flickered in her brown eyes.

"What?" I asked, confused.

"Oh! It's good," she smiled. "Aidan beat up Sam."

"No, he didn't?" I gawked.

"If the principal hadn't broken them up, Sam would've ended up in the hospital. Aidan worked him over good!"

"Did you see it?" I stirred uneasily in my chair.

"I saw the aftermath. Sam was bloody from his head to his toe."

"Why would Bane go after Sam?"

"Silly! Don't you know?

"No, I guess not." Jen seemed convinced about Bane's motive. I had my doubts.

"Bane whooped Sam's ass for spreading rumors about you."

I scoffed. "I seriously doubt that Aidan Bane was defending my honor. We don't even like each other as friends."

"Are you freaking blind? That boy never takes his eyes off you, and I think you like him too." Jen never worried about putting it out there. That was what I liked about her. I never had to second-guess her.

That night when the moon climbed the star-filled sky and the gentle chorus of cicada sang among the trees, I lay in bed with a book across my chest. No matter how hard I tried to focus on reading, my mind kept drifting back to this morning. I had crossed Sam off my friends' list. No love lost there.

Then my mind drifted to Bane. The hate in his stark blues and the imprint in my heart that he'd seared. I touched my lips, remembering the sting of his kiss. I tried to deny my feelings, but I had to face the truth. I liked Bane. The mystery that lay behind his eyes beckoned me. I reckoned I had a death wish, considering his temperament. Yet when I was with Bane, I'd never felt more alive. He had awakened a spirit in me that I never knew existed. These uncharted feelings were enthralling and frightening at the same time.

I tossed the book aside and rolled on my chest, squeezing my eyes shut. I wanted to think about daisies, puppy dogs, and fireflies. Damnit! I hated myself for my weakness.

FORGET HIM

$\mathcal{I}$ woke with a jolt, sitting erect. A stream of sunlight was hitting my face. I rubbed my eyes to clear the blur and swallowed down the dryness in my throat. That same dream returned, haunting me. My chest was heaving. Sweat dripped from my body.

The dream started with the faceless boy taking my hand and leading me down a dark corridor. His face remained obscured, but the ring he wore on his left hand was in plain view, a cluster of black diamond's outlining an oval eye. To my dismay, I stood in the center of a circle of black robes. Thirteen men. Always thirteen. Somewhere in the haze, a child's cry wafted in the chill. Shivers rushed over me as my mind carried me through the dream.

Then my eyes popped open, and the dream vanished. The effects never changed, always leaving me in an icy tailspin. I took a moment to collect myself, steadying my pulse.

A moment later, I heard pans rattling downstairs. Crap! Sara was home. I glanced at the time, 4:30 in the morning. School was out today, but I had papers to deliver. I scrambled to my feet, knocking off the covers, and darted to my bathroom.

When I finished dressing, I headed downstairs. The walk of death invaded my mind. After the brawl Sunday evening, I half expected

Sara to armed with an iron skillet. I entered the kitchen, and the smell of hot grease and batter hit my nose. Oh no, not again! I wanted to barf. With a frilly apron tied around her waist and a spatula in hand, Sara stood at the stove, making pancakes. I couldn't entirely blame my mom. I never bothered letting her in on my little secret that I hated pancakes. I appreciated the few times she'd made an effort to play mommy. Which brought me to wonder why the prodigal mother decided to return?

Sara glanced up at me, smiling. "Good morning!"

"Morning," I grumbled, still dragging my feet. I went straight for my favorite mug and poured a cup of black coffee. After adding creamer, I made my way to the table, blowing into my mug, while keeping one eye on Sara.

My mother's bipolar made her unpredictable, and then the fiasco on the front lawn still hovered between us. I wondered what she had up her sleeve. Rent was probably due.

I seated myself at the table, playing it cool, but underneath, I felt like a wound-up cat. Sara slid a plateful of pancakes in front of me, oozing with thick syrup. A burnt stench wafted up my nose as I stared at the melted butter running down the stack. I held back my cookies.

"I see you still use that ugly cup." Sara's eyes shifted to my mug and then back at me. It was no secret. Sara hated anything that reminded her of Dad, and that meant even this chipped cup, covered in faded red hearts. It was worth nothing, but to me, it was priceless. It was the last thing that Dad had given me before his unfortunate death. "Yeah, I always use this cup."

Sara joined me at the table. "I heard about the explosion at school." She sipped her coffee.

"Yep, me too."

"Glad you're okay." Sara cracked a smile.

"I'm thankful no one got hurt." I gulped my coffee.

Sara squirmed in her seat, antsy. "I'm sorry about Sunday," she confessed. "I only wanted to protect you, is all."

I knew my mother. Any act of kindness possessed an evil motive behind it. "Really?" I hardly looked over the rim of my mug.

"I was wrong to have jumped to conclusions." She held her gaze on her coffee cup.

I looked at the clock on the wall. "Gotta go. Work." I forced a quick smile and pushed off from the table.

"Wait!" Sara reached over, grabbing my arm. Her eyes seemed desperate. "Francis was wrong," she sighed. "I swore to Francis if he ever tried to hurt you again, I'd leave him."

"I can't talk. I'm late." I jerked my arm free.

"I'm going to be around more. I hope you will bring your boyfriend over, maybe for dinner sometime. I really like Aidan."

"He's not my boyfriend or even a friend."

That was when the charade dropped. The real Sara emerged like a snake from the grass. "You better find a way then, missy," she hissed. "He's the best chance you got!"

"This might shock you, but I do have other choices, college, for example." I set my cup in the sink and faced Sara. "I can talk later." The ire in my voice was just as intense as the pernicious glare Sara aimed at me.

As I ducked out the back door, I heard a plate fracture against the door's windowpane and glass shattering to the floor. I had a hunch that Sara meant that for me. Glad her aim was off this morning. Wearing syrup all day would've been a bad look.

After I'd finished my route, I headed home. My heart sped up when I whizzed past the corner of Saint Anne Street. The smell of crepe myrtle lingered in the air as I took a long whiff. Best fragrance ever! I rolled up into the drive. From what I could tell, it was empty. In any case, I still wanted to check inside before I could relax completely.

Moments later, I was standing in the kitchen by the back door. Just as I'd expected, glass and pancake intermingled and dripping down the door and onto the floor. Apart from not cleaning up the mess, Sara left the coffee pot on too. The aroma of burnt coffee and syrup perfumed the whole house. "Crap! It was gonna take a week to get that smell out."

With a long sigh, I flipped the coffee pot off and snatched the broom from the pantry. I started sweeping up the mess. The broken window needed some sort of cover until I could get it repaired. That meant I had to dig into my small savings, which reminded me of rent. Since Sara wouldn't give me the landlord's name, my hands were tied. The idea of giving up my money to her was out of the question. She'd blow it instead of paying rent. I suddenly wanted to hurl something. I didn't even know if I had enough to pay the full month. Maybe Ms. Noel had spoken to her nephew.

In the meantime, I'd asked my supervisor if he had any open paper routes available. I had been taking on a little more on the weekends, but it wasn't enough. Since school was out this week, I could use the extra hours to make a few more coins. I had my fingers crossed. The supervisor said he'd check the schedule and see. To me, that meant yes.

Later that night, Jen swung by to pick me up. She couldn't stop talking about a favorite hangout downtown, called Mother Blues. Though I'd never been, I knew the place. It was across the street from the Mudbug Café.

I never cared much for hot spots. I preferred the solitude of my bedroom or a quiet corner at a fleabag hotel. Nonetheless, I'd give it a shot. I'd probably drink a Coke and watch Jen play pool or foosball. Apart from Jen's bragging over her skills, she swore the joint had the best tunes and fried oysters in Louisiana. I'd take her word on the oysters and pass.

We entered Mother Blues with Jen leading the way. I took a quick assessment of the joint. Even though I'd never been to a bar before, I pictured this place similar to one—low lighting, nothing special. The main attraction was a few neon lights hanging on the wall and several pool and foosball tables centered under lamps that remotely lit the joint. Toward the back, I spied a snack bar and a few booths.

The place hustled with aimless chatter, blaring music, and pool balls snapping. Minus the liquor, it smelled of smoke.

Jen saw a couple of her friends and went off in their direction. I ambled toward the back, trying to pick out the heads that I recognized from school. I spotted a few, none I had a class with.

By the time I'd ordered a Coke, Jen had caught up. "Hey, I'll have what she's having," Jen called out to the cashier.

I took a long drag of my drink through the straw as my eyes washed over the spot.

"You likey?" Jen hollered over the loud music as she paid the cashier for her drink.

"It's cool," I smiled.

She nudged me. "I'll challenge you to a game of foosball."

Jen was at ease with herself here. Although I wasn't into games, I did enjoy hanging out with her. She was easy to talk to, and I found myself laughing at her jokes. Even though no one could replace Beck and Laurie, Jen was a close contender.

"Okay, let's do this then." I pushed off the counter. Off we went, sashaying our way to the far corner.

Jen slid the coins in the slot, and the game was on. She and I had played a couple of games before two boys from a neighboring town joined us. Jen and I teamed up together, playing against the boys in a game. Jen and I were fierce. We won three games out of four.

One of the boys took a liking to me. He'd been flirting with me throughout the match. When we finished, Jen and the dark-headed boy trailed off to the snack bar, leaving me standing with the tall blond. He was like me, shy. We both did more smiling than talking. When he finally mustered up the courage, he bent down close to my ear and whispered something silly, making small talk. I was smiling, enjoying myself until my eyes lifted, and all my blood rushed to my face.

Aidan Bane had just entered the building.

It was as if the room had frozen, and the only thing I could hear was my pounding heart. Bane saw me from across the room as our eyes crashed. Goosebumps popped up over my body. The boy had that kind of effect on me. He made no indication that he knew me. A sudden pinch of pain stabbed my chest. Bane's dismissal bothered me more than I cared to admit.

He joined a small group of guys over at a pool table on the opposite side of us. I didn't recognize any of the guys. They were somewhat huddled in a circle, all smiles and high-fiving each other.

Bane pulled out a cue stick from its sheath. I reckoned he must be pretty good at pool. Of course, it was in the genome of DNA that every rich boy was resolved to driving a Corvette, employing a butler, and comes complete with his own unique stick. No pun intended.

The blond boy drew me back. "You wanna sit down at a booth? I'll get you another Coke. It's on me," he smiled. The guy was more than mildly attractive. He reminded me of Logan, but I didn't foresee anything other than friendship. Yet considering that I was single, I might as well enjoy a little harmless flirting. I didn't need permission to do that.

"Sure!" I shyly smiled.

The boy guided me through the crowd to an empty table. Funny, I kept feeling two dark blue eyes beaming the center of my shoulder blades. It was starting to grate on me.

Jen and the other guy joined us. "Girl, you gotta try the fried oysters!" I looked down, and they both had a basket of some kind of fried nuggets. It didn't look anything like fried chicken, and the smell nearly made me barf.

"Thanks, but I'll pass," I grinned, holding my nose.

Jen and the dark-haired guy laughed.

Soon the blond boy returned with two Cokes and two hot dogs. As he slid in next to me, he pushed a dog and drink in front of me, "Here you go, pretty lady."

"Sweet! Thanks." We shared a short glance and a curt smile. Strange how no one had exchanged names, and even more bizarre, it didn't bother me enough to ask.

Thankfully, Jen and the two boys had the gift of gab. I sat and mostly listened. They didn't really talk about anything in particular. I was more than happy to sit back and listen.

Then the mood shifted when I caught a dark shadow in the corner of my eye. I should've known. Aidan Bane waltzed up to our table. "Good evening!" His smile stretched across his tawny face, revealing his signature, pearly smile. The chatter at our table stalled, and Jen and I shared a wry glance. Jen asked, being polite. "Hey, Aidan! When did you get here?"

"Oh, just now. I'm meeting a few friends here." Then he turned his eyes on me. "Stevie, could I have a word with you?" He nodded toward the door.

"Umm, I'm with my friends. Can it wait?" My insides were warring. I wanted to go with him, but the little voice in my head screamed… *don't go!*

He scratched his jawline. "I won't be long," he smiled, but it didn't reach his eyes.

I stared up at him, pausing. Then with a sharp sigh, I agreed. "Fine! Make it quick," The blond boy slid from the booth, cutting Aidan an evil eye as he let me out. "Are you okay?"

"I'm fine. I'll be back. Keep my spot," I smiled.

The boy cut his eyes one more time at Bane and then looked back at me and nodded. I was glad he didn't try to push Bane's buttons. I got the impression the boy felt a little intimidated by Bane's towering height. Just being in Bane's presence could make a person uneasy. He had that effect on folks.

I took the lead, heading outside. Bane followed right on my heels. I imagined he wanted to talk about the explosion. I'd rather pretend it didn't happen. It wasn't as if we blew the restroom up with a stick of dynamite. We just happened to be in the wrong place at the wrong time.

Then I recalled us landing in the empty football stadium clear on the other side of the school's campus. That little fact had me freaked out on so many levels. The explanation of how we landed hundreds of yards away was beyond my grasp.

As soon as we were far enough from earshot and out of sight from the window, I spun on my heels, glaring at him. "What now?" I was chomping at the bit.

"Who's the girl you're with?" He drawled casually, a tinge of green flavored his tone.

My brow arched, "Jen?"

Bane flashed a dark grin. "I meant the other girl."

Under the moonlight, his eyes were as sharp as a razor. I dragged in a raspy breath. "What do you want, Aidan?" This was the first time I'd allowed myself to call him by his first name. I braced myself against the building, arms folded to my chest, still feeling the sting of his words from our last encounter.

He stepped into my personal space. His fingers tenderly traced the line of my cheekbone. Regret appeared to be weighing heavily on his shoulders. He sighed. "I only want to apologize." The corners of his mouth tipped upward, almost smiling but then fading.

"Why the apology? You believe the rumors."

"Yes, about that," he inhaled deeply. "My behavior was quite deplorable."

Funny, even as mad as I was, all I could think about was his singeing kiss. No argument here." I wasn't giving him an inch. He could've called or come by my house instead of running into me by chance. But to be fair, I did tell him to stay away. "Do you know what caused the explosion?"

Bane's face remained courtly, too poised as if he was in a game of poker. "Quite a display, wasn't it?" He rubbed his jawline with his thumb.

I bent my lips to his ear. "How did we live through that without even so much as a scratch?"

He shrugged. "Stranger things have happened."

"Weird things happen around you," my eyes narrowed. "Why is that?"

"Such as," he countered, eyes full of obscurity.

"Such as every freaking breath I take!"

Bane was more than exasperating. He pressed me against the wall, our thighs touching. God! He smelled good too. "Can't you just let it go?" he whispered as he stroked a strand of my hair between his fingers.

I recalled his threat he'd implied at the firefly nest. Sorta hard to forget. "If I don't, are you going to dispose of my body underneath your house?"

"Princess." His voice was smooth as satin. "Your paranoia is starting to worry me."

"Sorry to bother you," I encountered.

Brittle silence settled between us as our eyes locked, frozen, unable to break free from each other. Why couldn't I just walk away and never look back? Forget him? Why did it have to be him? Aidan Bane was trouble. Yet, I abandoned all common sense when I looked into his sea blues eyes. Whatever this was between us, it was far more profound and more significant than anything I'd ever confronted, and I was terrified of where this may lead to.

Then the brief silence shattered as Bane replied. "You behave as if these minor things taint your propriety. Why must you persevere in these matters as if they are tethered to your ankle?"

"Do people where you come from talk like you?" I suddenly blurted out. Holding my tongue wasn't one of my virtues.

He scratched behind his ear. "Now you have a problem with my verbiage?" He tilted his head to the side. His warm breath felt warm against my cheeks.

"You talk like Grandpa's grandpa. I'm just saying."

Aidan threw his head back and burst into chuckles. When he came back up for air, he chimed in. Laughter still sparkled in his eyes. "You never cease to amuse me, Stevie Ray!"

I liked the way he said my name.

He reached out, tracing his fingers sensually down my arm. I held my breath, dropping my arms to my sides and stilled. "What are you doing?" I asked.

His hands slid to my hips, drawing me tighter against his muscular frame. I froze as he brushed his lips against mine and then to my earlobe, murmuring. "I'm having a lovely chat with my girl." He raised his blues back to me, "Is that a problem?" There were touches of desire glistening in his eyes.

Chills! Damn, chills!

"It depends."

He ignored my reply as his hands moved under my shirt, warm palms flushed to my skin.

Holy Jesus, aftershocks! I shivered.

"Depends on what?" He nudged my nose with his and then lightly kissed my lips.

I had to rescue my dignity and resist his advances. Where there were few rules in battle, fighting dirty wasn't beneath me. So, I used the parent card. "Depends on whether or not my mother comes out chasing you with a broomstick." I nodded across the street at the diner. "Lights are still on."

He cut his eyes over his shoulder and back at me. "I suppose that does present a problem." He blew out a sharp sigh. "Let's get the hell out of here." He flashed his signature smile, pearly white teeth, and dimples.

My heart wanted to say yes, but my good sense screamed *NO!* "I-I can't. I'm with Jen." Then the proverbial brick smacked me upside the head. I realized that Aidan Bane was after one thing, sex! I stiffened. "You don't hear the word "no," very often, do you?"

He came off with a sardonic grin. "Rarely."

"Well, let this one be your first." I stabbed my finger in his chest. "No! Nada! Not now! Not ever! You can't just pop up uninvited expecting me to dump my friends and leave with you whenever it suits your pampered ass!" I pushed off from the wall and stalked off, heading back inside to my real friends.

"I'm confused?" Bane yelled out, holding his hands in the air, irritated. "What did I do wrong?"

I paused with my hand on the glass door. My heated gaze collided with Bane's face. "I deserve better!" Then I disappeared inside. No matter how much I liked Bane, I wasn't going to let him use me.

Jen and the two boys, whose names I'd yet to learn, were sitting at the table where I'd left them. I reckoned by the look on my face, Jen knew I wasn't right. "Hey! Are you okay?"

I slid beside the blond boy and grabbed my Coke, sucking up the watered-down drink. "I'm okay." I looked away, trying to compose myself. Tears were welling, and I couldn't stop them.

I leaped to my feet and darted to the girls' restroom as tears streamed. I found the sign above the doorway reading in bold white, restrooms. I trailed off down the short hallway, rushing before anyone saw me sobbing. Just when I reached the door with the girl icon, I remembered the explosion. I froze. Since the blast, I'd been a bit leery of any public facility with stalls and toilets. Instead, I found the privacy of an old phone booth and ducked inside it. I just needed a minute to breathe.

Later that night, going home, Jen asked. "What happened between you and Aidan?"

"Other than he's a douche, nothing." I frowned.

"I saw your face. You were upset, man!"

I sighed and caved. "Bane was hoping I'd be his bootie call."

"That jerk!" Jen's jaw dropped.

"Yeah, I know!" I shook my head. "I said no, and that ended his short-term interest in me." I shrugged. Though inside, my heart was broken.

"It's his loss. Rite!"

"Rite!" Slang for 'I know dats right," I smiled back.

"You wanna stay at my house tonight? I have movies to watch. We can pop some popcorn, stay up all night." Jen dangled the tempting bait.

If it had been any other night, I would've taken Jen up on her offer. "It sounds great, but I have to work in the morning. A rain check?" I asked.

"Absolutely! Hey, I got asked out by Al. His friend, Cal, the blond one, I think he's crushing on you. Al mentioned going to the movies this Friday. We can make it a double date?"

I got the feeling this was a package deal. The boy Jen liked might not come if his buddy didn't get to come. I'd do it for Jen, anytime. The blond boy was cute and very sweet, a good distraction for an achy heart.

"Yeah, that sounds like fun. Let me ask my mom." I didn't have to get permission, but in case I changed my mind, I'd have an excuse to bail without hurting Jen's feelings.

OTHERWORLDLY

School started back up, and our short vacation had ended. It was Monday, and things seemed to be back to normal.

The worry of getting arrested subsided when the school and the fire inspector declared the cause of the explosion was a gas leak. I wasn't in any position to argue. Considering everything, anyone with half a brain knew gas wasn't even a factor. As I kept that little tidbit under my hat, I enjoyed my week off. Jen and I hung out, sometimes at her house and sometimes at mine. We didn't get to go out on a date with the two boys. Al called Jen and canceled. He'd caught the flu and was out of pocket for the whole weekend. Bummer, but it happens.

In my first class, English, I had a bone to pick with Sally. She started this crap between Gina and me. The length Sally would go to hurt her best friend blew my mind. It was time to settle the score.

When I walked into class, Sally was sitting at her desk, wringing her hands nervously. Good, I delighted in her anxiety. My eyes washed over Aidan's empty desk, and relief came over me. I had my hands full with Sally. I didn't need his interference.

I slammed my books down on my desk. A loud thud echoed over the buzzing discourse of the room, startling Sally. I stifled a laugh. "Hello, Sally!" I didn't bother hiding the anger in my tone.

"Oh, hey," she spoke meekly.

I stood, arms crossed, glaring at my non-friend. "What the hell, Sally! Why would you go along with Sam to hurt your best friend?"

Sally's shoulders slumped. After a handful of seconds, she finally turned around and faced me. "I didn't intend to put you in the middle."

"Then why did you involve me?"

Sally's whole body heaved with a long sigh. "Sam liked you, and I thought you two should hook up."

"I call BS on that, Sally! Tell the real truth!"

"Fair enough!" Sally held up her hand in protest. The facts commenced rolling off her tongue. "Gina doesn't have any problems getting boyfriends," she sniffed, wiping a dry tear. "Aidan wasn't lying about Gina under the bleachers. The boy she hooked up was someone I liked. Gina knew I had a crush on him too." She licked her dry lips. "So I went to Sam and told him about Gina. That's when he mentioned you." She squirmed in her seat. "Sam and I wanted to get even with Gina. We knew how much you and Gina didn't like each other, and… " she shrugged. "You know the rest."

I wanted to pound my fist into her face. "What a ratchet thing to do, Sally!"

"I guess." She kept wringing her hands, evading eye contact.

"Did you think for one minute that your idea might hurt me?"

"Sorry," she blurted out as if I was annoying her.

"You're sorry? Is that all you can say?"

Sally bunched her shoulders together like a dog hovering in a corner. "I thought you liked Sam."

"You and Sam set me up to get back at Gina. Have you bothered telling your BFF that little fact?"

"No!" She shook her head. "I don't plan to either."

"Oh! That's rich. Do you think Gina's gonna let this slide?"

"I don't know. I'm not Gina's keeper."

"Oh, really? You need to clear this up with your girl. Because of you and Sam, I have a target on my back."

"I said I was sorry."

Her cavalier attitude left me flabbergasted. "Sorry isn't going to fix this fiasco." I raked my fingers through my hair.

"I get it! It won't happen again."

"You're damn straight it won't!" I looked away. Staring at her pathetic face was like sand in my shorts. Saved by the bell, Ms. Jenkins walked in and ending our discussion.

It was a lose-lose situation with Sally. I reckoned remaining angry with her was a waste of good energy. To be real, I felt sorry for her. At first, I didn't see the connection between the two girls. They seemed so different. Now, it was as clear as a cloudless day. Sally had no backbone to stand up for herself, and she would do anything to get attention from the opposite sex. Gina fed off of Sally's insecurities. She used Sally to remind herself that she was the superior one, the blonde bomb. I think Gina and Sally deserved each other. They both were the worst friends that they possibly could be for each other and anyone else in their clenches.

When the teacher started counting row, Aidan Bane swaggered into the classroom late like he was the exception. He was the epitome of the bad boy that didn't seem to care about authority.

Ms. Jenkins tossed him a heated glare. He winked back, antagonizing her more as he made his way to his desk. I wondered why the teacher didn't order him to the principal's office. Maybe he got special treatment since his parents had deep pockets, or perhaps the faculty was afraid of him. I'd seen his temper in action. He was intimidating at best.

When Bane passed by me to his seat, he didn't glance my way. His cold shoulder bit too. He was driving me crazy. I'd never wanted to-not-want something so much in my life. Why did I punish myself? I sat through class, feeling like a ham sandwich. In front of me sat Sally, the Energizer Bunny with nonstop yammering, and behind me, Bane, throwing blue icicles at my back.

Finally, the bell sounded off, and Aidan whizzed past me like he was headed to a fire. Whatever! It didn't matter. Our little thing had ended. I frowned to myself as I gathered my books and headed off to the gym. Not my favorite class. Showering in front of strangers was the worst.

After gym, Coach Rosedale took me off to the side and asked. "Hey, are you up for a little extra cash?"

"Sure. What do you have in mind?" I liked the coach. She was tough but fair.

"The supplies closet needs a little rearranging. I got fifty bucks for you if you want the job?"

"Sweet! Yes, ma'am, I'll be happy to do the job."

"Great!" Her small brown eyes twinkled. "Come to my office after school, and you can get started then. The cleanup shouldn't take you more than a couple of hours, tops." She patted my shoulder and darted off in the opposite direction, down the hall.

Perfect timing! I needed the money. I worried the landlord might see the window Sara had broken and evict us for property damage. It had happened before. I checked the clock on the wall. Only two minutes to get to my history class before the bell sounded off.

School ended for the day, and the clacking of feet and the twaddle of laughter filled the halls. A sea of heads and backpacks headed out the front door.

By the time I finished unloading books at my locker, the halls had thinned. It was strange hearing the echoes of only my footfalls ricocheting off the lockers as I trotted off to the gym. When I made my way through the gym to the coach's office, I came to an abrupt stop, spotting a white envelope with my name taped to the door. I yanked it down and opened it. There was a key inside and a short message.

Stevie, please rearrange all the supplies. Wash the uniforms, sweep, and take the trash out. Come by here in the morning before school, and I'll have your money. Sorry to leave. Family emergency.

Thanks,

Coach Rosedale

A little disappointed, I assumed the coach would be waiting for me. Oh well, no biggie. I shrugged off. I didn't need her to hold my hand.

I snatched the key and tossed the paper in the trash, and off I went to the closet. I was humming a tune as I unlocked the door. It was a bummer that I couldn't use this extra money to buy a pair of earbuds. Music would be sweet right now. I unlocked the door and stepped inside, searching for a light switch.

"Ah! There it is." I mumbled. I reached up and flipped the switch. Immediately, the light flashed and extinguished. Blackness enshrouded me as I gasped, startled. "Crap!" I inhaled a whiff and instantly held my nose. A pungent order scurried up my nose.

Feeling around like a blind person, I dug my cell phone out and swiped the flashlight icon. I waved the small stream of light over the storage room, and my chin dropped to the floor. The coach had left out a few minor details. The whole place looked like a tornado had struck. Garbage scattered aimlessly, clothes thrown in a heap. Forget two hours. Cleaning up this mess was an all-nighter.

I rocked on my heels, debating. It was too late to back out. I'd tell the coach I'd gotten sick. A small measure of hope sparked. Then I remembered the broken window, and my heart sank.

With my shoulders slumped, I spun on my heels, getting a good look at the mess from the small stream of my cell's flashlight. I spotted a heavy-duty flashlight sitting on the corner of the shelf. A rush of relief and ire flitted through me. At least I had some light to work, and then, on the other hand, the coach must've known that the lighting was about to blow.

Feeling sorry for myself wouldn't get the job done. I tossed my hair out of my face and grabbed up the flashlight and flipped it on. The flashlight wasn't as bright as fluorescent lighting, but it was better than my cell. I found a basket in the back and started first with the laundry, stuffing it in a basket. I picked up the clothes and headed for the laundromat down a short corridor. That same tune from earlier ran through my mind, one of Charlie Puth's songs, I Warned Myself. I began to hum. Some music was timeless.

Unexpectedly, the room's warmth suddenly dissipated, and a cold breeze coasted up my T-shirt. I spotted a dark shadow moving in the dimness of my flashlight, and my breath stalled. I spun on my heels, shedding light over the lockers. I saw nothing! I eased a long sigh as a soccer ball rolled across the floor. Its echo flittered through my mind as I watched it come to a halt at my feet. "Paranoid much?" I laughed, giving it a swift kick.

I entered the small laundry room and tossed the clothes into the washing machine, dumped the soap, and turned the water temperature to hot. I slammed the lid down and headed back. I held the flashlight in front of me as it spread its beam across the floor. That was when I caught a silhouette of a man standing back in the shadows. Startled, I yapped, quickly flashing the light over the wall of lockers.

Still, nothing!

"I'm such a scaredy-cat," I scolded myself.

All at once, my gaze landed on a pair of black boots, stepping into the faint light. Shoes didn't move on their own. Panic welled in my throat. "Screw this!" I bit out. I made a beeline for the door. Just as my fingers clasped the door handle, fists gripped my hair and thrust me into the air, sending me sailing across the room, colliding into a pile of dirty clothes. The flashlight went flying, and total darkness devoured the storage room.

I blinked for a second as the peril sunk into my brain. I had to call 911! Hands trembling, I hurried, digging in my back pocket but quickly felt a sharp prick. "Ow!" I withdrew my fingers, feeling something wet and sticky. Blood! I must've crushed my phone when I hit the floor. Fear came gasping up my throat in a cold, panting fear. No phone meant I was at this creep's mercy.

In the next breath, a fist clenched a wad of my hair, dragging me to my feet. The pain was tormenting, but I fought, swinging at the air. A sudden burst of warmth struck my face. I swatted at the brightness as a voice appeared behind the light. "We meet again." The stranger's voice hummed like a machine as he revealed himself. I gasped. The man in black from the fair! He must've followed me.

Helpless, I dangled as he held me up from the nap of my head. My mind was wild of fright and pain. I begged. "Please, mister! Let me go." I sobbed.

"Have they left you ignorant?"

"They? Who's they?" I cried out. "Please let me go! I won't tell anyone. I swear!"

He unleashed a deep guttural sound like an animal. "I expected more fight from you. I'm rather disappointed."

"Please, just let me go!"

"It's a shame they did not teach you the histories of your inheritance."

"Mister, I'm nobody. You got the wrong person!"

"That's where you are wrong, angel."

I had to think fast if I wanted to survive. I started spitting out questions. "Why were you following me at the fair?" I blurted out. The longer he talked, the longer I lived.

"I represent an ancient faction. My mission is to watch you."

"Why would anyone hire you to watch me?"

"I am not a lowly mundane," he bared his jagged teeth. "However, I am a slave."

"I'm sorry! I'm sorry! I'm so, so, sorry! I'm only trying to make sense of this. That's all, mister." I spied the door, only a few feet away. I might have a chance to escape. Keep stalling, a voice in my head urged. "A prisoner? That's horrible."

"You can't imagine," he snarled.

I played the sympathy card. "Tell me more. I'd like to know." I tried pushing past the pain and sounding genuine.

"Does the word Illuminati mean anything to you?"

"No. I've never heard of it." I squeezed my eyes shut. Oh, god! I wanted to vomit.

"You're lying!" He shook me harder. "Your boyfriend is a member of *The Family*."

"Mister, I don't have a boyfriend."

"You are of great value to him."

"I don't know who you're talking about!" The stranger squeezed tighter, making me scream out. "I swear! I don't know!"

"You are quite an accomplished liar," he mused, "But not enough to fool me. I know you very well. After all, I've watched you since childhood. You are a hybrid, the property of the Family. You're no more human than I am."

"Look!" I swatted at his hand. "I don't know anything about this family, mister."

The stranger wrangled me closer to his frame, sniffing my body like a carnal beast, his nostrils flaring. "You smell quite delicious," he grunted. "You and I are going to have fun." He spoke against my hair.

Cold fear knotted inside me. No doubt, before he finished me off, I'd be begging for my death. "Please don't hurt me!"

"I'm afraid I cannot honor your request." He kissed my cheek. My stomach heaved. "You see, I must punish them for disgracing my kind. I must take revenge on them."

"Then go after them," I shouted. "Your beef's not with me." My eyes swept over the room, hoping to find a weapon in reach.

"Ahhh, I am doing just that. You are a priceless commodity to the Family, and yet they leave you unprotected. Such fools, they are!"

My whole life flashed before me. I wanted to live. With undeniable certainty, I had to fight. I blurted out the first thing that came to mind, "I don't believe you!" I screamed. "You're just some ugly circle-jerk who's forgotten to take his meds." I spat spittle in his face. "You schizo, crazy bastard, go back to the rock you crawled out from under!" If I angered him enough, maybe he'd loosen his grip.

In one swift move, he jerked my head so hard that pain shot down my spine. I nearly fainted. "I shall show you what I am." He broke into a prideful grin, and then it got freaky.

The stranger dropped his shades, revealing his eyes. The vision I had with Ms. Noel barreled through my brain. I froze, staring into the devil's eyes, a repugnant yellow, identical to cat-eyes.

Without warning, the stranger released his grip and laughter, pierced the dim light. He stepped back, shoulders straight and poised like a ballet dancer. As if performing on stage, he began a waltz, back and forth, in and out, vanishing and then materializing before my eyes. He bellowed darkly. "Now you see me. Now you don't." I watched in stunned silence as he disappeared in one spot and reappeared in another.

Then I seized my chance. I darted for the door. Before I reached the door, the creature clenched my hair and flung me with lethal force, slamming me against the metal lockers. I screamed, fighting for my life. My head pounded, my body coiled with agony. Blood saturated my hair, my clothes. I was a dead girl.

My mind began to slip into a tunnel, a dream-like state. Bane hovered over me, whispering. "You're safe now, Princess. I've got you." Warmth wrapped around my chilled body, and a faint glow encircled me as I drifted in and out of consciousness. A sense of calmness came over me. I closed my eyes as slumber came.

156

HEALING

My eyes flew open as I came up swinging, fighting off the monster that plagued my mind. When I heard Bane's voice, I calmed, stilling.

A sharp throb resonated from the back of my head, and the rest of my body ached. I tried to raise my head, but Bane, with gentle ease, held my shoulders flat on the bed. "Don't move, Love." His voice soothed me like a lullaby. I clung to it as if it was my lifeline.

I reached for the back of my head, and I flinched from pain. I shut my eyes, blocking bothering light. "What happened?" My voice sounded raspy.

Bane sat on the edge of the bed, his fingers laced with mine. My gaze lifted to his perfectly chiseled face. He was smiling down at me. "You took a good fall and hit your head. The doctor said you'd be fine after bed rest for a few days."

"I hit my head?" My brain felt full of cobwebs. "How did I get hurt?" I drew a blank.

"You slipped on baby oil at school."

"How did you find me?" Confusion swirled in my mind.

"I came back for my book bag, and that's when I found you on the floor."

"Lucky me, huh?" I tried to smile, but I flinched from the ache.

"You certainly are!" His blues filled with urgent affection.

"Where did you find me?"

"Hush, rest now. No talking. Worry about the details later," he declined his head gently kissing me on the forehead.

"Can you stay with me?" The thought of being alone terrified me. I didn't want to be clingy, but I needed him.

"Anything for my princess." Aidan slid underneath, throwing his arm over me, his body flushed against mine. He swallowed me with warmth and the feeling of safety. Aidan gently kissed my neck and my bare shoulder and moved to my heated cheek. Even with a muddled mind, I desired him.

I rolled over on my side, facing him as our eyes locked. My pulse began to race. I reached up and ran my fingers through his black curls. His eyes were glistening like the stars. He lowered his lips to mine and kissed me. It wasn't rough or possessive like our first kiss. This time, his kiss was gentle and sweet. Geez, I'd been craving those plump lips of his. I wanted to drink him down to the last drop.

I glanced down at myself and realized that a thin, white T-shirt covered my body. "Uh," I lifted my gaze, wide-eyed. "Did you undress me? I don't recall changing." Embarrassment colored my face a bright red.

Bane cuffed his hand over his mouth as his shoulders gently shook in silence. It had taken a minute before he answered. "I believe your mother had the pleasure."

"Oh," I replied softly.

Bane kissed me one more time on my forehead and exhaled a regretful sigh, "Rest now." He shifted his body to the side, gently throwing his leg over mine and pulling me close to his chest. I felt his warm smile resting against my neck.

Chills, dang chills!

A shaft of light pierced the window, showering its warmth throughout my bedroom as I blinked the morning haze away. It took a moment to gather my thoughts. I rubbed my eyes, yawning. I glimpsed at the clock on my nightstand and shot straight up out of bed. Crap! Eight in the morning, I have to get dressed. I scrambled to my feet. I had my paper route to run and school!

An unanticipated bout of dizziness struck, and I quickly eased back down on the bed. I sat on the edge, waiting for it to pass. I heard a light tap at my door. "Can I come in?" Sara stood, peeking through the crack.

"Yes," I mumbled, clenching my stomach. I felt like I might barf.

The door creaked opened, and Sara entered and lulled over to my bed. Sara held her mug in hand. I watched the steam curl from the dark liquid. "Don't worry about work or school today." She appeared friendlier than usual. I hoped she might be back on her meds.

"Mom, I can't afford to lose my job. I'm already late."

"No, you're okay." She sipped her coffee. "Stay in bed. It's not like you have somewhere to be."

"Huh... yes, I do. I have a job." I looked at her, puzzled.

"Take today off, is all I'm saying."

"Well, that sounds dandy, but that doesn't get the rent paid."

"Stop worrying! It's been handled."

A sudden dread washed over me. "Who paid the rent?"

Sara flashed a grin that was anything but sweet. "Someone very generous is taking care of our expenses. No more pinching pennies."

Maybe I needed a healthy dose of Drano to unclog my brain but... "I don't get it."

"A few minor changes have come into play."

Dread washed over me.

Sara went on to say, "I have a new job! I'm Aidan's caretaker. His parents asked me to watch over him while they are out of the States." Sara smiled like the daughter of Satan.

"Why would Bane's parents hire a stranger to watch over their precious son?" Sara had a knack for spinning tales.

"Gee! Thanks for the vote of confidence," she snapped.

"Sorry! It's hard for me to swallow. You can't manage your own self."

"Get used to it! They fired you, and I quit mine."

"I'm only late." I shook my head, scouting for my phone. "Where's my phone!" I snatched up a pile of clothes off the floor and started going through the pockets. "I'll let the newspaper know I'm running late. Problem solved."

A smug expression spread across Sara's face. "Your newspaper job has sailed, kiddo. When you sleep for three days, what do you expect." She spouted off, checking her hot pink nails.

"What?" I gawked at her.

"Baby oil? Slipping? Accident? Does any of these rings a bell?" Sara shrugged, taking a sip of her coffee.

I dropped my pants in the middle of the floor and glared at her. "I slipped?"

"Yes, right on that hard noggin of yours."

"Where's my phone?" I demanded. I didn't have time for these games. "I need my job!"

"It's too late." She sipped her coffee, lounging on the bed. "The job's already been filled."

"Mom, I can't believe this is happening."

"Did I not say things are just fine?" Sara's behavior seemed peculiar, even for her.

Then it dawned on me. "Has Bane been here?" Had I been dreaming?

"Yes! That young man stayed right by your side the whole time. He called his fancy doctor. Real rich too! The doctor drove right over here in a limo that stretched to the borderline. Anyway, Dr. Ashor left medication for you to take." Sara nodded over to the nightstand where a prescription bottle sat with my name printed on the label.

Apart from the evidence of the pill bottle, Sara's story didn't add up. I reached up and touched my head. "What kind of medication did the doctor prescribe?"

"Just something to make you sleep," she paused. "Why?"

"Did the doctor give a diagnosis?"

"Of course, stupid, you have a concussion."

"Did the doctor order any blood work or an X-ray?"

Sara shifted uneasily. "I didn't get all the details."

"Somebody isn't telling the whole story. Even I know giving sleeping pills to someone with a cracked skull can be fatal."

"Stop whining!" Sara threw her arms in the air, angrily.

"Aidan's generosity is a real good deal, missy! Not too many boys like him are going to cross your path. Take it while you can!"

"Wow! Are we into cliché's now?"

"At least I'm not riding a rusting old bike!"

Oh, Lord! I couldn't hold my tongue. "Is that what you did with Dad? Was he your opportunity?"

"Puttin' it bluntly, yeah, that was one opportunity I wished I'd passed up."

Ouch, that hurt! Not particularly what a child wanted to hear from a parent.

"Sorry to burden you."

"I'm sure you are," She retorted, glaring at me with murderous eyes.

I didn't get why she blamed me for her misery. "Why are you team Aidan after what transpired on our front lawn?"

Sara became edgy, nervous even. "Francis and Aidan both have settled their differences. Aidan promises to behave."

I laughed before I could stifle it. "What about charming Fran? Did he see the error of his ways?"

"Francis has no problem containing his distaste for those less than deserving." I knew her double meaning. Not only did Sara harbor resentment, but she also resented his presence. My mother feared Aidan Bane. "Anyway, I'm not here to argue about Fran. I'm letting you know that I'm okay with you dating Aidan. I invited him over for Sunday dinner."

"Huh, he's not my boyfriend, but you have a splendid time. I won't be coming."

"I'm afraid you don't have a choice. You're bedridden."

I shrugged dismissively. "Then I'll stay in bed and read. Despite what hope you have in mind, I'm the last girl on earth he'd ask out. I don't exactly run in his circle, Mom." I crawled back in bed, drawing my knees to my chest.

"Maybe his circle isn't as noble as you think."

My jaw dropped. I think Sara just complimented me. "Thanks, I think." I left it at that.

LONGING

*O*ne more day in the house, and I swore I'd combust. I thought I'd never say this but thank goodness for school.

Ms. Noel came to visit me every day since my accident, making sure I didn't want for anything. She was the only face I'd seen in two weeks. It seemed that Sara and Bane both had vanished from society. Okay by me. My life had changed since my accident, and I wasn't sure it was for the best either. Not having a job didn't sit well with me. I couldn't remember ever not working. On the upside, I'd been catching up on sleep.

Things were going too smooth right now. Sara working for the Bane's carried no weight. What sound-minded person would hire my mother as a caretaker? I wouldn't trust her with the cat. Though, I had no other recourse other than to accept her claim. I couldn't confirm this with Aidan. He had vanished. Nothing unusual. I needed to focus on other things more pressing. Like preparing for the bottom to drop. It wasn't a question of *if*. It was a question of *when*. Knowing Sara, it was inevitable to collapse.

I'd messed around and lost track of time. I had only ten minutes to get to school. I managed to gulp down a cup of scalding coffee before I dashed outside for my bike. The morning had a little nip to the air, but the smell of honeysuckle flavored the air. I drew in a whiff as I headed to the back porch. The sun was peeking behind the trees, and I could tell it was going to be a beautiful day.

My footfalls bounced off the wooden planks as I hurried along. I reached the back and stopped. "Where's my bike?" I spun on my heels, raking my eyes over the porch and the lawn. Then a disturbing thought came to mind. Did I leave my bike at school? Oh, geez! I threw my hands on my hips, ready to spit nails. "Crap! My bike got jacked." I tried to recall the events of that day. Sara swore I'd slipped, but I drew a blank.

I checked my watch. Only eight minutes to get to school before the tardy bell. "Where the hell is my bike?" My eyes slid over the backyard and halted on the garage. Maybe someone parked it in there? Dang! I balked. That old shed gave me the creeps. I'd been avoiding it since the day I'd parked my car in there. Now my beetle collected cobwebs and rust. I once hoped to have saved enough money to replace the tires. That dream died the second I lost my job. Now penniless, I didn't foresee any chance of ever tackling that hurdle.

I headed to the garage, detached from the house. It was old and sorta an eyesore, square in size, not much more than the size of an average bedroom and white painted shingles.

After a good heave, I managed to swing the lopsided doors open. The loud protest was a sure indication of the age and the smell of mildew. I coughed, peering inside, spotting the drawstring to the ceiling lamp off to the left, close to the back. I kept heehawing to go inside. Spiders and creepy crawlers dwelled in dark places like this. Faint light spilled inside, though it didn't reach the back corner where I spied my bike.

I rechecked my watch. Now, I had only five minutes to get to school. After mustering up enough courage, I slowly eased inside. I glued my eyes to the faint line of my bike and darted for it.

When I reached for the handlebar, I stopped dead in my tracks. "Oh, my God!" When I parked the beetle in here, it had flat tires. I squatted down and brushed my hand over the left-rear tire. "It's new!" I examined the other three tires, and I scratched my head, flabbergasted. All four tires were new.

How was this possible? Sara didn't have any money. I tapped my finger against my lip. Maybe Francis forked over the dough? But on a dishwasher's salary, I found that hard to believe.

I looked down at my keys. I'd ringed my car keys with the house keys. Overwhelmed with eagerness, I slid inside the car and turned the ignition, and the engine started with a gentle purr. My eyes dropped to the meter. The tank was full. That's weird. The last time I drove the car, the tank was empty. A wide grin colored my face. "Sweet!" I sang as I put the gear in reverse. With the radio blasting, off I sped to school.

Chances of beating the bell were slim, but this had to be my lucky day. I walked through the door of English, only a minute before the bell rang. I drew in a moment of relief as I made my way to my desk.

Sally appeared more than her usual chipper self this morning, smiling as I slid into my seat. "Hey," I said politely.

"Good morning."

Unexpectedly, a deep voice bristled against the back of my neck. "I see you got your car running." How did I miss Bane? Didn't I see his desk empty?

I turned halfway in my seat. "You are correct," I tossed a bright smile.

"I take it you have recovered fully from your fall?" His blues were magnetic.

"I'm better. Thanks." Suddenly a rush of questions churned my brain. "Hey?"

"Yes." He inclined his head closer.

"You found me, right?"

A smug grin played across Bane's face as he slid low in his seat, stretching his long legs from underneath the desk. His knee nudged my thigh playfully as his gaze held me captive. "You are correct." Now he was parroting me.

"We need to talk."

"Sure. No problem."

"Hmm, cool. Meet me during lunch at the oak. You know the one."

Bane suddenly sat up and tipped his chair close to me. "Let's cut class and go to my place," he winked. "We'd have the whole place to ourselves."

The boys on the next row over started snickering, eyes darting our way.

I narrowed my eyes at him. "Do you practice being a dick every morning in the mirror? Or does it come naturally for you?" I wanted to shove my foot up his hubris ass.

His breath tickled my cheeks. "I enjoyed our snuggling. I miss you." A vaguely sensuous light flickered in his eyes as if he held a secret.

"It couldn't have been that eventful. I can't remember a lick." I smiled with triumph.

The two boys burst into chortles. "Bane, she hates you, brah!" The redheaded boy teased.

"Nah, she loves me. She just doesn't know it yet." His blues danced, confident. Perfect timing, Ms. Jenkins walked in, and that ended any further tête-à-tête.

When class ended, Bane darted out the room. Sally lingered. She was up to something. Since that fiasco with Sam, I remained reluctant to let Sally back in my good graces. I learned a long time ago when someone stabs you in the back, you avoid them like the mafia avoided taxes.

I stopped off at my locker to unload when Sam decided to bless me with his company. He leaned against the metal, smiling. I recalled a time when I liked his smile and enjoyed his company. A scowl furrowed my brows. "What do you want?"

"Thought Old-Blue had thrown your body in the river," he paused. "Where you been, Chickadee?"

"Don't even try acting like you care," I warned. "You and Sally are hazardous waste to me." I spun on my heels to leave until Sam's fingers bit into my arm. I glared at him, fists loaded, ready to punch him. But without warning, my head started spinning, and everything became distorted like I was tripping on acid. Blurry visions flooded my mind. I began shaking as a burning sensation surged through me.

Sam's eyes bulged. He jumped back, dropping his hold. "You okay?"

"I have to go," I blurted out as I shoved him out of my way and shot down the hall. My heart raced, beads of sweat collected over the bridge of my nose, and my hands wouldn't stop trembling. What was happening to me? Was I having a mental breakdown? I needed to get outta here. I looked about frantically. Where could I go? Restrooms were out of the question. I whirled on my heels, heading to *my car!*

When I reached my car, I grabbed the key from my back pocket. My hands fumbled shakily, trying to hold the small key steady in the palm of my hand, but instead, I dropped it. The keys made a thud, hitting the gravel as the sound vibrated in my ears so loudly that it hurt. Everything appeared amped, the birds chirping, the trees rustling, the insects humming. My mind reeled frantically. "Damn!" I sobbed, sliding down to the asphalt. I huddled beside my car, drawing my knees to my chest. I rocked back and forth, terrified that I'd gone stark raving mad. I closed my eyes, hoping to shut it off, but the insanity continued to rack my mind.

I had no clue how long I'd been there when I heard familiar foot-steps. Bane kneeled beside me. A thin line between his brows deepened as he gently brushed his fingers across my wet cheeks. His worried eyes raked over me. "Princess, are you hurt?"

Tears streamed, "I don't know," I sputtered. "What's wrong with me?"

"I got you. You're safe." Bane whispered as he lifted me into his arms. I clung to his chest, keeping my eyes closed tight, resting my head on his shoulder.

I didn't know how much time had passed when my eyes opened. I jumped with a startle. Confusion poured over me as I eyed my surroundings, but the moment Bane's face came into view, I settled down.

We were sitting in his car facing the riverbank. I could hear the water trickled in the background, and the scent of fish and pine lingered in the air. The forest surrounded us, but this was a different spot than the Firefly's nest.

"Where are we?" My voice was scratchy and parched.

"We are at Tangi river." Bane reached behind his seat and yanked out a white sack. "I thought the solitude might give you a moment of solace."

"What happened?" I sat up. My mind felt muffled like I'd awaken from a ten-year sleep. "I remember talking to Sam. Did I faint?"

Ignoring my questions, Bane pulled out a can of Coke and a bottle of bourbon from a white sack. My eyes dropped to the label on the bottle, *Old Rip Winkle*. Seemed a silly name for alcohol.

Without an utter, Bane popped the can's tap, and a sizzle filled the car. I watched as he emptied half the soda out his window. It was not until he started filling the can with the bourbon that he spoke. "Not that I relish the idea of contributing to a minor." He went on to say. "However, whenever desperate times call for desperate measures, I ignore the customary dictate." His words exuded pomposity as his blue eyes locked with mine. He handed me the spiked soda, never breaking his solemn expression.

I stalled, not taking the drink. "I don't like alcohol." I stared back into his cold blues. His gaze never faltered nor did his offer of the soda.

"Fine!" I plucked the drink from him and threw my head back and downed a huge gulp. The cold liquid slipped down my throat. unexperienced with alcohol, I began choking as if I'd swallowed fire. "Geez," I croaked. "How do you drink this nasty stuff?"

"Feeling better?"

I scoffed. "Are you asking if I'm drunk?"

"Keep sipping, Love." He tipped the can to my lips. "You drink all your juice like a good little girl." He didn't bother to hide the sarcasm in his voice.

"I don't understand why you're force-feeding me this crap?"

"You had a panic attack."

"Panic attack," I repeated. Why didn't I remember?

Impatience crept into his voice. "Drink," he ordered.

I shot him a sharp glare as I unwillingly complied, tipping the can to my lips.

A tense silence enveloped the car as tall-dark-and-dictator continued to watch me. I took another swig, staring out my side window.

After a while, the burn subsided, and the bourbon started to warm my toes. I reckoned folks tolerated the awful taste for the effects.

Finally, I polished off the last drop. The best way to describe my condition was... *nice!* "All gone. Happy?" I smirked, turning the can upside down.

"Very," he replied as an expression of satisfaction gleamed in his eyes. He took the can and tossed it in the white bag.

"I have questions." My words slurred.

"Of course."

"Why haven't you answered my questions, then?" My forehead wrinkled, irritated.

"I am waiting for your query."

"Stop playing head games with me!"

Bane answered with staid calmness. "I never play with pressing matters."

167

"Why do you talk weird?

"Because I do not speak the offensive slang of a teenager, and I choose my words wisely, in your eyes, I am condemned." His eyes never left my face.

I rolled my eyes. "I just think if you used words in this century, you might be more likable." I shrugged. "I'm just saying."

Bane burst into laughter. His laugh was low and throaty. "Winning a popularity contest is the last thing on my mind." He tilted his head toward me and whispered. "You know, if you weren't besotted, I'd kiss you."

"Besotted? What does that mean?"

"Forgive me," he smiled to himself. "I meant tipsy."

"Are you even from this century?"

"Does it matter?"

"It's your fault that I'm drunk."

"I suppose it is." Bane ignored my accusation as he gently leaned in and kissed my flushed cheek. I shut my eyes tight, not able to stop myself from shivering. "What questions placate your beautiful mind?" he whispered as his lips seared a path down my neck, my shoulders.

Jesus! He was killing me.

I decided to stomp the brakes. "Stop touching me! I can't think." Apart from being loopy, doing the deed for the first time in a car didn't appeal to me.

His eyes gleamed like a tomcat finishing his dinner of cream, "If that is your wish."

"Whatever!" Geez, did he think his charm and dimples could make my panties drop? "Okay, since you asked, let's start with how you managed to keep from running me down that day I was on my bike, and let's not forget the explosion in the girls' restroom. How did that happen?"

Bane hesitated, measuring me for a moment. His carnal eyes made me squirm. "Why are you so hell-bent on knowing?"

"Why are you avoiding the answer?" His distrust chilled his eyes with reserve.

"Well," I pushed.

"Sometimes, it is best to leave well enough alone."

"So, you're not going to tell me?"

"You are better off not knowing."

"Can't I be the judge of that?"

"Let's just say you were fortunate that I have quick reflexes." He smiled, but it didn't reach his eyes.

I laughed. "Yeah, right! If you're a vampire or a stupid werewolf, maybe." I shook my head, disbelieving him.

"I assure you there are creatures far worse than your vivid imagination. I am neither one, yet I am not your typical man either."

An oddly primitive warning sounded in my brain. "So, you're dangerous?" I saw with my own eyes what he was capable of doing, coupled with other unexplained events that left me shivering in fear and yet thirsty for answers.

"When it is necessary, yes." Annoyance rose from his tone. "Shall we move to the next question?"

That single comment set alarm bells ringing. "You're not going to hurt me, are you?"

His dark brows shot up, surprised. "No. You have nothing to fear from me."

"You are always on my tail whenever I get myself into a fix. How is that possible?" By the intensity of his shoulders, I saw I was making him uncomfortable. Still, I had to know.

"You should leave it alone." His expression darkened with an unreadable emotion.

"You mean, I should leave you alone?" Strange and disquieting thoughts began to race through my mind.

"Some things may interest you, but it is not worth its hand of fate."

"Fate?" I found myself more than irritated with his babble.

He sighed impatiently, "Meaning death."

"Oh!" My breath seemed to have solidified in my throat.

Bane reclined back in his seat, studying me with his piercing blues. His hands clasped over his chest. "You ask a fair amount of questions."

"It's a bad habit of mine."

"Yes, I'm finding that out," he amused.

"You know what?" I snapped. "This conversation is tiring. Good riddance!" I tossed him a razor-sharp glare, unsnapped my seatbelt, and fled from the car.

I didn't care if I was lost. I had to leave before I went crazy. My dad used to say, a man without secrets had nothing to hide. I suspected as tight-lipped as Bane was, he must have a fleet of secrets.

I darted off, determine to get as far away as I could from this guy, but before I'd cleared the car, Bane had beaten me to the punch. With his arms folded across his chest in a dark stance, he stood, blocking me.

I jumped back, startled. "Geez!"

"Don't make me chase you." A sudden thin chill hung on the edge of his words.

Pivoting on my heels, I darted off in the opposite direction, but before my feet took flight, I collided into his chest. Bane was fast. Inhumanly fast.

"I wish to leave!" I attempted to pass him, but he sidestepped my move. I tried the opposite side, but then once again, he blocked me as if he knew my thoughts. I blinked, stunned. "What do you want from me?"

He gathered a loose curl in his fingers that had fallen over my face and brushed it behind my ear. "I'm not trying to frighten you." The sincerity in his blues confused me.

"You must want something?" I folded my arms across my chest.

"I want nothing," he whispered.

"Then why are you holding me against my will?" I spat.

Bane reached to caress my cheek, but I flinched from his touch. He inhaled a deep sigh and dropped his hand. "In my world, life doesn't afford choices. I do what I do because I am expected to. It is like breathing. I have no other option other than death."

"You talk in riddles. Can you just say what's on your mind?"

His flat, unspeaking eyes prolonged the moment, and then he revealed his truth. "I don't enjoy your company."

I hated to admit it but his admission bit. "Why? Because I'm not good enough to hang in *your* circle? After all, I am the pathetic bike girl."

He tipped his head upward to the sky, releasing a frustrated sigh. Then he focused back to me. "My aversion toward you has nothing to do with you. Yet it has everything."

"You're talking riddles." I inhaled an exasperating sigh. "Stop coming around if my company bothers you!"

"It's not that simple." His lips tightened.

I scoffed. "Yes, it is!"

"It's not possible," he paused as if he was struggling internally, "We are connected."

"That's your hormones talking, asshat." I shoved his chest. "Take me home!"

"This between us isn't over." He spoke defensively. "I've been fighting its lure, and I am failing. And," he gritted his teeth. "I never fail at anything!"

"I'm sorry, am I supposed to feel sorry for you?"

His lips tightened. "Perhaps if I show you, you will understand." In the next blink, he tossed his shirt off to the ground and jerked my hand roughly to his bare chest, pressing my palm against a warm patch of hair, and then he placed my other hand just under my shirt over my heart. "Listen," he growled.

Instantly, I flinched, trying to free my hand, but his ironclad grip overpowered me. I shot shards at him, forced to comply.

After a few seconds, he interjected. "Do you feel it?"

I gasped. Bane's heart was beating as erratically as mine, but simultaneously as in singular. Startled, I pulled away. "This is crazy!" I cradled my hand as if it were injured.

Bane's voice softened to a mere whisper, "Have you ever felt this alive before?"

"No," I answered, weirded out. Then I recanted. "I don't know!" I weaved my fingers through my hair. "This is your dilemma?"

"Yes," he bit out.

"You don't like me because of this," I glared at him, "But, you'd sleep with me?"

"At times, you do have redeeming qualities." The glint of humor flickered but quickly extinguished in his blues. "I don't want to hurt you. I'm not the kind of man that settles down with one woman. I never have, and I never will regardless of how much I want you in my bed. I will never make you happy. I don't foresee a future for us together."

"You're really a douche!"

"Name-calling isn't polite, Love."

"Go screw yourself!" I turned my back to him. Deep sobs racked my insides.

"Look!" he paused. "I don't like it any more than you."

"I'm sorry," I tossed over my shoulder. "I don't recall the ball and chain tethered to your ankles."

171

"Look at me, please." Did I hear Bane plead? "Look at me." His voice appeared gentle yet demanding.

When I wouldn't comply, he grabbed my chin and forced me to face him. "You're better off not knowing me." His blues were suddenly soft. "I'd rather hurt your feelings than ruin your life. You should have a normal life, marry a nice boy."

"You've been pursuing me! Only a hot minute ago, you were coming on to me."

"I'm a guy. What can I say?" He threw up his hands, half-shrugging.

I flashed him a dark smothering look. "I'm walking back." I tossed over my shoulder as I headed toward the road. Though, I didn't get far before he swung me into the circle of his arms and reclaimed my lips, crushing me to him. I wanted to fight, but I was helpless against his soldering kisses as I melted against his lean firm body. He was the master at getting what he wanted, and I was too weak to fight.

When he stopped, he released me with a jolt. I stepped back, over-whelmed with disgust. I took the back of my hand and tried to erase his singeing kisses.

"I can't deny that I want you. You're in my head, my blood, even my soul," he panted. "But we both know this will end badly." His eyes saddened. "For you, especially."

"That is the lamest excuse I've ever heard." I threw the words at him like stones. "Excuses, all excuses! The real reason is that I'm an embarrassment to you because I come from the wrong side of the bayou."

Bane's lips tightened. "That's not true!"

"Isn't it? Tell me the real reason why?"

He stood there, blanked faced. He couldn't even give me the cour-tesy to admit the truth.

"I want to go home!" Fury almost choked me.

"Very well," he glowered at me and turned away.

Bane pulled up in the school's parking lot and stopped beside my car. Seeing the stone line in his jaw, he was more than ready to dispose of me.

I held my eyes straight ahead as I spoke. "Thanks for helping me."

"Get some rest." His voice was strangely tender. "And stay out of trouble." The tip of his upper lip promised a smile, but the glint in his blues proposed antipathy.

"I can't make any promises. After all, I am a wayward teenager," I added with a slight smile of defiance.

"My princess, you are many things. However, wayward is not one." Our eyes locked for an instant. There was a spark of indefinable pain in his eyes. It touched me as much as it puzzled me.

Then the magic vanished as he withdrew a sharp breath and looked away.

I had feelings for Bane, a longing that I could no longer deny. I opened the door and slid out, shutting the door behind me.

School had let out hours ago. The sun was starting to slip behind the trees. My beetle was the only one left in the parking lot. I slid into my car, cranked it up and sped away. I glanced in my rearview mirror and saw that Bane sat with his car idling. It was not until I'd left the parking lot that I heard his car peel out down the street.

I withdrew an agonized sigh. I wanted to erase him from my mind. Just delete him off the page. The problem was… my heart had a will of its own. I sensed Bane was struggling with his own demons. He appeared as the white knight in shining armor, but underneath, he seemed to have a grave full of dark secrets. Something was off with him. The way he moved like lightning, always coming to my rescue. Then our hearts synced as one. What was up with that?

I pulled up into my driveway and made a beeline for the house. Not bothering with the light switch, I crumbled to my knees, sobbing in darkness. "Damn Aidan Bane and my life," I wept. "Why do I have to like a boy who hates me?" I pounded the floor with my fist. His words stung. I needed to face the facts. I didn't belong in his world—a high society world where people like me didn't fit.

After I finished sobbing, I dried my eyes, letting the quiet of the house soak into my weary bones. I stretched out on the wooden floor. I had other worries that were more important. Something strange was going on with me that had me rattled. I was finding holes in my memories. Weird! Maybe this stemmed from my head injury. That was a scary thought… *amnesia*. One thing for certain, I needed to steer clear of Aidan Bane. He needn't worry. I got the memo.

MAN-IN-BLACK

$\mathcal{B}$right and early, my alarm went off at 5 a.m. I slammed the snooze button and rolled on my back, staring at the ceiling. The room was as dark as the house was quiet.

I didn't want to face school, Sara, and especially Aidan Bane today. I thought about blowing school off. Then again, I'd missed so much lately. My grades were going to reflect my neglect too. I couldn't let that happen. I'd worked too hard to throw in the towel now. I blew out a puff of ireful breath. I rolled out of bed and proceeded to get ready for school.

When I drove up to Tangi High, there were only a couple of cars in the parking lot. I was early. I reached from the back seat and snatched up my bookbag. It was a pleasant morning on the warm side. Louisiana's weather was crazy like that. I decided to sit underneath the oak tree and catch up on schoolwork that I'd been postponing.

I shrugged my coat off, spreading it out flat on the damp grass and popped a squat. I eased a breath, lifting my eyes through the branches of the tree. Fall had set, and the leaves had changed to gold and bright orange. I loved this time of the year. I closed my eyes for a minute, letting the sun's warmth caress my face.

Then with regret, I cracked open my math book and proceeded to do my assigned lesson, calculus. With a little determination and work,

I knew I'd catch up. Besides, schoolwork would be a good distraction, keeping my mind off certain people that I preferred to forget.

All at once, I heard the sound of crunching grass. I snapped my head up and spied Jen making her way to me. I smiled. Jen's friendship meant a lot to me. "Hey! You're early too."

"I saw you and thought I'd join you."

"Sure! Have a seat." I patted the empty side of my coat.

Jen crossed her legs and flopped to the ground. "How's your head. You're looking good!" she asked.

"I'm better." I shrugged.

"I missed you yesterday. I thought I saw you drive up in your car, but at lunch, I didn't see you."

"Yeah, I was here for first class." I said. Unlike others, Jen knew how to keep a secret. "I had to leave. I had a panic attack."

"OMG! Did you go to the nurse's office?"

"No, Bane found me by my car collapsed on the ground, hugging my knees." A knot in my stomach tightened.

"Girl, that boy is in love with you." Jen breathed a dream-like sigh.

I burst into laughter. "You are a hopeless romantic, but you couldn't be further from the truth."

"I can't help it," she laughed with me. Unexpectedly, her mood switched to a more serious tone. "I'm curious about something," Jen paused, plucking up another blade of grass. 'How exactly did you hurt yourself?"

"I slipped on baby oil. Why?"

Jen's face suggested skepticism. "Aidan Bane found you, right?"

"Yeah, that's my understanding," I shrugged.

"Where did you fall?"

I didn't understand why all the questions, but I reckoned Jen had her reasons. "By my locker. Why?"

"I don't want to alarm you, but I think Aidan Bane is lying." There was a pensive shimmer in the shadow of her eyes.

An eerie feeling crept down my spine. "Do you know anything about my fall?" I set my book to the side, giving Jen my undivided attention.

Jen glanced uneasily over her shoulder and turned back to me, scooting closer. "This morning, I went to the gym to get some hoops in before class. I went to the closet to get a ball, but it was locked. When I glanced down at my feet, I noticed a strange substance smeared under the door." She paused, pulling another blade of grass. "I was curious to see what it was. So, I used a quarter to scrap at it. The tiny flakes were soft, crumbling like powder, unlike dried paint. I'm not a forensic pathologist, but it looked like blood. There's a trail of it going underneath the door." Jen stared me straight in the eye. "I think whatever is behind the door lies the truth to what happened to you."

"Let's go check it out."

"C'mon!" Jen bounced to her feet. "We don't have much time. We have to hurry."

"Lead the way." I rushed to my feet, quickly stuffing my books in my bookbag and shouldering it. We went straight to the closet. "Keep a lookout for me." Her eyes combed over the gym and down the hall.

"Okay," I whispered. I stood at the entrance, scouting for anyone approaching.

We had only a small window of time to investigate Jen's theory before the halls became flooded with students. I stood biting my nails as the seconds ticked, fearing we'd get caught.

Jen pulled out from her pocket a bobby pin. Like a thief on a heist, she twisted the metal into a thin straight piece of wire. I watched, holding my breath as she picked the lock. After a second, I heard a click. Jen twisted the doorknob and opened the door. "We gotta be quick," she whispered, waving her hand frantically.

I leaped to her side, gaping at her in awe. "How did you learn to do that?"

A mischievous grin veiled her features. "An old boyfriend taught me."

"That's a handy skill you got there."

"C'mon! Before anyone sees us," she urged.

In a fraction of a second, we both were standing in the center of the closet.

Without warning, blurred visions churned inside my head and seized my breath. Unable to take another step forward, I pivoted on my feet to exit the closet, but Jen touched my shoulder. "You're okay! I promise," she consoled me.

I nodded, teeth on edge, giving her the go-ahead. When we stopped, Jen pointed to a corner locker and said. "Someone must've taken a sledgehammer and went to town."

Shocked, I stepped up to the locker that outlined the shape of a body. I touched it with my fingers, tracing the cold metal laced in a dark crimson down to the floor. Jen asked, "Does this look like you slipped on baby oil?" My eyes slowly combed the closet. I couldn't believe my eyes. The only word that came to mind was... malevolence. The most disturbing of all was the considerable cavity on the floor, the perfect size for a head... *mine*. My stomach roiled as I stared at the wine-red in the crater.

"I was attacked," I gasped. "Bane claimed I'd slipped." But the second those words left my lips, I knew he'd lied. I suddenly wanted to know why?

As if plunged into a tornado, flashes of the violent altercation slashed my brain. I remembered! Down to the last dirty detail of the assault. I didn't slip on baby oil. I was attacked right here in this closet. The same, black-dressed man that stalked me at the fair, and to my astonishing horror, I knew him... or at least sorta.

As if it was yesterday. I was merely a child, eight years old, back at our old farmhouse in Oklahoma. I recalled how frightened I was, sitting at the top of the staircase, listening to angry voices that drifted to my bedroom and had awakened me.

Sara held the door slightly open. Even still, I saw through the crack two men, dressed in black suits wearing shades, standing on our porch. I strained to listen. The whispers were faint, yet I feared their presence.

When Sara closed the door and turned, her face was paled with terror. That night we left with the clothes on our backs. That happened ten years ago, right after the death of my father. The creature that had attacked me had a score to settle. My guess, it was with Sara, but then why did he attack me?

Odd as this sounded, the creature hadn't aged in ten years. How was that possible? How was any of this possible? Could there be a chance the black-suited men was the man my father was warning me about? A sense of peril hovered in the air. I needed to talk to Ms. Noel.

"Stevie, snap out of it! We gotta go!" Jen shook my shoulders gently, bringing me back to the present.

"Oh! Yeah, sorry," I stammered, blinking.

"Let's get outta here," Jen urged.

I nodded.

With no time to spare, I pulled out my cell from my pocket and snapped a shot the lockers and the dent in the floor. I'd just gotten my new cell yesterday at the feed store. I knew the camera feature would come in handy. Though, I didn't expect this.

I hurriedly slipped my phone back into my jean pocket and started to head out but halted when my eyes landed on a small object by my foot. I'd almost stepped on it. I picked it up, examining the small fiber. I knew what I had in my grasp, a piece of cloth ripped from my attacker. Now, I had proof!

Luckily, Jen and I got out before anyone noticed. We decided to part ways so we wouldn't drum up any suspicion. I thanked her and headed off to my first class, English.

I'd kept my little piece of discovery to myself. Jen had stuck her neck out enough already. If my attacker resurfaced, I didn't want Jen in this dangerous mix.

EVIDENCE

I warred with myself for about five minutes before I decided to ditch class. I had no other choice. I had to alert the authorities in fear that someone might tamper with the crime scene.

Less than twenty minutes later, I was rolling up to the Sheriff's Department. I rushed past the glass doors and marched up to the front desk.

A scruffy-looking deputy behind the counter approached me. His badge read, Bob. "Yes, ma'am, what can I do fer you," he drawled with a thick Southern accent.

"Yes, I'd like to report an attempted murder?" I checked my pocket for the cloth and phone. All the evidence needed, I smiled to myself.

He pulled his toothpick out of his mouth and gruffly asked, "Did I hear you correctly?" Dark snappy eyes glanced up at me under thick grayed brows.

"Yes, sir, you did."

The officer tossed over his shoulder, yelling, "Hey, Bubba! I gotta girl here that wants to report boyfriend abuse."

Then he cut his beady eyes back at me with the bit of a Pitbull. "Young lady, you can't bust in her' complainin' about your boyfriend 'cause you caught him with another girl," the officer yammered. "Now git the hell outta her' before I call your daddy!"

I fired back. "You have me confused with someone else!" I refused to back down. "I have a legit complaint." I kept my eyes leveled to his beady eyes.

A tall salt-and-pepper haired man stepped out from around the corner, tugging on his belt. By his thin-lined lips under his thick mustache, no one had to guess his mood. "What the hell is goin' on out her'," he demanded with the same Southern accent.

"This little smart mouth gul is wantin' to make a statement. I think this kid's boyfriend smacked her." The thick-wasted officer spewed spittle as he ranted.

"I didn't say, my boyfriend!"

The tall, slender officer held out his palm. "Hold on, miss!" He grabbed Bob by the arm and escorted him to the back out of sight. I could hear their voices but couldn't make out what they were saying. I stood there waiting impatiently.

Deputy Bob didn't return, but the sheriff, Bubba Jones, appeared from the back, making his back to the counter. "Sorry for my deputy. He's been going through some things at home. Now, young lady, how 'bout we fill out that report." The corner of his mouth tipped upward.

I nodded and followed his lead as he took me to his desk. It was a small station, and I doubted it was more than a two-man operation. The Sheriff pointed to a chair placed beside his desk. I took the seat without a word.

My nerves were off the hook. To keep myself from fidgeting, I clasped my hands in my lap. I reckoned after this, Bane would blow his cap. Considering he'd gotten caught with his hand in the cookie jar. I'd like to see him backpedal out of this lie. I have proof now.

Then a thought bore its ugly head... what if Bane knew my attacker? It made sense. Why else would he lie?

Sheriff Jones settled in his seat behind the desk and opened a drawer, pulling out a report form. He hooked his hat on a coat rack and gave a brief run with his fingers through his thin hair, and then focused back to me. "Okay," The sheriff sighed with a pen in his hand. "Let's start with your name and address, please."

"Yes, my name is Stephanie Ray, and my address is..." I gave him exactly what he asked for and waited to further the details of the crime.

"Tell me what happened." His face bore no signs of any preconceived opinion, unlike his deputy. He was thorough and to the point, probing with questions.

I started from the beginning down to the last minor detail of my attack. I thought how mind-boggling. Only minutes ago, I didn't have any recollection of my assault. I gave the officer a thorough description of my attacker, even the shades he'd worn.

Once I finished spilling my guts, the sheriff looked up from the report and asked, "Is there anything else you'd like to add to your story, miss?" His voice came across as flat.

"Oh! I almost forgot." I tugged from my back pocket my phone. "I have evidence! I snapped pictures." I offered, scrolling through the saved snapshots. My mouth dropped open. "I don't understand. I took pictures!" a sob surfaced in my voice. "I had them right here!"

"Maybe the shots didn't take. It happens."

"No! I double-checked." My voice grew to a shrill. "They were here! I saved them." I scrolled through my pictures again and cut my eyes back to the sheriff. "I know they were here!"

"Take a deep breath. I'm sure the pictures will turn up. I can get the snaps later." He furthered the report, "Anything else?"

"Oh, wait!" I dug into my pocket and drew out the tiny fabric. I opened my palm, revealing my treasured find. "Here!" I handed it to him. At least I had this for evidence.

He held it up under his desk lamp, examining it. "What is this?"

"It came from my attacker's suit. I think I ripped it off of him." I sat there quiet, wringing my hands.

His face twisted into a frown. "I wish you hadn't done that. Tampering with evidence isn't going to help your case." He scolded me.

"I'm sorry! I-I didn't think!"

He snatched up a clear baggie. "Try not to worry." A slight smile played across his face as he dropped the cloth in the bag. "I'll keep this," he stated as he held it up. "I need to log it in for evidence. Of course, I have to inspect the crime scene. I'll get back to you on my findings. Where will you be later today? I may have further questioning."

"You can find me at home."

The sheriff gathered to his feet. "I have your number and address, Miss Ray. I'll be in touch," he promised, extending his hand.

After I'd left the Sheriff's Department, I went straight home. I reckoned steering clear of the school would be best. Once I had solid proof, I intended to confront Bane.

My mind churned with confusion. What gain would Bane have lying to me? I shook my head, wading through all the sea of what-ifs. I pounded at the steering wheel. Grrrr! I wanted to scream at the mountaintops! I hated my life! I hated Tangi, and I hated Sara for insisting that we move to this godforsaken town.

Once I got home, I slowly climbed the stairs to my room. I went to my bathroom and opened the medicine cabinet. "Ah, good!" I took down the ibuprofen and twisted the lid open, shaking out two pills. I popped the small pills in my mouth and drank from the faucet.

Returning to the bedroom, I grabbed my book from my book bag, Macbeth, and settled in under the covers. I cracked the book open where I'd left off. Not exactly my favorite read, but an English assignment.

I never understood the big deal about Shakespeare. The language was out of date, and the stories were unrealistic. Take Juliet and Romeo; neither one ended well. They both lost their lives and for nothing. It was such a sad tale. While every girl in class sobbed, I rolled my eyes. Now we were studying Macbeth, a better choice. Still not my fav, but it was better than a miserable romance. Unhappy endings, I despised.

I must've fallen asleep. My eyes fluttered open, startled. After a few seconds, the cloud of sleep lifted. The doorbell was pounding in my ears. Some irate person was holding down the doorbell. "Dadgum!" I bolted up in bed, annoyed. "Who's blasting the doorbell?" Then it hit me. Sheriff Jones!

Throwing my feet off the bed, I darted downstairs, taking two steps at a time. When I swung the door open, my shoulders slumped, and my smile morphed into a bitter frown. "What the hell! Are you stupid?" Bane spewed curses under his breath as he stepped into my crawl.

I blocked the doorway, preventing him from entering.

"Excuse me!" My green eyes clawed at him like talons.

"Why didn't you come to me with your findings?"

Surprise yielded quickly to fury. "Why would I do that when you've been lying to me?"

"Stevie, you don't know what you've done."

"I don't know?" I stabbed his chest. "I was assaulted! You purposely hid that from me."

Bane roughly raked his fingers through his thick curls and blew out a burst of exasperation. I eased back, looking away. Bane's face was a glowering mask of rage. "You have put me in an awkward situation!" He threw his arms out. "Of course, how could you have known?"

"What are you talking about?"

"Never mind," he cut me off. "The harm's done. I'll just have to take care of it myself." He bit out the words as if this was my fault.

"You'll take care of what, Bane?"

"Don't worry your pretty little head. I got it," he snapped. "In the meantime, you needn't utter a word about this to anyone." He stepped up, grabbing my arms, roughly, only an inch from my face. "Do I make myself clear?"

"Let go of me!"

"You have no idea what you did," he repeated with contempt.

"I know I was attacked. Unless…" I suddenly bit my tongue. Bane was behind my attack! Why else would he stand here in my face, angry? It all made sense. Whenever the suit was near me, Bane wasn't far behind. A string of emotions surged: anger, fear, my heartbreaking.

"Unless what!" His voice swirled with acidity.

"Take your hand off me!" The sting of tears welled in my eyes.

"Fine." He dropped his hands to his side, "But I'm not leaving." Bane stood back, arms folded. His eyes were hardened and full of hatred.

"I'm done with your lies!" I threw my arm out, pointing to his car. "Leave my house!"

Bane leaned in and opened his mouth to speak, and then he stopped. Unexpectedly, the crunching of tires rolling over gravel snapped both our heads up, halting the argument.

A sudden feeling of relief flickered through me as the sheriff turned the ignition off and opened his car door. I withdrew a long sigh, wiping the moisture from my eyes. Bane glanced over his shoulder then back at me. His jaw twitched as we exchanged a silent glare.

Bane and I scattered apart. The liar went to the swing on the opposite side of the porch. I stayed just outside my door.

Bane sat swinging back and forth with his hands locked behind his head as if he didn't have a care in the world.

I torpedoed green shards at him, willing him to leave. I couldn't think of anyone right now that I hated more.

His lips pulled back a cocky white smile.

I frowned.

Once the sheriff reached the porch, his eyes cut to Bane and then to me. It was evident by the sheriff's pinched face and his precise movement that he knew he'd stepped into an argument.

"Good afternoon, Miss Ray." He politely tipped his hat to me, and then to the liar, "Mr. Bane!" The sheriff's voice lightened. "What a surprise to see you her', sir. I forget this is one of your rentals." The sheriff stepped up, extending his hand. Bane followed his gesture by gathering to his feet and complying with a hardy handshake.

"Yes, sir, Sheriff. I was collecting rent for my parents." Bane smiled as if the day was just peachy.

I stood there, tongue-tied. Bane was my landlord. That explained why Sara wouldn't fork over any information. I slipped a sideways glance at him, thinking this was one more mystery to add to the growing list.

Sheriff Jones cleared his throat, nervously fiddling with the ring of his hat. "Miss Ray, I'm not sure how to say this other than to say it," he paused, "I went down to the school and took a good look at the crime scene or where you claim the attack occurred."

I blinked with bafflement.

"There wasn't any damage to the lockers or the floor that you attested to in the report." He gave a short laugh. "I've seen my fair share of closets back in my day playing b-ball, and I didn't see anything backing your claims." A faint tug at the corner of his mouth suggested a smile. "Unless you have further evidence, I'm afraid this investigation is at a dead-end, ma'am."

My face glazed with shock. "That-that can't be possible! I saw that closet only two hours ago!"

The lines on the sheriff's forehead deepened. "The cloth you gave me comes from one of the basketball uniforms. Dr. Dunn showed me the torn uniform. I'm afraid the fabric didn't belong to your attacker. I'm real sorry, ma'am."

I held my hand out, "May I have the cloth back, please?" The spark of hope quickly extinguished. Nothing was adding up. I knew what I saw. Jen saw it too!

"I'm sorry, ma'am, but that little piece of fabric is the property of the school's. Dr. Dunn has it in his custody now. I'm afraid you'll have to speak to him concerning the cloth."

"What about my friend, Jen Li, she saw the closet too?"

"I'm afraid since there's no evidence backing your story, your friend's testimony is only hearsay."

After I'd managed to choke out, "Thank you," I spun on my heels and darted inside the house. I heard Bane's voice addressing the sheriff as I rushed upstairs to my bedroom. I flung myself on my bed and collapsed into a ball of tears, trembling as I sobbed.

I couldn't say how long I'd been in a state of a meltdown when I heard a voice through my tears. "Princess," a soft voice penetrated my mind like a small flicker of light in a dark tunnel, "Come here." His musical was velvety and kind.

"Bane," I barely mumbled. The fight in me had drained, and even if I ordered him to leave, I doubted he would've listened.

I held my eyes shut as he stretched out on the bed alongside me, drawing me tight, flushed against him. My head rested in the nook of his embrace. Like a fool, the gate of tears opened once again, and I quivered from the surge of despair.

Aidan kept tenderly stroking my hair and kissing my wet cheeks. It wasn't sexual, yet I trembled under his touch. I didn't understand his gentleness. He hated me.

After the clock's hand had spun a few more times than I cared to count, I was able to speak without stuttering. I needed to get this off my chest. "I know you lied," I blurted out. "I saw the closet." I stalled briefly, gathering courage. "What I don't understand is how I survived. The locker looked like a rocket missile had plowed through it, and the crater in the floor, with the dry pool of blood," I clenched my gut. The vision rendered me. "The impact should've crushed my skull."

Bane inhaled a sharp breath. "I lied to you to protect you. The attack is my fault." His lips tightened. "That's why you can't be around me. It's too dangerous."

"Your fault?" The vibrancy in his voice caught me off-guard. "You didn't hire him, did you?"

"No! God no! He attacked you on his own accord."

"Then why is it your fault?"

His expression stilled and grew grave. "It just is, my love, it just is." There was a pensive shimmer in the shadow of his eyes.

I wanted to know what he was hiding. I knew if I persisted, it would only cause him to shut me off completely. With regret, I moved on to the next question. "Can you tell me why he attacked me?"

"Don't concern yourself with matters that no longer exist. I made sure he will never bother you again." Bane grazed my cheek with his lips, and I shivered.

"You are the most confusing person I know. You hate me!" I tried to get up, but he pulled me back into the fold of his arms.

His sigh seemed conflicted. "Princess, I don't hate you," he bent his head down and gently kissed the corner of my lips, "Quite the opposite." The tenderness in his voice touched me.

"You make my head spin." I pulled away. "I recall you making it very clear that you didn't like my company."

"True… it has nothing to do with my feelings; for other reasons, my love."

Bane evaded questions like a cat evaded a pack of dogs.

"What is your reason?"

"Let it go, please." His blues pleaded, but it only infuriated me more.

"Help me understand! Do you think I'd forgotten last time?" I snapped, "Because the words you threw at me were harsh, mean and hurtful."

A muscle in Bane's jaw twitched. "I'm sorry to have hurt you, but you must not dwell about the minor details of your attacker."

"Dwell!" I shot up to a sitting position, holding back a truckload of curses. "That creature tried to kill me! The least you can do is fork over an honest explanation."

A chilled silence settled between us. Then Bane spoke barely above a whisper, "Justice has been rendered." He sighed as if holding some private news in check. "That's all you need to know."

"Rendered? That creep has been stalking my mom and me since I was a child. I have a right to know!"

"Let's just say," he kissed the hollow of my throat. "My family has connections, and you have nothing to fear." His lips moved farther down to the soft folds of my breast. "You and your mother are safe." His breath grazed my skin, sending me into a spiral. "He won't be bothering you any longer." Although his kisses were mind-blowing, his voice carried a certainty that ran cold in my blood.

"Did you kill him?" My heart throbbed.

For a brief moment, the silence loomed over us like a thick fog. Then Bane relented, "Yes." He dropped it in the still air.

Bane's confession threw me in shivers. The absence of emotion in his voice disturbed me. I struggled to remain coherent. "Is that why you didn't want the police to know?"

"I saw no point in bringing outsiders into a family situation. We are more than capable of handling problems discreetly."

"Hey! Did you clean up the-"

"As I said, we prefer to handle our problems in private."

"The Family? Your family cleared out that mess and replaced the whole wall of lockers and repaired the floor in less than thirty minutes." I gulped, shaking my head. "How is that even possible?"

"Will you give it a rest?"

"You speak of your family like they're the devil. And-and you took a man's life!" A faint thread of hysteria scoured my shaky voice.

"I did what I had to do," he spoke a matter-of-factly.

"Though, justified, you took that man's life!" I couldn't let that fact go.

"Did I tell you not to worry?"

I scoffed, "Oh, sure! That's easy for you to say when you've made me an accomplice to a homicide."

"I told you I have connections. No one will find out. However, you need to keep it under wraps. We don't need it to leak out."

I sighed. "Was it hard?"

"What was hard?" Bane's brows furrowed.

"I mean taking another person's life?"

Bane exhaled. "I did what I had to do. You said yourself it was just."

"Just or not, it can't be easy."

"I merely handled the problem."

He seemed tired, drained, and aloof.

"Oh, I see." I tossed a faint smile, but deep inside, I wasn't sure how I felt about our situation.

Lightly he fingered a loose tendril of hair on my cheek, tucking it behind my ear. His gaze latched onto mine. It was as if time had freeze-framed.

Then I confessed my secret. "That creature wasn't human?"

"Why do you say that?"

I wrinkled up my nose, knowing how ridiculous it sounded. "Hmm, the creature's eyes reminded me of a cat, and he did some kind of magic trick. He popped in and out of sight, like Bewitch."

The bed slightly shook with his laughter. "Don't go around telling folks that. They might think you've gone mad, Love."

"I wouldn't be too quick to judge." I nudged his shoulder with mine. "That man-creature spoke of weird things."

"Like what," Aidan sounded mildly curious.

"The creature kept saying I was very valuable to this ancient faction." I paused a moment. "He kept saying, the Illuminati." A wave of dread swept through me. "Is this your family?" I pushed.

"Princess, this man was a lunatic." He kissed my forehead. "You can't put any clout to crazy."

"Aidan, he seemed very sure of himself." I took in a sharp sigh. "Do you think there'll be others like him coming for me?"

"I believe you worry too much," he smiled. "The bastard is gone. I couldn't tolerate him any longer. Eating chips and ice cream was an abomination. Such a dreadful palate, I dare say." Humor sweetly favored his voice.

"Now you're teasing me." I scooted from his embrace, but he drew me back, crushing me to his lean body, tossing his leg over mine.

"Oh no, you don't." He smiled against my earlobe. "You're not getting away. We're having a fetching moment."

"There you go again," I said as Bane's body flushed snugly against mine, "talking like you're from another century." I smiled to myself.

"Oh, hogwash! The last thing I desire is sounding like one of these numbskulls around here." He leaned in for a light kiss on the lips.

Then a quick and disturbing thought surfaced, and I had to ask. "Have you ever killed before?"

The mirth in his eyes vanished, and something unrecognizable hid behind his glint. "Yes, I have."

With anticipation and half fear, I asked, "Was it justified?"

"Very much so."

I had to ask to clear the air. "Do I have anything to fear from you?"

Different than I first thought, I figured if he'd planned on hurting me, he would've already. He appeared to be a first responder, continually pulling me out of the proverbial fire, saving my neck.

"Have I ever harmed you?" His fingers clamped over my chin, forcing me to look at him. "Well?" His dark blues demanded.

"No," I barely spoke.

"You have no worries, Love." His voice was deep and comforting. Even still, he was as much a mystery as he was dangerous. Despite his darkness, I needed him.

"I think you feel like you have to protect me. Am I right?"

His dark brow shot up. "Why do you say that?"

"Why can't you answer a simple question?"

"The answer is yes." He slowly unbuttoned my blouse, exposing a lacy bra. The mere touch of his hand sent a warming shiver through me.

"Why didn't you tell me that you're my landlord?"

A humorous glint hid behind his blues. "I didn't see the need."

"I owe you rent, but I lost my job and… "

Bane interrupted me in midsentence, "You have no worries. It's been taken care of along with other expenses."

I quieted for a handful of seconds, thinking. "Am I your kept woman?" Quite a tantalizing thought, but I'd pass.

A sudden burst of laughter wafted into the air. "Of course you're not, silly." Playfully, he weaved his fingers through my curls and disheveled it into a rusty mess. I snatched his hand away while the bed shook with his laughter. He had an infectious laugh. Something I'd never grow tired of hearing.

I slid into my next question, "Why the generosity?"

"Isn't it obvious?" Our eyes locked like two magnets, and my breath stilled.

I couldn't read his mind, and with this back and forth crap, he-likes-me-he-likes-me-not, I stormed at him. "If it were obvious, I'd…" Suddenly, his lips recaptured mine, more demanding this time. Soon I'd forgotten my anger as our bodies intertwined together, curling to each other's form like a perfect puzzle.

My body arched to his as a soft moan slipped past my lips.

"You belong to me," he whispered against my ear.

Then as if a fog had lifted, following a long sigh, Bane gently lifted himself off me, though keeping me in the fold of his arms. He bent to kiss my cheek as he settled quietly.

I lay there with my heart thumping and clueless to what just happened. I wasn't totally in the dark about sex. I'd watched HBO and listened to past friends' talk, but this… totally blindsided me.

I thought that we were going to have sex. Crazy as it sounded, I wanted Bane, and yet, I felt relieved that he didn't push farther. Despite my jumbled mind, he left me craving more.

"May I ask you something?" Bane whispered.

I lay in his arms, flushed with embarrassment. "Okay," I whispered.

"Have you ever been intimate with anyone before?" His voice was soft and probing.

"Huh!" Oh, crap! I must've sucked. My heated cheeks deepened. "Nope, I haven't." I rolled on my side, facing away as I squeezed my eyes shut.

"You've never gone to second or third base?" he probed.

"Uh, no." Now my cheeks blazed.

"Apart from me, have you ever been kissed?" He kept pushing.

"Uh… I'm not sure what defines a kiss." I cringed, feeling stupid. I felt his silent laughter against my back. "A kiss is when two people join lips." I heard the amusement in his voice.

I flipped over facing him, flaming cheeks and all. "I was an unwilling participant."

He sighed. "I suppose I'm going to have to speak to Sam again."

"Why do I get the funny feeling there won't be much talking?"

Bane shrugged in his usual arrogant way. "I'm more the silent type. I'd rather demonstrate," he smiled.

"I think you covered that chat already," I sighed. "Sam attempted to kiss me, but he found nothing more than non-complying lips. It happened so fast that I didn't see it coming."

Bane withdrew a bothered breath. "Let me see if I have this straight. You lied to me about having sex with Sam?"

"I'm sorry. It hurt me when you didn't believe me." I shrugged. "So, I lied."

A shadow of regret crossed Bane's face. "You're not the only one who needs to apologize. I'm sorry for not believing you." Suddenly the tone in his voice darkened. "You don't know Sam as I do." He paused. "It would make me feel easier if you steered clear of him."

"How well do you know him when you just moved to town yourself?"

"Let's just say it's a guy thing. You know *locker room talk*." I could hear the acerbity in his voice. "When I think about the things he's …" Bane stopped in midsentence and then finished, "It makes me want to kick his ass all over again." His muscles tensed.

"You don't have to worry about Sam. I only liked him as a friend, and after that stupid stunt he pulled, I don't even want to be in the same room with him." I traced his brow with my thumb and smiled.

His stormy blues gleamed as if we were two star-crossed lovers. That was when I knew. I had fallen in love with Aidan Bane.

A bitter thought crossed my mind. I knew Bane didn't share the same feelings with me, and I hated myself for allowing myself to go there. He said that our relationship would end badly for me. I reckoned I was in for a crash landing.

After a while, when my pulse settled, I began to melt into Bane's arms.

It wasn't long before a gentle rise came from his chest, and a soft snore drifted to my ears. I stilled, listening to the sweet rhythm of his sounds. It wasn't long before my eyes drifted closed, and my thoughts meandered into a peaceful somber.

FRIENDENEMY

*S*aturday, when my eyes opened, my thoughts drifted to a fine stream of light. Hundreds of tiny dust flurries pirouetted aimlessly, basking in the sunshine.

Then memories of yesterday pillaged my thoughts.

My eyes fell onto the empty pillow where Bane slept last night. The only signs left were a faint woodsy scent and one long stem rose, red. I picked the flower off his pillow, careful not to prick my finger from its thorns and sniffed the delicate scent, "Hmm." I smiled, touching the rose petal to my nose. Roses always smelled like sweet pepper. A sense of giddiness licked through me as I released a heavy sigh. I wondered why he didn't wake me.

I thought I'd venture out today. Maybe do some window shopping. Ride my bike around. This time, it would be by choice. As much as I loved driving my beetle, I needed to conserve gas. Once the tank ran empty, I was back on my bike until I rob a bank. Just joking! Maybe.

I stopped by Ms. Noel's first thing to see if she needed anything from the grocery store. She gave me a small list, milk, bread, and butter. She added a few more coins for me in case I got hungry. Ms. Noel had a generous heart.

· · ·

Still, I hated taking her money. She earned only a few bucks selling her herbs and living on social security. No matter how much I protested, she insisted more. Reluctantly, I caved, taking her kind offer.

I'd grown to love Ms. Noel. After my silly accident at school and no longer with a job, I'd been making deliveries to her clientele. I didn't mind helping. It eased my guilty conscious and gave me something to do. Besides, Ms. Noel's arthritis seemed to be flaring up more than usual these days. She never said one word of complaint, but I saw it in her eyes and the stiffness in her walk.

I'd just stepped out of the Piggy Wiggly and mounted my bike when I nearly plowed into Sally. "Oh, hey." I didn't hide the vexation in my tone.

"Hi, there!" She broke into a broad smile. It occurred to me that I'd never seen Sally with genuine emotions. Her smile reminded me of a clown with a painted smile, crimson red, masking a frown. I think the real Sally stayed coiled in a dark corner, shivering from fear.

"Where have you been for the last few days?" Sally already had her nose to the ground, snooping like a hound dog. The girl had the schnoz for gossip. Everyone at Tangi High got the same treatment. There was no exception with Sally and her wayward tongue.

"Yeah, I'd been under the weather." I cuffed my hand over my eyes, blocking out the sun's glare.

"I heard you cracked your head wide open?" She smiled, though it didn't reach her eyes.

"Yep, that's what I keep hearing."

Oddly, my mentioning my accident felt rehearsed.

"You don't remember hitting your head?" Her thick brows slammed together.

She should tweeze those bushes, I thought snidely.

"Nope. Concussion." I stared back at her.

"Well, you're lookin' good." Sally's thick Southern accent struck me as odd. I didn't recall her having one.

"Thanks. Gotta go!"

I lifted my foot to the pedal and started to push off when Sally stepped in front of me and placed her hands on the handlebars, halting me.

"Have you heard," her voice spiked, "Sam and Gina broke up!"

"Sally, I ain't got time for this." I jerked my bike back to free her grip, but Sally didn't ease up. She clung to the handlebars like superglue.

"You wanna know who Gina's dating?"

"Let me guess," I tapped my finger on my chin as if I was mulling it over in my brain, "Oh, I don't know, the whole football team?" Okay, I'd cut below the belt. It wasn't like Gina didn't deserve it. The sting of her hateful words comparing my dad to roadkill still bothered me.

Sally giggled, flipping her wrist as if she were some kind of aristocrat with a fat pocketbook. "No, Texas!"

My brow shot up. "My name is not Texas!"

"Okay, sorry! Guess who Gina snagged?"

Sally's face hid behind the sun's glare, but I picked up a peculiar spark in her tone.

"Gina is dating the hottest guy in Tangi!" her excited voice bounced off my ears.

"Dating your brother doesn't count, Sal." Forget the shade-throwing.

I decided to sling mud.

Regardless of my twisted replies, they went sailing right over her head. It was like do or die, announcing the latest gossip. "Gina is dating, drum roll," she smiled. *"Aidan Bane!"*

My mouth dropped, and my surroundings became tunneled. Sally kept babbling, but her words were background noise to me. My stomach roiled.

All at once, Bane's words stampeded through my mind, *"I'm not a one-woman man, and I never will be."*

I told myself that I didn't care. I lied to myself. "Sally, I have to go!" When our eyes latched, I caught the smug glint in her eyes. I realized then that she knew I had feelings for Bane. After a moment of wallowing in her triumph, Sally stepped back, releasing her grip.

But I paused, overcome by a question I needed to ask, "How do you do it, Sal?"

"How do I do what?"

I wrung my fingers tight around the handlebars. I hated the notion of giving Sal her first bloody nose, "Hurting me! It seems that's your one mission in life. What have I done to cause this ongoing strife between us?"

"I don't know why you're attacking me." She shook her head as if she'd lost her way to the last donut shop. "Don't kill the messenger."

"It's, *'don't shoot the messenger.'*" I glared at her. "Get the cliché right."

"Sorry to hurt your feelings." She shrugged. "I didn't know you liked Aidan."

"Don't be coy." I rolled my eyes. "You're too hell-bent on telling me for this to be by chance."

Unexpectedly, a woman and a small child passed us, pushing a buggy full of groceries. Sally paused as she waited for the woman to cross. Then she cut her eyes back to me. "I thought you might wanna know that your beau is messin' around on you."

"Wait! A minute ago, you said you didn't know. Which one is it, Sal?"

"Well, it's kind of obvious the way you look at him."

I caught a quick glimpse of disdain.

"So, you tell me this… why?" I held my palm up. "Never mind!" I was annoyed at the transparency of my open feelings. Who was I kidding?

"Gina told me not to trust you." Spite ripped from Sally's mouth.

"I gotta go!" I swiftly pushed off on my bike, leaving Sally standing with her pursed lips. She and Gina deserved each other.

By the time I reached Ms. Noel's house, my anger had turned into racking sobs. I couldn't believe I'd nearly slept with him yesterday.

I dropped my bike by the curve in front of Ms. Noel's house and snatched up her grocery sacks. By the time I had raised my fist to knock, she'd opened the door. Her brows were dark with worry. "What's wrong, babee? Are ya hurt?"

"Not in the physical sense." I burst into tears once more and shrugged.

"Aw, come 'ere!" That was all she had to say for me to fall into her warm, consoling arms.

Ms. Noel somehow managed to get me inside and settled me down on the sofa. She prepared for me a cup of hot chamomile tea. After my second cup, my pulse simmered down. "Thank you, Ms. Noel." I smiled, even though I didn't feel like it.

"Ya know I'm a good listener if ya wanna talk." Ms. Noel sat in the rocker next to the couch. Quiet settled in the air for a minute as her worrisome eyes stayed fix on me.

"I know." My brows collided from another bout of tears. "I was talking to a girl from school, Sally. She's not exactly a friend," I inhaled a long sigh, "Anyway, she fed me some news that didn't sit well with me."

"And this has you upset?"

"Yep!" I tilted my head back against the couch, lifting my gaze to the ceiling. "My life has its fair amount of problems, but since I've met this boy, my troubles have escalated."

"How's so, Catin?" Ms. Noel's brows drew down into a triangle of confusion.

"For starters, he's my landlord." I shrugged dismissively. "Well, his parents are the owners."

"Oh mercy, that is complicated! I called my nephew, and he has yet ta get back ta me. I wanted ta ask him about that."

"That's not the worst. I heard Bane's dating another girl."

"Catin, it sounds like you like this young man."

"I wish it were that easy," I spat out with a bitter bite.

"What do ya mean?"

"I am inept when it comes to boys. I mean, I've never felt this way before over any boy. I had a crush on a boy back home, but we never dated."

"Aw, Catin, ya supposed ta be inexperienced at your young age."

"Ms. Noel, most kids my age have at least kissed, among a few other things."

"Chile, don't bother yourself over this boy. If he can't see how special ya are, then he doesn't deserve ya." Ms. Noel reached over and gently squeezed my hand.

My lips stretched into a barbed smile. "Bane admitted he doesn't like me. He also made it clear that he never settles down with one girl." I threw my arms over my closed eyes. "It just bothers me when I find out that he's dating a girl I can't stand."

"Maybe I should talk with this young man. He sounds like a low-down rascal," Ms. Noel chimed heatedly.

For a second, I stared at my hands, smiling inwardly. It was nice having someone care. I lifted my eyes to Ms. Noel. "That's why I don't get why I like him. I'm not into silver-spooned boys."

"You're not the first girl to have a heartbroken over a boy. There'll be better days!" Her faded blues gleamed, "Just don't do anything foolish."

I smiled awkwardly, embarrassing, sweet, and loving came to mind. "There's something else that's gnawing at me."

"What is it, babee?"

"I haven't been myself lately." I quieted a moment. "My memories have holes, days missing that I cannot recall. It troubles me." I sighed with a sharp nod. "When I slipped and fell, I reckon I must've hit my head harder than I thought. My brain keeps drawing a blank. I have patched memories."

"That is strange. Let me see if any herbs might help ya." She reached for my cup as she gathered to her feet. "Ya want some more tea?"

"I'm good. Thanks. I need to head home." I gathered to my feet.

Her eyes orbed. "Oh, wait! I prepared ya some dinner." Before I could protest, Ms. Noel had headed off to the kitchen, returning with a large brown sack, a tradition well known in the south. An easy smile lightened my face.

"You're my guardian angel." I kissed her lightly on the cheek, hugging her tightly.

"Chile, we're family," she smiled brightly, though her pearly dentures were missing today. I smiled back.

Later that evening, a storm rolled in, bringing ominous clouds. Thunder rumbled with fury, shattering against the windowpane as lightning streaked across the bruised heavens. Then came sheets of rain pounding the house.

I never liked thunderstorms, and this one wasn't any exception. I finally gave up and closed my math book. I wanted to kick myself for slacking. I was behind, and it kept growing. For some reason, I couldn't remember some of the formulas for my math lessons. Holes, more holes in my brain. I rubbed my temples as if that was going to make my memories return.

I climbed out of bed and went downstairs. Coffee sounded good. I headed for the kitchen. I fixed a whole pot and poured myself a cup. Then I sat in solitude at the small table by the window watching the rain.

Coffee was probably the worst thing to have before bedtime, but with the crazy weather tonight, I imagined I wouldn't be getting much sleep anyhow.

I stared out the window, wondering if I should take stock in Sally's claim. It didn't matter any longer. I'd decided to cut ties with Bane. Somehow, I'd find a way to pay rent myself rather than accept his charity.

Then an idea struck. Bane might be deducting the rent and utilities from Sara's paycheck. Maybe Sara wasn't lying; perhaps she was working for the Bane's after all. No point worrying about it now, Sara was predictable to a fault. Meaning, when she tired of this place, we'd be shoving off to the next hellhole. I sighed, shaking my head. The only thing holding me up from leaving was Ms. Noel and Jen.

Since my accident, slipping on baby oil and busting my head, my mind hadn't been the same. I had more daunting problems to brood about to last a lifetime. I decided to crawl back in bed with a good book, hoping that would relax me. Dressed in Bugs Bunny pajamas, I slipped in under the covers with one of my favorite books, To Kill a Mockingbird, a classic by Harper Lee.

I'd read only a few pages before I drifted off to sleep. It wasn't a peaceful sleep, quite the opposite. The same haunting dream that had chased me since my dad died returned with a vengeance.

I smiled at the cute boy, and he smiled back, taking my hand. As usual, I could only see his smile. His facial features were blurred.

When I glimpsed away, my breath caught. Deep male voices hummed in my ears. The words were unclear, but it sounded like chanting. Their cadence rose and dropped in a congruous psalm. A constant drip echoed like water dripping.

The boy turned to me, tugging at my arm. His lips moved, but I couldn't hear him. I strained to listen, still unable to make out his words.

Then he lashed out at me, his fingers bit deeply into the flesh of my arm, forcing me to follow. I cried out in pain, yelling at him to let go.

Ignoring my cries, he dragged me down a dark corridor. I'd angered him. Fright touched my spine.

Once again, I found myself standing alone. The faceless boy had disappeared. I turned around to seek an exit and froze. The same men in crimson robes with hands clasped standing in a circle of twelve. "Where was the thirteenth member," I murmured to myself.

An unfamiliar nudge urged me forward into the light. I stepped from the shadows, and as my gaze dropped, I realized I was wearing a bright red robe.

Hurriedly, I shrugged off the cloak until one of the men touched my shoulder. I winced from his cold, clammy palm.

In my past dreams, the robed men never interacted with me. Like a ghost, I was invisible. The dream had changed. Similar to the faceless boy, the robed man's face was a dark blur of movement.

The blur-faced man placed his hand on the small of my back and nudged me to join the circle. I stepped forward, joining the circle of twelve men, making a total of thirteenth robes.

My eyes fell upon a large gold-plated chair sitting on a platform. It took me back to medieval times, where kings sat on thrones. I spied symbols or drawings etched deep into the stone right above the altar. I recognized the pyramid with an eye centered on top. That very same eye I'd seen on the dollar bill.

The men began kneeling, bowing their heads. Confused about what to do, I shot a startled glance at the man who brought me to the circle, yet when my gaze lifted, the familiar boy stood in his place, wearing a black robe too. Though his face remained out of focus, my eyes drew to his dimpled smile. A reflection of something shimmered in the corner of my eye. My eyes caught his hand. Just as I'd expected, I spotted the same ring from all the other dreams, diamonds lining an eye.

The faceless boy tilted his head, whispering words in my ear. I smiled to myself. A tingling of excitement raced through me as his fingers trailed sensuously down my arm. Slowly, he raised my hand to his lips and kissed it.

Startled, I watched as the boy's brows drew together into a frown. He became incensed, shouting words at me, though only, his lips moved. Snapping my upper arm roughly, he forced me to take his hand. I shivered under his heated glower and followed his wishes.

Within the next breath, a blinding light flashed, and my surroundings morphed into something unrecognizable. I saw an outline of an unusually tall man. I couldn't see his face. Unlike the other blurred faces, he hid in the shallows.

An acidic frost raked down my back. I didn't understand what was happening. Frantically, my eyes combed over the black robes as their chins tilted upward as though they were praying.

"What is going on," I mumbled. A sudden hush wafted throughout the darkened chamber. I held my breath waiting for the dark silhouette to step into the shallow light.

When the beast bared its face from the darkness, I screamed at the top of my lungs.

My eyes flew open to blood-curdling screams, my screams. I lunged out of bed, kicking the covers, arms fending off phantom hands that crawled over my skin. My heart raced like a horse sprinting to the finish line.

I collapsed to all fours, panting. Sweat poured off my body, and I shuddered. For the first time in ten years, the nightmare had changed.

I dragged myself to my feet and eased onto the edge of my bed. I felt drained, zapped of energy. I brushed my hand over my arm and grimace. A sharp pain suddenly bit. I rolled my sleeve up, and my breath lodged in my chest.

Visions of the faceless boy charged through my mind. I recalled the grating pain of his fingers digging into my flesh and how angry I'd become. Still, it was only a dream. It wasn't real, but how could I explain the bruises on my arm, fingerprints?

I DIDN'T INVITE YOU

unday, the storm passed, and the sun, in its finest glory, peeked from behind the horizon. All life had returned to normal. The birds chirped happily. The bugs sang their songs, and I washed clothes and finally caught up with schoolwork.

I managed to finish my last lesson, snapping my book shut when Sara burst through the front door. She waddled in with a handful of grocery sacks, dropping them with a thud in the doorway.

I darted downstairs, and as I came to a halt at the end of the steps, my jaw fell to the floor. Sara ordered gruffly, "Well, stop standing there with your pie-hole opened! Come, help me!"

"Oh-okay!" I trailed off after her.

When I stepped off the porch, I stopped. "Where did you get the money for this car?" I gaped, eyeballing a red Ferrari.

"Stop gawking and just get the food," Sara snapped.

"Alrighty," I mumbled as I made my way to the back of the car.

Sara had the trunk wide open and noted several Piggly Wiggly sacks. "Mom, what have you done?"

A wicked smile crossed her lips, the kind of smile a killer made right before he decapitated your head. "You likey?"

"That's not what I asked," I clarified.

She squirmed for a second, most likely thinking of what lies to tell. "The ride belongs to the Bane family. Since I am such an indispensable employee, they're lettin' me drive their car. That's the perks workin' for the richest family in town."

"Uh-hmm, you want me to believe that the Bane's are letting you drive a brand-new Ferrari? Do you know how much one of those cars costs?" Doubt coated my voice like ice to the power lines.

"You don't have to believe me!" Sara gritted her teeth.

Whoops! There she went, confirming what I'd expected… *lies*.

Deflecting was a handy tool Sara used often. Side-stepping was Sara's defense. Whenever she'd get caught in her many lies, she'd use anger to stave off any exposure to her untruths.

I glanced inside the cab, no sign of Francis. "Where's your boyfriend?"

"He went to play cards with friends." She smiled, though her eyes remained icy. Sara never faltered with impatience toward me. Tonight, her agitation seemed more heightened than usual.

"Oh," I shrugged, shoving my hands in my pockets. "So, why are you here?"

"I'm cooking dinner."

"Dinner," I scoffed. Sara burned water.

Slinky-like a cat, in six-inch, red sole, Christian Louboutin shoes, Sara sauntered to the back of the car. The dress she wore fit like a second skin. "Yes, dinner." Her blood-colored nails glinted off the streetlight as she spouted orders. "Hurry up!" She nodded to the bags. "I ain't got all night!"

"Where did you get the money for all this?" I spied a box of dishes, plates, cups and cookware, pots, and pans. Suspicion flickered around me. "All this food and cookware must've cost a small fortune."

"Guess who's coming for dinner?" A seedy grin colored her face.

"Who?"

"Your boyfriend," she answered with a devil-may-care tone.

"What boyfriend?"

"Get that sack out of the passenger's side too. I bought you something nice to wear." Her gaze washed over me through critical eyes. "I don't want you looking like a street urchin," she tisked, "I brought makeup to highlight your green eyes. Your eyes have no life. They're dull as doorknobs."

Ow! That sorta hurt. I stabbed back. "Dad liked my eyes!" It's funny. I didn't look anything like either one of my parents.

"Your eyes are average. That's all I mean." Another shot to the gut.

I narrowed my eyes at her, still clinching the bags in my hands. "You never told me the real reason you're here?"

Sara briskly grabbed my chin, digging her sharp nails into my flesh. I bit back the sharp stab. "I'm not going to let you ruin this for me. Aidan Bane already has a wandering eye." She shoved my chin to the side. "This is your only chance to be somebody," she hissed. "This young man is accustomed to a certain quality of woman. Not some country bumpkin like you."

I glared at her, speechless.

Sara gathered a strand of my hair in her palm and turned her nose up at it, tossing it aside. "I wish I'd brought hair color. Too late now. I hope he likes redheads. I never got why the rave over the color red myself." Sara paused. "Well, what are you standing here for?"

Tears began to sting as I glared at the woman who claimed to be my mother. Sara may have carried the title, but she'd never fulfilled her position. "Sara, if you want to cook Aidan Bane a meal, go right ahead. I won't be here to cheer you on." I continued to say, "And I won't play dress up for you either." I shoved the bag of clothes at her. "I can stand on my own two feet without his help."

"Oh, really? Just how do you plan on doing that?" Sara drew back a sneer, flinging the white bag of clothes at my face.

I caught the bag and threw it on the ground. My face flushed with anger, "I plan to go to college! Maybe I'll become an attorney like Dad and live my life as I please."

Sara snorted a wicked laugh. "You overrate your father!"

"Whether I do or not, you should be proud of me for my aspirations. Proud that I don't need to prostitute my body out to a man in hopes he might toss a few coins at my feet." Rancor sharpened my tongue. "Get your own groceries!" I dropped the bags at her feet and stormed off, leaving Sara to her miserable, despicable self.

When I entered the house and locked the door, it took Sara no time to depart. I heard her slamming the car door and wheels peeling out.

I didn't understand why she was hell-bent on me dating Bane. Sara needed to realize that her daughter had plans, and it didn't involve a man's bank account.

Determined to forget Sara's hurtful words, I carried myself to bed and climbed in under the covers. I snatched a pillow, burying my face, and wailed until I fell asleep.

After an hour had passed, the doorbell rang. With dread, I carried myself downstairs, half-expecting Sara. When I opened the door, a dark silhouette in a trench coat, black, with a lopsided grin that spelled trouble, stared back at me.

Aidan Bane!

My brows collided. "What are you doing here?"

He held up several Piggly Wiggly bags in his grasp. "Did you forget something?" His blues twinkled with amusement.

"You still haven't answered my question."

"Pardon me for the intrusion, but I believe I am your dinner guest this evening." His dark brow perked, waving the grocery bags. "I presume these sacks are for tonight." He stood, devilishly handsome, shoulders ripped, straining against the fabric of his coat.

"I didn't invite you," I snapped a little more than I'd intended.

I could see the humor in his eyes as they gleamed, staring a hole through me. He was laughing at my indifference toward him.

"Must I beg?"

I bit my bottom lip, breaking my smile. "I'm not cooking."

"Then, I shall." His blue eyes glistened.

I blew out a long sigh, flipping a strand of hair from my face as I stepped aside. "Kitchen's straight back! But you probably already know that since you're the landlord." I leaned on the doorknob, frowning. Though secretly, I kicked myself for the sudden flurry of delight.

I followed Aidan as he took only a few strides to the kitchen. My steps were a bit slower as I admired his tailored fit jeans. Or for a better term, the way he was poured into them. The jeans framed the outline of his thighs and the solid shape of his buttocks. I bit down on my bottom lip, thinking if that strut of his could be bottled and sold to the mass market. If so, there'd be a lot of smiling housewives.

First shrugging off his coat and tossing it over a chair, Bane's glint caught the broken pane in the door. His brows dipped into a frown. "What happened?"

I shrugged, "Umm, pancakes and Sara."

His eyes bounced between me and the window and with a slight frown. "I'll get someone out here tomorrow to fix it."

"No. I'll get it repaired." I didn't know how but I'd manage. I didn't have a penny to my name.

"Don't worry about it. I'll take care of it." His eyes softened.

"Okay," I shrugged.

Bane turned his attention to our dinner. He first washed his hands and then started emptying the bags and laid the items on the kitchen counter to see what was on the menu for the night. Bane grabbed the frying pan from the box and set it on top of the gas stove. He then popped out a couple of T-bone steaks shelved with butcher paper.

Next, he foiled a couple of potatoes, tossing them in the oven and turned it on high. Moving right along, he emptied a bag of salad in a large bowl. He threw in a few sprinkles of white cheese, adding croutons and tossing the cold dish to a blend. Then he set the plate in the fridge.

I watched from the table, impressed that a rich boy knew his way around the kitchen. Of course, his other attributes were just as impressive. For a boy who towered over most, shoulders broad and threatening, he was light on his feet, moving with ease like a cat, fluidly and gracefully. His lean muscles flexing underneath his white shirt shot tingles to my toes.

My mind kept drifting to the last time we were together, the singe of his kisses. I almost wished that he'd pause dinner and usher me to the bedroom before I changed my mind. I snorted to myself. What a weak person I'd become, crumbling in his presence. I felt alive when I was with him, and yet, I didn't feel like I belonged to myself either.

Then Gina rummaged through my mind. Did I honestly want to know if he was dating another girl? I shook my head. If I believed this guy liked me for more than his amusement, I was fooling myself. I should end this now, tell him to leave. Though, there was that landlord thingy. That might make things complicated.

My eyes drifted to his hands, and I wondered.

All of a sudden, Bane spun around on his heels with two plates full to the brim. My eyes quickly bounced off his form-fitted jeans and jumped to his face. My cheeks rapidly heated.

He stopped in his tracks, eyes wide. "What? Did I forget something?" He stood holding each plate in his hand, brows arched.

Yeah, my virginity. Do not breathe that out loud. I warned myself inwardly. "Nope, looks swell." I faked a smile.

We settled down to eat in the kitchen. The table was as tight as Bane's car. His broad shoulders and height swallowed up the nook. The small table wasn't big enough for two people. Our plates clinked together, and his knees kept brushing mine.

I found myself liking the coziness. It was surprising to me that he didn't seem bothered by our lack of utensils. Short of supplies, we shared the one steak knife. Though, there wasn't much sharing. He did all the work, cutting mine up for me and even fed me my first bite. I had to say, it was adorable, and I found myself liking it more than I should. Setting my pride aside, I had to admit, the boy didn't disappoint. The steak was delicious.

Then I thought about Sara. Her hurtful words chapped my butt worse than a dog dragging his ass across a rug. I decided to kick off the night. "I hear you're dating Gina?" I bit down on a bite of steak a little too hard.

For a split instant, Bane's eyes mirrored surprise. Then he composed himself and replied. "Rumors circle this small town rather hastily." He flashed his tawny dimples. "I think they are a waste of precious breath if you ask me."

"I'm not sure you can call it wasteful when you get it straight from the source."

A moment of unease had passed before Aidan spoke. "Love, what can I say? I do have to keep up appearances." He smiled, taking a large bite of steak.

I hated his cavalier tone and the fact that he wasn't admitting nor denying. I looked out the window to compose myself. Though, it didn't do much good. Nighttime had fallen, and I couldn't see anything past my reflection. A sour, lemony face stared back at me. "My mother came to visit. You just missed her." I dropped my gaze to my plate and stabbed a piece of meat. "My mother thinks I'm too plain for a boy like you." I laid my fork down and lifted my gaze to him. "I want to know why you're here. I'm not even your type."

He followed my lead, laying his fork quietly on his plate. Politely, he patted his mouth with his napkin, putting the white linen to the side and rested his hands in his lap. When our gaze latched, his deep blues were far too piercing. "Sara doesn't see you through my eyes," he almost whispered.

Confusion plagued my mind. I couldn't be sure if Bane was teasing me or if he were serious. I responded as any logical female. "Huh?"

"Why do you do this to yourself?"

"Do what to myself?"

"Your mother is she always so abrupt with you?"

"Abrupt?"

"Yes. I think you don't give yourself enough credit. Most girls in your position would've taken up drugs and prostitution."

"Like Gina," I snapped.

"Gina serves a purpose," he replied with dark irony.

"Purpose, like how," I pushed.

"Must you insist on the answer to that?" The ire in his voice hummed in the air.

"Why Gina? There are a hundred other girls to date other than her!"

"Why do you think I'm seeing Gina?"

"Even Sara knows," I shrugged. "If you are, you are. Just own it." I hated myself for acting like a jealous girlfriend, but I couldn't stop myself.

"I'm not seeing Gina. She asked for a ride home. I was at Mother Blues playing pool with my cousin. Gina had been drinking. She and her friend, Sally, got into an argument. Sally left her ass stranded without a ride. I simply gave the girl a ride home."

"Aren't you the gallant one?" I suddenly wasn't hungry any longer. The air became thick, and guilt riddled my mind. I'd ruined the night with my petty jealousy.

A tense moment of quiet had drifted between us before he responded, "I am aware of Gina's comment concerning your father," he paused. His blues were intense, striking my heart, "She behaved maliciously."

My chin dipped down as I bit back the urge to cry. "I recall that day."

There was a faint glint of humor in his eyes. "Look, we didn't have the most pleasant beginning." He gathered to his feet and made his way to me. I glanced up into his face as he kneeled before me, gently taking my chin into his palm. His eyes stopped on the edge of my jaw.

His tone abruptly dipped into anger. "You're bruised and marked." His icy glare forced me to look away. "Who did this to you?"

I jerked my face from his touch. "It's nothing." I tried to pull myself to my feet, but Bane rested his hands on my waist, keeping me seated.

"Did Sam do this?"

I caught a spark of rage in his eyes.

I shrugged. "No."

Bane leaned back on his haunches. His blues darkened as he realized, "Sara!" His lips tightened.

Swiftly, he gripped my upper arm and gathered to his feet, dragging me with him. "Go pack your things! You're coming to my place. I'll have Jeffery come for the rest of your things tomorrow."

"I'm fine here?"

"I'm not leaving you alone," he growled.

"It's okay! I'm used to Sara." I tried not to make such a big deal out of it. "If she were on her meds, she would've never touched me."

He raked his fingers through his coal hair, sighing with frustration. He turned back to me. His fingers gently grazed my cheek. "Look at me."

At first, I resisted. I couldn't bear looking at his pity. After a moment, I slowly lifted my gaze to him. "I can't stay with you," I whispered, pushing down the knot in my throat. "If my mother blew up over me riding in a car with you, what will she do if I move in with you?"

"She won't bother you, I promise. I'll have a Fort Knox of protection."

Bane was only offering out of pity. "I appreciate your kindness, but Sara is my mom, and I have to deal with her myself."

His blues became harsh. "How well is that working for you?" Bane growled, stalking over to the fridge and opening it. His eyes combed over the selves. Only a few items stared back at him, a piece of pie and a covered bowl of gumbo, courtesy of Ms. Noel. Bane spun on his heels, turning his blaze at me. "This isn't living!" he shouted. Then he bolted to the cabinetry and started opening one door after another. "Your cupboards are empty! How are you surviving?" He turned his heated gaze back at me.

Swooned with anger, I realized he was right. Tears filled my eyes. "What do you expect me to do?" I wiped the tears from my face with the back of my hand. "I'm not rich like you!"

The inflexibility in Bane's blue eyes stole my breath. I flinched as he roughly swung me into his arms. "I know things have been difficult for you, but I had no idea it was *this* bad."

By the glint in his eyes, I knew he was judging me as though I was a stray dog, homeless and pitiful. I didn't want him to look at me like that. I wanted him to see me as his equal, but that was a far-fetched pipedream. How could he ever see me other than trailer trash? I was nothing. I had nothing! Even the clothes I wore were rags compared to his.

I jerked from his embrace. "I manage. I always have," I bit out sharply, trembling.

He slung his arm out, pointing to the empty cabinets. "This is not managing!"

"Look!" My eyes caught his storm-riddled blues. "Sara is my problem."

"She's not any longer. I'm taking you home with me!"

"Aidan, I don't need you saving me!" My heart pounded my chest. "I plan on looking for a job tomorrow. I can take care of myself."

"Starving is not taking care of yourself?"

He was right. Worrying about bills and food wasn't living. "I can't stay at your place. Sara works for your parents." I drew my arms around my waist.

"Come again?" His dark brows shot up.

"Didn't your parents tell you?"

"Tell me what?"

"Sara said your parents hired her to watch over you, a guardian. I assumed she was telling the truth. She was driving one of your cars."

"Princess, my parents and I are estranged and have been for some time. I have staff that provides my needs." His words had a ring of truth. "As for any car of Sara's, it is not one of mine. I assure you."

"I don't understand. Sara has to be working for you. Where would she get the money to buy all this food and drive a Ferrari?"

"I don't know what she's told you, but I can assure you that she does not work for me and never will."

"You said yourself that you had my expenses covered."

His brows drew in a puzzling frown. "What does that have to do with Sara?"

"I assumed you were deducting the cost from her paycheck."

"Princess, I've been paying your expenses and utilities since you moved into this house." His jaw tightened. "It was a prior arrangement with our families."

I stepped back, my eyes bright with shock. "What?"

"Look!" Bane's lips tightened. He stepped forward. Resting his hands on my shoulders. "I see Sara hasn't told you about the arrangement."

"What arrangement?"

"Stevie…" He stopped in midsentence.

"Oh, my God!" I saw it in his eyes. "What has my mother done?" I screamed at him.

"Look," he paused, "I'm sorry to break this to you." Behind his eyes, I saw undeniable regret.

"Explain what?"

He stepped closer, but I backed into the table. I didn't want him touching me.

"Can you calm down and have a seat? We need to talk." His hand extended to one of the chairs.

I ignored his offer. My feet stayed planted to the floor. There was no need to explain. I already knew. "My mother sold me to you," I barely whispered as tears welled. Before he could answer, I exploded, "Leave my house at once!"

He started to reach for me, but then he retracted, dropping his hand to his side. His throat bobbed, swallowing. I assumed he was holding back his distaste for me. Without a word, he spun on his heels and stormed out, slamming the door behind him.

Doused with rage, pain, and my heart ripping in two, with one sweep, I knocked the dishes off the table, sending them flying across the floor. Food splattered down the walls as I stood there with tears running down my cheeks. Always angry, always crying, when would it ever stop? I wiped the tears away with the back of my hand. I couldn't stay in this house another second. I rushed for my keys and darted to the garage.

WAYWARD WOES

*M*inutes later, I was in my car heading full speed down the dark roads, putting the house and my thoughts of Bane behind me.

I was utterly mortified. How could my own mother betray me? It was unfathomable. Sold to the highest bidder... *Bane!* What Sara had done was no different than sex trafficking.

Nothing made sense with Bane. I mean, why all the trouble, acting like a gentleman? He'd paid for services already. That night he stayed over, he could've had his way, but he didn't.

Sara was right. I wasn't pretty enough or good enough for him. I hated how much I cared about this guy! I wished I didn't care, but I did, and I didn't know how to stop.

I wondered how much my worth was? Suddenly the picture of that expensive car Sara rolled up in and all those groceries popped into my head. I can't believe anyone would pay that much money for a one-night stand.

I drove to Mother Blues. I needed a distraction or alcohol. Since I was too young to buy the stuff, apart from being penniless, I decided pool would be the safer alternative. I could stay outta trouble at a pool hall, providing I didn't get hit in the head with a pool stick, right?

I spotted Jen's car and parked in a spot next to her.

Jen always made me laugh, and right now, I needed a heavy dose of giggles.

When I passed through the glass doors, I noted the place was packed. I scan the area to make sure I didn't catch one dark head poking out among the others. My mind eased. Good! No sign of Bane.

I spotted Jen sitting in the far back corner by the last pool table, in a deep conversation with Sam. That's odd! Since Sam had played that terrible trick on me, Jen stopped speaking to him. I made my way over to her, "Hey, girl!" I smile.

"Hey! Long time no see, homey!" Jen jumped up and hugged me. I hugged her back.

"I know. Sorry!" I shrugged. My eyes fell on Sam's face. "Hi Sam," I spoke with less excitement.

"Hello, Chickadee!" He leaned over and hugged me. "Why the long face?" He grabbed up his pool stick.

I shrugged. "I don't know. It's Sunday?" A weak excuse but still an excuse.

"I know something that will lift your spirits." Sam carried a grin that stretched from ear to ear.

"Oh, lord. What?" I didn't need my spirits lifted. I needed a heart transplant.

"You and Jen should come with me to Speakeasy. It's a couple of towns over. It's sorta out in the boonies. Dark and ugly creatures hang out there." Sam deepened his voice for the dramatics. "It'd be fun. You know, takin' a walk on the wild side," he winked.

"Speakeasy? What is that?" Jen asked.

"It's a bar that only a select few get to see, a real treat. I go there all the time," Sam bragged.

I looked at Jen and asked. "Are you going?"

She shrugged. "I'll go if you go, but I can't stay long. School's tomorrow."

"Yeah, me too. I can't afford to miss another day." I bit my bottom lip. "You know, it might be fun to get away," so said the gal who never stepped outside the box. Me!

Sam drew me into the nook of his sweaty armpit. Yuck!

"Come on. We'll have a good ole time!" he flashed a lopsided grin. "I got your back. I swear on all the liquor in the Parishes!" Sam raised his right hand, mocking a sworn promise.

Jen burst into laughter. "Oh, you know he ain't lying when he swears on booze." She high-fived me, and I paused, mulling around in my head whether I should step on the wild side or go home. My eyes went back and forth between Jen and Sam as they both gleamed with adventure. I sighed, pulling out from under Sam's arm.

~

Before we took off, I grabbed an application from the cashier at the snack bar. I thought I'd at least apply. The worse they could do is say no.

For now, I was stepping away from careful Stevie and stepping into wayward Stevie like a nice pair of Stilettos.

We piled in Sam's truck. He insisted on being the designated driver. Jen and I both glanced at each other and burst into laughter. We both knew he was going to get tanked. We were cool with that. Neither Jen nor I cared much for the stuff. Jen and I decided one of us would be driving back. No sweat.

We passed a little town named Le Diablo. It wasn't much more than Tangi. Blink once, and you missed the whole patch of homes and a store or two. After a mile out of town, we ventured down a dirt road that had more craters than the moon.

When we finally reached our journey's end, we pulled up into a parking lot that was more beaten than the dirt road. Glimpsing over the cars parked around the joint gave me pause for concern from rusted out whoop-dee-doos to the crème-of-the-crop, cars filled the entire parking lot. What a strange mix of patrons, I thought.

The building appeared dilapidated, not much more than a beat-up metal box with nails and a few boards keeping it standing. The place gave me the willies.

Maybe we should try another place. I looked at Jen as we scooted out of the truck. "Hey, I'm not so sure about this place." I wrapped my arms around my waist as I kept eyeballing the joint. I watched as a couple staggered across the parking lot, arm in arm, headed to the shadows of the trees.

Sam bounced around the truck to our side, "What's wrong, Chickadee," he asked with a wide grin across his face. "You ain't likin' my friends?"

"Nah, man, it's where they hang their hat is the problem." I popped him in the chest with the back of my hand, pushing off from the truck and proceeded to the front door. Jen followed, and Sam followed.

When we reached the door, lively tunes were vibrating against the metal building. The air filled with static, making me intoxicated with a sense of freeness.

I'd never been inside a bar before, and this joint screamed of peculiarity. Little did I know that Jen and I were embarking on a secret world of weird and eerie.

Right when we stepped inside to a dimly lit corridor, Sam caught my arm and leaned into my ear. "If anyone offers you a drink, don't drink it. You'll live to regret it." He grazed my earlobe with his lips. Instantly, I tilted my head away. When Sam pulled away, I caught a strange stir behind his glint. It didn't give me the good kind of chills either.

I played along and nodded to Sam as I rushed to catch up to Jen. She'd reached the bouncer and was pointing to Sam. Sam reached over me and leaned into the thick-chested man's ear, shouting over the earsplitting music. The bouncer nodded for us to pass. He unlocked the gate and allowed us to enter. A slight tinge of regret pricked my conscious. I secretly had hoped the bouncer would've sent us packing.

Once we walked past the entrance, we entered into a large room with blaring music. It was hard to make out the tunes over the pounding sounds.

Neon lights hung on the walls, showering the bar with an eerie blue glow. The place brimmed with heads bouncing in every direction, dancing on the floor.

My eyes landed at the bar. Bright blue lights and liquor bottles lined the mirrored shelves. Standing behind the counter was a cute bartender wearing a hat and suspenders, no shirt. He moved fluidly, pouring drinks, keeping up with the massive demand. I slipped Sam a glance. He was already licking his chops for the liquor bar.

When I realized that the three of us were the oddballs at the party, I dropped my jaw, shocked. On the dance floor, my eyes washed over a sea of nude bodies. Shoulder to shoulder, shaking their junk, busting moves. My cheeks heated as I whipped around, facing the wall, my back to the dance floor, "Jen!" I tugged on her arm sleeve.

"Yeah," she yelled in my ear.

214

"These people are naked," I nearly screeched.

Jen laughed. "Yeah, I know! It's funny."

I glanced over at a table, spotting a couple wrapped up into each other. I jerked on Jen's sleeve again. "Look! Ten o'clock, at the couple in the booth. Girl! They're doing the deed!" The woman was giving the guy a lap dance, a very involved dance. Not something I wanted to watch.

Jen gulped down air, parroting me. She latched a hold on my arm. "What kind of place did Sambo bring us to?"

Jen and I started giggling.

"I think we should go!" I tossed a glance over my shoulder and then back at Jen.

"I think your right! Where's Sam?" Jen stood on her tippy toes, stretching her neck, peering over the bobbing heads. "I don't see him," she yelled over the music.

"Crap! He left us." My mouth tightened as I did a quick once over and then back to Jen's face. "You think he went to the men's room?"

"Nope, I think we just got punked!"

My eyes flew wide. "Aw hell," I yelped, brushing my gaze over the bar once more. "Hold on!" I dropped Jen's arm and stalked over to the bouncer.

When the burly bouncer's eyes lifted at me, he smiled as if he knew me from somewhere. He squatted down to yell in my ear. "Your friend left with another gul. Sorry," he spoke gruffly.

"Are you sure?" It would've been easy to miss Sam for all the traffic. Then again, we were the only ones dressed.

"Toots, Sam's a regular," he grunted out with a sideways grin. The kind of grin that left you feeling you needed to shower.

"Okay, thanks, mister!" I twirled on my heels, full of piss. If Jen and I make it out alive, I planned on killing that son of a bitch! I stomped my way back to Jen, ready to spit nails at our un-trusty friend. I leaned in, yelling over the loud music, "Sambo left!"

Jen's eyes widened. "That asshat!"

"That's what I'm saying!" I crossed my arms, steam rolling off my back. "What are we going to do?"

All at once, Jen's eyes lifted, a spark ignited. "Look who the cat dragged in," she smiled.

I snapped my head in the direction of her pointy eyes, and I choked on my breath. "Bane!" I whispered through frowning lips. He was glaring our way too, and not a happy look either.

Jen and I shared an uneasy glance. "I think lover boy is pissed at you."

"I think you're right." I kept my gaze even, watching the anger roll off his rigid body. The bouncer was speaking to him and snapping his eyes our way. The scowl on Bane's face grew darker by the minute.

"Damn! I don't remember Aidan looking that good in a white shirt. Nice biceps!" Jen whistled admiringly.

I nudged her arm. "Don't ogle too much! That's my man," I kidded.

Jen raised a brow. "Girl, that boy has it bad for you. He came here in the middle of the night to get you. Now that's love." She nudged me back.

"I reckoned," I faked a smile. Bane was acting on his sense of obligation. I reckoned he had wanted his money's worth before some other boy put his grubby paws on me—just the woes of wayward Stevie.

"Ought oh, here he comes," Jen announced, jerking on my arm sleeve, watching the stomping tower making his way to us.

"What the hell, Stevie!" He snatched me up by my upper arm. "You should never have come here!" His face was scarlet red, jaw tighter than a wound-up rubber band ready to pop.

"Let go of me," I hissed in his face.

Bane's gaze turned to Jen. "Good evening, Miss Li, or should I say good morning," he growled. "Do your parents know you're out this late?" His eyes were sharp and purposeful.

"Huh … " Jen tucked her arms behind her back, eyes wide. "My parents are out of town."

Bane scowled. "I can presume they don't know your whereabouts?"

Jen slipped me a sideways glance. "I swear I will never get into any vehicle with Sam ever again!"

"I'm glad to hear some of us have learned a valuable lesson." Bane's heated gaze collided with mine. "Let's go! I'd like some sleep tonight." He nodded to the exit door.

As we passed through the gate, Bane gave a sharp nod to the bouncer. "Thanks, my man, for calling."

"No problem, Mr. Bane. Glad to help." The bouncer winked at Jen and me. "You kids don't come back her' no mo'!" He nodded his head at us, the kind of nod that promised if we ever showed our faces again, there'd be hell to pay.

I picked up my pace, coming in behind the long-legged, angry Bane. I heard Jen giggling at the bouncer. I think he slipped her his phone number. I had one word to say to that... *jailbait!*

Bane jingled his keys, gripped in his palm down to his side as he angrily strutted toward the parking lot. Jen and I hurried along to keep pace with his long strides. It didn't take a mind reader to know that Bane was furious. I'd already stirred the hornet's nest with him earlier tonight when he left the house abruptly.

Bane had been holding a family secret and didn't share it with me until tonight. He might as well get his money back because I wasn't a participant in this arrangement he had with my mother. Speaking of which, I couldn't wait to see Sara. I had several bones to pick with her.

We'd reached the end of the lot, and I still didn't see his Corvette. I was starting to worry that he planned to shoot Jen and me, leaving our bodies in the sticks.

"Hey! Where's your car?" I asked, stretching my eyes over the lot.

Bane didn't utter a word. He kept his strut at an even pace.

When he clicked the remote, the headlights on a champagne-colored Rolls-Royce flashed. I gawked in disbelief. Talk about the granddaddy-mac of all wheels.

When we reached the car, Bane had stepped to the passenger's side first, holding both front and back doors open. He barked, "Get in!"

Jen and I shared a glance as we climbed inside the Rolls. Jen took the backseat. I wanted badly to crawl in there beside her. Nonetheless, the steamy driver shot me a grave look of warning as he held the passenger's door for me. Lucky me, I get to sit with grumpy.

Once the doors shut, a swirl of leather encircled me. I'd never sat in a car with such luxury. The bright red interior gave me a little dose of excitement. Discreetly, I brushed my hand across the seat. The leather was cool to the touch, and yet, smooth as a baby's bottom.

Bane reached his side, opening his door as a dim light flashed and smothered as soon as he shut the door. Before long, we were approaching the outskirts of Tangi, leaving Le Diablo behind in our rearview mirror. My gut told me that a heated argument was on the brink. By the hard line of Bane's jaw and the forbidding quiet that stirred between us, it was coming.

Despite Bane's foul mood, there was an upside to this. If he hadn't shown up, Jen and I would've been in serious trouble. Stranded in the middle of nowhere, at a bar that let just about any riff-raff come in was a recipe for danger.

My curiosity ran with me, wondering if Bane was a regular here. The bouncer knew his number. Then again, everyone knew Bane and his family. How was that possible when they were new in town?

I sat in my seat, staring straight ahead at the headlights swallowing up the road. The events of the night played through my head. Geez! I felt like a child, getting caught sneaking out. I huffed inwardly. Despite his indifference toward me, I had to make amends. I didn't want Bane blaming Jen for this. I started my spiel. "Look," I gulped, mustering up the courage, "I was the one who insisted we go. If you want to blame someone, then blame me." I glanced at his tense face.

Jen drew herself closer, sitting on the edge of the seat, propping her arms on the headrest. I flashed her a nonverbal cue to let me do the talking. She nodded and slipped back into the back. Not that I made things any better, "Look! I'm sorry you had to rescue us."

Bane kept his lips sealed, eyes glued to the highway.

I continued, "We weren't drinking… and we kept our clothes on!" I squirmed over that humiliating confession. I paused, trying to read his stone face. "Thanks for your trouble, but you can drop us off at Mother Blues. Our cars are parked there." I offered, hoping it would appease Sulky Sue in the driver's seat.

"I took care of your rides," he growled as he quickly pumped up the volume, Mozart.

Ouch! Apparently, he didn't feel like talking.

I invited Jen to stay the night, but she declined. Jen's aunt had called, instructing her to come straight home. The aunt would be there waiting. Someone contacted Aunt Betty and snitched. I had a sneaky suspicion Bane had something to do with that. I suspected the aunt would be reporting it to her parents.

Once we pulled up to Jen's house, I gathered by the dreaded look on her face she might be looking at a good week's worth of grounding.

With a heavy heart, I slipped out on my side and hugged my friend goodnight. "Man, I'm sorry!" I choked out an apology, tears welled.

Jen blew out a carefree sigh and swatted at the air with her hand. "Don't worry about me. I'll get extra chores and have my phone taken away for a week. A piece of cake!" Her sable eyes twinkled as she headed for her house.

I watched as Jen made her way down the sidewalk to the front door. Right before she stepped up to the porch, the light flipped on, and the door flew open.

"Yelp, that's a sure sign she's in trouble," I mumbled to myself as I watched Jen disappear inside the house. The light on the porch doused, and the shutting of the door wafted in the air. I felt terrible and a little envious too. Jen had a family who loved her. Pain tore at my insides. I thought of my home situation. I blew out a harsh breath, ready to face the reality of my life.

With a heavy heart, I slid back inside the car, shutting my door in silence. Still not an utter from Bane, he remained quiet the whole way to my house. I wasn't going to sweat it. I reckoned he'd speak when he got ready.

I leaned back in the cushiony seat, staring out the window. I liked the quiet and dreaded the consequences of my irresponsible behavior tonight. Though I doubted Sara would be waiting by the porch light like Jen's aunt. I sighed longingly. I wished I could talk to Dad.

We turned into my drive, and before the car came to a halt, I'd unsnapped my seat belt, my hand rested on the door handle, ready to flee the second the car came to a slow roll. I planned to get a head start, darting for the safety of a closed door. As I leaned into the door, Bane's fingers gently grasped my arm. "Wait," he called to me softly. "We need to talk."

Oh, geez! He sounded like my parent.

"Can't it wait?" I held my hand on the lever.

"I want you to come home with me. You can stay on the far end of the

wing, far away from me if you wish. You won't know I'm there if that's what you want. It's just," Bane's voice broke, "I'd rather you stay under my roof than leave you alone and unprotected."

"Unprotected?" My eyes collided with his soulful blues. There was a genuine concern behind his glint that grabbed my breath. "You worry about me?"

"Yes." His voice was uncompromising yet oddly gentle.

"I thought you were mad at me?"

A moment had passed before he answered, "Yes, quite so. However, I still want you under my roof out of harm's way."

I scoffed, "Who's going to hurt me?"

Bane leaned forward, so close that his lips were only a fraction from mine. Sensually, his fingers gently traced the line of my chin, trailing up to my flushed cheek. His blues were so full of pain and unquenchable warmth that I closed my eyes, fighting back the tears that threatened. When he spoke, his voice was tender, almost a murmur. "There are things in this world that most people have never seen and," he paused. "They're lucky. If they only knew the darkness that lurks amidst the shadows, it would be so terrifying that most would go insane." Gently, his thumb grazed my lips. "I only want to protect you. Will you at least grant me this one wish, please?"

I swallowed against the lump in my throat, knowing there was nothing simple about this man, but I'd allow him his wish. "Okay, I'll stay one night." I gave a faint smile. "Let me get a few things."

He tightened his grip, halting me. "Sorry," his blues flickered from the moonlight, "You're staying with me indefinitely."

I stared at him, gawking, "Indefinitely?"

"There is no coming back to this house. You're staying with me if I have to shackle you." The kindness in his blues had evaporated.

"That's kidnapping! I can have you arrested."

"Go get your things." His response held a note of irritation.

"I don't get a say?" I blinked back shock. "Am I your prisoner?"

"Are we going to argue all night?"

"Fine," I hissed. "You can deal with Sara."

"I believe I have." He drawled with distinct mockery.

"Whatever," I retorted darkly, jumping out of the car and slamming the door. I couldn't wait to find Sara. I can't believe she sold me into slavery. What a *mother*!

By the time I unlocked the door and stepped inside, Bane was on my heels. I quickly flipped on a light and jumped with a yelp when I felt something warm and fuzzy brush against my foot.

When my gaze dropped to the floor, I spotted a white ball of fur nestling up against my leg. "A kitty!" I sang, quickly gathering the kitten up into my arms. He nudged my fingers as his purr tickled under my touch. I smiled, softly hugging the kitten to my face.

Then it hit me. I glanced up at Bane. A faint smile played across his face.

My brows drew together, baffled. "You got me this kitten?"

Strangely, the debonair Aidan Bane nervously shoved his hands in his deep pockets, clearing his throat, "Yes, I thought you might like the company."

"When did you do this?"

"After I left, I went to pick up a few things for the house. I ran across a lady at the market, giving away a litter of kittens." He sneezed, suddenly covering his nose and mouth. "Anyway," he sniffled, "I took the last one." His blues twinkled, or it could've been his allergies.

"You-you-you did this for me?" I stammered over my words.

Then as if a veil dropped, his demeanor became aloof. "Get your things." His jaw tensed. "We have to go."

I hesitated, holding my questionable gaze evenly to his icy stance. It was duly noted that his air of authority and the stern glint of one who commanded instant obedience curled off his shoulders.

Boy-oh-boy, I smirked to myself. Bane was in for a surprise. He wanted me under his rule of thumb. I had other plans. Rules were for stuffy old women in high society clubs. I preferred a more straightforward approach, fly by the seat of my pants, and hope the landing didn't smart too much. That was the new Stevie, the wayward Stevie's take in life.

CASTLE MANIÈRE

 e brought my new furry friend, Snowball. I gathered by Bane's constant sniffling, he wasn't cotton to the idea. I figured if I had to stay at his place, the same rules applied for Snowball too. We were a package deal. Take it or leave it.

On the road to his house, we must've traveled twenty miles, deep into the countryside, before reaching his home. When we rolled up to a double gate, I nearly swallowed my teeth. Holy cow! The iron gates were like an impenetrable fortress. It reminded me of a scene out of a horror movie. Just past the black iron, we'd find a haunted mansion.

Bane punched a button on his key ring, and the giant gates crept open, allowing us passage. When we passed through, it wasn't long before a castle came into sight. Lights lined the stonewashed dwelling as if it were guarding some mid-century king.

"This is where you live?" I nearly choked on my breath.

"For the time being," Bane answered curtly.

"You live in a castle?" I felt like a misfit. This place was a palace where royalty lived and where common folk served. I reckoned I'd be the servant.

"Yes, some call it that." His voice came off flat. "I simply call it home."

I laughed in awe. "There's nothing simple about this place. You live in a freaking castle!"

"I think we established that already." His superiority was limpid. No wonder he stood out among everyone else. He was the real deal, an aristocrat that owned the air.

I eased back, sinking low in the seat. My palms felt clammy, and my stomach turned somersaults. "I think I'm going to be sick!" I grabbed my midriff, drawing my knees to my chest.

We came to a halt at the back entrance of the castle. After Bane cut the engine, he came to my side and held my door open. I guess he figured I was in shock. He took my hand and lifted me out.

He rolled his eyes over me, studying me. He barked, "when's the last time you've eaten? I recall you didn't eat at dinner."

"Huh, what day is this?"

Bane's brows pinched. "You must be joking?"

I opened my mouth to speak and then closed it. I rolled my eyes and skirted around Bane's question. "It doesn't bother me to go without food."

"That's not what I asked!" He bit down, lips drawn tight, "Never mind, I'll have Dom prepare you something."

We entered the side door, of course, the servant's entrance. We passed through a short hall. My guess, it was the mudroom connected to the main house. Only this wasn't a house. This place could fit fifty houses.

When we entered the kitchen, Bane pointed to a tall stool at the island. "Sit," he ordered.

The modern kitchen had all the stops. A large double door fridge, suggesting loads of delicious treats, and a gas stove built for a king.

"I'm afraid my chef, Dom, has retired for the night. I suppose I'm all you've got until morning." He forced a tight smile and twirled on his heels to the fridge. As he burrowed, half his body inside the oversized refrigerator, I watched quietly.

When he withdrew, his arms returned fully loaded with food, such as mayo, tomato, iceberg lettuce, and ham. I propped my elbows up on the black granite, resting my chin in my palm.

"I can make my own sandwich. I might be hopeless, but I'm not helpless." My eyes followed his skillful hands, spreading the dressing and adding ham, compiling lettuce and tomato slapped between two slices of whole-grain bread.

"Too late," his gaze lifted, catching mine as he slid the dish over to me. "Eat while I go get that..." he started to curse but stopped, correcting himself. "Pardon me, Snowball." He suddenly twitched his nose and rubbed it.

"Okay," I answered, chewing.

After I'd eaten and downed a cold glass of milk that I'd shared with Snowball, Bane grabbed up my bag, and we headed to the guest quarters. I carried Snowball in my arms. He was resting like a baby after drinking half my milk.

Instead of climbing the spiraling staircase, Bane insisted we take the elevator. Elevators and castles, oh my! On the third floor, we stepped out of the box and onto a hallway that stretched far as the eye could see, or so it seemed. Lighting dotted the limestone walls, shedding a soft golden glow down the corridor.

Bane stopped at the last door on the right and turned the doorknob.

"Here you are, home sweet home." He glanced down at me, one corner of his lip twitched, "ladies first." He held the door open. I caught his gaze and stepped past him into the room.

The suite had the feel of a man with expensive taste, dark paneling, rich, gold molding topped off with red Persian rugs. Thick fabric draped over the canopy bed, matching the autumn tones of the carpets and curtains. It had the style of a king.

I turned my focus back to Bane, "it's nice." It was exquisite, but not my taste. I never cared for dark rooms, even with generous lighting. I wouldn't dare complain and offend the noble host.

"You should have everything you need. You have your own bathroom, equipped with plenty of supplies, toothbrush, paste, soap." He gave me a quick smile. "If there's nothing else, I'll leave you to your quarters and see you in the morning," Bane started to leave.

"Wait! How do I get to school tomorrow?"

Bane tilted his shoulder toward me, partially out the doorway. "Jeffery will take you." His expression gave me no clue to his feelings.

"Oh, you're not going to school?"

"Yes, I think it's best if we aren't seen together in public, especially at school." He came off as aloof.

His words struck a sensitive chord with me. "Oh! And why is that?"

He shrugged. "I think, for the time being, it's best."

Confronting a polar bear would've been a piece of cake compared to him.

"You mean, best for you?" My hands rested on my hips.

"Stevie, we can talk tomorrow at dinner." His face was tense.

"What's wrong with right now?" I reckoned he didn't want to give anyone the wrong impression. Hooking up with the hired help was disgusting, and yet, he didn't mind playing grab-ass with me. Then, the arrangement flooded my mind. "I want to know more about the arrangement you and my mom have made behind my back?" I held my gaze to his.

Swiftly, Bane's fingers bit into my upper arm, shoving me inside the room. As he stepped inside and slammed the door behind him, he dropped his grip, though still glowering at me. "I swear your timing is impeccable," he hissed. "If you must know, then fine!"

"I have a right to know." My body trembled under his glare.

He roughly raked his fingers through his hair as he blew out his heated breath. After a moment, he cut his dark blues back at me. "I," he clenched his teeth, "Do not have the arrangement with your mother, Sara," he paused. "This contract was made between your parents and my family a long ago. I'm simply an unwilling participant." His repugnant words rolled off his tongue, cold-cocking me in the jaw.

I stepped back, stumbling, finding my back flushed against the bedpost. "Are you saying that my father agreed to this arrangement?" I barely spoke the words.

"Yes," he answered as though he didn't care if he hurt me.

"Arrangement of what?"

"I think you know the answer to that."

"Can you just answer one question for once?" I shouted, tears pooling. "I thought my mother sold me into sex trafficking, for Christ's sake!"

Bane scrunched up his face. "What a foolish thing to assume."

I could see the repulsion in his eyes. He hated me. "How could I not think that? My mother is driving a Ferrari! Hello! How else would she have gotten the coins?"

"The arrangement is a marriage." His words fell flat.

"Marriage?" My eyes widened.

"Yes."

"When is this happy event going to take place?" Sarcasm slid from my mouth.

"On Samhain, most folks know it as Halloween."

"Why that day?"

"It is a holiday for my family. It is a special day."

"Oh, what a perfect day! I'll be the one wearing black."

"I'm not in the mood for your cynical humor." There was a thread of warning in his voice.

"What? Are you not happy to be the groom?"

"It is not my wish," he whispered.

Bane's honesty struck me like a dagger to the heart. "So why agree," I scoffed. "Marriage arrangements are a thing of the past. Your family can't force you!"

"My family is very persuasive."

"Well, un-persuade them," I yelled back.

"You don't understand the precedence of this arrangement. There's no backing out now. Neither one of us can. We are bound to each other."

Chills crept over my body, "Like that stupid heart thing?"

"Something like that, yes." The muscle in Bane's jaw jerked.

"I don't care what promises my mother and father made with your family. I have a choice!"

"This may be hard for you to understand because you know nothing of your inheritance, but in our families, we don't belong to ourselves. We must abide by our duty."

"I'm confused. Our families? We don't know each other's family."

"Of course, you don't have an inkling of this matter! Your mother has kept you in the dark."

"Then let me in on this mysterious secret!" I shouted.

"Our union is for the greater good of the new system, the coming New World Order."

His words stirred an uneasy feeling down to the bone.

"You know what? You're jerking my string!" I clenched my teeth, angry and scared. "I need some sleep. I have to be up early tomorrow." I turned my back to Bane. I couldn't look at his face another minute.

"One more thing," he paused, his voice pinched. "I don't want you hanging around Sam Reynolds ever again. I hope I am clear."

My lower lip trembled as I scoffed at his bold demand. "Now you're dictating my friends?"

A sudden thin sheet of ice hung on the edge of his words. "I don't think you understand the severity of your situation."

I met his icy gaze. "I'm not your possession."

"As long as you're under my roof, you will do as I say." He stepped up only a breath from my face, looming over me. "End of subject."

"You don't get to call end-of-subject when it concerns me!" I stabbed him with my finger, "I control my destiny, bucko!"

Bane straightened his shoulders. His blues were sharp as a hawk's. "In our world, we have two choices; you can accept fate or resist and die." He drew in a sharp breath. "The sooner you realize that the better life will be for you."

I shuddered over his subtle threat. Despite my fear, I had to stand my ground. "Our lives aren't carved out of stone. We are free moral agents, able to choose our own paths."

"You are an idealistic girl setting yourself up for a great fall. A fall, I fear you will not recover from." There was a hint of sorrow in his voice. "I bid you good night."

I turned my shoulder to him. At this point, I hated him.

Before he stepped out, I twirled around, facing him, "Aidan," I called him by his first name.

He stopped, keeping his back to me.

"Just so you understand my standpoint, I'm an unwilling participant in this union too."

Bane simply nodded and then quietly stepped out of the room, shutting the door behind him.

I stood there for a brief moment staring at the closed door. The room was so quiet I could've heard a pin drop. I hated the silence and the way we parted ways tonight. I knew I was behaving like a total brat, but if I didn't push him away, he was going to break my heart. Besides, his kindness was solely out of duty to his family, whoever they may be. I wondered if his parents would be attending the wedding.

I couldn't do anything about my situation tonight. So, I decided a hot shower might help ease my frayed nerves. I stepped into the bathroom and gawked in disbelief. The black-marbled shower had so many gadgets that it took me a few tries before I figured it out.

I stood under the steaming water, letting the beads pulsate against my body. The swirl of clean soap encircled me, gardenia, I think. It felt wonderful, leaving my skin feeling renewed and soft. I stayed in the shower until the water ran cold.

When I stepped out, I spotted a white robe lying out on the counter, along with toothpaste, a brush, hair product, and a blow dryer. I shrugged on the heated robe, cinching the belt around my waist.

I spied a perfume bottle that struck my fancy. I picked it up and examined the diamond-crusted bottle. It sparkled like real diamonds. I whistled. "I've never seen anything like this at JC Pennies." I had to sample it. I jerked the top off and sniffed. "Nice!" I smiled to myself.

Why would a man have a woman's perfume? I bit my bottom lip, thinking. Good chance the fragrance belonged to a visitor. "A woman!" A little sting of jealousy struck. The idea of Bane entertaining another female chapped my butt like sand in my shorts.

I dabbed a little behind my ears and grazed my wrist with the tip. "Hmm," the scent hovered in the air. "Nice. A hint of jasmine!" I checked the name, Clive Christian. "Never heard of 'em.

"I bet the girl must be missing this stuff. Who knows, maybe Bane bought it for her."

All at once, jealousy coursed through me and the unthinkable happened. I poured the whole bottle down the drain. I giggled, thinking how wicked I'd become. "That's one gift that girl ain't getting from my shot-gun-husband-to-be." I stomped to the window and opened a small windowpane. "Man, I didn't realize how high we were." I glanced at the stars. They were bright against the black sky.

Then I remembered the perfume bottle still in my palm. With a good swift toss, it went sailing out the window, and less than a second, it crashed to the pebbled ground, and the sound of glass shattering was music to my ears. I laughed to myself. "Oh, what a shame, guess she'll have to get a new bottle now."

I climbed into bed and sank into the soft folds of the feathered mattress. The sheets felt like a little piece of heaven. I eased out a long breath.

Then the unwelcoming feeling of awkwardness pummeled my mind. I scoffed at the word guest. I think the term intruder might be a better description of me. What was I doing here? I was a misfit in the land of lavish riches.

How ironic? Bane was a king with no kingdom, and I was merely a peasant with no home. We had nothing in common. I liked hot dogs, and he liked caviar.

I'd be crazy to go through with this loveless marriage. Even though I had feelings for Bane, I certainly didn't want a marriage of convenience. Unlike him, I refused to honor a promise when I had no voice in the matter.

Then the thought of my father taking part in this atrocity broke my heart. I suspected Sara had a significant influence on his decision. Tears welled, and I wiped them away.

I thought of Bane. He'd spoken of a New World Order, and this marriage arrangement somehow benefited our families.

The only person I saw benefiting from this arrangement was Sara. She must've gotten a fat check. How else could she afford a Ferrari? Now I understood why this move felt different than all the others. Sara was living up to her end of the bargain, handing me over to my prearranged husband-to-be and collecting a fat paycheck for doing so. Betrayal and anger flitted through me.

I planned to find Sara tomorrow before this catastrophe gets any worse. She owed me an explanation. On the brink of tears, I bit my bottom lip hard, in disbelief of the lengths my mother would take. Sara's bargaining me off might be the breaking point where she and I parted ways for good. I knew Sara's illness caused her to make irrational decisions but selling me off into an unwanted marriage for a few bucks was unforgivable.

I buried myself into the fluffy pillow and cried. The stains on my pillow and swollen eyes bore evidence of my timorous night.

MEET THE STAFF

$\mathcal{M}$y eyes batted open when I heard someone's throat clear and the bed shifted. I snapped my head up, staring at a dark silhouette sitting at the foot of my bed. He was staring down at me with pursed lips.

"Well, sleepin' beauty awakes!"

I detected sarcasm in his Southern drawl.

I automatically tugged the covers to my chin. "Who are you?" My voice was parched and throaty.

The skinny man puffed out a cloud of smoke.

I coughed, waving the gray stench from me, wrinkling my nose. "Can't you find another place to do that?" I gagged. "I'm sure this place has a ton of nooks and crannies to hide that disgusting habit."

"Why would I do that when I can have a lovely conversation with your delicious self?" The caramel, skinned man's tone was void of pleasantries.

"Can you at least open a window and hang that thang out. It's choking me." I coughed, strangling.

"I don't mean to be rude, but if I hang my head out the window with a cig in my hand, Dom and the boss will string me alive." He drew in a long drag and blew it in my face. "No way in hell is I gettin' fired because of your delicate senses." The little snot disputed.

"Excuse me! I have a right to breathe, dude." I shot up into a sitting position.

"Gurrrlfriend, you might not have any rights after Mister Aidan finds that expensive perfume bottle smashed on top of his Rolls Royce. I'd never thought such a little bottle could leave such a large dent and discolor the paint." The skinny little snip eyed me up and down. "You sure is costin' that man a lotta money. Apart from the little fact that those diamonds are real, that perfume bottle that lies shattered into a million pieces was worth almost as much as the Rolls." He puffed on his cigarette and blew it into the air.

"Why do you think it was me? I'm sure I'm not the only woman in this castle that Master Aidan keeps company."

"*Pfft pleeeease!* Mister Aidan never receives visitors."

"I can understand why if you're depriving the guest of oxygen?"

Surprisingly, he laughed. "I'm Jeffery Noel, the butler. You know my aunt. She warned me how spunky you is. I was just messin' with you." His eyes danced with mischief as a faint smile lingered on his plump lips, though he didn't put his cigarette out. He patted my foot. "Come on. Get dressed. Dom has made you breakfast, boo." He bounced off the bed and pranced his way to the bathroom. I heard the cigarette sizzle and then the toilet flush. He stepped out from the puff of smoke and sauntered to the door. "Just get on the elevator and hit first floor. Follow the breadcrumbs, boo. You'll find me at the table, eatin'." He smiled. "Don't keep Dom waitin'. He's a cranky old soul when his food gets cold. You know how these ill-tempered chefs can be." He twirled full of sass and peacocked out the door. I sat back and laughed. "Hmm… so, that was Jeffery." I should've known he was Ms. Noel's nephew. He favored her a lot. Though taller than Ms. Noel and slenderer, he had her caramel skin and her round blue eyes.

Snowball startled me, meowing. He'd jumped up on the bed and came to me, nudging my hand for a quick scratch. "Hey, little guy! I bet you're hungry!" I smiled, raising my new buddy to my lips as I kissed him on the head.

∿

Following Jeffery's directions, I found myself wandering into the kitchen. Pots and pans covered the stove, and the smell of bacon and coffee wafted in the air. Instantly, my stomach growled.

My eyes fell on Jeffery. He was sitting at the island with his face drawn into a scowl. I'd noticed the stool beside him was empty.

Jeffery lifted his eyes to me and came alive, "Gurrrl, why you bringin' that damn cat into my kitchen?" His Southern accent was very apparent.

My eyes rounded. "Huh… he's hungry. I thought I'd give him some milk."

The older gentleman wearing the stained white apron spoke up. "Mademoiselle, pay no mind to him. Come! Sit, yes? I have breakfast prepared." He carried a thick French accent, and when he smiled, his deep browns sparkled like water in the moonlight. I instantly liked him.

I smiled back, shuffling my feet. "Thank you!" I was feeling a little uneasy with Jeffery's heated glare.

"Let me introduce myself. I am Dominque Florentine. You may call me Dom." He bowed as a smile stretched his pencil-thin mustache.

"Nice to meet you, Dom," I replied, smiling back.

"Vous êtes encore plus rayonnante que je l'imaginais." (You are even more radiant than I imagined). He spoke perfect French.

"Merci Monsieur," I grinned.

"Ah, a girl after my own heart!" His face gleamed.

Jeffery patted the stool next to him. "Chile, come sit right her' so we can have a good look at you." Jeffery smiled, but it was as phony as Sara's fingernails.

I tucked my chin down, feeling the heat across my cheeks. "All right," I breathed, climbing onto the stool. I still held Snowball tight in my arms.

Jeffery sneered at Snowball and cut his eyes at me. I returned the glare, daring him to touch my kitten.

Then I turned my attention to the chef. "Dom, what part of France are you from?"

Dom's soft browns were welcoming and engaging. "I come from a little place, South of France in Saint-Remy-de-Provence. It's a quaint town. The market on Saturdays is magnifique!" He bunched his fingers together and kissed them. "The market is where I first received my inspiration for the art of culinary. My home is rich with vineyards and rows of small Cafés." His eyes glossed. I understood homesickness. "There is no other place in the world like it, yes?"

"Je l'entends est belle et riche en histoire." (I hear it is beautiful and rich with history.) I smiled at Dom's twinkle.

"Tu parles bien le français." (You speak French well.)

"Thank you. I've taken it in school." Then I thought about Tangi. "What brought you here to this ghost town?"

There was a gentle stir in Dom's eyes, perhaps pondering of pleasant memories of a different time. "I came to work for Monsieur Bane when he purchased a nearby village close to my home in France." He placed a hot plate of simple eggs, a buttery croissant and bacon on the side with a tall glass of milk. I placed Snowball on the counter and shared my milk with him as Dom continued, "The village was no longer inhabited. Perhaps you've heard of it, Baux de Provence."

I gulped, holding my fork midway to my mouth. "Wait! Monsieur Bane

bought a whole village?"

"Oui! It is quite the picturesque village, perched on the edge of a rocky outcrop. However, the village no longer is thriving." He shrugged sharply. "Despite its state, it is a rare treat to wander the old streets and around the castle and quite the experience that will leave one breathless."

"It sounds wonderful." Although my mind still skipped like a broken record on the buying-a-village part.

A sick feeling came over me. If this dude had that much buying power, I wondered what he might be capable of doing if pushed.

Jeffery bolted out of his seat and stomped to the stove. His face soured, snatching up a plate and shoveled a generous side of eggs. He stomped back to his perch in an angry huff. "I suppose since Miss Fair-And-Lovely is the main attraction, I gotta get my own food." Steam curled from Jeffery's boney shoulders.

Dom rolled his eyes. "Jeffery, Monsieur Bane would expect nothing less of us. After all, she is our guest, and how often do we have the pleasure of entertaining guests?" Dom shot Jeffery a behave-or-regret-it-later glance.

The last thing I wanted was to get into a fight with Queen Jeffery. "Hey, I'm sorry! I don't mean to step on anyone's toes." My eyes widened, thinking I should leave. "I didn't ask to come here. Monsieur Bane insisted." My eyes darted between both men. "Clearly, I'm imposing."

I started sliding off the stool, but light golden fingers rested on my shoulder. Startled, I snapped my head up.

"I'm sorry, boo! Don't go. I just get a little crabby when I haven't eaten." He dropped his hand to his side. "I want you to stay. It's nice having a conversation with someone new rather than the present." Jeffery snubbed his nose at Dom.

Oh-boy-oh-boy! It'd be best to watch out for this skinny man.

I inhaled a slow breath. "Apology accepted, but don't come in my room again uninvited, especially smoking a cigarette!" I held my intended gaze to Jeffery's bugged eyes.

His mouth rounded. "I can't believe you blew the whistle on me," he shrieked.

Dom's expression froze with shock. "Jeffery, please tell me you did not do that!" His lips tightened, hands flew to his portly waist. "We agreed!"

Jeffery shook his head, excitable. "Dom, I swear, the bitch is lyin'!"

I laughed. "I'm not a bitch, and I'm not lying." I didn't lie about being a liar. Occasionally, I lied. Just not this time.

If an evil eye could kill, Jeffery would've been dead. "Hand over the pack!" Dom held out his palm, shooting fire at Jeffery.

"I can't believe you are going to take my smokes!" Jeffery's jaw dropped to the floor. "I am a grown-ass man!"

"I agree and qui manque de prudence!" (Yes, lack of prudence).

Holy hell, I started World War III! "Guys, I'm sorry! I shouldn't have said anything."

"No, don't apologize, boo," Jeffery huffed. "I'll hand 'em over. It's an expensive habit even though Dom paid for 'em." Jeffery tossed a spicy grin at Dom.

By the glance they shared suggested to me there might be something more than just co-workers.

Jeffery spoke. "So, tell us the juicy-juicy!" He wiggled in his seat, eyes sharp as a tack. "What's he like in the sack?"

My breath stalled. Crap! Payback was a bitch with my name on it.

All at once, a plate shattered to the floor. It had slipped from Dom's hands as shock seized him. He stood frozen, gawking at Jeffery in silence.

Ignoring the chef's reactions, Jeffery behaved unbothered with his elbow prompted up and his pointy chin resting in his palm, staring purposely at me. "Well," he pushed.

I smiled awkwardly, face flushed.

Dom spoke up, "Stevie, you do not have to answer that!" Dom's eyes fired bullets at the caramel-skin man. "Jeffery, you know better to ask such a personal question."

I stared back at Jeffery, "I'll tell you my darkest secrets if you tell me yours," I challenged with a perked brow.

After a quick pause, Jeffery moved on to another topic. "Jump up! Let me take a look at you." His eyes appeared sneaky.

"I'm eating, later, maybe," I smiled as I took a good size bite of eggs.

"C'mon! You can eat standing up. I want to take a good look at your lovely self," he smiled too sweetly. "Don't worry. You is not my type."

I couldn't hold it in. I laughed. "Okay," I smirked, jumping off the stool.

Jeffery raised his finger over my head and made a circular motion. "Turn around so I can get a better look."

I groaned, twirling in slow motion. I came to a halt staring at Jeffery's critical face.

He tapped his finger against his chin, eyeballing me. "You ain't model material."

I scoffed, "Thanks!"

"No, gurrrl, that's a good thang." His eyes washed over me from head to toe. "You got curves!" He jumped from his roost and stepped up to me. "You're not a stick, boo. I'm just sayin'." Jeffery lifted a strand of hair. "Your hair color is sorta the color of rust, not red and not brunette either. We get you some hair product and a good brushin' out that bird's nest, and your hair should shine like glass." His lips twisted. "Why ain't you wearin' your hair down than hidin' it up in that awful ponytail?"

I swiped my fingers over my hair. "The ponytail is easy."

"Gurrrl, you need to let me give you a new look." He air framed my body. "This look you got now is plum tired. We need to get you up to speed."

Ouch! That stung. My eyes dropped down to my clothing, raggedy jeans with gaping holes in the knees that I bought two years ago at Wal-Mart and a yellowish faded tank top, a wrinkled hoodie, and my scuffed-up Western boots. I withdrew a long sigh. "I-I..." the right words seemed to have vacated my brain. "I never have time," I shrugged, quickly changing the subject. "Have either one of you seen Bane this morning?" I climbed back on the stool.

"He was here earlier." Jeffery smiled, returning to his seat next to me. "He didn't stay long, just long enough to grab his coffee and skedaddled."

My eyes rounded, "Coffee! Do you have any left?" Oh, what I'd do for a cup right now.

"Oui! Pardon me for not offering you a cup earlier." Dom smiled, reaching for the coffee pot and pouring a heaping amount in a large mug. He returned to me carrying a side dish of cream and sugar with a hefty dose of hot caffeine. As Dom set the mug in front of me, I hovered over the curls of steam taking in the delicious aroma. A rich darkness, smooth with a fruity flavor. If the world went to hell in a handbasket, as long as I had my coffee, I'd be just fine.

"Thank you!" The coffee buzz would make this day go a lot easier. Unfortunately, it wouldn't help my living situation any. Even though Jeffery and Dom were starting to grow on me, I refused to be a prisoner. I needed to find a way out and do it fast. The one problem that kept nagging me was that I needed money.

"Gurrrl! You best swallow that shit! I gotta get you to school. Hustle, hustle!" Jeffery snapped his fingers. "Mister Aidan will have my butt if I get you to school late." Jeffery shoved me off the stool, nearly causing me to spill my coffee on myself.

"Chill dude! I'm coming!"

I took one more scorching gulp of my coffee, nearly giving my tongue a third-degree burn, and darted out the door following Jeffery.

By the time I walked into the garage, Jeffery had the Rolls roaring to go with a scowl on his face. I hurried along, jumping in the passenger's seat. Jeffery's brows dipped down, lips twisted into a sneer, eyes bulging as he glared up at me, "What the hell do you think you're doing?"

"I'm getting in the car." I looked at him, surprised.

"Gurrrl, you is supposed to be ridin' in the back, not with the hired help."

I rolled my eyes at him. "I'm just like you, Jeffery. I'm the hired help too but of another kind," I snapped. "Just drive."

"Hold the hell up!" Jeffery's eyes went wide as golf balls. "Is Mister Aidan keeping you here against your will?"

I flashed him a knowing glance without uttering a word.

"Does yo momma know this?"

I swallowed down the knot that persisted. "Yep, my mother set it up." I looked out the side window.

"Oh, my sweet Jesus! Lord have mercy on my lovely soul!" Jeffery ranted. "That explains a lotta shit!" He held his hand to his lips. "It ain't like Mister Aidan to bring guest home. He's never brought a girl home. The only ones we ever see are his uncle and that mofo cousin of his. Now that no good count cousin, you need to hide from him. He cray-cray as the loony bend and retched as the devil." Jeffery wagged his finger at me.

"After you drop me off at school, will you go by and check on your aunt?" I fiddled with my bag. "I don't want her to worry."

"Sure, boo, I need to check on her anyway." He patted my hand. "Don't you fret none. We look after our peeps," he smiled.

KISS MY EYES

I wished Jeffery had dropped me off a block from the school. Despite my protest, he insisted on depositing me at the front entrance. I wanted to crawl under a rock. The pointy stares and turned heads targeting my back were cringe-worthy. I reckoned it wasn't an everyday thing to see a rag doll stepping out from a Rolls Royce.

The second I entered English, Sally's head popped up, shooting her harsh eyes at me as if I was a dartboard. A frown had flickered across her face before she smiled. It had become apparent that we didn't care for each other. Part of me felt relieved, no more pretenses.

"Good morning!" Sally half turned in her seat, facing me.

"What's up," I half-heartedly replied.

"How's Aidan?" she asked casually.

I wondered how much she knew about my living situation. Rumors carried fast in a town that wasn't big enough to spit on. I got the impression Sally had heard. "Fine, I guess." I dropped my bag by my feet and settled in my seat.

Sally shrugged uncomfortably. "Glad to see your back, but I think Gina's pissed at you."

"What's new?"

"She knows that you've been hanging with Aidan. I don't blame her. They're *dating*." Sally emphasized the word dating.

"Can you knock it off? You're like chalk screeching across the board," I railed full force. "I don't give a rat's ass about what Gina thinks or if she's planning to kick my ass. Like she could," I scoffed. "Just turn around in your seat and shut up for a change! It actually would be a real treat to hear Ms. Jenkins instead of listening to your diarrhea of the mouth!"

"I was just giving you a heads up. I thought I was doing you a favor."

"Sal, you are the biggest liar ever! The only heads up you give," I fumed, "is the football team."

"You're still pissed at me for telling you about Gina and Aidan." She threw the words at me like glass shards.

"Sal, I don't understand you're motive. Were you hoping I'd kick Gina's ass?" I clamped my mouth closed, and then I decided to drive my point into her thick chest. "Maybe it's you who wants to kick Gina's ass, but you're too much of a coward to do it yourself." I was on a roll now. "I believe you hate Gina more than anyone else in the whole wide world." My brow arched, daring her to deny my theory.

"My friendship with Gina is none of your business!" Sally's ireful retort hardened her features.

"I'm right, aren't I?" I stared at her as her face beamed red.

"You're not perfect," Sally snipped.

I bit back a laugh. Sally surprised me. She did have a little backbone, after all. "You're right. I shouldn't have lashed out at you. I'm sorry." I bit my lip, pausing. "But you make it hard for me to like you. After everything you've done to hurt me, I'd be a fool to trust you again."

Sally's nostrils flared. I could've sworn I saw steam curling. I get why she didn't like me lashing back, but her dislike for me seemed to go much deeper. I hadn't a clue as to why.

Not a moment too soon, the teacher walked in when the bell rang, and that ended the conversation.

Sally turned to face the teacher. She didn't bother speaking to me during the rest of the class. It was a nice change.

After thirty minutes into class, Lord Aidan decided to bless us with his presence. Our eyes locked, and my heart lurched. He looked good too. The way his black hair fell over his face and his step, fluid and confident, capturing every eye in the room.

He'd dropped a small pink slip on the teacher's desk and didn't pause for his seat.

Ms. Jenkins cleared her throat and spoke, "Mr. Bane, this makes the third tardy this week. A hall pass isn't an excuse." The teacher's face tightened. "See that this doesn't happen again."

"No problemo, Teach." Bane flashed a cocky grin that could make a girl go weak in the knees and piss off a teacher. "I'll be sure to give Dr. Van your regards."

The class roared with laughter. Without another word, Ms. Jenkins blushed into an angry hue.

As Bane headed down the aisle to his desk, I tucked my chin down, burying my face into my English book. It seemed he preferred to ignore me as though I was a stranger.

Then an epiphany struck. It occurred to me that Bane had a dual personality. Here at school, he betrayed the typical bad boy with adamant defiance. Off-campus, his behavior displayed someone much different, older even. He was a mystery and one hard nut to crack.

He slid in his seat with a soft groan, the sort of sound that made your toes curl. Chills spread up my arms. Just hearing his voice and that signature scent of a woodsy spice sent my pulse to the stars.

He didn't even glance my way. After all, he didn't want anyone to see us together. A little burn trickled down to my gut. I sighed. I'd never been good enough to hang in his social circles, but how did I separate myself from him when the very air around him seemed magnified, and I was always getting caught in his snare.

The bell sounded off, and Sally scurried out the door.

I gathered up my load, stuffing my book and work inside my bag and shouldering it.

Bane was talking to one of the football players as I passed by him. He never glimpsed my way. I told myself it didn't bother me, but it did.

I stopped at my locker to unload when Sam snuck up behind me, tickling my waist. I leaped with a yap, books, and paper went flying. I turned around and slugged the crap out of his arm. "That's what you get for scaring me," I huffed as my pulse leaped in my throat.

Then Sunday night popped in my head, and I slugged him again. "That's for leaving Jen and me stranded, you jerk!"

I reckoned Sam wanted to redeem himself as he helped me gather up my books.

His puppy dog eyes glistened like black obsidian. "I had to take a piss."

"Did you use the outhouse?"

Sam's eyes orbed like bowling balls. "I looked hell and high waters for you girls. I finally asked the bouncer if he'd seen you two. That's when I discovered that Old Blue came and whisked you girls off on his broomstick."

"Now Bane's a witch," I rolled my eyes.

"No, not exactly." He unconsciously rubbed his arm. "I heard his family owns the joint."

My eyes dropped to his arm, and I gasped, staring at three deep bloody gashes from his wrist to his upper arm. "Oh, my God! Your hurt," my gaze lifted to Sam. "What happened?"

He swiftly drew his arm away, covering the marks with his sleeve, "Uh, nothin'."

My brows collided. "It looks like you got in a catfight."

"Don't worry about it." He patted my arm. "Hey, I got practice. See you later." He flashed a maquillage smile.

"Yeah, sure." I eyed him suspiciously. He sure did rush off when I mentioned the scratches. I wondered what happened.

When lunchtime hit, I went looking for Jen. I was on a mission and needed Jen's expert skills. Having her opinion would be helpful too. Just having her by my side made me feel more confident that I wasn't going crazy. She was the only friend I had in this entire school. I was grateful too.

Right outside the cafeteria, I spotted her heading for our tree. The same oak that Bane and I stood under on the first day of school. Jen and I usually ate lunch there if the weather permitted. It beat the cafeteria, sitting under the burning glare of Gina.

"Jen," I called out to her, heading toward her, out of breath slightly.

Jen's eyes lit up. "I see you survived the woes of punishment," she smiled. "How much time did you get?"

A little pain hit me in the heart. It wasn't easy admitting the downfall of a parent, "Yeah, getting grounded sucks." I shrugged. Right away, I shifted gears into another subject. Though I knew Jen wouldn't judge me, I didn't want to harp on my problems. "I need your mad computer skills. You up for the challenge?"

Jen paused a moment. Mischief filled her brown eyes. "What you got cooking in that brain of yours?"

"I want to Google Aidan Bane." I held my breath, hoping she'd be up for the task.

Jen laughed. "Girl, you don't stop!" She shrugged. "Let's go! I'm not hungry anyhow."

"Yeah," my eyes gleamed, "Me neither." We bumped shoulders, laughing.

Once we entered the library, we headed straight for the computer section, nicely tucked away in private cubicles, more private and out of earshot. I wanted to keep this under wraps. We picked the last one on the far end. Jen tossed her book bag down next to her chair and flopped down, fingers on the keyboard. She clicked on the Google icon. In the box, she typed Aidan Bane. I held my breath while the circle churned. "I swear the computer must be dial-up."

"I wish I had my laptop. This bitch is ancient." Jen groaned.

"The school should do upgrades. Shakespeare is too old." We giggled in a low whisper.

Finally, the search engine pulled up several pictures and a long list of Aidan Banes.

"Whoa! I guess his name is pretty common." I bit my bottom lip.

"There are a bunch, but look at this one," Jen clicked on one link that seemed to be the bio of a deceased person.

The circle churned for a handful of breaths, then finally, it stopped. We both gasped, staring at the new page and a picture that could've been Bane's twin.

"Oh my God," I barely breathed. "That has to be Aidan's great grandfather."

"Something all right!" she whistled low. "Read this, Stevie!"

I leaned in at the screen, scanning over the information. It was an obituary. The piece read,

Aidan Bane, age 23, of New Orleans, Louisiana, passed away on
February 25, 1918, died of Spanish influenza. He was born on August
21, 1897, in New Orleans, Louisiana. One survivor includes his wife,

Sabella Mae, no children. Mr. Bane was a student at Yale and a sorority member of the Skull and Cross Bones.

"Oh, my gosh!" I braced myself against the table. I was three shades of stunned. I expected a lot of things, but I didn't expect to find his twin. My eyes fell on Jen. "Do you think this is our Aidan Bane?" As soon as the question left my lips, it sounded ridiculous. Of course, it couldn't be. This man died at the turn of the century.

Jen shrugged. "I don't see how, but that guy in the picture could be Aidan's clone." Jen blew out a sharp breath. "Maybe the dead Aidan Bane had a kid by another woman that he didn't know about?"

I tapped my finger against my lips, thinking. "Possible, I guess. Hey, type in Skull and Bones." My curiosity was running with me.

"Yeah, that is a weird name for a Frat house." She laughed. "Those rich kids with Daddy's deep pockets usually are wicked."

I giggled, "Right, like that bar!"

"Girl, you know it!" She shook her head. "Freaky Freaks," Jen laughed, typing.

I grabbed another chair from the cubicle next to us and dragged it up beside Jen. After several ticks, the browser stopped with several hits.

Jen clicked on a link reading Yale's Skull and Bone, Conspiracy Archive. The front page displayed a large skull with crossed bones with crimson in the background, reminding me of a flag or an emblem like pirates.

As we scrolled down the page, our eyes halted on a black and white picture—the bi-line read, 1916. Thirteen men were in their Sunday's best, black suits and black ties.

In the front row, two gentlemen sat opposite sides of a table with a skull and crossed bones as the centerpiece. Behind the two seated, eleven other men stood, all heavily mustached. When my eyes gravitated to one man who stood nearly a head taller than anyone else did, I became grateful for the chair that saved me from falling to the hard floor.

Jen and I shared a shocked glance. For a minute, silence hung in the thick air as we studied the tall man's face. The only way I could explain it was that the guy in the picture had to have been Bane's doppelganger.

"Jen, this cannot be possible!" My heart raced faster than a Russian racehorse.

"Yeah, impossible!" Jen stared at the screen.

Dread washed over me. "No way!" I leaped from my chair, feeling electrified.

"Stevie, you gotta listen to this."

Jen drew me back to the computer.

She tossed me a quick look and began reading.

"The Skull and Bones is an ancient symbol with a powerful, clandestine connotation. Folks today have been misled to believe that the Skull and Crossed Bones signifies poison, but this is a calculated deception by the elite to hide its true interpretation. The Skull and Crossed Bones is an ancient instrument used by necromancers to gain satanic powers."

After Jen finished, she turned in her seat, staring up at me. When our eyes locked, we both mirrored each other's spooked gaze.

"What the hell is a necromancer?"

Jen's brows knitted. "Heck if I know." She placed her fingers on the keyboard and Googled the word. "It means sorcerer, a person who practices magic." She flashed a faint smile.

I scoffed. "I wonder if that includes the tooth fairy. If so, my life's crushed," I joked, pretending this stuff didn't have me rattled.

Jen laughed, "Yeah, right!" Then we sat in silence for a moment, mulling over our discovery.

I barely murmured, "Could this be Bane?" I shoved my hands in my jean pockets.

Jen sighed sharply, wringing her hands. "I don't see how it's possible. Still, how can we explain the look-alike thingy? This dude in the picture is not only the spitting image of Bane but has the same smile. Look at the guy's teeth."

I leaned forward, examining the image.

"Tell me if that ain't him?"

I shook my head, "Holy cow! He's got the same smile."

"Maybe he's like the Highlander! Old but hot as hell!"

I snorted, laughing. Jen always cracked me up. "Old and hot shouldn't even be in the same sentence."

"Yeah, that's gross." We both snickered, holding our hands over our mouths.

I checked my watch. "Damn, the bell's about to ring." My lips twisted into a frown. "Guess we'll have to pick this up next time." I shouldered my bag.

"Whatcha doing later?" Jen snatched up her bag and purse, following behind me as we left the library. "I might stop by for a moment after school."

"I'd love to have company, but I'm grounded," I lied. "Hey, I thought your parents grounded you?"

"Girl, that was yesteryear. I got out of it by saying a few Hail Marys' and swearing I will never go anywhere with Sam again," she laughed, "Which I don't even want to speak to that loser."

"Sam told me he'd been in the men's restroom."

"Oh no, he didn't!" Jen's eyes orbed, "That lying dog! He told me he went to his truck to grab his condoms. He made light of it by saying, 'no glove, no love." Jen stuck her finger down her throat.

"I can't believe that asshat!"

"Well, this has been very educational. We both know that Sam can't be trusted, and your hot boyfriend is old as hell."

I snickered. "Girl, go on! You know he's not my boyfriend. I'd never date a guy who's passed the age of twenty." We both laughed, but inside, I was kicking myself for lying. I was too embarrassed to tell the truth. How did I explain that my mother sold me for a few bucks, forcing me to live with a guy who hated me?

When the last bell rang for the day, I headed outside. No one bothered to let me know the protocol of how I would make it home after school.

I stood under the awning, rocking on my heels, biting my nails. I hated this feeling of homelessness.

After the last nail, I decided to put my own fate in my hands and headed to my house. How bad could it be? Two miles was a cakewalk. Ms. Noel would be happy to see me too. I no more walked a block and caught the Corvette pulling up to the curb. Yours truly rolled down the window and yelled out, "Hey, jump in."

His blues felt like red-hot darts shooting at my back. "Sorry, I prefer my bed tonight," I tossed over my shoulder, keeping my pace.

"C'mon, if you didn't like your room, there are plenty of other rooms to suit your taste."

I kept walking, keeping my eyes straight ahead. I wasn't in the mood to argue. Tires crunching over the loose gravel ricocheted off my ears.

I must've briefly blacked out for a second. When I looked up, Bane stood directly in front of me. His arms folded, brows dipped into an angry glower.

My eyes flew open, startled as I stopped in my tracks. "How did you get from your car to me so quickly?" I took a step back.

"I don't have time playing these schoolgirl games. Now get in the car," he ordered darkly.

"Hold on just a minute, buster! It seems you're the one playing games. You didn't say one word to me in English. Who's playing whom?" I threw the proverbial brick right back at his head.

"Stevie, I can't explain everything to you. I don't want certain people to get any ideas."

Bane really thought that was going to make me feel better. "What ideas? That you're hanging out with a poor girl?"

"Your social hierarchy has nothing to do with my distance." The bridled anger in his voice cut me to the bone.

"I get it." I threw the words at him like bullets. "I'm good enough for you when it's convenient, but I'm not worthy of your presence in public." I wanted to cry, but I swallowed it back, denying myself the aching urge.

For a second, his blues softened; then, he masked his expression as if he held some dire secret. "Look! You don't understand and, I don't have time to explain." A sudden thin chill hung on the edge of his voice. "You're coming with me whether you want to or not. You're not that heavy." His lips stretched back, revealing straight white teeth. "What's it going to be, Princess?"

"I don't understand why I have to stay with you. We don't even like each other," I countered icily.

"Get in the car, now!"

I drew in a quick breath, trying to wrap my dilemma around my head. If I ran, he'd catch me and drag me back. He outweighed me at least a hundred pounds. I crossed my arms, holding my gaze leveled to his even though I was quaking in my shoes. I blurted out the first thing that came to mind. "I have nothing to wear at your place. I need to go get my clothes."

"Jeffery has taken care of that." The insolence in his voice concealed little. "You're no longer living there. You'll be staying with me from now on."

My mouth dropped open. Startled hurt turned into white anger. "Who gave you permission to take over my life?"

"I think you know the answer to that." At that moment, I couldn't have felt more like a prisoner.

"Fine!" Curses flew from my mouth as I twirled on my heels, stomping to the car.

LA VIE DU CHATEAU

Once again, I found myself stuck in Bane's Corvette with the reticent torture of listening to his classical music blaring in my ears. This dude was a bundle of weird. What teenager listened to Beethoven and actually enjoyed it?

We finally arrived at his majesty's palace, halting at a barrier that reminded me of a stone boulder. Bane punched a button on his keypad, and the rock lifted, giving birth to a dark tunnel.

After a quick flash of darkness, we entered an underground warehouse that housed an arsenal of vehicles. I tried to keep my gawking down to a minimum, but damn! I couldn't stop myself. The collection had to have been one of the most expensive collaborations of metal on wheels in the world.

I slid out of the Corvette, gaping at the gazillions of toys. There were several different models of motorcycles, one I recognized, the classic Harley. An easy pick. Various foreign cars lined the warehouse, all in every imaginable color with shiny chrome. I spotted the Rolls right away, nestled next to my beetle bug sitting in the far corner.

Then I remembered Jeffery mentioning a broken perfume bottle landing on top of the Rolls. I snuck a quick glimpse at Bane. I wondered if he knew.

· · ·

All at once, Bane jarred my attention back to him when his fingers clasped my elbow. I flinched at his subtle touch. He was the last person I wanted touching me. I may not have to worry about my next meal, but when my freedom of choice got jacked, everything else paled in comparison.

We stopped in front of an elevator. Bane pressed the button, and after a moment, the bell dinged, and the doors parted. He nudged the small of my back, urging me to step inside of the box. I complied, rolling my eyes.

Bane punched the first-floor button and the doors closed. With a sudden jolt, my stomach lurched as the elevator engaged. I rocked on my heels, listening to the awful music.

Seconds later, once again, the bell dinged, and the doors slid open. We stepped out into a dark foyer. Bane took my elbow once again, leading me down a narrow hall and into the bright kitchen. I spotted Dom preparing dinner at the large stove and Jeffery sitting at the island reading the newspaper.

The king of the castle didn't waste any time shedding the likes of me. "Jeffery," Bane's voice was on the brink of snapping. "Can you escort our guest to her quarters? Give her the presidential suite on the east wing. I think it will suit her taste. See to her needs and make sure she is dressed for dinner tonight," he ordered as if I were an unwanted child. Maybe that was the norm for the elite. I did note he seemed distracted and a thousand miles away.

Once he finished instructing Jeffery, Bane dropped my elbow and left me standing alone without even a glance in my direction. I felt discarded like a cheap tramp after a Friday night bargain fest. I didn't get it. I was a nuance to him, so why bother? I watched as he disappeared around the corner, leaving me in the kitchen alone with Dom and Jeffery.

Jeffery glared at me like I'd stomped out his last cigarette.

"I should ask for a raise," Jeffery went on to say. "You bein' 'ere is addin' to my long list of chores." He slammed the paper down irritably, sliding off the stool.

Dom shot Jeffery a glare and then looked at me smiling. "Don't pay him no mind." Dom's eyes flickered warmly. "Jeffery's list of chores consists of gathering the newspaper and shredding it into a messy pile before Monsieur Aidan has had a chance to read it."

My eyes dropped down to the scattered paper over the granite. I smiled inwardly.

Dom continued, "If I didn't know any better, I'd swear that Jeffery had glued his butt to that stool." Dom's pencil-thin mustache stretched across his face, smiling.

I smiled back. I got the feeling that those two were going to make my stay here a little easier, even Jeffery and his snappiness. I dropped my book bag on the floor and made my way to the island. I climbed up on the stool next to Jeffery. "I do appreciate your hospitality." I directed my comment to the chef with the stained apron.

Dom placed a cold glass of Coke and a croissant sandwich in front of me that instantly made my mouth water. "Thank you." My eyes sparkled at the sandwich. All of a sudden, I realized that I'd missed lunch.

I turned to Jeffery and asked. "Did you go to your Aunt's house today?"

"I did and told her that you is pesterin' the hell outta me too!" Jeffery pursed his lips. "She sends her love and says to keep up the good work." He bobbed his head. "Any old hoot!"

I laughed. "I'm worried about Ms. Noel. I've been making deliveries to her customers. She needs help."

"I can take care of my aunt, don't you fret none, otay."

"Someone's a little snarky today." I smiled at Jeffery as I bit into my sandwich.

Dom smiled.

Jeffery's face twisted, eyes narrowed as he swiftly changed the subject. "Well… how did your day go at school today?"

I detected a suspicious tone to his voice. "Hmm… it went okay." I shrugged, taking a bite of my sandwich. The bread melted in my mouth as I chewed. I had swallowed before I spoke. "I did find something odd online." I took a sip of my Coke.

Jeffery perked up in his seat, leaning closer. "Oh! Gimme, gimme," he chimed.

I rolled my eyes. "This might sound strange, but I Googled Demon. I mean, Aidan." Whoops!

Dom smiled, and Jeffery laughed so hard he slapped his hand on his pants. "No, gurrrlfriend, you had it right the first time. That rich mofo hadn't given me a raise in two years." Jeffery twisted his lips into a sour face. "He should be glad I ain't quit."

Dom laughed, turning from the stove, facing Jeffery. "You should be glad Monsieur Aidan hasn't fired you." He arched a gray brow. "You do nothing but eat and bitch!" Something told me that Dom had Jeffery pegged.

Jeffery dropped his long chin, gawking incredulously. "What do you know? You don't know half the shit I do around 'ere!"

Dom retorted with just the right amount of spice. "Ah, the half I do see," he tapped the corner of his eye, "is enough to satisfy me a lifetime, ami!" (Friend)

"That's not what you told me last night!" He held an undertone that I didn't want any part of knowing. Jeffery decided to switch his focus back to me. "Boo, what were you sayin' about school today?" He used his sweet voice, yet it came off as underhanded.

I thought it might be best not to share my findings. My gut was warning me to wait, "Oh, nothing," I shrugged, "Just another day at school."

"Well, since your little secretive-self ain't got nothin' to tell, I guess I best take you to your new room." He stretched as he slid off the stool. "What was wrong with the first room? It didn't have enough elegance for your princess butt?"

My eyes narrowed. "My butt is far from royalty. If I had my way, I'd prefer sleeping on a park bench than listening to your mouth flapping." I snatched up my bag, brow arched. "If your butt ain't too proud, you think you could show me where I'm staying?"

Dom winked at me. "Jeff, I do believe you have met your match!"

"You hush up! Don't give this chile any ideas." Jeffery pursed his lips.

"I wouldn't dream of doing such a thing. I think this young lady is smart enough to figure you out on her own," Dom replied as he waved his wooden spoon, laughing.

"Let's get outta 'ere! I'm about to stuff that Frenchman in the trash packer." I bit my lip to hold my giggle, though I wasn't sure if he was kidding or not.

The light stopped on three. The elevator doors parted like the Red Sea. Right away, a cold draft skidded across my face. I felt like I'd stepped into the past. Dim lighting marked the tapestry that dotted the whole stretch of wall and century Old Persian rugs embellished the dark, stone floor.

Finally, we came to a halt, and Jeffery spoke his first words since we left the kitchen. "Here we are." Sarcasm churned in his voice, mixed with the jingle of keys, "Home sweet home."

We stepped inside, and a familiar scent of sweet pepper flooded my senses. A bouquet of red roses in a vase embellished a round table in the foyer. Crystal, I assumed. Unlike the other room, this one was light and full of sunlight. It felt more like a hotel suite than a dank bed-chamber.

The suite came fully loaded with the works, just like an expensive hotel room. I noted a large flat-screen television in the sitting room, and just off to the side, a bedroom passed the French doors.

I'd forgotten about Jeffery until he cleared his throat. He stood by the window. "Well, does this fit your taste buds a little better?"

His tone ignited a sudden feeling of ire. "Contrary to what you may believe, I'm not an opportunist. I explained to you my situation." I dropped my bag in a huff, glaring at the skinny man who seemed to have jumped to conclusions.

Jeffery's eyes softened as he made his way to the couch and eased himself onto the soft cushion. "One thing you need to know about me is that I can read people." He brushed the lint off his pants.

"I reckon you must think I'm a gold digger then."

He crossed his legs and sighed, meeting my gaze. "I did in the beginning," he flashed a self-assured smile. "I don't understand why he's holdin' you here when you clearly wish to be elsewhere?"

"I've been asking the same thing myself." I paused, debating whether I should ask. I decided to go for it. "Is your boss mental?"

Jeffery folded his arms over his chest, slightly kicking his foot back and forth. "You probably have discovered that Mister Aidan is a hard read. He's broody as hell and is a never-ending enigma." Jeffery's leg kicked a bit faster.

I made my way to a chair across from the couch. For the first time, I was getting a better understanding of the king of the castle. "What else do you know?"

"I know that Mister Aidan likes you." Jeffery studied my reaction as he kept his foot swinging.

I smiled back, disguising my shock. "How can you tell?"

"For starters, Mister Aidan is very protective of you." Jeffery dug into his pocket and pulled out a pack of Lucky Strikes. He patted his pants on both sides. "Damn! I can't find my lighter." He looked up at me. "You wouldn't happen to be a pyromaniac by chance?"

"No! Guess you're outta luck." I leaned back in my chair and tucked my legs underneath me.

"Well, since you ain't got no lighter, I'm leaving." He sprinted to his feet.

"Oh please! Can't you stay for a minute longer?"

Jeffery paused, eyeing me suspiciously. "Look! I can't hold off for a smoke, but I'll tell you this much." Jeffery headed for the door. "Somethin' is stirrin', and it's got me jumpy." His voice a near whisper. "My best advice for you is to stay the hell away from Aidan's uncle and that damn cousin of his. They's mo evil than the devil." He paused as his hand touched the doorknob. "Oh yeah," he said, one brow arched. "Mister Aidan expects you dressed for dinner at eight, sharp. I'll be escortin' you to the formal room." He started to leave but halted. Facing me, finger touching his chin, "Oh, by the way, keep that damn cat away from me. He's in my bedroom snoozin' on my fabulous bed." Jeffery scrunched his nose with obvious distaste. "You is cute with your red hair and dazzlin' green eyes, but this country hillbilly shit ain't workin' for you, boo. Burn that whole attire." He wagged his finger at me from my head to my toes. "Those garments is frightful." A devilish grin toyed with his plump lips. "I picked you out somethin' that will show off those killer curves of yours! Look beautiful tonight." With that said, he left, shutting the door behind him. I let out an angry screech. I hated snobs! I mindlessly ran my fingers through my hair. Jeffery was right. I looked like a scrounger. Even the hired help had more class than me.

I pulled out my cell, checking the time. It was only five. I had three hours to kill before dinner. I padded over to the Television and picked up the remote, staring at it. I didn't feel like watching a movie either.

Then the window caught my eye. I made my way over to it, tugging the sheer curtains back. The land stretched far as the eye could see. It felt as though I stood on the top of Mt. Everest. The clouds hovered low, dark, and ominous. A storm was brewing, just like my stomach was churning.

Though Jeffery didn't know the full scope of mine and Bane's arduous relationship, he voiced the very concerns I had. Why Bane's family was forcing him to enter into an unwanted marriage baffled me. Why would his family fork over money to Sara for a girl with nothing?

Then my mind flashed back to Ms. Noel's séance. I bit down on my bottom lip. I'd almost forgotten. She touched on the subject of some faction, vile and dangerous coming for me. For the life of me, I couldn't fathom who. What would someone want with me? I had nothing of value. To put the eerie cherry on top, Bane claimed he was protecting me, but from whom?

Suddenly, I yawned, and my eyes felt heavy. I decided a nap would be nice since I didn't get much sleep last night. I couldn't do anything about my situation now. I might as well rest up for dinner.

I went through the French doors entering the bedroom. As my eyes lifted, I halted, gawking in disbelief. It was as if I'd stepped back in the fifties. In the center of the room stood a white four-poster bed with a pink quilt and bold pink and gold pillows that matched the pink-bunny-rabbit wallpaper. I laughed as my eyes combed over the room. I reckoned this was Jeffery's attempt at humor. "What a funny man!"

I stepped into the bathroom, eyeballing white marble and pink towels and a matching terrycloth robe, pink of course. I bit my bottom lip, stifling a laugh. I spied the large garden tub that could've fit five large people. My eyes locked onto a trail of rose petals leading to the garden tub. Overwhelmed with delight, I drooled at the bath oils and various soaps placed beside the bathtub, and to top it off with a titil-lating lure; several white candles lined the floor with a soft glow.

"Hmm!" I tapped my finger against my lip. A soft laugh escaped my lips. "Jeffery lied about his lighter."

The tub was calling to me right in front of a picture window looking over the horizon. I quickly peeled off my clothes, and soon the bathtub swirled with rose-scented water as my excitement escalated. Wasting no time, I jumped in with both feet, sinking into the soothing magic.

A soft moan escaped my lips as I leaned against the cool marble and closed my eyes, letting the warmth soak into my weary muscles. A little piece of heaven.

A sudden bright flash of light flashed in my face. My eyes flew open, catching an angry streak of lightning ripping through the sky in the far distance. The clouds were building fast, growing darker and more menacing by the second. Another streak of light lit the bruised sky as thunder rumbled with ferocity. I jumped with a start as the crash reverberated around me.

After a second, I eased back and watched the display of fireworks until my bathwater grew cold. With a sigh of regret, I drew myself from the tub and stepped out onto a pink rug, snatching up the thick robe. I slipped it on and made my way to the bedroom.

It was as if a light went off in my brain. I shook my head, feeling stupid, of course… *the closet*. I'd forgotten about a practical thing, such as a closet.

I swung the double doors open, and there hanging all by its lonesome was a scarlet red dress. I spotted black heels on the floor. I reached for the sheer dress and examined it. "Damn!" I fretted. "There isn't much to it." I grabbed the shoes up, kicking both doors closed.

I spied a small pile of black on the bed and something shiny next to it. I padded over to it and picked up a diamond necklace and earrings to match. "Very nice, but I can't picture something of this elegant on me," I whispered.

I then turned my attention to the small black pile. I picked it up, holding it in my fingers. "Holy cow!" My eyes orbed. "This isn't underwear?" I was staring at a lacy bra and a matching thong. I felt naked already as my cheeks blazed. There wasn't much thread to either piece. Judging by the bra cup, I wasn't sure it would even hold my boobs.

Come to think about it; the satin dress didn't leave much to the imagination either. The back plunged low as well as in the front, and the length… There was no length? I think Jeffery just punked me with a shirt. Fright rolled over me. Dinner was a bust already. I couldn't wear this one-thread-count dress!

FLAMES OF MAGICK

*S*traight up eight o'clock, a faint knock came at the door. The dinner date had my nerves frayed. Wearing a spaghetti-strapped dress with a label that read Couture and the Louboutin heels made me feel more like an expensive hooker than a dinner guest.

I checked my hair once more in the mirror before I rushed to the door. I was unsure if my hair pinned up in a French bun would pass. "Oh well, it'd have to do," I mumbled to myself as I hurried to the door. I pictured Jeffery's sour face on the other side, waiting impatiently.

Nearly falling flat on my face, I managed to jerk the door open ready to wail into Jeffery's skinny ass, but I halted, gaping at the person standing at the threshold. Surprise siphoned the blood from my face. "Aidan!"

A moment of silence dropped as his eyes slowly roamed over me like warm melted chocolate, coating every curve and line of my body. He drew back a pearly smile of approval.

My cheeks flamed. "Is there a problem?"

"No problem where I'm standing, Princess." His deep sultry voice sent a spurt of warmth to places unmentionable as his blues continued roaming over my body, lingering a moment too long on the swells of my breast.

Instantly, I wanted to cover myself as I dropped my gaze to my hands.

Bane recovered his poise and spoke, "I thought I'd escort you to dinner." His blues danced. "Will you do me the honors?" He held out his arm.

"Hmm, okay." I flashed a faint smile, though I felt ridiculous in this outfit and makeup.

Even under duress, I didn't miss the tall, dark, and beautiful escort. Bane stood tall, poised, just the perfect combination of yummy in an Armani tux. A delightful shiver washed over me, and I blushed a deep hue.

"I hope your accommodations are more suited to your taste."

Then a quick sting hit me, bringing my attention to why I was here in the first place. "If you mean my taste as in held against my will, I'd have to say, yes," I tilted my chin in defiance.

"I am merely looking out for your safety. Surely you can understand my intent is in your best interest." Keeping a person a prisoner was not what I called protecting.

"Safety, my ass," With one sharp glower, I stalked past him.

When I reached the elevator, Bane touched the small of my back, nudging me onward. I looked up at him, a little alarmed. "Tell me we aren't taking the stairwell?" The thought of descending anywhere in these killer heels made the palm of my hands sweaty.

Bane inclined his head as he softly spoke in my hair. "I thought you might like having dinner on the terrace. The sunset is quite spectacular; the deep hues in contrast against the blue sky are never the same."

"Oh, I thought it was raining." Without thinking, I tugged at the back of my dress. There was a draft tousling the hem. The last thing I needed was baring my ass before the honeymoon. I rolled my eyes to myself.

Bane cuffed his mouth, shoulders slightly bouncing. "Yes, I heard the forecast. I assure you neither you nor I shall melt if the weather takes a turn for the worse," he flashed an impish smile.

After making our way down several dark corridors and climbing a small flight of stairs, we stepped out onto the terrace. Immediately, a cool breeze tousled my hair. A faint smell of rain hovered in the air, but what caught my breath was the sight before my eyes—hundreds of floating lanterns, coins of gold speckled the sky. The sun was just setting as a dash of salmon pink splashed across the dark blue sky. "It's beautiful!"

"I thought you might like it." There was a gentleness to his voice and mirth in his blues.

I stood speechless, blinking back my astonishment.

"May I have the first dance?" He held his hand out, patiently waiting.

"Uh," I bit my bottom lip. "I don't know how to dance."

A confident glint toyed behind his blues. "Then, I shall teach you." Abruptly, he swung me into the circle of his arms. I giggled when I collided against his chest.

He smiled back. "Just follow my lead." He huskily suggested, keeping his arm tight around my waist.

As if enchanted under a spell, I obeyed, first kicking off those ridiculous heels.

Then Bane glided my hand into position, and my breath ceased as I became acutely aware of every inch of his firm body flushed against the thin fabric of my dress, minus the thong. I wished I'd worn that thing now, although it wouldn't have mattered. I was ready to throw all my inhibitions over the ledge and give myself to him, no requirements, no expectations, surrendering my mind and soul and even my heart to him. It was official, I was putty in his hands, and when I gazed into those pools of blue, I found myself sinking further to a land of no return.

A vibrant piano played, no lyrics, no other instruments, just the strumming of the keys, soft and smooth. I recognized the song, *All of Me.*

Suddenly all my insecurities vanished, and nothing else mattered or existed except right at this moment. Bane and I together made perfect sense.

Despite my awkwardness, Bane moved fluidly, carrying me across the floor as if we were floating among the heavens. I wondered if he and I might find a way to love each other like my dad loved my mother. Did I dare step out onto the plank, taking a risk with my heart? All of a sudden, I shivered.

"Are you cold, Love?"

My cheeks blushed. "No."

When the music stopped, our feet halted. Our eyes locked as Bane's fingers grazed the line of my jaw. "You look quite fetching tonight." His eyes lingered on my lips. "I'm going to have to thank Jeffery for his keen sense of fashion."

Goosebumps covered my body as I giggled. "Yes, Jeffery does have a flare," I barely whispered.

The smile in his blues contained a sensual flame that ignited a stir in me. Without a doubt, if I weren't careful, I might fall in love.

"Dom has prepared us a simple dinner. One I think, will please your pallet." There were touches of amusement circling his mouth, trailing up to his eyes.

"I'm not that hard to please." I stepped away, gathering my heels.

Aidan led me to a quaint table. The table for two felt quite intimate, white linen with a single red rose sitting in the center in a slim vase next to a candle, the dinner plates shining like white glass, with napkins folded around the dinnerware. It was simple and yet elegant.

Bane slid my chair out for me as I took my seat, and he settled in his chair across from me.

A bolt of lightning struck in the far distance, but the violent crackle of thunder sounded as if it loomed directly over us. I jumped with a start, gripping my chest.

Bane smiled. "Don't worry. We have at least an hour before the rain hits," he winked.

"It's not the rain; it's the lightning that has me concerned." I peered above the lanterns.

"If you're uncomfortable, we can take our dinner inside."

"No, this is fine." I laid my hands in my lap. "I like this," I smiled.

Just then, Dom appeared with a dark bottle in his hands. The label read, Chateau d'Yquem, the year 1811. My eyes nearly popped out of my head. I wasn't up on my wines, though it didn't take an expert to know that the bottle didn't come from the local convenience store.

A white towel draped over Dom's arm. "I have the champagne you requested, Monsieur."

Bane's eyes sparkled. "Excellent!"

Dom corked the bottle with a pop and then poured a taste of the sweet liquid in Bane's flute.

I imagined like a French connoisseur, Bane tipped the glass to his lips and sipped, savoring the flavor. He nodded to Dom and smiled. "This is quite brut, perfect for the lady."

"Yes, Monsieur." Dom filled Bane's flute and then turned to fill mine.

I had to admit the champagne looked delicious with its golden color and the tiny bubbles fizzing to the top.

"Take a sip. It's delightful." Bane encouraged as his blues danced in the amber light.

"Okay." I picked up the long stem glass and sipped. It tickled my nose, and I giggled. I took another sip as it slipped down my throat much easier than the bourbon. "It tickles, but I like it." Suddenly, feeling the heat of his steady gaze, I dropped my eyes to my lap.

Mischief rested at the corners of his mouth. "Do you like the dress Jeffery picked out for you?"

"Yes, thank you."

"I'm not sure how to word this delicately." He paused, cuffing his mouth. "I think you forgot part of your apparel."

I gulped down air as my face burned. "How did you know?"

"Well, the dress is quite... thin." His amused gaze captured my uttered shock.

I began to stammer over my words. "I-I-I couldn't wear that string."

Hilarity poured from his blues like a waterfall. "I assure you I have enjoyed the view very much."

My mouth dropped open. "I wasn't trying to please you. I did it for comfort." I swallowed. "I mean, you can't think that I'd wear that damn string."

"By all means," he flashed a devilish grin. "Princess, do make yourself comfy as much as you like."

"I bet!" I snatched my flute and downed the champagne.

As if his eyes bored a hole through me, he asked, "Do I make you nervous?"

I felt like he saw right through me. "Do I bother you?" I held my gaze to his.

Bane raised his flute and replied, "Touche'!" Then he tipped the long stem glass to his lips and finished the bubbly.

I wanted to change the subject, so I blurted out the first thing that came to my mind. "What did you mean by New World Order?"

"Must we talk politics tonight?" He shifted in his seat.

"Don't you think I have a right to know since I'm part of the plan?"

"You do have a valid point." He poured him another drink. "Very well... The New World Order," he drew in a razor sharp breath, "Is a centralized economy."

"For the entire world?" I asked.

"Yes," he answered.

"I don't see how that's possible."

"It's more plausible than you think. World leaders are working toward a utopia where everyone under its umbrella will live in peace and harmony."

"The government is corrupted and then getting other world leaders to agree... Plus, you have the nation's debt to consider." I didn't mean to burst his bubble, but let's keep the dreams grounded.

"You may be surprised." There was a mysterious glint behind his blues.

"You said our union has something to do with a new system. I'm confused."

"When the time comes, I will explain. However, for now, you will have to trust me."

It frustrated me to no end how he kept keeping me in the dark. I wondered if he thought I was too dumb to understand. So, I went straight for the jugular. "How much," I blurted out.

His dark brows shot up, "How much what?"

"How much did your family pay my mother?"

His face pinched. "Does it matter?"

"Yes, I want to know how much I'm worth."

He leaned back in his chair, studying me under his stern gaze. "Your mother will live very well for the rest of her life if she doesn't squander it all away."

I felt the sting of betrayal. How could a mother sell her child? "Why did your family pick me?"

"Why do we breathe," he came back at me, taking a drink of his champagne.

"Come on! Can you at least tell me how our families knew each other and how this arrangement transpired?"

All at once, Bane's shoulders went rigid. His face transformed from playful to strained. "Our families are connected."

"I remember you said we're not blood-related. If we don't share the same kinship, then what are we?"

"We are not related." He sat up straight. "I use the term family loosely." He reached over grabbing the bottle from its sheath of ice and poured himself another glass. After he'd finished, he held the bottle up, offering me another. I declined by bearing my palm. He placed the bottle back on the ice and snatched his glass up, tipping it to his lips and draining the glass.

"Can you explain to me what the term means?" I felt like a child tugging at his hem.

"Our bloodlines belong to a very ancient collection of thirteen families. Each family with different bloodlines. Our histories go back centuries to a secret society that only a few have had the privilege of knowing."

"Where is this family you speak so highly of?" As far as I knew, neither one of my parents had relatives.

The line in Bane's mouth tightened a fraction more. "Your mother wasn't ever part of the Order. However, your father, Jon, was a member."

"Wait! My father has living relatives?"

Bane's lip tightened. Then he explained, "Yes, he once was a member."

"Once?" I shook my head, baffled.

"Jon possessed a rebellious spirit. He fell in love with a worldly woman, an outsider of our kind… your mother."

"Worldly? What do you mean?"

"Sara is an outsider, a nonbeliever and not the Family's choice."

"I don't understand." All at once, needles bristled against my neck.

"They refused to give your father their blessing. As a result, he defected from the Family and married your mother against the Family's orders."

"My father's family didn't like Sara?"

"No. The Family had someone else in mind."

I shook my head, appalled. "What is it with these people playing God?"

"To preserve our bloodlines is essential to further our goals. Our bloodlines keep us strong."

The direction of this conversation became more disturbing by the minute. "It sounds to me that my father did a smart thing by leaving. I would've left too."

"And if so, how would you plan to make your get-a-way?" He smiled darkly. "You have intrigued me."

Quietly, I watched him guzzle down his third glass. "I don't have an escape, but I sure as hell won't comply with some stranger's plan for my future." I tilted my chin in defiance. "I guess I'm like my father in that way." I reached over, snatching the bottle from the ice and bypassing my flute. I tipped the bottle up to my mouth and gulped several swigs. I needed some liquid courage.

Bane's eyes were sharp as a double-edged sword. "Shall I order you a bottle?" He wasn't making a peace offering. Rather the opposite. I sensed he resented my independence.

"Thanks, but I have my own." I smiled with a smirk, holding the bottle up as though I was toasting. I bravely met his grave stare. "So, are you saying my father and your family made this arrangement?"

"You are partially right," his jaw twitched. "They have arranged for us to join in union. Partners, for a better term."

"Partners for what?"

Irritation painted his face. "Can you not read between the lines? Must I spell it out for you?"

"My father was an attorney. I'm sure he knew his way around a contract. So, I'm going to ask you one more time… what does the term union mean?"

"It means that we marry and bring forth children."

A soft gasp escaped my lips. "Children? My father agreed to this?"

"Why do you keep torturing yourself?" Bane sighed with exasperation.

"I want to know," I hissed.

"Some things are best left alone."

"I disagree!" My voice rose, baring my anger. "I mean, I'm only half of the Family's bloodline. Why me?"

"I don't think you are ready for the full disclosure." Briefly, his face softened. Then the iron mask quickly returned.

"Whether I'm ready or not, I have a right to know." I stared at him, searching for the meaning behind his words. "Can you at least tell me when I have to spread my…?"

Bane interrupted my sentence. "Vulgarity does not suit you, Princess."

"What are you going to do? Tie me to the bedpost. Have your way with me just like your family has instructed?" I leaped from my chair and slowly and seductively made my way to him. The wind kicked up my hem, revealing a flash of bare skin, but I didn't care. I had a point to make.

My fingers tugged at each strap of my dress one at a time, slipping off my shoulder and down my arm, shrugging the soft fabric into a red puddle on the ground. I stepped out from the satin, making my way to his majesty.

Bane's face appeared cool as a cucumber as I moved to my bra, unsnapping it and shrugging it off to the floor into the pile with the rest. Barring only the diamond necklace and earrings that grazed the soft swells of my body, I was ready for the plucking, willing and drunk. I suddenly halted, grabbing the table for support as the ground spun underneath my black heels.

In the next wave, I fell into Bane's arms as he shielded my naked body with his jacket. "Princess, I appreciate the offer, but maybe when you are more yourself." Amusement flickered through his voice as his eyes locked with mine.

My words slurred; even still, the effects of the alcohol didn't waver my heart. I desired Bane in the worst way. I craved his touch, his flaming kisses, and most of all, his heart. Through the haze of drunkenness, I whispered three words of doom, "I love you!"

FORGET-ME-NOTS

$\mathcal{I}$'d awaken in my suite, blinking at the pink rabbit wallpaper and Snowball curled at the foot of the bed, purring. A lamp still burned, giving the room a soft hue of light. My mouth felt like sandpaper. I groaned, sitting up. I felt like I'd gotten an ass-kicking.

Until I threw off the covers and swung my feet over the bed, I didn't realize someone had changed my clothes. Men's pajamas, I presumed by the looks of it. The black garment swallowed me up, several sizes too large, but thanks to the drawstring tied around my waist, the pants hugged my hips. I sniffed the fabric and recognized Bane's scent. Spice and a woodsy mix penetrated my senses.

Then the flood of the night charged through me. My brain might've been hazy, but I would never forget the most embarrassing night of my life. The dinner ended with my weak attempt at sexy. "I can't believe I used those three words!" It was one thing going the full Monty, coupled with three little words that were so profound and utterly mortifying, it made me loathed myself even more. I dropped my head in the palm of my hands. I was the most pathetic virgin ever.

I stumbled to the bathroom in search of ibuprofen. The buzz of alcohol had passed, and in its place, a killer headache had taken residence. I searched through the medicine cabinet and found nothing. I looked in every nook and cranny throughout the suite only to come up empty-handed. I huffed, wondering where else to look.

I spied my cell, sitting on the table in the foyer. I snatched it up and checked the time. Three in the morning! I laid it back down on the dresser. Maybe I could find something in the kitchen.

Bane might not approve of me wandering the castle at the wee morning hour, but tough titty! This kitty needed drugs. I marched to the door and gave it a good tug. I frowned, just as I'd expected, locked. My first thought was to kick it down, but then I had a better idea.

I remembered Jen using a bobby pin to unlock a door. For the life of me, I couldn't remember why we were breaking into the school's property, another hole in my brain. Oddly, I recalled her nifty little trick. Quickly, I ran my fingers through my hair and found a pin. I twisted and pulled at the small wire until it was one long strip of metal, just like Jen had done hers. I bent down and eased the wire into the keyhole. I twisted it and poked around until I felt something click. I quickly gathered to my feet, withdrawing the bobby pin. I held my breath as I grabbed the knob and turned it.

To my delight, it gave under my grasp. It worked! I bounced on my feet, clapping my hands together. Then I realized noise carried in these hollow halls.

I had to be careful. A guard might be lurking. I listened for any noise, nothing. I checked under the door for any shadow passing, nothing. Slowly, I cracked the door open, just enough to peek through. I saw no signs of life. The corridor appeared to be empty.

Barefooted, I quietly crept out into the hall. My heart pounded in my chest. I eased the door closed behind me, careful not to make a sound. Tip-toeing to the elevator, I kept my eyes sharp and ears opened for any invader.

I entered the elevator, reaching to punch the black button to first floor but stopped. I bit my bottom lip, feeling a rush of mischief. Two words came to mind... *2nd floor.* I suddenly wanted to know the mystery behind it. I punched the second button. In the next breath, the elevator stopped, following a sharp ding, and the doors parted. I eased my head out, sweeping my eyes in both directions. Bingo! No sign of a soul in sight. I nearly squealed with euphoria.

I darted off to the left, padding lightly through the dim corridor. A sudden burst of thunder roared, and a streak of lightning spilled from the beveled-pane windows. I jolted, throwing my hand over my mouth to smother my squeal. After a minute, settling my pulse, I moved on.

The floor didn't look any different from the other two. I saw nothing out of the ordinary or extraordinary about the second floor. I tried opening the first door I came to, but it was locked. I made my way down the corridor, trying entry after entry and found nothing open.

Bane had everything on lockdown. "All this for nothing," I murmured under my breath. I wished I'd stayed in my room and called for room service. My headache had intensified. The adventure turned out to be a dud, and the excitement had vanished. I just wanted to find some ibuprofen and go to bed.

I headed back to the elevator. I thought I'd try the kitchen. I might find a bottle there. At least, I could get a snack and something to drink. My stomach was starting to sound like *The Star-Spangled Banner*.

Without warning, the elevator doors dinged, and I froze. Who'd be up at this hour? Quickly, I ducked into a dark corner. My back flushed against the wall, holding my breath.

I listened as footsteps approached. When the intruder coiled the corner, I felt my face go ashen. Shock flitted through me. It was Dr. Van Dunn, the principal! What was he doing here? I quietly watched as he passed by, nescient to my presence. The stench of his cigar filled the hall. I quickly clamped my palm over my mouth to hold my gagging.

He came to a halt at the last room at the end of the corridor. A faint sound of knocking echoed past me. After a second, the door opened, and a stream of light gushed into the hallway. I heard a familiar male voice. Then in a split second, the door shut with Van disappearing inside. Voices muffled.

I leaned back into the shadowed corner, easing air back into my lungs. If I were smart, I'd high-tail it outta here! Forget that this night ever happened. Which one did I want to pick, A: smart or B: reckless? I took a quick glimpse down the hall, biting my bottom lip. Of course, I chose B.

I crept to the door where a thin wafer of light dappled the floor from underneath. I had a nagging feeling that something was up with Van's visit. It seemed suspicious that the principal would be visiting a student at this hour.

So, like any savvy eavesdropper, I quietly leaned into the door and pushed my ear to the cool Mahogany wood. It was like an acoustic. I could hear everything.

. . .

"I hope you have just cause for getting me out of bed at this ungodly hour! It's a shit-storm out there." An older male's voice growled as he moaned, following the swish of a cushion. I assumed it was Van.

I heard a different chair squeak, perhaps wheels rolling across the floor. Someone was sitting in an office chair, possibly behind a desk. Suddenly a deep voice, young and velvety, pierced through the door. Bane! "Sorry to disturb your beauty rest, uncle, but this couldn't wait. I didn't want you seen."

"Yes, one of many secrets we must keep." I recognized Van's voice. I recalled the sarcasm in his tone far too well.

"Shall we get down to business, or are we going to argue all night over semantics?" Bane's voice was forceful, sending shivers down my spine.

"No argument here." The older man wheezed. A heavy smoker, I presumed. "I do need to chat with you over my man, Zak. You didn't have to kill him. He's been a loyal servant to me for years."

"Loyal, you say?" Bane's voice sounded angry. "That bastard nearly killed the girl. I simply gave him what he deserved."

"Oh, lighten up! Zak was having fun with the hybrid."

"Lighten up," Bane snapped, "If that spineless Crypt had succeeded, where would your plans be today?"

"Perhaps I trusted him too much." I heard Van puff on his cigar and blew out the smoke. "No need to cry over spilled milk. The hybrid is fine and ripe for the picking."

"She's not fine! To clean up your mess, I had to dust Miss Ray and her friend, Jen Li. Do you know the long-term effects of Angel Dust?" Bane roared.

"So, what if you wiped her memories! Soon, she'll be dead, and we'll have her powers!" Van laughed wickedly. "Problem solved." The older man's cavalier attitude sent a cold chill deep into my bones.

"If you had taken care of the crime scene, I could've spared both girls and convinced the girl she had a bad dream."

"You worry far too much, nephew." Van drew in a raspy breath. "Let's move to the real reason you sent for me."

I heard boots slide across a hard surface and then drop with a loud thud. Bane must've had his feet propped up on the desk and then planted them swift to the floor.

"I'll just get right to the point," Bane exhaled. "I do not wish to extract the *girl's powers. It is against the Family."*

Van scoffed. *"The hell with them and their Order! Do you prefer to be bound to this girl for the rest of your immortal life?"*

There was a shift in Bane's tone, the same harsh voice I heard when he attacked Francis. *"Don't worry about whom I'm shackled to when we have bigger concerns,"* Bane paused. *"I think it's in the Family's best interest that we stick to our original plans. We only get one shot."*

"You can't back out now! We've already committed treason," Van's voice exploded with rage.

It sounded like a fist slamming onto the desktop and a chair on rollers crashing against the wall.

"Dear Uncle, I am not the traitor," Bane hissed, *"I have merely followed orders."*

"You're a yellow-belly coward," Van fired back just as fiery.

Bane laughed darkly. *"Now who's calling who names, Edward Van Dunn? You are the one wanting to take the girl's life as if she's the sacrificial lamb."*

"Isn't that what she is?" Van pointed out sharply, *"The lamb that our brotherhood has created. Is she not the one?"*

There was a brief silence. Then I heard Bane speak. *"Yes, she is the Family's creation."*

"DuPont, if we back out now, we are dead men. I want … " Van's voice swirled with desperation. *"I need her powers."*

"I don't understand why you are hell-bent on taking the girl's life," Bane argued.

"Her death won't even be worthy of a notch on your belt. For Pete's sake, don't you see the bigger picture here?"

"You think it's going to be that simple?" Bane pushed.

"No, of course not, but in the end, we will have conquered our most valued treasure. We can do this!"

"What you feel is a hard-on, Uncle."

"Don't worry about my jollies. You owe me, DuPont!"

"Uncle, I know you're hungry, but there is more at stake here."

"Oh, good God, man! What is more important than having the wheel of power at our feet?" Van pointed out unsavory.

"It's difficult for me. I feel the girl's powers increasing every time I touch her, and my desire to mate with her is growing. She's in my head. I can't stop thinking about her. Jesus! Our hearts beat as one!" Bane exhaled sharply. *"I*

don't know how much longer I can hold out." I detected disgust in Bane's voice. "I can't take her life. Do what you want to me, but I won't do your dirty work."

Van shouted, "She's our ticket to freedom!"

"I do not wish to be a party to your diabolical scheme, and I wouldn't be if you were not blackmailing me," Bane paused, "If she ever comes into her full abilities, she could eliminate this whole galaxy. Hell, you know as well as I there was no gas leak in the girl's restroom. Stevie did that all by herself. I'm telling you, she is one powerful hybrid!" Bane hissed, "It would be wise not to show your claws to her."

I heard Van laugh. "You're in love with that little Dream Angel."

"Don't be absurd; the only one I've ever loved is myself."

"Then why do you care what happens to her?" Van asked, sneering.

"It's biological. The girl is my mate for life. Since her powers are developing, so have her pheromones. It's near impossible for me to refrain from my natural urges."

"Good God, Du Pont! Don't blow this. If we are to extract her powers, she has to be a virgin."

"Don't you think I know that you vile pervert!" Bane's voice was harsh and angry.

A heavy sound of someone blowing out smoke filled the room. Van was smoking. "Have you given the vessel her installment?"

"Yes, Sara has received payment," Bane snapped.

"Have you told the hybrid who killed her father?"

Silence fell between the two men. Then I heard Bane exhaled. "I haven't told her yet."

"Dammit, Du Pont! We have to do this on Halloween. You need to get it together and quick!"

A shadow flickered back and forth under the door. Bane must be pacing.

"Then you know what you must do next," Van coaxed.

"Yes. I am thoroughly aware of what steps I must take next. You act as if you're my master. Have you forgotten that I'm older than you?"

"That may be true. However, you need to start taking your position more seriously. Do your job! Depose of the mother. She's utterly useless. For the life of me, I don't understand what Jon Collins saw in that whore."

Bane scoffed. "We don't always get to pick who we fall in love with."

"Good God, my man! You've gone soft for that twat."

"Don't worry about my feelings or where my abstinent heart lies." Bane

sounded like he wanted to strangle Van.

"Oh, I don't worry, Du Pont! I have faith that you won't let me down. As long as you follow through with our agreement, I'll keep your dirty secret to myself and the proof in a locked safe." Van inhaled a ragged breath. "If you betray me, I will report my findings to the Council. They won't tolerate insubordination regardless of your reasons." Pure evil resonated from Van's voice.

A soft gasp escaped my lips. Déjà vu blasted through brick and mortar and into the hidden caves of my mind. For several minutes I stood frozen, feet glued to the floor. I stood there reliving every horrible event that had occurred since Bane had come into my life.

Every frightening detail that had happened to me barreled its way to the forefront of my skull. Bane knowing my father's murderer, the man in black attacking me, the closet, my injury, the cover-up. I even remembered when I was a child, the night the men in black came to visit Sara in the middle of the night. It was so clear to me as if it happened yesterday. It was shortly after Dad's death. The men in black were warning Sara. I recalled trying to hear their muffled words. Whatever reason they had that night, it set Sara into a tail-spin, and we'd been on the run since. Ms. Noel was right! What a blind fool I'd been.

It all made sense now. Bane's bad boy image was a charade and his interest in me was a lie too. It was all lies to lure me into their insidious trap. Bane, Dr. Van, and my own mother were all plotting my demise. How could I have not seen this? Crap! They used my own mother to get at me, and she fell right into their laps for her selfish greed. That was so disturbing on so many levels. I couldn't wrap my head around it.

Oh, my God! Jen was in danger too. They didn't just drug me, but Jen got caught in the crossfire by helping me.

Footsteps and shuffling knocked me back to my present state of reality. If they caught me, I was dead. I quickly sprinted for cover. I noticed a door leading to the stairwell. Past the door and up the stairs, I darted for the third floor. I had to get out of here! I needed to grab a few things from my room and snatch up Snowball. I have got to find where Bane hid my car keys too. I had to warn Jen and find Sara! Then I was putting this devil-may-care town in my rearview mirror and getting the hell out of Dodge.

SECRET PASSAGES AND
UNEXPECTED ALLIES

*W*hen I coiled around the corner, my heart somersaulted and crashed into my ribs. I froze. I remembered closing my door. So, why was it wide open? Maybe I didn't close it all the way. Regardless of what I kept telling myself, I knew with certainty that someone was in my room waiting for my return. I bit my lip, indecisive. What if I turned around back to the stairwell and fled on foot? Then I'd be leaving Snowball behind.

I took a deep breath to calm myself. I'd just lie about my whereabouts. It wasn't as if I'd never fib before. Not my best feature but it came in handy now and then. I eased my steps toward the door, stretching my ears and eyes for any hint of who might be lurking in my room. One eye slipped past the threshold, and I gawked in disbelief at the last person I thought to see, relaxing on my couch… *Jeffery!* I stepped inside, arms crossed, with an uncompromising glare aiming at my suspicious visitor.

"Well, the prodigal child decides to return." The sarcasm in Jeffery's voice only pissed me off further.

"Jeffery, what are you doing in my room at this hour?"

"Oh, I thought since you'd gotten a little tipsy on the terrace that you might be a little hungry. I just got in myself. I have a busy social life, but you wouldn't know that cuz you've never asked." He glared at me through his sooty lashes. "I would've been here sooner, but something tells me that your sweet little face wouldn't have been here to greet me." He smiled, scrunching his shoulders together, sighing, attempting to play innocent. "So, whatcha been doin'?"

I narrowed my eyes, ready for whatever he threw at me. I made my way to the chair by the window. "Not that I have to explain myself, but I had a headache and went looking for some ibuprofen." I flopped down into the cushioned chair.

Jeffery tossed me a small box. "I figured you'd need these. Guess I was right." A smirk colored his face.

I caught the box and glimpsed down at the label, ibuprofen. "Thanks," I answered in an even tone. Nice gesture but I wondered what tricks Jeffery had up his sleeve.

"I saw a particular person's car when I pulled up into the drive. I was concerned about you. That uncle of his is mean as a Tasmanian Devil!" Jeffery paused a minute, studying me. "You look a little bothered, boo." He tapped his finger on his chin, eyes sharp and judgy. "Are you okay?"

I propped my elbows on my knees, laying my face in the palms of my hands. Confliction rode heavily on my shoulders. If I told Jeffery, he'd do one of two things, A: tell Bane, or B: help me escape. "I know this sounds like I've gone mad, and maybe I have, but Van and Aidan are making plans to kill me." I licked my lips. "I need to get out of here! Can you help me find my car keys?" My eyes pleaded with Jeffery.

"Gurrrlfriend, you're puttin' me in a sticky spot, which most of the time is a good thang but not this one."

Tears started to collect as I stared at Jeffery in dead silence. He paused, taking in my dire face, and then his lips pursed, shaking his head. "Never mind, boo," Jeffery rolled his eyes, "I'll get your keys. Mister Aidan has them in the kitchen in the junk drawer." He bounced to his feet. "Get your stuff, and don't forget that mofo cat. I don't get paid enough to take care of no stinkin' cat!"

～

Moments later, I'd changed my clothes and had everything packed, including Snowball, tucked in his special kitty carriage. With our guard up and hands full, off Jeffery and I went.

"I know a back way that no one takes. It's the servant's entrance. Mister Aidan doesn't care which way Dom and I travel throughout the castle, but whenever his uncle or that mofo cousin of his comes a-knockin' I hide in these old secret passages. C'mon, we need to get to steppin'. Pick up those mofo legs, gurrrl," Jeffery snapped, jerking my hand, and nearly making me fall on my face.

"I'm stepping! I'm stepping!" Jesus! I mumbled under my breath at that coco-buttered man. I think that was Jeffery's flare. He had the arrogance of a queen bee, like the land of nectar, golden honey, gooey and sweet, yet in the same breath, he'd sting the crap out of you. A required taste, I had to agree.

We hurried through a door leading into a gentlemen's parlor or a more current term, a drawing-room, dark mahogany wood-paneled walls, and crimson winged-back chairs placed around a gambling table. The room screamed man cave, and it reeked of cigars and sweat.

Jeffery ran to the large bookcase that covered a whole wall. He tipped back a book from the case, and a hidden door screeched open. I gawked in disbelief. I thought things like that only existed in books and movies.

Hand over fist, Jeffery halfway dragged me into the small opening. "Pay attention, gurrrl! You gonna put both our heads on the choppin' block," Jeffery urged as he closed the bookcase behind us.

My eyes orbed, terrified. "Are you kidding?"

"I never kid about my lovely head." He twisted his face. "That came out wrong," he huffed. "Let's git!" He tugged on my arm, dragging me down a dark, narrow passage.

I covered my mouth, coughing from the cloud of dirt flying in my face. "How do you see? There's no light and," I coughed, "the dust?"

"Stop your bitchin'!"

"I'm not complaining," I snapped back.

"Shush," he jerked on my arm even harder, making me pick up the pace, "Voices carry down 'ere!"

"Sorry," I half-whispered and choked on a mouthful of dirt.

After several corners and spirals of stairwells, I felt like I was on a roller coaster. My stomach churned with queasiness from ingesting all the dirt but then we stopped.

Jeffery tapped three times on the center of a wall, and another entrance opened. We passed through it and down another corridor that was less dusty with more light.

When my eyes adjusted to the light, I realized we were standing in the kitchen.

In a flash, Jeffery dashed to a drawer. Hurriedly, he drew out my keys and jerked on my wrist, dragging me to the warehouse. We rushed through double doors and down another corridor. My lungs were screaming for air, but there wasn't any time to waste for something as little as breathing. I'd do that once I'd made my get-away.

Once we reached the elevator, Jeffery punched the G button. Seconds later, we stepped out into the warehouse. Not missing a beat, Jeffery kept my feet plugging on.

When we reached my beetle, Jeffery halted abruptly. He shoved a handful of cash into my hands. "Boo, take this! You'll need it. Don't tell anyone where you're goin'. Just get the H. E. double L. outta 'ere. That uncle of Mister Aidan's is one bad mofo. I'm tellin' you when white folks are mean, you don't want to cross their path. So, you run, boo, run your ass off, and don't stop until you is in China." Jeffery snatched me up into his arms and hugged me. "Go on, git the hell outta 'ere before any of those mofos see you."

Tears came to my eyes, "Thank you, Jeffery! I don't know what to say."

"You say nuffin! Go on now, git!" Jeffery opened the door for me and handed me the key. "Follow the arrows, and it will take you straight outta 'ere. You don't need a password to leave," he smiled, but it didn't reach his worrisome eyes.

A moment lingered as Jeffery, and I gave one more silent farewell, then I dove into the beetle, sliding the key into the ignition. The beetle started up, sounding as loud as ever.

With no more time to spare, I released the brake and slammed it into first gear. I was off in a flash, and the taste of bitter freedom caressed my parched lips.

I checked my rear-view mirror, and Jeffery was still standing, watching as I sped away. I'd misjudged him. He'd been my friend all along. It touched my heart, and I'd be forever grateful for his kindness. I opened my palm and looked at the wad of money. I gasped in shock. The cash appeared to be all several one-thousand-dollar bills. Crap! Did they make bills that large?

Jeffery advised me to get out of town, but with Bane and his uncle and all their resources, they could pluck me from anywhere. Where could I go? Who could help me find a solution? The police would be out of the question. Bane owned the locals. Besides, I learned my lesson from the last time.

Then it hit me! Ms. Noel!

UNTOUCHABLE

*I*t was the worst storm of the year, and it had to be the one night that I decided to make my get-away. If I thought the hailstorm couldn't get worse, I soon discovered how naive I was.

Thunder roared, breaking sound barriers, and lightning crashed, shooting hot streaks of light across the ominous sky, hemming me in from every direction. Winds howled as the blinding sheets of rain pummeled my Beetle.

I sped down the countryside as my car rocked like a baby's cradle. The headlights were hardly enough to see the dark road ahead, but it didn't deter me from speeding. I feared my car might get swept away by raging floodwaters, coupled that with towering pine snapping in two. I had no other choice. I prayed to make it to Ms. Noel's in one piece. I checked my rearview mirror. No signs of another car's headlight. At least I had that advantage.

My gut told me that once Bane and his uncle discovered that I was gone, they'd come looking for me. My best friend right now was momentum. It was a race for time. My heart pounded against my chest as I floored the gas pedal.

Finally, I began to see specks of light ahead. I was almost there to Ms. Noel's. I turned onto the main drag and sped past the diner and onto Saint Anne Street.

I could see Ms. Noel's house now in plain view. Suddenly, my lungs expanded, and I could breathe. The porch light was on as if she had been expecting me. Quickly, I pulled up to the curb and tugged on the break. I knew I should hide the beetle, but that would have to wait. I wanted to get inside out of this torrential downpour before Snowball and I drowned. At that instant, a bolt of lightning struck, shattering all around me. The black sky lit up, electrified, and enraged. I jolted with a squeal, and Snowball hissed. We both felt the peril in the atmosphere.

I grabbed up Snowball, who was shivering with fright and tucked him under my hoodie. I flung the door open and leaped out, making a mad dash for Ms. Noel's covered porch while thunder nipped at my heels. Poor Snowball dug his claws into my chest, meowing and hanging on for dear life.

The second my feet hit the porch, Ms. Noel, dressed in a housecoat, stood holding the screen door open. "Chile, hurry! This storm is the devil makin' babies," she hollered over the pounding rain.

"Sorry for coming at this hour." I shivered, standing in a huge pool of water. Snowball, just as wet, lay trembling in my arms. "I didn't know who else to turn to."

"Babee, no bother. Let me take Snowball, and I'll get him some cream. In the meantime, you rest on the sofa." Ms. Noel's smile soothed better than any cup of chicken soup.

Ms. Noel headed for the kitchen with Snowball, and I made my way to one of the rocking chairs by the fireplace. As my mind began to unwind, I started shivering. The shock was beginning to set in, and the sting of the cold rain and everything else that had gone down from the moment I set foot in this town began to seep into my bones. The trembling wouldn't stop, and neither my teeth chattering. I leaned over, arms stretched, letting the warmth of the fire soak through to my weary bones.

Ms. Noel returned with a hot cup of tea and a dry blanket. She always knew the perfect remedy. I smiled up at her. "Here, babee, wrap this around ya and drink some of this tea. It'll calm ya nerves." She patted my shoulder and seated herself on the sofa. "I knew ya be comin' tonight," she smiled warmly. "The devil is out tonight and is ready ta play."

I shrugged with a bitter laugh. "Did the devil have blue eyes by chance?"

"Catin, the devil has many faces." Ms. Noel drew in a thoughtful expression. "Remember that God don't like ugly. Hmm uh, he sure don't."

"They're coming for me, Ms. Noel!"

"Chile, who's coming for ya?" Ms. Noel's face became fraught with worry.

Chills trickled down my spine as the conversation plunder through my brain once again. "I overheard Bane talking to Dr. Van." I gulped, "Dr. Van, the principal, is his uncle!" I nervously swallowed. "Remember the séance?" I wrapped the blanket tighter around my shoulders.

"I sure do."

"I think Bane is the faceless boy in my dreams, and he and his uncle are coming after me. I think they're the people my father was warning me about. They believe I have powers of some sort. It all sounds crazy!" My voice shot up an octave. "They plan to kill me!" My head was spinning. "I haven't figured it all out yet!" I stared at her wide-eyed. "You're right, about Sara. The-the-the stalker, he's the reason why Sara's been running all these years." I gasped, feeling the shiver of panic. "Bane knows the stalker. His-his-his name is Zak, the man in black with the shades!" I gulped air, "Or it was his name. Bane killed him after he attacked me." Catching another wind, I yammered on. "I didn't slip on baby oil. Zak attacked me. Bane and Sara both have been covering it up. Bane used some kind of drug on me to make me forget."

"Lord, have mercy!" Ms. Noel's eyes expressed shock.

"That's not all." I paused. "Sara sold me to Bane! I think she is in on the plan too." I raked my hands through my damp hair.

"Lord, sweet Jesus! I knew that woman's heart was black."

I swallowed against the ache in my throat. "And I haven't told you the worst. Bane's been protecting my father's killer." Knowing this about Bane hurt more than the threat of death. Take my life, torture me until I can't scream any longer, but aiding and abetting a fugitive, my father's murderer, was such an unfathomable betrayal that I'd never forgive him. Ever!

"For goodness sakes, Chile, are you sure that's what you heard?"

"Yes! I'm certain! I heard it with my own ears."

"You don't worry none! We have help." She flashed a promising smile. "Visitors are coming to help."

My brows furrowed. "Who'd be coming at this hour and in this storm?" I pulled the blanket tighter as shivers covered my body.

"You just rest ya eyes, on the couch. Ya going ta need all the strength ya can muster. There's magick in the air tonight, and it's mighty angry." She patted my knee.

A cold dread spread over me as I nodded my head. It had been a taxing night. My eyes were starting to grow heavy, and another bout with a headache lingered. I gathered to my feet and leaned over Ms. Noel, hugging her generously. "Thank you! You're the only person I have in this whole wide world that I can trust."

Ms. Noel smiled, eyes twinkling in the embers of the fireplace. "Babee," she patted my arm, "Of course, I will protect ya."

Out of a dead sleep, my eyes popped opened and locked onto two silhouettes hovering over me. Instantly, I gasped and bolted straight up, arms flailing, fighting off blurred faces in black robes. The dream had returned with impeccable timing.

"Stevie! Stevie! It's me, Jen! You're safe." She gently shook my shoulders.

I stopped as Jen's voice pulled me back; still, my breathing was erratic as my heartbeat. "Sorry!" My eyes were droopy, and my brain was just as hazy. I rubbed my eyes to try to shake off the drowsiness.

As I lifted my gaze, I spotted a tall, slim figure standing next to Jen. My eyes widened with surprise, "Sam!"

"Hey, Chickadee," he said as he busted out into a full grin.

"What are you doing here?" I rubbed my eyes, batting them to clear my cobweb brain.

Jen and Sam shared a disparaging glance.

Surprised washed over me as it hit me that they were the visitors.

"I have to warn you!" I rushed with urgency. "Jen, Bane drugged you! He did the same thing to me too, with something called angel dust." Terror ripped through me, "And Dr. Van is Bane's uncle!"

In a subdued manner, Jen eased herself onto the sofa next to me, resting her hand on my shoulder. "Yes, I know about Dr. Van." She glanced up at Sam. "And the drug, angel dust. The effects aren't as harsh on me. I gained my memories back after a couple of days," she paused. "This may be hard for you to believe, but Sam and I come from another dimension. We have been sent here to watch over you," she smiled oddly. "I wanted to tell you, but we were forbidden from our source to reveal our true identity."

I didn't recognize this person who looked like my friend. "Say that again?" My eyebrows collided.

Sam interjected. "We're your guardians, Guardians of Light."

"Come again?" My eyes bounced from Jen to Sam.

Ms. Noel stepped in. "Babee, listen to what they sayin'."

I nodded at Ms. Noel. "Okay, explain, please."

"We're here to protect you," Jen softly confessed.

"How can you protect me?"

Jen held my gaze. "I know it's hard to believe."

I interrupted. "You think?"

Concern toiled in Jen's eyes. "This may sound preposterous, but you're not human."

My eyes flew open as I gawked at her. "Come again?"

Jen's eyes softened. "Let me explain."

"Yeah, please do before I go into cardiac arrest!" I had wacko men wanting to chop my block off, and my friends were spooling tales from the land of Oz. Good grief! I sure as hell wasn't in Texas anymore.

All of a sudden, a streak of lightning crashed, and the whole house sounded like an explosion. With no warning, darkness swallowed up the light. I jumped with a sharp yep, clenching my chest. I settled back down, but my pulse continued to race. If it had not been for the kindling fire, we'd been sitting in the dark.

Ms. Noel asked, "Babee, are ya okay?"

I nodded, "As good as expected." I pressed my lips into a smile, but it was only a mask.

"Let me get ya something a little stronger ta drink. I save this for emergencies." Ms. Noel hightailed it to the kitchen.

Jen spoke up. "Considering everything that has transpired recently, you need to know the truth."

My eyes met hers. "Okay, I'm listening."

"Sam and I don't have all the details of how they created you, but what we do know is that you possess special abilities."

"Abilities?" I felt like I was in a tunnel, voices echoing all around me, "Like me blowing up the girl's restroom at school?"

Jen's face lit up. "That was you!"

Sam chimed in. "Damn straight, that was you, gul! You got some strong energy."

I threw my palm up. "Bane and his uncle are planning to kill me. They want to extract my … " I raised my fingers, gesturing a quote, "powers from my body." I jumped to my feet, shaking off the woolies. "It's all too weird."

Ms. Noel returned from the kitchen with a small glass filled with a transparent substance that looked like water. "This should make you feel better, babee," she handed me the glass. "This is what we here in Louisiana call hooch."

Sam's eyes ignited. "Oh, man! Now that's the stuff." He broke out into a greedy grin, nearly licking his chops.

Ms. Noel flashed a warning glint at Sam. "Don't you be gettin' any notions, young man, this white dog ain't to toy with." She shook her head at the puppy-dog-faced boy. Then she turned to me. "Drink it slow, Catin. It will rest you real nice."

"Thank you, Ms. Noel." I tilted my head back and downed the clear liquid. Suddenly I began gasping. "What is this?" I choked out, my throat blazing.

"That's moonshine!" Sam looked like he was salivating.

"No offense, but that stuff tastes awful," I choked.

Sam shot a mischievous wink. "That stuff will burn holes in your tummy."

"Thanks for the warning," I coughed out, my throat burning.

Sam moved in closer, dropping to his knees on the floor next to me. He went on to say, "We know that magick courses strongly through your veins. Old Blue and his uncle believe that if they take your powers, they'll gain supremacy over the world."

My brows drew together with confusion. "I don't understand."

Jen joined in. "They call themselves the Illuminati. They have been in circulation for centuries, all the way back to the Knights Templar, although the ones that exist today, unlike their former fellow brothers, are not of the light."

"Wait! Bane said my father was a member but defected. Van referred to a man with the last name of Collins. My dad's last name is Ray."

Jen shrugged. "We aren't aware of your father. I'm sorry I can't be more helpful."

"I may never know the truth," I said.

Jen pressed on. "What I do know is that the Illuminati are insidious creatures, masterminding a conspiracy to rule the world. They are the elite behind a frenzied campaign for World Dominance and a New International Economic Order. With supreme ultimate power at their beck and call, they are in the driver's seat. They have infiltrated the government, the banking system, the White House officials, every drug lord, and every organized crime from here to the land of no return. These Satan-worshiping fanatics bring destruction, famine, and global war."

Sam picked up where Jen left off. "Simply put, the Secret Brotherhood plays humans against one another as if it's a game of chest. They call all the shots, who lives, who dies. They are a bunch of sociopaths with big guns."

I sat there numb with shock, speechless.

Sam sat back on his heels, his face drawn. "Chickadee, unless you come into your massive artillery, ammo loaded, you ain't got much of a chance."

Jen snapped her head up at Sam. "Don't say that to her!"

His arms flailed. "It's the truth. Why lie now?"

Feeling a cocktail of fear, pissy and face down in the gravel, I butted in, "Why the trouble then, if I'm as good as dead?" I inhaled a sharp breath. "I might as well go back to the castle and offer myself up on their demonic altar." I raked my fingers through my hair. "Isn't there a protection spell that will keep me safe?"

Sam shared a glance with Jen, and with a long look on his face, he replied, "These diabolical men are lords of the underworld. With their untold wealth and treasures, they have the power to purchase even the devil." He stared at me, allowing me to digest this atrocity. "These occultists are convinced that their destiny is to enslave mankind. They have their hands deep in the black cookie jar of magick, and they will use any means to achieve their goal."

I scoffed. "Look, I won't deny that there's some weird freaky crap going on, but some of this stuff is whacked."

Ms. Noel interjected. "Evil has many faces, babee."

My attention fell upon Ms. Noel, "Do you believe there's a conspiracy?"

"It seems this young man who has watched over you appears to be up to no good! Whether he's part of a secret brotherhood or he's the devil himself, I think you might want to keep your distance." Ms. Noel never wavered from telling the truth, and I trusted her.

My gaze dropped on Jen and then to Sam. "Is there a solution?"

Sam sprinted to his feet and started pacing vehemently. With each striking pace, he mumbled incoherent words. He was struggling internally.

"Are you okay, Sam?" Jen asked.

He stopped dead in his tracks. His fist cuffed, raised to his lips, his eyes shifty, nearly black. "I have an idea that might stop the Family from coming after you, or at least keep them from killing you."

"I'll do anything!" I pleaded.

Sam rubbed his stubbled jawline as he paused momentarily. "I do have an idea, but you won't like it." He made his way over to me and dropped down to his knees, grabbing my gaze. "If you sleep with Old Blue on Samhain by the stroke of midnight, you will become infused; your essence with Aidan's spirit will unite as one. This act will bind your powers, but you will be bound to him forever, and forever is a very long time."

I laughed. "You mean I have to have sex with Aidan?"

"You are still a virgin, right?" Doubt blanketed Sam's face.

I rolled my eyes. "What do you think?"

Sam blew out a long wind of breath. "Good thing, Chickadee! That's your free ticket."

"I don't understand how having sex with Bane will defuse this nightmare!"

Sam flashed a sly grin. "Have you ever heard of sealing the deal?"

"Will you get to the point, please?" I snapped.

"If you merge yourself with Aidan, the two of you will become untouchable. You know, joined at the hip."

"What else are you not telling me?" I held my breath as a sinking feeling washed over me.

"The catch is that lover boy ain't exactly an angel." Sam leaned closer to me. "Aidan's lineage traces back centuries. He's part of the Malchut Beit David, meaning Kingdom of the House of David. Most know it as the Davidic Line."

"David in the Bible?" I asked as my brow arched.

Jen placed her hand on Sam's shoulder and interjected. "Histories reveal that dark magick runs deep in Aidan's family on both sides."

"The Davidic Line was the bloodline of Christ." I shook my head. "I'm not sure I'm following you."

Jen explained. "History doesn't always paint the complete truth. Some histories got lost in transition. In this account, the House of David, there were others connected to the Davidic Line that took another direction, a much more sinister path."

I rubbed my temples. "I'm not sure I can take much more of this."

Jen patted my hand, smiling and then proceeded. "On Aidan's mother's side, the Davidic line, David had a distant relative born at a much later time, after Christ's birth… Anne Montchanin."

"What does an ancestor have to do with what I'm facing?" I asked.

"Bear with me." Jen smiled. "Anne was a medium. She consorted with the spirit world."

I shrugged. "Ms. Noel's a medium. She's the purest person I know."

"I agree, but Anne didn't consort with the light. She summoned evil. Anne was barren and wanted children. As an act of desperation, she sold herself to the darkness," Jen paused. "This is Aidan's linage."

I didn't want to ask, but an inner voice persisted, "And his father's side?"

Regret smothered Jen's face. "They say on his father's side the bloodline runs to Beelzebub."

I gaped at Jen and then at Sam and Ms. Noel. "Isn't that the…"

Sam grabbed my arms so that he could force me to look into his face. "The Illuminist is tainted with pure evil blood, deviled blood."

"Hold on a damn minute!" I jerked free of Sam's grasp. "My father was a member of the Family. He was good." He was going to take that back, or else he was getting a black eye.

Sam cocked an eye. "Was he? From what I've heard, he's done some pretty low-life things that made him a real hardnosed dick." Sam's words stormed at me with a flurry.

I sprinted to my feet, fist white-knuckled to my side. "Take that back, Sam," I railed. "That's my father you're attacking."

Sam bolted to his feet, meeting me toe to toe. "Why should I? It's the truth. If he had not defected, none of this would be happening."

"How can you say that?" I gaped. "If my father hadn't met my mother, I wouldn't be standing here."

Sam towered over me. "That's my point. We wouldn't be in a war, fighting to protect you."

I stepped back. "Are you saying this is my fault?"

Sam took a step forward into my personal space, "Inadvertently, yes."

What a dickweed!

Jen stepped in between us. "Sam, we didn't come here to argue over who did what!" Jen placed her hand on Sam's arm to calm his temper, but instead, he flung her arm off, all while he kept his heated gaze on me.

I slid my gaze to Jen. "It's okay. I'm leaving." Without a glimpse in Sam's direction, I sidestepped him and reached for Ms. Noel, hugging her. I smiled. "I need to go find Sara. I should at least warn her that she's in danger too. Can I leave Snowball with you until later?"

"No problem, babee. You stay safe, now!" She hugged me back. "Let me know where y'at. I'll worry."

"I will!" Tears welled.

I started for the door. When my eyes lifted, Sam was blocking my path.

"We're not finished." Sam's eyes had taken on a predatory expression.

"Oh, we are finished." My words were stern and precise. I tried to step past Sam, but his fingers bit into my upper arm.

"I said we ain't finished." This time, he spoke in a low, grunted tone.

He was on my last nerve as my temper started to boil. Then suddenly, Sam jerked his arm away as though he'd touched a hot burner. He held his palm as seeping blisters rose. Curse words streamed from his mouth. His heated gaze shot at me. "You burnt me!" His eyes were full of shock.

I shook my head, freaking out. "I didn't do that to you!" This hostile person I didn't recognize.

I started to bail until Sam called my name, "Stevie!"

I paused with my hand on the doorknob, keeping my back to him. "What?" My voice was sharp.

"If you decide to bind yourself to Aidan, you have to do it at the stroke of midnight, or else you lose everything, yours and Aidan's powers and possibly your lives."

I paused a moment contemplating this absurdity in my head. I replied curtly, "Thanks." Without further discussion, I snatched up my hoodie and flew out the door.

MOTHER'S LOVE

*A*s I hurried down the steps shrugging on my hoodie, a light coming from my house caught my eye, and I halted. Rain poured off my hoodie, hindering my vision, but the soft glow penetrated through the sheets of rain like a beacon.

I hadn't given it much thought where to look for Sara. Maybe she'd returned looking for me. I needed to warn her about my findings. I didn't understand why she sold me to Bane, but I didn't want to fight with her either. I wanted to wish her well and be on my way. Despite Sara's betrayal, I honestly wanted her to be happy and well. Life was too short to harbor ill-will. I hoped she and Francis leave town also. It was not safe here. I spied Francis' old car parked outside, no sign of the red Ferrari. All of a sudden, I wanted my mother.

Hovering from the gushing rain, I tromped through the mud, half-blinded by the cold rain streaming down my face, my eyes were set on the little white house that I once called home. I scurried up the steps and reached for the doorknob.

Against the howling winds and pounding rain on the rooftop, I heard faint cries as I closed the door behind me. The sobs were coming from the kitchen. "Mom!" A profound sense of worry flurried through me as I rushed to the kitchen. My pending troubles somehow didn't seem as important. All I could think about was my mom.

When I entered the kitchen, my eyes fell upon Sara, slumped, her face buried in her hands, seated at the table. Tissues scattered across the floor like white dots. I rushed to her side and kneeled before her. "Mom, what's wrong?"

Sara sniffled. Her voice appeared frail. "It's Francis," she choked through tears, "He's gone." Sara began weeping deeply. My mother's whole body shook.

"Where is he? I'll call him." I pulled my cell from my pocket.

"He's gone," she roared.

"Mom, don't worry about him. We need to leave. Where're your things?"

"Will you stop?" Sara hissed. "Francis didn't leave me, you idiot! He loved me."

"I don't understand?"

Sara dropped her hands from her face, aiming her heated glare at me. "Francis is dead, murdered!" Her accusing eyes sent chills spiraling down my spine. Without warning, my stomach roiled, and I couldn't stop the hurl. I dashed to the sink in the nick of time.

Weak and shaking at my knees, I rinsed my mouth and made my way back to the table. I eased down into a chair next to Sara. I pushed past my bout with queasiness and asked. "When did this happen?"

"This morning. I'd left Francis to take care of our–" Sara stopped, apparently to hide her shenanigans.

"How did Francis die?" An old acquaintance came to mind that I hadn't thought about in a long time, Charles.

"What difference does it make? He's dead!" Sara choked, barely able to speak, "I found him when I'd returned. He was lying in a river of blood. It was horrible!" She began sobbing, shoulders shaking.

Something told me that this nightmare was like a merry-go-round of eerie. I sat back, mulling over in my head about Charles and his unexpected death. "Mom, how did Francis die?"

"His throat was slit," she wailed.

"Charles was killed the same way too."

Sara didn't have to confirm my suspicions. I read it in the newspaper clippings she'd been hiding.

"Why are you bringing up Charlie? I'm heartbroken over Francis," she snarled, baring her teeth. "Stop badgering me with all these harebrained questions!" She pulled away from me with her back to me.

"I know Charles died the same way. Why can't you admit it?"

"What do you want me to say?" Sara hurled over her shoulder. "Yes! Charlie's throat got slashed." The venom in her voice spewed, "Happy now?" I didn't know why, but it felt like the blame shifted to me.

"Mom, don't you think it's strange that both Charles and Francis both died with their throat cut and then Dad's death too? That's three men who have been in a relationship with you who have died in cold blood." I rose to my feet and stepped softly in front of Sara, kneeling. "Do you think someone from the Bane's family has been tailing us?" She had to know it was Bane.

Sara's gaze finally latched hold of mine. Her eyes filled with rage. "It's you and your father that I have to thank for my miserable life!"

My eyes dropped to Sara's hands. She was holding my cup that Dad had given me before he died. I spotted the picture of Dad from my nightstand too. The only two things I had left of Dad's. The cup was hard to miss with its red hearts and a small chip that had broken off the handle. The mug and picture contained no value, but to me, they were priceless. Everything else, Dad's photos but that one, all his possessions, Sara had burned. "You went digging in my nightstand and found my picture. You got my cup too."

I spotted the half-empty bottle of Jack Daniels on the table. I should've known. I wished I were dealing with sober Sara. "Did you know that I never wanted children?" Deflecting my question, she spoke in an incoherent voice, almost a whisper, "Jon insisted. The doctors thought I had a blood disorder," she looked me straight in the eyes, "It was easy. Blunt trauma to a new pregnancy is an effected method of birth control." Her lips twitched into a sneer as she laid the cup on the table and stuffed the picture back in her pocket, returning in her hand a pack of cigarettes and a small box of matches. She struck the match and lit her cigarette, taking a huge drag and blowing the smoke into the air.

I quickly gathered to my feet and stepped back out of her smoke range. I learned a long time ago that it was best to keep my distance when she was in one of her moods. I leaned against the counter, eyeballing her cautiously.

"Your father just wouldn't give it up." She took a second long, thoughtful drag on her cigarette. I watched in silence. The cherry of the cigarette illumed. Quietly, Sara flicked the ashes on the floor as she blew out a long stream of gray smoke. Then her odious eyes targeted me. "Not until someone from Jon's family approached me did I reconsider giving your father a child. The gentleman was a distinguished diplomat of Jon's family," she flashed a wicked smile. "I only agreed to do it for the money. I never wanted you, and I am glad to be rid of the burden." Her eyes caught mine. "Why are you here anyway? I handed you over to him."

"Don't worry. I won't be staying." Raw and primitive grief overwhelmed me. "You sold me to a monster!"

"What's a few bruises when you have the world at your feet." Sara raked her eyes over me as her mouth twisted in disgust. "I think you got the better deal. You're as frumpy as they come." She took another drag off her cigarette and then broke down sobbing, tears streaming, "Francis is dead! What am I going to do now?" Sara pressed her hand over her face and wept.

Without thinking, I made a step toward her, but then my inner voice stopped me. I wanted to wrap my arms around her, to console her, but my better sense warned me against that notion. Sara wouldn't have welcomed my embrace. Instead, my getting in close range of her might provoke her into a physical altercation, the last thing I wanted. A sense of hopelessness devoured my mind, my whole existence. Even though I reminded myself of Sara's illness, it didn't make her words hurt any less.

Suddenly, Sara flung the cup across the floor with all her might. I stood there gaping incredulously. She had taken my cherished mug, the last gift Dad had given me, breaking it into shards covering the floor. In a frenzy, I dropped to my knees, tears streaming, as I swept the ceramic shards into my palms, hoping to salvage it.

Then unhinged anger coursed through me. I jerked my gaze up at Sara, slowly rising to my feet. "What did Dad and I ever do to deserve such loathing from you?" My fists clenched to my side.

Sara's eyes shot at me like razors. "I never wanted this life." She clamped down on her lips, and then she released her venom. "I thought Jon was wealthy. Good God!" she scoffed. "He went to an ivy league college, Yale, for Pete's sake!" Sara threw her arms up, enraged. "How the hell did I know he'd planned to disown his family," she sputtered. "The son of a bitch didn't tell me until we were married." Sara snorted a laugh. "The honeymoon from hell, no electricity, no water and no luxurious get-away. I. Hated. Him!"

"I don't understand how you can be so heartless. I feel like I've been spinning my wheels in the mud. All I've ever wanted from you is your love, but you're incapable of such a human emotion. You can't see past your freaking nose. You've never been a mother to me! You love that liquor bottle more than you love yourself!" Whether it stemmed from her mental illness or her sociopathic nature, it didn't matter any longer. I was done.

"That's right! I didn't act like your mother because I'm not. We are not even blood. Oh, knock that look off your ugly face," Sara's face twisted into a scowl. "You had to have known that I wasn't your biological mother."

"What?" Shock rampaged over me like an avalanche. Suddenly, I felt something wet in my hand. I glanced down. Blood was dripping from my right hand. I'd been gripping a broken piece from the mug, tight in my fist. I dropped the shard to the floor, standing in a stupor.

"I didn't stutter." Acerbity interlaced her voice.

"Did I ever know the real you?"

"I'm tired." Sara evaded my question. "I assume you know the way out." Her voice was empty, cold, and unfeeling. She rose to her feet, a bit shaky. "Go make a life for yourself with that young man. He cares about you." Without another word, she finished destroying the last possession I had of my father… *the picture from her pocket.* She dropped the torn chunks to the floor and snatched up the half-empty bottle of Jack and moved past me, heading for the stairs. I gapped at my only picture of Dad, tears streaming down my cheeks. How could she be so cruel?

Silently my eyes gravitated to Sara's back as I watched her drag herself upstairs. As if Sara had aged ten years in mere minutes, her shoulders slumped, she appeared broken and withered. Funny, I once thought of her as beautiful, glistening blonde hair and sparkling hazel eyes, full of life. Now, she seemed old and haggard.

Despite her disdain toward me, I stilled loved her. She was my mother, good or bad, blood or not. Once I heard her bedroom door shut, my mind spiraled out of control. Raking my fingers through my damp hair, I didn't have a clue what to do next. Leaving her wasn't an option.

Then it hit me. Call me crazy or stupid, but the one person that came to mind was the only one who made sense... *Bane!* I tugged on my cell from my pocket. I held my breath that it might not be soaked through and useless. "Oh, God!" It lit up. My hands trembled as I punched his number.

On the first ring, he answered, curses poured from his lips, "Where the hell are you?"

I swallowed hard. "I'm at my house. I need you to come here as soon as you can. Bring the angel dust."

"What?" He became silent.

"Just bring it!"

I heard him breathing on the other end. Then he replied. "I'll be there shortly. Don't leave, do you understand me?"

"I'll wait for you but come alone." I sternly demanded. Then I heard a click, and my phone went dead.

I collapsed to the wooden floor, drawing my knees into a fetal position. The coolness of the wood seemed to comfort me as I shut my eyes, trying to close myself off from the world. Regardless, my mind wouldn't stop. No one could help me now. Not even Ms. Noel. I had to look to Bane for the answers. If it was true that he wanted me dead, then so be it. I'd do anything to get past this nightmare.

I opened my eyes and slowly eased to a sitting position. Every part of my body protested in pain. I'd fallen asleep, but it felt like a house fell on me. Straightaway, a loud banging came from the door that could have awakened the dead.

I picked myself off the floor and darted for the living room. I flung the door open, and there stood Bane, looking angrier than ever. He stood mountainous in a black trench coat, a couple of unruly curls hung in his face, water dripping off his body, eyes dark and menacing.

He stepped in, pushing past me. With his back to me, he breaks the momentary silence. "I'm assuming the dust is for your mother." He pulled out a small bag of glittery white powder.

My eyes dropped to the strange substance. "That's what you used on Jen and me?"

"I don't have time to argue with you. Where is Sara?" He flung over his shoulder, his voice forceful and grave as the storm.

"Look! I just want her to forget about today." I paused. "Francis was murdered. She's taking it hard."

Our eyes collided. "I'm quite aware of Francis' misfortune. Wait here." He turned to head upstairs. Quickly I fisted his sleeve, halting him. "I'm not letting you out of my sight around my mother!"

"Either you want this or not?" His glint reassured me his patience was threadbare.

"Sara needs to forget Francis. She can't handle another tragedy, another loss." The knot in my throat squeezed.

"Why do you bother with her? Sara doesn't deserve your kindness."

I struggled to keep my voice from quavering. "Sara's my mother. Isn't that enough?"

For what seemed forever, Bane and I stood, locked, eyes frozen on each other. Even after discovering his true intentions and protecting the murderer of my father, my heart ached for him. How sick was that?

Bane broke our trance and started up the stairs. His snappy words drifted behind him, "Let's get this over with before I change my mind."

I stayed right on his heels as we both entered Sara's room. Just as I'd expected, she had passed out, laying spread out on the bed, half on, half off. I spotted the liquor bottle on the nightstand. She'd polished it off.

Bane started to make his way to Sara's side until I wrung my fingers around his coat sleeve, tighter this time. He spun around, glaring at me. "What now," his voice was emotionless, and it chilled me.

"How well are you up on your pharmaceuticals?" My eyes darted to the small bag of sparkles clenched in his palm. "What the hell is that stuff." My conscience gnawed at me.

Bane's blues were as frigid as the North Pole. "This isn't your run-of-the-mill drug. It's not even known to mankind."

"Though not entirely," I hissed.

"It's a mystical component made of rare fey jewels. It's crushed into fine particles like sand or dust."

"It looks like glitter."

A glint of sarcasm pranced in his blues. "Princess, this is not glitter, and it isn't a fairytale either. This powder, known as angel dust, can wipe out an entire race. It's no toy, Love."

"I know it will wipe a person's memories." I shot him a baleful glare. "Can you erase her memories of Francis without killing her?" I had a sick feeling about this, but I feared if Sara didn't get relief, she might commit suicide.

"I'll give her enough for her to sleep a few days. With the amount of liquor she's ingested." Bane nodded to the empty bottle. "The worst scenario is that she'll wake up with a hangover."

I raked my fingers through my tangles. "Okay! Do it and then get rid of that fairy crap!"

Bane nodded. His face void and remote as he made his way to Sara's side, I watched in silence.

There were tale-tell signs that even in Sara's sleep, she mourned deeply for her loss. I hoped the dust would give her time to heal so that when her memories returned, she might be stronger to handle the grief.

I watched as Bane carefully dropped a few sprinkles in his hand and chanted words in a strange language that I didn't recognize as he made odd hand gestures and then gently dropped the dust over Sara's body. Though I didn't understand one language, I sensed the words impacted a strong connotation.

As soon as Aidan finished, he was swiftly on his feet and down the stairs, heading out the door. I ran after him, yelling, "Stop!" As if my words fell upon mute ears, he kept going. It wasn't until I reached his car did I catch up with him. "*Du Pont!* I overheard your conversation with your uncle, Van!" I was panting, rain beating my face, blurring my vision. I kept talking to his back. "If you want my life, then take it!" I yelled. "I have nothing else to lose." A dagger to the heart would've hurt less than his betrayal.

Bane pivoted on his heels, glaring at me as if he wanted to devour me.

"Well! What are you waiting for? Here I am. Take me!" I slung my arms out.

In a millisecond, Bane charged me like a bullet before I had a chance to flinch. In one instant flash, he'd spun me into his arms. The best way I knew how to describe what happened next was... as if scooped up into the eye of a tornado, cinched tight in Bane's arms, we spun around and around, at speed beyond anything I'd ever experienced. I felt like *Dorothy* in *The Wizard of Oz*, minus the house.

ONLY YOU

 hen we came to an abrupt halt, I quickly concluded that I wasn't in the Land of Oz; instead, Bane and I were back at the fireflies' nest, or so it seemed.

The atmosphere appeared thicker, with no breeze. The trees were calm, and the bugs were quiet. My head spun in circles like Ring-Around-the-Rosy. I stammered over my words, "What-what-what-did-did-you-you do?" Immediately, my stomach roiled, and I darted off to the nearest bush.

Bane stood by my side, gently stroking my back, but I was still hurt and angry with him. I wanted to punish him. Jolting up, I swung at him, knocking his hand away. "Don't touch me!" I screeched. "You've been hiding my father's murderer from me all this time!"

"Stevie," his face appeared torn. "Please, let me explain."

"Why bother? Don't you have me penciled in for a beheading? My compliments to you and your precious Uncle."

"Will you please come and have a seat with me?" His soft velvety voice sent quivers down my spine. I opened my mouth to protest, but all at once, an eerie feeling hastened me to stop. I peeled my eyes away from Bane and combed over the trees. Something was off about this place. It was as if I'd been copied and pasted into a picture. Even the forest appeared strange and unnatural.

I spotted the fireflies flickering in and out from amidst the dark shadows of the pines. I recalled the display was spectacular and weirdly very much like last time. Aimlessly the fireflies descended from the trees. The tiny glow-balls gathered in a line, gracefully making their way to us. How odd, I thought. Why aren't they under the trees, protected from the storm?

I noticed the rain had stopped. Did the storm pass? My eyes dropped to my feet. The soil was dry as a bone. I peered up at the cloudless sky. The stars were glistening brightly. I looked at Bane. "Where are we?"

"We are in another dimension." His ironic tone alarmed me.

"Dimension?"

"It is an altered reality, parallel to ours."

"This isn't the same fireflies' nest?"

Bane shrugged. "I thought," he smiled tightly. "It would be the safest place for us to talk." He gently took my hand, guiding me to a soft patch of grass where a plaid, red and white blanket spread out over a patch of green.

A picnic basket filled with assorted crackers and cheese laid on the blanket as if we were having a picnic. My eyes gravitated to a long neck bottle of red wine and two long stem glasses.

We seated ourselves on the blanket. Bane snatched up the bottle and uncorked it. A loud pop wafted in the still air. Very skillfully, he held the bubbled glass in his fingers and poured it half full. He handed the glass to me. I hesitated, thinking that this felt more like a dream. Then I forced a faint smile and accepted the drink. I sniffed its dark rich aroma and lifted the glass to my lips, taking a small sip. Its taste lingered a moment on my lips, a tartness that I didn't recognize. I peeked above the rim and caught Bane watching. I flushed slightly and said, "It's nice. Thank you."

Bane smiled back. After he poured his glass, a long sigh followed. "Where shall I begin?" His blues looked straight through me as if he were searching for my soul.

"You could start with how we got here?"

"I suppose you might as well know." His grave expression made me edgy. "In the world of the extraordinaire, it's called shifting."

"What do you mean?"

"Have you ever watched Charm?"

"*Ooooh!*" my eyes widened. "How is that even possible?"

"It's an art I have mastered for centuries." He took a sip of his wine.

"Jesus! Centuries," I gulped.

One corner of his lip quirked. "My lineage comes from a long line of Druids, and I am immortal as well. I... hmm, don't age."

"You've been drinking too much Kool-Aide," I half-laughed.

"You think I'm making this up?" he asked. "Then tell me how we got here?" A gratifying glint lingered behind his eyes.

"Druids are wizards, right?"

"You are correct."

"Did you work your magick that day I nearly became the deer in the headlights?"

"Yes."

"Hey, did you magically fix my car?" I didn't know why I hadn't questioned this before now.

Bane cuffed his mouth and paused, clearing his throat. "Hmm, no, I paid for the repairs."

"Oh," I bit my bottom lip. "Thank you," I whispered.

Bane flashed his lopsided grin. "You're welcome."

"Did you use magick on me that day I nearly tied one on with Gina?" I held my breath.

"Yes. I used a small smidgen of angel dust to slate your mind, momentarily." His face remained solemn.

"The night we encountered Francis... "

Bane interjected. "I was protecting you."

"Why have you kept this from me?" I shook my head, frustrated.

"I carried doubt that you were ready to hear the truth."

"Did you cast this forest and the picnic?" My eyes washed over the blanket and goodies.

"Yes."

I drew in a deep breath and exhaled. I might've looked calm on the outside, but on the inside, I felt like an erupting volcano. "How old are you?" I recalled him boasting to Van about his age.

"I'm three hundred years old. Give or take." The corner of his lip tipped upward, pushing a smile.

"That explains your weird speech," I mumbled, letting my eyes wander over the soft glow of the fireflies. My gaze slid back to Bane. "This may sound loony but is your bloodline tainted with the devil?"

Before answering, he laughed in a jovial way. "Hmm," he cleared his throat. "It appears that someone has been whispering in your ear. My bloodline goes back far. Hence, just as anyone, I do not have control over who my ancestors were. I will tell you this much... my bloodline runs strong with magick. It has come in handy from time to time. Regardless of my lineage, I am grateful for my ancestors' gifts despite their inherent nature."

"Oh, okay." I decided I needed to get to the heart of my questions. "I want to know who killed my father." I narrowed my eyes at him.

"I know you want to know about your dad's death and rightfully so. However, I'd like to know what you heard while listening in on my conversation." Bane grabbed an apple from the basket and started tossing it back and forth, from hand to hand, his dark blues fixed on me.

"Oh, that!" I swallowed. "I didn't set out to snoop."

His brow arched, "Oh, really?"

I rolled my eyes. "Okay, yes. I did go snooping, but I didn't plan on stumbling onto your private conversation."

Bane's blues sparkled under the soft glow of the light, a shine of suspicion. "And," he urged.

I looked down, pulling up a blade of grass, strange how it felt real under my fingers. "I know your uncle is the principal, Dr. Van. His real name is Edward Van Dunn. You both talked about an Order and the Family."

He changed his seating position, resting his arm on his leg. "Go on. Tell me everything." He encouraged with a stern tone.

"I heard you both refer to me as a hybrid." I snatched up my glass of wine and hurriedly took several sips. I gently wiped my mouth with the back of my hand. "You and Van discussed my abilities." I tugged on another blade of grass, hiding my eyes under my lashes. "You claimed your urges were growing stronger," I rolled my eyes. "Something to do with controlling yourself." Coming clean with that little hot fact pretty much torched my face.

I got the impression Bane was hiding a wide grin as he dropped his chin, slightly nodding complacently.

"I overheard you say it was me who blew up the girl's restroom," I recalled how we landed unharmed in the football stadium. "I know your uncle wants you to dispose of my mom. Van called her a vessel, whatever that means." I grabbed my glass and polished off the drink.

"It seems death knocks at my door a lot. Not in the natural sense, first my father's death, then Charles, a boyfriend of Sara's, and last but not least, Francis." I looked at him, full of skepticism. "I suspect it might've been someone in the Family."

He cocked his head to the side as if surprised. "Why do you think it's someone from the Family?"

"Because I remember the MIB," I nearly shouted as I shot green bullets at him. "They've been following Sara and me since I was a child."

His brows knitted, "MIB?"

I rolled my eyes, "Men in black. Your guy, Zak, was tailing me at the fair that night I ran into you."

"That explains your jumpiness. Why didn't you tell me then?"

"I didn't trust you and obviously with good reason." I looked away at the stand of trees. "I recall the attack. That monster was going to kill me." I shivered from just thinking about what could've happened. "Your uncle ordered him to stalk me!" I half-whispered. "You knew I was in danger, and you didn't do anything to stop it!" I turned my back to him. I couldn't look him in the eye. How could I have cared for him when he'd been involved in a conspiracy to kill me? Yet that wasn't the worst. Knowing he was protecting my father's murderer shattered my world completely.

An insufferable silence enshrouded us. The intensity was so thick you could slice it with a butter knife. Finally, I couldn't stand the quiet any longer. I tilted my chin to the side, keeping my back to him as I began an arsenal of accusations. "Will I die by your hand or some executioner from the dark ages?" To my ears, I sounded full of piss and vinegar, but if the truth were told, I was already dead.

Unexpectedly, Bane swept me into his embrace. At first, I fought him, twisting in his arms and arching my body. I sought to get free. He was the last person I wanted to touch me.

Yet when I lifted my eyes to his beautiful face, there was unspoken anguish churning in his blues, and I calmed.

"Please stop saying that." He rested his forehead against mine. His breath was warm as he spoke, "I didn't know that my uncle had you tailed. The thought of that bloody Crypt touching you made my blood boil. I won't apologize for ending his life; I'd do it again a hundred times." He bent his head back, pulling my eyes to his. "I'm not taking your life." He gathered my chin in his palm. "Since the moment I laid eyes on you, I've been trying to protect you. To keep you from-" His voice broke.

"How can you be protecting me when you're embarrassed to be seen with me?"

His brows shot up. "I'm not ashamed of you."

"Then why did you have Jeffery drive me to school and throughout the day, you blew me off as if I didn't exist?"

"I didn't want Van coming after you. If he suspected that I had any interest in you, I feared he would've come after you. That's why I kept my distance."

"You don't mind being seen with me?" Could my assumption have been wrong?

"Are you kidding? I can't imagine having anyone else by my side than you." His voice drifted into a whisper, "*Only you.*"

"You said you didn't like my company, and you're not a one-woman man!"

"Yes, at first, I didn't want to like you, but then-" he paused. "Then I found myself caring more for you than myself."

"You care about me?" I barely whispered.

"Of course, silly," he kissed my hand, "I would not have gone through all this trouble, keeping you out of harm's way if I had not cared." He paused as a smile played across his lips. "However, you didn't make it easy on me."

"If what you're telling me is true, then why are you hiding my father's killer?"

"Once you know the answer, it will change your life forever. There won't be any going back, and I refuse to dust you again. So, you better be damn sure this is what you want."

I hesitated. Was I willing to step off the cliff? I inhaled and exhaled pointedly. Out of respect for my dad and the turmoil that his death had caused my family, I had no other choice. I whispered the only answer I could. "Yes, I am sure."

Bane's eyes softened. "Princess, the answer has been right under your nose all along," he smiled. I wanted to melt into his arms and pretend the world was one big happy place. Yet, no matter how much I tried to look through rose-colored glasses, the reality was too profound to deny.

"I don't understand."

"Think about it." Bane's gaze searched deep into mine.

All at once, like a house dropping from the sky, I knew. Bane was right! I barely whispered the one word. "Sara?" I looked to Bane, searching for a plausible explanation. "Why didn't I see it?"

"How could you have known. You were a child."

"How long have you known?"

He reached for my hand. His fingers were warm and strong as he grasped mine. "Come back to the blanket and sit with me." His brows drew together in an agonized expression.

"If Sara had been so unhappy, why didn't she just leave?"

"I will explain everything. No stone will go unturned. You have my word. Please, join me." I nodded as he held my hand, leading me back to the blanket.

Bane blew out a disquieting sigh before he started. "Your father, Jon, once belonged to the same secret society as I, known as the Illuminati. We have many names and assume secrecy at all costs. You are one of us. Your true last name is Collins."

"No, it's not. Ray is my last name."

"Stevie, until a few hours ago, you thought my surname was Bane. It is our custom to hide our identity from outsiders. However, your father had other ideas for not taking his last name."

"I can only imagine."

"He chose to use his middle name to break free from the Family."

"The Family?"

"Yes. As I once explained, the Family is a collective of thirteen families, all different bloodlines. The chosen thirteen each brings a particular talent or skill to the table. Jon was a master at law. He graduated with honors at the top of his class at Yale. He was a member of the Skull and Cross Bone fraternity, quite an impressive resume, a genius."

"Wow! I'm beginning to wonder if I knew my dad at all."

"You knew the parts that counted the most, Princess. He had a big heart, and it showed. Jon was a stand-up man. He voiced his opinions rather boldly. He didn't hide the fact that he didn't approve of the Family's unique traditions. Jon had different ideas for a New World Order, ones set apart from what the Family envisioned. When he realized he couldn't persuade the councilmen, he decided to break ties. It wasn't a hard decision.

. . .

He had fallen in love with Sara. The Family became enraged with Jon. It is forbidden to become unevenly yoked with unbelievers. The Family demanded that he dissolve his involvement at once. That was the deciding factor for Jon defecting."

"What did he do?"

"Jon eloped with Sara and moved to a small town in Oklahoma."

"Eufaula! That's my childhood town."

"Yes, however, as the story unfolds, Sara was very displeased with her circumstances. Blind to Jon's decision to break free from the Family, she had much bigger plans. Of course, why would she think otherwise? Snatching a Collins boy, she'd hoped it would've put her on the map among the elite's social circles."

"Sara, in her moment of weakness, mentioned that Dad disowned his family."

"Yes, once Sara discovered the truth that your father no longer possessed wealth, she became enraged, although she didn't leave him. As an alternative, she found another avenue to the Family's fortune.

"Sara is a resourceful person."

"I think that's an understatement. As I was saying, after a year of marriage, Jon and Sara started trying to get pregnant, or at least that's what Jon wanted. Sara was on an entirely different page."

"Yeah," I scoffed. "Sara's on Sara's page. That's the only page I've ever known."

"Sadly, I agree."

I felt a sudden prick of anger.

"Anyhow, the Family kept a careful watch over Jon. They were aware of his extensive knowledge of the law. They didn't want any surprises. However, the Family did discover something of value that could benefit them greatly, Sara's penchant for money. Shortly after that discovery, they soon unveiled a dark secret that Sara was secretly causing herself to miscarry. It was her sick way of getting back at Jon for denouncing his family's fortune."

I couldn't fathom the lack of humanity Sara's possessed. "She admitted to me about the miscarriages."

Bane stopped and drew my hand into his palm. His blues filled with tenderness. "Do I need to give you a break?"

"No! I'm fine. I just need to hear this." I smiled, though my bottom lip quivered.

He exhaled. "Let me get through this appalling story so I can stop torturing you. As I was saying, the Family seized the opportunity by approaching Sara with an irresistible offer. They presented a blood contract to Sara."

"Let me guess. She took their offer?"

"Yes. The Family sweetened the deal for Sara to refuse. Through the unscrupulous persuasion of The Family, Sara pressured Jon to seek a doctor, an in-vitro fertilization specialist. Since Sara was a master at lying, she was more than convincing. As everything went accordingly, Jon agreed. What Jon didn't realize is that Sara had brought him to the Family's appointed doctor, an influential member of the ninth members of the councilmen. Dr. Astor is renowned for his advanced science, top in his field. He is beyond light years ahead in alien technology and advanced pre-implantation genetic cloning."

I gaped. "Cloning?"

"Yes. The Family Order has connections that far exceed any of mankind's primitive technology. Their scientists are renowned for their evolutionary research in genetic engineering, alien engineering."

"Alien! Like big ugly bugs?"

Bane cuffed his hand over his mouth. "You and bugs, I swear," he laughed. "It's more like celestial."

"Angel stuff?"

"Precisely. The Family calls you, Project Dream Angel."

"An angel," I gaped at him, stunned.

"Yes," he answered.

"How is that even possible?"

"I'm getting to that part," Bane smiled. "As I was saying, once the blood contract solidified, Sara was locked into an in-frangible agreement."

"What is a blood contract exactly?"

"A blood contract is no ordinary legal document. It is a contract under dark magick. Sara literally had to sign the contract in her blood.

"Why blood?"

"Blood magick is very powerful. After all, it is the source of life. Without it, one dies."

"Did Sara understand the risk?"

"Yes, but it didn't matter. Wealth was the deciding factor for Sara, regardless of the consequences. Anything after that concept didn't seem to concern her."

"I reckon the Family wanted to use Sara as a lab rat?"

"I'm sorry but yes," he paused. "This wasn't normal in-vitro fertilization, our doctors have been researching and running tons of trials. However, all have failed. Since Sara agreed to take the plunge, she was the first human to be tested. The doctors busied themselves getting everything perfect for the trial to be successful. With the art of technology under an environmentally controlled chamber, the scientist extracted DNA from your father, Jon, and extracted DNA from a celestial being. With help from the alien advancement, we were able to create a special sperm and inject it into a celestial egg. Once the embryo had developed to term, Dr. Astor transferred the embryo into Sara's womb."

"So, Sara's not my biological mother?" I took a sprightly breath.

"Yes, that is correct."

"What the hell am I?"

"You are amazing." Bane hesitated as if to soften the blow. "We refer to you as a genetically engineered angel. We call you Dream Angel."

Shock swirled in my head. "I'm not human?" Despite how insane this sounded, I believed Bane.

"Not entirely. You are a fraction."

"Sara was okay with carrying a freak?"

"There is nothing about you that is even close to an abomination."

"I think I'm pretty close to it." There were so many uncertainties that it made my head swim, and yet, I felt free for the first time. "All my life, I'd been a misfit, and now I know why."

"You're not a misfit. You're remarkable," Aidan's eyes met mine. "Where was I? Oh yes, everything was going without a hitch. Sara was following the rules. Jon was impervious to Sara's lies, and her routine checkups on the surface looked like a normal pregnancy. The baby was growing as any healthy fetus. Then there was a complication." Aidan's lips tightened. "In Sara's third trimester, the doctors detected her CBC count was off. They also noticed a difference in Sara's behavior. The test revealed a change in her DNA. This surprised the doctors. No one saw it coming. The celestial fetus infected her with a virus that altered her genetic makeup. Since this experiment was new, Dr. Astor didn't know if after the baby's birth, the damage might reverse itself or if it was a permanent condition. Even though this was unexplored territory, Dr. Astor suspected it was highly improbable."

"Is that why she's-?" The word couldn't pass my lips.

"A sociopath, partly," he paused, "Which brings me to your father's end."

I cringed, "My mom is ill because of me!" Tears welled, spilling down my cheeks.

Bane gathered my chin in his fingers. "You are not responsible for Sara's illness." He tilted his head back and let out a frustrating groan. "Look," his eyes caught mine, "I didn't want to tell you this, but the infection only enhanced Sara's flaws. She wasn't a Samaritan before the affliction. So, don't beat yourself up for her impropriety."

"Sara said I ruined her life! At first, I didn't understand what she meant, but now it makes sense. "

"Sara may have been affected by the virus but she still had free will. She ruined her own life. I know you loved her but she wasn't the best person before she met your father," Aidan continued. "Still under contract after your birth, Sara had the responsibility to care for you. As your handler, she was to see to your needs. Secretly keeping Jon out of the loop, the Family set up a bank account in Sara's name; a very substantial cash flow."

"Wait! Sara had money all these years? While Dad was alive and even after his death?"

"Yes. The Family provided well."

"She let me go without food. The simple staples to live." My eyes narrowed with anger. "That explains how she was able to collect all her expensive clothes. I thought her many boyfriends paid for her expensive things."

"Sara mishandled the money. That's why Zak and his comrade came to your house that early hour when you were a child. Sara had been gambling. She'd lost a large consumption. Zak left her a message of warning, and that's why she was running."

"Jesus! How could I have not known?" My eyes flickered to the forest and then sliding back to Bane. "Sara wanted the rest of her money."

"You're correct. A clause in the contract states that upon your eighteenth birthday, Sara is to relinquish you into my care. After the final transaction, Sara would receive her payment."

"You agreed to this?"

"One doesn't argue with the Family. You simply follow orders."

"Wow! That's very disturbing!" My stomach knotted.

"You may find it hard to accept, but it is the Family's way, our way."

"Sorry, but I'd never stoop to such barbarity."

"Never say never. When push comes to shove, instinct kicks in, and you will find yourself doing anything to survive."

"I'm beginning to understand a lot of things."

"Anyhow, Sara began to get careless. Jon stumbled upon her stash of expensive jewels and designer clothing. This set Jon into a fury, launching a full-blown investigation into Sara's whereabouts. In only a matter of days, Jon discovered an account in her name with a generous cash flow."

"How much?" I asked.

"Pardon?"

"How much did my mother get?"

"Her fee was arranged in two installments, half the money after your birth and the final payment when you were deposited."

"You still haven't answered my question."

"Sara received twenty million."

"Wow," I breathed harshly. "I can't tell you how many times I'd missed meals because she claimed we were broke." My eyes drifted to the fireflies for a moment, then back to Bane, "Your money?"

"No! The Family paid."

"Where is this mysterious Family?" Strangely, I'd never seen anyone except his uncle.

"The Family stays in hiding from each other. The only time we gather is during emergencies. It is easier to keep our anonymity."

"Oh, I see."

Aidan sighed. "Jon confronted Sara over his findings. Of course, Sara denied having the account, claiming it had to be another Sara Ray. Jon was steps ahead of her. He'd had Sara tailed, confronting her with incriminating pictures. As expected, this prompted Jon, demanding a divorce and custody of you. Sara knew Jon's wily ways of the law, and she knew he'd have the upper hand. It wouldn't be hard proving she was an unfit mother. Often Sara had been seen keeping company with truckers."

A new and unexpected pain surged through me. "Good God! I had no idea."

"You were a mere child then. How could you have known?" Bane reached over and caressed my back. "I'm sorry to inform you of these deplorable accounts."

"No, it's okay." I nodded. "Go on. Finish, please."

Aidan furthered the story. "Sara became paranoid that if Jon followed through with his threat, the Family might break the contract, leaving her penniless."

"There's no silver lining to this story, is there?"

"I'm afraid it gets worse." He sighed. "As the histories read, Sara sought out an undisclosed associate of the Family. As a supporter, he helped Sara. He materialized a car, saturated with dark enchantments, and it was Sara driving the vehicle, ending your father's life upon impact. Jon didn't see her coming because the car was invisible."

My whole body went numb. "That explains why the police couldn't find any evidence. Oh my God!" The story seemed so preposterous, yet I knew it was the truth. I snapped my head up at Aidan. "Did Zak help Sara kill my father?"

"No. Zak and his companion merely advised Sara that she still had to comply under the binding contract despite Jon's death. She'd been keeping company with a particularly shady character. The Family wanted her to understand they were watching and would not tolerate any foul behavior."

"That's the reason we left that night. I remember how she ushered me into the car, and we sped away with not much more than the clothes on our backs. It was like yesterday. All this time, I blamed the illness for her restlessness." I inhaled a ragged breath. Then I had to know. "If you'd known about all this concerning Sara, why didn't you stop her from killing my father?"

"If I'd known, I would've stepped in, but I had no idea. I discovered this recently when the accounts fell into my lap. The Family keeps a record of every event that has transpired since the beginning of time." Bane paused, "You must know that I would lay my life down to protect you."

"I know that now." I shrugged. "It's just I've been living a lie most of my life."

"Yes, Sara was trying to hide. She didn't know the Family had tagged both of you."

"Tagged?" I didn't like the sound of that.

"Yes, implants, a tracking device," Aidan spoke calmly.

"That explains how Sara and I were easily found," I bit my bottom lip, thinking. "Do I still have an implant?"

"No, that dissolved the moment you became eighteen."

"Oh! So, I can't be tracked now?"

"Correct." He faintly smiled. "You are under my protection. I do things differently."

I scoffed, "Like locking me up in my bedroom?"

"If I'd told you not to wander the halls at night, would you have listened?"

"Probably not, but I still don't understand why you needed to lock me in my room?"

"I did it to protect you. I didn't want you running into the unsavory creatures I sometimes consort with."

I reckoned whether I agreed with him or not, I needed to move on to the next question, "So, now what? Where do we go from here?"

"I'm speaking with the councilmen tonight," Aidan sighed. "It's our yearly meeting, Samhain. Most know it as Halloween."

"Isn't this the night we're supposed to marry?"

"Those plans are on hold. I'm planning to turn my uncle in for treason. They may charge me as an accomplice. Regardless of the outcome, I won't allow my uncle to take your life."

"I don't understand why he wants to hurt me? Is it because I'm different?"

"Remember, I said you are a genetically engineered angel?"

"How could I forget," I half-laughed.

"The purpose of your creation is to bridge the gap between life and death. Through you, we can create a world free from sickness and death. Even famine would be a thing of the past. We call it The New World Order."

"That sounds great, but I don't see how one person can change an entire planet."

"It won't be an overnight change. It would be up to you and me."

He paused. "Since we are a perfect match, our children would be immortal, never to face sickness or death. They would live their life as intended, humankind living in perfect harmony, never dying or growing old."

"So, the Illuminati created me to fill the new world with healthy children with you?"

"Yes. We are spirit mates. Unlike humans, you don't have a soul. You have an essence which makes you even more unique."

"The Family calls me Dream Angel, and I'm an angel?"

"Yes, you're correct."

"And we are spirit mates like made to be lovers?"

"Yes."

"That sounds like hormones?"

Bane flashed a lopsided grin. "Our hearts are joined as one. Is that not proof enough?"

I thought of Logan. I didn't feel this static charge I have with Aidan. "I reckon we do have a connection."

Bane took me into his arms and claimed my lips.

When he pulled back, his eyes appeared saddened. "I will never forget you, even in my death." Tears slipped down my cheeks. "We have to go. I have to be at the castle to meet with the council and confront Van."

"You can't put your life on the line for me." I searched his eyes, terrified of the outcome.

"I have to stop Van from hurting you." Tenderness touched his blue eyes.

"If you reveal to the council that you had conspired with your uncle, they will kill you."

Aidan's jaw tensed. "I don't see another way around it. Once the council is aware of my uncle's scheme, they will arrest him, and you will be safe."

He gently tugged me to my feet and gathered me into his arms. "Hang on, Princess," he smiled down at me as I shut my eyes tight. The whirling struck, stealing my breath, but this time it didn't seem as violent.

In a blink, we were back on Saint Ann Street in front of Ms. Noel's house. The storm was fierce as ever. Lightning crackled across the dark sky as thunder rumbled, rain hitting us sideways.

Aidan pulled from his pocket something small and shiny. He clasped my hand, placing it in my palm and closing my fingers around it. His voice was loud over the hammering rain and hallowing winds. "I want you to have this in case I don't make it. I'm sorry for my part in this tragedy. I wish we could've had more time together." He gathered my chin into the palm of his hand. "You mean more to me than you'll ever know, my love." His blues churned with sorrow.

I opened my hand and saw a key. I jerked my gaze back to Aidan. My brows furrowed, confused. "What is this?"

"It belongs to a safety box at the Savings and Loan bank downtown. I've collected bonds; enough money for you to live on for the rest of your life."

"Aidan, are you saying you're going to die?"

"Anything is possible. That's why I want you to get the hell out of here. Don't stop until you are far away. Do you understand me? No argument! I don't want you anywhere near the castle. If Van sees you, he'll kill you."

"Aidan, I can't leave you to face Van and his minions alone!"

"Love, I am more than capable of taking care of myself. Trust me and go find safety!" He gathered me into his arms, molding my curves to the contour of his lean body and crushed his lips to mine. I returned his passion with just as much fervor. The rain was rolling off our faces, but it didn't waver our trance.

Then in the next instant, without another word, he'd vanished. He was gone just like that. Maybe forever. Tears welled as I blinked back the reality of our love ending before it had a chance. I crumbled to my knees as surging water gushed over me.

I had to pull myself together and get out of sight. I stumbled to my feet, struggling against the rainwater pulverizing my body. If I didn't take shelter, I would surely drown. As the relentless rain pounded me, I shoved the key Aidan had given me in my pocket and dove into the driver's seat of my car, quickly closing the door behind me.

My fingers had gone numb as I fumbled with the key, jabbing it into the ignition. I paused, staring outside at the downpour pummeling everything in sight, the wind whipping the trees back and forth, the swelling drainage ditches. The water was collecting fast, and I was terrified that my small car would wash away. I stalled, unsure what to do. Traveling in this storm was suicide.

Chances of me escaping Aidan's uncle were slim to none. Then why run? Shouldn't I stay and fight? Sam's suggestion came to mind. Could Aidan and I infused our powers together and save ourselves from his sinister uncle? I shook my head, laughing, on the verge of hysteria. If there were an ounce of truth to Sam's theory, I had to act on it.

Doused in a dark coating of weird, I believed this strange world existed, and with some uncanny fate, I'd been brought into the folds of this calamity whether I was up for the challenge or not.

Accepting that fact, I had to address the next imminent question … did I want to be shackled to Aidan Bane Du Pont for the rest of my life? I reckoned, since both our lives were on the line, it was a small price to pay. The illogical was logical. I had to find Aidan before it was too late. I couldn't stand by and let him die for nothing.

I hastily turned the ignition. The motor churned but wouldn't roll over. The more I tried, the more the engine dragged. "Crap!" I gritted my teeth, muttering curses. I slammed my shoulders back into the seat and took a long breath, giving it a rest for a minute. Then I tried the ignition once more. This time, I got the clicking sounds of a dead motor. "Son of a bitch!" I pounded my fist against the steering. "Now, what do I do?" Tears clouded my vision as I wiped my eyes with the back of my hand. "Of all nights, my car had to stall!"

I glimpsed out the window. Streaks of rain lined the windshield. Raging water surged on both sides of my little bug. I knew Saint Ann Street would soon swallow me up. If I stayed in the car, I'd drown.

Somehow, I had to get to Aidan's and pronto. How did I do this on foot? Then a light went off in my head. I spotted Francis' car. I bit my bottom lip. Half the time, Sara left the keys in the ignition. A spark of hope lit the fire under my ass as I flew out of the car, fighting through the mud and raging water. I forged ahead for the Cadillac.

THE OTHER WOMAN

*D*aylight had broken, but the storm hovered over us in darkness. The sun had vanished behind the bruised clouds, hopeless and gloomy. It was as if the heavens had reined havoc upon us, unfortunate souls.

The whole idea of racing off in a dead man's car through this godless cyclone had to be bat-shit crazy. Yet here I was with insanity strapped to me like a chastity belt barreling down the flooded streets, praying I made it to the castle safely.

I kept my eyes on the road and my foot on the gas, plowing through the rainstorm. Even though Francis' car was a heavy lug that weighed a ton, I could feel the tires hydroplaning. Rain hindered my vision even with the wipers on full speed. I jumped with a start when a blast of thunder roared, and lightning ripped across the sky. I was terrified, but I didn't let my fear stop me. I kept plugging on. I had to get to Aidan before it was too late.

Coiling around a bend on a back road, using poor judgment, I turned the wheel too sharply. Before I corrected the error, the car went into a tailspin. I slammed on the brakes, which I soon realized my huge mistake. Out of panic and fear, I screamed, shutting my eyes tight, knowing that I was about to wrap this lug around a tree.

It all happened so fast. I slammed my head into the steering wheel, knocking me silly. Pain pierced through my muddled brain as I touched my forehead and drew back something sticky and wet. My eyes dropped to my fingers. Blood! Soon everything became a blur.

When my eyes opened, I was lying across the seat of Sam's old Ford truck, my head in his lap as he sat in the driver's seat.

The first thing that prompted my attention was the throbbing pain from my forehead. I touched it and quickly withdrew. "Ouch!" I squinted against the pain. "What happened?" I groggily asked.

"Chickadee, you smashed into a tree. You'll be okay. A little blood never hurt anyone." Through the light of the cab, I glimpsed up at Sam's bright smile. I was glad he found me.

Then I drew in a sharp breath, jolting to a sitting position. "How long have I been out?"

"I don't know. I found you conked out."

"What time is it?"

"10 o'clock."

"In the morning?" my voice hovered on the edge of hysteria.

"Huh! Chickadee, you must've hit your head harder than I thought. No, evening."

"Holy crap! Sam, I need you to take me to Aidan's castle. I have to find him before it's too late." My eyes pleaded with him.

"Too late for what?" Sam's face expressed confusion.

"I don't have time to explain. Can you help me or not?" I snapped.

Sam paused, eyeing me suspiciously. "Do you think that's wise considering everything you know about him?"

"Yes!" I wrung his coat into my fingers, making him look me straight in the eyes. "I know I sound like a raving lunatic, but you have to listen to me."

Sam's eyes sparkled with excitement as he replied, "Batten down the hatch! It's gonna be a bumpy ride." He turned the key, the engine roared. He grabbed the gear with vigor and shoved it forward, hitting the accelerator. We were on the road headed to the castle. "How did you manage to wrap your car around a tree?"

"I lost control going around the bend. Everything else after that is a blur."

"Why are you out in this shit-storm?"

I gaped, "Have you lost your mind? You do remember our lengthy discussion at Ms. Noel's, right?"

Sam glimpsed at me, taking his eyes off the road for a second. "I'm sorry for the things I said about your dad, man."

"Don't worry about it." I bit my bottom lip. "I know you don't trust Aidan, but I do. Call me stupid, but my gut tells me to believe him." My eyes studied Sam's face.

His eyes churned, holding my gaze. "Right or wrong, you have to follow your gut," he smiled, gunning the gas.

"Thank you, Sam! Thank you from the bottom of my heart."

I sat back in my seat, inhaling deeply as the sense of urgency hovered over me. I was grateful for Sam's help and understanding. Perhaps, I judged him too hastily. After all, he was my guardian. All the bad behavior had been a masquerade to fool everyone. It made sense and eased my mind knowing he could be trusted. The long stretch of road was treacherous, sharp winding curves that threatened death. The relentless rain still hammered us hard, but we forged on, determined to reach the castle.

After a fight through this crazy storm, we reached the gates of Castle Manière. Strangely, the gates were wide open. The gates were always closed.

"Sam, have you ever been here before?"

"I came to a summer party. I don't remember much afterward. Too much booze," he said with a wink, grinning. "By the way, there's a Halloween party tonight."

"Here at the castle?" Why didn't I know?

"You didn't know? Old Blue invited everyone." Sam glimpsed out his window. Though the clouds remained angry looking, the rain had slowed. "If I were a bettin' fellow, I'd wager that the party got canceled."

"Maybe, but then why are the gates open?" I stared at the iron fortress.

"Good point," he said as we passed the gates and rolled down the winding drive.

All at once, Sam's eyes hitched to something down the drive. "Looks like some kind of party happening 'ere." Sam nodded up ahead.

I followed his lead and nearly dropped my teeth. Several cars lined the drive. Not just your everyday run of the mill, Buick's either. These cars were the crème de la crème. "Whoa!" I whistled. This must be the

Family that Aidan mentioned, the Family that only came on important occasions. An unexpected dread paled my face.

"Yep! I'd like to drive that cherry-red Bugatti." Sam's eyes glossed with longing. "That there car happens to be a Rembrandt, limited edition. Sweet, ride too!"

"You sound like you've gotten behind the wheel in one." I thought it was sorta weird, considering his truck was a dinosaur.

He exhaled. "Nope, just read about it in a magazine."

Soon, we were approaching the front entrance. "Sam, stop here. I don't want to draw attention." I didn't say why or whom I intended to avoid, I figured for Sam's safety, he might be better off not knowing.

Sam pulled off back into the shadows where no one could see us. "Do you want me to tag along," he asked. "In case you need backup?"

"No. Go home." I smiled. "This is something I have to do alone. I appreciate your help." I leaned over and wrapped my arms around his neck, planting one big kiss on his cheek. I drew back, smiling. "Thank you so much for rescuing me!"

"No matter what, Chickadee, you're my gul!" Sam smiled, though a flicker behind his glint appeared unusual. I shrugged it off. This storm had everyone jumpy.

"Okay, wish me luck!" I tossed one last smile before bolting from the truck. I made a dive for the bushes planted against the castle. I'd blend in with the shadows of the brush, going unnoticed.

Luckily, the rain had ceased, but the ground remained saturated and muddy. I stayed low to the mud, on my hands and knees. By the time I found Aidan, mud would be pouring from my pores. On all fours, I ventured off to find Aidan Bane Du Pont. After crawling over the roots and creepy crawlers, I finally came to a window filled with light. It was high, almost too high for me to reach. I looked around to see if I might spot something to stand on, a broken tree limb, anything. "Ah!" I spotted a couple of bricks only a few feet from me, hiding under a bush. I grabbed them and placed them under the window. It gave me just enough height that on my tippy toes, I could see just above the sill.

My heart skipped a beat as my eyes soaked in the festivity. I felt like a child peeking around the corner at the grownups. The grand room boasted with a decent crowd of people, chattering about merrily. As far as I could tell, there was no Halloween party here. What laid before my eyes reminded me of the movie Gatsby. The women dressed in glittering gowns that flowed like liquid glass around their legs as they sashayed across the floor. Each lady came with her arsenal of jewelry, diamonds that glittered from their earlobes to their ankles. Judging by the size of the jewels, these housewives invented the Ritz.

The men in their tuxes blended as penguins huddled for a leisure sunbath. It was easy to separate the tall from the short and the thick wasted from the lean.

Waiters carried trays of assorted finger foods and long stem glasses filled with a light gold bubbly beverage offering up to the guest. Lively music vibrated the glass pane. I noted a stage of dancers. They seemed out of sorts, like strippers busting in on the president's daughter's ball. They stuck out like a sully, sore thumb.

One male dancer featured in the center of the other dancers wore only a strange headdress that resembled a ram with two horns. Apart from being nude, the male dancer was breathtaking as he was eerie. His body gleamed of bronze skin, smooth as porcelain.

The other dancers were men and women, scantily dressed. Five, I counted, encircled the one with the horns, kneeling before him, stretching their hands over his body, touching him intimately. I wanted to look away, but I couldn't peel my eyes away. Frozen, I watched as the indelicate dancers engaged in a lustful frolic. And I thought cable was racy.

Moving right along, I eased down to the next window, spotting more couples dancing as laughter wafted in the air, and generous amounts of champagne gilded every diamond-marked hand.

I took a slight interest in watching one older lady, dressed in a bold print gown. Too bright and loud, she reminded me of Sally. I laughed to myself. The portly lady, white-gloved and carrying a tall stem glass in one hand, was attempting to edge her way through the cluster of guests and lacking grace. She stumbled about, bumping into others, spilling her drink onto a couple of ladies that looked like they wanted to strangle her.

I watched for a moment longer and nearly forgot why I was here. I slid my gaze to the other side of the room, and my breath stalled. I gawked in disbelief. Tears stung as the suit of foolery slipped over me. I spotted Bane dressed in a tux dancing with a beautiful blonde. I couldn't help admiring her elegance and poise as they glided across

318

the floor in one smooth, fluid motion. I watched as Bane and the woman gazed into each other's eyes like star-crossed lovers. He smiled at something she whispered in his ear.

An unexpected bout of jealousy bit me like a two-headed snake. Feeling the sting of betrayal, I was pissed, humiliated, and hurt. I risked my life for a man that had made a mockery of me. I suddenly felt conscious of my clothing, covered in mud. Whatta fool I'd been. I didn't belong here, and I didn't belong in a world filled with over-stuffed pockets.

I pulled from the window. I couldn't watch any more. I'd seen enough. Sara was right. I was frumpy and undesirable. I reckoned I deserved whatever I got for being the biggest idiot in the freaking world! I hated him, but I hated myself more. I wiped a tear away with the back of my hand, smearing mud over my cheek.

I took in a long sigh. The venture was over, and the kindled romance had ceased like the rain. The sooner I left this town, the better off I'd be. Maybe Ms. Noel would join me.

Shoulders slumped, spirits shattered, I started to turn away and look for Sam, then I caught a flash in the corner of my eye that stopped me in my tracks. I cut a hard look back through the window. I noticed that all the men were heading out, leaving the party.

I panicked, thinking I'd spotted. After a few heartbeats passed, I relaxed. The tuxes were venturing off in another direction, a remote area of the castle, it seemed. I had to know where the men were heading? I watched as a sea of black and white gathered in an assembly exiting the grand ballroom and abandoning the women.

I spotted Aidan, still holding the blonde's hands, kiss her on the cheek. His face glowed with genuine affection for her, an endearment he'd never shown me. The young woman held his heart. It hurt me to watch, yet how could I not. They looked good together, both blue blood, beauty equally matching beauty. As for me, I was the girl looking in from the outside, where I belonged.

The men were quickly diminishing, and my insatiable curiosity was imploring me to follow. Swiftly, I moved farther down to the next window, seeing that the men had disappeared. I inched down to a couple of other windows and stopped.

I heard a loud voice shouting angry words. I recognized the voice. I eased up to the sill of the window and peeked barely above the rim.

My mouth dropped open as my eyes widened with fear. Dr. Van Dunn was speaking to one of his MIB. This one I didn't recognize. Not making a peep, I listened to their conversation.

"I have a sneaky suspicion that my nephew is planning to abort our plans. That Judas-kissing bastard," Van railed.

"Yes, master, and you wish me to find the girl and bring her to you?" The creature's words were robotic, cold with no inflection to his speech.

Chills pirouette down my spine.

Van growled. "Yes, bring her to me! I'll be down in the dungeon in a coterie with these idiots. Bring the girl to the warehouse and contain her there until I arrive."

"Yes, master."

"Whether or not my nephew wishes to deny our alliance, I'm taking the girl's powers. After I obtain the girl's magick, I'm coming for my nephew next. I think it's time I get rid of that pesty immortal."

Stepping off the bricks, I dropped to my knees, raking in as much oxygen as my lungs demanded. Van's hard-knock determination sparked a deep-seated fear in me that left me reeling. If I didn't know panic before, I certainly did now.

Crap! Whether I wanted to or not, I had to find Bane! Where the hell would I find the dungeon? I assumed there was an underground chamber. I bit my bottom lip, thinking. Come to think about it, Jeffery mentioned the castle had hidden passages all through its inter-dwellings. "That's it," I murmured. There had to be a hidden door leading to the dungeon. I nearly jumped with joy!

I quickly took off toward the back of the castle. What I knew about history and midcentury castles was that attacks started from the front. Why else would they have a drawbridge and water to divert takeovers? A back door or trap for escape would be in the least conspicuous place. I figured the hatch leading below would be ancient as hell and at the base of the castle wall. I hoped my hunch was right. I wasn't looking forward to scaling a sixteenth-century castle.

With only the moonlight for my guide, I plunged onward. I followed the line of the castle, hoping to find the secret door. My hand brushed across the jagged stone, hoping to find anything that might resemble a trapdoor. Corner after corner, ripping vine after vine, I saw nothing that indicated a secret entrance. I retraced my tracks and again came up empty-handed. I rested my hands on my hips, sighing with a feeling of defeat.

I leaned against the stone and gazed over the pea-green meadow that stretched as far as the eye. The moon was full and cast its silvery light over the tips of the hills. The land was plush with rolls of green carpet. It was beautiful.

I trekked through the thick lawn, heading for a large oak, the only tree on the premises. Not looking where I was stepping, my shoe caught and down I went, face first.

Frustrated, I flipped over on my back, kicking with anger. Wet to the bone, chilled and enshrouded with mud from the top of my head to my big toe, I just wanted to go home and sleep until never came. One swift kick to the ground, and my foot hit something hard. I yapped from the sudden pain, but then my eyes widened with surprise.

I blinked, looking at my foot, and there it was. My mouth morphed into a huge O. I bolted up, diving for it. My hands banded around something cool to the touch and felt metal.

I began ripping away vine after vine, down to the soil. I started shoveling mud with my bare hands. I didn't care if I dug to China.

Out of breath, my muscles aching, I sat back on my heels in disbelief as my findings stared back at me. "It looks like a lever, a door," I whispered excitedly.

Flat against the ground like a storm cellar door, although it looked like something from the stone ages, the wood appeared almost petrified. By its tattered wear, I assumed it was fragile. Still, it was a door, and I bet it led to the secret chamber that Bane's uncle described. I wiped away the mud off the lever as best as I could.

My eyes combed over it, examining its style. I'd never seen a doorknob like this. It certainly matched the castle's age, yet how this door and the latch survived all these centuries baffled me.

I marveled over the mechanics of the door. The best way I could describe it was that the latch consisted of a horizontal bar held in a vertical loop, with a fastener attached to the doorframe. No argument, the thing was older than time, but none of that mattered. The only thing that concerned me was whether the years had rusted it to ruin. I reckoned there was only one way to find out. Holding my breath, I banded my fingers tightly around the latch and gave it a stout tug. At first, it didn't give as I strained against it, teeth grinding, face colored red. Then suddenly it released its iron grip, sending me backward off my feet and landing on my derrière. "Ouch," I shrieked in pain, quickly rolling off my rump.

Then my eyes blinked back at the lever. Gathering to my feet, I grasped the handle and heaved the wooden door. It roared with defiance, but I had a stern determination that I was getting my way. The door dislodged as I flung it open. A thick cloud of dust burst into my face. I dropped to all fours, gasping and choking. Stale air and old dirt had the reek of manure and tasted even worse. "Yuck!" I hacked up the foul-tasting grime.

After clearing my windpipe, I rose to my feet, wiping the smut off my face with the back of my hand, only to make it worse. What an awful mess I'd become, looking down at the caked mud and layered dirt. "Stop being such a big wussy!" I gritted my teeth. "Good grief! I was freaking out over a little smut!"

I shook my shoulders, shrugging off my paranoia as I stepped up to the berth in the ground. Cobwebs and darkness blanketed the cavity, preventing me from getting a good look. I stepped back, repulsed. I realized the risk, stepping off into that black hole. Snakes and alligators were just the cherries on the whipped cream.

I pulled out my phone and slid the bar across, and that was when I realized the battery had died. "Damn, damn, damn!" I twirled on my heels, banging the phone against my forehead in a temper tantrum. I wanted to stomp the phone to oblivion. Forgetting to charge my cell appeared to be a death wish. With a long huff, I stuffed the useless phone back in my pocket, cursing words that would've made a sailor blush.

I dropped to my knees, hovering over the hole. I reached down, swiping at the cobwebs. I couldn't look at the sticky stuff, and I nearly lost my cookies when the gray icky stuff clung to my hands. I quickly raked my palms over the blades of grass. It took several takes before I got the tangled web off my hands. "Yuck!"

Taking a deep breath, I forced myself to stick my head through the hole. Forcing my eyes to open, yet holding my breath, I leaned in through the hole and peered inside. With the little light the moon reflected, I spied stairs.

With no flashlight, not even a match, I couldn't gauge how far down the hole went. I felt confident it wasn't a water-well, spotting the stairs.

I worried about the condition of the steps. As far as I could tell, the stairs looked like cobblestone and mortar. I had no idea if the old stones would crumble under my feet. There were so many scenarios that each was as equally dangerous. If I reached the bottom in one piece, would I meet the infamous uncle and his diabolical servant, the MIB?

Or would I find myself in a den of poisonous snakes or snapping alligators? I shuttered over each possible synopsis. "Crap!" I bounced to my feet, stepping away, my fist cuffed to my mouth.

Hysteria was only a breath away. I inhaled deeply and exhaled, dragging in as much courage as the night air allowed.

I stared at the black hole. Either I take the plunge or turn myself over to Van. I twirled on my heels, searching the ground. I needed something for backup, protection. My eyes landed on a long stick under the oak. I hurried to it and snatched it up. I grabbed a rock, tossing it in my hand.

Cutting my eyes back at the hole, I glared at what I must confront. I just needed to do it, not give any thought, but dive, feet first. "I. Can. Do. This!" Teeth gritted, in one long stride, I dove into the belly of darkness

THE KNOWING EYE

"Oh, geez!" I froze. Needles bristled my neck as if I were dangling on a tightrope blindfolded.

Submerged into complete utter blackness, I was on the verge of delirium. The story of Jonah and the great whale plagued my mind. "Okay," I inhaled the stale air, "I can do this," I softly coaxed myself.

I placed my hand on the jagged wall. Instantly, I felt cobwebs sticking between my fingers. I jerked away, drawing my hand to my chest. "C'mon, no wussy-pussy," I snorted to myself. I inhaled a deep breath and settled my palm against the coarse stone. The other hand clenched the long stick as I waved it in front of me, feeling for any obstacles. As far as I could tell, the path appeared to be unobstructed, but it was narrow.

I stretched the stick to the right as far as I could and discovered nothing but air. No wall on that side. "Great!" One slip and I'd fall to my death.

I tossed the stone, listening for its echo. Several seconds passed before I heard a loud thud. I had a hunch, it was fatal.

If I stayed close to the wall, I should be okay. Well, in theory. I steadied my feet and felt a rough surface that I assumed was cobblestone. It was uneven and unsteady as I heard small pebbles tumble down the steps and fall off the ledge. I'd have to ease down, testing each step before I bared my weight on the next. "Okay, so far, so good," I blew out a breath.

On the count of three, one foot at a time, I eased down, once step at a time. My balance was as sturdy as possible under the circumstances. I took another step, descending farther into the abyss.

Before I realized it, I'd gone down several feet. I peered above my head to the entrance. The hole had grown much smaller and dimmer. I was sinking farther down into the bowels of blackness. I still had no idea how far I had to go before I reached the bottom. Although no doubt, if I fell, it'd be the end of me. I sunk deeper, palm flat against the wall, my stick in front of me guiding like a blind person.

Just when I started to feel confident, I made an error in judgment, stepping too heavily on a loose rock. The stone gave out from under me, and I dropped my stick off the cliff. I felt myself slipping, but I couldn't correct the fall. I tumbled down several feet. I landed with my upper body on the cobblestone as my legs dangled off the edge. My heart raced as I held onto a sharp rock, but my grip was slipping. I had to act fast. With all my might, teeth clenched, I swung my leg over onto the stone, hoisting myself back up on the steps. I rested against the wall, heaving air into my lungs. I thanked my lucky stars that I was still alive.

Then I remembered my stick, my trusty guide. Curses flowed. I was so pissed at myself. Despite my frustration, I was stuck. Whether I went up or down, it was treacherous.

With fear and determination, I slowly rose to my feet, my back flush against the wall. Steady on my feet, I continued to descend deeper into blackness. Suddenly I halted. I felt a flat surface, and in the far distance, I heard an echo that sounded like water dripping in the distance. The sound felt so familiar that the hairs on the back of my neck bristled. I inhaled a dusty breath and reached out, knocking the cobwebs away. Just past a few feet, I felt only space. My pulse kicked up a notch as I slowly made my way, one step at a time, hands groping whatever blocked my path.

Then all at once, my fingers touched a barrier on each side of me. I gasped! A corridor! The passage was narrow but more than enough room for me to pass. I eased a breath, relieved that I was on a flat surface, no more crumbling steps under my feet. Still unaware of what lied ahead, I proceeded with caution.

There was another mass of cobwebs as I swallowed down a full-blown panic. I fought fearlessly, bush-hogging every clinging web that slapped my face. As I made my way further down the corridor, I spotted a dim light flickering ahead. The dripping water echoed louder now. From what I could tell, I was approaching an opening, possibly a chamber. I picked up the pace with new zeal; my eyes fixed on the small light.

As I coiled another corner, I stopped dead in my tracks. My heart lurched as if I'd stepped into my dream, the very same dream that had been haunting me since childhood.

The small candlelight held only a dim glow, mostly shadowing the chamber. My eyes washed over an assembly of thirteen men draped in black hooded-robes, all facing a high-point panel of nine men dressed in stark white robes wearing gold masks. I assumed they were the councilmen, Bane had mentioned. Soft whispers wafted through the atmosphere as I strained to listen.

I crouched down, keeping back in the shadows, and crept closer to the front, hoping to get a better look. I found a shadowed corner and ducked behind the water fountain. I crouched low, hidden in the shadows, peeking past the edge of the basin. I remained as quiet as a mouse.

On the far left, there were carvings on the wall. With the faint lighting, I had a hard time making it out. The petroglyphs were old symbols and drawings cut out of the stone, very similar to Egyptian art, highly symbolic. I recalled reading that symbolism played a significant role in establishing those in power and order. Each symbol of Egyptian gods and goddesses was omnipresent in Egyptian art. How strange to have these markings on the castle walls.

One carving drew my attention; the depiction came from a mix of different animals. I assumed some mythical creature stemming from pagan religion. The carving though a bit worn, had seen better days. Still, I could make out its contour. I found it fascinating and eerie at the same time. Its head had the shape of a serpent. Resting on top of its head, laid two horns like a beast. The body was scaly, resembling a dragon. The front feet were feline, yet its hind feet were razor-sharp talons, as deadly as the creature's scorpion tail—what a strange beast.

Above the panel, I noted a glowing eye in the center core of a triangle sitting on top of a pyramid. Chills wrapped its sharp claws around my spine as I realized that the eye was the same eye on the back of a dollar bill.

"Holy hell," I murmured silently. "What have I gotten myself into?" I held my hands flush to my chest, feeling my erratic heartbeat. Why did I get the feeling that somehow the eye carving here and the eye in my dreams were connected?

All at once, I heard feet stirring, and a loud thud hit the ground. I spotted two black-robed men carrying white sticks. What the hell! I strained my eyes to catch a better glance. Then it struck me. "Holy cow! They were carrying bones! Human bones! My blood ran cold as I watched. The two men set the pile in a pit in the central core of the chamber and started a blazing fire that rose high as it licked its way to an opening in the ceiling.

Then things began to shift fast. On the side closest to me, I spied a five-pointed star carved into the cobblestone floor as it began to separate. Out from the bowels of its grave came a throne gilded in gold.

The men in robes gathered around the giant fire as the men in white robes rose to their feet. Hands joined, faces lifted to the flame, they all commenced chanting.

The cadence rose higher as the intensity grew. The words were unclear, but I didn't have to understand. Deep to my core, I knew it was pure malevolence, and it sickened me.

I wanted to run, but my feet lodged to the ground.

When the chanting stopped, silence spread amidst the robes. A loud crash like lightning scoured the chamber as dark, ominous clouds grew with a fierce wind, howling. The men had fallen to their knees, bowing, arms spread, and palms flat to the floor as if in prayer. "Prayer to what?" I asked inwardly. The fire thickened, dancing, swirling, expanding, shrinking, and licking the sky.

I watched in terror as a creature stepped from the center of the blaze. Unlike anything I'd ever witnessed, the creature possessed the shape of a man engulfed in flames. When the life-form cleared the fire, his body morphed into something unfathomable.

I couldn't call him a man or even a human. No human could walk through roaring fire unscathed. Suddenly, I recalled the dancer with the horns earlier. It hit me; the creature was a deity, a god they worshiped.

How did I describe this creature when I didn't believe my eyes? His scaly body had to have stood at least ten feet tall. The horns he wore appeared as his crown, and a protruding tail that was as threatening as his piercing fangs sent crippling chills down my spine. The beast's feet were talons and his hands, claws of a lion's. He was hideous.

Repulsed and terrified, I wanted to run for my life, but I feared for my life and Aidan's life too. I had to know if this monster planned to kill Aidan.

Without any warning, I heard a familiar voice rise from above the deadly quiet. I raked my eyes over the chamber until I spotted Aidan. My heart lurched for him. Oh, my God! I feared for his life.

Cloaked in black, he stood tall in front of the golden throne where the beast sat, holding a scepter with the tip carved into a snake. I steadied my eyes on Aidan as I listened.

"Rise, my brothers," the creature's strange mechanical voice shouted. *"We are gathered here tonight to feast!"*

A quiet stir washed over the chamber as the black and white-robed men rose to their feet, now facing the beast.

"My brother Du Pont, it is good to see you once again. I understand you have something to purge among this good fellowship of brothers." The creature spoke with authority.

"Yes, wise one, your presumption is correct." Bane kneeled before the beast.

"Then get on with it, for we have a celebration to revel in our success," the creature hissed, pounding his scepter against the stone floor.

"Thank you, omnipotent one, for allowing me to take the floor." Aidan's voice rose among the men and spoke with confidence. "It has come to my attention that there are some among us who wish we should proceed with another direction in obtaining our New World Order." Aidan's face's voice was dark and grave. "I have been blackmailed into following orders I wish not."

Loud chatter spread like wildfire in a dry wheat field.

All at once, the beast leaped to his feet, stomping his scepter against the floor, demanding obedience. "Be quiet, you imbeciles!" The creature snarled with loathing. He glided his eyes over the cloaked men and then cut his baleful gaze back to Aidan. "Now, proceed with your grievance, my brother." The creature seated himself back onto the golden throne.

"I have been a long-time servant to our cause, working toward our new

system, where mankind's world and the mystical realms can live in peace and harmony. We are at the threshold of profound change, and I desire to do my part."

"And your part, my brother is?" the creature asked.

"The girl, the hybrid, has been entrusted to my care. She has been promised to me in a blood contract," Bane hesitated. "The girl is our one true answer to bring forth perfect health and harmony to our worlds! Lord Cruis, we should embrace this awe-inspiring chance and allow this precious gift to live and fulfill her destiny."

Suddenly, emerging from the scarlet robes, a man rose and approached the beast. "I am truly sorry for speaking out of term. If I may be so bold, I'd like to approach the council?" The man encroaching was Van.

A hush scurried over the robes.

"Brother, Dunn, you better have a good reason for this disruption!" The creature's threat solidified the cluster of robes.

"What my nephew is trying to say is that we must go forward as planned with the hybrid. However, my nephew has expressed his concerns with the young girl," Van exclaimed. "The child is not accustomed to our way of life and may not be a willing prospect. I fear to say," Van spoke fluidly.

The creature leaned forward, his eyes targeted Van, "Why do you speak this?"

Bane stood silent, shoulders straight, face unreadable.

"The girl has had a dreadful life. Living with an alcoholic host has taken a toll." Van's voice was sharp and angry. "I have reason to believe the hybrid is not stable. Rumors have surfaced that she is a drug addict. If this is true, she is a contaminator and must be dealt with accordingly," Van spewed his lies.

"Has the hybrid lost her virginity?"

"Yes, I believe my nephew, sire, have compromised her purity."

The creature cut his eyes at Bane. "Are these claims true, Brother Du Pont?"

The slew of black robes stirred with busy chatter.

In a flash, the creature sprinted to his feet, snapping his deadly tail at the cloaked men. "Quiet you, feeble half-wits." He railed with indignation. The chamber settled, and the creature turned his attention back to Aidan. "You may answer the question, Brother Du Pont."

Aidan cut his deadly eyes at his uncle and then back at the creature before he replied. "The girl remains pure. I'll not hide my true feelings any longer,"

Aidan bellowed. "In the beginning, I desired no part of the hybrid. She's rebellious, willful, and has a short fuse of a temper." An echo of laughter spread among the robes. "Seeing past her flaws, I have had a change of heart, and therefore my wishes have changed as well. Cruis, great almighty, I wish to do my duty for the good of the cause by taking this young woman into my house of protection." Aidan stood tall and courageous.

Van shouted at Aidan. "You bastard! How can you betray me? You ungrateful ..."

Aidan remained silent, though carrying an angry scowl.

The chamber exploded into a restless clamor, feet shuffling frantically, fists raised in the air. The white robes and their gavels pounded with great force. The voracious noise penetrated the air.

The creature lifted his scepter high above his head as lightning shot out amidst the robes. In a hot flash, bodies scattered, heads ducking, men falling as their bodies go limp.

Then a sudden rush of silence fell, and the chamber stilled, eyes wide with horror. The creature paused, eyeing every robe carefully before he took his seat. "Brother Van Dunn," the beast addressed him with renowned disdain, "Another outburst and I shall have you for dinner."

The uncle nodded in silence, his jaw working.

"Brother Du Pont, I expect you to take the girl under your wing tonight. We all need to do our part. A new world rid of sickness, death, and famine."

Van leaped to his feet, taking bold steps closer to the throne. "Please, great ole one, you must hear me out," Van pleaded.

The creature snapped his eyes at Van. "If I allow you the floor, will you accept my decision once and for all?"

"Yes, Cruis, of course," Van answered swiftly.

The creature turned his attention to the white robes, "Do you agree with my decision of hearing Brother Van Dunn's argument?"

In a collective voice, the white robes agreed, shouting, "Aye!"

Cruis nodded his head for Van to proceed.

"I am not blessed with immortality as my nephew. Of course, I use that term loosely, Brother Du Pont has lived for three centuries, and I am still working on one." Soft chortles of laughter bubbled from the robes. "Yes, I am merely a human in our brotherhood. Please allow me to speak on behalf of my human brothers and my brothers, who are of the gods." Van began to plead his stance. "Let us share tonight a wondrous gift." His arms stretched apart, *welcoming.* "Let us partake in the girl's essence, and we all rule as gods! We won't need to wait for her offspring to bring forth perfect harmony to our system. Let us take what belongs to us now and relish in the delight of ever-lasting life," Van roared as he searched through the sea of robes.

"What good is a kingdom when you have no courtiers?" Aidan challenged Van. Then he addressed the robes, "If we abort our original goal, we will be facing extinction! Will gods rule over each other?" Aidan cut a hard glance at Van and then turned his focus on the creature and the white robes. "This," Aidan pointed to his uncle, "Are the ramblings of a desperate, aged man, craving attention like a suckling baby crying for his mother's tit." Aidan's voice caused a shutter throughout the robes. "The girl belongs to me," he fisted his chest, showing dominance. "And it will be a cold day in hell if anyone challenges me." With a predatory stance, Aidan stood tall and threatening.

The creature tapped his chin as he appeared to ponder over both men's arguments. "You must ask yourselves why these lowly ones deserve a second chance. Humans are each other's worst enemies. They destroy everything in their path. Because of their hard-headedness, they are plagued."

Aidan spoke up. "I believe the girl is the answer to our prayers, sire. We, the Illuminist, created her for this sole purpose. It is our true destiny to enter a New World Order free of pestilence and war," Aidan shouted with fervor. Excitement soared among the robes as they bellowed their support.

Van scoffed. "My dog knows more tricks than that bitch you want to bed!" Vile spewed from Van's mouth.

"Silence, old man! I've had enough of your insidious lies," the creature lashed out.

Immediately, Van bowed his head as if in remorse, though I had a sneaky suspicion, it was far from what he held in his black heart. "Forgive me, sire."

The creature stood up, gripping his scepter in his right hand. "The councilmen and I will grant this wish to Brother Du Pont. If this hybrid does not comply, your punishment will be death." The creature narrowed his black eyes. "Are we clear, Brother Du Pont?"

"Yes, sire!" Aidan gave a curt bow and exited the floor.

The creature, Cruis, turned his evil gaze on Van. "For your treason and lies, Brother Van Dunn, I shall revoke your privileges as a member of this Brotherhood. You shall remain disfellowshiped until I decide you have learned your lesson." The creature roared, "Be off with yourselves," the creature lifted his gaze, "This meeting is adjourned."

The robes began chanting. They dropped to their knees, kneeling to the creature as he stepped back into the blazing fire and vanished.

All at once, the atmosphere became airless. My lungs were begging for oxygen, and I had to get the hell out of this crypt and fast.

TREACHERY

On all fours, I crawled back to the passage I had entered. Once I reached the dark corridor, I leaped to my feet and made my way out like a bandit on crack. As I rushed for my life, a rhythm of prayers hovered in the air. The sickening sound made me nearly vomit, but I pushed it down and did some serious talking to my legs move.

Finally, I reached the stairs, and up I climbed, praying I'd gone undetected. Plunged into total bleakness, once again, I found myself groping, inch by inch, my way back to freedom.

With no warning, I heard footsteps approaching, and panic struck. Whoever was coming was gaining on me and fast. Holy crap! I'd been caught. My lungs tightened as my heart raced. Trapped, I had nowhere to hide; I did the only thing I knew to do… *run!* Devoured in complete darkness, I rushed, step after step. All I could do was keep moving, praying I reached the entrance.

Without warning, a beam of light struck my back. I stopped dead in my tracks. I'd been found. I prayed it wasn't Van. Wondering if I could jump, I peered over the ledge and gasped. The drop had been a bottomless pit that ventured far past the light. I was doomed. Like a gun to my head, I turned with my hands in the air, squinting against the bright light. My breath lodged in my throat as I braced myself for the worst.

"Chickadee! What the hell are you doing down in this hole." The friendly voice pierced from behind the flashlight.

I cuffed my hand over my eyes. "Sam! Is that you?"

Sam dropped the flashlight to his side. "Is there another fella that calls you Chickadee?" he smiled.

I rushed to him, throwing myself into his arms and planting a huge kiss on his lips. "Sam, I can't tell you how happy I am to see you!"

"I think you just showed me." He lingered a moment as our eyes hitched. "What are you doing down in this crypt?"

The accounts of what I just witnessed flooded my mind. "Sam, we need to get out of here, pronto!" I grabbed his hand. "I'll explain later."

"I get the feelin' you're right." He slightly bent over the edge, shining the light down over the ledge. "Dadgum! I sure would hate seeing anyone fall onto those spikes.

"Come on, Sam! We gotta go, now," I urged, tugging his hand.

"Yes, ma'am!" Sam held the light in front of us, guiding us back to the entrance. In a few minutes, we were out of the rabbit hole, bent over dragging in hordes of fresh air. I'd never swallowed so much dirt in my life.

After a minute of clearing the dust, Sam spoke up. "Gul, what possessed you to go down that hole?" His voice seemed full of irritation.

I reckoned, I had him worried. Good ole Sam. I smiled to myself. With not a lot of time to explain, I took the easiest route. I lied. "I fell down the hole."

"Was this trap open when you fell?" He eyed me suspiciously as he lifted the tattered door to the entrance and closed it up, latching it back.

"Hmm, yes," I lied. "I don't even remember a door being there. I was walking along and tripped." That part wasn't a lie. I felt terrible not telling Sam the whole truth, but my gut warned me to keep it to myself.

"You're not hurt?"

I looked down at my filthy clothes. "No. I'm good, just dirty," I laughed.

Sam wiped my nose with his finger, drawing back a film of dirt. "I'd say you look like you've been mud wrestling." He flashed a seedy grin, "A good look on you." He raked his wolf eyes over me quite boldly, making me squirm uncomfortably.

I changed the subject quickly. "Where're you headed?"

"Oh, I figured I'd hang out under this oak in case you fall into another trap." Sam broke out into a broad smile, but it didn't reach his eyes. It struck me as peculiar. On second thought, I shook off the notion. Why wouldn't I trust him? He was my guardian and protector.

"Sam, thank you for being here for me."

He gently squeezed my shoulder. "I got your back!"

"I understand why you behaved the way you did. You were under-cover." I let out a ragged sigh. "I appreciate your advice. I've decided to go through with the infusion spell."

"You're going to complete the bonding ceremony with Aidan after all? Risk everything?"

I'd made my decision. It was my turn to save Aidan. "Yes, risk and all."

"Are you sure you're makin' the right decision?" Doubt veiled his voice.

"I have to do the right thing." I couldn't turn my back on Aidan now. He'd risked his life to save mine.

"Gotcha, Chickadee!" Sam snatched a piece of grass out of my disheveled hair and smiled. He tossed his thumb toward the oak. "I'll be right here waitin' if you need me." He leaned in and hugged me. When he drew back, there it was again, that strange glint in his eyes.

I blew it off. This night had everyone on edge. "Thanks, Sam! You're the best."

A sense of urgency swallowed me as I feared I'd be too late finding Aidan. Despite seeing him with another woman, I sensed that Aidan had been protecting me all along. I was confident he wouldn't betray me now, so I had to step up to the plate. Van wasn't going to stop until he got what he wanted. As long as I stayed a virgin and my powers unprotected, Van was a grave threat. If he succeeded in taking my essence, whatever that meant, he might become unstoppable, which meant Aidan was in jeopardy too.

The way I saw it if I could stop Van in his tracks by giving myself to Aidan, then why the hell not? It was merely a means to stop this night-mare that seemed to imprison Aidan and me. If such a little thing as giving up my virtue meant saving our lives, it was a small price to pay. Chills covered my arms. I needed to find Aidan, and the best person who could rally him up for me would be Jeffery.

Huddled in front of the kitchen window, I spotted several wait-staff in black and white uniforms coming and going with silver trays filled with hors d'oeuvres. I spotted Jeffery wagging his finger at a young waiter. I couldn't hear a word, though Jeffery's jaw was flapping just as hard as his finger-wagging. He hastily grabbed the white towel from the young waiter's grasp. Jeffery dotted his face with a cloth. I laughed. When did Jeffery ever work up a sweat?

The young waiter mostly nodded his head, and then Jeffery waved him on, dismissing the young man. In a huff, Jeffery spun on his heels, pushing his way through other staff members. Most everyone was neck-to-neck, shoulder-brushing-shoulder, hustling to keep the guest flushed with food and drink.

It was not until Jeffery's eyes landed on me did he stop. His eyes grew the size of baseballs, and his chin nearly hit the floor. Discreetly, he pointed to the side entrance. The servant's entrance!

Not wasting a second, I crawled over roots and mud until I reached the back door. Keeping out of sight, I ducked behind the only bush by the entrance... *a rose bush*. After tonight, I'd never feel the same about the flower. "Ouch!" I mumbled huffily.

With a loud bang, the side door opened and out stepped an agitated Jeffery. His back faced me as I slid from behind the tortuous thorns. Quietly, tip-toeing, I tapped him on his back. Jeffery jumped with a start, screeching. "Lord, have mercy on my delicious soul," He shrieked like a woman, his hand clutching his chest. "Gurrrlfriend, I swear, you have no idea what I've been through tonight. That deranged cousin of Mister Aidan's is going to be the death of me yet!" Jeffery fanned himself with the towel. "Stay the hell away from that ugly mofo scoundrel!" Jeffery drew in a deep drag off his cigarette. Then he raked his eyes over me and halted on my face.

Like a light switch, Jeffery's face soured. "What the hell happened to you?" he eyed me from head to toe. "I know you is a bit raggedy, but dang gurrrl, please tell me that you haven't tract that nasty filth in my kitchen?"

"Will you shut up a minute?" I peered around to see if anyone was in earshot. "Aidan's uncle is looking for me." I spit out. my mind suddenly switched subjects as my eyes landed on Jeffery's cigarette. "I thought you said you were quitting,"

Jeffery puffed on the cigarette and blew the stream through his nostrils. "Gurrrl, I had quit for a whole two days until tonight. I had to use this as an excuse so I could meet you." He held up the cigarette. "This shit is your fault, seeing you here with a price on your head, and that mofo cousin of Mister Aidan's, I swear on my momma's grave, you both have gotten on my last nerve. I needed a smoke just to get me through this terrible night. I got blisters waitin' on all these snooty white folks. And. I. Hate. Stuffy. White. Rich. Folk too," Jeffery hammered away.

After he puffed again on his cig and withdrew smoke, I managed to jump in. "Sorry to hear your troubles, but dude, I need to find Aidan!" I rushed my words.

Jeffery eyed me critically. "You gonna go see him lookin' like a frightful mess. Gurrrlfriend, don't you wanna keep the man?"

"My clothes are the least of my troubles. Where is Aidan?"

"Well, if your sweet little self must know, he's havin' one of those secret meetings. They have 'em every Halloween, some superstitious shit about appeasing the dead. I never got that, but whatever floats their boat."

"Jeffery," I interrupted abruptly. "Shut up and go find Aidan. We're in danger."

Taken aback, his mouth popped open and then closed. "You ain't playin'," he studied my face for a second.

"No, I'm not. Can you get Aidan for me, please?"

He drew on his cigarette as the cherry deepened to a fiery red. He dropped the cig and stomped it out with his foot. "I guess I best go get him." He went to reach for the door, but I stopped him, "Wait! I almost forgot."

Jeffery stopped and turned to face me. His brows dipped down full of piss and vinegar. "What now?"

I stepped up to him and leaned closer to avoid anyone from listening. I pulled out of my pocket the key and placed it in his palm. "Take this key. I want you and Dom to get out of here as fast as you can. Aidan gave this key to me."

Jeffery's eyes went bug-eyed. "I know exactly where this key comes goes. I was with him when he opened up the account. Do you have any idea how much money is in this safety box?"

"Right now, I don't care. I'm more worried about you and Dom's welfare. You took a risk in helping me escape, and Dom has been nothing but kind to me. I'm returning the favor. Promise me the two of you will get the hell outta dodge."

"Are you sure you want to give this to Dom and me?"

"Yes! Please go find Aidan." A tear escaped and ran down my cheek.

"Ah, honeychile, don't cry." Jeffery started to hug me but halted. "I'd hug you, but I ain't gettin' Armani dirty." Instead, he patted me on the shoulder like I was contagious with a disease.

I laughed as I wiped the fallen tear with Jeffery's towel.

"Listen here," he caught my gaze, "Go past the pool and hide in the guesthouse. The key is under a pot plant by the door. I'll have Mister Aidan meet you there," Jeffery hesitated. "Don't go and get yourself killed," he warned. "We got some serious shopping to do when all these mofos leave. Gurrrlfriend, you're in desperate need of a do-over." Jeffery scrunched up his nose.

"Jeffery, I love you too!"

LILIES OF DECAY

*J*ust as Jeffery said, the key was under the plant. As soon as I unlocked the door, I dove inside, shutting the door behind me. I leaned against it, trying not to freak out. My chest heaved, screaming for oxygen. The air felt stifled in this little cottage.

The problem wasn't the room. I was beginning to doubt myself. What the hell was I thinking? Did I really believe that he'd sweep me into the embrace of his arms, and we'd ride off into the sunset happily ever after? I should be more inclined to believe that the blonde in Bane's arms earlier tonight would be the one. Did I need a brick in the head for me to realize that he hadn't been entirely honest with me? Then the comment he'd made to that creature, "she belongs to me," did I want to become his possession? Mistrust began to spread like venom. I wrapped my fingers around the doorknob. Maybe I'd been too hasty. Leaving with Dom and Jeffery or even with Sam sounded more logical.

"Forget him; I'm outta here!" I turned the knob, but something stopped me. I heard a shuffle in the shadows. My breath stalled. I wasn't alone.

When my eyes lifted, all my fears and doubts had vanished. "Aidan!" He stepped from the dark into the moonlight, beautiful and tall as ever. I ran into his arms and melted. Tears streamed from relief that I'd found him. "Hey," I pulled from his embrace, "I'd been standing here for several minutes. Why didn't you say something?"

He flashed that lopsided smile that always stole my breath. "You were so beautiful standing there in the moonlight. I found myself lost."

I studied his face for a moment. Charming, but it didn't seem like him. Then again, he was under a lot of pressure. "Hmm, I've been thinking." I bit my bottom lip. "Can you pop us somewhere safe? We need to talk."

"Sure! Where to," he smiled down at me.

"I don't know. You usually decide." That was odd. Aidan always took the lead.

"All righty then, hang on, got just the place."

All righty? Has Aidan changed his speech pattern, or could this be his true self? "I'm hanging."

Aidan pressed me against his chest a little too hard, and I gasped. "Lock your hands around my neck, babe." His voice swirled of sensuality. "I wouldn't want to drop you."

I followed his advice with my eyes shut tight. In the next breath, we were floating in some kind of draft. It was so different from the other times, and not nearly as extraordinary.

We stopped abruptly. I opened my eyes, and we were standing in a field of lilies. As far as my eyes could see, I saw stark white with dark, emerald green underneath. The sun was setting, and a deep pink splashed across the sky.

"Are we in a different dimension?"

"Dimension?" Aidan's eyes appeared baffled.

"Hello, wake up!" I air knocked on his forehead. "You were the one who told me about altered realities." I stared at him, wondering if he'd wiped his brain with angel dust.

"Oh, yeah! I remember. Sorry, I've had a lot on my mind tonight."

"I see." It was evident Aidan wasn't going to mention the secret meeting. His holding back pissed me off. I never was one for holding my tongue, and I reckoned no point in changing that little idiocy now. So I plunged into it feet first, "Aidan, why are you acting like this?"

He jumped back as if I'd stabbed his big toe. "Gul, what's your problem?"

"I found your secret dungeon, and I watched that vile creature come out of the fire."

Aidan just stood there gawking.

I slugged him in his arm. "Why are you playing stupid? I saw you with my own eyes."

"I don't remember what the dickens you're talkin' about, but don't hit me again," he gravely warned.

Funny, I didn't recall Aidan having a Southern drawl. Then he did just threaten me. "Or what," I challenged.

"Or I'll knock you off your big feet."

"Tell me the truth, or I'm leaving!" I crossed my arms, holding my gaze to his.

"How about we start with you taking off your clothes and spread 'em wide for papa!"

"Ugh! Don't speak to me like I'm one of your whores!"

"I'll talk to you, bitch, anyway I choose."

Had I been blind to his true nature? I scoffed. "This conversation is over!" I spun on my heels, heading to god-knows-where.

As I brushed over the field, a startling realization hit me square in the jaw. The sun hadn't moved. The atmosphere was void of air, no wind tousling my hair or the treetops. It was as if everything had frozen in time. Then there was the silence, no birds chirping, no crickets singing, and the scent hovering smelled of decay. Nagging pain in my gut told me we weren't even on earth.

I cut a hard look back at Aidan. "Where are we?"

A virulent grin seized his face, "Wouldn't you like to know?"

"Actually, no, take me back, now," I demanded.

Aidan slowly circled me, hostile and menacing.

My heart hammered against my ribs as I eyed his every calculated step.

"Aidan, why are you behaving like this?"

"I'm giving you what you want." His eyes darkened dangerously.

"Yes, you have been very generous to me, but can we take this down a notch? You're scaring me."

Aidan tilted his head backward and released a deep belly laugh. Chills dawdled down my spine. "I like scaring you!"

"Just take me back!"

"Do you think leaving will right this apocalyptic doom you have created?" Cords in his neck jutted out.

"I didn't ask to be born, and I didn't ask to be bound to you either," I shouted.

"Shut up! Undress or else I'll tear your clothes off your body myself, and when I'm finished ripping your insides apart, I'll leave you for dead!" He flashed his pointy teeth.

When did Aidan's teeth become jagged and sharp like a piranha? I jumped back, losing my balance and falling to the cushion of flowers. Only I landed on something sharp. I drew my hand back and saw blood. My blood! Since when were daisies sharp like glass. "What the hell kinda place did you bring me to?"

He leaned down over me, looming in my face. I smelled his whiskey breath. "I'm only going to say this but one more time. Take. Your. Clothes. Off!"

I rose to my feet, meeting his perilous gaze. "Screw you!" I turned my back to him, and that was when I'd made my worst mistake.

Before I knew what hit me, I was on my back, and Aidan was throttling me. Violently he began ripping my clothes off. I did the only thing I knew to do, and that was to fight back, arms swinging, fingernails digging, feet kicking as hard as I could against his incredible strength. I screamed for mercy at the top of my lungs. Back in the haze of my mind, I recalled Sam's warning, and I desperately wished I'd listened.

In return for my pleas, he wrung his fingers around my neck, squeezing the life out of me, shutting off my oxygen. I pounded at his arms fiercely to free from his steel clenches, but he was far more powerful.

Deprived of air, the burning in my throat and lungs morphed into a scorching fire. I felt my life slipping away as he bore down his hold. The light grew dimmer by the second, and my will to fight weakened as my body grew numb. I vaguely felt his release of my throat.

By now, he'd forced my clothing off my body. The shredded cloth lay in a pile next to me. Exposed under his violent prison, as if I was in a tunnel, I watched as he unfastened his belt and unzipped his pants. A sick coldness enshrouded my body as I sank into unconsciousness, fading to the point of oblivion.

Then suddenly, I was jarred back to my harsh reality, and only the burning agony in my gut kept my senses alive. In a last-ditch effort, I began thrashing. I reached up and drove my thumbs into his eye sockets.

For a quick breath, he loosened his grip as he clutched his face, howling. Right on cue, I kneed him, dead center in the groin. He doubled over, groaning. "You stupid bitch!" His face knotted, drool dripping from his mouth and clenching his crotch.

I rushed to my feet, darting for the safety of the trees, but before I could gain momentum, he toppled me to the ground. My feet flew out from under me as I smacked my head hard on a sharp rock. A sudden bout of pain struck as something sticky and warm began to drip down my face. *Blood!*

Every cell in my body screamed with searing misery as I wrapped my fingers around my neck, gasping for air. So much pain; blinding pain.

"Whore, I'll teach you not to run from me!" That's when he reared back with his iron fist and crushed my jaw with such force that it seemed inhumanly possible.

For a second, I blacked. When my senses returned, I begged for the sweet release of death. "Kill me, why don't you?" Racked with anguish, I couldn't take much more.

Swiftly, Aidan threw me down on my back, jarring me back to the present, forcing my legs apart, my mind spiraling as my death became more imminent. He outweighed me better than a hundred pounds and was much stronger. Rape filled his face, and hatred diseased his heart. Under my racing mind of all things to wonder, it didn't make sense for Aidan to take my life.

All at once, I heard a loud crack, and an unbearable stab quickly followed. I tried to scream, but my throat burned too much. My arm. Oh, dear god, I couldn't move my arm. I think it was broken. *Oh, god, just kill me!* I shouted in my head. I couldn't stand the misery. The excruciating torture seized my breath. When I opened my eyes, the lilies were gone and, in its place was decay. Skulls and bones everywhere. Now I understood the stench. The field was an illusion.

"It's your fault that I'm in this mess in the first place. If you'd not moved here, everything would've been fine." Aidan rambled, madly. "I hated you from the moment I laid eyes on you, Chickadee!"

Chickadee? Wait! "What the hell," I gasped. "You're not Aidan! Y-Y-You're Sam! How did you … "

Suddenly, it was Sam's voice piercing the atmosphere. "That's right!

You fell into my hands so easily. It almost seems unfair." His dark eyes churned with malice.

A rush of relief washed over me. I'd reached the end of the line. I welcomed death. I never imagined my ending would be so vile and violent. I wondered if I'd see my dad. Would he be there at the gates of heaven welcoming me? I smiled to myself. That would be wonderful. No more worries, no more disappointments, all sadness melted into nothing. Death was tranquil, serene.

Thrust back to the present, Sam rose up over me, grinding his body against me. Somehow, he'd dropped his pants to his knees, and he didn't shy away from his manhood as he groped himself. Sam shot a wicked smile. "You like what you see?" he moaned, trying to force a kiss upon me.

I took his lip between my teeth and bit down hard. I tasted blood in my mouth and spat it back into his face. He jolted back, touching his lip and drawing back blood. "You whore!" he railed as he backhanded me. It hurt like hell, but I wouldn't give him the satisfaction.

"Aidan will hunt you down. You're dead!"

"My cousin has my father to worry about. I hope he finds me," he boasted. "I plan to leave your remains on his doorstep," he growled. "I'm going to make sure no one gets your essence!" He smiled ominously.

"So you're Aidan's cousin? Who is your father?"

"Van is my father, Chickadee! The very one who wishes your death," he sneered.

"Get off me," I hissed.

"Why would I do that? We're having such fun. Besides, you're gonna be dead in a few!" He flashed his jagged teeth, sharp and unnaturally shiny.

I closed my eyes as Sam poised himself. I prayed for a speedy death.

Abruptly, something snapped within me, like a tight lever releasing its grip. A dark flash shot past me, and a roaring sound assaulted my ears.

Out of nowhere, a shadowed figure sent Sam spiraling into the air and crashing to the ground in a bloody heap. Losing consciousness, I forced my eyes open and saw Aidan crouched in a war stance standing over me. He snarled with savagery as he rose tall and fearless.

I attempted to ease up on my elbows, but I'd lost too much blood, and I had only one good arm. My head felt heavy, and it was even harder to hold a thought. Death promised. I laid there, surrendering to its sweet beckoning call.

WE BELONG

S lipping in and out of consciousness, I couldn't tell if I was dreaming or if it was real. The lilies returned, and a bed of soft flowers comforted my broken body.

Two male voices pierced the atmosphere as I drifted in and out of a dream state, listening...

"Sam, I warned you not to go near her," Aidan roared as he charged Sam, launching him several feet away with one powerful druid blast of white lightning.

Sam tumbled backward, slamming into the ground. He jolted to a sitting position, shaking off the sting, blood dripped from his mouth. "Come on, Cuz!" He staggered to his feet, taking the back of his hand and wiping the blood from his lips. His breath sounded short-winded. "I was just having a little fun with her, is all."

"You've done enough harm. I'm ending this now!" Bane's voice spurred from blind rage.

"Aw, Cuz! We're family. Where's the love?" Sam's voice appeared shaken.

"It left when you kidnapped Stevie! You crossed a line, dear cousin, and now you have to pay," Aidan promised gravely.

"I've been paying all my life!" Sam's mad laughter bounced around my brain. He'd fallen into the pool of hysteria. "My wonderful father has made me into the creature I am today, a psychopath," he paused, "And for something that wasn't my fault, you punish me by taking my life?"

Bane's voice, though powerful, filled with despair, "Do you think being in this family has been easy for me, for any of us," he shouted. "Your father has been blackmailing me for a long time now. My beloved cousin, we both have our story to tell."

"How about we sit down and break bread, Cuz?" I pictured Sam smiling as he extended an olive branch.

"Nah, I think we've said enough. I have to stop you from hurting any more women. It has to end here."

"So, it's just like that? No second chances!" Sam growled. "I remember you made an error, and my father took you under his wing. He hid the truth from the Family to save your pathetic ass!" Sam bit out in anger. "I get caught with my pants down over some inept girl, and now your hell-bent on killing me?"

"Enough is enough, Sam! You're damaged goods. No one can control you. If the Order doesn't act and stop your madness, you're going to blow our cover. Your conspicuous behavior has gone beyond reason. You must be dealt with."

"Oh, and you, my cousin, an assassin, has never harmed a soul or taken a woman against her will?" Sam argued.

"For the record, I've never forced my affections on any woman. As for my murders, they were justified!"

"Of course, you claim justice!" Sam's mad laughter echoed. "Your blood is tainted, Prince of Darkness."

"My cousin, I wish I could say I'm going to miss you, but I'd be lying."

"If you kill me, my father will come for you!" Sam threatened, grasping at straws.

Bane scoffed. "So be it. Let your father come. I am following direct orders from the council. They asked me to handle you. Sorry Cuz."

Out of nowhere, an explosion erupted that was so blustery it fueled everything in its wake. From the trees snapping to the leaves and branches falling like bricks, raining from the heavens to crashing to the ground, the atmosphere rumbled ferociously.

I lay helpless as I feared the outcome. I listened, though I slipped back and forth from unconsciousness. Silence swallowed the field of lilies. I opened my eyes for a second as I spotted a thin wafer of what appeared to be something burning, wafting into the dark sky, drifting high above the towering trees until it dissolved.

My eyes closed as peace engulfed my thoughts. I drifted afloat into

347

nothingness. My lungs opened, no pain, no sadness, fear had ceased. Only sleep, deep sleep.

Unaware of my surroundings, I felt warm arms embrace me. I heard a deep throaty voice filled with worry. "Princess, I take full responsibility for this."

"Aidan?" Did I hear a sob?

I was nestled against his chest as he confessed. "I should've stopped him before it came to this. I'm so sorry." His heart thundered violently, beating as fast as mine. "I'm going to make you better," he whispered.

When my eyes fluttered open, I gasped, my mind muffled. I didn't know if I were dead or alive. I began to wiggle until I heard a gruff voice.

"Lie still. I'm trying to heal you." I glimpsed up at Aidan's face, brows knitted tight, face strained with concentration.

I gasped, taken aback. "What are you doing?" My eyes filled with fright as I jerked away, confused, and terrified.

"It's okay! Lie still."

I recoiled, remembering Sam's vicious charade. A minute passed before I could comprehend that the man before me was the correct Aidan Bane. I relaxed, trusting him.

A golden swirl of magick engulfed me, penetrating its warmth down to the bone. My eyes dropped to my arm. Bane's hands flushed against my skin as a bright light spilled from underneath his touch. Somehow, my body began to ease from the pain and strangely mend.

"Sam looked identical to you. How is that possible?" My head ached, and my mind fought through the cloud of confusion. Had I'd been dreaming?

"Shush," Bane coaxed, faintly smiling with weary lines coating his forehead. "I can't heal you if you keep fidgeting."

I nodded. My voice had returned, and the burn in my throat had vanished, though my throat was parched. Even my head no longer hurt. I flopped my head back to the cushion of what felt like cloth, closing my eyes, letting the warmth soak into the pores of my body, mending all the broken pieces.

As though Lazarus rose from the dead, life spread through every cell of my body. The pain had taken absence, but I remained light-headed and weak.

After a few moments, the warmth stopped, and I heard Aidan shuffle, sitting back on his heels. I opened my eyes and saw how drained his face looked. Taken aback, my eyes drew in his taunt features. His lips were a light blue, and his skin almost gray, "Are you okay?"

"I'm fine." His breath was short. "Just give me a minute. Healing is quite taxing." A weak smile appeared on his pale skin.

"I'm sorry!" I reached out and touched his cheek. "I should've listened to you." Guilt swelled inside me.

"No need to apologize. How could you have known?" Though his smile was faint, the color in his face was returning, and his breathing eased.

"Where are we," I mumbled. My eyes raked over the forest. "We're back with the fireflies, the altered reality. What happened to the field of lilies and dead people, skull-bones everywhere."

"The field was an illusion Sam created. It doesn't exist, like dimensions."

I glimpsed around at my surroundings. I was lying on the same picnic blanket, the basket and wine bottles still in tack. "Did you change the scenery, or did we pop here?"

Aidan stifled a laugh. "You watch too much, Bewitched," he grinned. "I don't recall ever popping anywhere. I shift. It is similar to time travel. Creatures like us have the gift."

"I get it, shifting in and out of different dimensions." I burrowed my brows, baffled. "How did Sam shift?"

"Sam is fey. Part fey and part human." Bane grimaced. "Sam isn't capable of creating dimensions. His father 'clipped his wings' for lack of a better term."

"How can Sam be your cousin and Van, your uncle, since you are centuries older?"

"If we give each other titles, it makes us appear less conspicuous to outsiders."

"Are you blood kin to them?"

"No. The Order is part of the thirteen bloodlines. I am the last of mine."

"What did Sam mean by Van taking you under his wing?"

"Because I appear young, I must keep the appearance as such. Van acted as a guardian over me. It was only in pretense, nothing more."

"He was blackmailing you. There has to be more to the story," I pushed.

"My love," Aidan paused, "Will you allow me to handle Van?"

I gazed into his tender blues, and I decided to let it go for now. "Okay." I bit my bottom lip. "Can I ask you something else?"

Bane blew out an exhausting sigh. "Go ahead. Something tells me you'll ask even under protest."

"Sam came with Jen to Ms. Noel's house and claimed he and Jen were guardians. I believed him."

"Sam most likely eluded both your neighbor and Jen. Fey are known for such trickery. It was an enchantment."

"So the lilies and bones are make-believe too?"

"Yes, it came from his black heart. That's why it reeked. The Family had no founded evidence until recently, but we discovered that Sam is a serial rapist and a murderer." Bane paused. "I'd suspected his criminal behavior for some time, and that's why I didn't want you around him."

I rose to my elbows. "With a father like Van Dunn, I understand why Sam was so damaged."

Bane's face tensed with sorrow. "Not everyone turns evil from a bad parent. Take you, for example."

I laughed. "I'm not perfect. I lie sometimes." I bit my bottom lip.

"Yes, I am well aware, and let's not leave out that stubborn streak of yours," he smiled.

"Was it different for Sam?"

"In Sam's case, it was more nature than nurturing. His fey nature overrode his human side. He was void, no conscious. Fey are unpredictable. None are good," Bane sighed. "Sam really couldn't help himself," he blew out a long sigh. I caught a glimpse of sadness in his eyes. "I need to get you out of here."

"Good idea." I forced a faint smile. My heart hurt for Bane. It couldn't have been easy taking Sam's life. "Aidan, you did the right thing, taking Sam's life."

His jaw twitched. "Sometimes doing the right thing isn't the easiest."

"I know." Quiet settled between us for a few seconds. "Which brings me to something that's been weighing on my mind."

"Which is?" A glimmer deepened his blues.

"Don't get mad." I sighed. "I watched the secret meeting in the dungeon. I saw that blood beast step from the fire." I caught his gaze and held it to mine. "I heard everything."

Bane's blues darkened, his face unreadable, "Go on."

I licked my lips. "If we infuse our powers together, your uncle's attempt on my life would be futile. You'd be appeasing the beast and the councilmen, and we'd both be safe."

For a long minute, Bane stared at me blankly. I reckoned he was mulling the idea around in his head, and then he blurted it out. "Do you know what the spell entails?"

I swallowed hard, fighting off my uneasiness. "Not entirely, but I do know it involves losing my virginity." I shrugged, feeling the heat in my cheeks deepened.

"That's only a mere part of it, Princess." He searched my eyes. "If we do this spell, it will bind us together, forever. One cannot live without the other. No man or creature can separate us. Neither you nor I have the power to sever our ties." He held his gaze to me. "Are you ready to take that plunge? There's no going back."

"Will it protect us, both?"

Bane hesitated as he studied my face. "Yes. However, are you a willing participant?"

"I ask you the same thing. Are you?" No argument, I wanted to be with Bane. I just wasn't sure he wanted the same. Then I thought of the other woman. "I mean, I know you have an interest in someone else. I saw you with her tonight. I don't expect you to hang around afterward."

"What are you talking about, Stevie?" His brows arched.

"I saw you dancing with a beautiful blonde."

Aidan threw his head back and burst into laughter.

"What's so funny?"

"Silly, of course, I love her with all my heart!" his blues danced.

A sudden stab to the heart hurt worse than anything Sam or the MIB had done to me. "Oh, I see," I spoke, looking away.

Bane took my chin into his fingers and forced me to look at him. "The blonde is my sister, Helen," he smiled.

My brows shot up. "You have a sister?"

"Yes," he stared into my eyes. "I'm with you. Only you." His whisper was soft as silk.

"Then, I'm in if you are." I bit my bottom lip as our gaze locked.

He drew in a sharp breath, fingers raking his coal-black curls. "We have to do it tonight at the stroke of midnight for the spell to work." He grasped my shoulders, forcing me to look directly into his face. "We won't be using protection. It has to be completely uninhibited for the spell to work."

His blues were so piercing that my breath caught. This was one of the biggest decisions I'd ever make in my life. It was larger than life itself and grander than Aidan and I ever imagined. Even still, I wanted to do this for so many reasons. "I understand the consequences, and I don't care. I want to do this." I held my gaze even to his.

A faintly eager glint flashed in his eyes. "Okay, we have work to do, so we need to go."

All at once, Aidan cuffed his hand over his mouth to stifle a grin. "Hmm, as much as I love the view, Princess, I think you might want to cover yourself."

My gaze rolled down the length of my body, and my cheeks flushed. "Oh, geez, I forgot." I hid my eyes under my lashes.

"I certainly didn't." He flashed his sardonic smile.

Without another word, very gentlemanly, he shrugged off his white shirt and draped it over my naked body. Gathering me into his arms, he lifted me to my feet, and we shifted into the bliss of another dimension.

We twirled fiercely for only a minute, spinning and spinning, feeling sucked through a vacuum and coming to an abrupt halt. Our feet landed on solid ground, steady inside an unfamiliar house.

"Are you alright?" Bane held me on my feet, his face taunted with concern.

I grasped my forehead. We'd stilled, but my head continued spinning. "How do you get used to that? It's like motion sickness on warp speed."

Laughter burst from Bane, a rich, smooth laugh that I loved hearing. "My love, I forget you are new to my world." He bent his head to mine. "There's a shower in the back. Go clean up, and I'll be right back with food."

"Wait! You're leaving me?" Fear needled my neck.

"I have to get you something to eat." Aidan kissed my forehead.

"Can't you conjure it up with druid magick?" I felt a panic attack brewing.

"What we ate and drank at the fireflies' nest wasn't real substance. That's why the alcohol didn't affect you." He kissed my left cheek. "You need actual food in your stomach. We shalt have you going into shock." He gathered me into his arms and hugged me tight against his bare chest. The feel against his shirtless chest and my bare breast sent a delightful wave down to my core.

"Where are we?" I tilted my head, catching his gaze.

"This is an extraordinary place, a place that only I know. We are miles away from any creature, man or beast," he smiled.

I shook my head and smiled back. "Aidan Bane Du Pont, you are full of mystery."

"That I am," he grinned

"Hmm, while you're out, will you check on Ms. Noel and Jen? I won't relax until I know they're safe."

"Consider it done," he winked. "Now go get a shower," he demanded as he playfully slapped my rump.

MAGICK'S IN THE AIR

*M*agick sizzled in the cool air.

I stood in the mirror, attempting to brush out the tangles. After several futile tries, I gave up and settled for disheveled hair. There were more important things than my wild hair.

A wave of apprehension swept through me. I knew that after tonight, life would change forever. So much was in the balance, our lives, our future. If Bane and I didn't follow through with the right timing and the right spell, we'd still be vulnerable to Van. Our lives depended on everything.

On the plus side, if we infused our powers together, Van couldn't touch us. That was the theory anyway. I knew it sounded farfetched, but how could I deny it as well? I didn't see any other way out.

Another big question, did I want to lose my virginity to this man? It was more than just losing my virtue. Chills covered my body. To be honest, setting aside the peril we had against our backs, I'd still give myself to him. I loved Aidan. For the first time in my life, I was utterly in love. I sighed, staring at myself in the mirror, draped in a towel.

I needed to get my butt out there. I had no idea of the hour. We were at a time crunch, literally. With three deep inhales for bravery, I stepped out into the main room, trembling.

In the corner of the cottage, the fireplace caught my eye. I watched as the flames crackled. Then my eyes landed on the bed, white linen, and the cover turned down. Oh, my! My breath caught.

My eyes shifted to Aidan as chills rushed over me. His body rippled with muscles. Not huge like a bodybuilder, but like a baseball player's, lean and taut. My eyes slowly trailed down his abs, eyeing a thin line of hair that passed the band of his pants, spiking my curiosity.

Unaware, I was startled by a throat clearing, "Pardon me," he smiled. "Come eat." he nodded to a tray on the bed. "Oh, your friends are well and safe in their homes."

I smiled back. "Thank you." I turned toward the bed, eyeing the tray.

Food was the last thing on my mind as my cheeks blazed.

"Make sure you drink the wine. It's loaded with sugar, and it will ease your nerves." There was a hint behind his words as he tossed a towel over his shoulder, heading for the bathroom.

"Okay." I sat on the edge of the bed, staring down at the tray. The only thing that interested me was the dark liquid. Eating didn't appeal to me. My stomach churned with uneasiness.

I managed to down the full glass of wine, but as for the food, I mostly pushed it around on my plate. I never cared for eggs.

I glanced over by the fireplace and noticed on the floor a white circle against the dark wood. Inside the circle, a five-point star, also white. Two points erected at the top and one at the bottom. White candles burned at each point. I slid off the bed and padded over to investigate.

"What the hell?" I walked around the perimeter of the circle, careful not to smear it.

At that instant, I flinched. Aidan had come up behind me and goosed me. I turned to face him as our eyes collided, a smile played upon my face as I drank his deliciousness. His compelling blue eyes, the firm contour of his lean muscles, and the confident set in his shoulders sent shivers to my core. Still wet from his shower, his messy black curls fell loosely over his face. I bit my lip as my eyes drifted south, spying beads of water sliding slowly over his well-defined abs, ending at the towel wrapped low at his waist. He looked like he'd been sunbathing for days, sun-kissed to a golden brown.

Aidan cleared his throat, jarring my ogling. My gaze snapped back to his face. There were touches of humor encircling his mouth and spreading to his blues.

I broke the uncomfortable quiet. "Where do you want me?" Oh, geez! That did not come out the way I meant. I hid my gaze under my lashes, cheeks burning shamefully.

"You may enter through the opening in the pentagram, but you have to leave your towel here," his brow arched.

"Huh, right now, in front of you?" Nervously, I swallowed.

Humor toyed with his expression. "Princess, it's not like I haven't seen you naked." His eyes swept over me as he drew back with a lopsided grin.

"Okay," I exhaled. This was one time I wished for the dark. "Hmm, can you turn around, please?" I rolled my eyes as I clung to my towel.

Bane smiled, his blues bouncing with amusement. Not uttering a word, he turned his back. Silently, his shoulders shook.

Whatever, dude!

With reluctance, I dropped the towel, gathering my arms tightly to my breast. I didn't know why my bareness bothered me now when only minutes ago, I was utterly nude. Good grief! I was about to hand over my virginity, and all I could think about was if he thought I was fat. "All naked."

Bane slowly turned to face me, and my eyes locked with his as he dropped his white towel too. I reckoned, he was trying to make me feel more at ease, but standing close to him, completely exposed, made me even edgier.

"Shall we enter," he asked as he extended his hand to the opening.

"I guess." At this point, my heart was hammering so loud, I couldn't hear myself think.

I followed his lead and passed through the opening to the inside of the star. Bane entered after me, closing the opening with a short piece of white chalk. I focused on the fireplace as I listened to the chalk scrap across the wooden floor. I waited, standing in the center for further instructions.

After Aidan finished closing the circle, he turned to me. I tried not to let my eyes wander south, but they had a mind of their own. He was stunning, standing there in the candlelight before me. Every line of his hard body sent waves of ecstasy to a place deep within me. Not having a lot of comparisons, I reckoned I wouldn't have any complaints. He was ready for me, and the thought made me tremble. "Hmm, where do you want me?" I asked again as my voice quivered.

Aidan's brows drew together. "Are you sure this is what you want?"

I nodded, "Just nervous!" I forced a smile.

He stepped up to me, his warm breath caressing my cheeks. A vaguely sensuous light passed between us. "We can take it slow," he whispered, "We have time." His finger tenderly traced the line of my cheekbone. Silence lingered as his gaze was as soft as his caress. "You're so beautiful." His velvet voice was low and purposely seductive.

"Thank you," I said stiffly.

Still holding my arms tight against my breast, Bane gently tucked a strand of hair behind my ear. "Let me see you." A faintly eager look flashed in his eyes.

I nodded, unable to speak or peel my eyes from his. As soon as his reaching fingers touched the warmth of my hands, I felt safe.

"Ah," he murmured, "Much better." His blues brightened with pleasure. I stood there, frozen with a mixture of unchartered feelings swirling in my head. I held my breath in silence as he slowly and seductively slid his gaze over my body with approval. When his sensuous eyes returned to my face, my cheeks burned. "You're breathtaking, love."

It was easy to get lost in those pools of blues. I tilted my chin, lips parted, and before I realized it, Bane had claimed my lips, crushing me to him. Oh, geez! His tongue sent shivers of desire charging through me. One hand slid down my stomach to the swells of my hips. His touch was light and painfully teasing.

I pulled away, feeling a wave of apprehension. "Uh, are we going to do this on the floor?" It suddenly dawned on me the bareness of the floor, no pillow, no blanket, just the bare, hard floor.

"Yes, the spell is very specific." Bane's eyes smothered me with tenderness.

I couldn't possibly understand the full meaning of this act. I hardly knew anything about my inheritance. I only knew what I was told, a lab experience with angel DNA.

One thing I knew was that I wanted to be with Aidan as long as he'd have me. Nothing else mattered.

"It's getting close." Bane touched his forehead to mine, his hands resting on my hips. "Princess, are you sure this is what you want?"

I nodded, reassuring him that I did.

"Alright, then," he sighed, "Let's take our places." He stepped up to the one point of the star. "Here," he drew my hand. "Lie here, arms straight out, even with the side points of the star. Your legs will be spread out even with the two points at the end."

I gawked at him in disbelief, "Really?" I didn't envision it like this.

"Love, no one but me will see you."

I rolled my eyes. "It just seems to be more for show than ... " I covered my breast with one arm and the other spot with my hand. "I'll do it."

Just as he asked, I laid down on my back, flushed against the cool floor in the position he instructed. I shut my eyes tight, embarrassed of my exposed body.

Aidan joined me as he sat with his legs tucked under him, knees at the crest of my core.

My eyes flew open as I caught a flicker of silver and instantly gasped. "What are you doing with a knife?"

"We have to bind our blood. I slice my palm, and then you slice yours. Then we grasp each other's hand together, binding our blood as one." Aidan paused, his face pinched, "That's when I enter you. It's going to hurt, but the pain will only last for a second."

A tingling bristled against my neck, "How much pain?"

Bane's face twisted, "Because it's quick and harsh, it will hurt," he gave pause. "I'm not going to soften the works of the spell. You need to understand the full ramification of what we are doing." His explanation, though with good intent, didn't help with my anxiety.

"How many virgins have you taken?"

"Not as many as you think." The corner of his mouth tipped upward, suggesting a smile.

My heart sunk, thinking about what the uncertain future held for us. "So, what are we?"

"What do you mean?"

"Where will we go from here, from this night?"

"Oh, our future. We get married and live in bliss."

The shock of his announcement hit me full force. "This is one strange proposal," I laughed.

Aidan smiled like a cat that had eaten the canary. He was taking pleasure in my reaction. Suddenly, the humor dropped from his face. It was time. "Let's proceed."

All of a sudden, my breath stalled.

Aidan opened his right palm, and with no hesitation, he grasped the hilt of the blade and sliced a cut in his palm. Cupping his bleeding palm, he gave the knife to me.

I followed his lead by running the sharp blade across my right palm. My hands trembled so much it was hard to steady the knife. Somehow, I managed as I flashed a weak smile. In the next breath, we tied each other's bloody hands, extending our arms to the ceiling. Aidan began the incantation in a language I didn't recognize.

Following immediately, without a chance to catch my breath, he sealed the spell, fast and furious, thrusting himself inside me. The pain was so blinding, my insides felt jammed to my throat. I muffled my screams as tears streamed down my cheeks.

In the next breath, the room began spiraling; lightning shattered around us. Dark magick crackled in the air. A mighty electrical charge shot between us. When my eyes lifted to Aidan's face, his eyes glowed like marbles of fire as an explosion licked through us, leaving us both quivering.

When the spell finished, the candles blew out, and even the fire doused. The cottage stilled, and Aidan and I both collapsed. Our hearts pounded against each other as we both heaved for air, lying in each other's embrace.

THE ROSE

*T*he endless night had finally grayed into dawn when my eyes opened. Slowly, fighting a throbbing headache, my memories began to seep back into my skull. Aidan must've carried me to bed last night. I no longer felt the cold floor against my body. Instead, I lay in a soft cloud of feathers on the white linen bed.

I stretched and yawned as a sudden soreness struck the lower region of my body. "Ow!" I muttered, drawing my legs to my chest and rolling over to face Aidan.

To my disappointment, his side was empty, and the only proof he'd slept next to me was the slight dent in his pillow and the rumpled sheets. The cottage was still, and he was nowhere in sight.

Then I spotted a note with a long-stem, red rose on the nightstand. I scooted to his side and snatched up the note and the rose. I sat up, legs drawn to my chest as I tipped the rose to my nose and inhaled the aroma of sweet pepper. "How sweet," I whispered to myself. I snatched the note and unfolded it. The first thing that came to mind was a Dear-John letter. My eyes brushed over the words,

Getting breakfast. Be back shortly.
Forever Yours!
Aidan

I didn't know why but seeing the note lying there felt as if the rose's thorn had stabbed my heart. Why didn't he wake me? I sighed, feeling like a possessive girlfriend. Last night was wild. The spin-tale crazy crap, a storm of fireworks that charged through us and leaving us panting in each other's arms.

My eyes drank in the quaint room. It was fair in size yet tiny as an ant in comparison to the castle. Over by the front door, which I hadn't a clue if the door was an actual entrance, I spotted a stark white love seat, a coffee table made of distressed wood, and a vase sitting in the center filled with pink roses. Fresh, I assumed. On the other side, I spotted an overstuffed couch in the same theme color nestled in front of the fireplace.

My brow arched when I noticed no traces of burning wood.

By the bed, another vase filled with deep purple hydrangeas placed on my nightstand.

Funny, I didn't see Bane in this little house at all. I wondered if he'd conjured up this quaint little spot. The cottage's décor appealed more to a woman's taste. I recalled him mentioning that no one knew about this place.

I scooted off the bed and padded my way to the bathroom. I probably should shower before he returned.

Once I had finished showering, I walked out into the room when I spotted Aidan sitting on the couch by the fireplace. I noticed he'd found new clothing, jeans, brown leather boots, and a sweatshirt. His signature woodsy scent lingered in the air.

Feeling awkward, I still had the same towel from last night wrapped around my body.

Aidan's head snapped up in my direction. His blues sparkled. "Good morning, Princess. I trust you had a restful sleep?" I loved his perfect smile. I just wanted to fall into it.

"Yes, thank you." I made my way to the other side of the sofa and seated myself. I fiddled with my hair, still wet and dripping.

I noticed that Bane seemed preoccupied with the newspaper. The silence grew, and so did my uneasiness. "Umm," I cleared my throat, "Where you've been?"

He poked his eyes barely over the rim of the paper. "I went to get our food and clothes. It's over there on the table, hot coffee too." He nodded over at the bed. "Everything you will need is lying on the bed." He tossed a curt smile and went back to his newspaper.

"How considerate." My voice bounced off more agitated than I intended.

Aidan arched a brow and dropped the paper on his lap, giving me his undivided attention. "Is there something on your mind, my love?"

"I'm just feeling a little uneasy about where we go from here."

Aidan drew out a long sigh, "Are you having second thoughts?" His blues were like a chisel chipping away at me.

"No," I paused. "But I would've liked waking up next to you this morning. You could've at least awakened me before you left. "

He smiled. "I'm sorry. I didn't want to disturb you."

"Oh." Now I was acting like a possessive girlfriend. "I'm sorry too. I guess I'm a bit on edge."

"It's fine, love." There was a faint glint of humor in his eyes.

I wanted to change the subject. "So, we are safe from your uncle's clenches?" I couldn't let go of this nagging feeling that something was off.

"Now that we are linked, Van can't touch you. I imagine he'll be fuming for a while, but he won't go against the councilmen now that they know about his defiance."

"So now that we have this bond between us, we can't ever be separated?"

Bane paused for a minute, eyes sharp as a tack. "Do you wish part ways?"

"No!" I was startled that he'd asked such a question. "Do you think I would've agreed to last night if I wasn't in this for the long haul?"

Bane's eyes softened. "I don't think the works of last night has completely hit you, my love."

"Then help me," I insisted.

"It will take time. Be patient." Aidan smiled, yet it didn't reach his eyes. He went back to reading his paper.

My eyes shifted down to my lap and then slid to the fireplace, trying to gather my thoughts. Then I fixed my gaze on Bane's face. "I have questions."

The paper ruffled as he folded it and laid it on the other side of him, "For example?"

"For example, did you ever meet my father?"

"No, but I knew of his good deeds. He was a Samaritan."

"Really, like how?"

"Jon believed in the good of people. If a person needed his services and didn't have the money, he'd handle their case anyway. That was one of the good things about him. Unlike the Family, he didn't need money."

Tears began to surface, but I held them in check.

"Did my father know that the Family had chosen you?"

"Yes. Jon was informed."

"Did my dad know that you were a druid and immortal?"

"Yes, he knew."

"Why didn't my dad meet you?"

"The Family would not permit it, some technicality in the contract."

"Did my father approve of you as my chosen mate?"

"Quite frankly, I think that's why he agreed."

I sat back, baffled. "Then why did Dad change his mind?"

"I think when Jon realized the great lengths that Sara had gone to betray him, it opened his eyes, and he proceeded to stop her."

"Why does Van hate my father?"

Aidan drew in a sharp breath. "Hmm, who knows with my uncle? Your father was a well-liked man, and those he stood firm against hated him. Van and Jon had butted heads a few times. I think Jon saw Van's turpitude."

"Why was Van blackmailing you? What was he holding over your head to force you to partake in his rebellion?"

All at once, Aidan's expression tightened. "Love, in my world, our world, sometimes we are forced to make harsh decisions, decisions that those on the outside might not understand," he smiled, but it didn't reach his eyes. "Can we leave it at that and trust me for a change?"

I smiled, even though my heart ached for him. I could see in his expression it was a painful memory that he didn't care to rehash. I just needed to trust him that some secrets were best left alone. "Alright, I'll pass on that one," I paused. "You and your sister make wonderful dance partners. You both looked close." I still felt a little sting from watching them dance across the floor. Maybe it was because I felt more of an outsider and inadequate to be an equal partner.

A sparkle danced in his eyes. "Ah, yes, Helen."

I felt my neck bristle, "Just Helen?"

Aidan sighed. "Helen Claire Du Pont."

"Her name suits her. She's exquisite." A stab of jealousy struck my heart.

"Yes, for a sister, I suppose." The warmth of his smile echoed in his voice.

"I have more questions." I'd rushed my words before he closed me off again with his nose back in the paper.

He replied, "And?" He appeared open with my probing questions.

"Who was that creature? I saw him step from the fire?"

"The creature is a mythical dragon. He comes every year on Samhain to speak to us. We call it the Feast of Beast. On this night, the walls between different worlds are at its thinnest. Creatures such as Cruis can cross over into our dimension."

"He killed one of the men in robes. I saw it with my own eyes." I shuttered reliving the vision.

Aidan's lips tightened as he folded his hands and laid them in his lap. "That is a prime example of your lack of understanding. Lives are expendable in my world. Death is often a learning tool."

"What's there to learn after death? It's permanent!" I crossed my arms.

"What would you have me do? Strike the mythical creature that is immortal?"

"I reckon not, but I want to know why the man in black attacked me." This question I wasn't wavering on.

Aidan shifted, facing me. "Zak wanted revenge against Van for holding him prisoner. I found out later that he'd planned to attack you that night at the carnival, but I showed up in the nick of time. Crypts are creatures of darkness. They never do well in the company of humans. My uncle held him down from acting upon his true nature, and simply, Zak decided to take his revenge out by getting rid of you. He knew Van had banked on your essence."

Ice slinked down my spine. "Lucky me!" I frowned. "I have another question about your eyes? Last night when we were in the throes of the spell, your eyes blazed. What was that?"

"It's part of druid magick. The more powerful the spell, the more intense the fire becomes."

"Does it hurt?"

"No, it's not hot at all. It comes from the energy of the earth. This planet flourishes with electricity."

"Oh, will my eyes fire up too?" That was one ability I'd like to have.

"Possibly," he replied as he shrugged. "Concerning your talents, we are still on the trial basis of how far advanced your abilities will grow."

"Where does my magick come from?"

"Yours is a derivative of angel magick." Aidan leaned over and tucked a strand of hair behind my ear. "It's different from earth magick."

"I keep hearing I have powers, but the only time I've seen any hint of such was the explosion." I shrugged. "I'm still trying to understand that."

Bane sighed. "We can't be certain the full measure of your gifts. Right now, we can only speculate. I think as you become older, your abilities will manifest."

"I have the DNA of both my father and an angel. How is that even possible?" Trying to figure that out made my head spin.

Bane clasped my hand and squeezed gently. "I know how difficult this is for you," he hesitated, "How does mankind procreate?" he smiled. "Our scientists have advanced technology; alien technology that far surpasses anything humans can fathom."

"Is that why you became angry with me for going to the police because I'm... *different*?"

"I thought we covered this, but yes." He leaned closer to me. "If the hospital had discovered that you were not human, it would've started a catastrophic mess. The Department of Defense and the CDC would've jumped on you, and well, you can only imagine the rest."

I dropped my gaze to my hands in my lap. "It makes sense, but how did my pictures disappear on my phone?"

"Our world is cloaked. Humans cannot see our magick. We are hidden from their eyes."

"Then why couldn't I see the pictures?" I stared at Bane, not quite sure what to make of this.

He shrugged. "I'm not sure. Perhaps since you are young and coming into your gifts, your abilities aren't reliable."

I shook my head, feeling the impact of a world full of the strange and the unexplained, "But Jen saw the closet too."

"My love, I don't have all the answers. Perhaps, your friend Jen is a seer."

"What is a seer? Never mind, I don't want to know. I want to know if I'm immortal."

"At this point, we can only speculate, but we believe you will have a long life."

"Now, I have a question?" There was eagerness in his eyes.

"Ask away. I'm an open book." I squeezed my waist.

"Where's the key I gave you?" Bane gently tapped the tip of my nose.

Oh hell, any question but that one. "Eh, don't get mad, but I wasn't sure if either one of us would make it through the night alive. So, I made a rash decision to give the key to Jeffery." I bit my bottom lip. "I wanted Jeffery and Dom safe."

"I didn't give you the key to give it away. I wanted you to leave town." He drew in a long breath. "I didn't expect you to be willing to agree to the spell. That's why I didn't mention it. I'd hoped to have appeased the councilmen to buy us more time to disarm Van." He blew out a harsh breath. "Even if it meant killing the cad."

"So, you think this is my fault?" I gawked in disbelief.

"Not entirely. If you had just left-" Aidan didn't finish his sentence.

"I thought this was what you wanted?" I blew out, feeling the sting of shock.

A shadow of disappointment crossed Aidan's face. "You'll soon find out that there isn't a solution without consequences. We just need to make the best of an unpleasant situation."

I leaped from my seat. I was irked by Aidan's admission of regret. "If you didn't want me last night, you should've said something. I promise you, it wasn't a bed of roses for me either. It hurt like hell!"

Aidan gathered to his feet and made his way to me. I could feel his breath, brisk my shoulder, as my back remained turned to him. It was hard to stand my ground when I wanted him to love me back. "Will you look at me, please?" His fingers took my arm with gentle authority.

Swallowing the sob that rose in my throat, I turned to face him.

"I'm sorry." His blues were tender as he whispered. "I didn't mean that I regretted being with you. I meant that I wished it had been more natural. There was no tenderness last night. It was harsh and savage. I'm sorry you had to experience your first time like that. I wanted your first time to be a cherished memory, special."

I faced him, tears bordering in my eyes. "Where do we go from here?" I wasn't sure I was ready to face a lightless future without Aidan.

He touched my trembling lips with his thumb. "I thought I'd round up Jeffery and Dom, get my key, and we all would go somewhere far from here, out of the clenches of my uncle and the Family."

"Then what?" I swatted his hand away. I wasn't giving in that easily.

Amusement flickered in his eyes. "We get married." His fingers brushed my collarbone, lingering.

My eyes narrowed. "Stop that!" I pulled away.

"Stop desiring you?" His voice was deep and sensual.

There was a stir of longing, a yearning in my heart.

"Is there something wrong with wanting to make love to you?" Bane fingered the tip of my towel, tugging at it gently. The smile in his eyes contained a sensuous flame.

"Will you be making love or just having sex?" I held my gaze, denying my body's response to his tender touch.

A smile ruffled his mouth. "Perhaps, I should demonstrate." A mischievous glint in his blues apparently had a double meaning, and I was powerless to resist.

Suddenly, he lifted me into the cradle of his arms, and in the next blink, he eased me down on the soft bed. Aidan stripped his clothes off and dropped them to the floor, where my towel somehow ended up too. He climbed into bed next to me. Gently he gathered me into his arms as he whispered in my hair. "You are even more beautiful in the light." Aidan's lips kissed the pulsing hollow at the base of my throat.

A delightful shiver ran through me. This seemed so different from last night. Gentle, arousing, more... *loving*. Bane moved back to my face as he feather-touched my lips with a tantalizing persuasion that sent waves through my whole body. I wanted him, and I needed him even more.

Then things got heated. Aidan took my mouth with intensity, and I returned his kisses with as much desire, succumbing to the forceful domination of his lips. "You belong to me," he whispered, between kisses.

His hand moved under the cover to skim my hips and thighs as his fingers searched for pleasure points, slipping his hand between my thighs as my body arched from his skillful touch. "Holy, Toledo! What are you doing to me," I murmured, my breath panting.

"I'm making love to you," he softly spoke, his singeing kisses trailing down toward the lower region of my body.

"I love you, Aidan Bane Du Pont. I have from the very beginning, and I will love you forever." I weaved my fingers through his thick black curls and brought his lips back to mine, kissing him hungrily as if it were my last dying breath.

Soon our bodies were in exquisite harmony with one another, exploding into a downpour of fiery sensations. The real world spun and careened on its axis as our lovemaking reached astronomical heights.

When it was over, we laid in each other's arms, gasping in sweet agony. Love flowed between us as our hearts pounded against each other. Wrapped in the nook of his arms in a silken cocoon of euphoria, I found myself happy, blissfully happy.

My gaze lifted to his as I whispered. "Can I ask you one more question?"

Bane blew out a restless breath. "Only one more," he teased.

I smiled to myself. "Will I be spouting wings?"

Suddenly a burst of laughter filled the air. "My love, you're not that kind of angel." Then he leaned in and kissed me. "Sleep, my love. You've worn this old man out."

I giggled, biting my bottom lip. "This time was much better. It was sweet."

Aidan popped one eye open. "Just sweet," he huffed. "I demand a do-over," he teased, squeezing his arms around my waist, drawing me closer.

A soft laugh escaped my lips. "Okay, okay. It was hot too."

"That's much better. Never tell a man his lovemaking is sweet. It offends his manhood and a few other parts I shall not mention." He kissed my shoulder and then the top of my head. "Now, sleep, my lady," he smiled against my ear.

I giggled to myself, and before long, my eyes grew heavy, and I drifted off to a peaceful sleep.

DUPLICITY

I heard the sheets ruffle, and my eyes fluttered open. My gaze landed on Aidan getting dressed. "Do we need to get up?" I roughly whispered, taking in a sharp breath, trying to push through the haze of sleepiness.

He leaned over and kissed me gently, smiling as he drew back. "Stay in bed. I have to find Jeffery and Dom to get the key. I shouldn't be too long." He zipped up his pants and shrugged on his sweatshirt.

"Can't I go with you?" I sat up with the sheet drawn over my breast.

"I'm quicker if I go alone." He sat on the edge of the bed and shoved his boots on.

"Why the rush?" I didn't know why, but I felt an uneasiness about him leaving.

"When I return, we can go anywhere you wish. I promise." His blues glistened like cobalt.

I sighed. "I guess."

Aidan reached over and gave me one quick peck before he sprang off the bed.

"Aidan, I don't have a good feeling about you leaving," I blurted out as disquiet grated my insides.

"I assure you that I'll have the boys fetched and returned to you before you realize I am gone." He sauntered over to me and drew my chin in his hand as he eased down on the edge of the bed next to me. "I'll be fine. I promise." A strange glint behind his eyes struck me wrong. He sighed. "I should warn you, though."

"Warn me about what?"

"Princess, in my world, one can't take anything for what it seems." He lowered his chin and captured my gaze. "Believe only half of what you see and nothing of which you don't. Keep that close to your heart, and you will survive," he smiled, quickly kissing my forehead.

"Huh?" I shook my head. "You're giving me a child's riddle."

"I have to go. No time to explain." He leaned in quickly, kissing me on the lips, and then he vanished.

"Crap! I hate his disappearing act," I huffed. There was not a lot to do around here. My eyes washed over the quiet cottage. I decided to get dressed. So, I shoved off the bed and traced off to the bathroom and showered.

Momentarily, when I returned with only the towel covering my body, I made my way to the chair where Aidan had moved my clothing. I held up a white slip dress with clusters of beads and paillettes on its bodice. Soft ruffles swirled elegantly around the skirt. I ran my fingers over the velvety material. It was exquisite. My eyes dropped to the shoes, gentle heels in a muted tone matching the cluster of beads on the dress.

Aidan thought of everything; I noted a hairbrush, hair product, and makeup. I laughed to myself, mindlessly raking my fingers through my tangled hair. He even thought of the lingerie matching the dress. I sighed. I couldn't put my finger on it, but for some reason, I felt out of place.

I loved him, but I still felt unsure whether I fit in his world. Granted, his life could be ugly. That was no problem for me. My world hadn't been the easiest, either. Even still, after our infusion and love-making, it didn't ease my misgivings.

Oh, well, too late to change my mind now. Regardless of my insecurities, I wanted to be with Aidan more than life itself. So, if I wanted to stay with him, I needed to stop feeling inadequate. We had our whole life to decide together. I wondered where he planned for us to go. I reckoned the sky was the limit.

I finished getting dressed, and by using the hair product, brushing out the tangles or at least most, I made myself a cup of coffee and settled down on the couch. I sipped my coffee. It was perfect, bold, and hot. I set the cup on the coffee table and picked up the newspaper.

First, I read the horoscope. I checked mine first, Gemini. I sipped my coffee while reading. I laughed out loud. According to my horoscope, I was going to take a journey to a far distant land. Even the stars aligned with Aidan and me. I flipped through to the cartoons and scanned over them.

Then it caught my eye. The headlines of the paper in bold letters stared back at me. My heart stopped.

Woman Found Dead

During search and rescue, Sara Ray found dead at her residence.

Mrs. Ray died of an unknown drug overdose. Police are calling it a homicide.

Unprecedented shock slammed into me full force like a head-on collision with a meteorite. I lurched to my feet, dropping my cup of coffee as it splattered creamy liquid over the white rug and my dress.

"Oh, dear God! How could this be happening?" Then, as if an ocean of water dropped on my head, I realized that all this time, while Aida was in bed with me, he knew about my mother's death. Why didn't he tell me? He left without a word.

Struck with grief, I began pacing. My gut like a fist pounding away. Why did I ask for Aidan's help? What was I thinking, dusting Sara with some sort of alien drug? I didn't want her dead. I only wanted her to forget her pain. I watched Aidan give her a small bit. I had taken the drug too and came out okay. Even after Jen had gotten dusted, she didn't have any complications. Then again, Sara was older and an alcoholic. I recalled him saying that the drug was no toy. I assumed he knew the safe amount of dosage. Could he have mistakably misjudged the amount?

Suddenly, I recalled the conversation Aidan had with his uncle that night at the castle. Van wanted Aidan to get rid of Sara. I heard Aidan agree. He'd been working under his uncle's iron fist for some time, for reasons beyond my understanding.

Where was he? I sped up my pacing. It had been longer than an hour. I needed to get to my house and find out about my mother. "I can't believe this is happening."

A soft knock appeared at the door. I froze. At first, I thought it might be Aidan returning, but no, he wouldn't have used the front door. Then I recalled him saying no one knew this place. The knock came at the door again, louder this time. My neck bristled. Who could it be?

Abruptly the knocks became more aggressive. Bang, Bang, Bang! I jumped back. Sheer black fright swept through me. Crap! What should I do? I bit down hard on my bottom lip. The pounding was becoming more explosive as the door rattled from its hinges.

What if Aidan was in trouble and he sent someone to warn me. If I were left here in this god-knows-where cottage, I'd die from starvation. What other choice did I have other than to open the door? It was apparent whoever was on the other side knew someone was here.

I inhaled a deep breath and edged my way to the door. My hand hovered over the doorknob, fretting if his uncle might be on the other side. I touched the knob, shut my eyes and counted to three. "One, two, three!" I swung the door wide open and froze in shock. "W-w-what a-a-are you doing here?"

"May I come in, please?" Sally smiled sweetly. That childlike voice of hers was worse than a hundred and one sticks of chalk simultaneously.

"Why should I?" I folded my arms, narrowing my suspicious eyes. I smelt a rat.

"I thought while you're waiting, it'd be nice for us to chat." I detected a little vinegar in her tone.

"How did you find this place?" I cut my eyes beyond Sally and saw nothing but a forest of towering evergreen. There wasn't even a pathway leading up to the door. I looked back at Sally. "Something tells me you didn't walk." Skepticism rolled off my tongue.

Sally flashed that stupid grin of hers. "Aidan asked me to speak with you." Her voice oozed with syrup.

"Aidan?" Disbelief poured over me like thick molasses. "Why would he send you?"

"Well, I don't mean to toot my own horn, but I'm quite a reliable source when I need to be." Her brow arched. "Are you going to allow me in, or are we going to have to do this on this tiny ledge you call a porch?" Smugness gleamed across her sugar-caned face.

I stood there, eyeballing her. The girl appeared different. She carried her shoulders straight; confidence radiated from her whole demeanor. Reluctant, I stepped aside and let her pass, although I didn't trust her shifty eyes. I kept the door open, standing in the threshold of the door. It didn't feel quite right cooped up in the same tight quarters with this peculiar chick. I planned to keep my distance until I figured out what this bitch had up her shady sleeve.

I leaned against the doorframe, not taking my eyes off the unwelcomed guest. I noted, Sally didn't hesitate to make herself comfortable on the sofa. A little too comfy, in my opinion, but I kept my mouth shut and watched as I steadied myself for any of her shenanigans.

She smoothed her bright pink dress as she sat, back straight with perfect poise, white gloves, and purse out of the fifties. It was official; she'd gone off her rocker, or judging by her weight, maybe she broke the damn rocker.

Sally began her spiel, and it was a doozy too. "Well, your boy asked me to speak with you first. He has some rather impertinent information for you."

"You spoke to Aidan," I asked as my brow shot up.

"Of course, how else would I be here," she giggled, which sounded fake.

"Where is Aidan?" Could Van have captured Bane and under duress, force him to tell my whereabouts? I prayed that wasn't the case.

Sally ignored my question as her eyes drifted to the newspaper. "Oh, I see you've been reading the latest news," she tisked twice, "Such a misfortunate mishap. I'm terribly sorry for your loss."

Sally was full of crap. There was nothing genuine about her. It would be a cold day in hell before I discussed my mother with her. I remained silent, listening with a healthy dose of caution slapped on a sandwich of mistrust.

"I'm sure it's going to be difficult after your horrible loss. Especially after the police find evidence of the drug." It was as though Sally was in my head, but when our eyes met, I saw apparent loathing in her dark eyes. "For the life of me," she carried on in her sweet voice, "I'll never understand how such a young child can pull off so many murders?"

Talk about left field. Hell, I think this witch flew off the field with a broom tucked between her legs.

"What child are you talking about?" I gawked at her in disbelief.

"Well, there are certainly enough motives to reach the heavens if you don't mind my candidness. Why, after all those years carrying that dirty little secret of your mother's naughty deed, it's no wonder you snapped. Knowing your mommy committed such a heinous murder sent you, you poor thing, over the ledge," she smiled.

"Sally, have you gone mad," I hissed. "I think you should leave." I didn't know what game she was playing, but I wasn't standing for it.

As if my words fell on deaf ears, Sally continued with her poison, "And then all those men, you certainly didn't want your father replaced by another man, *a new daddy*!"

"You're really reaching now!"

"No wonder you snapped, you poor thing. When you discovered your mommy was abandoning you for her newest lover, that's when you lost complete control. Why it was more than you could handle."

Sally's Southern drawl seemed more profound than ever. "Last but not least, in a last desperate attempt, you knocked off your mummy by poisoning her. You just became enraged and turned psychopath. I suppose when you kill one person, it must get easier with the next."

I gaped at this crazy person in front of me, my fists white-knuckled to my side. "If you believe I am a killer, I doubt you'd act like you own the place."

"Oh, I have no reason to fear the likes of you. Aidan wouldn't let you hurt me." Her eyes narrowed, full of loathing.

I stepped forward. "I don't know what rock you crawled out from under, but I suggest you go back to it," I snarled.

"That's not the way to treat your host when you are a guest."

"What?" I shook my head, baffled. "I don't have time for this, Sal. Get out now before I throw you out!"

"I can't leave," her eyes widened, "I have to give you a message from Aidan." She sneered, "You know now that Aidan knows about your murders, he wants nothing to do with you. That's why I'm here," she laughed with this disgusting throaty snorkel, "I know it's lame, but I'm your worst nightmare!"

"Van sent you here, didn't he? Aidan's uncle put you up to this?" My heart pounded in my throat as I looked down my nose at Sally.

"You silly girl, Uncle Van would never get between a husband and his wife's squabble."

"What did you say?" Did I hear her right?

"You heard me," she smiled, "I'm Aidan's wife."

I strangled on my spit.

"All this," she pointed to the décor of the cottage. "Does any of this look like a man's cave?"

I didn't answer her but glared at her absurdity.

"I decorated the cottage myself. My husband prefers other things." Her gaze fell upon the bed.

"Oh, I know. Aidan and I enjoyed the comforts of the bed *several* times." I threw the match on the gasoline as she ignited.

"Shut up!" she hissed. "My husband wanders from time to time, but he always comes back like an obedient dog."

"Really?" Picturing Aidan controlled by Sally was a hard swallow.

"We've been together for a long time. I'm as immortal as my husband. My real name is Sabella," she boasted.

"What is your middle name?" The obituary that Jen and I stumbled across on the Internet struck me suddenly.

"Why it's Mae, Sabella Mae Du-"

"I know, Du Pont." I couldn't help the acid in my voice.

"Did you come here to flaunt your marriage and that fat diamond on your finger?" The rock was so large I imagined she had to use a bulldozer to lift her hand. It was over the top, just like her bright color attire and syrupy voice.

"Well, I have to admit it has been fun. Like all good things, it must end."

"Sal, say what you have to say and then get the hell out!"

"I love your directness. It's one of your better qualities, setting aside the fact that you slept with my husband." Sally shot darts at me.

"I'm not a homewrecker!" I screamed. "I don't believe he's married. Especially to you. I stayed with him at his castle, for Pete's sake!" I wanted to band my fingers around her fat throat and squeeze.

Her eyes took on a gleam like glassy volcanic rock. "Of course, you're not a homewrecker." A sudden thin chill hung on the edge of her words, "You walked right into our trap, silly girl."

Panic like I'd never known before welled in my throat. "Sal spit it out!" I fought to hold my fragile control.

"Aidan only wanted your powers. He didn't want to share them with his uncle. He knew if he took your virginity under a sex spell, he'd gain your powers." Sally flashed an icy smile.

"Wait! How did you ..." I stopped myself and said, "I don't believe you!" I was on the brink of lunging at Sally. "Aidan cares about me. He proposed marriage. Is that somewhere in your plan too," I scoffed, challenging her.

"Are you that naive? Don't you think if he had intended to marry you, he'd have a ring on your finger?" Her brow arched. "Where's *your* ring?"

"Maybe, he hasn't gotten it yet."

"Aidan had to do what he had to do to get your powers. The marriage talk was more or less pillow talk."

"Well, he did a good job. He did it twice." I could see my words stabbed at her when she flinched.

"I think your service is over here. I'm done with this conversation." A flicker of loathing hid in Sally's glint.

"Are you forgetting something?" I asked with a slight smile of defiance.

"Whatever could that possibly be?"

"You've forgotten that Aidan and I have fused our powers. We are as one. I am just as powerful as he is. Maybe you should watch your mouth." My eyes shot bullets straight to her black heart.

Sally swallowed nervously.

Ah, there I had her, right where I wanted her. A scared little pussycat!

"I'm done with this boring conversation." She dragged her over-weight body to her feet. "I'll be sure to tell my husband how you squealed like a pig when I ram that dagger through your man-stealing heart." She strained to gain control again. As much as she tried to prove her point, the real fact was I'd frightened her, just like the little coward she'd always been.

I laughed. "You can't kill me, bitch, without killing Aidan." Oh, dear, God! I hoped I was right.

Her eyes widened with surprise as her mouth popped open and close.

377

With renewed strength, I basked in the knowledge of my power. "I'm a genetically engineered angel." I straightened my shoulders back as I edged closer to Sally. I spoke with calm, "You can't kill me! I won't kill you, but I will throw you out of here, and on the way, I'll enjoy pounding your face with my fist."

I seized my chance. I dove for Sally's throat. I was only inches from strangling her.

But my efforts were abruptly halted by an iron-clad clench. It was as if I'd been wrangled and roped like a wild animal. My gaze dropped to a man's arm snaked around my neck, holding me flush against his broad chest.

"Sally, what is this?" Fear reigned and took possession of every cell in my body.

"We're taking you to where you belong."

"Where I belong?" my brows collided as fear ripped through my mind.

"Yes, with all the harden criminals in a cell locked behind bars," she scoffed. "You're a murderer, and you're going to get exactly what you deserve!" Venom oozed from Sally's voice as her laughter hammered my ears.

"I'm innocent! I didn't murder anyone, you lying bitch," I spat, gnashing my teeth to get at her.

"Aidan, my love, be a sweetheart and get rid of the trash?"

"Aidan!" My mind went wild, needing to know if he'd been a part of this atrocity. My eyes trailed down my captor's arm. He was male. I could feel his erection pushed against me. His hands, beautiful, long fingers, and strong, wearing a *ring*, the same ring in my dreams, an eye in the center with diamonds encircling it.

I tried to twist to see his face, but my silent captor kept me pinned, prisoner to his grip. "Let me see your face!" I screamed, kicking, and trying to bite at him. He was stronger than me, and my attempts were unavailing.

I didn't have to see his compelling blues, his firm features, the confident set of his shoulders, to know my captor, the faceless boy, which I'd been dreaming since my childhood. The woodsy scent, even the gentle flow of breathing I knew far too well to doubt who held me captive. Aidan had deceived me into believing someone like him could love a girl like me. What a fool I'd become.

In the next breath, something sharp prick like a needle stabbed me in the neck, and suddenly, I began to feel my mind slipping away. In the background, I heard Sally laughing, sick, depraved laughter, but it didn't bother me. My mind was shutting down as her voice grew distant. Peacefulness swept over me like I was floating in the ocean, just drifting aimlessly. Then darkness swallowed the light.

DAUNTLESS ANGEL

THE ANGEL SERIES BOOK 2

ASYLUM

$\mathcal{S}$ally made good on her threat. The Supreme Court of Justice found me guilty for the three murders charged against me. My whole life went down the crapper before I could say, "I'm innocent." I was framed. Headlines in the news nationwide read,

CRAZED DAUGHTER SNAPPED

Teenage Girl, Stephanie Ray Collins, Turned Serial Killer Leaving a Trail of Murders!

Despite my protest of innocence, somehow, the State had hard evidence against me. If you asked me, they pulled it out of a rabbit's ass.

According to the State's officials leading this witch trial, it was an open-and-shut case. I pleaded no contest to the charges by the advice of my crappy attorney, Bernard Valdez. He promised if I didn't fight the charges, Judge Xavier LaMotte would show me mercy and likely give me a lesser sentence. I took his word for it against my better judgment, and I fell right into the devil's hands.

As ironic as it sounded, the prosecution claimed that luck was on my side. Under the circumstances, living with an insane parent who murdered my father, the court-appointed psychiatrist, Janet Dubrow, deemed me as someone who snapped…*a crime of passion*, if you will.

As my fate fell into unrelenting hands of the officials, the State's prosecution charged me as a juvenile for the murder of my mom's boyfriend, Charles Dodson.

The judicial system finding a ten-year-old child capable of committing such a heinous crime, slicing a grown man's throat from ear to ear, was inconceivable to me.

Charles stood a firm six foot four and weighed over two hundred pounds. The crime they charged against me was an impossibility. A child weighing less than a hundred pounds and less than half his height could not have carried out such a forceful assault.

After eight years, the evidence miraculously appeared out of thin air. The state's argument seemed weak and unrealistic. However, the prosecution claimed they had damaging evidence against me. All their claims were based in fairyland. The national news headline read that the police found a bag of my bloody clothes and the knife with my fingerprints, stuffed away in Sara's closet. When I unpacked her closet, I didn't come across any such bag. The bad simply didn't exist. At that point, I knew that due process I'd read about was not in the cards for me. Justice had left the building and I had to fight the devil alone.

Any imperative clue proving my innocence slipped past their dirty noses. My attorney, Bernard Valdez, the state prosecution, Laurent Marcos, and Judge LaMotte, ignored the fact that at the time of Charles' death, I was at school sitting in plain sight, first row.

These outstanding pillars of society turned the other cheek and ignored anything that would've cleared my name.

Apart from Edward Van Dunn, Aidan's uncle, I reckoned several members of the Illuminati were aiming for me. The hardest one of all to swallow was my mom, Sara, playing a part in this atrocity. She had no problem keeping a crypt of secrets from me, but the idea that money was the fuel that flamed her motivation sent me reeling.

My stomach churned with bitterness every time I wondered how easy it was for my own mother to throw me to the wolves for a few coins. Unfortunately for Sara, her diabolical plan didn't save her life. She'd died before she'd gotten the chance to wallow in her wealth.

For the murders of Francis Bonnel and Sara Collins, my mother, I got off with an insanity plea. It could've been worse and knowing that little fact seemed to soothe the nightmares somewhat.

Somewhat.

The federal judge sentenced me with no chance of parole to live the remainder of my life at Haven Hospital, located on the outskirts of Bayou L'Ourse, an asylum for the violent and criminally insane.

I was the youngest in history labeled a serial killer, the second woman charged as such. The first woman received the gas chamber. I supposed luck had my back in a very wacko way.

Then unexpectedly, a dark cloud was lifted, and my nightmare ceased, or so it seemed. On my twenty-first birthday, the US Court of Appeals, the Fifth Circuit, overturned my conviction. I was exonerated of all charges.

A release order was set in motion, granting my freedom. All charges were mysteriously dropped. Though I knew better than anyone, it was a crock of shit, but I'd take it to get out of this hellhole.

It was an early spring morning when the doors of the reformatory opened. A cool breeze tousled my tangled hair. The sun peeked just above the horizon.

I haven't had a whiff of fresh air or a glimpse of the golden sun in three long years. I inhaled the fresh air and savored the sweet taste of honey.

I had no idea where I was going. There was no one to call. I was alone and abandoned, but I didn't care. I was free. I made my way, one slow step at a time to the exit gate. Movement was difficult and painful. Every joint in my body screamed with agony. I couldn't say when the last time I'd taken a stroll. I wasn't allowed outside my cell. Considering my daily dose of drugs, I wasn't much for socializing, let alone sitting up or even standing without assistance.

I think the medical staff wanted me incapacitated. The staff feared they couldn't contain me. After all, I was a danger to society and to myself. So, they kept me locked away in the dark, forgotten and away from everyone. It felt as if they were hiding me.

Hallucinations were no surprise. I was practically a breathing pharmacy. Majority of the time, I stayed in a state of confusion. Discerning between reality and illusion became hard for me. Dr. Phil Good made sure of that. It wasn't hard, void of thought and desire. I was a dead girl inside. I hated myself for not having the guts to stop breathing.

The gentle sun felt soothing against my pale face as freedom caressed my dry, cracked lips. When my eyes focused on a tall, dark, figure by the exit gate, I first thought my mind was playing tricks.

Though I wanted to check out, something in the back of my mind kept knocking me back to life or at least forcing me to breathe.

I was stuck on this demented carousel, a merry-go-round of insanity, and I was never getting off either. I knew who was responsible for my unlucky fate. I didn't have to have my palms read to know, and it didn't take a genius to figure it out either.

This was the work of the *Illuminati.*

Was any of this real? Did Aidan and his treacherous charms trick me into believing a lie... *a genetically engineered angel*? I scoffed at the absurdity. Could I have imagined him, and like my mother, be insane?

It didn't matter now.

No. I might be insane like my mother, but even a lunatic couldn't have conjured up this tale. The cold hard facts was that I was a gullible girl who fell in love with a charmer who played a very cruel joke at my expense. I fell right into his trap. I hated Aidan Bane DuPont, but I loathed myself even more.

In a screwed up way, my rage toward him kept me alive. If that was what I was, then breathing didn't prove life, not in my case.

Then my world took a turn. Funny, how quick the flick of a Bic could overturn a federal ruling? For three years, the Federal Judicial System marked me as a menace to society. They were determined to keep me locked away forever, until my twenty first birthday.

I had awakened that morning with papers slapped in my face. I'd been acquitted of all charges.

Like a domino effect, everything started to fall into place. The prosecutors filed a motion to drop charges based on the assigned shrink's testimony that I'd shown great improvement through treatment. Strangely, I couldn't recall one time speaking to the good doctor. However odd and peculiar as it sounded, the Louisiana Board of Pardons and Paroles dismissed the charges, claiming that I no longer posed a danger to others or to myself. It was uncanny how conveniently they arrived at their decision this late in the game.

To put it plain and simple, the Board knew and I knew that it was a farce. I was framed. Mere putty in their vile hands and there was nothing I could've done to have stopped them. Not even an angel had that kind of power.

Whenever the Illuminati came for you, they buried you so far under there was no point of return until they decided otherwise. The Order called the shots. If they wanted you dead, you were a goner. They played God because they were.

As I approached the exit, I spotted a tall figure watching me. The glare of the sun blinded my sight. I could only make out a silhouette. It was not until I came into focus that my cloudy mind began to open like tiny drops of water to a dry flower. Slowly his face came into view.

Suddenly, I froze. My knees nearly buckled under me. At first, I thought my mind was playing tricks, but no, he was *real*. I thought I had lost everyone.

"Chile, it is so good to see you!" Jeffery held out his caramel arms.

I stopped for a second, taking in the sweet vision. "Jeffery, is that really *you*?" It was all I could say.

"Damn straight it is!" he smiled brightly.

I dropped my small bag and shuffled into Jeffery's arms, melting against his warm chest. His arms squeezed tight around my shoulders, holding me close. Tears began to stream. "I can't believe you're here!" I feared since the charges, everyone had abandoned me. After all, I was a serial killer, a danger to society.

"Ah, boo, I could never desert you. How you are?" Jeffery's forehead lined deep with worry.

"I'm better now," I croaked through tears, wiping my cheeks with the back of my hand.

"Gurrrl, you've gotten so skinny!" Jeffery held me at arm's length, eyeballing me from head to toe.

"Food was kinda sparing in there."

"To see you like this just breaks my heart, boo."

"I thought you had," my voice cracked, "forgotten me." I sucked in a deep breath, holding what mind I had left.

"Honeychile, Dom and I have been tryin' to help you since the day they put you in this mofo place. We hired the best attorney money could buy."

"Really! I had no idea." Shock surged my frail body.

"It was a nightmare. Dom and I were denied visitations. In fact, we were banned from the premises."

"Why?" Astonishment touched my pale face.

"That's what we tried to find out. Our attorney couldn't get anywhere with those rascals!"

I softened my voice. I didn't want any of the hospital's staff to over-hear me. "They set me up, Jeff," I licked my dry lips. "I didn't kill anyone." Those words hadn't caressed my lips since that day Aidan and Sally had drugged me.

"Boo, I know you is innocent, and apparently, you must have a fairy godmother. Some powerful mofo pulled some ironclad strings to get you exonerated."

"What? They told me I was getting off for good behavior."

"Gurrrl, you'll believe anything. No insane murderer who's killed several folks ever gets off. Boo, did they's assigned you a parole officer?"

"I don't think so."

"Of course they didn't! 'Cause they know you is innocent." Jeffery's face crinkled into a wake-the-hell-up smirk.

"I guess I'm a bit out of touch." My sluggish brain had trouble processing all this.

"It's okay, you is comin' home with Dom and me." Jeffery patted my back.

"Oh, I can't impose." I shook my head in protest. Although, I was homeless, dropping my troubles on my friends was a liability I couldn't allow. If the Illuminati had enough power to incarcerate me for crimes I didn't commit, then they might go for round two? Which meant anyone I associated with could become a target as well. I couldn't let that happen to Jeffery and Dom.

"Gurrrl, did I not tell you, you is family?"

I scrunched my nose up, "Jeff that might not be a good idea." I stepped back, shaking my head. "Wherever I go evil follows."

Jeff rolled his eyes. "Now you is actin' cray-cray! No mo' lip. You is comin' to live with Dom and me." Jeffery rested his hands on his hips with that divatude that only he could do. "I never say a damn thing I don't mean. So come on! Your home is our home. No, really. I ain't lyin'. It's *yours*. You paid for the house."

"What?"

388

"Remember the key you gave me?"

I just stared blankly.

"Anyway, boo, you is rich, a billionaire times a billion! Mister Aidan made sure you could own the world."

"Wait! I *have money?*" My words felt like an echo.

"Uh-huh, and that's an understatement! Now come on. We is goin' home. I'm hungry. Dinner's gettin' cold."

"Home! Where do we live?" I tried to push through the cobwebs shrouding my brain.

"New Orleans! Where else is there?" Jeffery grabbed my small bag as I latched onto his arm.

HOME SWEET HOME

hen we rolled up into the drive of our home in Jeffery's Lincoln, my eyes froze. I stammered over my words. "T-t-tis-this can't be our house!"

"It sure is. We live in style. There's no better place than the Garden District." Jeffery bubbled with pride. "I told you, *les bons temps rouler!*" (let the good times roll!)

"I hope so, Jeffery. I truly hope so." I endeavored to put on a happy face, but in the core of my spirit, my glee had taken absence. I didn't want to be a Debbie Downer. I wanted to believe better days were ahead.

Despite my good intentions, I had my doubts. I might be physically free but my heart still was shackled. I didn't know if I'd ever recover. I reckoned time would tell.

I blew out a raspy sigh as the memories of that day rushed through my mind. Sally's sick laughter still lingered in my ears as much as the sting of Aidan's arms wrapped tightly around my body.

To this day, my brain seemed riddled with holes, and because of that, the seeds of doubt were planted, giving me pause to Aidan's involvement. My captor's cowardly face remained obscured while his hand bared a diamond ring. The very same ring that haunted me in my dreams ever since I was a child.

Then everything went black, and my life came to a screeching halt.

That was my last memory of that shattering day. When I'd awakened, shackled, I realized that my happiness had ended forever.

Jeffery parked the car in the garage that was off to the side toward the back of the house and cut the engine. He then turned to me with his bright face, "This is it!"

"Huh, what?" I stared at Jeffery as though I was listening to him underwater. His voice sounded muffled.

"Stevie, you sure you're okay?" Jeffery scrutinized my facial expression as I stared back at him blankly.

"I just need rest." The strength I once had seemed to have been depleted. I reckoned when the drugs washed out of my system, I'd feel better. Still, I doubted the old Stevie, full of piss and vinegar would return. She died the day Aidan and Sally had taken her captive.

I reckoned I'd have to deal with that later.

Now I had to face the hard facts. I paid a heavy price for my faith. As a result, the only thing I understood was revenge, it was the air I breathed. Torment was the fuel that kept me going. Anger was my inspiration. Yet the force beneath my feet was... *rage*.

If I were smart, I'd move on. With the wealth that had been kindly bestowed upon me, I should make a new life for myself, leave the past in the past. Nevertheless, no amount of money could buy my way out of this baleful maze.

My gut kept telling me that Aidan's family wasn't finished with me. After all, I took away their precious chance of world domination by infusing my powers with Aidan. I prayed my instinct was wrong. I wanted to be done with them, once and for all.

A gnawing memory kept tapping at my brain, a flash of visions I couldn't recognize. It felt as though I'd forgotten something, but what? Could it be another bad memory of that hospital locked away in my drug-hazed brain trying to dig its way to the surface? If so, I preferred for it to remain buried, or even better...dead.

"Boo, let's get you in the house." Jeffery came to my side and opened the door. He gently slid his arm around my waist and eased me out of the car. I guessed I was weaker than I thought.

"I'll have Dom fix you something good to eat. You startin' to look more pale, even for your white lily skin." He smiled sweetly, but by the bags under his eyes, I think he could've used some of his own advice.

I worried that I was the source of his sleepless nights.

As we made our way to the house, I couldn't peel my eyes away. It was breath taking. A vision only in a magazine. Majestic and mystique, the century old mansion stood tall as if it were awaiting for our arrival, merely painted white, with black plantation shutters embellished the narrow windows along the front porch.

Ancient avenues of oaks lined the street, offering its cool shade as crepe myrtles colored the air with sweet perfume. The wonderful scent reminded me of Saint Ann Street, my old neighborhood back in Tangi.

This house, in comparison to my previous home, was no small fry. After all, it didn't get much better than the Garden District. Jeffery led me past the wrought iron fence, leading up a flight of brick steps that seemed eternal and just passed the steps, on the porch hung oversized ferns swaying gently to the light breeze.

The yard was small, yet its luscious green was inviting. Suddenly, I yearned to run my bare feet across its thick carpet. I couldn't remember the last time I'd felt the cool touch of grass between my toes.

Tears began to sting, and I quickly wiped the moisture from my eyes. I wanted to hang on to my last shred of dignity until I was in private.

On the left side of the porch, I noticed a white-wicker swing with fluffy pillows of yellow and on the right side a wicker table with multi-colored chairs matching the flowers from the garden.

When we entered the house, the aroma of food floated in the air. Instantly, my nose kicked in from the delicious tang, taunting my growling stomach. Dom must have been stirring up a big meal. I couldn't wait to eat. The perks living with a chef.

Then my attention shifted to the grand foyer. A sweetness scented the room of gardenias in a glass vase, centered on top of a round table made of dark Mahogany, under the three-tier chandelier.

I stood there for a moment, gaping at the elegance. This was beyond my imagination. Stunned for words, I twirled around, slowly taking in the awe.

As Jeffery nudged forward, we entered into the sitting room. Sunlight filtered through the windows, bringing a wonderful warmth to the room. I spotted a grand piano sitting in the corner by the picture window. Soft accented chairs and a white stuffy couch nestled the cozy fireplace, in conjunction with bright Persian rugs adding color and elegance to the dark-wooded floors. Artistic paintings hung strategically on every wall, lending the home that good old Southern charm.

"Jeff, everything is so amazing." Tears began to fall regardless of my effort to hold them back.

"C'mon. Let's get you some food, then I'll show you your room upstairs. Dom and I fixed it up nicely for you." Jeffery smiled, trying not to show his unease.

"That sounds great." My smile felt hollow.

Suddenly, a faint meow came from underneath the piano. I glanced down and caught a glimpse of a large white puff of fur rubbing against the stool. My eyes went wide. "Is that…?"

"It sure is, and you best be thankin' me too. That damn cat and I do not get along. He's nothin' but trouble," Jeffery grumbled.

Surprisingly, I laughed, and Jeffery's eyes glistened. It was nice to see his old spark back.

As soon as Snowball heard my voice, he came running to me. I grabbed my beloved cat into my arms and nestled him against my chest. His gentle purr felt soothing. I'd forgotten how much I loved that sound.

This time a flood of tears poured down my cheeks, not sad ones but joyous ones, the kind I hadn't had in such a very long time. I was home. I lifted my eyes. "Jeff, thanks!" I could barely speak above a whisper.

His deep-golden face beamed as he leaned in giving me a quick squeeze. "C'mon before Dom decides to skin me alive. That cranky Frenchman has been waitin' all day to see the likes of you. Besides, I'm hungry."

Unaware, for the first time in a long while, I felt numb. Numb was good.

Hence, regardless of how good everything seemed right now, I wasn't fully myself. It would take time to heal. My mind seemed to drift into nowhere-land, a vast desert of sand and tumbleweeds. I had no idea how long it might take to recover…*if ever.*

I possessed a stockpile of troublesome, but there was one thing I was certain of that being here in this lovely home with Jeffery and Dom was the right path in my recovery, or at least for now. I still needed to be mindful of their safety and the risk they were taking having me in their presence.

When we stepped into the kitchen, I was swooned by several mixtures of spices, kicking up my grumbling stomach a notch. I paused taking in the delightful aroma. Common to most Southern homes, the kitchen was at the back of the house. The bright gallery came equipped with all the modern amenities blended with that old-world charm. The Wolf-stove seemed to be the focal point of the room, and the oversized stainless steel refrigerator promised a heavy stock of assorted foods. I especially liked the pictured windows bringing in the outside to the indoors. The space had everything one would need, inviting and cheery as the rest of the house.

Dom, in his white stained apron, turned from the stove, and quickly his pencil-lined mustache stretched across his face into a bright smile. "Oh, how wonderful! The mistress of the house has returned." The chunky chef gathered me into his arms and hugged me tightly. He then held me at arm's length, eyeing me from head to toe like a father inspecting his soiled child from a day's play. "Look at you!" he tisked, making a clicking sound with his tongue. "You must eat. Come. Sit," he urged in his heavy French accent pointing to a round table directly in front of the far-left window. He pulled a chair out as I followed his lead and sat down. "I have made a feast for you, but I think perhaps you might eat something not so rich for the tummy, yes?"

Before I'd uttered a word of protest, Dom padded off, in short, returning with a bowl. He placed it on the table in front of me. "This is much better. Eat," he insisted, air swatting me.

I glanced down at the steamy curls drifting to my face and savored its salty aroma...*chicken soup*. Instantly, a smiled touched my lips as I looked up into Dom's gentle face. "It smells delicious. Thank you." I reached for my spoon.

Jeffery sat a glass of milk and a mug of Coca-Cola on the table beside me. He patted my shoulder, "Boo, drink both of these," he advised. "You is startin' to look even more pasty than normal." Disquiet painted his face.

My hand instantly touched my face. "I am?"

Jeffery's nose crinkled. "I know you is naturally pale but *damn!*"

My good friend always knew how to flatter a girl. Some things never changed.

I flashed him a black look.

Jeffery was right. My skin looked haggard. During my confinement at Haven, the food provisions severely lacked. In fact, I couldn't recall eating, unless drugs were part of the food group.

Only a unique type of employees worked at Haven. *monsters*, I called them. Not your typical Southern-hospitality kind of folks. Their behavior was pernicious.

I assumed the Family handpicked each and every employee. I couldn't imagine any decent person working in that torture chamber they called a hospital.

I shivered. The abuse, a vision I wanted to forget.

I once feared the men in black. That changed the minute I stepped foot in Haven. The men in white were far worse, the *orderlies*. They took the meaning of sinister to a whole different level.

Even under my murky mind, I recalled how the boys in white got their rocks off. Every round, they gathered around my bed cheering on the nurse who had the pleasure of administering the drugs. Because I didn't cooperate, the boys took great enjoyment holding me down and prying my mouth open and stuffing a fist of meds down my throat.

I hated them and plotted their death, with a simple butter knife. I took some sick pleasure envisioning their murders. I never acted on it, but just the same, the desire persisted.

The orderlies often reported to the charge nurse, Betty, concerning my defiant behavior. Unfortunately, my reprisals fell upon unsympathetic ears. Nurse Betty favored her staff, condoning their ill-patient care.

After her precious boys kept coming back with busted-up lips and scratched-up faces, the nurse took matters into her own hands. That was when she pulled out all the stops, shackles, and a straitjacket.

Several months later, the doctor begrudgingly took a moment out of his busy schedule of snorting coke and watching porn in his office to examining my festering foot. It was the latest topic among the orderlies. The heavy shackles were too tight, cutting off circulation. From the lack of proper cleaning, infection set. If I'd been anywhere else, I would've been hospitalized. Ironic though, I was in a hospital. If that was what one called it.

Dr. Phil Good and Haven feared imprisonment for their sadistic care. Thanks to the doctor's paranoia, he ordered the nurse to remove the shackles, and I received the proper medical attention.

Betty and her minions didn't seem too pleased with the doctor's orders. Despite the doctor's wishes, they were determined to keep at least half of me constraint. Happily abiding by the orders of Nurse Betty, the orderlies kept me in a straitjacket for safety measures.

Still, I took some sick delight laughing in their faces when they had to remove the oppressing steel.

❧

I looked up with my spoon suspended. Two pairs of worried eyes were mirroring my every move. "Guys! I'm fine," I attempted to convince them, but I didn't want to sound ungrateful either. After all, they could've left me at the gates of that appalling hospital. "I mean, I really, really appreciate all the trouble you both have gone through for me. I'll be okay. So, stop worrying!" I forced a smile. To be honest, I might've been trying to assure myself that as well.

Dom reached across the table patting my hand. "Why don't you let us do what we do best?" He smiled, stretching his pencil mustache even thinner.

"I'm sorry." I dropped my spoon into the bowl of soup and withdrew a faint sigh. "I don't want you guys to fuss over me." I couldn't be more grateful for their endeavor to nurse me back to health, but I had nothing to give back. I was empty and barren.

"We want to help," Dom smiled warmly.

I hesitated for half a second then I spoke up. "I have to ask. It's been on my mind for a while." I paused. Dread washed over me. "Have you heard from Aidan?" I blanched, fearing whether or not I really wanted to know.

Jeffery and Dom shared a strained glance. Jeff took the lead and answered. "Boo, we ain't seen Aidan," he inhaled a sharp breath. "Since that night you were kidnapped and all sorts of spooky mojo shit has happened." Jeffery's oval blues bugged.

"Like what?" My heart skipped a beat.

"For starters, that whole damn castle vanished, foundation and all." Jeffery face paled as if he'd seen a ghost.

I gawked in surprise.

Then Dom added, "We haven't heard from Aidan since the disappearance. His cell phone goes straight to voice mail. Everyone has disappeared, and we have no explanation to why. Even his uncle Van

396

and his son, Sam, have vanished off the grid." The taunted wrinkles in Dom's forehead were stark.

I sat there in silent shock. It was no secret that Aidan's Uncle Van and Sam were not my favorite subjects. Sam was a psychopath and a serial rapist, and his uncle wasn't any better.

I couldn't vouch for Van's whereabouts. Although, I knew what happened to Sam. Aidan took his life. Though Sam's demise was abrupt and violent, it was justified. He was going to rape me and leave me for dead. Aidan saved my life by killing Sam before he'd finished me off but not before Sam had badly beaten me.

If it hadn't been for Aidan and his Druid magick, I would've died. I reckoned that was one thing I could be grateful for. "How is it possible for Aidan to be *MIA?*"

Jeffery chimed in. "That's an understatement! We have no mofo idea. We *is* still scratchin' our heads. I got a sneaky suspicion that his family used that voodoo shit and poof, castle and all those mofo jokers went bye, bye. Apart from Aidan, I hope none of them return."

Dom interjected, scolding his partner. "Jeff, you're too superstitious. There has to be a logical answer to their whereabouts."

"I beg your *pardon!*" Jeffery gaped, "Where the hell have you been, mister?" Jeffery started wagging his finger in Dom's face. "Explain to me how that damn castle vanished, Mr. I-Believe-In-No-Ghost? Even the rosebushes disappeared," Jeffery pursed his lips in a huff.

Dom kept his composure as he gently countered, "Clearly I don't have all the answers, but don't assume without facts, *ma chère*. Nothing around here is ever as it seems."

"Well, you need to stick to what you know best, cooking," Jeffery retorted with an extra dose of sour-cream.

Suddenly, I started to laugh, hysterical laughter. Both the men forgot about their tiff and shifted their wide eyes to me. At that moment, I'd lost my senses. I couldn't catch my breath. Soon Dom and Jeffery joined in, and the room filled with insane mirth.

It felt good to free this strange emotion inside me. The peculiar hilarity seemed odd to my ears, a sound that jumped ship since the asylum.

Even so, with no warning, my mood changed like the wind. I started to sob, and the house became still. For a brief moment, my two friends gaped in stunned silence.

I was a mess. The drugs were flushing out of my system faster than I'd expected and reality was forging through.

Looking down the barrel of a gun was hard to swallow. My life was a train wreck. I wasn't sure what was worse, dead inside or alive and despicable.

TIME LOST

*A*fter we had finished dinner, Jeffery found a perfect excuse to leave the dishes for Dom while he dragged me upstairs.

At the end of the hallway, we stopped at a door. "What's the hold up," I questioned, reaching for the knob. Like a streak of lightening, Jeffery threw himself against the door, blocking my entrance. My brows furrowed, confused.

"Oh, no you don't, gurrrlfriend!" He waged his finger. "Not until you wear this." He pulled out a pink scarf out of his pocket, waving it in my face.

I snatched it out of his hand and grumbled. "All right, I'll put it on if you take that damn smirk off your face."

The tips of Jeffery's mouth stretched to the Grand Canyon. "Let me help. Turn around." He twirled his finger over my head. "No peeky-poo," he advised as my back was to him, "Or else I'll slap your white-lily hands till they turn black." He cinched the knot as my head jerked backward. "You know, once you go black you never go back!"

Good grief! I rolled my eyes as I rubbed my head. "Whatever!" I couldn't see it, but I felt my friend's smile of triumph.

With Jeffery's guiding hand, I stepped through the threshold, sightless by the scarf that was cutting off brain cells.

It was *that* tight.

If I even acted as though I might peek, Jeffery jumped on it like a fly on crap, swatting my hands. Sometimes Jeff could be one real *mofo*.

"Okay, you can open them now." Jeffery beamed as he jerked the scarf off my head. I suddenly felt circulation to my brain.

When my eyes opened, my breath stalled. I stood gaping into a large room. "Holy mother of God, this is my bedroom?" I turned to Jeff, astounded. "No way!"

"Way! Dom and I spruced it up ourselves. Do you likie?"

I gulped. "Uh, yeah! It's *sick*!" I latched my arms around Jeffery's neck and squeezed.

"I suppose sick means you like it."

I glimpsed up at my friend with a wide smile, "It means you *rock*! I *adore* it." I quickly reached up and kissed him on the cheek.

"Okay, now you is gettin' too grateful. You know I hate that cuddly-kissy-kissy shit." Jeffery rubbed his cheek.

Funny, I found myself laughing, an actual laugh. "You haven't changed a bit."

"Oh, yes, I have!" Jeffery pursed his lips. "Now I belong to the snotty, rich-bitch society instead of waitin' on 'em." Jeffery waved his hand. "I got refined too. I can hold my little pinky out drinking nasty, hot tea, eating a stale crumb cookie just like those gossipin' old biddies. I even got hats that can run circles around those old women, and I do mean literally."

I shook my head. Who's he fooling? He hadn't changed one bit. I laughed to myself. I wouldn't have it any other way.

Slowly combing my eyes over the room once again, I started to pinch myself. It all seemed too good to be true. The bedroom was more than enough room, yet it was warm and inviting.

Like all older Southern homes, it had a blazing fireplace on the far wall. Muted overstuffed chairs cozied-up to the hearthstone, perfect for reading a good book by the warm fire. The room was adorned in gentle, soft creams with just the right touch of mint green and light lilac.

When my eyes fell upon the canopy bed, my heart sank. Staring at the white netting took me back in time to *Aidan's cottage*. Memories, I didn't care to revisit, if ever. Maybe later Jeffery wouldn't mind if I removed it. I'd wait to ask him later. I didn't want to spoil the moment for him.

I glanced into his beaming face. I think he was more excited than me. Seeing his joy made me love Jeff even more than I already did. I couldn't be more grateful to the guys for the trouble they went through to help me.

A sudden pain struck, bringing me back to the reality that my being here might not be in the guy's best interest. Everything was quiet for now, but I didn't know how long that would last.

Shaking off the willies of my past, I drew my attention back to the present as I padded over to the window hiding behind sheer curtains. I drew the drapes back and gasped. Below was a garden full of bright colored veggies. It was enchanting. Breathtaking cherry-blossom trees full of soft pink buds swaying in the breeze. I spotted an array of flowers that dotted the fence with every color imaginable.

For a second, my breath stalled until Jeffery tapped me on the shoulder. I quickly drew in a breath and glanced up at my friend. "Hey, there's more stuff to go bug-eyed over." Jeffery tugged at my sleeve.

"I'm coming," I tossed a gentle smile.

"I saved the best for last." Jeffery smiled and opened the double-door closet.

I gaped as though I was gazing into a wonderland. Mom's closet came to mind, but this closet was the mother of all. I turned to Jeffery. "You did this for me?"

"I sure did, boo. Of course, I hope you'll let me borrow some of this divine fashion," Jeffery teased.

I entered the closet with my hand brushing along every delicate item. The closet seemed endless. To top it off, it smelled of brand-new clothing with the tags still attached. Moving on, the built-in shelves contained rows of designer shoes such as Louis Vuitton, Manolo, Gucci, and Christian Louboutin. The chiffonier was stocked full of scarves, jewelry, accessories, and even Victoria's Secrets apparel and PJs. Speechless, I didn't know what to say. Did I fit the role of royalty? I came from rags, and now I lived in a home fit for a queen. This all seemed too good to be true.

Spinning on my heels, I glanced up at my dear friend. "You must've spent a fortune!" I whistled. "Why spend your money on me?"

"Chile, it's not *my money*. You is the billionaire, and you need to look like one. Those rags," Jeffery scrunched his nose, "are wretched. No offense." His face soured at my choice of ensemble...*prison clothes*.

I looked down at my clothing and turned to the full-length mirror in the corner. One quick glance and I staggered. The girl staring back appeared broken. "I'm pretty pathetic, aren't I?"

Jeffery's eyes moistened. "Ah, boo, just give it time. Dom will fatten you up, and those green eyes of yours will sparkle again. Real soon! You'll see." He wrapped his golden arms around me and I melted into his chest and sobbed.

I was the ghost of a person who once lived. I'd lost weight, my eyes were dull, and my hair lacked luster. I pulled from Jeffery's embrace, wiping the tears from my cheeks.

Then anger nipped. Aidan and his family had stripped me of my spirit. Now I had to put the pieces back together. I wasn't sure I had the strength.

Jeffery spoke up, drawing me back to the present, which I gratefully appreciated. "You ain't got nothin' to fret about. Just think of me as your personal stylist." Jeffery twirled like a high dollar model, strutting down the catwalk.

Oh lord, personal stylist! Jeff's taste was, well, extreme. I had to admit he did a fabulous job picking out the new clothing, on the other hand, I had my reservations about him dressing me. "Huh! We'll see." One could say my taste teetered on the reserved side.

"What," Jeffery shrieked as he placed his hands on his sassy hips. "Child, I know my skills!"

"Yes, you do. It just ain't mine. I'm just saying," I shrugged.

"My style *is* definitely a step up from yours," Jeffery eyed me like his bestie. "Gurrrlfriend, *pffeaseeee!* I'm gonna make you look good!" He snapped his fingers and twirled. "When I'm done, folks around 'ere are gonna think you is royalty, as you rightfully are. Hash-tag that, sistah!"

Oh, brother! I thought inwardly. I saw that we had a lot of lost time to make up.

UNWANTED GUEST

I glanced over at the alarm clock. Damn, two in the morning. My eyes wouldn't close. How ironic. For the past three years, I'd slept like a baby on cold metal. Sleep was easy then. Of course, I had a constant cocktail of drugs pumped into me, twenty-four-seven.

But tonight, not even my Sealy mattress could subdue my spinning head. I flipped my lamp on and sat up, drawing my knees to my chest. I spotted Snowball at the end of the bed, curled up, *sleeping*. What the hell? Everyone, including the cat was sleeping but me.

I felt restless. Something I haven't experienced in three years. I couldn't stop thinking about my mom. I'd had only a minute to process her death before my life had been jerked out from under me. Now, accepting Sara's death didn't resonate with me. It was as if she'd merely moved to some forgotten town, getting her hooks in another boyfriend, and living it up on his dime and nickel. Any day now, she'd show up at my door like a stray cat. Yet logic said otherwise. My heart ached with regret. We didn't exactly have the best relationship. I was angry back then and now I didn't know what I felt. How did one cope with the loss of an abusive parent? I reckoned I'd have to learn as I go.

Then I thought of Dad. The whole concept of Sara killing Dad shook my core. Could I come to terms, knowing that Sara's selfishness cost my dad's life? Did I have any other choice? I had to accept the truth and find a way to move on. How did I do that when my heart wrung with pain?

I had trouble deciding whether I hated Sara or *pitied* her. Placing all the blame on her didn't seem fair. She had no control over her mental state. A human carrying a celestial fetus was a serious mistake, and her payment... she contracted a disease that altered her brain, turning her into a sociopath.

I blamed myself as if I'd committed the murder. I should've never been born. An experiment that should've never happened. A freak of the Illuminati's creation best described me.

The Family created me in an undisclosed medical lab. How exactly scientist concocted an embryo between my dad's DNA and a celestial creature's DNA blew my mind.

What kind of creepy monster did the Illuminati create? I shuddered over the thought. I had no clue to the kind of powers they bestowed upon me. I once heard I had powers of mass destruction. I prayed the rumor was a lie. It only made me feel more like a freak. I thought superheroes were invincible. I certainly wasn't. Rather, a pathetic weakling fit my description more appropriately.

Powers? That was a joke on me. I scoffed. Where were my powers when they took me against my will? My captors, the Family, in the name of their cockeyed justice, I knew they had the upper hand. I paid the price for their insidious sins.

That was when I came to stay at the lovely, Haven Hospital. After getting comfy, I accepted my lot in life. The drug-induced coma felt like a god send, anything to ease the misery. I was a dead person with a pulse. I had no family. No friends to call. I was utterly alone, facing a life sentence for crimes I didn't commit.

The only thing that reminded me that I was alive was the deep-seated tick that kept clawing at me. A lost memory, perhaps? For the life of me, I couldn't recall what. I eased out a wry sigh.

I glanced about at my new surroundings. The beauty and riches seemed like a dream—but it was real. I was home, surrounded by people who loved me.

Then why wasn't I happy? Our material needs were more than plentiful. Yet not even an infinity of cash could fill the void in my gut. Facing the fact that my mother had sold me into slavery nearly destroyed me, but the treachery that splintered my heart had been dealt by the man I gave my heart to... *Aidan Bane DuPont.*

I get why the Family and Sally turned on me. What I didn't get was what did Aidan have to gain? That night at the cottage, we entangled our spirits as one, infusing our magick forever. So by betraying me, didn't Aidan betray himself? Nothing added up.

Then that following morning, the bottom fell out. Sally and her anonymous co-conspirator abducted me. Although I never got a glimpse at my abductor, I sensed it was Aidan. His touch, his scent, I knew without having to see his face that it was him.

Now my mind swirled in doubt. I reckoned there was a huge part of me that didn't want to believe he'd stoop to such a monstrosity. I began to rub my temples, trying to ease a pounding headache.

The funny thing that I couldn't figure out was why did Aidan need to subdue me with an injection? Whoever held me, stuck me with a needle to knock me out. He could've just as easily used the angel dust or his druid magick. But to use something that was so human like as a simple needle didn't seem like him at all.

So much mystery plagued my mind. Another mystery, how did Aidan and the castle mysteriously disappear without a trace? How could a castle vanish in broad daylight? I shook my head, bewildered.

There was no rhyme or reason to this madness. Even the last words Aidan had spoken before he left my side that faint morning. I recalled his words as if it were yesterday... *'believe only half of what you see and none of which you don't.'* His riddle played in my mind like a broken tune. What did it mean?

The truth may never rear its ugly face. Despite my gut instincts, there was one piece of fact I couldn't deny, Aidan had abandoned me.

I threw my legs over the edge of the bed, aggravated. I thought maybe I'd grab something to drink and visit the garden. Wearing only a white-cotton gown, I threw on a shawl over my shoulders and tiptoed down the stairs, careful not to wake the house. I went straight for the subzero fridge and grabbed my favorite drink, Coke, before heading out back.

A soft breeze gently tousled my hair as I stepped outside onto the patio. The aroma of pine and cherry blossoms delighted my senses. I kicked off my slippers and wandered out to the garden. The grass beneath my toes felt cool and invigorating. I spotted a swing nestled under an old oak tree in the far corner, apart from the garden. I glimpsed high above the leaves and whistled. "Wow! An old fashion swing. What a quaint little spot." A smile stretched across my face. It reminded me of my childhood. My father use to push me on a hand-made swing he'd built from leftover wood. Gosh, I'd forgotten.

I slipped into the swing and pushed off. I felt like a child again, toes touching the starry sky. I didn't want to be anywhere but here. I felt... *happy*.

Suddenly, I heard a rustle, obscured behind the tree line. A chill snaked down my spine. I stopped as I searched among the trees. *Nothing.* Then a shadow moved. I sighed. "Whew!" It was Snowball scurrying from under the hydrangeas. *Paranoid much?* I laughed as I watched my cat scamper off.

Then abruptly, I heard footsteps approaching fast. I leaped from the swing, scanning the garden and the thicket lining the fence.

Nothing.

Out of nowhere, echoes of footfalls pierced the air. Leaves crunching under someone's feet. I pulled the shawl tighter over my shoulders. My eyes raked over the stand of trees once more. Nil, no one. "I should go back in the house," I whispered.

I took three steps and halted. There, under the moonlight, stepping from the shadows, an outline of a person in a cloak, tall and very beautiful. My blood iced.

"Hello. Let me introduce myself." She slipped the crimson hood down, though, not extending her hand. Without warning, the air became chilly. "I'm Aidan's sister, Helen, and my brother lost his life because of you." Arrogance resonated in the way she tilted her sharp chin. The mark of a true Illuminati, but her crass arrogance didn't register. I was stuck on, "Aidan's d-d-dead?" I gawked at his sister as a strong mistrust squeezed my lungs.

"Of course, how rude of me. You didn't know." Enmity coated her words with sweet honey. "You must forgive me, you were away." She gave pause. "I hope you enjoyed your stay." She smiled, but it wasn't your usual welcome-home smile. There was wickedness behind those cherry lips. A fury, I didn't want to tangle with.

"I didn't kill your brother."

"I'm sorry. I must have not made myself clear. I didn't say he died by your hands. *I said* you were the reason," she hissed like a serpent ready to strike.

"I dearly love chatting about family, but let's cut to the chase. How does an immortal die?"

"Why should I divulge any information to you," she snorted.

If it involved a heart, I doubted she would've understood, but I tossed the dog a bone anyway. "I once loved your brother."

She sniffed haughtily. "Do you think my brother loved *you?*" The tall beauty snickered under her breath, "You *stupid* girl! That night at the party, he only intended to fulfill his duty, his promise to the Family. My brother couldn't *wait* to be rid of you."

Her words burned like acid, but I swallowed the angry bile down. I refused to show weakness. After all, that was what she wanted. So I replied with my own special brand of venom. "It doesn't matter now. He's gone. Another one bites the dust. *Next.*" I shrugged, smugly.

The vixen blonde clenched her teeth. "My brother was clever. He fooled *you*, didn't he?"

I wanted to stomp the smirk right off her elegant-but-wicked face. Rather instead, I threw a little shade with a smile. "Apparently, he wasn't clever enough. He's dead."

"Shut up," the blonde beauty roared, cornering me against the fence, "Say that again and I'll end your pathetic life right now!"

A smile tipped the corner of my lip. I'd struck a chord all right. I knew mocking the dead was not in good taste, but with all the shade-throwing, I figured a little mudslinging at her hind-ass was well deserved.

Still, there had to be more to her coming here than flaunting my past. "Why are you here, Helen?" I eyed her suspiciously.

The blonde assumed a posture of superiority. "Are you bothered by me?"

I laughed. "Bothered like a cockroach, but that's an easy fix." A deep, seedy grin played upon my face.

"Careful what you say, hybrid!"

Her idle threat didn't frighten me. She couldn't do anything to me that hadn't already been done. "So, are you here to announce Aidan's death? You're really starting to bore me," I feigned a yawn.

"Not exactly." Her eyes filled with dark portents.

"Why are you here at this ungodly hour, then? I have nothing else to give."

"You're right! Now that my brother's gone, our long-awaited goal is null and void. We made a mistake relying on a useless human."

I was done with this futile squabble. "Well, Helen, it's been lovely, but I'm leaving. I'm sure you can find your way back to the rock you crawled out from under."

"Stupid hybrid," she sneered. "I didn't come to revel in your release from prison or your very generous cash flow, courtesy of my dead brother. I've been sent by the Family to give you a message."

I shook my head, exasperated. "There's nothing you or your family can say that will interest me. Go home," I demanded. I understood the Family's powerful reach better than anyone, and I knew when to pull out of a game that I was no match for.

"I'm more than happy to leave, but first, I have to deliver a word of warning."

"Go home," I gushed, side stepping the blonde. I had one intent... *leaving this bitch to wallow in her own spurious threats.* I was done. "You have nothing to say that's worth my time," I threw at him over my shoulder as I headed straight for the house.

"They'll send someone far more dangerous than me," the blonde called out. "I think, for your sake, you should listen."

I stopped dead in my tracks and slowly turned, facing Aidan's sister. I narrowed my eyes, not caring that she saw my disdain. "Then get on with it," I snapped, "So I can be done with you and your damn family *forever.*" I hated her and everything she stood for.

The blonde's face twisted as if she'd bitten into a rotten apple. "The Family sent me here to tell you," she paused. "Don't go sticking your nose into things that is none of your affair. If you don't heed to our warning, your life," she hesitated, "and the life of those close to you will suffer greatly. I hope we have an understanding?" The frost in her voice sent chills over my body. I fully understood between the unspoken lines.

I stood there thinking of the different ways I could snap her neck but my curiosity slammed into first place. It seemed suspicious to go to this much trouble for little old-hybrid me. I tossed an amused smile. "It sounds like *your* family is a little paranoid."

The blonde's lips curled in disgust. "Paranoia is not our forte. You should be mindful of where you step. I'm sure you wouldn't want to find yourself back in that hospital." Without another word, the blonde beauty in the scarlet cloak disappeared from sight. My gut told me chances of becoming bosom buddies with Aidan's sister were slim. Suddenly, a cold breeze swept through me. I quickly gathered my shawl tighter around my shoulders. It was time to head back inside. The sooner the better too.

SEE NO EVIL

*W*hen the later morning arrived, I needed a U-Haul to drag myself out of bed. After the encounter with Aidan's sister, my mind kept repeating questions like a bad rerun. Suddenly the sting of tears threatened. If only I knew how Aidan died. What if he'd fallen victim to his family as I did? I shook my head, feeling the weight of guilt. Could I have been wrong? It wasn't a stretch, suspecting Sally and her bag of tricks. Then who was helping her? The man who held me felt like Aidan and he smelled like him. I recognized his manicured hands. I questioned if there was chance it could've been an imposter but that was impossible. Sam was dead. He was the only one that could cloak Aidan. So, what was I supposed to believe?

One truth I was certain as I lie here alive... it proved that Aidan's theory was incorrect. One *could* live without the other. My breathing was proof. Strange though, Aidan was never wrong. He didn't make mistakes. After living 300 hundred years, I reckoned one learned to master perfection.

I raked my fingers through my hair. Believing his death was unfathomable. Frustration, pain, and rage smothered me. All I could do was lay my face into my palms and sob.

After a long good cry, I wiped the tears from my face and pulled myself together. I decided to go downstairs while the house remained quiet. Once I reached the kitchen, to my surprise, the aroma of piping hot coffee filled the air. Dom had set the coffee maker for 6 a.m. I wondered if he'd overheard my conversation with Helen.

I sensed more problems on the horizon. Aidan's sister showing up at our house unannounced with no good intent, proved more than ever that my presence here was a threat to the guys. If I stayed, I was putting them at risk.

I got a nagging feeling this wasn't the last I'd hear from the Family. Helen's threat rode on my shoulders like a heavy feed sack. I had to do something. I couldn't let her or that despicable Order harm *my family*. Yet the Illuminati had the strength of gods. They were everywhere. No escaping their clenches if they wanted you.

Somehow I had to figure out a way to keep them at bay. My family meant everything to me.

It was a nice morning regardless of my run-in earlier. I stepped out into the lawn, and right away, I spotted the vegetable garden roped off. I padded over to it as an admiring smile crept across my face. The leafy patch left me breathless. Everything was in a nice neat row. Assorted vines covered the soil in thick blooms. The garden definitely had Dom's marvelous touch. There were onions, spinach, tomatoes, rosemary, and ginseng root. *How odd*, I thought. Ginseng was a magickal plant used in certain rituals. Ms. Noel kept a supply of it all the time. I learned of its use by watching her prepare it for her customers. I wondered if Dom knew of its properties.

I made my way back to the tree swing. I refused to let a vile creature as Helen deny me the right to certain joys in my own home. Despite her opinion of how I obtained the house, it didn't matter to me.

I earned this house with my own blood. Whether I stay here or not, this home belonged to the guys and me. I'd guard and defend this place like Daniel Boone fighting for the Alamo. We might go down in a blaze, but not without a good old-fashioned fight.

Come to think about it, I should find a weapon. At this point, my so-called powers were useless. Having protection might not be a bad idea just in case we have more uninvited visitors.

I slid into the swing and pushed off. As I climbed into the great blue, higher and higher, the cool morning breeze caressed my face. The tension in my shoulders lightened. This very moment gave waking up a delightful purpose. I'd much rather do this all day than confront my troubles. Soon, I would have to come down and find a solution to keep The Family off our backs. The complexed question was how? What would be their kryptonite? If I discovered their weakness, I might have a chance in stopping the almighty beast. The world would be a safer place, and so would my family.

With no warning, footsteps approached, jarring me from my thoughts. At first I stiffened. Flashes of my recent encounter flooded my mind, but when I spotted the on comer, I quickly relaxed by exhaling a Down-At-The-Heel sigh. "Oh good God! You startled me," I gasped in relief.

"Stevie, I'm sorry. I didn't mean to frighten you. I wanted to bring you this." Dom handed my shawl to me. "You will catch your death of cold out here," he scolded me.

I dug my heels into the soil to stop the swing. "Thank you." I reached for the soft, shawl and wrapped it around my shoulders. It had belonged to Sara. It was the only thing I had of hers. "You don't have to fuss over me. You're not my employee."

"Perhaps, but it is what I do best." Dom stalled for a second, peering over at the roped-off garden. He nodded over his shoulder. "You like my vegetables?" he smiled, a sense of pride yet his eyes seemed troubled.

"Yeah, the garden is sprouting." I fixed my eyes on the lush patch and lingered a moment and then back to Dom.

"Oui, I overheard your conversation earlier this morning," he stared out into the garden. "That intrusive creature needed tossing out on her sweet derrière."

"You know Helen?" My brow arched.

"Knowing, *non!* It is not necessary. The girl is trouble. It is like a poisonous viper. You may not know the species of the reptile, but you know not to get near it. She is nothing like her brother. Aidan, through all his faults, he had a heart. This girl is as wicked as her black magick."

It seemed Dom knew more about the Family's inherited practices than I'd given him credit for. Obviously, Jeffery and I underestimated him.

"What do you know that you're not telling me, Dom?" My inquisitiveness tickled the hairs on my back.

"My beautiful child, I may play the role of naïveté, but I am far from ignorant."

"Wait," my eyes orbed. "You know about their... uh, special talents?"

"I've seen plenty of strange, unexplained things around that family to know they are not in the same gene pool of let's just say, the commonalty." Dom's accent seemed more profound than usual.

"But I heard you argue with Jeffery."

"*Oui!* I prefer to leave that little tidbit apart from my life partner." His mustache tipped upward. "You know how he gets with certain subjects. Protecting him is for his best interest and our peace of mind, yes?" Dom winked, flashing a lopsided mustache.

A faint smile caressed my lips. "*Oui* on that one!" I paused with a more serious note. "Dom, just how much do you know about Aidan's family?"

"I've been wondering when you were going to ask that question." He nodded toward the house. "Why don't we go inside and discuss this over breakfast? You look like you can use another cup of coffee and something nourishing to eat, yes?"

"Sure, lead the way." Whatever Dom knew excited me and frightened me at the same time. I might as well brace myself for the worst.

Until I stepped inside, I didn't realize how nippy the early morning had been. The warmth rushed across my face, and the smell of bacon aroused my appetite.

Jeffery had already arrived, sitting at the table, holding his fork erect. I recalled how Jeffery got his panties in a wad at mealtimes. I laughed to myself. Some things never change.

Dom had gone all out preparing breakfast with a fine table spread with fresh fruit, a popular treat in France, baked buttery chocolate croissants, scrambled eggs, and crisp bacon.

Apart from the delicious eatables, the best part about this wonderful feast had nothing to do with the food.

My glance bounced around the table at the two faces sitting across from me. It touched my heart to be sharing this beautiful morning with my two best friends in the whole wide world, and for that, I felt honored. They truly were my family. I think Dad would've approved.

For a short while, we ate in silence, then Dom and Jeffery shared a strained glance. Dom went to clear his throat, a discussion was about to commence. I dreaded it too. I withdrew a deep sigh and laid my fork down, waiting for Dom to start.

"Oh, for God's sake," Jeffery huffed. "Just say it. We're gonna become petrified wood before you get around to it!"

I stifled a laugh.

"Jeffery! Where is your patience?" Dom's voice dipped down into a scolding tone. "We can't just blurt it out. The poor girl has been through enough. We don't need to pour salt on an open wound."

"Well, it's better to throw the whole container of salt all at once than to drag the misery out sprinkle by sprinkle on a festering sore!" Jeffery folded his arms, pursing his lips.

"I'm getting to that part if you'll settle down." Dom gave his long time but annoying partner a disconcerting glare before focusing back to me. "My sweet, Jeffery and I are very concerned for you. You have awakened some very powerful enemies once again. We are fearful for your safety."

Jeffery squirmed in his chair. I reckoned he needed to excuse himself and go seek out the gentlemen's restroom or he was a bundle of nerves.

I could relate. My teeth were on edge too. "Yeah, after the visit from Aidan's sister, I've been thinking about getting a weapon." A tight smile snagged the corners of my mouth.

Dom whetted a gentle smile in return. "Let me first say, nothing happens by accident. The Family is quite crafty. Throughout history, any catastrophic event that has been written, the Family has been the masterminds behind it. Wars and famine are not by chance. It is the Illuminati's ploy to bring mankind down to his knees. Even the death of your father was no accident. His deflection cost him his life by the hands of someone he trusted… *your mother.*"

All of a sudden, I felt regret squeezing my lungs. "Where is my mom's grave? I'd like to pay my respects."

There was a hint of sadness behind Dom's eyes. "The Family took your mother's body before Jeffery and I had discovered what had happened."

"Was she given a proper burial?" My appetite began to dwindled into a sharp pain.

"Obviously, you were not informed. I am sorry to tell you that your mother's body was cremated."

"No!" My eyes burned with tears. "I didn't get to say my last good-byes." A swirl of mixed emotions hit me.

"We inquired of Sara's ashes, though, we were too late. The Family had disposed of her remains."

"What right did they have to do that? She was my mother! They didn't..." I paused, calming my temper. "I appreciate your efforts." I shrugged. "I don't expect Aidan's family to show me any kind favors." I glanced at the garden to compose myself.

"Jeffery and I apologize for not..." Dom trailed off.

Jeff interrupted. "We did everything we possibly could." He reached over and touched my hand.

I flashed a short smile. "I know. You both have been a huge blessing. Thank you both for everything." My eyes glided between two sets of troubled eyes. "I have so many questions spinning in my head. Where do I begin?"

Dom cleared his throat. "Hopefully, I can assist you with some of your dilemmas."

"Anything that can help, I'm grateful for it." I leaned in closer. Dom had my full attention.

"You see, for the first time since the beginning of man, there is something the Illuminati fears."

I coughed out a short laugh. "That crazy occult isn't afraid of anything. They're on the top of the food game and we're their meal."

"Ah, that is what they want you to think. They fear much." Dom held an impish grin.

"I find that hard to believe."

"Stevie, the Family is terrified of you."

I almost laughed. "They locked me away in an insane asylum, framing me for murder. The Family is like God."

"I know it must seem as so, but please allow me to explain," Dom smiled.

"Please do." I shifted in my seat, feeling a wave of dread.

Dom began. "As history foretells, the Family are the ones who created the secret society. Let me explain." Dom moistened his lips. "The first sector of scientists who began experimenting with genetics were the ones who actually created Frankenstein. Of course, not as the movie but something much more sinister."

"I'm not liking the sound of this."

"Oui, the Family can be quiet intimidating."

"That's an understatement." Chills shimmied down my spine.

"Oui! They are very dangerous. Although, they are not the most feared. Any power they cannot mimic or possess terrifies them. That one…" Dom slipped Jeffery a furtive glance, then back to me, "is you, mon chéri." Dom extended a gentle smile.

I crinkled my nose. "Wait! You know?"

"Oui. Jeffery and I figured it out. The Family would have not gone to great lengths to capture you if you were a mere human. They would've simply taken your life."

The churning in my stomach deepened. "Speaking of death," I hesitated. "There's something I just discovered." I raked in a piercing breath. "Aidan's dead." I spat it out as if it burned my tongue. "His sister shared this with me early this morning." I had a gut feeling that Aidan's death and the disappearing castle was linked. It definitely had strange and eerie stamped all over it. When I lifted my eyes, I saw Dom's and Jeffery's stunned faces. It pained me to see the starkness in their eyes. I went on to tell what I knew. "She refused to go into any details." I shook my head, frustrated, and baffled how his death could've happened.

"Jesus, take me home, *NOW!*" Jeffery began fanning himself like he was about to faint.

Dom quietly torpedoed a calm-down scorn at Jeffery before he commented. "I'm not sure I can believe everything this woman says."

"Yeah, me either, but you haven't seen Aidan since his castle vanished. It certainly appears as if… " I choked on those last two words. I couldn't say the words. I feared if I did, then I'd have to believe it. I wasn't ready to accept Aidan's death.

"Yes, it all seems incredulous. The last time we saw Aidan, it was that night when the two of you were together in the pool house." Dom cleared his throat. "I went looking for you to make sure you were safe. When I saw you with Aidan, I assumed everything was fine."

"I sure as hell wasn't okay," Jeffery sang. "I got tied up and locked in a mofo closet by that rascal, Aidan's cousin, Sam. I hate dark places, and I hate that boy even more." Jeffery crossed his arms in a stew.

"That nasty booger was hiding around the corner, waitin' for you to leave before he jumped me."

I clutched my chest. "That explains how Sam knew where to find me," I half murmured to myself. "He must've heard our conversation." My eyes slid over to Dom. "That night when you came to check on me, it wasn't Aidan you saw. It was Sam. He had the ability to mimic anyone."

"Oh dear lord! We had no idea." Dom's face took on a look of fright. "When I saw you in his arms, Jeffery and I assumed you were safe. We are so sorry!"

"Don't blame yourself. How could you have known? The real Aidan saved my life," I paused. "He killed Sam for hurting me." My eyes slid to Jeff. "You don't have to worry about Sam ever again."

"Lord have mercy!" Jeffery chimed. "Never in my life have I wished a fella dead, but that sadistic mofo, I'd happily sweeten his tea with rat poison and be smilin' in his face while he's downin' it and askin' for mo. Huh-hmm, I sure as hell would!"

I reached over to Jeffery. "He's gone, so maybe you should save the poison for the real rats." I smiled, but it was strained, and right away I went to the next question. "Did Aidan ever catch up with y'all the next day? He left me at the cottage to find you."

Jeffery and Dom looked at each other with confusion. "No. He never showed up," Dom continued. "We tried finding out what happened to the two of you, but the Family had stepped in and brushed everything underneath the rug. Coupled with Aidan's disappearance, Jeffery and I didn't have a clue to your whereabouts. It was not until we saw your face broad-cast over the news did we realize what had happened."

I wrapped my arms around my waist, trying to hold off a panic attack. "I'm very sorry for what I've put you two through these past three years."

"Don't worry yourself," Dom encouraged. "It wasn't your fault."

"It hasn't been easy on you guys either," I shrugged bitterly. "You both can rest assure that I won't be stirring up any hornet's nest. Whatever his sister is protecting, she doesn't have to worry. I plan to keep my distance from her and that wretched family, *forever*." I tried to ease the guys' worries. On the other hand, I expected nightmares over Helen's threat.

417

A person filled with raw fear was unpredictable and highly dangerous. If I were Helen, I'd watch my step. No way in hell would I let her
or the Family hurt Dom and Jeffery or take me back to that sadistic
hospital.

"Yes," Dom continued, "Regardless-of-your-noninvolvement, it
appears that the Illuminati is feeling uneasy having you free. Not too
many people can rattle their chain as you have, my dear."

"Those cold hearted bastards aren't afraid of me." I found that hard
to digest. "The Family thinks of themselves as the almighty."

"Contraire, my child, you are a force to be reckoned with, and
because of this very fact, I am certain that Helen's visit has a hidden
agenda. What we must do is find out *what*."

"I think it's clear. They want me out of their way, dead or alive."

Then all at once, Jeffery erupted, "If they could've taken your life,
you'd be stiff as a board rotting in some unmarked grave right now.
Lucky for you those evil-white-ugly rascals is terrified of you. Why do
you think that hospital kept you shackled and comatose? After all, you
is the most badass mofo out there... *a genetically engineered angel!*"
Jeffery snapped his fingers, full of swag.

"I rarely ever say this about Jeff, but he's right, yes," Dom admitted.

"I don't feel supernatural. Rather, I feel helpless, which is pretty
human in my book."

"Right now you are vulnerable. For this reason, we need to take
measures reassuring your safety. A trainer can help you learn self-
defense. As for tapping into your angelic magick along with your druid
gifts, we can't be much of assistance there. However, we will find a way."

"Druid?" Surprise, shock, and stun, all rolled in one, attacked my
brain. "I'm not a druid!" I shook my head. "No way!"

"Can you be certain of that?" Dom's brow shot up. "You are your
father's daughter."

"My father, Jon?"

"*Oui!* Your father comes from the druid bloodline."

"I had no idea," I said.

"Why do you think the family arranged for you and Monsieur
Aidan to join in union?" Dom asked.

My brows suddenly collided. "Does the Family believe in plural
marriage?"

"Why do you ask?"

"I understand that Aidan is married to Sally."

Dom's face took on a look of surprise. "Stevie, I've worked for Monsieur Aidan for many years. Not once has he mentioned a wife. You were the only woman in his life."

I raked my fingers through my hair, blowing out a sigh. "I'm not sure what to believe anymore."

"I do know that the Family had arranged for you to be married to Monsieur Aidan. They would have not allowed another woman to cause problems. They knew that with your magickal abilities and Aidan's druid magick, your children would be immortal. Sickness and death will be a thing of the past. Some refer to you as the new-age Eve."

"Eve! That's the first I've heard *that*," I squirmed.

"Yes, that does seem extreme." Dom cuffed his mouth, hiding a laugh.

"That's just icky! " I shuddered.

"I know this is daunting." Sympathy filled Dom's gentle brown eyes.

I averted my eyes to the large window, wishing I had never left the comfort of my swing. I straightened my shoulders and slid my eyes back to Dom. "Now that Aidan is no longer with us, the Family doesn't have much hope for a perfect race and a one-world government." My stomach fluttered like butterflies as I thought about the past and an imposing future I faced. Still nothing was matching up.

"Oui. It does seem their future is at a disadvantage now." Dom rubbed his mustache, thinking.

"What about the infusion between Aidan and me? Shouldn't I be dead too? If Aidan was truly dead, then that theory was a fallacy."

"Nothing is certain, chère. Aidan's theory could've been wrong."

I shook my head, "Aidan didn't make mistakes. He was too careful."

"True," Dom curtly answered.

"I don't know." Now I was really confused.

Dom went on. "There were other trials than you. Different. Although, sadly, the mothers died during birth. The children who successfully survived had a blended mix of fey DNA, like Sam."

Jeffery blew out a sharp sigh. "That explains why Sambo was so mean!"

"Yeah, Sam." Goose bumps popped over my arms.

"Boo," Jeffery butted in. "Don't you fret any over that no-good count. He was plum evil." Jeffery's voice trembled with fear.

I shrugged. "Anyway, how did the fey become involved with the Illuminati?"

"Well," Dom went on to explain. "You've heard of the Nephilim giants?"

"Yes, my dad read the Bible story to me when I was a child."

"Then you know the Nephilim was the offspring of the angels and the daughters of man?"

"Yes, I remember." Dom had my attention. I couldn't see what the Nephilim had to do with Sam's kind.

"Did you know that the giants were the gateway for the fey race?"

My brow arched. "Really! How so?"

Dom began, "As the story foretells, the giants are evil in every sense…"

I interrupted, "Are you saying the giants still exist?"

"Non, not the ones from the ancient world."

"Was there another world?"

"No, the same earth, just another period. It was called the Time of Ole, the biblical era, the world before the flood, " Dom clarified.

"Oh, I vaguely recall the tale." Flashes of Dad reading to me as a child wafted in my brain. It was such a long time ago that I'd almost forgotten.

"*Oui!* During the Time of Ole, angels walked among man. Some were friends with Noah. Of course, their relationship took a drastic turn when the angels took the young daughters of man. This angered the humans and enraged the angels' creator. Angels and humans having relations were forbidden in the ancient world. Angels were not meant to have human desires, even more so to produce offspring children… half-angel, half human. In the eyes of their creator, it was apostasy, an unforgivable act. As for the aftereffect, the angels were punished for their disobedience."

"What sort of punishment?" Curiosity bristled my neck.

"Since the celestial beings were perfect creatures with eternal life, they faced eternal destruction for the act of treason. However, first, their creator had to set an example for the heavenly body to see the consequences for their ill behavior. Until their allotted time, the rebellious angels were marked as an outcast and bound to the earth, no longer permitted to enter the heavens," Dom explained.

"I'm confused. Am I one of them, half human and half angel?" I glimpsed over at Jeffery, who was starting to go pale. I slid my Coke over to him. Without delay, he snatched it up and down it like it was a shot of whiskey.

"No, you are not half human and you were not conceived by a human. Your design is quite different."

"Then I don't understand why you are telling me this."

"Please allow me to clarify," Dom smiled.

I nodded silently.

Dom continued. "The Nephilim reached adulthood very quickly. Soon the giants followed in the footsteps of their angelic fathers and mated with humans and every other creature as well. Subsequently, the children of the Nephilim created a new race called fey. They're referred to as Seelie." Dom paused, giving me a moment to let it sink in.

"So the fey have survived all these centuries?"

"Funny you should ask. The Nephilim offspring received protection by the Illuminati."

"I thought the first Illuminati formed a secret society in the early seventeen hundreds as the Knights Templar?"

"The Illuminati have been in existence since the beginning of time. Actually, Cain was the catalyst for the Family's true beginnings. Cain became the true founder of the occult. Of course, it has evolved since then but it is still the true beginnings."

"This just seems uncanny, all wrapped up with a pretty pink bow on top," I cringed.

"Now that you are part of the world of extraordinaire, you can see it has many faces. It's something you mustn't ever reveal to anyone nor forget."

"Don't worry. I will take this to my grave." I just found a whole new freak-out. I squeezed my waist trying to hold it together.

Dom smiled, but it didn't reach his eyes. "The Illuminati had always been interested in science. The Family realized that they had something exclusive, so they agreed to provide shelter to the young fey if they agreed to abide by the sealed contract."

"What is it with this damn family and contracts," I scoffed. "So the children of the Nephilim survived the flood?"

"That is correct," Dom said.

"What happened to the original giants and their mothers?"

"The giants didn't have as much luck as their children. Even the Illuminati knew they couldn't coexist with the Nephilim. However, they did extract DNA from the adult Nephilim, however any further dealing with them had ceased."

I wrinkled my nose, unclear. "Dom, how did the Illuminati know about DNA back then?"

An impish glint hid behind Dom's eyes. "The angels, of course. They assisted in mankind's creation."

"I guess that makes sense," I shrugged, picking at my cold food.

"It does seem incredible for man to have such advanced abilities that early in time. However, before mankind was even a thought, the know-how of science was always there among the angels." Dom sipped of his coffee.

"So, you were saying about the giants?" I propped my elbow on the table, still playing with my food.

"Yes. As I was simplifying. No one succeeded in reigning the mighty giants into submission. For this reason, the Family left them and their birth mothers behind, sealing their fate once and for all. The deluge took their lives."

"What happened to the angels?"

"They took their true spirit form."

"How did the Illuminati and the offspring of the Nephilim survive?"

"The fallen angels assisted in carrying the old ones to the highest peak, sealing them off in a cave where the water couldn't penetrate. When the water receded and land resurfaced, they came out, though weak and thin. They survived by feasting on others who didn't have as high of a position. The lesser ones were much more expendable."

"How did you come across this information? This isn't in the Bible accounts," I asked, puzzled.

"You are correct. The Illuminati have kept historical records from the beginning of time."

"I remember Aidan saying something about how they kept meticulous documentation of my father's death, but I had no idea that their accounting went back to the beginning of man's existence."

"Man's existence began long before Adam and Eve," Dom flashed an erudite grin, "But that story will have to be told another time. How I came across the accounts, well, when you have worked for someone for as long as I have, a trust is established. Many of their secret meetings, I served their meals, and was permitted to be among the black and white robes. Eventually, they trusted me with a key. At night, when the house was quiet, I'd sneak down to the hidden chamber and snoop through their records."

"Aidan explained the books were protected by black magick. How were you able to get past that?"

"Yes, they are very protective of their scrolls. It is *their* bible."

"Then how were you able to go unnoticed?"

Suddenly a roguish grin hid under his mustache. "I had the key to unlock the protective spell. Like I said, they trusted me."

I gawked at Dom as if he were the cat that ate the canary. "If you had been caught, they would have… "

"True, but I managed to stay under their notice."

"I should be taking lessons from you." I smiled with a newfound respect.

"I do have a few tricks up my sleeves," he grinned back, and then he took a long-winded breath. "What I've discovered is astounding and quite disturbing."

"Do tell!" I eagerly encouraged.

Dom furthered his story. "After the deluge, another race of fey began. This time, the new fey became the offspring of the angels and the adult children of the Nephilim, creating a much more distorted fey, the Unseelie."

"Wait! Are you saying, the new fey mated with grandpa?" Right away my stomach roiled.

"*Oui*. To humans this act is disgusting, but angels are supernatural beings as well as fey."

"Holy crap! I'm condemned as they are." All of a sudden, sheer fright swept through me.

"Non, non," Dom shook his head. "You are not of their sort."

"What makes you so sure?" I bayed, stunned by the possibility of my origin.

"You were created in a lab. The angel's DNA you share did not have intercourse with a human. You were born by the manipulation of technology. Alien advancement. That is why they refer to you as *a genetically engineered angel*," Dom reassured.

A moment of silence settled between us as I stared out the window, mulling all this in my brain. Then a question struck. "Okay, then why the history lesson?"

"I think it's important for you to know the Family's past, present and future. It may save your life someday."

"All right, I'll listen." I wanted to close my ears. It was just one more thing to add to the list of reasons to hate the Family.

"I suspect their grand scheme of things is much larger than ridding the world of sickness and death." Dom withdrew a strained sigh. "I'm afraid they are creating an army."

I glanced over at Jeffery, and his expression had changed from bulging eyes to tongue hanging. Was he going into shock? Drool was collecting at the side of his mouth. I scooted my chair over as I eyeballed him. "Holy crap! Fey on steroids."

"Oui! A mass production of super-strength fey."

"So, if they are creating an army of fey, why didn't they contain Sam? He was like the hulk when he turned to his true nature." I shuddered from the flashes of that horrendous night.

"I think they decided to use him as a decoy.

"What do you mean?"

"Sam had mastered the skill of trickery. Unfortunately for Sam his life ended abruptly. As Sam became progressively worse, no one could control him. Simply, he needed to be handled."

The hairs on my neck began to prickle. I knew that term too well. "The Family *handled* my father." I felt sick. "I know about the Family terminating Sam."

"Yes! However, his death had a double-edged sword. They appointed Aidan as the eliminator. When Sam found out, he became enraged. He fell into the Family's hands, as they had hoped." Dom pushed aside his cold coffee.

"I think I know what you're leading to. Sam sought out revenge against Aidan by coming after me." It was all too clear. "Aidan played along, convincing me he'd saved my life, confessing his dying love for me as we rode off into the blazing sunset." I took a moment, letting this sink in. "The Family orchestrated that attack. It was a ploy to get me to trust Aidan, but why? What did the Family want from me?" I shook my head, mystified. "Every event that transpired since I stepped foot on Louisiana's soil had everything to do with a master plan to catch me at my weakest moment." I'd been a fool. "I played right into their hands," I murmured mostly to myself. Stunned, I palmed my face, feeling the impact of the veracity. Just when I thought I had washed my hands of that family, I found myself still in the same deadly whirlwind. I thought it was over. Rather, I'd just begun. I raised my head, catching Dom's gaze. "Was I ever in real danger of Van taking my powers and leaving me for dead? After all, he was the reason I volunteered myself to Aidan."

Dom's face became smothered in sorrow. "There are still many mysteries surrounding your capture. I think there is more to uncover. However, I do believe Monsieur Aidan refused to join Van's master-plan to take your powers. When Van realized Aidan's betrayal, he went into a rampage. However, for some unknown reason, the Family intervened."

"What does the Family want from this vicious ploy?"

Dom shook his head. "Whatever reason they have, it is enough for them to have locked you away. I find it quite suspicious to drop your charges and set you free."

I sat there numb with shock. Dom reached over to his untouched glass of Coke, pushing it directly in front of me. I grabbed the drink and gulped it down quickly, wishing it had a kick to it.

Then it hit me like a head on collision with a freight train. I slammed my glass down with force. I looked straight into Dom's eyes with an abrupt awakening. *"They wanted me pregnant."* Suddenly, my heart skipped several beats. "Oh, my God! I have a child!" I bellowed. It wasn't a question, *it was a statement.* I shot to my feet in a whirlwind of panic. My chair flew backward, crashing to the floor. I could barely ask the heartening question. "Do you think my child is still alive?" My heart felt like it was going to break in two.

Dom hesitated, his eyes shifting, thinking. "Yes, the child has to be! Why else would Helen warn you to stay away? They must be hiding the baby."

"I have a child," I whispered. Those monsters had my baby. What if they are hurting my child? With my eyes wild with worry, I glanced over at Jeffery, rocking, and hugging himself. I desperately wanted to join him. "It's all clear to me. That's why Helen was trying to frighten me. They don't want me to know. Those conniving, devil-dealing, bastards!" I shouted to the rooftop. Rage and fear shot through me as my head spun with all the possibilities.

"What did Helen say," Dom asked, disquiet colored his face.

"She warned me to stay away or else." I cringed as my mind rushed over her sinister words.

"Or else what?" Dom stared at me parroting horror.

My face grew ashen. "She threatened my life and both you and Jeffery too."

"Oh, my! Aidan's sister is quite a catty one." Dom tapped his finger on his chin. "We need to take precautions. An alarm system, perhaps."

"Or I can move. If I'm gone, they'll leave you and Jeffery alone. Besides, no high tech alarm system is going to keep this girl out. She's gifted." I picked my chair up off the floor and sat it upright. Though I was too antsy for sitting. I began to pace.

Dom refuted. "No. We won't let her run your life or ours' either. This is your home. We will deal with this as a family."

I stopped and faced Dom. "It's too dangerous. Me taking chances with my life is one thing but I can't have you and Jeffery stepping in the middle of my mess."

Suddenly Jeffery snapped out of his coma and sprung to life.

"You ain't goin' nowhere! That white-no-count-high-priced-ho ain't kickin' you out of our home. Besides, you got the bank account."

"Jeffery!" Dom gaped.

"I was just sayin'," Jeffery shrugged, his face glistened with innocence.

Dom flashed Jeffery a I'll-Deal-With-You-Later glance. Then his eyes slid back to me. "Stevie, I know your heart must be breaking."

"My heart has already been fractured a long time ago. This"—I clenched my teeth— "This has me enraged!"

"If this helps any, I believe Aidan cared for you." Dom's face softened.

I threw up my hands in disgust. "There's no excuse that can cover his treachery. I lost three years of my life, framed for crimes I didn't commit. I lost my mother, my father. I lost my innocence. I lost my will to live, and the biggest loss ever—losing my child, who may or may not be alive." I took a deep breath, calming my rapid heartbeats. Then remorse struck. I shouldn't have taken my anger out on my friend. "Dom, I'm sorry." I peered outside the window, easing my breath, slowly. The breeze was blowing lazily as the trees swayed gently back and forth. I wanted to find my way back to the swing and forget the woes that beseeched my spirit, but my mind kept jumping around like a rock skipping over water. Then I knew what I had to ask next. The answer beckoned me, and I could no longer deny its thirst. I held my gaze on the trees, eschewing eye-contact with Dom. "Do I have the DNA of a fallen angel," I boldly dared.

Dom gave a startle gasp. "I think you are better off not knowing."

"I disagree." My heart lurched.

"I can't be certain. However, I do have my suspicions."

"Do you think this angel was an accessory to stealing my child?"

"It's possible." By the distortion in Dom's face, it was plain to see that he was warring with himself over whether or not he should reveal the truth.

With no warning, Jeffery slammed his white-knuckled fist onto the table, bringing both Dom and me to his full attention. "Dom, if you don't tell her, *I will*," he threatened. "She needs to know the whole truth!" Before Dom could gather a full sentence, impatient Jeffery bellowed like he was a one-man band. His eyes latched onto mine. "*Yes*! You have *mofo-bad-angel-blood* inside you, gurrrl." Then Jeffery used his indoor voice. "But that doesn't mean you is bad. Just a little spicy."

Dom threw Jeffery a lemon glare.

"Holy crap!" My knees buckled. Quickly, I grabbed the table for support.

"Chile, don't go and break your neck. Let me help you." Jeffery glided me back into my seat. "I'll get you a refill." He snatched up my glass and shuffled off.

Then I focused back to Dom. "I'd like to know his name." It suddenly became crucial for me to know the other side of my bloodline.

"A name, oui. I haven't met this creature, only stories, and I pray I never do."

"Is there a way to call upon him?"

"No, I refuse to help you there!" The anxious look on Dom's face told me he knew. "Stevie, you arc treading on very deadly ground. This is not the time to be dauntless," he warned. "You must leave him alone!" Deep lines etched across Dom's forehead. "Do you understand me?"

"I need to know his name! He might can help me find my child." Tears welled up. Dangerous or not, I needed to find this fallen angel.

Then Dom gathered himself from the table, and before he retreated upstairs, he turned to me and announced, "Against my better judgement, I'll give you his name but you must tread carefully. He is not to be trusted. Mustafa. The dark angel's name is Mustafa."

TROUBLE KNOCKS

*A*fter the past few weeks, I'd grown tired lying in bed, feeling sorry for myself. Sooner or later I had to leave the sanctuary of my bedroom and face the world.

I'd decided to take Jeffery's advice and join him on a night of painting the town red. Nothing better than a little music and a whole lotta liquor to lift the spirits. I didn't make a habit of drinking. Sara, my mother, had problems with the stuff. I refused to follow in her foot-steps. "But sometimes, a girl's gotta let loose."

The relentless worry that I might have a child wandering God-knows-where hurt worse than cutting out my bleeding heart. I reck-oned, I'd take Jeffery's advice and take a break. He wanted to show me the bright lights of New Orleans. I finally caved.

After a long bath, I threw on an oversized towel and went to my own personal department store called, *the Closet*. I had no idea what to pick out. Too many choices. I looked through garment after designer garment until I came to one outfit. I held the dress up, examining its threads. "Hmm." Jeffery might actually be a fashionista after all. The mini dress shimmered in black sequins, cut to hug my hips. The front dipped down revealing far more than I liked. It was the little black dress that could. And of course, hooker-heels, black-pumps embell-ished with gold spikes. "Crap!" I held up the shoes. "I hope I didn't break my neck in these puppies!"

I made my way to the cosmetics area and seated myself in front of the lit mirror. I glared at my unruly hair. As I held the brush in my hand, I stared at the young girl before me. A stranger at best. The gentleness in her eyes had vanished, but something else took its place. Grit, perhaps? Who was this girl, a shadow of the person she once was? The sparkle in her green-eyes had returned, but behind that shine laid a deep-rooted sadness. I wondered if she would ever find happiness?

Focusing on the present, I gaped at my hair with a snit. At least that part of me hadn't changed. The mess on top of my head was still unruly and defiant. I decided to make the best of it. I took the blow-dryer and ran it through my hair every which way. Messy was what I wanted, and messy was what I got. I did some teasing to give more fullness and height. Bed-head hair seemed to fit my outfit perfectly. Wild woman on the prowl. Quite appropriate, I thought.

I blinked, empty, examining the final results. She looked nothing like me. No amount of makeup, hairdo, and name-brand clothing could hide my despair. So much had happened in the last three years to fill a century.

I might have a child out there. I didn't know why, but I sensed a girl, no more than a toddler. I wondered who she favored more, Aidan's blue eyes and black curls, or my freckles? Tears began to build and I pushed them back. One thing I knew, I couldn't sit on my thumbs any longer. I had to find her.

I remembered that morning at Aidan's cottage like it was yesterday. Sally's intrusive knock at the door, listening to her cruel accusations of crimes I didn't commit. If I'd known what I knew now, perhaps I could've stopped her madness. Though, I was outnumbered. Sally didn't execute my capture alone. Apparently, Aidan had assisted her.

Having firsthand experience of Aidan and his bag of tricks, such as the angel dust or his druid magick, it didn't make sense of why he resorted to something as mundane as using a needle. It was out of his character. Though whether I wanted to face this or not, he was part of the scheme with his family, most likely his uncle, to trick me into giving up my powers.

A frosty shudder shot through me like a heavy blizzard. I rubbed my arms, trying to knock the chill off. During my lovely stay at Haven Hospital, I dreamed of Aidan's beautiful face whispering sweet nothings into my ear. I tasted his salty kisses on my dry lips, but it was only a dream. A dream that only fools dreamt.

Despite everything, my heart still ached for him. I'd turned into a sniffling fool. How could I love a man who's heart was black? I wiped a fallen tear.

There were far more important things to worry over than the loss of a Janus-faced man. My voice of reasoning drew me back. I planned to start snooping around. If I had a child, I'd find her. The best place to start would be Haven.

Jeffery met me downstairs. He knew some of the hottest bars on Bourbon street. After all, he'd lived here in New Orleans most of his life.

After arguing over transportation, Jeffery, and I both agreed driving would be a buzz-kill. Neither one of us wanted to be the designated driver. We'd planned on doing some heavy drinking. We considered taking the streetcar, but the ride would've taken too long, so we chose to take a cab.

Soon, the two of us in our wild attire and sparkling ensemble, made our way to the infamous Bourbon Street.

The late-spring evening was as sultry as a midsummer night, and it didn't take long for my clothes to start sticking to me. The worse part, Jeffery didn't know the streets as well as he'd bragged about. Go figure!

"Jeffery," I huffed from walking, "I'm not taking another step. I have permanent blisters after tonight."

"Come on, my favorite bar is down one more block." He tugged on my arm.

I jerked back. "That's what you've been saying for the last five blocks! Pounding the pavement isn't my idea of a good time in this sweltering heat."

"Don't get your panties in a bunch, Ms. Swingin' Dixie." Jeffery swatted at me.

"Hey," I jabbed myself, "I'm not the one with a Dixie."

"Oh, you think your cute don't you? That's just tacky," Jeffery pursed his lips.

"I tell you what, let's trade shoes. My heels for your flats." I arched a brow, challenging him.

"You is cray-cray? I ain't wearin' them suicide heels."

I gaped. "You insisted I wear these pumps!"

"Yes, I did 'cause I wasn't gonna wear 'em on *my* fabulous feet. Them thangs will give me bunions."

It took everything I had not to smack him upside the head with one of my bunion-making-heels. Instead, I glared at him with my arms folded.

"Look, c'mon. There's a bar across the street. See the neon sign?" Jeffery pointed. "Let's go to this joint!" He pulled on my sleeve.

"If you chicken out, I'm hailing a cab and calling it a night."

"Shut your mouth! You said pick one. Did I not do that?"

I just rolled my eyes. What was the point in arguing?

There we were, standing directly under the bold neon sign that read *Mephistz*. I flashed a sidelong glance at Jeffery and asked. "You come here to a biker's bar?"

Jeffery scoffed. "I come here all the time. Now quit your bitchin'. We found a bar." He gave me a little shove through the entrance door.

Once inside, a rush of smoke and careless chatter bathed my senses. The lighting was dearth, only the soft glow of candles dotted the darkness. It was nothing special. Although, the joint held a sizable crowd.

Jeffery and I made our way to the bar. I reckoned that was where we'd start, as I didn't see any empty tables. No sweat, I'd rather sit at the bar anyway. We sat at an angle for a better view of the crowd.

Jeffery leaned over into my ear and shouted over the prattle. "I'm not sure I wanna drink anything. I refuse to drink from a spotty glass." Jeffery's lips twisted into a pout.

I laughed leaning back in his ear. "You've been hanging out too long with those old biddies playing Pinochle."

Jeffery barked back. "Gurrrlfriend, at least they wash their chubby old hands. I doubt the waitstaff her' bothers to bathe." Jeffery eyed a scruffy, long-haired man carrying a tray of drinks as he zipped past us.

I started to jab Jeffery in the ribs but froze.

As if all else had ceased, a strange vibration flickered through me. A swirl of tunes that I could not identify. Yet, it was like catnip to a cat, I had to investigate it. "Order me a drink," I tossed over my shoulder to Jeffery as I slid off the stool.

Before he'd uttered a word of protest, I'd been swallowed up into the smoky crowd.

Possessed, I obeyed, following the music's trail as if I'd been enchanted by the pied piper himself. I was powerless to resist.

My eyes gravitated to the center of the room where couples were dancing. Seductively their bodies moved in rhythm with each other as though they were making love.

Suddenly, a delightful shiver ran through me. I knew I had to join them.

When I stepped onto the floor, I paused. Closing my eyes, I let the melody weave its magick into the pores of my heated skin like a cold piece of ice on a sultry night. I tossed my hair back, surrendering myself to its seduction.

My hips began to sway back and forth as though I was enticing a long lost lover. The spellbound music carried me to a place far away, and I surrendered as it ravished every inch of my body.

Without warning, the music stopped and the enchantment quickly vanished. My eyes popped open, and there standing before me was the most intense gold eyes I'd ever seen. He stood facing me, tall, rawboned, and beardless with an ingenuously appealing face. His long, velvety blonde hair reminded me of a wheat field. He wore a T-shirt, white, showing off his bronze tan and a firm toned body. Gorgeous didn't seem to justify his beauty. However, his gold eyes impaled me as his mouth drew tight and grim.

I didn't catch Jeffery walking up behind me until he band his fingers around my upper arm. He whispered. "Let's get the hell outta her'. *Now!*" his voice was urgent as he tugged on my arm a bit rough.

"Why do we need to go?" My eyes remained glued to the tall-blond-and-broody. "I like it here."

"Hell to the *NO!*" Jeffery huffed. "Does your white lily ass not see we ain't welcomed?

"I think your friend is a wise man." There was a silken thread of warning in his deep voice. "He's right. Your kind doesn't belong in here."

I lifted my sooty lashes and realized that I'd become a spectacle. Every eye in the joint targeted my back. My cheeks flushed, and at that moment I wanted to be invisible. I knew I could do either one of two things, A: duck my tail and run, or B: stand my ground and go out with a blaze of glory. "Last time I checked, this bar is open to the public." I ramrodded my back straight and tilted my chin upward.

The stranger's jaw clenched. His eyes slightly narrowed. "I see." A smug smile tugged at the corner of his lips. "You're a brave girl or just stupid."

Laughter drifted in the air.

"What is your problem?" I challenged. This dude needed to go back to the bar and take up where he left off, polishing glasses.

The irate stranger took a step closer, our noses nearly touching. His warm breath played upon my flesh colored cheeks. "Little angel," he hissed. "Leave while you still can." The glint in his eyes appeared predatory and Jeffery and I were invading his turf.

Suddenly, the atmosphere was stifling, and I couldn't breathe. I latched hold of Jeffery, "Let's go." I scoffed at the stranger with a scornful retort. "Sorry for trespassing, asshat!" Amusement danced in his eyes. Yet, he remained silent and with a strong flavor of hostility.

Several blocks later and added blisters to my feet, Jeffery and I found a resting spot where we felt safe enough to stop. We spotted a bench and flopped down, taking a load off, and heaving for air.

Sweat pouring down my face and aching feet, I refused to take another step. I knocked my pumps off and begun rubbing my feet, wincing over the pain. At that point, I swore off heels. Barefoot was the new trend for me. I'd take my chances stepping on glass any day of the week opposed to wearing torturous heels ever again.

"Gurrrl!" Jeffery jarred me from my moment of self-pity. "What just happened back there?" Jeffery's breath came in short puffs.

I blew out a long sigh of bewilderment. "Heck, if I know. The music had some sort of spell on me." I shook my head in confusion.

"Hold up! I didn't hear any music." His mouth dropped opened in disbelief.

"You didn't hear that uncanny music? It's was like a drug, hypnotic like." I stared at him. Surely it wasn't my imagination? It was the most bizarre thing I'd ever encountered.

"Nope. It really looked eerie too! All those strange people dancing to air."

I started to wonder if I'd lost my mind. "Holy crap! For real?" Shock veiled my face.

"F'sure," Jeffery mirrored my bewilderment.

"That's really bizarre," I shook my head. This whole night had been a bust. That bar and that gold-eyed stranger was the cherry on top.

Expect the unexpected in this peculiar city where voodoo and creepy people frolic together.

"Gurrrl, I didn't have to hear it anyway. You were a seductress, center stage. You sure as hell surprised me. I didn't know you had sexy moves. Your sensuous dancing almost brought the house down."

"Jeff, hush! I was just dancing." I tried to brush my humiliation under the proverbial rug.

"Don't be embarrassed. All that yummy testosterone in that bar was makin' me woozy too!" Jeffery started fanning himself. "They all had their eyes on you, gurrrlfriend! Including that angry-hot-as-hell-hunk of man."

I rolled my eyes. "I didn't notice. I was too busy staring down the grudge. Did you see his angry eyes?"

"Um-hmm! I sure did, and some other parts too!" Jeffery crossed his legs, swinging his foot and pursing his lips.

"Jeffery, have you ever heard the phrase too much information?"

"Maybe, but that don't mean I'm gonna stop sayin' what I'm thinkin'."

"Give it a rest. This night has been bad enough." I couldn't help but feel a little rattled, and that music seemed to have drained my energy.

"Not all was lost tonight. Something good came out of this excursion. Well, two things actually," Jeffery corrected himself.

"And what may that be?" I held my breath. With Jeffery, it was like Cracker Jack's. You never knew what you were getting.

"Okay, Miss Smarty-panties. First, we got out alive, and secondly, that guy is *h-o-t*. Delicious with a hot-fudge sundae and a huge, juicy cherry on top of a mountain of… "

"I get it! I get it! He's *fine*." I covered my ears. "I learned a long time ago looks aren't everything. You didn't see his snappy eyes? He acted like a real asshole."

"Well, if I recall correctly, Miss High and Almighty, you were a bit snippy yourself."

"*ME!*" I couldn't see how this was my fault. "He was rude, *first*." I clarified. "All up in my grill, trying to intimidate me. I should've cold-cocked him."

"Maybe, but he saved our lives. Did you not see the dark stares we were getting'?"

"He threatened us!"

"Well, now that you put it like that, you do have a point, but that mofo was *fine!*"

"Then, Jeff, you date him. I'll go back and get his number for you." I started to push off the bench, but abruptly, Jeffery grabbed my arm.

"No, no! That's fine." He threw his hands up in protest. "I can admire that lovely man from a distance, a very *far* distance."

I stifled a laugh. "C'mon," I nodded toward a different direction. "Let's not make this night a total bust. I don't know about you, but I could eat a beignet right now."

"Girlfriend, you read my mind. Besides, it wouldn't hurt for you to put on a little weight. As for me, I'm black and fabulous. I can eat anything I want and never gain a pound."

I rolled my eyes as I started my way down the sidewalk to Café Du Monde. They made the best beignets in New Orleans.

STRANGE AND EERIE

*A*t 4 a.m. I'd awakened with a start. A tree limb kept scratching at the windowpane, making me jumpy. Even Snowball, appeared edgy. I finally gave up on sleep and went down to the kitchen to fix a cup of hot cocoa. Maybe it'd take the jitters away and I could finally get some shut-eye.

Moments later, with my piping-hot cocoa in my favorite heart mug, I went outside to the back garden. A light breeze tossed my hair and the air smelled of crepe myrtle. I drew in a deep breath. I loved this garden. It gave me a sense of serenity and peace. I'd never get enough of this luscious patch if I lived to be a hundred.

I sat at the small table and sipped on my cocoa. My eyes washed over my mug. When I was a young child, my dad bought a mug much like this one for me. It meant more to me than just a simple mug. It was a little part of him, a memory I cherished.

My mother on the eve of her death, out of jealousy, she shattered the original mug into pieces. It was the only thing I had left of Dad. Mom wanted to punish me. She was so angry that night. I would never forget the disdain in her hazel eyes. I was looking down at a woman that had lost all hope and will to live. I think that was why she opened to me. Harsh but truthful. She never loved me because I wasn't her child. I really belonged to no one unless I considered the Illuminati.

Sara's cruel words continued to haunt me. She hated me as much as she hated Dad. Sadly, those were the last words she'd spoken to me before her demise. She blamed me for all her woes. A part of me agreed, her human body wasn't equipped to carry an alien fetus. Hence, it damaged her mind. Enough of the past. Too much pain. I exhaled. I finished my last drop of cocoa, then I thought about the swing.

A little fear hit me, yet I dug my heels into the soil and made my way to my favorite spot. Screw Helen and that hideous Family! If they really wanted me, they'd find me, regardless. I refused to let them take everything. I jumped into the swing like I had so many times as a young girl and pushed off, letting the cool wind caress my face. I closed my eyes, gliding to-and-fro. The crickets were singing and the tall oaks rustled through the gentle breeze. I heard a mockingbird chirping in the distance.

A smile crept across my face. I could spend the rest of my life right here in this spot, contented. A long sigh followed. It was only wishful thinking; too many dragons to slay and not enough time in the day to slay them all.

I trembled over what the future might have in store for me. With mistrust bouncing off my shoulders, it was time to set my plan in motion. I needed to find a way inside Haven and to their files. It wouldn't be an easy task. I suspected the Family had me under surveillance, watching my every move from afar. To pull this off, I'd have to slip under their radar.

I suspected any record of my child's birth might be encrypted. I had news for them. Their idle threat wasn't going to stop me from finding her birth certificate. Paper trails always had a way of coming out in the wash. Even if the paper might be a little soggy.

What if Van was behind the kidnapping? My worst fear. I could only hope that my suspicions were wrong, but if I were right, God help that son of a bitch.

Something else had my mind baffled. Why hadn't they killed me? Whenever the Family finished with their lowliest subjects, they guilefully eliminated the nuisance. They disposed of my mom. *So why would they keep me alive?*

Considering Dom's theory, I seriously doubted they feared me. They were too powerful and imperious to be intimidated, even by their own creation... *me.*

Last but not least, another mystery to throw into the brewing pot... the angel, *Mustafa*, who I shared DNA with, if he truly were evil, did the apple fall far from the tree? Should I take Dom's advice and stay clear of the angel?

On a positive note, could this creature be an ally, helping me find my daughter? Even though no one would ever take the place of Jon, my human father, Mustafa might be able to help me. No argument, I needed directions on how to embrace my inner angel. It might even be cool if we became friends or family, if that were such a thing among our kind. I wondered why he hadn't ever tried to contact me. Perhaps the Illuminati wouldn't allow it. I reckoned my guess was as good as any.

On the dark side of the coin, if Dom were right about this angel's stance, did I want to take such a dangerous risk? I shuddered over that concept. I was beginning to feel as if my life was heading for another collision.

I sighed, thinking about my real dad. I wished he were alive today. He'd tell me what to do. I exhaled a disquieting breath. No matter how hard I wished, nothing could bring him back.

Then that bar, Mephistz, came to mind. Everything about that place screamed Déjà Vu, the music, its seductive lure, like an intoxicating drug. Yet strangely, Jeffery didn't hear a note, and that golden-eyed beauty, why the hostility? Maybe he recognized me. After all, I was a known felon. Though, I sensed my reputation had no bearing on his aversion toward me. It didn't matter. I had no plans of going back to that bar.

I bit my bottom lip, thinking. I thought that later this morning, I'd take a trip down memory lane to Tangi. I'd like to check out the empty field where Aidan's castle once sat. I reckoned dropping by Ms. Noel's was in order too. I hadn't seen my elderly friend since that day I was taken. Maybe she could help. Ms. Noel had an uncanny way of knowing things which may lead me to my child.

∾

By eight o'clock that morning, I had dressed in a white tank top and jeans, slipped on my sneakers, and threw my backpack over my shoulder before heading downstairs. Even though my trip was no more than a couple of hours away, I made sure I had everything I needed: a few snacks, water, and a GPS system on my cell, and last but not least, my trusty dagger, tucked in its sheath, strapped to my inner thigh. I couldn't say why I chose a knife for protection over a TAZER or even a gun. I reckoned it called out to me. I found it in a little antique shop full of all sorts of oddities. The shop clerk even said he had other knives like this coming in. He claimed they were rare and gifted. I had no idea what he meant. I liked the knife and I wanted the others that matched.

I paid the man on the spot. The cold steel wasn't cheap but I didn't care. I had to have them. At least it was some form of protection. I doubted the knives would kill Helen or any of the Illuminati, but it might slow them down long enough for me to get away. Either way, I never left home without my blade.

I zipped downstairs to find Jeffery. I needed a favor, and I was certain he wouldn't mind.

~

"NO *mofo way*," Jeffery screeched.

"You mean to tell me you don't trust me to drive your Lincoln?"

"That's right! I don't let anyone drive my *baby*."

"Have you forgotten? I bought that *damn* car!" Hitting below the belt often didn't happen, however, sometimes a girl's gotta do what a girl's gotta do.

"Oh, now that's just tacky!" My unyielding friend slapped his hands on his hips, staring me down. "The only way you is gonna get my car is if I'm driving it. No further discussion." Jeffery glared back at me in a lock down stance.

Then as if a brick had fallen from the sky and struck my head, I'd forgotten. I had money! "Fine! Can you take me to the nearest car dealer? I'd like to buy my own stinking car."

Jeff rolled his eyes. "Miss Thang, do you even have a valid driver's license?"

Damn! Now Jeff's trying to parent me.

"Well, Mister, Fancy Pants, I don't know," I admitted. Then the fight halted, and we both burst into laughter.

After I renewed my license, Jeffery and I went directly to the nearest Ford dealership. With cash in hand, I paid the ear-to-ear-grinning salesman one fine price for one very special Mustang. This little sweet sports car fit me perfectly. I really didn't care for those obscene luxury cars, and somehow, me driving one didn't seem right, so I thought a cherry-red, rag-top Mustang would be the perfect middle ground.

Reluctantly, Jeffery didn't want me trailing off by myself and getting into trouble. Of course, he knew how to drive a good point into the ground. In fact, his words would ring in my ears for some time.

"Is you outta your ever lovin' mind? You is sticking your nose where it doesn't belong at that haunted, vanishing-into-thin-air castle is plum stupid and insane," Jeffery rambled in a fiery rage.

"I can handle it. I have to do this, and *no*, you can't go! I have to do this alone." I stood my ground with determination strapped to my hip.

"Fine! I don't care much for driving your brand-new Mustang any ole how!" My friend pouted like a five-year-old.

"Wait! You won't let me drive your oversize, slow-moving-heavy-priced-heap, Lincoln, but you expect me to let you drive *my* Mustang?"

"That's beside the point." Jeffery crossed his arms, refusing to see the correlation.

"It is the point! You're not driving my car with the top down in your ridiculous satin, bold-pink suit, black bowtie, waving at all your high-society stuck-up bitches."

"Now that's below the belt. I'll tell you like I tell Dom, you just ain't got the flair for fashion like I do."

Oh, Jeffery had flair, all right. I just wasn't sure about the fashion part. "Jeff, my dear friend, no one can do flair like you!" I smiled with an impish grin.

"You know that's right! Now may I take my friend for a test drive?"

Off I went down the wide open road with the top down, my hair to the wind, and the soothing sounds of the engine purring beneath me. It felt as sweet as milk to a suckling baby. The taste of freedom on the highway couldn't have been more invigorating. Skipping out and finding adventure away from all my troubles seemed perfect for my ailment.

In any event, I didn't have the luxury of leaving for long. There were too many loose ends in my life. Sooner rather than later, I had to confront my imminent uncertainties.

I withdrew a pensive sigh, staring at the long stretch of highway. How did I wrap my head around the uncorroborated speculations? I felt so disconnected to a world I hardly believed existed, and worse, I was a stranger to my own child. I wished I knew her name. It would be more tangible. I blew out a frayed breath. I must be crazy, wanting to dive in blindfolded over a child's existence that hadn't been confirmed. What if this was a wild goose chase? Despite my dilemma, I had to seek my hunch. I'd never forgive myself if I didn't try to find her. I couldn't move on until I found the truth. I had no choice.

This wasn't going to be easy. The Family wouldn't like me digging into their affairs. After all, they took great measure in sending Helen to deliver a message, hoping to convince me to back off. The Great Oz had spoken. I laughed to myself. Since when did I ever listen to any advice?

Where do I start? Vital records, maybe. Most birth records were public. My gut told me that mine had been destroyed. So where did I start looking? If my calculations served me right, I had the baby nine months later from the date that I first arrived at that hospital. I must have given birth during heavy sedation.

Whatever drugs they used, it had to have been very potent to have kept me oblivious to my growing belly. Any memories of a pregnancy or giving birth, I drew a blank. Nothing. How could a woman not know she'd given birth to her own baby? Anger stirred within me.

That family, through their entire existence, has brought nothing but death, millions in their wake, and yet they continued to survive like a cockroach.

If they took my child, they'd pay dearly, reining havoc on their miserable souls. I supposed that was the angel inside me.

 ~

Pulling up to the main gate of the castle, my mouth fell open. This couldn't possibly be the right place. What once reminded me of a mighty fortress now laid before my eyes weathered, only a gate swinging half off its hinges, creaking back and forth. It was as if it had been adrift for years. Even the paved drive had eroded with potholes and cracks. How could something so magnanimous turn to ruin so fast? It had aged far past its time. This couldn't be natural. I suspected dark magick had been in the works. Its rotten decay reeked in the atmosphere.

As I inhaled the breath of caution, I drove past the entrance and followed the well-trodden path. When I reached the end of the driveway, I stopped abruptly. The most unnerving part of what lay before me was what I couldn't see. Nothing but a field of weeds, no evidence of the castle nor its foundation.

"This isn't possible," I mumbled as I eased out of my car, combing the area for any unwanted visitors. The Family might not take too kindly to trespassers. I reached down to check my trusty dagger. Protection had become a necessary evil. I patted my steel for reassurance.

I made my way over to the center of the vacant field where the castle once stood in its imposing glory. Golden broom-sedge and marigold flowers had grown amok up to my knees. No sign of life besides a squirrel or two stirring among the trees. I stood in the middle of a field of weeds, slowly twirling as in slow motion, taking in the whole panorama. I couldn't believe my eyes. "Talk about pulling up root," I grumbled.

I shivered as an icy breeze blew through my hair. The vacant field of weeds swooned of eeriness. I wanted to look at one more spot before I left. I waded through the high weeds trying to find the marked spot only by a few paces from the ancient oak tree that once shaded the rear of the castle. I kicked around hoping to stumble onto the same metal knob, the door leading to the encrypted chamber. Surely it hadn't vanished too. I got down on my knees, yanking up thorny vines in the spot that I swore was where it had been last seen. Nothing. I sat back on my heels as my eyes raked over the soil. It was gone like everything else. I gathered myself to my feet, peering the stand of trees. I wrapped my arms around my waist as this terrible feeling of someone watching washed over me. Though there were no signs of anyone or anything stirring amid the brush, only a crow perched on a low branch of the oak, cackling. He seemed distressed as though my presence disturbed him. Oddly, I saw no other birds.

A rush of chills spread over my body.

Then it came to mind how terrified Sara became over the sight of a black raven. Looking back, she might've had a good reason for her fear.

~

I couldn't get out of there fast enough, kicking up the dust as my tires sped away. Leaving that godforsaken place in my rearview mirror eased the tension in my lungs. I never wanted to look back ever again, but I couldn't cast it aside just yet. I had a child somewhere out there. Until then, I was stuck in this world of peculiarity.

Since I was near Tangi, I needed to visit Ms. Noel. I worried she might not be very welcoming. The last time we spoke, I'd stormed out of her house, leaving her to deal alone with Sam and Jen. Now I had a shady past. Folks were funny about people like me, especially violent felons. Even though I was innocent, in the eyes of the law, I was a hardened criminal.

Despite my past, I wanted to take a chance and visit my dear friend. It would be nice to see her pleasant smile again and catch up on old times and present too.

Setting aside my visit with Ms. Noel, uneasiness clenched my gut. The small house I once lived in, only a door down from Ms. Noel's, was a sore spot for me. Too many bad memories beseeched my mind. It was the last place I'd seen Mom alive. Facing my feelings over my mother's death wasn't something I wanted to confront. I felt responsible for her death. If I hadn't asked Aidan to give her that stupid dust, she might still be alive. A tear escaped, and I quickly wiped it away.

There were so many questions unanswered. Did Dom have the straight truth about Aidan's involvement in the Family's master plan? Should I have ever trusted Aidan? If he could leave out the crucial part about his longtime marriage to Sally, what else was he hiding? If the dead could talk, what would Aidan say?

Did I ever think Aidan truly loved me? I did. I saw it in his eyes. He revealed so much through those deep blues of his. At times it was like gazing into a crystal ball.

Now the answer to that question seemed like light years away and I seriously doubted that I'd ever know the truth. Only he could clarify his feelings and he was gone forever. I had to accept the reality that I had no other choice but to assume the worse. The worse being that for the sake of his family, he turned his back on me, so what good was a love like that?

I wondered why he died such a needless death. He was loyal to his family. Why would they dispose of him? Besides, the man knew how to take care of himself quite efficiently. He was an immortal. Aidan had walked this earth for many years, more than several lifetimes than any human. I was certain that throughout his long life, he had encountered a few life-threatening altercations, and in the mist of doing so, he'd mastered skills in surviving. So then, what caused his death? Good question. With any luck, the answer might lead me to our child, or whether the toddler existed.

Then I thought back to that morning at the cottage, Aidan's last words to me, a riddle, "Believe only half of what you see and none of which you don't." What did it mean? I drew in a harsh breath. All these unanswered questions were bringing on a pounding headache. My brain lately did nothing but swim in a whirlwind of confusion.

Funny, the one good thing that came from all this atrocity was that I no longer had the nightmares. When my freedom had been taken, the dreams stopped. *Strange*, I thought.

To be honest with myself, all these fairytales seemed nothing more than a twisted castle in the sky. Regardless, I had to keep my mind wide open. If I wanted to remain alive, I had to accept that there were dark forces lurking about, watching me.

If I were going to hold on to the last shred of sanity, I had to push aside my disconcerted feelings for Aidan, bury them so deeply that they could never resurface. I needed all my focus on finding my child. Aidan was gone forever. Things were different now. The old Stevie died with him. The new Stevie was less fragile, a change for the better, I think. For the sake of our child, I had to keep my mind on the target. That meant steering clear of any distractions, including a moment down memory lane.

One fact that I'd take to my death was that the men in my life that I loved ended up dead. I couldn't face another loss. It just wasn't worth the pain. The heart was too treacherous for me. After all, it nearly killed me. I was dead on the inside. Death just had reached my heart yet. I almost welcomed that day.

Did I think I'd ever trust another man enough to let him close to me? Could destiny have someone else in store for me? I hoped not. Aidan shattered my heart and there wasn't any more of me to give.

~

Soon I turned the corner onto Saint Anne Street, a place I once called home before I was arrested. I slowly pulled up into the drive and put the car in park. I kept it idling as I raked my eyes over the old house. It had aged so much. Vacant and withered, the house appeared abandoned and weather-beaten. Weeds ran amok and the paint had cracked and peeled, exposing rotten boards. I exhaled biting my bottom lip. I had to go inside. I flung the door open and quickly jumped out. I feared if I hesitated, I'd coward.

My stomach churned as I approached the house. I noticed the steps leading to the porch were in despair. A couple of the boards had rotted in two. I eased around, stepping lightly until I reached the porch. I stood before the door. My hand paused, barely touching the metal knob. I held my breath giving it a twist. To my surprise, the door creaked opened. My heart hammered as I forced my feet to move past the threshold into the empty room. I stared up at the interior stairs. I swallowed hard, rocking on my heels.

Before I realized it, I was standing at the threshold of my mother's bedroom. The last time I'd seen my mother alive, she was in this room, sleeping off a fifth of Jack Daniels. She was distraught over losing her boyfriend, Francis. He'd been murdered, his throat had been slashed.

Aidan was standing on the other side of Sara's bed with a white bag in his hand. He called it angel dust. A very powerful drug unknown to humans, fey gems crushed into a fine powder.

I froze, pausing as my eyes washed over the empty room. It was nothing like I remembered. The curtains were torn, half-way hanging from its rod. Between the cobwebs and dust, it appeared as though no one had ever lived in the house. All the furniture was gone just like the charm and warmth.

Suddenly I felt stifled. I couldn't get out of there fast enough. I ran down the stairs and out the door as quick as my legs could carry me. I leaped into my car, put it in reverse and floored it.

Two doors down, I stopped in front of Ms. Noel's house. I waited a moment as I clinched the stirring wheel, trying to pull myself together.

I should've left well enough alone. I inhaled, trying to shake off the shivers.

I placed my hand over my eyes, squelching through the sun's glare, and there Ms. Noel stood, waiting for me. Some things never changed. When I reached the top steps, she instantly grabbed me up, like I was the prodigal child returning home. For the first time since my release, I let myself have a good old cry. I supposed it was past-due. A flood of tears came as I lay in my old friend's embrace. I wept like a baby. Finally, after what seemed like forever, we both pulled ourselves together and went inside.

Once my eyes adjusted to the dim lighting, I became startled. I knew the house had aged but *condemned* hadn't crossed my mind until now. As my eyes swept over the living space, it was apparent that the house was in a disarray.

The ceiling buckled like it was waterlogged and there were cracks around the doorway, suggesting foundation problems. I feared at any moment the house would come crumbling down right on top of us.

When my eyes landed on Ms. Noel, she attempted to brush off my worries. "Oh, babee," she waved her hand. "Don't mind this old place. It's just like me. Some things are more droopy these days is all," she flashed a toothless smile. I didn't expect anything other than her upbeat attitude. Nothing seemed to rattle her constant smile.

From the lack of care for my dear friend and her deficient living conditions, she couldn't stay here any longer. "Ms. Noel, pack your things. You're coming home with me," I insisted.

"Oh, that's nonsense, chile. I can't leave my home. This old house and me have lived too long together for me to just walk out on it." Ms. Noel patted my arm.

No way in hell could I leave her in this sort of living conditions. "Okay, I'll tell you what I'll do. How about you come with me for a little vacation while I make arrangements to repair your house?" I smiled brightly.

"Nah! That's too much trouble. Don't be frettin' none over me. I'm just fine where I'm at, babee."

"Ms. Noel, I can't leave you here. This house is unsafe. I can't believe the city hasn't condemned your house."

"Don't worry, chile. I threw away that old yellow paper that some uniformed man posted on my front door. Stop your frettin', I have magick protecting my home. No city feller is gonna come and remove me."

Right at that moment, I spotted a bright-yellow sign kicked halfway under the couch. I picked it up and quickly scanned over the letter. I was right about my suspicions. The Board of Health had declared this house condemned.

"Ms. Noel, the city is demanding for you to leave your house in less than two weeks. If you don't come with me, you'll end up homeless. I can't let that happen."

"Babee, I can't turn my back on my home. This old house has watched over me since childbirth, and all my belongings, I can't leave behind my crafts. Why some of my spirit books are traced all the way back to my ancestor, Marie." Ms. Noel appeared distraught.

"Don't worry. I'll hire someone to pack up all your possessions and move it all to my house."

Suddenly, Ms. Noel's shoulders slumped as she gave in to a defeated sigh. "I guess I don't have a choice."

I felt terrible. Even worse, I feared this house collapsing on top of her. "Don't worry. I have more than enough room for you, and besides your favorite nephew lives with me too!" I squeezed her hand gently. Ms. Noel just nodded her head. "Let me call a moving company and get things rolling. Then I'm going to take you out to eat." I smiled, trying to hide my worries. "Are you eating, Ms. Noel?"

"I eats when I feel like it, but lately I haven't been feelin' much like cookin'. This house gets too hot, and I'm just ailing too much lately."

I didn't like the sound of that. I suspected her meals were infrequent. She appeared a bit pale. I feared her health had waned a great bit since last I saw her. When we return to New Orleans, I planned to get her in to a doctor. The sooner the better. Since money wasn't an issue, I'd see to it she got the best medical care possible. It'd be nice to put this money to good use.

When we returned home, there were swarms of family members, young and old, waiting for Ms. Noel's arrival. When Jeffery laid eyes on his great aunt, tears streamed down his cheeks. He had no idea how bad her living conditions had become. Supposedly, a local family member promised Jeffery to look after Ms. Noel and swore she had things under control by frequently stopping by to check on her and running errands to the grocery store, even cooking for her as well.

448

Come to find out, the money Jeffery had been sending only got as far as the kinfolk's pocket. Not one penny went to Ms. Noel. Upon discovering this, Jeff nearly spit nails, and I was right with him.

Evidently, when I'd called home to let the guys know that Ms. Noel would be staying with us for a bit, Jeffery and Dom contacted a few of the family members. Then those folks called other family members, and before we knew it, our yard and home swarmed with people from all over the state, an overdue family reunion.

Dom and Jeffery went all-out with decorated tables set outside in the lovely garden, filled with platefuls of every delicious dish imaginable. Many brought gifts and their own special dishes as well. There were at least ten different sides of Southern fried chicken from various family members. Plus, there were hot-water cornbread, collard greens, potato salad, mustard greens, macaroni and cheese, corn on the cob, barbecued ribs dripping in spicy sauce, mudbugs, catfish, shrimp gumbo, and mouthwatering desserts. A feast for a queen, indeed, but the best part of all was watching Ms. Noel's face gleam with pure happiness.

It was *her* special day. Dom seated her at the head of the main table as the queen she deserved to be, and everyone gathered around her with hugs and kisses, welcoming her home. I stood back, quiet to myself as I witnessed the love and devotion everyone expressed for this wonderful lady. I'd never seen so many smiles and tears all in one place at the same time. There wasn't a dry eye in the house, including mine too. I felt blessed to be part of this happy event.

Even with all this wonderful joy, a part of me felt sorrow. A sense of loss tugged at my heart—the loss of my parents, a lost love, and possibly even the loss of a child I'd never cradled. A yearning began to stir within me. I found myself craving the soft touch of my baby, a child stolen, taken against my will. My eyes brimmed with tears, and I pushed them back. "No," I said to myself. "I won't do this today." Today belonged to Ms. Noel and her family. My day would come, just not today.

In the morning, I planned to call around and see about getting Ms. Noel in to see a physician. With a doctor's care and Dom putting her on a healthy diet, she'd be as good as new in no time at all. Another thing I should add to the list was Jeffery's fashion designer. I imagine his aunt could use some new garments as well. I wanted to roll out the red carpet for this sweet lady, give her the best of everything.

～

That late evening, after everyone had gone, Ms. Noel finally said her good nights to everyone and went to bed in one of the guest rooms downstairs that we had planned on making a permanent bedroom for her.

After I had washed the last dish, Jeffery caught me off guard. In one swift sweep, he'd grabbed me up and hugged me so tight he nearly knocked the wind out of me. As he held me, he spoke through choked tears. "Thank you so much for bringing my aunt home." He sniffled. "You don't know how long I've been trying to get her to come live with me. No matter what you say, once my aunt gets a notion in her head, you can't talk her into nothin'!" The genuine gratitude in Jeffery's tearful eyes touched me.

Tears began to sting my eyes. "Don't beat yourself up, Jeff. She's here now. I'm going to get her in to see a doctor tomorrow. She's going to get the best care money can buy. With Dom's cooking and your coddling, Ms. Noel will be as good as new." I gave my friend a tight squeeze back.

"Stevie, thank you."

"For what?" I placed the last dish in the drain.

"If it hadn't been for you, I wouldn't have this sweet life I have now. It's because of your generosity that I don't have to worry about my aunt's care. I appreciate everything, and I love you, and gurrrl-friend I never say nothin' I don't mean. Just like I won't hold it against you that you're not fabulous and black like me, of course." Jeffery teased as he did his twirl, prancing like the best.

I rolled my eyes and laughed. That's my Jeffery. "Of course." I smiled brightly. "To be honest, I'm not the one you should be thank-ing." My voice dipped into a more serious note. "It's Aidan who is responsible for all this extravagance." I shrugged my shoulder, feeling a little sad. "I reckon that's one good deed he did for us."

A glint of sadness flashed in Jeffery's blues. "I miss him, you know." Jeffery paused. "Do you?"

I withdrew a long sigh and dropped the towel over the sink. "The

Aidan before the betrayal, I do." I glanced down at my feet, trying to collect my raw emotions. "There are times I want to smack him hard upside the head for tricking me. Then there are times I wish I could feel the comfort of his arms around me once more. He had a way of making me feel safe and secure." I felt a knot in my throat surfacing. "Still, even that was a lie."

"You may find this hard to believe but I believe he loved you. There were times when you wasn't lookin', I'd catch him watchin' you. He had a smile on his face. With that said, even when a person loves you, it doesn't mean they is good for you. With Mister Aidan raised in that no-count family, they screwed up his mofo mind." Jeffery shook his head.

"What happened to him?" My breath caught as my curiosity rose. Aidan wasn't known for sharing a lot of his personal stuff.

"Gurrrl, you don't *know*?" Jeffery's eyes rounded to saucers.

"Know what?" Now I really wanted to know.

"One could say he finally flew over the coo-coo's nest."

"Why do you say that?" Instantly, I felt the sensation of a spider crawling up my back.

"He killed his parents, boo!"

I think my heart needed a jump-start. "W-w-what?"

"Gurrrl, his parents were monsters, torturing kittens, sorta shit. He just snapped."

I stood as if I'd been shot and waited to fall. "Oh my God! It all makes sense." I half whispered to myself as my eyes bounced around the room and then back to Jeffery. "That's what Van was blackmailing him over, the murder of his parents."

Jeffery's mouth flew open. "Lord have mercy! No? I didn't know. That's some screwed-up crap."

"Yeah, Aidan is a mountain of mysteries." I blew out a deep sigh and asked, "Do you think he had partnered up with Sally and the Family to frame me?"

"Boo, I'd like to say no, but Mister Aidan was a hard man to get acquainted with. He pretty much kept to himself." Jeffery appeared baffled, shaking his head.

"I'm with you on that one." I bit my bottom lip. "It seems that Aidan had a dungeon full of hidden secrets."

"Uh, hmm! It sure does." Jeffery rubbed his neck, thinking.

"Yeah, I reckon we can't really know a person." I picked up the dish towel and started wiping the counter robustly.

"I didn't understand why Mister Aidan kept letting his uncle come around. He didn't like him no mo than he liked his cousin, Sam," Jeffery's face twisted. "Hell, I got lots of family I'd shoot on sight if they even looked like they is comin' to visit." Jeffery grabbed up a cookie and took a large bite. He paused, chewing before he spoke. "I don't know why I am surprised about Van's underhandedness. He and that whole family is the devil."

"Tell me about it," I scoffed. "I know that better than anyone." I quickly folded the towel and laid it on the counter.

One huge question kept circling my brain, if the death of Aidan's parents was what Van was holding over his head, then I had to wonder if Van had something to do with his death, but how could a mortal kill a powerful druid? An immortal druid at that. I grabbed a raisin cookie and shoved it in my mouth. There were so many possibilities and untold truths surrounding the Family that it left my blood feverish with fear.

"Jeffery, when did you learn of Aidan's parents' death?" I rubbed my hands together to knock off the crumbs.

"The eve of Halloween, the night before you were taken, I over-heard Aidan and his uncle in a heated argument."

"That's interesting." I dropped my gaze down at my feet, remembering that night far too well. I lifted my eyes back to Jeffery. "Do you think their fight might've had a correlation to my getting framed and Aidan's death?"

Jeffery shrugged. "With that family, boo, anything is possible."

"Don't I know that!" I shivered thinking how my life had taken a terrifying turn that morning at the cottage.

"Gurrrl, it's nonsense to try to figure those mofo folks out. Forget them! It's the past, and Aidan's gone. There's love out there for you. Now you needs to get out there and find it!"

"I don't know. I just don't believe it's for me." I shrugged sharply.

"Don't be stupid! You're young and beautiful. You have this really huge heart, and I think you deserve to have true love. The sort of love that wiggles your toes. Your one true love who will lay his mofo life down for you. That's the love I'm talkin' about," Jeffery snapped his finger with perfect flare.

"When you find that kind of love, let me know." I grimaced. "I don't put much stock in that soul mate stuff. Look at my parents. My father's love for my mother cost him his life. Look what love has cost me. Three years in a mental institution for murders I didn't commit, and I may have a child at the mercy of those sociopaths." I stopped. I had to put a cork in my brewing emotions. It was wearing me down something fierce. I felt her spirit pulling at me every waking minute. I thought my heart was going to rip in two. My face felt heated. I took a deep breath, slowing my heart rate down along with my temper. "Jeffery… love has too high of a price for me. Besides, I don't have anything to give!" I spun on my heels facing the sink. It was like an electrical charge of emotions surging through my body. I wasn't angry, I was enraged. I felt like smashing something.

"Chile, I feel your pain"—Jeffery gently touched my shoulder—"but one of these days, you're going to want to get back on that horse. I promise you, and this time, it's going to be the real mofo deal." I glanced up at Jeffery's twinkling eyes.

THE PROMISE

*E*xhausted from the day, when my head hit the pillow, sleep came in only minutes. It wasn't until 2:00 a.m. I'd awaken from a stir at the end of my bed. My heavy lidded eyes slowly opened as I spotted Ms. Noel sitting down at my feet. Startled, I sat up, intaking a curt gasp. I rushed, asking, "What's wrong?" Alarm flooded my hazy mind.

"Oh, babee, I couldn't be better. I wanna thank ya for today. It was very kind of ya to bring me to my family."

"Ms. Noel, it's not necessary to thank me. Let me help you back to your room. You need your rest."

"Nah! Don't worry ya pretty little head about me no more. I'm gonna be just fine. In a minute I'm goin' home, but before I leave, I want to tell you somethin'."

A sudden spurt of panic jolted me. What did she mean she was going home? *She must be delirious*, I thought. I strained my eyes from the faint moonlight wafting through the window. I could see only a thin outline of Ms. Noel in her nightgown, "Remember, your home is with us now," I reminded her though I was getting this eerie dread.

"No, I don't mean this home, babee. I'm talkin' about my home upstairs."

Upstairs? Something was off. "Ms. Noel, we're on the second floor." I started to reach for the light, but something stopped me.

"Now you need to listen to me because I don't have long before they come fer me," she whispered in a low voice. My brows puckered, baffled. "There's a young man with gold eyes."

"What..." I stared at her, wondering if I might be dreaming.

"Hush, Babee, listen," Ms. Noel scolded me.

Okay. I'll hear her out, and then I am calling 911.

"The gold-eyed man came to me in a dream. He wants me to tell you to seek him out. He can help you find your baby, honey."

My throat went dry. How did she know about my child? Then again, Ms. Noel had an uncanny ability of knowing a person's deepest secrets. "Wait! How do..."

Ms. Noel interrupted, not allowing me to finish.

"He saved your life that night at that gin joint with the strange name. Jeffery and you had stepped into a world that only few have witnessed. The gold-eyed man stepped in to protect you both. Stay close to him. He will guide you through your journey."

"I don't understand." My eyes blinked with incredulity.

"Babee, I have to go now. They're calling me. Take care of that nephew of mine. Give him my love. I love you too, babee."

"Wait! Ms. Noel. Let me help you to your room." I slipped from the covers and slid out of bed. When I turned back, I realized I was alone. The end of my bed was empty. "Ms. Noel," I called out, mystified. Quickly, I flipped my bedside lamp on. The light shed its glow around the room, but I saw no sign of a living soul. Chills tickled my neck. I flopped back down on my bed, releasing a nervous giggle. Could I have been dreaming?

With no warning, an icy breeze fluttered through my hair. I wrapped my arms around my waist as I rushed to close the window, yet to my surprise, I found it was closed shut.

Before I had a chance to digest what had happened, I heard blood-curdling screams coming from downstairs. It was Jeffery! I panicked. With no time to consider, I fled downstairs, taking two steps at a time, following the bloodcurdling cries.

As I reached the guest room, I stopped. There stood Dom at the bedside of Ms. Noel, consoling Jeffery as he lay over his aunt's limp body. She had died in her sleep. Right away I went to Dom's side to help with Jeffery. At this point, we couldn't do anything for her. Ms. Noel had passed.

Just seeing the pain in Jeffery's eyes broke my heart, and I felt the sting of tears myself, but I held mine back. Right now Jeffery needed our strength and breaking down wouldn't do anyone any good. Even still, I felt stunned. The death of Ms. Noel didn't feel real. Only moments ago, she had been talking to me.

The coroner announced Ms. Noel's death at 1:55 a.m. How could that be possible? She had awakened me at 2:00 a.m. Had I been speaking to Ms. Noel's ghost? I shivered. Maybe I should keep this to myself. I might've been dreaming. A very vivid dream, if so.

Since the passing of Ms. Noel, Jeffery wasn't handling it very well. His relentless weeping kept Dom and I busy. Her death had heartbroken all of us, but it hit Jeffery the hardest. I took it upon myself to handle the funeral arrangements. For Jeffery and the family, I wanted nothing but the best, and the best meant the traditional New Orleans *jazz funeral.*

Down here, folks did things in a large way. I'd never seen a procession where the grieving family danced to a lively band parading down the streets of the city. Some attending came dressed in bright colors of gold and purple with feathered hats. Men in top hats marched alongside a glitzy horse and buggy, carrying the coffin.

Jeffery and Dom were at the head of the march as the line of family members and friends went back for more than a mile. Many came from all over the state, from people Ms. Noel treated with her special herbs to folks she'd greeted in passing.

Watching Jeffery fall apart had tugged heavily on my heart. I knew he blamed himself for his aunt's death. I wanted to comfort my dear friend and reassure him it was her time to go. Maybe after things settled, I should tell him about my visit. I think it might help Jeffery deal with his loss. After all, she did give me a message for him. I should honor her last wishes.

The funeral had been quite emotional, not a dry-eye throughout the day. Poor Jeffery was a broken soul. It took several of us peeling him off his aunt's coffin before they dropped her into the ground. Jeffery's deep belly cries nearly ripped my heart out. I'd never seen him so distraught. Dom had the patience of an angel. He never left his partner's side.

After the procession, folks came to the house. A few family members, while eating some of Dom's famous desserts, told stories

456

about Ms. Noel. I gathered by the pleasant tales, she was a well-loved woman by everyone. It had been a sad day and yet, a day of celebration.

~

It was twelve o'clock midnight, and only a few folks were stirring about on Bourbon Street. Strange, I thought. The city that never slept must be taking a nap.

I stood in front of the neon sign that read, *Mephistz*. The very same bar Jeffery and I were abruptly asked to leave. I must've lost my mind because here I stood once more, a glutton for punishment. Stupid, I know. I was about to make the same dimwitted mistake, only this time I had a completely different purpose. Tonight had nothing to do with partying.

Rather, I came to follow through with a promise I'd made to a dying friend or, should I say, dead. I shivered, but that wasn't my only reason. If this stranger with the gold-eyes had any information leading me to my child, I had to take my chances.

I looked down at my hands. They were trembling. Quickly I hid them behind my back. With these tight satin leggings and a clingy blouse I poured my body into, I didn't have any hiding spots. Aside from my uneasiness about this bar, I sensed something different about this golden-eyed man. In my short life, I'd been in the face of some dark-hearted sons of bitches, but this one had me quite intrigued.

"Okay," I said to myself, "On the count of three."

When I entered the bar, it hadn't changed any since my last visit. Nothing out of the ordinary. Even though the joint was empty of patrons, a thick cloud of smoke like fog wafted in the air, coupled with a pungent scent of sweat and liquor. Typical dive.

I made my way over to the bar. An older man bartending came over to me. "What's your poison, little lady?" He flashed a smile with a profound whistle. I suspected dentures. I returned the kind greeting with a curt smile. I tried to mask my jitters, though I got the feeling this guy saw through my charade. "Just Coke tonight. Thanks." There was low music in the background playing, a radio, I think. The tunes were much different this time. I was relieved. I needed my mind clear.

He tossed another lopsided grin.

"Where's your friend," he whistled.

"He's home. I came alone." I pushed out a smile.

"Oh, I see." The bartender seemed suspicious as he lazily popped the cap and handed the Coke to me, still in the bottle.

"What? A girl can't go to a bar alone?" I squirmed a bit.

The server nodded politely. "Depends," he answered curtly, his face unreadable.

"Depends on what," I challenged.

"Depends on what you're looking for." He picked up a glass and tossed the towel off his shoulder and began rubbing the spots away. His eyes looked familiar. Too intense for a man his age. "Looking at that Coke, I say you're here on business." A smile ruffled his mouth.

"Whata smart gentleman you are," I smiled. "I'm looking for a man about six foot four, blonde hair to his shoulders, late twenties, golden eyes, nice looking." I surprised myself on how I popped off details about the dude's appearance. "He was here that night." I took a quick swig of my Coke, trying to play it cool.

"And what would a nice lady like you want with this person?" The server began rubbing the glass a little faster like he was trying to start a spark.

"Isn't it obvious," I threw the question back at him. I didn't feel like explaining myself. So I tried to pull it off like I had the hots for the guy.

He laid his glass down, flipped the towel over his shoulder, and looked me straight in the eye. "Nah, that ain't it." Then the corners of his mouth tipped slightly upward, hinting at a smile. "Not that he wouldn't be flattered by your offer." He shot a knowing wink.

It seemed this guy knew far too well how to get a rise. "Is your friend afraid of a little girl?" There was a drift of challenge in my voice.

The bartender's eyes narrowed.

I felt the heat of his glint as I dropped my gaze. Though when I lifted my eyes to meet his, my breath lodged in my throat. It was as though a veil had lifted and *poof...* the golden-eyed dude stood in the bartender's place. My brows shot up with astonishment. "W-w-what just happened? Where did the old guy go?" I stared at him in disbelief. "Wait! That guy's not you?" *Please say no! Please say no!* All right, I was having a weak moment. I had to admit the golden-green-eyed guy had some serious eye candy going on and was way too hot to be a dirty old fart.

"Maybe, maybe not." He flashed his pearly whites.

A tingle washed over me. I had to stay focused. As stately as he might be, I refused to become ensnared again by a man, so I ignored my weakness. "Someone sent me here, saying you could help."

"Really. Like what sort of help?" He dropped his towel and glass and leaned over the bar on his elbows, inching closer to me. I pulled my shoulders back, distancing myself.

"I need to find someone."

"Look Freckles, that sounds like a job for the police." The man rose back up and began wiping the same glass, dismissing me. He clearly wanted no involvement.

I pushed forward. "The police won't help."

He suddenly stopped rubbing the glass as our eyes locked. "Why will the authorities not take your case?" His eyes now held a note of interest.

"Because I need to infiltrate the Illuminati." I dropped it in his lap like an explosive bomb.

He leaned in again, only closer, dropping both the glass and towel. I now had his undivided attention. "What could that family have of yours that you're willing to lose your life over?" All the air went out the door, and an icy stillness seized the joint.

At that point, no need to beat around the bush; either he was willing to help or not, so I blurted it out, "My child." I stared back at him as a faint glint of shock took hold of the stranger's expression.

He stood frozen. Then suddenly he hurled a glass across the room, shattering it against the wall. Shards flew from the explosion.

I flinched from his sudden reaction. Coming here might've been a huge mistake.

"Who sent you to me?" Anger hardened his features.

Awkwardly, I cleared my throat, "Ms. Noel, my friend." I stepped back.

Though agitation still lingered, he seemed to simmer down. "How is Ms. Noel," he asked as he ran his hand through his thick hair.

"She died. We buried her only a few days ago."

"I'm sorry to hear that. She was a good woman." He went back to wiping another glass, only more vigorously. "However, she was wrong." He still continued polishing the glass.

"Wrong about what," I spoke up sternly, hoping to mask my uneasiness.

He looked up at me with exasperation strong in his eyes. "There's nothing you can do. The child is dead."

His cruel words cut down to the bone. I narrowed my eyes. "Sorry to have bothered you, whatever your name is." I was wasting my breath. I turned to leave.

"Val," he said to my back. "Short for Valor, and you are?"

I faced him and said, "Stevie."

"Stevie, where is the father of your child?"

"Dead," I said flatly.

"How did he die?"

"I don't know." I stood tense.

"Did the Illuminati do it?"

"Perhaps." I shuffled my feet. I didn't know where he was going with this.

"Were you married to him, or was he just a boyfriend?" Strange that he'd ask such a personal question. Why would he care?

"You want the truth?" I faced him, shoulders back, ready for whatever he threw at me.

"Yeah, I do." He appeared more than curious.

"The father was neither."

His brow arched. "Neither? You don't look the type for a one-night stand."

"Look, mister, either you'll help me or not. I don't see where it's your business about my love life."

"Does your deceased lover have a name?"

"Yes," I said with ire hanging on the edge of my tongue.

His brow shot up, obviously waiting for me to say.

I rolled my eyes. "Aidan Bane DuPont."

The golden-eyed man smirked. "I've heard of him. He's part of the Illuminati family."

"Yes."

"And this child of yours is Illuminati?"

Now my temper started to surface. "No! The child is mine." I pointed to my chest, in a huff. "I gave birth to her, not that vile family!"

"Okay, okay!" He stuck his palms up in defense. "I get it. You're a mom, and you want your child back."

460

"Are you going to help me or not?"

"Hmm...let me think about it," he paused as though he was mulling it over in his head. "Yeah, about that... NOT a chance in this lifetime, lady!"

"Why didn't you just say that in the first place then."

"Well, let me save you from the trouble. There's nothing in this universe that can penetrate the forces of that forsaken occult. The child is as good as dead, and the sooner you face that fact, as harsh as it seems, the better off you are and everyone around you."

Talk about blunt! "Listen! I didn't come here to get a lecture, *you jackass*! No one knows what that family is capable of doing better than me. Whether you help me or not, I'm getting my child back! Got it?" I had my fist flinching at my side, ready to start swinging.

Instead, the ground started shaking underneath our feet, and our argument came to a sudden halt. When our eyes exchanged, there was a mirrored shock. Abruptly losing control of my footing, my feet flew out from under me. It happened so fast I had no time to catch my balance.

Expecting a sharp pain shooting up my backside from the hard concrete floor, I found myself nicely tucked against the gold-eyed man's chest as he held me steady. The rumbling ceased, but my heart picked up where the vibrating floor had stopped. For a moment, I felt flustered. When our eyes locked, he had a curious gleam in his unusual eyes. He whispered. "What the hell are you?"

Then I remembered his little masquerading trick and his swift speed rescuing me from the fall. "I could ask you the same thing," I threw back at him. The speckles in his golden eyes shimmered, stealing my breath away. I was putty in his grasp. Crap!

THE DEVIL'S DEN

hata freaking jerk! I spilled my heart out to him, practically begging for his help, and all he could say was, "Get out!" No explanation. Nothing! And he couldn't just ask me politely. Compared to last time, he'd been as sweet as a Pitbull, which was a step up to this. To make matters worse, he had the nerve to carry me out and drop me dead center on my ass on the sidewalk, and his last words, *"Go home, Freckles. I told you not to come back."* He then hailed a cab and left me there as he disappeared back into his damn bar. I didn't understand why Ms. Noel sent me to *him*. She was wrong about this jackass. There was nothing nice about him. If you called self-absorbed and arrogant "nice" then I'd pass on this one. I didn't need his lousy help anyhow.

That following week, we did our best to get back to our usual routine. Of course, the whole house continued to mourn over the loss of Ms. Noel. Dom kept us fed and did everything he could to comfort his longtime partner of twenty plus years. It touched me seeing how Dom lovingly cared for Jeffery in his time of grievance. Family support played a huge part in getting over the death of a love one. Ms. Noel would be greatly missed but in time, the pain of loss would ease for Jeff and Dom. She would've wanted it that way.

In the meantime, I decided to do some of my own detective work. Of course, I kept it on the down low. If Dom and Jeffery caught wind of my plans, they'd lock me up in the wine cellar and throw the key away or, even worse, insist on coming with me. Sweet, but not smart. I had to do this all by myself.

Haven Hospital, I figured, would be my best place to begin. Like most hospitals, a filing system was a given. I assumed Haven attained records of their patients as well, and with any luck, they had a file stashed away of my child's birth. It may be a mission impossible, but it was my only shot.

I gave in to a bleak feeling. Would the Family be careless enough to trust Haven with valuable files? Chances were slim. There might be a clue... anything that could lead me to the whereabouts of my child.

Breaking into Haven was a cinch. The hospital never kept up with modern times by upgrading to computers. They stored everything on hard copy. That meant any old sap with a little motivation could get easy access to their archive.

I had a solid plan on how to get my hands on that file too. Well, sorta solid. At least when I played it out in my head, it seemed rational with only mild risk.

∼

When 1:00 a.m. rolled around, I headed down to a well-known spot that drew in a particular type of crowd. A speakeasy, New Orleanais' slang for bar, located in the Upper Ninth Ward district. A dive I wouldn't take even the infamous Jack the Ripper to on my worst night. No worry though. I could handle myself. If I could survive the iniquity of the Illuminati, anything else was a piece of cake.

I discovered this place during my stay at Haven. Back then, it didn't mean anything to me, but now, it might just be what the doctor ordered. I overheard a couple of orderlies talking about a bar they hung out at down at the Bywater area, south of the Mississippi River. After listening to the orderlies' lewd chats, I figured it must be a sleazy dive. Judging by their character, I couldn't imagine anything else.

I overheard one particular fat cat bragging about being a regular. Seeing that it was a Saturday night, with any luck, the bastard might be getting his jollies off at this dive tonight. Since he worked at the hospital, he'd have easy access to the office, meaning he could steal my file. I thought if I sweetened the deal with a generous incentive, it might

463

motivate him. I heard he had a gambling problem and was hard up for cash. It sounded insane but dangling the rabbit in front of this fat son of a bitch just might be my ticket to getting my hands on the file and finding my child. It was a long shot. Those employed at Haven were and twisted just like their prototype, the Illuminati, but if I could appeal to the orderly's greed, he might be inclined to help. After all, money was the root of all evil. This creep was greedy *and* evil. He should play right into my hands.

When I saw the weathered sign hanging from a rusty chain, the words were barely legible. It read, *The Devil's Den*. I thought, *how fitting*. There were dives and then there were *dives*. For safety reasons, I didn't want to become conspicuous. To hide the fact that I was a girl, I found an old baseball cap and a sweatshirt that should've been thrown out long before now. I even went as far as tying down my boobs, making me appear flat-chested and less curvy. Since I was sweating like a pig under all this clothing on the hottest night of the year, my stench should repel any admirers.

I strolled in like I owned the place, yet, bile rising up in my throat as I nodded to strangers. No one knew the difference as far as I could tell.

The joint spilled over with loud blaring music and crowded bodies, shoulder to shoulder with all sorts of creepiness. Personal space at this dive didn't exist. Stepping into New Orleans nightlife had its risk, but this rat-infested bar took front and center. My eyes raked over the place. Talk about strange bedfellows. The smell was different here than at Gold-Eyes' bar. The stench of liquor, sweat, and sex filled my senses. *Yuck,* I wrinkled my nose, offended.

There were tables centered around a lit stage and a silver pole right in the middle of it with a nude girl spread-eagled, begging for tips. On the other side, there were more intimate settings behind sheer curtains, providing obscurity. I was right. It was a strip joint. I noticed that all the eyes were glued to the nude women, which meant less attention on me. Now all I had to do was find my guy.

I cleared my throat, hoping my voice didn't sound too high-pitched. With caution, I approached the husky guy behind the bar. I figured if anyone knew this cat, the bartender would. I leaned over the counter, standing on my tippy-toes, waving down the server. I didn't want to shout out the name. The element of surprise would give me an edge.

"Hey, do you know Joe Harrell," I spoke over the loud music. The man wasn't much to look at, but by his size, I summed him up as someone not to piss off.

"What's it to you?" He smacked his gum, eyeing me suspiciously. Why did all bartenders ask the same questions? Did they learn this at Bartending School?

"It's worth a little somethin', somethin'." I flashed an impish grin, slipping him a crisp one hundred dollar bill. The bartender eyed the cash, then he cut his gaze back at me.

He snatched the money into his grubby hand and nodded toward the back at the last curtain in the far corner. "Joe's over there. One of our girls is with him. You're welcome to join him." The bartender grinned, flashing his rotten teeth. My lips curled into disgust. I didn't even bother with a reply.

I craned my neck looking for the back of the lounge. The lighting, like every other bar, was dim and smoky. Pulling myself off the bar, I inched my way through the sordid crowd. With each step, I kept running ideas through my brain of options other than this one. It was just my luck, I kept coming up empty-handed. Balls against the wall, I had no other choice. I drew in a biting sigh.

When I reached the last cubby, I jerked the curtains open. Sure enough, there he lay, half-naked with a young girl that could've been my younger sister. A minor, I assumed no more than sixteen.

It was obvious that I'd interrupted something by the glower on his face. "Hello, Joe! Remember me," I sneered, oozing sarcasm. The orderly pulled himself up into a sitting position, grunting like a stuffed pig.

He glanced up at the half-naked girl as she gathered what little clothing she possessed, covering her body. "Honey, why don't you go get me a cold one," he croaked in a deep throaty voice as he reached over and slapped her ass. I took one look at the scared girl, and right then, I wanted to castrate that dirty perv.

I side stepped the girl as I leaned in half whispering in her ear. "Take this and get the hell outta her'. I best not see you in this rat hole again. I slipped her a wad of money. "Go home," I ordered.

The girl's eyes widened, shocked. She gave me a quick nod and clenched the green roll to her chest as if her life depended on it. She smiled, though, I could see tears welling in her brown eyes. I watched briefly as the young girl took off in the direction of the front door. I felt relieved knowing she was getting out of this dump.

Jolted back to why I was here in the first place, a gruffy voice impaled the air. How well I remembered that shifty voice.

"Hey! I know you!" The orderly's beady eyes slithered over me from head to toe. Creepy bumps whittled up my spine. "Fancy seein' you here. You must've missed Old Joe. You and me had some good times." He winked. "Doubt you remember. You were stoned." He grinned, flashing his nasty teeth.

Then it hit me. The bastard had *his* way with me during my drug-induced stay at Haven. A sudden spurt of rage coursed through my veins. Instinct took over as I flew into that disgusting animal with murderous eyes. His sick laughter echoed in my ears. It reminded me of a pig's gurgling after a throat slashing. Without thinking, I struck him hard with my fist. I got a few good licks in before he bounced me off of him like a rubber ball, slamming me into the brick wall.

He leapt to his feet, spitting out blood. "Since you ran off that little sweet filly and ruined my night that it's only fair you take her place." His voice was filled with lust.

At that moment, I wanted to cut his testicles off and cram them down his throat. I needed to stop this fiend from hurting anymore girls. Without hesitation, I lunged for his throat with my dagger in my hand. The pig acted faster than I'd expected. Swiftly, he dodged my deadly swing as he yapped, "You stupid bitch!" His face had gone blood-red. "I tell you what," the pig gritted his teeth, "I'll give you a little reminder of the fun we had back at your old home, Haven."

Without delay, he grabbed me, thrusting me down on the dirty floor, my dagger went flying out of my hand as his body fell on top of me, crushing my lungs. If I didn't get this cow off me, I'd suffocate. That wasn't the worst. Every raucous part of his body pressed against me. I wanted to vomit but I feared I'd aspirate.

Crap!

Suddenly, he rammed his fist clipping my chin, knocking my face sideways. Pain shot through my body paralyzing me. He must've dislocated my jaw. Dammit, that hurt! As the blows kept coming, blood spread over my face. My mind started to faze with each steel blow.

Then the fight shifted and I was in trouble. In one strong jerk, he started ripping my clothes off! I screamed, yet no one came to my aid. I cursed him as hard as I fought back. I took some sick pleasure knowing that this time I wasn't easy pickings.

In a last-ditch effort, I took my thumbs and pressed hard into his eye sockets. I tried slamming them back into his pea-sized brain. He howled a string of curses, palming his face. He loosened his grip for a brief second. That was all I needed. I scrambled for my dagger, only a few inches from my reach. I clasped my fingers around the hilt and lunged for his jugular.

The orderly had fallen backward. Not wasting a moment, I flew to my feet, aiming for that animal's throat once more. Until that pig bled out onto the floor, I had no intention of stopping.

Without warning my body was propelled off my feet. Someone had a hold of my pants, dangling me in midair. "What the fu…!" My eyes fell upon the last person I'd expected to see… *Gold-Eyes*.

"Put me down!" I shouted. I could hear in the background that filthy pig screaming his lies.

"I didn't touch her! That crazy bitch tried to *kill* me," he shouted into the crowd that had gathered around. But the one voice who caught my attention, was the one holding me back.

"Put me down! That pathetic swine deserves to die," I growled.

"Not until you simmer down, girl," Gold-Eyes spoke with authority.

"Simmer down," I raged. "That disgusting worm tried to *rape* me! You freaking simmer down," I screamed at him while he continued holding me captive. With an exasperating exhale, my captor, in one clean sweep, disarmed me, taking my knife away. And as if I were a feed sack, he threw me over his stalwart shoulder. I pounded his back and kicked, cursing him all the while, but he made no attempt to free me. "I swear you're next if you don't let me at that fat brute," I cursed through gritted teeth. He ignored my threats as my defiance didn't faze him. His silence infuriated me.

It was not until I'd reached some unknown apartment on the top floor above the dude's bar did he release me. "Sit down over there on the couch," he barked at me as he sat me down in the middle of what I assumed was his pad. By then, I didn't have any more strength to fight, so I flopped down on his leather couch. It felt cool to my back, which seemed to calm me.

He disappeared to the back, returning a few minutes later with an ice pack and something else that seemed to catch my interest. My eyes went straight for the shot glass and the Jack Daniels in his other hand. Without a word, he filled the small glass to the brim and handed it to me. I gladly accepted the gold liquid. I downed the whole thing in one gulp. Though it was known to be a smooth liquor, it burned like hell going down, but the warmth soon spread to my toes. I laid the glass down with a bang on his coffee table.

Apart from my raw throat, I uttered, "More!" I wiped the liquor off my mouth with my arm sleeve. Without a word, he grabbed the empty glass and poured another full shot and handed it back to me. "Thanks," I choked out, giving him a quick glance. Gold-Eyes grabbed a kitchen chair, dropping it in front of the coffee table, directly facing me. In one stride, he swung his long leg over the chair and sat backward in the seat. He crossed his arms over the back of the chair and focused his attention on me. It was then he'd broken his silence. "What happened back there," he asked in a placid voice.

I leaned back, placing the ice pack on my face. I winced from the sting. Then, I shot the stranger a dark smoldering look and said, "Why do you care?" I still felt a tinge of anger.

Apparently, my comeback struck a nerve. "Look, you little hellcat! You nearly got yourself killed. That place is bad news."

"I can handle myself," I snapped.

"Uh, yeah. You handled yourself really well tonight." His expression grew serious. "What's a nice schoolgirl like you going out to a roadhouse full of depraved creatures, who'd rather eat you than look at you?"

"Look! This is my problem." I frowned with cold fury.

"Besides, the last time I asked for *your* help, you dropped my ass on the sidewalk and walked away. Why concern yourself now?"

"Freckles, you're not as tough as you think." He didn't hold back the ire in his tone.

I didn't have time for any lectures. I leapt to my feet but stumbled. The liquor rushed to my head, making the room spin. *Crap! I'd forgotten to eat.* My nervous stomach had been churning something fierce all day. Suddenly, my stomach roiled as I fought not to vomit. I raised the back of my hand to my forehead, feeling sicker by the minute. "It's late. I have to go home." I slurred my words as I staggered toward the door. Gold-Eyes gently grabbed my arm, reeling me back before I reached the door, or did he catch me before I fell? My mind was a bit muffled.

"It's nearly two in the morning," he said. "Sleep in my bed. I'll take the couch." He smiled but it didn't touch his eyes.

That morning I'd awakened to a throbbing headache and stiff muscles. I couldn't tell which hurt the most, my face or my head. Right away I picked up the aroma of bacon. I could hear the sizzling. I thought, how *strange. When have I've heard Dom cooking from downstairs?*

Then my memories slammed into my brain. *Holy crap!* I was at that bartender's apartment and in his bed half-naked. Startled, I jumped up, landing on my feet, yet wobbly. The liquor from last night still lingered.

Talk about a cheap drunk.

I never was much for holding my liquor, not that I'd had many nights boozing it up. Obviously, I'd passed out. I noticed my change of clothing, or lack of. The Band-Aid wrap had been removed along with my torn sweatshirt and jeans. Now draped over my body was a jersey shirt that definitely wasn't mine. It hung on me like a curtain, and it had some sports team across the front with a number on the back.

Yuck! I hated sports.

I peered through the glass doors and spotted a blanket and a pillow lying on the couch. The dude must've slept there last night. *Whew!* I took a breath. That made me feel a little better, although I wasn't too sure how I felt about him undressing me.

I opened the French doors and entered into the small living room. The apartment was smaller than my bedroom. It screamed "man cave," but it had its charm.

I heard a cheerful voice coming from the back of the flat, "Good morning!" I round the corner following his baritone voice meeting his stunning smile in a very small nook, no more than a ten by ten. The kitchen, I presumed. There wasn't much to it. A small fridge, a stove, and an oven with only two burners, a small sink and a table hinged to the wall that folded.

Looking at the dirty dishes in the sink and two plates full of eggs and bacon, clearly, he'd cooked breakfast. My brow shot up in question. Why the fuss? We certainly were no match in heaven. We hardly tolerated each other's company.

"Did you sleep well?" he flashed a lopsided smile, pulling me away

469

from my thoughts. A scowl crossed my face. I wished he wouldn't do that. I hated dimpled smiles, and his teeth were too straight. Shouldn't he be doing this for his girlfriend?

"I need to get home. Where's your phone? I can call a cab." I sounded aloof. What was the point with the nicey-nice?

"I'll take you home, but first you need to eat."

I made a sour face.

"Come on! I cooked all this food. The least you can do is eat." His brows creased like I'd hurt his feelings. Damn! Why did he have to be so sweet?

I snarled at the food. "I'm not big on breakfast. Got anymore Jack Daniels? For my killer hangover." I shrugged. *Geez!* He didn't have to stand there gaping.

When we sat down at the small kitchen table, it felt too intimate. The breakfast table only seated two places, and our knees kept brushing against one another.

I suppose he was trying to be a courteous host. He even went as far as setting two aspirins by my plate and a glass of OJ. Apparently, his guests didn't get alcohol for breakfast. Bummer!

Halfway through the eggs and bacon came the annoying questions. "So, how did you know Ms. Noel," he asked, making light conversation.

"She was my neighbor back in Tangi," I replied, staring down at my plate, playing with my food rather than eating it. I felt his penetrating gaze on me that it made me shift in my seat. I kept my eyes fixed on my plate. My headache behind my eyes was growing worse. I just wanted to go home and sleep off this hangover. Besides, I didn't want to get chummy. Keeping my distance meant no mess.

"I'm sorry to hear about her passing." His brittle smile softened. "How did she die?"

"Uh, her blood sugar dropped in the middle of the night." I continued pushing my food around on my plate.

"So, why did you go to *The Devil's Den* last night," he smiled benignly, as if dealing with a temperamental child.

"It's personal," I curtly replied. Then I heard his deep sigh and a fork falling onto the plate with a hard *ding*. What was with this dude breaking dishes?

"Look! I'm sorry I put you out on the street," he admitted with irritation.

Now he had my attention. I looked up from my plate. "Are you apologizing for both times?" I glared at him with a raised brow.

"Yeah, I guess I am." His voice held a note of mockery.

"Why did you throw Jeffery and me out of your club that first night?" I stuffed my first bite of eggs in my mouth. Chewing helped to distract my temper.

"I know your kind," he blurted out.

I sensed a secret behind his glint as I blinked with silent shock.

"The music." He went on to explain. "It affects our kind." One corner of his mouth was pulled into a slight smile.

"I have no idea what you're talking about," I denied. I wasn't sure I could trust him. If my secret got out, I'd end up as some government lab rat. No thanks.

"You don't lie very well, do you?" He smirked, not intending a reply. "Humans can't hear the music. It's on a different frequency."

My brow arched. "What? Like a dog whistle?" I mused, but inside I was freaking out.

"No. More like celestial." He gazed at me with a half bland smile.

"Celestial?" This had to be some fluke. How else would he have known? "You mean an angel?"

"Exactly. The music appeals to our spirit. It's like catnip to a feline."

"The music?" This time I dropped my fork and gave him my full attention.

"Yes, the music." There was something hidden in his smile.

"And you're like me?"

"Well, not exactly," he paused.

"My beginning came from divine creation, not man-made."

"Divine creation?" I tried staying cool. Instead, alarm swallowed me whole.

"That's correct."

"Created by God?" Was he insane?

"Yes, we are a race of angels. Our kind are called *Zophasemin*. Zop for short."

"*Zop*? That's a funny word." I forced a smile.

He paused, fixed on my face. "Don't be flippant with me. I know who you are. The streets are full of information about you."

"Sure! And my mother and father are fairies." There was nothing like adding a little sarcasm to having breakfast with a stranger.

"Actually, your mother was your host. You were not conceived naturally." He leaned back in his chair, with a cocky glint like a wolf that had made his first kill.

Icicles slid down my spine. "I haven't a clue to what you're meaning." I'd deny this to my grave.

His mouth twisted wryly. "Are you going to skirt around the truth all morning?" The speckles in his eyes stood out more than usual.

I glanced down at my untouched food and exhaled a deep sigh. Was I crazy for wanting to know more about my origin? I lifted my gaze and looked him straight in the eyes. "Tell me more." I'd hear him out. See what he had to say and admit to nothing. The less I say, the better. But he sure had caught my curiosity. Were there really creatures like me?

"Like myself, you are celestial. You could say you're ninety-nine percent celestial. You do have a small portion of human DNA and something else that I can't put my finger on."

"What makes you think I'm some freaking creature?" I studied him suspiciously.

It looked like he held back a laugh. "Like myself and my race, we can see human aura. With you, not only do you have an aura, you carry effusion, which is the outflow of celestials."

"Effusion? I've never heard of that."

He raised an eyebrow. "It's like a translucent mist or Essence, for a better word."

"Do I have that... ?" Damn I sounded too eager.

"Yes, along with your aura as well."

"What does my aura look like?" My heart pounded against my chest. This dude better not be jerking my leg.

"With every human, it's different. Your aura is a rose, but when you get angry, it turns a deep purple. Effusion is more of a sense rather than a color."

"That's interesting." I didn't see colors or sense any effusion.

"Your aura is very soft, but your effusion is much stronger, more like one of us."

I might as well put down my shield. I had to know. "Why don't I see this myself?"

"The only thing I can conclude is that you haven't tapped into these senses in your brain. It should come naturally," he shrugged. "It's possible that your human side is blocking the outflow of your effusion, kind of like a cold with a stuffed-up nose. I wouldn't worry. It will come in time. After all, you are strong," he reassured me.

"If I'm like you, then why did you throw me out of your bar?"

"The others would've sensed you were mixed, part human." His face was solemn.

"That doesn't explain why you kicked me out of your bar."

Suddenly his lips thinned like a razor. He cleared his throat nervously. "Most Zops' look upon the mixed as the Nephilim giants, impures or inbreeds."

"So! Nothing's wrong with diversity." The insult pierced like a dagger through my heart. "My father's blood was pure and good!" It all didn't seem fair. At last, I'd found a race like myself, and yet, I was revered as an outcast.

"I'm sure your father was an exceptional man. As it may be, to the imperial, it is irrelevant. A pure-blooded Zop looks upon the spawn of angels and humans as an abomination."

"*I'm* not an offspring." I pointed to myself.

"I know it's hard to understand our ways, but regardless of how you were brought into this world, the fact is, you are not created in the divine light. For the Zop, they perceive you as tainted."

"Do *you* think as they do?" My eyes tightened. I didn't know why I suddenly cared about his opinion.

"Well… let me see. I broke up a fight that you were about to get your pretty little head sliced off in and could have damn well gotten myself killed, and I'm sitting here with you in my gracious home, and I never allow anyone in my humble abode, not even a woman I'm bedding." I felt my cheeks flush over that vision, not that I cared.

He continued, "I gave you my bed, which I missed dearly last night, and last but not least, I cooked you breakfast. I never cook. Not even for a woman who has shown me great affection." His gold eyes sparkled. "Did I answer your question?" He seemed amused while he waited for my reply.

By his starkness, a tingle spread over me but it bothered me. I

473

wanted to run rather than yield to a long forgotten emotion this stranger had aroused within me. A sensibility I preferred to steer clear of. Then a thought crossed my mind. If he wasn't interested in bedding me, then what did he want from the disgusting impure? "So," I asked. "Let's stop with all this chitchat and just say what you really want."

"I want nothing," Gold-Eyes said, revealing only a stone face.

"Then why waste your time on telling me all this? Why didn't you let the pure Zop have their way with the girl on the wrong side of the heavens?"

He paused. I couldn't read his thoughts. "I don't know. I felt responsible for you," he shrugged.

"Responsible? Yeah right. I've heard that before," I scoffed. "So, why did you set me out on the sidewalk when I came to you for help?"

He ran his fingers through his somewhat messy hair and let out a deep sigh. "I know the Family probably better than you. We go back a long ways, too much history. Don't care much for 'em either. I know how they work and how they think. Your friend is right, sending you to me," he paused. "However, my days of fighting the Family are over. I keep to myself. Like I said, too much history." His jaw twitched. It was obvious he felt the backlash of the Illuminati as much as I did.

Unanticipated, a spark of hope glimmered. Perhaps if I offered him an incentive, he might be inclined to help me. The inspiration for most was money, and by the meager furnishings of his apartment, he probably could use a few bucks. "Name your price," I blurted out. "I can pay you for your help." I dangled the bait. Everyone had a price.

Quickly, his face twisted into anger. "You think I'm doing all this for *money*?"

I shrugged without answering.

"I don't need *your* money," he snarled, jumping to his feet. "I think you've worn out your welcome! Don't ever step foot in my bar again. I won't protect you if you do." Gold-Eyes reached over, grabbing me up in one sweep, carting me out the door and down the stairwell, halting at the sidewalk. Once again, he deposited my ass on the sidewalk. Then he put two fingers in his mouth and whistled at a taxi that was approaching.

The cabbie had no more stopped and rolled his window down when Gold-Eyes shouted, "Take this girl home, and don't bring her back." He then placed a wad of money in the man's hand. The driver nodded, "Yes, sir!"

My face was beet red from shock. Okay, getting put out twice on the sidewalk was starting to become a habit, yet this dude didn't know me very well. I was worse than a pesky gnat. The word *no* to me only meant a challenge. I'd be back. *I ain't afraid of him or his kind.*

DEFEAT I WILL NOT

$\mathcal{J}$t was not until Jeffery's eyes nearly popped out of his sockets did I realize I'd returned home that morning in only a football jersey. By my lack of attire, I was certain a few questions rose between Jeff and Dom.

Escaping their queries only lasted until that evening. The interrogation commenced when I came down for dinner. Only seconds had passed before Jeffery started a flood of questions as we seated ourselves at the table. "What did you do last night? I dare say it must've been... hmm, interesting," Jeff inquired, sweetly. Dom remained quiet, only rolling his eyes now and then.

"Oh, out and about," I answered lightheartedly.

"Well, I might not know the out part, but I sure can guess the *about* part." Jeffery eyed me suspiciously. Dom just cleared his throat, glaring at his partner.

"Yeah, and what might that be?" I didn't want to tell the guys what I'd gotten myself into last night.

"I sure do like your jersey. Been watching any football lately," Jeffery asked nonchalantly.

I scoffed. "Nope, not one."

Then ole Jeff let it rip. "Gurrrl, if you don't spit out what mess you got yourself into last night, I'm gonna turn you over my knee and whoop yo' ass until the damn cows fly! Forget the mofo flyin' pigs! You had Dom and me up all night worryin' over you! For all we knows, you is lyin' in a ditch dead."

I held my head low and slumped my shoulders. I knew Jeffery would've made good on his threat, and worse, I deserved it. "Guys, I'm sorry. I was looking into a hunch of mine, and it kinda backfired."

Jeffery eyed me suspiciously with one brow raised. "Well… from what I can tell, it looked like thangs went pretty damn good. Who's jersey you wearin' this morning, missy?"

My cheeks felt like fire. "It's not what you think."

"What am I thinkin' then," Jeffery challenged.

"Hmm, you know." I rolled my eyes. "A friend loaned me his shirt. I sort of had a little scuffle last night, and my clothes had gotten a bit torn, that's all." I shrugged my shoulders and took a bite of my pizza, feeling the heat of four eyes on me.

Jeffery and Dom shared a cheerless glance. Dom spoke up. "That's some scuffle. I see your bruised face. *Yes?*"

Damn! The makeup didn't work. "Well, about that… I sort of fell into a… hmm, door."

Jeffery chimed in, "Uh-hmm, and that damn door just jumped right out in front of you too." Jeff's voice was full of cynicism.

Dom, with his wise patience, intervened. "Stevie, Jeffery and I care about you and your safety. When you stay out all night and come home the next morning… pardon for my bluntness… looking like a tom cat with your hair a mess and barely dressed, we fear you may be behaving recklessly. We are only worried. You can understand, yes?" Dom's voice of reason never failed to set me straight.

A deepening hue of shame struck me tenfold and I let out a defeated sigh. "You won't like what I have to tell you. First, it's not what you think. I don't have a lover." Talk about embarrassment.

"A lover is our least worries. We fear far darker things, my sweet." Trepidation spilled over into Dom's voice.

"I don't mean to trouble you. It's just I can't go through life not knowing if I have a child. I owe that to myself and especially to her even if I die in the process."

"Her? Do you know for certain you have a daughter?" Surprised flitted through Dom's soft eyes.

"No. It's just a gut feeling."

"What can we do to help you," Jeffery's voice appeared genuine.

"Oh, no!" My eyes widened in alarm. "I don't want either one of you in the middle of this. I can't have any more bloodshed at my expense. I love you both too much to let you get involved with my problems."

"But my sweet," Dom interjected. "We are already involved, simply by association. We are in this together."

"Maybe so," I shook my head, "but I'm still not going to ask for your aid. I can't ask that of you. I think as long as you both stay neutral, the Family will leave you alone." I stood my ground. There was no way would I budge on my decision.

"The friend who loaned you the shirt, is he or she helping you," Dom asked.

"Not yet, but he will." I had a mischievous glint in my eyes.

Jeffery went pop-eyed. "Oh my god! You've been keepin' company with that drop-dead gorgeous man from that mofo bar. Gurrrl, you can't deny it! It is written all over your face."

"It's not like that!" my cheeks blushed.

"Uh hmm… chile, you is lyin'! You like him." Jeffery pushed vehemently.

"Trust me when I say there is no love there. I mean nada!"

Jeffery rolled his eyes, bobbing his head in a rhythmic motion, full of attitude. "Uh hmm… If you say so, boo."

I bit my lip, doubting if I should ask this, so I just blurted it out. "Jeffery, I need your advice on something."

"Sure. What might that be?" My friend slowly sipped his hot cup of java, not taking his eyes off me.

"How to seduce a man?"

Without warning, Jeffery showered us with his coffee, and Dom's face paled. For folks who were not parents, they sure did act as such.

That night before I left the house, Jeffery, and Dom both gave me strong instructions, or more like rules. Jeffery wanted to go with me to make sure I didn't do anything stupid. I had to do some fast talking. I assured him my plans were mildly risky, and if I was going to get a man's attention, I didn't need my good friend tagging along. A third wheel was never good when you're trying to seduce a man, and since I was green behind the ears when it came to the men's department, I didn't need a wrench in the plan.

One thing I felt for certain, celestial or human, they both understood sex. So I was going back to that bar this time with my guns loaded. If I could catch Gold-Eyes' attention, he might be more persuaded to help me find my daughter. I had to try.

When I stepped out of the cab at the bar, I heard wolf whistles by a couple of dudes passing by on foot. I instantly tugged on my short dress, questioning Jeffery's choice of attire for tonight. He swore this would do the trick. So far, by the looks I got from those two strangers, Jeffery might be right. The dress was a bit too bold for my taste. It clung to my curves like second skin. Normally I'd never wear a garment as such, leaving so little to one's imagination. The color, a bold red with a plunging neckline screamed s-e-x. I thought any minute my boobs would flop out. I worried the dress might slide up and reveal my tiny thong, which rode up my ass. Such uncomfortable garb for no one to see. The spike boots that came to my knees reminded me of hooker heels, which equally matched my wild hair and cherry-red lips that made me look like I'd been stung by a bee. I fit the perfect description of a lioness on the prowl. I guess in a way I was on the prowl, but for another kind of hunger.

I stalled before going inside and took a long breath. I tucked my boobs in for reassurance and entered the bar. A daunting thought crossed my mind, what if this didn't work?

I ducked in a shadowy corner and watched as customers mingled about, just like any other night. The bar was humming with chatter. Maybe I should try this another night when it wasn't as crowded. On second thought, if I backed out now, I may never get the courage again. So, I lifted my chin in defiance, straightened my tight dress, and made my way through the smoke-filled nightery. "I hope I pull this off, otherwise I'm going to look ridiculous," I mumbled to myself.

As expected, it was dark, and the stench of strong perfume and whiskey wafted in the air. My hands were trembling like an alcoholic having dry heaves.

Then a bitter thought appeared, I was among my own kind, yet I had never felt more as an odd girl out, or in my case, angel. I had to pull myself together. An enchantress didn't tremble like a coward.

My eyes combed the dim place, trying to spot my target. If he were the kind of male I sized him up to be, he should fall for the bait, *me*. I listened to Jeffery's instructions on how to walk seductively. I hoped I had the swag down, even still, Jeffery put me to shame.

Unexpectedly, that mood-altering music began playing. The tunes were different this time, yet it had the same effect. I attempted to tune it out, running a catchy song I'd heard on the radio today, but its lure was stronger than my will. The song beckoned my sensuality. How could I refuse something that seemed as natural as breathing? "Screw it!"

As I edged my way through the crowd, I spotted Gold-Eyes behind the bar in the amidst of a conversation with a couple of very beautiful women, but once his eyes landed on me, the women were cast aside as his hunted gaze quickly adhered to me. A moment of triumph wheeled my heart. For some unsung reason, the notion of him with another woman struck a chord with me.

I flashed an enticing glance his way as I seductively swayed my hips, raking my hands through my hair, tossing it into a dishevel as I ambled my way to the dance floor. While the music infused my spirit, I discarded my inhibitions and moved into the role play of a seductress.

When I glanced up at my target, our eyes locked. The corner of my cheery lips tugged into a faint smile. I began to let the music possess my mind and body. My hips began moving back and forth, letting the music make love to me. Hypnotically, I gave myself over to its force. Like an enchantress, I taunted every eye who so dared gazed upon me.

When my eyes opened, there he stood, a glint in his eyes that was much different than before. Desire, perhaps?

My breath caught. I'd forgotten how beautiful he was. He reminded me of a king, awaiting his mistress. His golden eyes ravished over me from head to toe. I teased him back with a titillating smile. Then I reached for him, and he took my hand, gathering me into his strong arms, up close and *very* personal. The warmth and comfort of his firm body against mine gave me a tingling sensation and his scent, sweat and oddly enough smelt like a field of wildflowers, that nearly set me off into a lustful tailspin.

His hand pressed against the small of my back, drawing me tighter. As his sweet breath taunted my bare neck, my heart pounded against my chest.

Then he whispered in my ear, "Do you have any idea what you're doing to me?" His voice was thick and husky.

"Why don't you tell me," I softly teased, throwing my long locks of hair over my shoulders. My hands began to comb his firm chest as my eyes eagerly washed over him. Swiftly, he lifted me up onto his hip, and we began to dance. It was hot and dirty as our bodies pressed against one another. I surrendered myself, letting him carry me away into the spellbound music. His sensual touch sent chills over my body and I found myself yearning for something that had taken absence since that night with Aidan.

Before I knew what was happening, he leaned in and kissed me, devouring my lips like a man starving. I thought he was going to take me right there on the dance floor. Yet, the most frightening part of all… I desired him as much.

All of a sudden, he withdrew. I opened my eyes, still under the spell, confused, murmuring, "What's wrong?" Then my eyes landed on his thin lined frown. Before I could gather my senses, he'd swept me up, over his shoulder, my bare ass in the air, ushering me out the front door. It happened so fast that I conscientiously couldn't make heads or tails of what had transpired between us, until he'd deposited me on my ass at the sidewalk, and I was gulping down the city's air. Then I realized my fate. The spell had vanished. I knew my attempt had failed by his unyielding jaw. Crap!

"What the hell just happened in there?" He pointed to his bar as he towered over me with his face low enough that I'd felt the ire of his breath.

I knew this wasn't going as I'd hoped. The passion in his eyes had elapsed, and in its place came hostility.

I tried to play up to him. "I don't know what you mean. Can't a girl take a shine to you?" I puckered out my cherry lips. Apparently, luck wasn't on my side. It seemed my scanty attempt of flirting only inflamed Gold-Eyes temper.

"Do you have any idea what this"—he waved his hands over my curvy body without touching me—"does to someone like me?" His jaw flinched.

"You don't like my dress?" I fluttered my eyelashes, awkwardly. I think I hit an all-time low of making a fool of myself.

"It doesn't matter what I like. This isn't you!" His tone came off as if he were parenting a child.

Despite his inflection, he was right. Nonetheless, I didn't want to hear it. "Don't talk to me like I'm a kid!"

"You are a child," his curt voice lashed at me.

"Like hell I am!"

He gave a deep throaty laugh. "Yeah? Just how old are you, and don't lie. I'll know if you're not being truthful."

I got in his face and declared, "Old enough to fu… !" Before I could finish my smartass-*adult* comment, he jerked me up and in one sweep, opened a taxi door and threw me in the back seat. I was certain he'd gotten a good view of my lacy, red thong as my short dress climbed up my ass.

He tossed the driver, the same one from last time, a wad of cash, and gave him strict orders. "Take this half-clothed little girl home. Directly home. If she even looks as though she's coming back here, I want you to report back to me immediately," he commanded with authority. The cabbie simply nodded.

Then Gold-Eyes turned his angry blaze back to me. His face twisted with annoyance. "Little girl, you've got a lot of nerve coming up in my bar, trying to seduce me. Keep your ass at home! Go to school and behave yourself." He then slammed the door shut.

He was sending me home, and I had to get his attention. So I screamed. "Wait!" Frustrated, tears streaming down my face, "I need your help. I can't do this alone. You're the only one I know who has a chance in finding my child. Ms. Noel said you could help me!"

"What does a feeble old woman know?" He clenched his teeth. "Go home! You're too young to be playing these games."

Despite his resistance, I wasn't giving up that easily. "You think I'm a child. I'll tell you what I am." I hung my head out the window, trying to jar his attention. "I'm a mother determined to find her lost child," I yelled through choked tears. "Even if that means sleeping with you!"

Disconcerted, Gold-Eyes kicked the tire and ran his fingers through his blond hair. Clearly his hesitance exacerbated his dilemma only worse. I could see his struggle, but then he drew back. His face became stoic. "Freckles, I wish I could help you, but I can't." With that said, he nodded to the driver, and before I could say anything else, the taxi sped away.

I watched the growing distance from the rearview window as we both stared back at each other. For a second, I thought I'd caught a glint of regret, though I must've been wrong. He stood frozen, watching my departure, with no attempt in recanting his decision.

After we had turned the corner, I faced back around, feeling the full effects of defeat. Every hope I had was left back there standing at the curb. I should've known using my sexuality wouldn't have changed his mind. What a fool I'd become. He didn't have to worry about me any longer. I finally got the message. I was going to have to do this on my own.

I put on my determined face. I couldn't allow this little bump in the road stop me. For tonight, I just wanted to wallow in my pity.

ALLIED

$\mathcal{W}$hen I'd arrived home, I managed to get past Dom and Jeffery noticing me before I could scurry upstairs to my bedroom. It was not until the next day after lunch when Jeffery sought me out. I assumed they had figured out that last night didn't turn out the way I'd hoped since I'd been hibernating all morning.

I was still in bed, lying low under the covers, when a soft tap came at my door. I bit my lip, reluctant to answer. I knew stalling would only delay the inevitable. Giving in to a recalcitrant sigh, I groaned, "Come in." I didn't really feel much for talking. Setting aside my foul mood, I owed them a reassurance I was still alive and fine as one could expect under the circumstances. The door opened slightly, and Jeffery's head peeked inside.

"Is it safe for me to come in?" he whispered.

"Yes," I replied, tugging the coverlet over my head.

Jeffery stepped in and sauntered over to my bed flopping himself down on the edge. "I take it things didn't go as planned." Jeffery patted my foot, followed with a consoling smile.

I peeked over the blanket. "You could say that." I let out a shameful sigh.

"Gurrrl, I know a little voodoo that can take care of this jerk! It works too! I've used it a time or two." Jeffery's chin lifted with pride.

I giggled shaking my head. "That's not necessary. I doubt a magic spell would sink into his thick skull anyway." I sat up, drawing my legs to my chest. "He wouldn't even hear me out." My heart sunk like an anchor at sea.

"The dress didn't get him stirred up?"

I scoffed. "That's an understatement. At one point, I thought he was going to take me right there in front of everyone."

"Gurrrlfriend, I can't imagine any straight man refusing you!"

"I don't understand him," I shrugged, feeling the burden of rejection. "We were kissing, and then all at once, he was hurling me into a cab, ordering me never to return." I shook my head. "How can I ever show my face after that fiasco?" I drew out an exasperated breath. "I blew my chance. He'll never help me find my child now," I swallowed back the tears.

"Oh, boo, I don't think it's as bad as you think."

I hugged my knees close to my chest, regretting last night. What was I thinking? I cheapened myself, using my body to entice a stranger. Me sexy was a joke. I frowned to myself as I shrugged in reply.

"Now listen!" Jeffery wagged his finger at me. "I know things didn't go quite as planned for you, but don't give up just yet. It sounds to me this guy cares about you more than you think. It's obvious, he stopped himself before he ruined your virtuous reputation."

"My virtuous reputation!" I laughed bitterly. "Oh, the dude cared alright! He dumped my ass on the sidewalk!"

"Was that before or after he kissed the hell out of you?" Jeffery's lips pursed.

"It was after."

"Did he approach you, or did you approach him?"

"He came to me," I moaned into my pillow.

"Where at the time did this encounter take place?"

"On the dance floor."

"And were you dancing like that night we were together?"

"Uh… yeah." My cheeks blistered with embarrassment.

"Uh-hmm! Gurrrl you hooked that man line and sinker. He's into you, but it sounds like you might've frightened him."

"That's not it. I don't believe Gold-Eyes is easily intimidated."

"Wait! What did you just call him?"

"Gold-Eyes," I said, confused.

"Boo, did you ever find out what his actual name is?"

"Yeah. Briefly, we exchanged names."

"So, has the man ever called you by your first name?"

I rolled my eyes. "No, not that I recall." I didn't see Jeff's point.

"What *does* he call you?"

"Hmm… Freckles," I confessed.

Jeffery burst into laughter. He laughed so hard I thought he was going to break a rib. *I* on the other hand, didn't see the humor. I sat there silently, waiting for him to let me in on the joke. "Gurrrlfriend," he wiped the tears of laughter from the corners of his eyes, "That man may not know it yet, but he has fallen for you! He gave you a pet name. It's called an endearment." Jeffery's self-assured grin stretched from ear to ear. "Men aren't that creative. They don't waste time on mushy stuff unless they really like you. If he's calling you a name, such as Freckles, you have done a cha-cha on that man's heart, gurrrl."

"You once claimed I'd done the same thing to Aidan." I forced a smile, though weak with sadness

"Yes, and I still do. Nowhere is it written you can have only one true love. Although sometimes with love comes heartache. It ain't always pretty with a pink bow, boo," Jeffery smiled. "This one is different. You'll see," he winked.

"You didn't see his inflamed face and hear the asperity in his tone," I said. "If he had any interest in me, he'd be more obliged to help find my child." I waved my hand, dismissing my crushed faith. "It doesn't matter now. Finding my child is more imperative than winning favors from a man I hardly know. I can't allow any more distractions."

"It isn't always that simple."

"Either way, he's not knocking at my door offering his gallant hand." I turned over on my side and pulled the cover over me. I didn't have the patience or the energy to discuss this any longer.

Jeffery patted me on the leg. "I think he'll change his mind. Some folks have to let the idea settle a bit before they make a firm commitment. Let's not forget the Family's position has less than honest practices. They is complicated as they is ugly with bad juju. Just be patient, he'll come around. Mark my word!" With that said, Jeffery left my room, shutting the door quietly behind him.

SURPRISED GUEST

he next day, I decided to get down and dirty, close to Mother Nature. My mind was tight with thought of how to proceed with my next plan. At Haven, the nurses' shifts changed at twelve midnight. They were usually busy scurrying about with their routine for the night. I thought if I went disguised as a nurse, I could slip in the office where they kept the files, find my case, and slip out before anyone realized they'd been robbed. It was a weak plan, but it was all I had. I wished I had Aidan's ability to pop in and out of thin air. It certainly would make my mission easier. Unfortunately for me, I guess that was one talent I didn't inherent. A big disappointing bummer if you asked me.

Today I promised Dom I'd help out with the garden. There was a good bit of work that needed to be done and he needed an extra hand. I didn't mind. It felt good working the cool soil. I sensed a connection to the earth's richness, getting my hands dirty and grit under my nails. I started with sowing a small patch for the fall vegetables. The rows I dug out weren't perfectly straight, but Dom said the plants didn't care about precision. As long as they had plenty of dirt and water, they'd grow. I decided gardening was my new passion. Dom seemed to appreciate my unskilled aid too.

Jeffery didn't like getting his manicured hands ruined or for that matter, doing anything that meant menial work. I often wondered how he managed the trade of a butler. I suspected Aidan didn't expect Jeffery to carry out the traditional role. Though, Jeffery was very loyal. I sensed there was a kindred spirit between Aidan and Jeff by my conversations with both men. For Dom and Jeffery, my heart went out to them that neither one had a chance for closure with Aidan's death. Although Dom or Jeffery never discussed much at the dinner table, I sensed the loss took its toll on them more than they revealed. It certainly affected me, even knowing of Aidan's betrayal.

Any who, apart from unpleasant memories, it was a wonderful autumn day, great for planting. A shift in the weather stirred the trees, bringing in a brisk coolness as the sun caressed my face with its consoling warmth. I felt enlivened. After being confined at Haven for three long years, not allowed a simple glimpse of the sun's golden rays made this day a wondrous treat that I'd cherish for the rest of my life.

It was great working in the garden, but my time with Dom was especially endearing. I'd discovered he was quite well-read of the medicinal use of plants. He reminded me of Ms. Noel in that way. I'd obtained quite a bit of knowledge from watching her prepare common herbs such as jimson weed for asthma. It was in high demand during the flu season.

Near twilight and many rows of new seeds planted, leaves raked into piles and burned, my face had become beaten by the sun's kisses. Dirt and mud had spread from my bare feet to my hair, I was a frightful mess. The hopes of ever becoming clean again would take several washings, yet I didn't care.

Dom had finished for the day and left me to myself as he went inside to prepare dinner. I wasn't ready to give the day up and decided to finish up a few more spots. I had my heart set on planting a few more flowers such as periwinkle, lantana, and marigold along the side of the house. I thought I'd touch up the veggie garden with a little more tilling. It was important for the plants' roots to have room to flourish.

I think I enjoyed the garden even more than Dom. There was something special about this patch. My troubles seemed to dissipate while digging my fingers into the soothing dirt. It was the best medicine for a heavy heart.

I found myself humming to a favorite tune while hunched on my knees in the middle of the flower bed, digging with a handy trowel. I thought I'd plant the lantanas against the house first since they would grow the tallest, then the periwinkle and set the bright gold and orange marigold last to line the flower bed. With my small garden fork, I worked the moist soil until it loosened. I prepared small holes for each flower. Then I dumped each plant one by one out of its little plastic cup and dropped the flower and its roots into the individual hole. Lastly, I packed the dirt around each stem so the rain wouldn't wash it away.

Out of the blue, I heard Jeffery's throat clear. I thought, *oh dear, what does that man want now? All day he's been bugging me about everything underneath the sun.* I didn't even bother to look up at him standing behind me.

"Jeffery, not now! I'm busy!" I snapped, irritated. Whatever he wanted could wait. I wasn't going to the store for him looking like a mud wrestler. Then I heard his throat clear again. *Ah, hell!* I twisted around, not giving a thought to my state of appearance.

Stunned, I realized it wasn't Jeffery as I held my hand over my eyes trying to block out the sun's glare. The sun blotted my view of the tall stranger's face. I froze, unsure who stood before me. After my visit with Helen, I wasn't too fond of unannounced visitors. Then he smiled. I swallowed down shock, staring at a lopsided smile that not even the sun could hide.

"Gold-Eyes?" I called, doubting myself.

He gave way to a snort as he sidestepped, blocking the sun's rays, coming into full view. "I hear mud is a great skin care." His eyes glistened, raking over me from a mud covered face to my black feet.

Startled, I leapt to my feet, losing my balance. Gold-Eyes reached out, but not fast enough before I'd fallen onto his chest. I hadn't noticed his white shirt until my hands had landed on him. I instantly jumped back, stammering over my words. "I-I-I'm s-s-so sorry!" Instinctively, as though my brain had stopped, I quickly started rubbing the mud off the front of his shirt, only making it worse. Under the muse of his golden eyes, I had no doubt he thought of me as a blundering idiot.

He grinned wide, wiping the dirt off his chest with no avail. He chuckled. "It's fine." Then he paused as our eyes hitched for a silent moment. Right then, I realized how much I loved his speckled eyes. Whenever he smiled, the gold glistened. "You...um...wear dirt well."

He commented as he let out a soft laugh, something I'd never heard him do.

I was quite thankful for the shroud of mud, hiding my blushing cheeks. I composed myself as best I could under the circumstances and asked, mystified, "Why are you here?"

He pulled his eyes away for a second and then looked back into my perplexed face and relented, "I'd like to reconsider helping you."

My eyes orbed. "You're serious?"

"Yeah," he scratched his chin. "I guess I am." His full lips gave a half-tugged smile. Without a second thought, I sprung into his arms, mud and all, and something magical happened. His lips pressed against mine, then gently covered my mouth, kissing me. The gentleness of his lips was a delicious sensation. Not demanding or possessive. But sweet and tender. Yet, sensual. When it ended, it was as though time had stood still. A quiet understanding came between us. His gaze roved and lazily appraised me. My cheeks blazed as I nervously giggled. "Umm, your shirt!" I deflected.

He glanced down at his once-nice, clean shirt, and slipped me a sideways glance. "Yeah… I guess I'm staying for dinner. Since you got my shirt dirty, I think it is only fair you wash it." He grinned, impishly.

I bit my bottom lip. "Yeah, you're right," I paused. "Jeffery can wash it," I smiled brightly.

I had left the men downstairs to their discussion over sports and male interest as I hurried to take a shower. After the hot water had run its course and a ton of dirt followed the trail of water down the drain, I jumped out grabbing a clean towel and wrapping it around my dripping body. I quickly brushed my teeth and attempted running a brush through my defiant hair. My face was a bit red from the sun, so I didn't bother with makeup. Tonight, I decided to be me, barefoot and bare face. No glitz or glamour.

When I came downstairs, I had on my old tattered blue jean cutoffs and a simple tank top for a relaxing evening with a new dinner guest.

Jeffery had loaned our guest one of his T-shirts. I think he had a sneaky reason behind his generosity. The shirt had to have been two sizes too small. It hugged every defined ripple in Gold-Eyes' washboard stomach, along with the short sleeves hugging his biceps. I had to admit, it was quite distracting. I found myself kicking Jeffery several times under the table. Gawking at the dinner guest displayed a lack of manners and sparked a deep embarrassment that I'd preferred to keep to myself. Nonetheless, I had to thank Jeff later for the T-shirt. *Nice thinking*, I thought.

After the wonderful meal Dom prepared, a true Louisiana meal of mudbugs, fresh corn on the cob, and boiled potatoes, we settled down in the sitting room for a beer. I hated the stuff and preferred sweet tea. Jeffery decided to entertain us with his recent piano lessons. I smiled, clenching my teeth through the torture of "Bridge over Troubled Water." Never once in tune, I discovered that the screeching of chalk across a blackboard was much more enjoyable than Jeffery butchering a perfectly good song.

On the other hand, our guest, Gold-Eyes, was gracious enough to keep himself together and managed a kind smile.

Once Jeffery finished, he stood and took a bow as if he had played a profound performance equal to Mozart or Beethoven. Needless to say, I felt a yearning to have my foot up Jeffery's backside.

"Bravo, bravo!" we all cheered. Despite the encore, I think we all secretly hoped he wouldn't insist on a repeat. Setting apart from Jeffery's enthusiasm over his newfound hobby, I thought about cutting the strings in the piano. There was only so much one could bear.

Before long, Jeffery lost his interest in the piano and moved on to the paintings on the wall. He loved his taste in art and loved showing off his modest knowledge of the artists as well. Dom allowed Jeffery the floor. He sat back passively and joined in the conversation whenever Jeffery stopped for a breath. Dom didn't seem to mind. I think he appreciated Jeffery's flair for life. When we got into the mid part of the evening, I interjected by nudging our guest. "May I have a moment with you in private," I asked, half whispering.

Gold-Eyes' smile dwindled down into a slight tug at the corner. "Certainly. I'm all yours." I couldn't help feeling a little nervous. I gave him a tight smile and took his hand. As we rose to our feet, I announced to the guys, "Hey, fellas. I need to have a moment with Gold... " I stopped in midsentence. It occurred to me that I'd forgotten his name. I glanced up at my guest, and there appeared a little grin taunting at the corner of his mouth.

Jeffery saved me from total humiliation by butting in and doing the honor of officially introducing us. He cleared his throat. "Let me have the pleasure. Stevie, I would like for you to meet Valor Cross." Jeffery very gallantly pointed to our guest. "Val for short, and Val," Jeffery glanced at me, "I'd like for you to meet the one and only Stephanie Ray Collins. Stevie for short." Jeffery's blue eyes sparkled with mirth.

My cheeks were flushed under the humorous gaze of Val's eyes. I hid behind my lashes as I mumbled. "Nice to be on first-name basis."

"Likewise, Freckles." His voice was deeply rich, yet playful. Goose bumps covered my arms. The good ones.

Dom and Jeffery didn't help the matter any when they both snorted laughter. Some things never change.

Jeffery thought it'd be more private for our guest and me to sit outside on the front porch. We were far away enough from anyone's earshot.

The full moon caressed us with its silver light and a nice evening breeze rustled through the trees while a faint scent of crepe myrtle caressed the evening. Mockingbirds were chirping among one another, a sound I never grew tired of hearing.

I didn't want to sit in the swing. It brought back too many memories of a time that I didn't care to revisit. I supposed there may be some residual feelings still lingering over Aidan. Why else did I still get a tug at my heart whenever something reminded me of him? Perhaps in time, the pain would ease.

So I went and sat down on the top step, and Gold-Eyes followed, sitting down next to me, stretching out his long legs. He never questioned why I chose the steps and not the swing. I was grateful.

The house sat on a hill where we could see all the way down to the end of the street. The Garden District was breathtaking. Tree-lined sidewalks with rows of stunning Victorian homes standing in their glory. A delightful sight I once thought only existed in magazines. Sometimes I had to pinch myself to make sure this was my life. I sighed, sadly. Despite the remarkable life that had been bestowed upon me, if given the choice, I'd give up all of this to have my child back.

Gold-Eyes, or I should say Val, cleared his throat and brought me back to our pending discussion. I glanced up, but not before I could veil my sorrow. His speckled eyes softened, and I knew he had caught a glimpse of my sadness. I quickly looked away, but it didn't matter.

He saw my heavy heart. Even though, his eyes filled with a gentle ardor, he didn't ask why the sad face. Instead, he wrapped his arm around me and hugged me tenderly. We shared a moment of silence. Then with a deep sigh, he began probing me about my plans.

"Do you have any idea where you want to start looking for your daughter?" His tone was serious and direct, stirring the air with nobility.

"Yes, I have it all planned out. I want you to break into Haven Hospital and steal my file," I confessed.

Val gulped the last bit of beer down and crushed the can with his bare hand. "Uh… you don't ask for much, do you?"

"Well… unless you have another idea, it's the best I've got." I didn't look him in the eyes. Rather, I kept my eyes focused straight ahead. "I figured Haven hospital will have my medical documents. Just maybe the birth might be in the same file."

"Wait! The guy at *The Devil's Den*, he worked at that hospital. You had planned on bribing him… "

I didn't know if he was asking a question or stating a fact. "Yeah. Unfortunately, I didn't get that far." I picked up a pebble and threw it at the mailbox down at the iron gate. *Ting*. It bounced off the box. Then a curious question hit me. "How did you know I was there?"

Val shifted, hesitating before he answered. "Mac, the bartender recognized you, so, he called me. My friend knew you were in over your head. That place is not exactly a spot for the weak at heart."

"You think I'm weak?" I snapped my head at him, glaring.

Val paused briefly as he searched into my eyes. "No. I don't, but I do think you jump before you think," he smiled. "It took some gumption to do what you did. Still, stupid." His eyes gleamed with what appeared as admiration.

"Yeah, it's starting to become a bad habit of mine," I smiled to myself.

"Tracing off to those back alley joints is asking for trouble."

He didn't have to tell me. I knew far too well about creatures lurking in the shadows. Then it dawned on me. "How did your friend know me?" I stared into his face. Something I just realized… I liked his chiseled chin and his strong jaw. He was handsome, though, different than Aidan. Aidan had swagger and the arrogance to match. Val seemed more grounded, yet a leader with dignity.

"To be honest, it wasn't much of a secret. Mac saw you that night I threw you out of my place. Our little encounter sorta developed into a hot topic among the regulars," he paused, tinkering with his keys. "I'd sent a warning to the locals to ban you," Val tossed a short smile. It was disturbing enough that our tiff ended up as gossip. The banning part, I didn't care about, yet there was more than what he was telling.

"What's the other reason?" Our eyes locked. The gold specks in his deep green eyes glimmered under the moonlight.

"My friend knew I had a fondness for you."

"Oh," I said, surprised. I didn't know what to say. "Uh… thanks," I said awkwardly.

He exhaled a long breath and returned to the subject. "So you need me to break into this hospital?"

"Not exactly." I tucked a loose strand of hair behind my ear. "I think with your ability to copycat other people, you can masquerade as one of the orderlies. All you have to do is find the file, grab it, and get out."

"Do you know the layout of the hospital?"

My face squinted like I'd eaten a bug. "No. Not entirely." Crap! Why did he have to ask that? "But that orderly at *The Devil's Den* knows."

"You think that fat bastard will help you after you tried gutting him?" Val snickered to himself.

My eyes shot up, orbing into balls. "I didn't try to gut him! I was aiming for his throat," I clarified.

Val threw back his head and belted out a robust laugh, deep bass. "Oh, that makes a whirl of difference then." He scratched his chin, grabbing my eyes. "Is that the best idea you got?"

"With the right price, I think he could be persuaded." I might be naive about a lot of things, but greed was an easy thing to spot.

"How much?"

"Whatever it takes." An impish grin grazed my lips.

"You're that rich?"

"Yep," I replied.

For a brief moment, our eyes locked. A hush rendered. With a long sigh, he exclaimed, "That guy, the father, he must've hurt you pretty bad." It wasn't a question. It was an observation. I didn't answer. I didn't have it in me. I looked away, peering off down the street.

"Okay, I'll get the layout, and you, my friend, will stay put. Safe out of harm's way."

"Oh, no! I'm going with you. I didn't say I wanted you to do this alone." Sitting on the sidelines was out of the question. I was in this 'till death.

"We're going to do this my way, or else I'm walking."

By the stern glint behind his eyes and the tightness of his lips, he wasn't going to budge. Even still, my stubbornness got the best of me.

"I'm in this with you, all the way."

"Sorry," he smiled. "My way or the highway, Freckles." He stared back at me with an inflexibility set in his jaw.

I paused a moment to collect my cool. I needed his help, and I didn't have many other options. In fact, he was it. I had to take it or leave it. "Okay," I withdrew a defeated breath. "Agreed, but one more thing?"

His shoulders stiffened. I knew he was dreading my next request. "Will you teach me how to fight? You know, street fighting?" Like I said, why beat around the bush?

My new friend shook his head and grinned.

Then he looked me straight in the eyes. "You never cease to amaze me. I'll teach you. Be at my place bright and early tomorrow morning." Then he hesitated. "If I train you... don't expect me to powder puff it. I'm going to treat you like a man." Val leaned in with his lopsided grin. "I hope we have an understanding?" His eyes were solid and firm.

"I wouldn't expect anything less,"

"And oh! Don't wear those damn cutoff shorts. They're too distracting. Wear sweats and pull your hair up too."

Talk about blunt. "Alright, I will, if you stop calling me Freckles," I bargained.

Val snorted a laugh and shook his head. "There are no deals in war, sugar," he stated, handing the crushed beer can to me. "Gotta go." He rose to his feet, pausing as I stood up on the top step, our gaze, eye to eye. I thought he was going to kiss me. I saw he wanted to in the gold speckles of his warm eyes, but he pulled away. Instead, he softly slugged me in the arm, like a little sister. I reckoned that was best. If the truth be told, I wasn't ready to move on just yet. My head was still swimming from what Aidan, Sally and that whole blasted family had done to me. I may not ever get over it. That was a fact I had to face.

I watched as he trailed down the long steps. Once he reached the iron gate, he turned back to me and called out. "I like you better with no makeup. Your freckles stand out." He tossed me a sideways glance, dangling his keys in his hand. Without another word, he straddled his Harley and rode off. My eyes followed him until he was out of sight.

Funny he should say that. Tonight, I *was* me. No fancy clothes or hairdo... just me.

ELUSIVE DREAM

I couldn't fall asleep that night. Worry kept clouding my mind. As much as I needed Val's help, I found myself concerned over the target I might be putting on his back. After all, he had nothing to do with this fight. He knew the Family. I wasn't sure what that entailed but any dealings with the Illuminati couldn't be good. Whatever his experience was, he possessed knowledge of their operations. So it wasn't like he was going in blindfolded. Surely he could take care of himself. Still, I was asking a lot.

Odd how he changed his mind when he was dead-set against getting involved. I wondered if the money had persuaded him, though, he didn't mention his price. If money was his motivation that was fine. I preferred to keep our relationship business. Personal might become a hindrance. I had to keep focused on finding my daughter.

That early morning, I sat in front of the mirror at my makeup station. Staring at my disheveled hair, I thought change was past-due. A new look with a new attitude was just what the doctor ordered. Quickly, before I changed my mind, I reached in the drawer and pulled out a pair of scissors. In only a few clean swipes, the lustrous locks fell to the floor in a heap. Once finished, I looked at myself in the mirror. What was left caressed my heart-shaped face. *Quite fitting for the present Stevie*, I thought. Now Val couldn't complain about my hair getting in his way.

After I'd showered, I went to *The Closet*. I shook my head. Only Jeffery would think to name a closet, but I had to admit, it was impressive. I looked through each piece of clothing, and nothing came even close to what Val instructed. "Nothing sexy." I tapped my finger on my lip. I snatched a pair of black leggings and Val's jersey. The leggings were tight fitting, but the T-shirt, three sizes too large, covered all the sexy parts... my boobs and butt. What else could there be?

Time was running out, and I didn't want to be late on my first day. If he thinks I didn't take this seriously, he might change his mind. So once I finished dressing, I took the stairs two at a time. No time for breakfast. So, I grabbed a piece of toast and headed out the door. Both the guys were still asleep. This evening when I get back, I plan on apologizing to Dom for missing his morning feast. Breakfast in this house was a holiday. I needed to make more effort to be here. Dom worked so hard keeping up this lovely home. He wouldn't have it any other way. Regardless, I needed to show more gratitude.

When I arrived at the bar, I took the back stairwell to his apartment directly above his establishment. For some strange reason, my heart began pounding at my chest. I drew in several deep breaths to calm my pulse. I started to knock, but as I raised my hand, the door flew open, and there he stood dressed in a white T-shirt hugging his beautiful six-pack and exposing his well-formed biceps. A little thrill shot through me, though the excitement was short lived. By the starkness in his eyes, I sensed agitation. "You're late," he barked.

"I am not!" I answered sharply. "You told me early. I'm up before the damn rooster's crow," I retorted while I stormed past him. I brushed against his arm without budging his footing.

"I told you to wear sweats. What's this?" He tugged on his jersey that I brazenly had worn. I jerked it out of his hand and snapped back. "It's fine. No skin showing. What's your problem?"

The playfulness in Val's face from last night had vanished and a mean-eyed green monster had taken possession of the dude's body. "That shirt defines every curve. And the pants? What were you thinking?" His hard eyes raked over me from my flip-flops to my boobs.

"I thought it might be a smart move to use my best features to throw off my opponent." My hands rested on my hips, shooting him a challenging glare.

Val's eyes flashed with humor for a second until his attention drew to my hair. "What is this?" He snatched a short curl.

I swatted his hand away, feeling annoyed at his fault-finding. "I'm just trying to be one of the boys."

"I think that's impossible, Freckles." His eyes sparkled, with one corner of his mouth tipping, suggesting a smile.

"Whatever," I shot back, trying to hide my rosy cheeks. "Are we going to get down to business?"

Val's eyes combed over my body with a lopsided grin followed by a deep breath. "C'mon." He opened the door waving at me to exit first as he followed behind. The whole way downstairs, I felt the heat of his eyes glued to my ass. It was obvious to me by his slow-moving feet taking deliberate care in each step down as his footing echoed in the spillway. I was grateful my back was turned to him. My face blistered with embarrassment.

We finally stopped in front of a metal door that read, Private. My nerves were getting the best of me. I'd been in plenty of fights during school, but I had no concept of how a Zop fought. I eased a fretful sigh.

Val jiggled his keys as he stepped in front of me, unlocking the door. Holding it open, he spoke for the first time since the top floor. "Ladies first," he mused. I assumed his good mood stemmed from his gawking at my ass while descending three damn flights of stairs. I think shopping later is in order for an over-size pair of sweats. I rolled my eyes at him as I entered.

When we stepped into darkness, he flipped the lights on. My breath instantly stalled. "Wow! Talk about souped-up!" I whistled. "This has to be at least ten thousand square feet?" I twirled in a slow circle taking in the full panorama.

"Yep, actually a little more." A proud smile stretched his lips. Obviously, the warehouse had a vital purpose for him. Then my face twisted with curiosity and confusion. "What does one man do with such a huge place."

Val's brow shot up. "Oh, there are many things one can do in a facility such as this," he replied with a hidden undertone. I wasn't sure I wanted to know the entailment.

The dwelling reminded me of something out of the dark ages. It was rustic and smelled of men, sweat. The vast room was dimly lit and appeared built solid with large wood beams from the ceiling to the floor that reminded me of a centuries-old warehouse. The word gym didn't quite give it justice. As my eyes raked over the spacious place, it left me chilled. I remembered my studies of European history, how the Middle Ages were known of torture techniques that were less than humane. The devices used in that barbaric period were inconceivable, and even harder to believe there were people who enjoyed conjuring the most gruesome devices.

If my memory served me well from my studies, I recognized one device that was called a Judas Cradle. It looked like a wooden stool, only the seat was shaped into a sharp cone, not flat and certainly not meant to be used for casual sitting. They would strip the person down to bare skin. Then, hoist the prisoner up and drop him on the sharp spear ripping his rectum. The picture in my mind was quite disconcerting. I noticed another device called the Rack. It was believed to be the mother of all torture devices. It consisted of a wooden frame with two ropes fixed to the bottom and another two tied to a handle in the top. I remembered reading about how the torturer would turn the handle as the ropes pulled on the victim's arms, dislocating the bones, creating a loud cracking sound. If the torturer kept turning the handles the limbs were torn right off the body.

I flew into Val, appalled. "What the hell kind of place is this?" I turned on my heels, heading straight for the doubled doors.

Val grabbed my arm, halting me. A lopsided grin flipped up as he exclaimed, "In my world, sometimes we have to resort to drastic measures."

Sick to my stomach, my snappy eyes shot up at him. "You got to be kidding? After all these centuries, you, a Zop, have to resort to such barbaric methods out of the dark ages?"

"I know this is hard for you to understand, but the world of the extraordinary is cruel and savage. If you want to stay alive, it would be best for you not to forget that." The glint in Val's eyes gave me a jolt. This was creepy no matter how I looked at it.

My eyes drifted to the far wall where a long line of weaponry stood erect in glass cases. Before I realized it, I was standing in front of one of the cases eyeballing it with curiosity. In my history lessons, I'd never read anything about swords. Each one had a unique design. Some of the etching was worn and faded.

My eyes fell upon another device encased by itself that reminded me of a skewer. Strange how it hummed as if it was singing my name. As I examined the eerie spear, I assumed by its weathered condition, it either had been ill-treated or it was very old.

I turned to call for Val, but he had been standing behind me. His step was light as a thief. It reminded me of Aidan, and a slight prick tugged at my heart. Without hesitance, I pushed my memory away. I forced my focus back to my more recent interest. "What is this?" I touched the glass, peering at the object, curious of its strange effect it held on me.

"It's very ancient. According to legend, it's cursed. It's deadly to anyone who uses it."

"Like hexed?" I whispered, mesmerized, unable to peel my eyes away.

Val's eyes brimmed with mystery as silence hovered between us briefly. "Have you ever heard of the Sword of Destiny?"

"No. I haven't." My eyes blinked with incredulity. A forceful urge to know more washed over me.

"The name was given by a Roman soldier after piercing the heart of Jesus of Nazareth."

I glanced at the sword and then back to Val, gaping. "You're kidding?"

"I only wish," he snorted. "The relic has mystical powers. The kind that can wield the world to one's will." The expression of disgust masked his face like a bruised blanket of fog.

"Holy mother of god! And you keep it here?" My mind reeled with fear and astonishment.

"Yep! It's not going anywhere. I made sure of it."

"What if someone steals it," I had to ask.

An uncanny darkness flittered in Val's voice. "They're a fool if they do."

"Why do you say that?" I thirst for more.

"Simple. Anyone who uses the blade dies once it leaves their possession. The sword has left a trail of kings and dictators dead in its wake. They say that's what happened to Hitler," he shrugged. "That's why I keep it in the box. It's held captive by a protection spell."

"Holy cow! If this fell into the hands of the Illuminati it would kill them. Like the black plague, it'd wipe every one of those sons of bitches right off the face of the earth."

Val's face soured. "The curse doesn't affect the Order. They are immune."

"How is that possible?" I gawked with disbelief.

He swallowed hard as though he was pushing down vile. "If you are as evil as the curse, the curse is useless. It's like a vaccination. Once you've been exposed to the virus, you become immune."

"Oh my God! The Order can never get their hands on this spear!" the small hairs on the back of my neck stirred. Then a question aroused my curiosity. "Can the sword kill one of them?"

Val's left brow flickered slightly. "Yes. In some cases, for example, those gifted with magick, it is the only thing that can kill one of those black-hearted bastards."

"Oh my!" my pulse was kicking. "I hope your spell will keep the sword safe. Good for our side to have this weapon but not so good if it gets in their hands."

"Precisely," he grimaced, staring at the sword. "I plan on keeping it out of their reach." He placed his hand on my shoulder. "Let's get back to why we're here," he gestured, extending his other hand to the opposite side.

I lingered for a moment still staring through the glass, unable to free myself from the spellbound sword. Whatever enchantment adhered to it, I sensed it was insidious and very powerful. It was as though the sword was screaming my name. I shivered over the thought of what evil lurked from this weapon.

I pulled myself away and trailed after Val to the center of the room where mats lay, spread out on the floor. As we halted in the middle, Val waved his fingers at me. "Give it up!" he demanded in his deep voice.

My brows knitted, baffled. Without thinking, I blurted out, "Like hell if I will!" He cut me off, rolling his eyes.

"No, not that." He grinned, mischievously. "Your knife, please." The gold speckles in his eyes sparkled.

"How did you know?"

He grinned like a young boy discovering hidden treasure. "Hmm… in your walk."

"Smart-ass," I retorted. Val remained staring at me with his open palm.

"Sorry, but my knife stays on me." There was no compromising when it came to my blade.

"I've seen how swift you are with that thing, and I value my neck, and a few other precious parts, too well to trust you with that dagger. *Hand it over!*" he knitted his brows daringly. "Unless you want me to take it?" A mischievous light danced in his glint.

I entertained the thought, tempting fate, but I relented. I didn't want to wound him before I got my first lesson. I took a deep breath and blew it out. "Okay but turn around. You've seen enough of my ass for the day. Must I give you bare skin as well?"

He flashed that roguish crooked smile of his and teased. "Why be shy now? I saw exposed skin that night you wore that red dress… nice lacy thong."

I felt a rush of heat to my face. "I thought you said I was getting the same treatment as the boys?"

Val laughed. "Fair enough," he groaned, turning his back.

Keeping one eye on him, I slipped down my leggings to my ankles. Good thing I didn't have to give him a peep show, I wasn't wearing any panties. After I'd unstrapped my trusty blade in its sheath and clothed myself, I cleared my throat. "Okay, you can look now."

When Val twirled on his heels, facing me, I slapped the loaded sheath into his opened hand. A glint of victory glittered in his eyes as he tossed it over on a table in the corner. I folded my arms, feeling the blunt end of irritation.

If he saw my discomfort, he didn't let on. "Now, let's get down to business." He eyed me carefully as if I were a horse for sale. "What are your abilities?"

I blinked, taken off my feet. "Excuse me?"

"Zophasemin have special gifts," he shrugged. "You know, supernatural abilities. What can you do?"

"I-I don't know," I stammered. It had never occurred to me that I might have a gift.

Val's brow arched. "Wait! You haven't developed your powers?" He said that like I had a contagious disease.

"What part of *no* do you not get?"

His brow flipped up. "Where were your parents while you were growing up? Did they not teach you anything?" Val's comment really grinded against my last nerve. I decided to sandblast his ass with my whole life's story. I didn't know why, but I felt I needed to explain.

"I had parents! Unlike yours, mine were human." I furthered my story, "Like you once said, my beginnings started in a lab. My mother... or should I say my *handler* who posed as my mom for eighteen years never revealed my true identity."

Val listened quietly.

"It began when my mother, Sara, for some unexplained reason kept miscarrying. Although, she held her little secret from my father, Jon. Sara was very resourceful. She went behind my father's back causing her miscarriages. Anyway after several failed pregnancies, she convinced my father to see the Family's renowned specialist, Dr. Astor. The Family and Dr. Astor guaranteed their medical breakthrough would work. Only one hitch. Before they started the treatments, the doctor and the Family insisted that my parents sign a blood contract. You probably have heard of this sort of agreement. It is sealed with magick, dark, and impossible to break."

"Yes, I am aware," Val nodded, encouraging me to further my story.

"As cunning as the Family was behind my father's back with my mother's help, they sweetened the deal by offering Sara a ton of money if she'd allow additional experimenting to the fetus outside the original agreement. Without any details to what the scientist planned on doing, Sara didn't bother getting the lowdown of the risk. The money seemed to be her primary interest."

As I kept spilling my horrible story, Val's face became more drawn.

"All parties agreed that once I reached the age of eighteen, I would be relinquished to the Family."

I noticed Val's jaw twitched, though, he remained quiet.

"When I was eight years old, my father started having second thoughts. He privately consulted Dr. Astor, asking if the contract could be breached. Jon, once a family member of the Illuminati, was excluded from an addendum to the blood contract, only involving Sara and the Family. They knew my father wouldn't have agreed. His values were impeccable, directly the opposite of his family, the Illuminati."

Val cracked his knuckles as the tension in his face grew.

"My father stumbled onto the truth and became a liability, threatening my mother's chance of becoming a millionaire. Once my mom received word of my father's cease and desist order, she approached the Family asking for help. The Family had invested a great deal in me. According to them, I was their true fountain of everlasting life. They considered me as their savior. As a result, they became an accomplice in murdering my father. Sara was afraid he'd screw up her plans and the Family agreed."

I kept on spilling my truth. "According to the Family, my DNA had been genetically engineered, infused with celestial and human nucleotides, creating a unique genetic code. Then, as an embryo, I was implanted into a vessel, Sara. How they managed to conjure that up goes beyond my understanding," I gave pause, inhaling a long breath. "I knew nothing of my true nature or that damn Family until I became the ripe old age of eighteen. It was not until then when I discovered my truth birth, and my life changed forever. My 'loving' mother agreed to hand me over to those monsters once I reached adulthood. She made good on her promise. She delivered me into the hands of the Family for a huge sum of money."

"Freckles," Val interrupted. "I didn't know the whole story," his eyes softened.

"Yeah, it gets better," I went on to say. "I was sealed to be mated with a chosen member of the Family, Aidan Bane Du Pont." I held my breath, struggling to admit this out loud. "I fell in love with him knowing he was dark and very secretive, but he pursued me until I could no longer deny my heart. Aidan convinced me that he loved me and assured me he didn't share his family's antics. I believed him." I averted eye contact, not wanting to reveal my vulnerability. "Certain members of the Family, set out to steal my essence. In order to save myself and Aidan, I believed if I gave myself to him our powers would lock together. I once thought this act would prevent anyone from taking our lives, that we would be safe from the Illuminati. I know better now."

Val stood there with his arms crossed, listening intently as I continued.

"I couldn't have been more wrong. I was set up. The morning after I'd given myself to Aidan, he and his wife, Sally kidnapped me, framing me for murdering my mother, and her two previous boyfriends. Proof of my innocence never mattered. The Family was gunning for me. I was sentenced to a lifetime in an institution for the criminally insane. Three long years I stayed in a small cell, drugged with no hope of ever seeing daylight. Every day they forced me to lie in a pool of my vomit and feces."

I paused, questioning why I was telling this stranger my whole life.

Come what may, my hesitation didn't stop me. "It wasn't much of a party staying at Haven Hospital. The first year I was contained in solemn confinement. The hospital claimed I had violent tendencies. Placing me into the mainstream would've been too risky." I sneered at my next words as I spit them out, hoping for some relief. "I believe their real reason had to do with concealing my pregnancy. The Family wanted it to remain a secret. So, they kept me pumped with drugs through the whole duration." I didn't wait for Val's reply. "If they couldn't extract my abilities, then they'd take the next best thing, my child." I looked away. "That's my theory," I shrugged, but underneath I was reeling. I'd hoped that he might somehow gain an understanding of how damaged I'd become, but at that point, I couldn't go any further.

As expected, my human side snapped. I started shaking. Tears began streaming down my cheeks. Every nerve in my body felt on fire. I collapsed to the floor, covering my face with my hands, weeping hysterically. I think at that moment, I'd lost my mind. My whole body shuddered.

In the next breath, I felt the comfort of two stalwart arms drawing me into a blanket of consoling warmth. Val held me silently in his arms as I shook from the flooding tears, which wouldn't cease. I heard his soft voice in between my sobbing, easing my open wound. For the first time in a very long time, I felt safe, which I thought would be an impossibility after Aidan's betrayal.

It was a good while before the tears dried, and all the while, he kissed my head and cooed with soft words of love.

It was much later when I woke up to find myself alone in Val's bed. Even through the dimness, I recognized his room. I must've dosed off most of the morning. I yawned into the pillow, and I suddenly picked up his scent. A long-forgotten stir began to rise. The reality of being alone pained me, and I couldn't stand the feeling. I wanted *him*. I called his name. "Val," I whispered with a sleepy voice.

"Yeah, coming," he called back to me. He entered the room, bringing me carryout soup. "Hey. Sleeping Beauty is awake!" He smiled brightly.

"What time is it," I asked, rubbing my eyes and yawning.

"I don't know. About eleven."

"In the morning?"

"No, night." Val laid the soup on the nightstand. "I thought you might like something to eat." He started pulling the lid off the soup.

"Don't…" I asked.

He glanced over at me. "Don't what?" His eyes implied confusion.

I reached over and tugged on his T-shirt, pulling him into the bed with me. All I wanted was to feel his arms around me once more. I craved his touch, his scent. I yearned to taste his sweet lips. It didn't take much of a tug either. He hungrily followed my request. The soothing pressure of his weight on top of me felt wonderful. It didn't take long before I had found myself lost in his kisses. They were much different than before, more possessive.

His hands drifted to my bare skin underneath the jersey, and soon the shirt found its way to the floor. Shortly after, his T-shirt followed, showing exactly what I'd expected, a beautiful six-pack against his tawny skin. His hands were devouring, and I began to thirst for more. After he unsnapped my bra, he gently slipped off my leggings, leaving me totally bare. His pants were unzipped, showing a trail of hair underneath. Soon off they joined the pile of clothes on the floor. Before long, we both delighted in each other's climbing desire.

My hands trailed over his firm body and his hands began to sizzle over my hot skin. I couldn't remember if making love to Aidan felt as exciting. This Zop was definitely growing on me, and here I was in the heat of passion, yearning for him to quench the fire that grew deep within me. He was hot! Obviously, I wasn't his first. His hands and kisses were too skillful.

As he worked his magical hands over my body from my breast to the lower region, I moaned for more, arching my back. I guessed by his sultry eyes, he wanted me as much as I wanted him. It was freeing, lovemaking with no expectations, no commitment, just uninhibited passion. I savored in this new awakening.

Then it happened. Val lifted his head as our eyes hitched. In his husky voice, he whispered, "I could get used to sharing my bed and sharing my life with you." Unexpectedly, he broke the rules. Briefly, he paused. "I'm falling for you, Freckles." I pulled away, searching into his gentle eyes for the reason why he'd gone soft on me.

My brows knitted as I rose up on my elbows. Val didn't move, still hovering over me. "Come on! Let's not do this!" I nearly grimaced.

Disappointment twisted his face as he exclaimed, "I tell you I'm crazy about you, and that's all you can say?" I could see the hurt and disappointment in his eyes. Better to let him down now than to string him along.

"You don't have to make this into a mountain. Relax. I'm not looking for any sort of commitment with you. We're friends and business partners with occasional benefits. Isn't that what you guys dream about? Sex with no chains?" I got a little sarcastic. Yet the instant it left my lips, I regretted it. I was really starting to act like a bitch just a tad too much these days.

Val pulled himself off me and turned his back to me, sitting on the edge of the bed. I lay there, feeling a bit exposed and confused. Trying to make sense of this, I asked, "Why are you upset at me?" I reached out to him and gently nudged his back.

His head tilted to the side, looking over his shoulder. "You can't even call me by my name. My name is Val. Say it," he demanded.

I didn't get why he was behaving like I'd stomped on his petunias, but okay, whatever. "Val! Val! Val! Happy?" I sang out, glowering at him as he faced me.

Countenance covered his silent face.

Then he broke the quiet tension. "I can't do this." He ran his fingers through his honey-colored hair. "I refuse to share my bed with you as long as you have feelings for *him*."

Wow, where did that come from? "What difference does it make? Aidan's dead!" My comeback felt harsh and too cold. Even still, I didn't get why he had a problem with my past lover.

"It matters to me! I won't have you like this."

"Like what? Naked in your bed?" My voice spewed with aggravation.

"No! I mean I won't make love to you until you're over Aidan, free and clear!" His golden eyes burned through my heart. Hence, an uncomfortable quiet fell between us. Then he gathered his clothing and, with strain, he snapped. "Get dressed. I'll take you home."

Oh no, he just didn't!

Irritation burned through me. "That's okay! I wouldn't want to trouble you." My voice dripped with ire. "I can catch my own cab.

Hey! Maybe it'll be that same driver you've often thrown cash at, ordering him to get rid of me." I laughed with scorn. "I'm not good enough to hang in your bar, and I suppose that goes for your bed as well. That's just rich," I hissed. As I angrily snatched up my clothing, the bravery of nudity disappeared along with our passion expiring. Suddenly, I rushed to cover my body from humiliation.

Val's eyes softened as his voice filled with sadness like he'd lost something precious to his heart. "That's not it, and you know it!"

"Then tell me your reason. Why?"

"Sometimes there's more between a man and a woman than just sex."

A pain of guilt struck me. At the same token, it made me even angrier. I couldn't help how I felt. "Don't judge me! I know all about letting go and trusting. I did that and look where it got me! Prison," I screamed. "I never want to give another man that much power over me ever again!" I took in a barbed breath. "If you want more, then you need to look elsewhere." I stared coldly into his longing eyes, but my words of endearment wouldn't come. So I did what I knew best. "Fine! I'll call my own cab!" I grabbed my cell.

As I gathered my things, I kept my back to the marred guy in the room, but then it quickly came to me why I was here in the first place. I knew I had to swallow a little pride. Losing my chance at finding my daughter wasn't an option. Whether I wanted to admit it or not, I needed him. I suppressed my anger in order for me to talk to him calmly. I cleared my throat, "I still require your help. I'm willing to pay you handsomely for your trouble." I held my breath, waiting for his response.

Quiet settled for a brief moment. Only his splintering sigh drifted in the dim room. "I don't want your money." His words sounded hurt, yet deliberate. "I keep my word. If I say I will do something, I do it, regardless. Give it to charity," Val replied crassly. I felt the blaze of his words. It wasn't what he said, but the tone. Shame flushed my cheeks. I couldn't look at him. I felt bad enough. He continued. "Be here in the morning, early," and he disappeared, leaving me alone to my loathsome self.

. . .

509

Riding in the cab home, an ache deep within my gut knotted. I hated leaving him like this. He wanted more. It was apparent in his wounded eyes. The past Stevie would've fallen head-over-heels in love with him. He had all the right ingredients to make a perfect boyfriend... easy on the eyes, strong and protective, and far too considerate to waste on me. Not trying to beat myself up, but I knew the 'we' part wouldn't work.

I should not have let my guard down, yet I'd wanted him, plain and simple. I wiped a tear away. Despite my selfish desires, if I allowed myself the luxury of caring, Val would be getting the short end of the stick. I was only a fragment of a woman. As long as my past continued to merge with my present, I'd never be whole. I might as well face it. Until I found peace within myself, I was not my own. I withdrew a glum sigh. The only thing that mattered right now was finding my daughter. Anything outside of that was pointless.

MIASMA

$\mathcal{W}$hen I arrived home, Jeffery had been waiting up for me. I suppose both Jeffery and Dom had been concerned for me after I'd missed all three meals today. A guilty feeling hit the pit of my stomach. I'd forgotten to call. I withdrew a deep sigh. After years of having very little to eat, missing meals didn't seem that big of a deal to me. I assumed since I was only a smudge of human and more celestial, my body didn't require a lot of nourishment. Growing up with my mom, my lack of need to eat turned out to be a blessing. We didn't have much more than the shirts on our backs, even more so with food.

I followed the light to the kitchen where a renowned foot was tapping vigorously against the hardwood flooring. I rolled my eyes and murmured, "Good grief!"

Jeffery's voice echoed from the kitchen, "Gurrrl, get your butt in 'ere!" he called out sternly.

My breath caught in my throat. "Oh mother of God! Is he pissed at me too," I mumbled?

Once I seated myself across the table from Jeff, he placed in front of me a steaming bowl of soup. It was my favorite, chicken and dumplings coupled with Dom's famous Dee-Dee rolls. The bread was so moist every bite melted in my mouth. It was the modern-day manna. It was *that* divine. I didn't waste any time digging in.

"Thanks, Jeff! What's up?" I asked, peeking over the curls of steam

511

while I blew into my spoon. I noticed the worried lines on Jeff's strained face.

"Dom's been sick today with worry. I sent him to bed with one of my sleeping pills. Well, actually, the pills are his. I just borrowed them. Any hoot, I hope your evening went well?"

All at once I felt like a kid again under fire. There was a pinch of sarcasm in Jeffery's tone. "I had better." I shrugged, drowning my memories of the day in my dumplings.

"We had a visitor today." Jeffery kept tapping his foot, and soon his fingers joined in.

I knew right away this couldn't be good. "Who?" my breath chilled.

"Oh, it ain't that horrid clan," Jeffery chirped as if he'd read my mind. "Someone you will never guess in a million years."

"Just end my misery and cough it up already!" I grumbled as I dropped my spoon into the soup, making it splatter onto the table. I reached for a napkin and started dabbing.

Jeffery's face soured as though he'd smelled something poignant. "Chile, you need to stop bein' so snippy!" he lectured, full of attitude.

"Sorry. It's been a rough day," I squirmed in my seat.

"I'd love to hear about it, but you have a visitor!" Jeffery sounded agitated.

"Jeff, I love you, but can it wait until morning? I'm just not feeling it."

"No, ma'am! It sure as hell can't." Jeffery's lips pursed. I knew whenever my friend made that tart face, he meant business. I might as well grin and bear it. My only hope was that whatever it was that he needed off his chest didn't last into the wee morning hours. "Shoot," I conceded.

"Okay, Miss Stevie, smarty-pants, close your eyes. It's a surprise!"

Without a clue, I heard soft footfalls coming behind me, not heavy like Dom or loud like Jeffery but light and quick like an athlete. Like a shot I felt cool hands over my eyes and a soft voice following. "Guess who!"

Immediately, I knew. I twirled around in my chair, and there stood my good friend, Jen Li. I hadn't seen her since that stormy night at Ms. Noel's.

Jumping to my feet, I embraced my welcomed friend. We shared in mirth and tears of joy. "I can't believe it's you!" I stood back, gazing at Jen, still in disbelief.

In life you only have a few true friends, and that described Jen in a nutshell. "Your friend, Jeffery, looked me up." She nodded to the oddly quiet man, tapping his foot, feverously. "I had no idea you were living here in New Orleans. I'm going to UNO here. I got a scholarship in volley ball, so here I am, a college student." She smiled, flashing her bright white teeth against her brown skin.

That's funny. I could've sworn Jen played basketball. I chewed on the inside of my lip, thinking. If my memory served me well, she preferred the more aggressive sports. Suddenly Jeffery caught the corner of my eye. His cheeks had bloated as if he was holding back vomit, and his eyes were glazed. I'd be the first to admit that Jeffery had his weird moments, but this was really strange even for him.

Suspicion began to stir.

"How did you end up here?" Jen broke my train of thought.

"Well, I came to stay with Jeffery and Dom." I smiled, trying to put on a good face.

"Jeff told me about your mom's death. I had no clue!" Jen reached out, placing her hand on my shoulder. "I'm sorry I wasn't here for you. I had no idea where you had disappeared to. Even Sam was struck with bewilderment." Jen's face seemed genuine, but Sam died before I'd disappeared.

Perhaps she had the days mixed up. I kept forgetting it happened more than three years ago. It seemed like yesterday. "Yeah… uh… a lot of things have changed. When did you last see Sam?" I held my watchful gaze fixed on her.

"Let me see." Jen tapped her lip with her index finger, thinking. "It was the next day at school."

Unearthly chills slithered down my spine. Why was she lying? "Are you sure you have the right day?" I tried to be inconspicuous.

Jen's face etched with incertitude. "No, wait! It was Halloween night at Aidan's. Sam took me home. I had a little too much to drink. You know me! Partee-hardee!"

That was peculiar. Firstly, Aidan didn't throw a Halloween party for the public that night. Only members of the Family were invited. Secondly, the Jen I knew didn't drink. She was a health nut. "How late did you stay?" I played along with heavy caution.

"Oh! We shut the party down," she bragged. "I don't know maybe three in the morning." She tossed an impish grin.

Creepy bumps popped up over my arms. "That's really odd," I replied.

"Why do you say that?" Her fine tweezed brows arched.

I wasn't sure who this person was standing before me, but I knew who she wasn't. I kindly smiled. "Aidan didn't have a party for his friends. There was an event that night but it was for family only." I watched her body go rigid.

"Wow," she swallowed. "You know, I was pretty drunk. Maybe I have it confused with a later party."

"You might have gone to another party, but it wasn't with Sam."

Her eyes grew like marbles. "What do you mean? Of course I was with Sam. We were dating."

If I had any doubts before, I certainly didn't have them now. "Jen, you never dated Sam. Gina was his girlfriend."

"That two timer! He was dating her too?" she feigned shock. "I'd love to give him a piece of my mind."

I sucked in an inaudible breath. "That's going to be hard to do. Sam is dead." I swallowed a pinch of guilt. Casting logic aside, I couldn't help feeling somewhat responsible for his death.

"He died?" her chin dropped.

I glanced down at my feet, then back at her shocked face. "Yeah... actually he died on Halloween night, three years ago." The tension in my jaw ached. "You see it would be an impossibility for Sam to have taken you home that night or any other night following."

"Damn! I'm really confused," she giggled as she scratched her head. Then her eyes latched onto mine. "How?"

Crap! I didn't want to tell her the truth. "A car accident," I lied.

"A two car accident?"

I shook my head. "No. No other driver. He wrapped his car around a tree," I lied again.

"Man-oh-man, that blows!" Jen made a whistle.

"Yeah, life's been... surreal," I confessed, feeling the mockery in my voice.

Then swiftly, Jen switched the kernel as though Sam's death hadn't registered with her. "Are you still dating Aidan?" Her lack of reaction to Sam's death seemed unlike her. The old Jen would've expressed her shock and asked a flurry of questions

"No, I haven't seen him since high school." The topic for discussion with this girl was getting more bizarre. Now she was team-Aidan!

"Aw, sorry to hear that. I'd hoped you two would've gotten engaged." Everything was off with this conversation, including Jen's unexpected visit. I slipped a sideways peek at Jeffery. His face had drawn pale, and he was unusually still. If I were a betting woman, I'd make a wager that this visit had the mark of the Family. If Jen was under a spell, we needed to help her.

"Do you remember that day when Sam and you met up with me at Ms. Noel's?" I searched deep into her brown eyes to see if there was a small glimmer of recollection, though, I saw nothing supporting my suspicion. If Sam had put her under an enchantment, why hasn't it expired after three years?

Jen wrinkled her nose, then she asked in an off-beat voice, "Ms. Noel?" she tapped her finger on her chin. "Wasn't she the owner of the diner?"

I remained calm. "Yeah, her! Fairly young, had a bunch of kids. We'd babysit for her from time to time. Remember?"

"Oh, I sure do! Those kids were brats too," Jen affirmed, staring vacantly at me.

I turned my attention to Jeff. He still carried that trance like stare. I shook his shoulder, hard. After a moment, Jeff blinked. It was as if he'd come back to life. "Lord have mercy! Did I sleepwalk again?" He shrugged his shoulders, blinking his heavy lidded eyes.

"Wake-up, boo. I got a question for you," I insisted in an unruffled voice.

"Hurry-up! I'm tired," Jeffery growled. "I just can't stay up like I use to."

"Jeff!" I rested my hand on his shoulder. "Tell me again how you got in touch with Jen?"

"Oh, Lord have mercy," Jeffery exasperated. "Why would I say that? The gurrrl *found* us. She came knockin' on our door this evenin' all prissy-in-pink, insistin' to see you. I couldn't chase the bitch off with a broomstick. She wouldn't leave."

Now that was the Jeffery I knew. "Where's Dom?" I rushed.

515

"He's upstairs, sick," Jeffery tossed his hand toward the stairs, seeming unfazed.

A cold stir crept over me, nothing was adding up. Immediately, I faced my suspicious guest. My eyes churned with mistrust. "Who the hell are you?" I felt for my knife. Damn! I'd forgotten it. I'd left my blade at Val's. Without being too obvious, I scanned the room for anything I could use as a weapon.

The only way I could best describe the passage before my eyes was as if I were in another person's dream, and I was a mere by stander watching. In a flash Jen's body began to seize, thrashing violently, face distorted. Next, her body exploded, shattering fragments of something like glass in every direction. Quick on my feet, I lunged across Jeffery with my back to the flying shards, shielding us both as we toppled to the floor. My whole backside was bathed with an unknown substance that felt wet and cold. *Blood,* came to mind. Instantly I touched my neck and drew back the moisture on my fingertips. I glimpsed down, gawking. It was only water. WTF? When my eyes lifted, I gasped. There were hundreds of tiny molecules floating aimlessly in the air and evaporating into vapor.

Then in a quick blink, the murky mist vanished, leaving no proof of existence. All evidence of Jen was gone.

"What the hell!" Jeffery leaped to his feet.

Alarmed, I urged, "Go check Dom!" A bone-chilling expression colored Jeffery's face as he sprinted up the stairs.

In the meantime, I scoped the kitchen-cabinetry for an easy weapon. I went through several drawers before I found Dom's goodies. My eyes nearly went bug-eyed as I gazed down at the Shun knives, high-quality made in Japan. I realized then that I wasn't the only one in the house with a knife fixation. I admired the glimmering collection, smiling. Quick with ease, I locked my fingers around the hilt of a thinner blade. Itching to test it out, I tossed the chef's knife in my palm, getting a feel for the steel. It was perfect, nicely balanced with a little heft.

Without warning, screams emerged from upstairs. Thrust from my thoughts, I dashed in the direction of the bellows. When I reached the threshold of Dom's bedroom, my breath lodged in my throat. Jeffery was leaning over Dom's body, screaming blood-curdling cries. Shear panic slammed into my chest. Then my lungs expanded once my eyes landed on the lump on the floor. Dom had been bound by rope, gagged with duct-tape. He was alive! "Thank goodness," I breathed, grateful for the wall holding me up as I filled my lungs with air.

Hysterical, Jeffery sobbed. "Oh lord have mercy! Did I do this to you?" Jeff's shaky hands weren't much use loosening the tight rope.

I fell beside him offering my aid. "Hey boo, let me do this. Your hands are trembling." Jeff nodded, still weeping as he sat back and let me take over the task.

My hands weren't much better. Thank the stars that I had Dom's razor sharp knife to do most of the work. Willing my hands steady, I began sawing the rope in two. "The Family did this," I hissed through clenched teeth, fiercely working the blade back and forth.

Once I freed a very shaken chef, Jeffery assisted Dom to the lounge chair by the large window. Tears welled as I watched poor Dom rub his wrist. I sat back on my heels, releasing a winded breath. "Are you okay, Dom?"

Dom nodded, his face pale and drained. "Oui! I will live." He gave a wry smile. Apparently, he was in a little pain, the rope had made thin-lined cuts. I think in a day or so, the cuts would be a faint mark, but the memory of tonight, I feared may linger for life.

"I can't believe I did this to you," Jeffery cried. "I swear I don't remember tying you up."

"Jeff, I'm fine," Dom insisted, breathing a bit heavy. "You were under a spell." He soothed his distraught partner. Then Dom's eyes shifted to me. Determination was irrefutable in his jaw. "It is imperative that we take measures protecting ourselves. This can't wait, I fear."

Guilt began to abrade my gut as though I had an ulcer. "Guys," my voice quavered. "I am so sorry!" I ran my fingers through my short curls. "As long as I live here I'm endangering your lives. I should find another place."

"Nonsense," Dom barked. "You're staying here, and that's final."

"If I stay, we need to hire big, beefy guards that know how to use an arsenal of weaponry," I countered.

"I second dat," Jeff conferred as we broke down and started laughing over Jeffery's remark and the eldritch night.

Apart from the short moment of humor, I knew my next move was unavoidable, contacting the one person who understood the Family's darkness probably better than me... *Val*. I pulled out my cell phone

517

from my bra and speed-dialed. My heart pounded as I counted the rings. Finally, he picked up.

"Hello." A little chill washed over me as I heard his drowsy voice.

I blurted out, not worrying if I sounded desperate. "I know you're mad at me. You have a right to be, but something bad has happened. It's got the boys and me scared. Can you please come over?" Dead silence fell for what seemed like an eternity. Then I heard something familiar… a sigh.

His voice was deep from sleep. "Let me get dressed and I'll be right there." *Click.*

I placed my phone back in my bra and looked up at the guys to find two sets of eyes targeting me.

Jeffery decided to chime in. "You just amaze me. You treat that poor boy like dirt. Then you call him in the wee morning hour, askin' him to get out of his nice, warm bed to help you out. With no questions asked, he comes to your rescue. Gurrrl, you better start treatin' that man better," Jeffery scolded me, wagging his finger in a heat of fury.

I popped off, "How do you know his bed's warm?" By the curl of Jeffery's lips, I surely thought he was going to chase me down with the same broomstick he threatened Jen with.

Less than half an hour later, we heard the doorbell. Even though we were expecting Val, the chime sent us jumping out of our skin. After making sure the guys were settled, I scurried downstairs to the front door. I saw through the glass Val standing patiently with his hands in his jean pockets, rocking on his heels. A little spurt of excitement struck as I realized how cute he looked with his disheveled hair. He had that "just rolled out of bed" look. It was a good look for him. Chills etched down to my toes. The good kind. I swung the door open, and before I could contain myself, with no given thought, I threw myself into his arms. He held me back for only a split second before his comforting arms tightly wrapped around me. As I began to melt into his consoling warmth, my body started trembling and tears began to streak my face. Geez, this was not how I pictured this. I wanted to portray strength rather than a display of some sniffling milksop. Val seemed to bring out the sappy side of me.

I choked through the words, "I think the Family is trying to hurt us." My voice filled with unhinged fright.

Val craned his neck, combing the area of the house to see if he spotted a glimpse of any suspecting shadow lurking around the skirt of the house. Then speedily, he ushered me inside and closed the door behind us, locking the bolt. "What happened?" His gold eyes filled with worry.

I wiped the tears off my face with the back of my hand and began telling him the accounts of the night. By the time I finished, Jeffery walked up behind me and interjected. "Uh-hmm! It was like Jasper the friendly ghost. I tell you! The girl just turned pale-white, and her body went *poof!* It was like out of a horror movie," Jeff spoke in his high-pitched drawl. I was glad he decided to come downstairs and join us. After all, he spent more time with Jen than I did. He may recall something that could be helpful. Yet on second thought, whatever that creature was, it had Jeffery under some hex.

Val stood there in silence, taking in our tale of the night. I turned to Jeff and asked, "Is Dom okay?" Concern saturated my voice.

"He's still shaken, but this time, I really did give him a sleeping pill. He should rest good with *that* pill," Jeffery said.

"How about you, boo?" I rubbed his upper arm, consoling him. "Are you okay?" I smiled. My heart went out to him. I knew far too well how he must feel. Though, Jeffery might find it hard to accept that he was under a spell. We were all merely puppets on a string when it came to the Family's mastery.

"I think I'm done trippin'." He drew out of his pocket a crisp-white napkin and dabbed the sweat off his forehead. "I sure ain't drinkin' no mo Kool-Aid."

I glimpsed at Val, hiding a suspicious smile behind his fake cough. I wanted to laugh too, but I didn't dare. I didn't want the wrath of Jeffery's broomstick on my tail. Just the same, I had to give it to old Jeff. He could make any fright into comedy. That was what was so special about him.

"Fellas," I suddenly felt a rush of chill. "I think we have been cursed." My eyes bounced between both men.

"Now let's not jump to the gun just yet," Val advised. "What purpose would someone have to hurt Jeffery?"

"I'm guessing it was a trap for me, but the plan backfired," I answered.

"Why not just tie up both men and surprise you with an ambush?" Then his steady gaze slid to Jeff. "No offense, my man."

"None taken. Though you did give me a good idea… uh, never mind." Jeffery quickly masked an impish expression on his face, then he focused back to the conversation. "C'mon! Let's get some food. We can talk in the kitchen."

Jeffery laid out a batch of Dom's homemade chocolate-chip cookies and made a strong brew of coffee. After seating ourselves at the table, sipping the coffee and sinking our teeth into the fabulous, gooey cookies, Val broke the gleeful silence reminding us why we were here in the first place. "Oh, I almost forgot. Your knife. I thought you might want it back," Val smiled.

My eyes perked. "I sure could've used this earlier. Thanks!" I took my dagger still strapped in its sheath and held it close to my chest. I promised myself that I'd never leave it again. Tomorrow, I planned to go get the others. A girl could never have too many knives.

Val continued. "Okay." His gold-eyes pointed at me. "Tell me why you think this had anything to do with the Family and dark magick?" By the hard lines in Val's face, I was certain this strike was larger than I'd initially envisioned. I was frightened too.

"Who else would stoop to such a low," I reasoned.

"Have you two ever heard of a *miasma*," Val asked.

Jeffery and I shared a glance, and in the same breath, we both bellowed. "*Nooo!*"

"Well,"—Val took a deep breath. "I think what you all experienced was the work of an evil mist known as miasma."

"That name has spooky stamped all over it," I quavered.

Jeffery broke in. "Forget the mofo spooky! Whatever that girl was, it stunk worse than any skunk I'd ever come across." He pinched his nose, twisting his lips into a scowl.

"Come to think about it, I noticed a smell too. I kept thinking the stove had a gas leak. Weird!" I grimaced. "I don't know why I didn't mention it."

Val interjected. "Stevie, you may have been under the enchantment, like Jeffery."

"Your right. Now that I think about it, I wasn't myself." I wrapped my arms around my waist, trying to ease my nerves.

Val continued. "My friends, what you have encountered is a rare type of incantation," he rubbed his bristled chin, thinking. "What is strange to me is that the cast is seldom used to harm anyone. However, its foul odor can clear a herd of elephants."

"A spell that stinks! That's just rich," Jeffery groaned.

"It's a very powerful incantation," Val went on explaining. "Whoever worked the spell is a craft master. Not just anyone can conjure a miasma."

"What did you call it?" It sounded like a childhood disease.

"It's pronounced as mē'azmə," Val emphasized the sounding.

"Let me see if I understand you correctly. What we saw tonight was not my friend, it was a miasma." Suddenly I felt as if I was sinking into a black hole.

"That's correct," Val confirmed. "Your friend might've appeared real, but in truth, you were merely seeing a hologram."

"Do you think this mysterious craft master is trying to harm us?" I knew for the sanity of my family, I needed to open my ears and take heed. Yet, I alone may not be enough to protect them.

"It's possible," Val sipped his coffee. "In spite of everything, I can't be certain." He set his cup down and sighed, "By the same token, I do suspect that the miasma was sent to spy."

My brows furrowed. "Spy? How?" I felt the hairs on my back stiffen.

"A miasma," Val furthered, "is similar to astral projecting. Rather than a flesh and blood human materializing before your eyes, the craft master remains anonymous, hiding behind the miasma."

"Talk about hiding in the closet," Jeffery rolled his eyes.

"More like a coward, if you ask me."

"A dangerous coward, if you will." Val ran his fingers through his hair. "I think I might better stay until dawn. Don't bother finding me a bed." Val rose from the table. "If you and Jeffery will excuse me," he nodded. "I'll be busy ridding the house of bad energy and working protection spells," Val turned to Jeffery, crunching on a cookie. "You got any sea salt and sage? White candles and purified water, I'll need as well."

"I have sea salt and sage, and if you consider my finger in the water purifying it, then I got that too," Jeffery joked, or at least I assumed.

I was ready to get this project started. We couldn't rid this house of bad juju fast enough.

"Oh," Val turned a serious eye on me, "It's time you meet our kind."

My breath stalled. "I thought you said the Zophasemin hated me. Remember, I'm impure?"

"True. Don't worry, I have it handled. This is my gang. They follow me and will do whatever I ask."

"So you're a gangbanger?" I asked.

"No, sweetheart. I'm the leader of the Zop. No one messes with me unless he has a death wish and that includes following my orders."

And there it was. Val the great leader, assuming a posture of superiority by that lopsided grin of his. I didn't see that coming. Then a thought hit me "Val, did you order your gang to leave me alone?"

Jeffery watched in silence, still nibbling on the same cookie.

"Oh, the lady calls me by my name. There's a first!" Acid coated his baritone voice.

"There's no need to be so sensitive."

He snorted a curt laugh. "Sensitivity is what sets the Zop apart from the rest."

"Oh, and you kicking me out of your bed was a tradition?" I crossed my arms over my chest, glowering.

"Now who's the sensitive one? I just chose not to make a whore out of you. I like to think of myself as a gentleman." Val's soft eyes abruptly hardened.

I hated fights, but I never backed down from one, and I wasn't going to change that tradition now. I gathered to my feet and pushed off from the table. My hands fisted to my side. "For your information, your hind-ass, that's my decision. I think a woman should have the same freedom as a man, sleeping with whomever without being pegged as a *fille-de-joie*." I glared angrily at the towering demigod, a giant at six-four, against my small frame of five-five. "Furthermore, for your information, I don't go jumping from bed to bed. I've only had one partner in my life, and that was a one-time deal, so watch what you call me!" I glared at the mighty man.

A strange noise disrupted our heated argument. Both Val and I halted turning in the direction of the galling sound. It was Jeffery chomping on popcorn, sitting frozen and bug-eyed. We had forgotten we were in mixed company.

Unfortunately, Jeffery didn't' get to see the ending of the show.

Once he saw the blaze of Val's face, he quickly scattered upstairs. I, on the other hand, had to finish the heated discussion with one irate Zop.

I twirled on my heels with fire in my glint. "Do we have to continue this *pointless* argument?"

"Stop avoiding the inevitable. I get that you're afraid to admit that you have feelings for me," Val charged.

"Don't be ridiculous!" I slammed back.

"Really! Is this how it's going to be?"

"I have no idea what you're referring to," I denied, vehemently, wishing I'd escaped with Jeffery upstairs.

"Stop being coy with me. Admit it! You don't call me by my first name because you're scared of letting that tender heart extend pass your nose.

"Actually, I never call my employees by their first name." There went my smart mouth.

When I saw the anger in his eyes ignite, it took me back a step or two. My once-gentle Ben didn't seem so gentle any longer. He paused while never lifting his scowl at me. He leaned in, lowering his voice to a mere whisper. "He really hurt you, didn't he? I know deep down this isn't who you are." His words tortured me. "I didn't want to just have sex. I wanted to make love to you. You are deserving of nothing less."

I stood there frozen, unable to speak. How stupid could I have been to overlook this? I think at that point, I'd hit my lowest low. I had been too wrapped up in my own selfish desires that I'd forgotten to consider Val's feelings. What a selfish fool I had become.

I started to reach out to touch his face, but by then his face glossed over, closing himself off to any further conversations in relation to our intimacy issues. I knew any attempt on my part would be futile. I dropped my hand to my side and stood there staring back at him in silence.

As if our discussion had never come into play, he went on to say. "You might want to make another pot of coffee. It's going to be a long night and even a longer day," he hesitated. "I'll be outside if you need me." I stood frozen, watching him exit the house.

Obviously, he felt hurt. I didn't know what exactly he wanted from me. If he wished for my heart, I'd gladly give it, but he was asking the impossible. My heart stopped beating a long time ago.

DISCOVERY

The golden dawn was just peeking over the horizon when Val stepped back into the house. He'd finished smudging the exterior with sage. By his drained face and damp hair from the cold dew, I began to grasp that this ritual was an intricate venture. The rite demanded hours, and considering that he'd had little sleep, the tall order had taken a toll on him.

Ms. Noel once explained to me the importance of a protection spell. The cleansing could only be performed by the craft maker, someone with a particular kind of magick. Any other caster standing in the energy-field might disturb the sacred ground, contaminating the incantation.

Keeping that in mind, and the huge argument between Val and me, I thought it might be wise to steer clear. Besides, right now, I hated myself. Val was right, my mind seemed to linger in the past. I wasn't sure if Aidan had anything to do with it, but I was certain my child did. If he couldn't understand my plight, I didn't see our relationship blossoming into anything significant.

Val didn't waste any time getting to the interior. Since the same rule applied, I stayed in the foyer, sinking into a comfy chair, and keeping out of the way. Quietly, I listened to his gentle footfalls as he moved willowy throughout the mansion, chanting an ancient language.

After a short time, my eyelids grew heavy and soon sleep crept upon me. Hours had passed when a soft tap on my knee awakened me. I opened my droopy eyes and there, bigger than life and kneeling before me was Val. His face appeared weary and his beautiful golden eyes were blood-shot, but a sweetness had replaced his angry glint. I instantly smiled, and a thrill shot through me. I was happy to see he wasn't mad at me any longer.

An aroma of breakfast drifted through the house. I knew right away Dom was back to his old self, preparing breakfast for everyone. My French friend loved early mornings. He had us all beat with age, yet, he often worked the longest and hardest. Jeffery, I'd decided, was an immutable fixture collecting dust.

"Are you hungry," Val asked.

"Yeah. I could eat." I stretched and yawned.

Val flashed a crooked grin, extending his hand. I smiled back, taking him up on his kind gesture. As he hoisted me onto my feet, I lost my balance, falling into his arms. Whether it was an accident or Val's intention, I'd never know. Although when our eyes met, we froze as if time stood still, lost in each other's captivating breath. His hands rested on my hips, a slight caress of his thumb brushed against my bare skin, right above the waist band of my pants, spreading goose bumps over my body. Visions of the past night in his bed came rushing in. My breath hitched as I watched Val slowly begin to lean in for a kiss. Only a fraction from my lips, when Jeffery peeked his head around the corner clearing his throat that echoed throughout the house. Val and I both jerked back, startled as Jeffery amused. "Food is gettin' cold!"

With disappointment riding shirt-tail, our trance faltered, and the enchantment broke. I withdrew from Val's arms and followed Jeffery.

At the table, everyone seemed quiet and into their private reflections of the night before. Dom cleared his pallet and addressed Val. "Thank you for your help. We are very grateful."

The left corner of Val's lips quirked into a brief smile. "Don't mention it. I'm glad to help," he paused, switching to a more serious note. "It is crucial for us to find out why this unknown presence is targeting you good folks," Val advised.

Dom joined in, saying out loud what I was already thinking, "I think we won't have to look very far to find this scoundrel."

"I suspect everyone at this table assumes that the Family is responsible," Val disclosed. "However, this miasma isn't their style."

I jumped on the wagon this time. "If it's not the Family, then who is it?"

"I believe it's a sole entity haunting you for its own personal reasons," Val speculated.

Funny, I just realized that I'd never seen Val in his own element, strong and confident. I felt enamored.

"Oui," Dom agreed. "Do you have any idea why we are being targeted?"

"No. Not yet," Val went on to explain. "That's why we need to get to the bottom of this black magick. I think if we find the motive, we'll find the person behind all this hex-spying."

Jeffery butted in with a shriek, "Hold the hell on!" He raised his hand in the air like he was about to give the sermon on the mount. "Can those evil mofos see us in the bathroom?"

Dom rolled his eyes, Val and I shared glances but quickly diverted our eyes off in another direction to avoid an explosion of uncontained laughter. Val cleared his throat, pushing down the mirth. "Bro, just make sure you're covered-up when you do any... extracurricular."

I couldn't hold it any longer as I spewed over the brim of roaring laughter.

Val and Dom somehow kept their composure.

"That's just fine, missy," Jeffery fumed at me. "I have a broomstick with your name on it," he pursed his lips.

"I'm sorry, boo," I snickered, nearly breaking a rib. I wiped the moisture from my eyes. "I couldn't help it," I snickered again.

Jeffery folded his arms, his face blistered in ireful silence.

Dom took the table and asked, "Do you have any suggestions of how we can find this mysterious malefactor?

Then I intervened, straightening my shoulders back, taking a much more serious tone. "There is someone I suspect who might be behind this ploy. She's well trained in the arts of magick. I saw her vanish with my own two eyes, and she detests me."

"What's the girl's name? I can get my peeps to check her out," Val asked, sipping his coffee.

"Helen DuPont," I revealed.

Val's sip suddenly spewed forth, shooting poor Jeffery in the face. Jeff shrieked, springing from the table and running for his bathroom, leaving a trail of curses in his wake.

Dom followed after Jeffery and I snatched a napkin for Val. When I handed him the towel, I arched a suspicious brow. "Do you know this bitch?"

Val's voice was raspy, burning from swallowing the coffee down the wrong pipe. "In passing," he coughed out.

"Uh-hmm. Sure there's not more to it?" My voice lanced with mistrust."

"Hmm... I know *of* her." Val dabbed the dark liquid off his once white T-shirt. By then, Jeffery and Dom had returned. Val quickly moved on to the next subject, his voice still hoarse. "I have made arrangements for one of my fighters to help. He's going to stand guard. No one leaves this house without him. Everyone sticks together, even if it's the market or the *bathroom*."

Jeffery flinched, holding his hand up, waiting for permission to speak.

Val nodded his head, acknowledging Jeff.

"Does your guard have to stand over us in the bathroom? I mean," Jeffery shifted in his feet. "I like company, but even for me, that's just a bit TMI."

"Affirmative, bro," Val gibed. "I will personally see to it that my fighter never leaves your sight." Val slipped me a sideways glance and winked.

I held back the laughter that begged for release. Dom, as usual, shook his head, keeping silent.

"You are one cruel mofo," Jeffery huffed. He pivoted on his feet, stomping up the stairs as curses wafted throughout the mansion.

Later, the doorbell rang, and we all jumped. Val assured us it was one of his fighters that he'd requested for duty. He went to the door and brought his sidekick to the kitchen, where we all waited. The Zop-fighter wasn't quite as tall as Val. He was shorter and boxier, more compact. His features were dark hair and deep-brown eyes, nice look-ing, yet he paled in comparison to his leader. Val stood at least a head taller and was leaner, although, they both could've passed for giants. "Hey, everyone! This is Razz. He'll be watching over you until we correct the problem."

Razz nodded his head without speaking a word. His expression was stern but with ease until his eyes landed on me. He quickly stiff-ened, eyeing me with caution. As you know me, I never back down. I eyed him back just as equally cautious. The young Zop appeared a few years younger than his commander. By his stance, he reminded me of an English bulldog.

Then a bizarre incident happened. They began to exchange conversation in their native tongue, a strange, foreign language. I gasped when I realized I understood the words. Before I could contain my excitement, both Zops' eyes switched to me. I quickly pulled myself together, confessing, "Silly me. I bit my tongue. Ouch! It hurts. I'm gonna go check it out." I lent a tight smile. Talk about awkward.

As my back turned, I couldn't help the fat grin that spread across my face. I understood their alien language. Wow! On the other hand, I didn't care much for what I heard from the shorter Zop and his opinions of me.

Val didn't waste any time assigning me to my new regime. I had to learn how to, as Val called it, stretch my abilities. First, I had to do a stupid breathing exercise similar to learning how to push within your gut, like a singer. Best part of the training, the Commander in Chief, Val, allowed me the privilege of practicing in the garden.

The assignment was tedious, mundane, and uninspiring. I kept checking the time as it dragged by. After a while of uneventful stretching, I decided to take a break. I went straight for the swing.

Time elapsed. I didn't care. I was happy, swinging back and forth with my toes reaching for the white-puffy clouds in the sky. I leaned back, eyes closed, enjoying the crisp cool breeze brushing across my face, and inhaling the scent of lantana and moist soil.

Then my little bit of happiness abruptly halted in midair. Startled, my eyes flew open. I'd found myself locked in an iron embrace, facing two very angry gold eyes.

"What do you think you're doing?" Val's voice had a healthy dose of exasperation slapped between two slices of bread with me in the middle.

"I'm taking a break," I snapped. "I've been out here since the crack of dawn." I tried squirming out from under his grip, but my attempts were futile. He was much stronger.

His brows knitted. "Do you think my exercise is too tough for your tender behind?"

Oh, no he didn't! Them's fightin' words, as we say in the south.

"That tender *be*hind you're referring to," I spat as I struggled to free myself from his iron-clad hold, "is as tough as *you* and any of *your* gang!" My eyes blazed at my captor. Then abruptly he dropped me, causing me to land on my ass with a thud. "Ow," I mumbled.

I scrambled to my feet, fist loaded, ready to fight. Obviously, Val sensed my irritation, as he'd not bothered hiding his smirk. I first wanted to smack him. On second thought, what was the point? He'd just dodge my blow, and with my luck, I'd end up over his lap with my ass exposed to the palm of his hand. He had turned into a brute. I wanted my gentle Ben back. This tower looming over me with the fragrance of acerbity was not my sweet Val.

"No breaks! You are Zophasemin, it's time you start acting like one."

There was something almost predatory in his tone. I didn't like it one damn bit either. "My weak humanity is what drives me. I am proud to claim my human side. After all, I am my father's daughter. Don't you *ever* forget that," I hissed, shoving my hands into his chest, though, he might as well have been a mountain. He didn't even waver against my thrust.

Without warning, the grand warrior, Val, burst into a roar of laughter. Unaware, I heard another source of chuckles on the back of my neck. I twirled on my heels to find the Zop fighter, Razz, shooting a shard grin down at me, leaning against *my* favorite tree. That was all it took, I simply snapped. "What's so damn funny, *Zop*?" Before I realized what I was doing, I thrust my dagger straight at him, missing his head only by half an inch. The blade notched the tree, making the metal chime. My eyes flashed fire, that same burst of flames like Aidan's as I confronted my foe. "*I understood every word you said last night, Razz. I'd tread lightly if I were you,*" I spoke with clarity and confidence. Apparently, the Zop had a problem with my druid blood. He'd made it clear if it weren't for his Commodore, he would've enjoyed killing me with his bare hands. He looked upon me with disgust. He even went as far as to insult my father, and for that, I *hated* him.

Both Zops stood frozen in stunned silence. *Good,* I thought. "I'm hungry," I announced, "I'll be in the kitchen if you care to find me." Without another word, I left them there with their gaping faces.

I heard Val bark orders at Razz to stand watch. I high-tailed it to the house. I needed distance between those two lugs and their stupid Zop pride.

When I stepped into the kitchen, Dom and Jeffery had disappeared, leaving the table set with a delicious spread of cold cuts, various sorts of cheese, pickles, lettuce, and chips. It wasn't fancy, but I liked it this way... simple.

I'd already taken a seat at the table with my sandwich in hand when Val strutted in from outside. After washing his hands, Val sat down in the chair next to me. It appeared that his eyes were filled with wonder. I held my breath, trying to hide my snarky grin. Nonetheless, my pride didn't lesson the effects of my piqued feelings. Val should've never brought that creep into my home.

Finally, he broke the unbending quiet. "How long have you been speaking Zophasemin?" Catching a sideways glance, I noticed that Val had a glint in his eyes like he'd caught my hand in the cookie jar.

I first swallowed my bite, then I answered, eyeing my food. "I haven't a clue to what you mean. I can't speak Zophasemin. I only understand the language, and it was not until I overheard the two of you babbling in your native tongue did I realize I could interpret it." I refused to face him as I took another bite of my sandwich.

"Then explain to me," he pushed. "How you were speaking *my* native tongue just moments ago?"

The corner of my lip tipped into a sneer. "I was *not* speaking your stupid language," I vehemently denied, still keeping my gaze to myself.

"Stevie, you spoke our language better than *any* Zop."

I snatched up a chip and popped it in my mouth as if I were unfazed. "Maybe you need to clean the wax out of your ears, Commodore. I only understand Zop."

Val blew out a harsh sigh. "I think the only right thing for you to do is apologize to Razz. You nearly ended his life with that knife of yours." He bit down into his sandwich, taking almost half. It seemed his bite was bigger than his bark.

"*What* the hell!" I snapped my head up, facing the golden beauty, clenching my teeth, sparks flying mad. "I can't believe you," I screeched. "First of all, how can you bring that jerk into my home when he wishes nothing more than to rip my heart from my chest? You're not protecting *me*. You are putting me in harm's way with that beast who walks the grounds aimlessly."

"You're wrong. Razz won't go against an order. Forget what he thinks!" Val tried to blow this off like I was having a P.M.S. moment.

"It will be a cold day in hell before *I* ever apologize," I avowed. "You made a bad judgement call, Commodore."

Val lowered his head for a second and took a jagged breath. "I'm sorry. I didn't have much of a choice."

"You have a choice. Don't invite him!"

"Look! You might as well get used to not being the most popular among our kind." How could he truly understand my stance? After all, he was the perfect Zop.

"For your information, I'm good with unpopularity. I've had that all my life. It's the Wanting-My-Head-On-A-Silver-Platter part that I'm having an adjustment problem with."

"I'm sorry, Freckles. I did warn you. It's our way. I can't change tradition." Val's jaw tensed, but his eyes were elsewhere. I suppose he had other situations more pressing than my little ole life.

"*Our* way," I stormed. "Excusez-moi! *Not* mine! I'll never hate someone merely because of their origin."

"I understand you haven't been raised in our culture. We are a proud race. We wish our kind to stay whole and pure."

"Oh my God! That's the real reason you pushed me out of your bed," I stormed. "It has nothing to do with my heart belonging to another!" My green eyes threw shards at him.

"Don't be ridiculous," he scoffed. "Now you're acting like a woman."

"Ridiculous! Is that anything like a Zop female," I struck back.

"This conversation is over," Val demanded as anger rolled off his body.

"I'm sorry, but I'm not one of your soldiers. Answer my question," I ordered fiercely.

"Which question? You ask so many, it's hard to keep up," Val met my heated stare.

"Did you not want me in your bed because I'm part human," I repeated through clenched teeth.

Val blew out a wind of frustration. "The human part wasn't an issue at the time. I wanted you to myself. I didn't want to share you with another, even if he was dead. I meant what I said." He halted his words briefly. I saw the struggle in his face. "However, after considering this connection you and I share, I believe we are better off as friends. My culture and customs are very important to me. This is who I am. If I gave you my name in marriage, I would bring shame to my kind, and worse, our children would be outcast as well as you and I. I don't want to do that to you or my unborn children. There's no future for us, and I think you would be better with a human or a druid."

I sat there dumbfounded, staring at him. What was it with these guys and their freakin' family ties? I didn't know why his words stung so much, but they did. Why would he say that to me? I never planned a future with him. I didn't dare. In fact, I never gave him any indication that I expected us to become a couple. Now that he'd admitted openly that we had no future, assuming that I'd expected more, it set my teeth on edge. "I guess this means I won't be getting a ring?" Sarcasm sugar coated my words.

It didn't help matters any when he smirked at my reply. "Guess not," he relented stiffly.

Then I let him have it. "I never asked for any commitment from you. As far as I was concerned, you were a mere entertainment. So don't get all worked over with worry that you're going to crush me. I never thought of you as a permanent fixture anyhow." I pushed from the table and charged outside. I needed a distraction, anything to get my mind off the burn of Val's words.

I made my way to the tree where I'd left my embedded knife, deep in the bole of the oak. In one angry jerk, I ripped it from the grasp of the tree.

Suddenly, my attention shifted to footsteps behind me. I twirled around with my trusty knife in my hand, ready for whatever came next.

"You're pretty good with that knife," Razz addressed me in his tongue.

To my surprise, I replied back in his native language as if I'd been speaking it my entire life. "My throw was off. I was aiming between your eyes," I eyed him cautiously.

"I heard you're a spit fire." His hunted eyes raked over me sending eerie chills over my body. "I suppose if I were in your skin, I'd be a bit angry too." The Zop stepped closer into my personal space. "Our ways may seem unfair, however, it has worked for our race for centuries. It's nothing personal."

"None taken. I know my place, but you need to know yours as well. Don't get me wrong, I do appreciate your assistance. However… this is my home and my family. You will respect my position as long as you are here. I hope we have an understanding." I held my proud chin high.

"Fair enough, impure." His dark glint made me want to coil, but I refused to cower under his condemnatory eyes. "Know this as well, if I ever catch you out and free of my leader's protection, you are fair game."

My brows knitted in confusion. "I don't get how you can hate another only because he or she is different."

"It is not another. It is impures we detest."

"Why do you hate us so much?"

"Mixing our kind with yours is forbidden."

"Who instills this idiocy in your head?"

"Our creator, naturally."

"A creator who is prejudice?" I couldn't wrap my head around his barbaric belief.

" My creator is *righteous*. Your kind wasn't meant to exist. We are pure. Our kind does not destroy each other in war. Rather, we stand together as brothers, whether we like each other or not. Humans are wasteful and selfish. War is used for greed. Zophasemin are selfless. We would lay our life down for our brothers. Tell me, would your humans do the same for you?"

"For the most part, you are right. Humans at times can be very self-absorbed, yet not everyone. Unlike your kind, mankind was given a choice, a freedom to decide for themselves. There is nothing far greater than the gift of freedom, to choose your own destiny. So my answer to your question is… I'd lay my life down in a second for anyone I love, and those two humans inside my house who have been gracious enough to feed *you* would return the favor to me at any given moment. It's called humanity." I ended the conversation by walking away. I'd had it with politics and self-righteous pricks. The human part in me was really starting to make me proud. Screw these prideful Zops. They should watch themselves. They were on my turf.

HIDDEN TREASURE

*A*ll week it had been miserable. By all the bruises and body aches, one might wonder if I was the redheaded stepchild. Val was beginning to think my human side affected my Zop side. He tried everything in *his* powers to awaken my dormant abilities, but instead, he got the human side of me cussing at him.

I did have some gifts. I was quick on my feet and swift with a knife. I'd gotten very good with my aim. I hit my target nearly every time. At least I had that going for me, even still if I ever came up against a creature of supernatural abilities, my chances of winning were slim.

I decided I needed a human break. I didn't feel I was getting any closer to reaching my goals or finding my daughter. I wanted to decompress. So I headed for Bourbon Street, plenty of action there. It was a Friday night, and it was certain the streets would be bustling with folks.

A little guilt pricked my conscious as I had snuck out like a grounded teenager. Val gave Razz strict orders not to let anyone leave the house, and that order especially was directed at me. If the truth-be-told, the Zop soldier didn't give a rat's ass if I choked on a carrot stick. In fact, if it were left up to him, I'd be dead by his doings.

Funny though, why did Val seem different? He was full-blooded Zop. He didn't appear to be offended by my anomaly. Rather, he protected me. I couldn't figure him out. He hated my kind, yet he came to my rescue, standing guard over my house for days and teaching me to fight. Val didn't have to do this. So why the big deal about my birth? Should I be punished for something I had no control over? I had no say in my birth no more than the color of my skin. Why couldn't the Zop nation abandon their prejudiced ways? Perhaps pride made them blind?

And there was no argument, Val was prideful, arrogant, too confident, kind, gentle, sweet... I shook myself hard. *'No niceties!'* I warned myself inwardly. It made me weak. I had to remember he was nothing more than a device for helping me find my daughter. I shouldn't forget the Zop leader stood with the enemy. His *kind*. It seemed my list of adversaries kept getting longer, and my friends kept dwindling down.

Still, I didn't understand what came over me the other day at lunch. Val denying any future between us really stung. It felt like a stab through my heart. I didn't see us as a couple, so why did I get all irked?

Soon my cab stopped, and I reached over the seat and handed the driver his fare. I slid out and shut the door behind me.

Stepping up on the sidewalk, I breathed in the surroundings. I adored downtown, the Spanish architecture with bold yellows and various shades of orange, the jaunty music and neon lights. It was my little piece of king cake.

The tourists were starting to stir. Chatter was growing as the crowd thickened. The spirit of good times hung in the air. The whole street seemed on fire tonight. Jazz music flowed onto the street. People were merrymaking, hopping from bar to bar, boozing up for that splendid hangover the following morning.

Certain hot spots here weren't exactly for the fainthearted. Unfortunately, it didn't matter how tough of a stomach a person had, most didn't have a clue to what lurked in the dark shadows.

Speaking of which, I planned to steer clear of Val's bar. First, I didn't want word to get back to him that I was hanging around in the French Quarter, and two, I didn't want to run into one of his Zop comrades. Losing my head tonight wasn't an option.

Wanting to be left alone, I wasn't in the mood to attract any interest, so I wore a tank top and my cutoff jeans. I didn't bother with makeup. To hide my face, I wore a cowboy hat I'd had for years. It was pretty beat-up and tattered. I figured it'd help me to blend in with the crowd.

In case there was some trouble, I came prepared. Hiding under my shorts, I strapped my dagger to my thigh, an easy reach for the unexpected.

It was not until I had walked about halfway down the street that I came upon a new-age bookstore. It read, *Magie Noire*. I knew what that meant Black Magic.

It continued to read, *"Tarot Readings, Spells, and Herbal Magick."* A sign hung in the door reading open.

The small bookstore reminded me of the one in Tangi, so I decided to explore it. I had a few bucks on me. No telling what I might find.

I pushed the door open, and the bell jingled as I entered. Once the door closed behind me, a strong whiff of incense, sandal wood, hit my nostrils. The scent carried me back to a simpler time, memories of Ms. Noel. I paused a moment, trying to adjust to the dim lighting. I missed my elderly friend. Looking back, I'd rejected Ms. Noel's unconventional beliefs. I think now I'd take it quite differently. After my world had crashed three years ago, I learned the hard way that with age comes great wisdom. I wished she were still alive so I could tell her that too.

Jarring me from my thoughts, strings of beads rattled, alerting me to the clerk returning from the back. A dark-skinned lady came out and greeted me with a warm smile.

"Welcome, my friend! Feel free to look around. If you need my assistance, just call." She spoke with a deep Jamaican accent.

I smiled back. "Thank you. I'm just looking." I couldn't help but admire her attire. It was quite impressive. The material appeared to be cotton, but it was far from ordinary. The garment wrapped around her whole body in bold blue, purple, and bright orange. To match, she wore some sort of cloth wrapped around her head. It was as lovely as the dress. I loved her gold loop earrings too. It seemed to go with her style very well. My eyes trailed down to her feet, and oddly, she was barefooted. *That's the way to be,* I admired. I hated wearing shoes too.

I moseyed down the aisle, thumbing the books. I think the store carried every book of witchcraft, voodoo, and spells that ever existed. The shelves scaled all the way to the ceiling. Next, I browsed the candle section, tarot cards, and magickal herbs.

When I came to a display, my eyes rested on one item that stood out from the other trinkets. I'd seen this root before. The plant had been carved into an ugly doll. I was so drawn to the weird thing that I couldn't stop myself from picking it up. I brushed my hand across it, noticing the rough texture of the strange bauble. The color wasn't any better, it reminded me of tobacco spit.

I knew I must've appeared totally out of my element when the storekeeper interrupted. "Dat tis a poppet," the lady spoke in a heavy accent.

I jumped, startled. I didn't hear her approach me from behind. "Some call it an Obeah doll much like voodoo. In the hands of the wrong person, it can do great harm." She pointed to the strange carving. "You mustn't touch the doll." She eyed me with caution. I didn't take the lady as confrontational, rather instead, she seemed direct.

"Oh! I didn't mean any harm." I quickly laid the doll back on the shelf. "It's just so… unusual." I clasped my hands behind my back. I felt a little uncomfortable, like a child getting scolded.

"I am certain you did not mean to bring ill, but before you handle any-*ting*, you must know its origin. You must handle a poppet very carefully. One wouldn't want to spread bad juju onto another," she quieted for a moment, gazing deeply into my eyes as if she could see every dirty secret I'd ever possessed. I began to shift a bit, feeling the unease. "You are different. Not fully human, *no*," she asked as if it was a common question.

I blinked with surprise, "I'm sorry?" How could this stranger know me?

She softly giggled. "Honeychile! You heard me. No worry, mon. You will come to me when the time is right."

"You remind me of a friend I once knew." I tossed an uneasy smile.

The lady paused, then her forehead creased with curiosity. "What does a young girl as yourself need with such a powerful tool like *tis*?" Her accent was as strong as her deep-brown eyes were penetrating.

I snorted a short laugh. "You wouldn't believe me if I told you. I don't want the doll, actually. It reminded me of my friend. She once used these dolls, and…" I choked in the middle of my sentence.

"Your friend… she is gone?"

"Yes, she passed away a few months ago. She is greatly missed."

"I am sorry for your loss. You have lost much for someone so young."

The lady seemed to have read me well. It was almost eerie. "Yes, I have," I replied curtly.

The lady paused, eyeing me like I was a tea-leaf reading. I started to shuffle my uneasy feet from the presage she seemed to hold over me. "I have a gift, very special. I've been *waiting* for you to stop by." The lady turned and made her way to the back, past the string of beads, disappearing from sight. I began tapping my foot nervously listening to the string of beads clattering. I thought about making a clean get-away as my eyes bounced back and forth from the back to the door, but my curiosity rendered me. I waited holding my breath.

Soon she reappeared with a small white box in her hand. "This belongs to you," she smiled, opening the plain box. Inside laid a necklace with a stone. It was beautiful, like flickers of fire with glimmering gold. It reminded me of Val. I brushed my fingers across it. A sudden hum came from within the stone. I gasped as I glanced up at the lady. "Yes," she spoke softly. "It is called Angel Fire."

"It is beautiful," I nearly choked with amazement.

"There is more to it than its beauty. It calls to your true name." The lady smiled as though she possessed a secret about my life.

My brows knitted. "What do you mean?" A bit taken aback, I questioned her motive.

"Oh, don't be afraid," she laughed. "I'd recognize you anywhere, my child." She extended her hand and introduced herself. "I am Mardea."

I took her hand and shook it, but I sensed an uneasy stir. I pulled my hand away and responded cautiously. "Glad to meet you. I'm Stev..."

The dark-skinned woman interrupted. "I know who you *are*." Thrown off my guard, she clarified her intent. "No worry, mon. It is not I whom you should fear, Essence. I am on your side, and lately, I hear you could use a little support," she smiled kindly at me. "'Tis necklace is a talisman. It will help you tap into your magick. There is a blockage deep within you. It is a binding spell, coupled with several others to mask over it. Someone doesn't want your powers to emerge.

My eyes orbed. "Who would do such a thing?"

"I don't know. Though, I can tell you dat they wish to fool you into *tinking* you have no abilities. Don't let them trick you! You are very powerful, so you must wear this stone at all times. Never take it off, my child." The lady fastened the necklace around my neck as I stood there uneasy, holding my hair up.

My fingers grasped the stone. "I don't understand. How do you know me?" My mind swooned with trepidation.

"Someone close to you asked me to keep this necklace until you came. He's a loyal believer of the old ways, and he wishes to protect you from your powerful enemies. Wear tis. Never take it off or the spells will return."

"I'm confused. Who left this for me?"

"I'm sorry. This person wishes to remain anonymous."

I shook my head in bewilderment. "How do you know you have the right person?"

"I saw you in a vision." The dark-skinned woman smiled.

"Did this person give a name," I asked with urgency.

"My child, you already have the answer." She seemed surprised by my asking.

I had to take a stabbing breath. "What did this admirer look like," I asked as chills skated across my skin.

"He was very well dressed. It was obvious he had money. His features were tall and dark, very handsome, but his most outstanding feature were his blue eyes." The woman watched my reaction closely. "He referred to you as Princess."

Right then my breath caught in my throat. My hands started trembling. This couldn't be possible! "When did he give this to you?"

"Hmm... only weeks ago."

Holy crap! Could it be... Aidan?

"Please tell me what all you know. I must have every detail!" My urgent voice submerged in panic.

"He did give me a message to give to you." The lady's dark eyes held a secret that I had to know.

"Please, what did he say?"

She hesitated, unsure she wanted to reveal her mysterious messenger. "He said it was not he who betrayed you... and one more." The lady gave pause.

"What else," I pressed impatiently.

"Dat your daughter is alive."

I staggered over her last words. How could I believe this stranger? I tightened my eyes with disquiet. "This must be someone's idea of a joke!" Now I was pissed. "Lady, what game are you playing?" Doubt colored my fear.

She smiled to herself as if she recalled a private joke. "He told me you would accuse me of lying, so he gave me something only you would know." The lady went back behind the counter and reached underneath and brought out a glass jar with holes punched in the lid. "Here." She slid the Mason jar across the counter to me. "He said this should be proof enough."

I gasped. I couldn't believe my own eyes. Inside the jar took me back to a time I once wanted to forget, a firefly fluttering about.

Then I fainted, collapsing to the floor.

FEATHERS RUFFLED

"**W**hat the hell were you thinking, Stevie!" Val screamed, his face blood red.

I'd never seen him this angry before. I felt every inch of his wrath striking me, flinching each time. Damn, damn, damn! I would've gotten away with it if I hadn't passed out. Just my luck! "Calm down! I'm fine." I rested my hands on my hips. I was cloudy on the details of how Val found me. When I had awakened, I was back home in my bed. It was not until later when I'd joined everyone in the garden that I'd been struck by the big goon's temper. From one corner of my eye, I saw Dom and Jeffery cringing. From the other corner of my eye, I saw Razz gloating. I hated that *Zop*.

"You were not only putting yourself in danger but everyone else in this house as well. The very folks you vowed to give your life for!" Val's words hit me hard like closed a fist to the face. He was right about that part. I turned to Dom and Jeff. "I'm sorry, guys. What I did was selfish. I won't do it again. I promise." My eyes glistened with tears.

Jeffery spoke up. "It's okay, honey, but I hope you got lucky, b'cuz I don't understand what possessed you to be so stupid." Jeffery tossed a little shade at me. I couldn't help but laugh. Jeffery always had a way of making light of the worst situations.

"Oh, I got lucky, but it's not what you think," I smiled through my tears.

"Lardy sakes! This I gotta hear," Jeffery rolled his eyes. He was such a drama queen. Dom tossed me a short smile, and Val glared at me. Razz's eyes tensed with suspicion which I'd just about blew a gasket when my eyes stopped on him. Honest to God's truth, if I had to look at one more scowl from that piece of trash, Razz, I was gonna snap.

"Look, Zop!" My heated eyes turned on him. "I've about had it with your freaking glares on my back. You got something to say, then say it!" The soldier needed an attitude adjustment, and I swore one more smirk from that son of a Zop, and I was going to give him an adjustment.

The Zop soldier began to speak in his tongue. "I have plenty to say, whore! I think my leader has gone soft. It is forbidden for any Zop to mix with such company as yours. We waste our time and energy standing watch, protecting a spoiled brat who doesn't care for anyone but herself." Razz spat at my feet. "Go back from the rock you crawled from out, fallen angel. No Zop will ever accept you. You are foolish if you think my leader will ever claim you. The only use you offer is on your back. Our leader would be wise to remember his place." Razz's eyes simmered with hatred. I glanced at Val. His jaw was set in stone as his whole body exuded the force of authority.

"You are insubordinate, soldier," Val stepped between us. "Stand down, or I'll show you how soft I truly am," he gravely threatened.

Then the Zop turned his inimical position on his commander. "Why should I when this inbred has challenged me?" His eyes bore repulsion, aiming at me.

I had enough of the Zop's bellyaching. I stepped up. "Let's see what the asshole's got!" I challenged, standing with my shoulders straight. "I'll fight him!" Even through the rush of anger, my internal voice screamed, *crazy bitch, you're gonna get killed!*

Val turned to me. "Do you think you're ready for combat?" His eyes were tight. Clearly, he feared for my safety.

"I'm ready as I'll ever be," I said as I glared at the hostile Zop.

"You remember everything I've taught you?" It seemed as though Val's eyes were searching for a way out.

The way I saw it, I had no choice. Fair or not, I had to confront my enemy. Like it was second nature, I honed in on my very large opponent.

"All right then, let the fights begin." Val met Razz's heated stance.

"I give you permission to engage in this duel only with your fist. There will be no weapons, nor will anyone lose their life today. Do I make myself clear, soldier?"

"What's the fun in a few bruises and a busted nose?" There was a deep-seated edge of hatred in Razz's voice.

"You'd do well to follow an order. If you break it, I'll kill you myself. Do we have an understanding?" Val's eyes glistened with malice.

"I give you my word," Razz promised, gritting his teeth.

Then Val turned to me and reached his hand out. "Hand 'em over," he curtly ordered. I grimaced as I pulled the knife from my boot and slapped it into his hand. Still it didn't satisfy him as he stood there with his hand still extended and his brow raised. *Geez!* I rolled my eyes. I really needed to get a new hiding spot. Reluctantly, I unbuckled my other knife that had been tucked under my shorts and tossed it to him.

"Now you can fight," Val announced.

I sucked in a healthy dose of oxygen and released it slowly. In my combat training with Val, he taught that breathing in a fight was vital for stamina. If you become winded, you lose your concentration and strength—two very important tools if you were to survive. I rushed through my mind over all the techniques that I'd learned as Razz and I crouched down circling one another.

We swapped insult after insult. I think what made him lunge first was a cheap jab about his momma forgetting to teach him manners while she had an overactive hobby of lying on her backside. I didn't know why, but comments about a dude's mom got a rise every time. I scoffed in his virulent face, watching his face blaze with violent intent.

Oddly, it seemed the bigger the Zop, the slower the responses. When he lurched for me, it seemed as though he moved in slow motion. With little effort, I dodged him by side stepping. It was funny when he slammed his face down onto the gravel. My laughter was like a sonic boom as I stared at Razz's butt sticking up in the air and his face flat into the sharp gravel. Though my mockery made him enraged as he took me by surprise. This time, I wasn't as quick. As a consequence, I paid for it when he thwacked me down to the ground. My head hit first, throwing me into a burst of pain while he threw himself on top of me, pinning me underneath him.

The Zop's weight was crushing my lungs. He had to weigh a good hundred pounds more than me. We were unmatched, to say the least. By his smirk, it was obvious that he knew he had the advantage. I knew if I didn't get out from under his iron grip, he was going to pound my face until I was dead. I refused to give him that satisfaction.

Before I had a chance to brace myself, I felt a sharp jab to my left jaw, then my right, and then my left again. His blows were so forceful I felt my jaw snap out of socket and pop back in as he continued to cold-cock me with his massive fist. I had to stop him soon, or else there wouldn't be much left of me to beat.

Suddenly the blows stopped, following a sharp pain at the nape of my wet, sticky head. He'd grabbed my hair and nearly jerked it out by its roots. I gritted my teeth to keep from screaming out from the pain. The Zop leaned in with his foul breath and whispered in my ear, "I bet you like it rough. Maybe I should take you, like my friend at the hospital when you were too drugged to scream. Unlike him, I like my humans screaming, and with you, I'd make you do more than holler." His depraved voice sickened me. I forced myself to look directly into his twisted face, yet my training hadn't prepared me for this. I drew in a sharp breath, startled by his oil-like eyes, no white, no pupil, only a fiendish black.

Then the sudden rush of memories of that hospital jarred me back to my pending danger. I used the anger to unfurl my powers as I released the beast that resided within me. What happened next, I couldn't say. I may have blacked out. The best way that I could describe the way things went down was that my essence had awak-ened. As the consuming force grew, it devoured my entire being. Stevie vanished, and a monster had taken her place. It was similar to that experience with Aidan in the girl's restroom, but this... this felt like the Granddaddy Mac of Hiroshima.

It all happened so fast. A sudden burst jolted me like lightning, pushing its way out, then it came back to me. In one easy sweep, I freed my arms. I felt this searing heat surge forth through my hands. It was like fire, only it didn't burn. Streams of light forged as I shoved my hands against Razz's chest, blasting him onto the hard ground like a rocket missile.

Blood and sweat streamed down my face, but I didn't let little things like that stop me. I jumped on that bastard, and I began beating his face, returning the favor. After his face started looking more like raw hamburger, I topped my next blow with my knee, violently thrusting between his legs. As he doubled over, squealing like the pig he betrayed, I laughed in his face. I regretted I couldn't castrate him. Sorry but not sorry, I took delight knowing he'd be out of pocket in the lovemaking department.

Suddenly the party halted. Before I had a chance to make my next move, Val snatched me up and held me back. "Enough! You proved your point," he ordered.

"Like hell I have," I shrieked, fighting to get loose. "That son of a bitch threatened to rape me. He was in with that pig, *Joe* from Haven! He deserves to die," I hissed through clenched teeth.

"Are you sure?" Val stood tall, in control as his one arm held me tight.

"Yes! He just admitted to it in my ear," I hissed through clenched teeth.

"Enough fighting for one day! You proved your worthiness." He clasped his hand on my shoulder. "Go get cleaned up." Val stood firm. He turned to Jeffery and Dom. They were quiet spectators with blanched faces, gasping at the violence that just transpired.

I felt awful that they witnessed my fight. I realized from this event today that even though we shared a house together, our worlds were very different. They were not accustomed to violence as I had become accustomed to. I think in the future, I should be more mindful.

Val addressed Dom and Jeffery. "Take her in and see to her wounds. I'll be in shortly. I have some business first," his face was dark and hardened.

I had a feeling he wasn't too happy about Razz's threat. True, we were in a full-blown brawl, but rape was *rape*. I suspected that this act was as forbidden in his culture as in the human's world. I didn't care what Val decided to do with that disgusting jerk as long as I never had to lay eyes on him again, or else I might do all the innocent girls out there a favor and kill him myself, the racist bastard.

GIFTS FROM THE DEAD

"**H**old still," Jeffery ordered. "Gurrrlfriend, he worked your face *good!*" Jeffery gently swabbed my face with alcohol. I tried not to flinch, but that stuff burned like a mofo.

"Ow! Can't you be easier?" I leaned away grimacing.

"Gurrrl, you amaze me. You fight a man who is more than double your size, and you is bitchin' over a little alcohol on a little old scratch? Chile, go on!"

I took in a deep breath. "I know but he had it coming."

"Gurrrl, you could have waited until he dozed off and got 'em with the cast-iron skillet? That's how my mama used to get my daddy, and let me tell you, it worked too! Daddy learned to sleep with one eye open and never stray again. He liked to roam a bit too much. Yo know, *water always runs to the river*, that's what my mama would say." Jeffery dabbed the cotton ball with more alcohol.

I stiffened from the burn, then I exhaled, feeling very human. "I'm sorry that Dom and you had to see…" I couldn't get my sentence out from the sudden wincing.

"Dom and I were terrified for you. We had no idea how you were gonna fight off that big old ugly mofo. Val needs a good tongue lashin' too! Dom and I is mad as hell at him. He should've never allowed that beast to touch you. Zop's tradition or not! I don't care. That fight should've never happened." Jeffery seemed adamant about his standing. He seldom wavered in his opinions. Something I wished I could instill in myself.

"I never wanted him here." I flinched again from the alcohol.

"Well… I think I've done as much as I can." He tossed the bloody cotton ball in the trash can. "You're lucky that these wounds are superficial. That animal could've killed you!"

"I know. It's me and my big fat mouth," I agreed.

"No, bitch! It's your big fat temper!" Then Jeffery snorted a laugh. "You sure did surprise Dom and me. You whooped that Zop's ass," Jeffery emphasized as he high-fived me. "Lardy have mercy! What was that glowing stream that shot from your hands? Dom and I thought you were gonna set the place on fire! You is one mofo, dauntless angel!"

I shook my head, still stunned. "It just felt like a herd of wild mustangs needing to be set free. It was the most awe-inspiring thing and the most frightening experience I've ever known." I shrugged my shoulders as I reached for my angel-fire necklace, still latched to my neck.

Dom entered my room with some hot, soothing tea and some chicken soup. Leave it to Dom to think of the perfect remedy. Tea, food, and sleep were exactly what I needed, though I was too stoked. I suppose the effects of the fight wore heavily on me. Every time I thought about Razz's threat, I got pissed-off all over again.

"This will make you feel better, *oui*?" Dom placed the tray over my lap as I leaned back in bed. I didn't know what the big fuss was about. I only had gotten a few scrapes and bruises. No broken bones, not even a busted nose. Then I remembered the beating of my life from Sam. If Aidan hadn't found me when he did, I would've died. I shivered over the memories, memories of Aidan and the feelings he stirred within me.

I smiled, hiding my spike of sadness. "Thanks Dom, but I'm fine. Really! It's the other guy you should worry about," I winced.

"I don't think so. I hope he suffers *très*!" (*greatly*) Dom spoke with apparent anger in his voice. "Your friend should've had Razz removed from our home long before now."

Dealing with the ominous presence from the Family hadn't been easy for the guys. A sudden stab of guilt struck. "I'm sorry, Dom. I didn't mean to put you two in the middle of this toil."

"No," he said with vigilance, "It is not for you to apologize. You did nothing wrong. That creature had abhorrence for you the moment he set eyes on you. Constantly making anti-Semitic comments at you in your own home is unacceptable. You, no worry! End of discussion. Sleep now, yes?" Dom smiled and patted me on my foot.

"I love you, guys." Getting a bit misty-eyed, I pushed through the biting pain and smiled.

Dom and Jeffery had left me to rest, but before I dozed off, I overheard a conversation outside my door. Jeffery had pulled Val to the side. It sounded like he was giving Val the what-for talk.

"You should never have let that beast come to this house to begin with. He nearly killed Stevie, but I'm sure glad she showed him! That mofo deserved a good wallopin'"

"I'm truly sorry for Razz's behavior. I give you my word, I will handle him accordingly."

"Good, cause if y'all come up into my house again, threatening my girl, I'll take a buckshot to your lovely ass," Jeffery warned. "You need to protect her from trash like that. She's a good person, and she deserves nothing but love and devotion. You understand me?" I pictured Jeffery wagging his finger in Val's face. I almost giggled.

I heard Val's voice. "Yes sir! I will lay my life down for her. That's how committed I am to your girl."

"You make sure. Any-oh-how, I doubt your soldier will have the balls to come back here. My gurrrl neutered that Zop!" I heard Jeffery snapping his fingers.

Then Val gave way to a short laugh. "Yes, sir. Indeed! That little woman is as fiery as her hair."

That was the last I heard before I drifted off to sleep.

When my eyes finally opened, the house was quiet. I glanced at my alarm clock, and it was two in the morning. The lights were out except for the night light I kept on my dresser. I glanced around, and my eyes landed on Val sitting in the overstuffed chair next to my bed. I smiled to myself, listening to his gentle snores and watched the rise and fall of his chest as he slept, but from the way he was hanging out of the chair, he looked miserable. The chair didn't accommodate his size very well.

Most of his long body hung over the chair. I took a deep breath, watching. There was a sense of peace watching him sleep. Without thinking, I reached over and nudged him. His droopy eyes opened slowly, and he glanced over at me.

"Hey. Come lie down with me. I promise to behave," I flinched from the painful stiffness. My face had taken a good beating from Razz.

Val stretched and yawned, then he turned to look at me. Our eyes locked for what seemed like forever, then with a deep sigh, he whispered. "I think I can help your injuries." He slid over to the bed and pulled me into his warm arms. I welcomed him as his citrus scent engulfed me. He leaned in without putting his weight on me, and he mumbled something in my ear as he brushed his hand gently over my body.

Immediately, a vibration sensation came over me, penetrating throughout my body. When he finished, a soothing calm settled, and the aches and pain completely vanished. After he murmured sweet nothings in my ear, my eyelids became heavy, and soon I drifted off to sleep, nestled in his caressing arms. The last thing called to mind was a gentle kiss right before my thoughts slipped into a peaceful slumber. I remembered thinking how easy it was being with Val.

MARDEA

*L*ater that morning, I began to arouse from a dead sleep. As the haze of yesterday came to mind, my eyes slid over to Val. Obviously he'd been waiting for me to wake up. He sat relaxed in the chair by my window, sipping a fresh brew of coffee. With the sound of my sheets stirring, his eyes slid over to me. A cheery smile stretched across his face as he spoke. "Good morning, Rocky!"

"Mornin'," I mumbled as I rose up on my elbows, spying his coffee. "Is there any coffee for me?" I almost salivated for his cup.

"Yep, a potful."

"Well, where is it," I said, a bit muddled.

"Oh! You meant do I have a cup for you?" Val attempted to play innocent as his eyes rounded. I glared at him, puzzled.

"I guess. I have to go get my own," I said, feeling a bit pestered.

"I suppose." He sipped, acting as though he was disinterested.

I stared at him as a tinge of annoyance began to grow. I pondered a moment, trying to access his peculiar mood. Then I blurted it out. "What the hell has crawled up your ass this grand morning?" my eyes narrowed.

"Oh, you caught that, huh?" His eyes met mine as equally.

"I guess I did," I bit back.

"Shall you go first, or shall I squeeze it out of you?" Val's eyes hardened.

WTF! "Don't I at least get a cup of coffee before you start in on me?"

"What possible reason would I have to start on you?" His mouth had set in stone.

I'd had it with this guessing game. "How about you just spit out what's on your mind? I haven't developed mind reading, *yet*. Just fill me in on the blanks already!"

"Hmm… where shall I start?" His eyes nearly bore a hole through me. "What were you thinking, going to that bookstore?"

"Are we back on that subject?"

Val just stared at me in silence.

I rolled my eyes. "'Cause I could. It called to me. I don't see what's the big deal."

Val snorted a laugh. "The necklace you're wearing, it reeks of powerful magick. Black magick."

"It does not," I barked. I couldn't fathom that this little stone came from a dark place. "The lady at the bookstore gave this to me."

"Who gave the necklace to *you*?" his brow arched.

"I told you, the clerk!" I skirted around the truth. I wasn't ready to reveal my source. Strange though, I felt like I'd cheated on Val with another man.

"That's all? Just that ugly necklace?" Val watched me skeptically.

"No. There was a message for me." I bit my bottom lip.

"Which was?"

"My daughter is *alive*." I couldn't stop myself from smiling.

"And this unknown person confirmed this?"

"Yes!" I threw my legs off the bed, sitting up, excited. "We can't keep wasting time. We have to get into that hospital and find my records. I know… "

Val cut me off with a wave of his hand. "Whoa! Hold on!" He leaned forward, bracing his elbows on his knees. "We are going to do this when I say so. I'm not going in there half-cocked with no backup. It all has to be well planned."

"What's there to plan? You can change your face. Go in there looking like one of the guards, ingress, egress. It's that simple."

"It's more complex than you think. What if the real person I'm mimicking is there? Also, I need to know where they keep their files. I doubt they keep their records in plain sight. They're too crooked to be that stupid. Remember, I have to leave with the file without getting noticed."

"When will you have the plan in order?" My heart felt like it was going to leap out of my chest.

"An anonymous ally is getting it for me. I'm meeting with my informant tonight."

"Sweet! Where are we meeting this person?"

"Hell no!" Val bounced in his chair, his face red again. "We aren't going anywhere. I'm doing this alone."

"You can drop me off at the corner. I'll stay out of sight."

"Absolutely not! Do you want to scare off the only lead we have?"

"No, of course not."

Val sat there with an odd expression, staring, as if he were trying to blueprint my mind. "I have to know who gave you that necklace. This time I want the whole truth, or you can find someone else to help you."

I rolled my eyes, tugging the covers off me. "What's the big deal? It's a *necklace*."

"Did the stone come from *him*?"

My eyes orbed. How the hell did he know? "That's impossible! He's dead." I closed my eyes. I couldn't hide anything from Val. He seemed to hold some truth serum over me, not that he deserved to know about Aidan. He had no claim on me. Still, I felt it was only fair to come clean.

"Okay! Yes," I blurted out. "The clerk didn't give his name but she described someone that looked like him." I looked away, feeling the sting of guilt.

"I'm guessing that Mardea's been keeping in touch with your ex-lover hasn't she?"

"Wait! How did you know her name?" *I didn't recall the storekeeper ever introducing herself.*

Amusement danced in Val's golden eyes. "I told you once, I have spies everywhere."

I glared at him in shock. What was the point of hiding the details of my little discovery? "She didn't know his name, but she gave me proof." I squirmed, feeling a bit uneasy.

"And?" It was only a solitary word, but I could feel Val's agitation loud and clear.

"The Jamaican lady gave me a jar with a firefly." I sighed. "Aidan and I shared a special place in the forest, a nest of fireflies." I tossed a shameful shrug, unable to look Val in the eyes.

"I see," his jaw twitched.

I sat there in silence. I didn't understand.

"Why are you acting mad," I asked straight out, even if I didn't want to hear his reason.

"Oh! You think I'm jealous of *him*? A man who is dead," his eyes were sharp. "Do you want to know why I wouldn't make love to you?"

"Yes," I whispered.

"I sat watching you sleep. I don't know why, but I have this strong need to shield you." His face took on a look of deep regret that puzzled me. "Anyway, I heard you cry in your sleep... and it was *his* name you called out."

"I'm sorry. I don't have control over talking in my sleep." I sat there, lost for words. How was this my fault?

"True, but it can be a window to what's really in your heart."

"When are you going to understand that Aidan is my past?"

"That's the problem. As long as you still love this man, you will never be open to another. That's the reason I couldn't sleep with you." Val paused. "If I can't have your heart, then I don't want any other part of you. Freckles, it's all or nothing for me."

I shook my head. He was starting to wear my nerves thin. "Bull-shit," I attacked. "It's not my past that keeps us apart. In fact, Aidan has nothing to do with the reason we are not together. How can we be together when your kind despises me? Remember? I'm a dirty impure!" I threw myself off the bed and stood in front of him white fisted and half-naked with only a T-shirt barely covering my ass. I didn't care. I wasn't in the mood for shyness today. Val's eyes combed over me, painfully slow. He stopped as our combative eyes met.

"We seem to have some obstacles to hurdle." His mocking lips tugged at the corner of his mouth.

"Look! I can't erase Aidan, and I wouldn't want to if I had a choice. If it were not for him, I wouldn't be who I am today, but... he's my past, meaning, my feelings are buried along with his death. He's gone and you're here. All I know is when I'm awake, it's you I think about, *not* Aidan. It's your arms I crave. It's your kisses I long for. It's your touch I yearn to feel. I only want to share my bed with you... only you." The pain behind my eyes was clear. "For now that's all I have to give, Val." I whispered his name. I felt if I let his name escape my lips, I'd lose myself, forever. Regardless of my insecurities, it was time I stopped letting my past dictate my future. I had to face it. Spite our differences, I had feelings for him.

Val eased out of the chair, making only one stride to reach me. He was so close I could feel his warm breath on my face. Gently with his thumb, he began caressing my cheek. My breath stalled just when I thought he was going to kiss me, instead, he murmured. "Sorry, that's not enough for me, Freckles. Like I said... it's all or nothing." And with that said, he pushed past me and left my room, shutting the door.

In a fit of rage, I picked up his coffee cup off the nightstand and hurled it at the door. It shattered into a million pieces, splattering coffee all over the door. "Gold-Eyes, you're an insufferable ass," I screeched watching brown liquid slowly drip down the white door. I was done, done, done! Done with men, period!

DARK ANGEL

THE ANGEL SERIES BOOK 3

PRELUDE

*S*o much had happened in last three years. It felt as though wherever I went, death followed. First my dad, killed by a hit-and-run driver. My mother's fiancé Charles, the poor man, lay in his own pool of blood caused by a throat slashing. France died by the same fate. And last, my mom. She died by a drug overdose. All were surrounded by suspicion and all the fingers of justice pointed to me.

I had been railroaded by the Illuminati, the Family. All the murders were pinned on me. I was innocent, but the good old justice system saw it differently. They tucked me away in a nice asylum for the criminally insane and threw away the key. They didn't stop there. The medical staff kept me under a drug haze for the duration of my stay.

Then the unexpected day came when I was set free. Supposedly, I'd been cured of my insanity and no longer was a threat to society. What really happened was the Family stole my newborn child while I was drugged, laying in my own feces.

When I was released, Jeffery and Dom saved me. They took me in and explained that the key Aidan had left me made me into a billionaire. My quality of life had improved, yet I yearned for my unknown child.

Shortly after my release, Aidan's sister, Helen came for a short visit. She had a message from the Family for me to keep my nose out of their affairs. She also announced Aidan was dead.

After visiting a psychic, I received a note with Aidan's handwriting, stating our daughter was alive. And my search began. I had to find my daughter and Aidan.

I found help, Val. An angel like me, or sort of. I was created in a lab by humans with alien technology. Val and his kind were created by the divine. I was viewed as an impure, hated by my own kind. But I'd deal with them later. First, I had to find Aidan and then I'd find my child.

I wasn't sure if I could trust him any more than I trusted the Family. He betrayed me, not telling me he was married to Sally. I wasn't sure I believed her, but I had no proof proving her wrong or right. I didn't see his face. I reckoned all things would come out in the wash, although it was going to be one long hard wash before I reached my end.

Those bastards could call me dauntless angel. I wasn't backing down until I got my child back. Fuck 'em!

BLUEPRINTS TO MY HEART

*S*ince my tiff with Val that last morning, I hadn't heard from him in over a week, not even so much as a phone call. If I didn't know any better, I'd think he was avoiding me. I threw my cell down on the kitchen table, annoyed and flopped down in a chair, shoulders slumped. Giving way to a defeated sigh, I felt abandoned. That made me one grumpy girl. Not even the aroma of Dom's delicious coffee perked my spirits.

I understood Val's frustration. I didn't know what he expected from me. I couldn't undo my past with Aidan any more than Val could change his heritage. Why couldn't he just accept that we both have baggage?

This yearning inside me felt worse than blisters on my heels. Regardless of my heart's desire, I had to face the reality that whether or not Aidan was included in the equation, the fact remained that Val and I didn't have a future together. I had to keep Val's best interest at heart. I couldn't stand back and watch him become ostracized by his race on my account. It would be too selfish for me to put him in that position.

To be fair, even if I wanted to, I couldn't make a decision of where my heart lied. My stomach knotted. When I'd walked into Mardea's bookstore that evening, little did I know that my life was going to change course. Meaning the already sticky triangle just became more complicated.

If the storekeeper, Mardea, was telling the truth, that meant Aidan was alive, and he had our child in his safe hands. That certainly changed everything. Perhaps all my pending questions would come to a light.

Considering all things, I couldn't exclude the Family. It hadn't left my notice that they could be setting a trap. Regardless how this scenario played out, I needed to watch my back. An act of haste could get me killed, and worse, lose my child forever.

Before I proceeded forward with my search, I needed to know if Val had come across any vital information. Not knowing had my gut in knots. If I were a betting girl, I'd wager that the Zop leader took it upon himself to seek out Mardea and confront her. Val made it very clear that he didn't trust her, nor did he care for the necklace either.

Despite Val needing time to simmer, I had to see him. The walls of the house felt like they were closing in on me. I couldn't wait any longer. I was going insane. If he didn't want to come to me, then I'd go to him.

One hour later, I stood in front of Val's bar, trying to settle my nerves. I watched the orange colored neon light flash above the door reading *Mephistz*. A cool breeze tousled my hair. Not exactly pleasant, unless you liked horse manure.

I wasn't sure if my uneasiness came from the possibility of running into Razz or confronting Val. Either way, I planned to pull up my big girl panties and confront my eschewing friend.

I'd rushed to get here. I threw on the first pair of raggedy jeans I could find, a light tank top, my scuffed-up cowboy boots, and my western hat. Makeup took too much time, so I splashed some water on my face and brushed my teeth. I figured I looked perfect to hang out with the scumbags who frequent the bar. Obviously, the Zop clan was not my fav. I had a problem with prejudice pigs.

I brought backup, my trusty dagger. I never left the house without the steel. I'd gotten pretty handy at throwing. I could hit a snake at thirty feet. It'd be nothing to thrust a blade between one of these jokesters' eyes.

Chin tilted in defiance, I entered the bar like I owned the joint. Wasting time wasn't my forte, so I directly went straight to the bar. A young man behind the bar approached me. The glint in his eyes told me he knew my kind, an impure. "What will it be?" His disdain was apparent.

"I'll take a beer, dark draft, and Val, if he's around," I flashed a sugary smile.

The guy smiled without it touching his eyes as he slid a large mug my way. "Sugar, he's over there," he nodded past my shoulder.

I pivoted on my heels, immediately dropping my beer. "That son of a bitch!" Gawking incredulously, I stood there, beer spattered over my clothes. "What is *she* doing here?"

Then I heard the bartender snort behind me. "It's one of those on-again-off-again affairs."

"She's not a Zop. So, you approve," derision spilled forth from my tone.

"My approval doesn't matter. Just glad his *girlfriend* doesn't stink like an impure."

I scoffed over my shoulders at the bartender's dig. I wasn't going to dignify that comment with an answer.

It wasn't hard spotting Val. His blonde locks stood out among the crowd. He was in the center of the dance floor, dancing seductively with her. Their bodies locked together tight. A sinking sensation washed over me, like I was falling into a black hole. I couldn't rip my eyes away as I watched.

A lopsided smile seemed glued to Val's face. I knew that look. He once looked at me that way, but something was different. His face gleamed like a man in love. Apart from me, the whole world knew, including the hired help.

Their bodies pressed together, swaying to the music, there was no question, they'd shared more than just friendship. All this time, he'd never mentioned a girlfriend, but one thing I couldn't deny—I had to confront this bitch once and for all. Before I gave it another thought, my dagger left my hand. End over end, it sailed through the air past the crowd, right on target, the dagger nicked *his lover's* ear.

It all went down so fast. In one instant, she yapped, grasping her bloody ear. The room fell silent, following only a second later by an echoing thud, piercing the wall clear on the other side of the bar. I smiled to myself. I got the results I wanted, Val's attention and that bitch's hands off him.

Seeing the girlfriend's starkness only sweetened my endeavor, until

I became keenly aware that every eye in the joint had my back for a target. Despite the potential of getting mobbed, the only pair of eyes that I'd concerned myself with was the livid gold ones glaring at me. One glimpse of his steel jaw and I knew I'd crossed the line. At this point, a fight was inevitable, but his anger didn't seem so important. I wanted to know what he was doing with *her*.

I kept my feet planted to the ground and teeth gritted, staring back as Val charged straight for me.

Now in my face, he towered over me with a six-foot-five fierceness, consuming and threatening. My heart hammered against my chest.

I raked in my fear. I couldn't let a little thing as death stop me from confronting him. I stiffened, bracing myself for the storm.

"Just what the hell do you think you're doing?" Val wailed through clenched teeth.

"Oh… just playing with my little old knife." I flashed a mischievous smile.

Then *her hand* snaked around Val seductively, trailing the line of his chest. Obviously, she knew his body very well. It took everything I had not to beat that despicable woman with my bare fist.

As I expected, the bitch interjected with a sultry coo. The sound that would prompt me into having my memory wiped in order to forget. "Fancy meeting you here, Stephanie," she purred with acid.

"You must be on break," I snarled "Rumor has it that the corner's a bit slow these days. I hear they pay whores well, but only if they have all their teeth. You might want to offer a discount." I taunted as if the devil sat on my shoulder.

She snorted a tight smile. "What the hell are you talking about? I have all my teeth."

The blonde had no clue. "Yeah! Not for long." I spat her name as if it carbonized my tongue, *"Helen!"*

I etched my hand to my second knife hidden in the back of my pants. Helen had the speed of a cheetah and claws to match. I wasn't about to let my guard down.

Val stepped between us, blocking me from any chance of taking down the blonde. "Helen," he ordered, sternly. "Stay put! Let me get rid of this nuisance. I'll be back shortly." He winked at her. Then Val turned a cold eye on me, swooping me over his shoulder, carting me outside to the sidewalk *again*. It was starting to become an annoying habit. Once more, I seemed to have found myself left on the curb like an empty milk-jug.

When we were out of earshot, he set me down roughly. Shaken off balance, I fell, landing on my keister. Disenchanted, I took note that he didn't bother to offer me his hand to help me to my feet. Instead, he hovered over me with veins in his neck standing out in livid ridges. "Can you not take a hint," he blasted me. "If I wanted to talk to you or see you, I know exactly where to find your pampered ass."

"Yeah, I see why you haven't been returning my calls." Without delay, I shook off the embarrassment and sprang to my feet. "What are you doing with *her!*" I snapped, resting my hands on my hips.

Val's eyes tightened as he leaned closer. "I know what it must look like," he barely whispered, "But sometimes desperate times call for desperate measures."

"What," I scoffed sarcastically. "You getting laid?" The ache of betrayal struck. A pain I knew too well.

"It's not like that, Stevie," he whispered heatedly.

"What is it then? You sleeping with the enemy?"

"Not exactly," Val sighed deeply as he weaved his fingers through his hair. "Helen and I go back a long ways."

"Is she the discreet person you were hiding from me?" I hissed as I jabbed a finger in his chest.

"I didn't tell you because I knew how you'd react."

"If you can't be honest with me, how can I trust you?"

"I haven't deserted you," his voice rose, no longer a whisper.

"Oh, really? If I hadn't thrown my knife, I think you would've taken her right there on that filthy floor!"

"If I didn't know any better," a lopsided grin stretched across his face, "I'd say you're jealous."

"Is that what you think?"

"Yes, I do." Val's eyes glistened.

"You're wrong!" I denied emphatically. "What I have a problem with is that *Helen is* Aidan's sister! That bitch is just as evil and part of that disgusting family and most likely she knows where my da... " Then it hit me. Damn, how stupid could I be? I picked my hat off the ground and shook the dirt off. "I blew it!" The acidity hit me.

Val scratched his day-old stubble. "Maybe not. With her, it's hard to say." His eyes turned gentle.

"What happened to the first plan, mimicking a staff member from the hospital?" My brows knitted in confusion.

Val blew out a long sigh. "A couple of my Zops and I went to Haven. We found their files, but no sight of yours. The Family is not stupid. Do you honestly think they'd leave such salient information lying around?"

"No, of course not. I had no other recourse." I felt overwhelmed with disappointment. "I guess we're on plan B?" I attempted a forced smile.

"It looks that way." There seemed to be something else lingering behind Val's voice that I couldn't put my finger on. Although my finding out what would have to wait. We had to go into plan B before a certain person became suspicious.

"Okay, let's make this look good." I acted before I'd given him time for-my-meaning to sink in, as I hauled off and sucker-punched him in his square jaw. His face flew to the side, blood splattered from his busted lip. Then I launched curse words at him. "You dirty bastard! Don't *ever* call me again," I shouted, making this feigned squabble look real.

Without hesitance, I lunged into the backseat of the cab parked by the curb. Apparently, it had been waiting for me, the same driver as always. Though, not surprising. This time, *I* paid. I watched from the rearview window as Val rubbed his jaw with stun written over his face. A tight smile lit my face. There was a part of me that took some pleasure in socking him. I guess this was becoming a bad habit, clocking the men in my life. I shrugged. It could be worse. I could have to cook.

That night a storm blew in raining sheets of steel, pounding the rooftop. Limbs from the oak tree kept scraping the window and casting shadows in my bedroom. And then adding the lightening streaking the menacing sky and thunder roaring, it all kept me buried under my blankets shaking. Storms in this weird state had no mercy for its inhabitants. That was the one thing I disliked about Louisiana.

Giving up on the fantasy of sleep, I high-tailed it downstairs to put on a kettle of water to heat. I figured a cup of Dom's chamomile tea might soothe my restlessness. I'd just settled down at the table, looking over one of Dom's gardening tip magazines, when I heard light footsteps. I peeked over the rim of the mag, and in walked Dom, dressed in his night robe.

"Hey, Dom!" I smiled warmly. "You couldn't sleep either?"

"Oui," he answered in short. "Jeffery will be joining us momentarily. We want to show you something." Dom's face seemed strained.

"Okay." The magazine no longer held my interest as I tossed it aside and folded my hands. Dread had a bad habit of knocking at my door too frequently these days. I took a sip of my hot tea, trying to hold my panic in check. My fingers started strumming the table to keep myself from a full-blown breakdown.

The clock's ticking echoed through the house relentlessly. *Tick-tock-tick-tock.* Time seemed to stand still as I kept checking the grandfather clock. Unable to stand the wait any longer, I caterwauled, "Oh, for heaven's sake! What the hell is it?" I exhaled an irritated breath.

I'd no longer evinced my impatience when I'd heard Jeffery's bare feet padding down the stairs. My breath stopped in my throat. I wasn't sure if I was relieved to have the suspense end more than hearing the disquieting news. The minute Jeffery shuffled into the kitchen, my worries ballooned. My eyes homed in on a white envelope, grasped in his hand.

"Don't get your panties in a wad," Jeffery snipped. "I ain't breakin' my mofo neck!"

"What is so important that it can't wait till morning?" At that moment, I wished I were anybody but me. My stomach clenched.

"You'll see… " Jeffery buzzed, "But you need to chill! We want to see too!" Jeffery huffed, handing the plain envelope to me. It was nothing out of the ordinary. Merely a plain white envelope addressed to me. "It was left on our porch step today." Jeffery urged me to open it by swishing his hand at me. "Open it!"

"Okay!" I glared at him. I tore open the envelope and pulled out a letter. I unfolded it and began reading it silently:

My darling, Stevie,

. . .

I have our daughter. I finally managed to escape the clenches of my family, but Dawn and I are still in hiding and must remain for an undisclosed time until it's safe. Be patient my dear. We both want you with us. We are family, and she misses her mother. Go to St. Louis Cemetery tomorrow at midnight. Meet me at Marie Laveau's tomb. Wait there, darling. Don't tell anyone of our plans, and especially the Zophasemin you've been keeping company with. Trust no one. I love you, and I can't wait for you to be in my arms and meet our child for the first time.

Forever love,

Aidan

Wide-eyed, I looked up at Jeffery and Dom. Their faces were etched in curiosity as they sat in dead quiet, staring at me. Jeffery broke the stupor between us first. "What does the letter read?" His voice rose an octave.

I sat there for a minute, trying to decide what I should say. If I revealed the details, I might put them in danger and risk losing my daughter forever. That wasn't an option. I squirmed for a believable lie while I feigned a smile. "Oh, this is a reminder from Val. That's all." I shrugged, nonchalantly. I wadded the letter up and stuffed it in my pocket.

I sensed that Dom and Jeffery didn't believe me by the glance they shared. Dom cleared his throat and added, "As I always say, '*Chacun a son gout*'" (Each to his own). However, if there is something risqué you are embarking on, you should inform us." Dom's gentle eyes glistened with concern.

"Guys," I sighed sharply, "Sometimes it's best to leave well enough alone." I pulled from the table.

"Wait," Jeffery called out. "At least leave a note for us to find. If you encounter any trouble, we need to know your whereabouts."

"That's a good idea! I'll make sure to do that."

"Excuse me, missy," Jeffery's chagrin pierced the atmosphere.

I knew that tone all too well. "Yes." I tilted a sideways glance, not fully facing Jeffery.

"Where shall we look for this note," he asked very innocently.

"Oh no, you don't!" I stared at my friend. "If I tell you where the letter is, you won't wait. You'll snatch it up as quickly as my back's turned. I'll have it in a place you'll least expect, and when it's time to read the note, there will be a sign. You'll know when it happens." I grinned.

Jeffery threw his hands up in disgusted resignation. "You is too sneaky for your own *mofo* good! Don't go off gettin' yourself skinned alive, chile! There is tacky people out there who will cut you as to look at you." Jeffery let the anger pour.

I took a deep breath and said, "*C'est la vie*, Jeff!" (That's life) I shot back.

"You, my friend, are becoming more of a diva than even me." With that said, Jeffery pursed his lips and left the kitchen, stomping up the stairs like a jilted lover, leaving a trail of curses in his wake.

Shortly after Jeffery's departure, Dom pulled from his chair and began with a gloomy sigh, "We knew what we were getting ourselves into when we opened our lives to you. We are well aware of how the Family operates. They are a *bete noire*." (a black beast) Dom gave pause. "Jeffery and I have *avoir le coup de foudre* (fallen in love with you). We only want what's best for you, my dear." Dom came around the table and squeezed my shoulder and made sure I looked into his warm eyes. "Don't shut us out completely." He smiled, and without another word, he went to seek his disgruntled partner.

I swallowed the knot that lodged in my throat as I listened to Dom's footfalls fade. I never doubted Dom's and Jeffery's devotion. Still, it was nice hearing it.

Though my decision might've been right, it wasn't an easy one. Despite my better judgment, I felt guilty. They both have stuck their necks out for me. That was all the more reason why I had to protect them at all cost.

THE TOMB

*O*nce the relentless rain had past, a brisk chill followed. I couldn't stop shivering. I stood in the center of St. Louis Cemetery in front of Marie Laveau's tomb. I was early, only a few minutes before midnight.

Strangely, the night appeared dead, not a stir of wind nor a soul in sight, or a black cat prowling. Flowers, beads, and Jesus candles marked the legendary Marie's grave. One candle was still burning low. The soft light casted shadows, bouncing off the tomb. The boneyard didn't need any help with eerie, hairs pricked the back of my neck. As my eyes washed over the graveyard, I took note of row after row of weather-beaten tombstones. The old yard had an unquiet beauty. Yet, it didn't ease my tension any.

A bad feeling washed over me. I worried I might be walking into a trap. Ambushed or not, I still would've come. Nothing was going to stop me from finding my child.

Apprehension rode heavily on my shoulders, if this wasn't a ruse, and I was truly meeting Aidan for the first time since that morning at the cabin, then this would change everything. Could I accept Aidan back into my life? The last time I'd seen Aidan seemed so long ago, yet the pain still stung like it was yesterday. Memories rushed through my mind, and just for a minute, I doubted my gut's warning. Despite his involvement with Sally, I couldn't erase his imprint, his passionate kisses, the warmth of his embrace. Did I still love him as Val believed? I wished I had an answer.

I released a sharp sigh. This wasn't the time to sort through my problems. I had to keep a clear head and be prepared for whatever I was about to confront.

For backup, I followed through with Jeff's suggestion in case things went south. Luckily, Jeffery didn't have a clue that I knew about his *less-than-tasteful* activities. A ponder, I'd rather not reminisce about.

It was the one certain venture, I could count on that Jeffery would do. Every morning like clockwork, Jeffery would steal away to his quaint little cubbyhole for a few moments of basking in his favorite magazine.

Before the tire tracks were cold, I seized my shot when Jeffery left the house for a spot of tea with a few socialites. As soon as the coast was clear, I snuck into his private nook, placing the note inside an earmarked page of his brown-paper-covered magazine. Although, I was riddled with guilt, invading his privacy, I couldn't think of a more inconspicuous spot. Still, there were drawbacks. I'd forever have that unsavory vision burned into my brain. Totally gross!

If my plan panned out as I'd hoped, by the time Jeffery took his break in the morning, he'd already discovered my note, instructing him to alert Val. I felt if anyone had a chance finding me, it would be him.

I had to admit, Val had become my rock. He deserved more from me. Unfortunately, I was a mess.

If Aidan were alive, there were unresolved issues that needed to be dealt with before I could make any decision, whether it was Val or Aidan. I wished my resolve were that simple as drawing sticks.

Of course, it never works that way. Since Aidan and I shared a child, it made things much more tangled. I had to think about what was best for her.

Whichever way I chose to look at this, I couldn't forget my mistrust for Aidan. There was too much deception that had transpired between us for me to let my guard down.

It was different with Val, despite our disparity. Perhaps, his clan might soften toward me if their leader showed mercy upon me.

Then again, I haven't been exactly great girlfriend-material. Sharing my heart seemed difficult for me.

Then there was Helen. What if Val had feelings for the blonde? The thought stung like a switch to bare legs.

I checked my watch again, eleven fifty-seven. What if no one showed up? What if Aidan and Dawn were captured? What if I was a sitting duck? I shook my head. I needed to stop with the what ifs. I needed to stay alert and prepare for the unexpected.

Abruptly jarring me from my thoughts, I heard a shuffle of feet, moving over loose gravel. Swiftly, I ducked behind the large grave marker, stretching my ear over my pounding heart. I glimpsed at my watch, twelve midnight. They were encroaching, fast. I held my breath, listening.

Then the shuffling of feet stopped. I peered around the tomb and gasped. My face stricken. All at once, an urge of rage gushed through my veins. WTF? I came out from behind the stone, standing firm in my feet. I should've known. "Well, *Helen*, fancy seeing you here. I'm beginning to wonder if you've become my biggest fan. You seem to keep popping up." My eyes narrowed with a heavy dose of disdain. Sleight of hand, I reached for my dagger, tucked underneath the band of my pants right below my tramp stamp. I grasped my fingers around the knife's hilt ready to spring into action.

Helen scoffed. "Don't flatter yourself. I'm here to follow through with my promise."

"She keeps *her* promise." I mocked. My suspicions were right. I'd been set-up. Funny, though, Helen may be in for a surprise. Since last we met, I'd sharpened my skills. I kicked an empty beer bottle, feeling edgy. "And pray tell what promise you are referring to, Aidan's-little-sister?" I hit a nerve as she grimaced.

"I warned you not to stick your nose where it didn't belong."

"I haven't a clue to what you're referring to." Could Helen have sent me the letter? Perhaps drawing me out was the only way she could get me alone.

"Don't play coy with me. Why must you keep trying to dig up something that doesn't concern you?" The blonde's lips curled with contempt.

I sighed, exasperated. "Look, we don't care for each other. I get it. Let's cut to the chase. Just tell me what I already know." *Keep calm!* I coached myself.

"Why make it easier for you?" Helen stood tall like a goddess. I wondered how someone with such beauty and grace could be as equally wicked.

"Despite popular belief, your brother had feelings for me. I think he would want you to do the right thing." My face pinched tight. "I know about my child. I gave birth during my stay at Haven Hospital. To hide my growing belly from me, the Family made sure that I had an ample amount of drugs pumped daily into my body." My voice broke. "You must... you must know your brother would never approve of such cruelty?"

Helen clapped her hands in a mock applause. "Hooray, hooray! It's a girl!" She was not congratulating me. Her tinged tone oozed with menace. "You should've moved on with your life. Forgot the child. You may be her fleshly mother, but she doesn't belong to you."

"A girl," I mumbled to myself. Anger hit me like a bullet. I lurched forward, veins in my neck were standing out in vivid ridges. "I am her mother," I hissed. "She is *not* a commodity. The child belongs with me!" I tightened my fingers around the dagger, white knuckled.

"Since we're being honest with each other," she suddenly deflected the subject, "Your new boyfriend, Val, spoke highly of you. He laughed at how lousy of a lay you are." She cackled like a crow, lying.

I shook my head in annoyance. "Are we deviating from why we are here?"

The corner of her mouth tipped with indignation. "I think Val is very much part of this meeting." A predatory glint appeared behind her eyes. "After all, I have something you want and you have something I want."

I scoffed. "You want Val?" I laughed to myself. "Val is his own man. I have no claim on him."

"Of course you don't," she tossed a smoldering grin. "You could never hold a man of such station. You couldn't even keep your position with my brother."

I laughed back in her face. No point in arguing with her caviling insults. "Are we going to stand here the rest of the night swapping jabs? Really, I had more faith in you, Helen. It's not my fault if you can't keep a man."

Boiling steam appeared to rise from her incensed face. Damn, what a Kodak moment, I giggled to myself.

"Laugh at this, whore," she sibilated. "I have *your* child!"

My laughter wedged in my throat. My body woodened. "Your bluffing!" She was baiting me. I drew in a deep, slow breath, holding my wit.

"Maybe," she paused, smiling, "Maybe not."

"You're wasting my time." My fist tightened into balls down to my side. I turned to leave but stopped at her words.

"Aidan and your daughter are being contained as we speak." Her face lit with bitter triumph.

"How do I know you're not lying?"

"Because the truth hurts more than a lie." Her demeanor gave no hint of deception. I still didn't trust this bitch.

"I want proof." I waited, caution set in my stance.

Not uttering a word, Helen nodded to the left, from behind the shadows, one of her barn-side guards revealed himself with an iPad in his grasp. He halted by her side, waiting for further instructions. "Show her," she ordered, brusquely. The brawny guard stepped closer to me, almost too close, pressed play and handed me the tablet. I snatched the device abruptly from his beefy hand, my patience spent. My pulse was erratic as my eyes were glued to the screen. Everything surrounding me ceased, the only focus that mattered was that small device.

Only moments later, I heard laughter, a child giggling. My stomach clenched as my eyes watched the screen. A little girl about three years old was blowing out candles, it was her birthday. She had dark hair like Aidan and green eyes like me. In a small voice, I heard her call out, "Daddy," and that's when all my doubts vanished. Aidan appeared beside her. He looked happy, smiling, while helping her blow out the last candle. The angelic child reached up to hug her father's neck, and then the picture went blank.

My head snapped up at Helen. "Where are they now," I demanded through snarling teeth. It took every ounce of strength I had not to throttle this evil vixen.

"Finally, I have you rattled." She dangled a wicked grin.

I didn't reply, though, the flame in my eyes gave me away, rage like no other.

"What did I ever do to deserve such horrendous treatment from you and your iniquitous Family?" It would take me an eternity to understand such cruelty.

"You have no clue." She smirked. "This doesn't have anything to do with you. It has to do with *your* father."

"My celestial donor?" My brows furrowed, confused.

"No, not Mustafa. I'm referring to your human father.

"You're tormenting my child and me because my father defected from the Family?"

"They never told you?" a slight inflection touched her voice.

"Told me what?" I held my hand steady on the hilt of my dagger.

"Why am I not surprised?" she smiled darkly, sending chills down my spine. "I am Aidan's adopted sibling." She hesitated. "I am *your* blood sister."

My chin hit the floor. "You're lying!"

"I'm different from you. My blood courses strong with druid blood. I am like my father, Jon."

"Jon Collins is *your* father?" I stood like I'd been shot, waiting to fall.

"I'm disappointed." Amusement crossed Helen's face. "I assumed my brother would've told you."

"I don't understand." I couldn't believe my ears. How could I have not known?

"I suppose I have to enlighten you on our family's history."

"I don't need a history lesson," I hissed through clenched teeth.

"Oh, but you do." Her brow arched. "You see… before your mother came into the picture, there was someone else, *my* mother."

Whether I wanted to admit it or not, there was a ring of truth. "Go on," I coaxed.

"Once Jon finished law school, he was promised to wed my mother, Lilith. The Family had arranged their union long before Jon's and my mother's birth.

"Prearranged marriages are from the dark ages. Why would anyone agree to such a burden?"

"In our family, we honor tradition. It has kept us in existence for centuries. Our magick flows strong in our blood. It is imperative we keep our bloodline pure. Which brings me back to our father."

"What happened? Did my father marry your mother?"

"Jon and Lilith were inseparable. She loved our father. Jon, not so much."

"He hated the Family's lack of propriety. He was a good man. I'm sure it had nothing to do with your mother."

"You couldn't be more wrong," she sneered. "Our father eloped with your *worthless* mother. Not only did he abandon his family, he deserted his fiancé and unborn child, a child that was *fully* his," Helen shrieked, tears welling up in her eyes.

"He'd gotten *your-your* mother pregnant?" I'd stammered over the words. "This...this couldn't be possible." I raked over my mind to recall if my parents had ever mentioned another child before me. I drew a blank.

"It's true," she wiped a stray tear. "My father, our father, had forsaken me."

"If this were true, my father must've had a reason for leaving your mother. He was an honorable man." Despite my distaste for Helen, my heart went out to her.

"Our father was a coward," Helen spat. "Rather than living up to his obligations, he left the Family, refusing to marry my mother. Jon didn't care about her or his unborn child. He was selfish!"

I shook my head, denying her tragic tale. "You couldn't possibly be his child. My father couldn't have children."

"Are you that naïve? My mother cast a spell against him after he ditched her at the altar."

I gawked, disbelieving.

"Oh, don't look so surprised, little sister!" Helen's eyes narrowed with hatred.

"I don't believe you," I railed. "My father wouldn't have left his own flesh and blood behind."

"Forgive me for tainting the image of your perfect Daddy, but you should know who your father truly was."

I get her grief, whether it was true or not, but what did I have to do with her Daddy issues? "Let's say I give you that. I don't understand why you're dragging my family and me into this?"

"For the sins of the father, the offspring must pay the transgressions."

"Because of an act of another, you intend to punish me by taking *my* child?" My heart went out to her but holding my child hostage was playing with death.

"It's like a double-edged sword. If you will, an eye for an eye." Her lip twitched. "The child is quite amazing. She possesses great powers, much like her mama and," she pronounced each word precisely, driving the knife further into my heart, "we intend to utilize your little girl's abilities until we drain her *last* breath."

"Oh, hell no!" I lurched forward in reach of the blonde. "Over my dead body, sistah," I hissed, ready for a bloodbath.

"Careful what you wish for. This time there will be no mercy. The Family spared you once due to my brother's pathetic plea. This time, his begging will fall against muted ears as he sits and rots in his cell."

"Aidan *is alive?*" My heart stopped!

"After my brother escaped our clenches, that's when he sent you the letter. Personally, I feel he's wasting his time on trash."

"Tell me where they are," I snarled like a lioness crazed for her lost cubs.

"Well, sister dear, my adopted brother, your ex-lover," she rebuffed, "is a bit under the weather. You see, he received quite a beating for his disloyalty. A lesson he truly deserved. He needed his priorities set straight. Placing his loyalty to you first makes the Family very angry. After all, the Family is a very jealous god."

"*God*? That's a bit grandiose even for *you*, Helen." I was done. "Tell me where they are if you want to live!"

She ignored my threat. "One is never too pompous when it is true!" Her eyes shot acid at me.

"Tell me where Aidan and my child are," I demanded with a hard-line glower.

"Don't worry, little sis. You'll reunite with your lover and child soon enough." Helen's lips curled with insolence.

"If you have harmed them, I'm coming for you," I threatened with grave intent.

"Your child is safe for now. She's having her milk and cookies." The wicked witch smirked. "We're preparing her for the celebration tonight. Since we were unable to drain you of your gifts, we'll just take the next best thing... *your daughter*." Her lips pursed like the kiss of death.

Alarm torpedoed my chest, nearly knocking the breath from me. "If you value your life, you'll let my child and Aidan go free, *unharmed*." I spoke with a steel calm. At this point, I wanted to end her pathetic life, yet I knew that would be a grave mistake. I'd never find Aidan and my child if I took her life now. I had to be patient. She didn't meet me in this cemetery just to gloat.

"*Tsk, tsk,* such sisterly love."

"Let's save the love for later, dear *old* sister. Set them both free, and you can have me. Take what you need from me, my life, my freedom, my powers. Leave Aidan and Dawn out of it!" The way I saw it, I was a stranger to my daughter. She knew her father, and by what I saw on the video, she loved Aidan dearly as I loved my father. I refused to take the only thing she knew.

"Oh, I'd love to take you up on your offer. However, there's a slight problem." Helen sneered. "When you screwed my handsome brother, the two of you fused your powers, locking your strength together as one. You're bound to Aidan forever. One can't live without the other."

Holy mother of god! It was true. We *were* sealed. It wasn't a lie. The real deception wasn't between Aidan and me. Rather, the Family concealed the truth from both of us. "I can assume since I'm standing erect, you're telling the truth about Aidan?"

"You catch on fast."

"What do you want?" I met her murderous glare equally while I waited for her to make a move. She better get ready, it wouldn't be without one hell of a fight. I suspected she had brought more than one goon. Like my daddy would say, hope for the best and prepare for the worst. Tonight, I came packin'.

"There are many things I desire, one of which is for my dead daddy's favorite child to suffer. I wish for my brother to look upon your once-beautiful face after it's mangled. After I'm done with you, he won't think of you as his precious princess." Then, she saved the worst for last as she pierced my heart with her foreboding words. "To top it off, while you lie helpless, you'll have the pleasure of witnessing your daughter's life force being stripped from her body." The frothing-out-the-mouth blonde just crossed the line.

A calm came over me as I began to speak with precision. I knew with certainty what was about to go down. "Three years ago, you and your family had the upper hand over me. Back then, I had a lot to learn about *your* world. Since that time, I have learned a thing or two. As a result, I've been forced to learn particular skills. So, if you don't mind me speaking candidly, let me explain exactly how this ambush is going to transpire. First, I plan to take out all your guards, one by one." Her two escorts had stepped forward into the dim light. I expected that much. I had sensed her squires' presence lurking among the shadows.

I nodded to the man on my left. "John Doe over here has a slight vision problem that he failed to tell you. He'll be my first target. I'll take out his good eye, leaving him blind and no use to you." Helen's mouth flopped open like she was catching flies. "And when your second man, Don Juan, lunges for me, I'll have my second knife stop him in midair. The knife will penetrate his skull, killing him on impact before he hits the ground. Afterward, I think you and I should have a sisterly visit. You're going to take me to my family." I stared at her with full intent of my threat.

Suddenly an epiphany struck. At that very moment, clarity rang louder than the Liberty Bell. I understood my true purpose. The Family never intended for me to create a new world. They wanted to create an army of supernatural soldiers. For lack of a better word… assassins. A large numbers of souped-up warriors taking the world by storm, ridding the earth of innocent people they deemed as weak. This was their abominable plan from the beginning. *The New World Order.* A world of perfect people just like them, vile, and evil, and unholy immortals with everlasting life. Wow! That was taking ambition to a whole different level. I hated it.

I looked over at the woman claiming to be my blood. I saw pure fear in her eyes. I smiled with joy, knowing I was about to carry out my threat. Then, with no thought given, I went into action. In only a matter of seconds, both guards were faced down in a puddle of blood with no sign of life from either one.

My eyes whipped around at my beautiful sister. Frozen, she glared at me like a frightened pig before the slaughter. As I turned to her, I felt my essence surge forth. In the blink of an eye, I had my arm grasped around her throat, tight, with my dagger pressed against her jugular.

"Tell me where they are," I hissed in a deadly whisper. The blonde tried to wiggle loose, but her efforts were futile. "I'll say this just one more time before I end your pathetic life. Where are they?" I demanded, desperate, but determined. She started to speak but stopped as something hard struck the back of my head. Pain shot through my mind, and in the next breath, everything went black.

LOST AND FOUND

*W*hen I came to, it took a moment for me to gather my senses. Soon the harsh memory of how I'd gotten here flooded my foggy mind. A sharp pain shot from the back of my head, confirming I'd been shanghaied. Go figure! I sat up wincing. By the throbbing ache in my right side, I most likely had a few broken ribs. My left eye was swollen shut, gnawing like something fierce. I flinched when I sighed. Such cowards to beat me while I was out cold. No doubt, this was the work of my lovely sister and her goons. Good thing I've had practice getting my ass kicked. I laughed, flinching.

As my one good eye adjusted to the dimness, I realized my holding cell wasn't much more than a few sprigs of hay scattered over a cold, dirty floor and iron bars. Oddly, it was as though I'd fallen back in time. It was medieval in every sense, dark and musky. No bedding, no pot to piss in, not even a chair to rest my wary bones. Just a dirty floor. Animals got better treatment than this.

I eased myself against the stonewall, drawing my knees to my chest, trying to focus on anything besides my claustrophobia. Since Haven, solitary confinement became my own living hell. The staff loved tormenting me by confining me inside a ten by ten box, crunched up, with no provisions. If the authorities had ever caught them, the hospital would've been shut down immediately.

I pushed up off the floor, bracing myself against the wall. The blow to my head must've been a humdinger, judging by my dizziness. My headache was blinding. I managed to limp over to the bars. With the one good eye, I stretched my one eye to see if a guard might be on watch. I saw nothing, but my vision was hindered. "Hey," I bellowed. "Anyone out there!" The echo of my voice was the sole reply. No sign of a living human, only a faint trickle of water vibrated off the wall, down the corridor. Funny, I remembered that eerie drip from Aidan's secret chamber. It was like déjà vu. Though, I shrugged it off. I had enough on my plate to worry about than some stupid flash back.

I grasped a bar in each hand and gave it a good tug. Pain shot through my entire body as I flinched. Regardless of how superhuman I might be, those bars weren't budging. It'd be wise to stay alert for anyone approaching. Though my eye-sight was hindered, I still could hear.

I drew in a torn breath, regretting my hasty decision. How stupid could I've been? I shouldn't have lost my temper. If I hadn't let my hardheadedness get the best of me, Aidan and Dawn would be safe, free from Helen and that vile family. Damn it!

I laid my face in my hands and began sobbing. I yearned for my child. She deserved to have her mother. "Is there something wrong with wanting to hold your own child?" The tears streamed down my cheeks and stung like hell from the cuts on my face. I didn't care. I welcomed the pain.

I wiped the tears from my face with the back of my hand. It still wasn't too late. I had to pull myself together. If I wanted to save Dawn and Aidan, I had to draw strength from my inner powers. I sensed the essence earlier. Somewhere in the depth of my core, it patiently waited.

I must've dozed off when I heard the jingle of keys and footfalls approaching. Alerted, I pulled myself to my feet, thankful my pain had eased slightly. I privately thanked my angel genetics for that. In my world, fast healing was a welcomed thing. I leaned against the wall to balance my wobbly legs. I stilled, barely breathing, staying calm as I listened. Whoever was coming, I braced myself, expecting the worst.

Suddenly, I remembered my necklace. I reached for it. It was gone! I dropped to my knees on the floor, scurrying for it, hoping it had fallen.

With no light and an injured eye, I came up empty-handed. My worst fear was that someone took it. "Crap! I'm screwed," I murmured to myself as I rose to my feet.

When the footfalls halted, there stood my loving sister.

"I hope you are enjoying your stay." Even through the faint light, her smug face shined like a beacon.

"I'd definitely recommend this spot. The bed's soft as a feather."

"We pride ourselves on our Southern hospitality." She smiled, harboring a wicked glint behind her sooty lashes.

Time was closing in. I had to reason with this woman. "Let's make a truce, Helen. Free Aidan and my daughter, and I'll do anything you want!" To beg for myself was out of the question, but to plead for my child and her father, there was nothing I wouldn't do for their safety.

"Why should I do *you* any favors," Helen snarled.

"Don't do it for me. Do it for the sake of an innocent child. For Pete's sake! Do it for your brother."

"Tsk, tsk! Where's your inside voice?"

"I left it at the cemetery with my patience." If I could've shot fire from my eyes, I would've smacked her right between the eyes.

Helen arched a brow. It surprised me with all that Botox. "I read in the Bible once that patience is a virtue."

I snorted. "Bible school! You didn't combust?"

"My, my, aren't we cranky when we wake up from our nap."

I didn't bother with a retort. We could do this till she grew a wart on her nose and flew off on her broomstick, for all I cared. Instead, I'd preferred saving my energy for things more productive, like snapping her neck.

"I hope your guest will put you in a better mood." A nefarious glitter tainted Helen's blues. I knew my sweet sister had some scheme up her sleeve. I cautioned myself.

I heard high heels approaching and getting closer. When the heavy clanking stopped, my eyes landed on the visitor. I blacked out with rage. In half a blink, I reached the bars, grabbing a fistful of hair. I intended on snapping that bitch's neck. And damn near did! Until Helen shot me with some sort of souped-up TASER that knocked me off my feet, throwing me back onto the hard floor. The stun gun might've prevented me from killing the visitor, but it didn't stop me from taking a fistful of hair.

Simultaneously, screams belted forth and a vindicated grin played upon my swollen lips. Despite the discomfort from my backside, I found delight in her agonized face. I called to her. "Lucky for you I'm on this side of the bars," I snarled. "No damn stunner will stop me from killing you, Sally!" Pushing past the twinge, I pulled myself to my feet with newfound strength.

"I can't believe you ripped my hair out," Sally bellowed, grasping the crown of her head. "I have a bloody bald spot now!" Tears gathered in her eyes.

"Come a little closer," I taunted. "I'll gladly give you a matching one."

"You're an animal!" Sally roared like a hyena.

"I guess I am," I spoke calmly. I could feel the rumble of my powers trying to surface. "Where have you been all these years, Sal?"

"Raising *your* bratty child." She shot me a smothering look. "That child's insufferable, just like her mother."

"You can always give her back, since you stole her from me in the first place." I reached down the back of my pants and eased out my dagger. I grasped the hilt in my hand, hidden behind my back. I had only one shot. There were two targets. Hard decision, I thought. Until I saw the keys dangling on Helen's hip. If I took Helen down, with any luck, she'd fall close enough to the bars where I could snatch the keys from her body. If I decided to take down Sally first, though her death was overdue, my chances in getting the keys would be unlikely. Helen wouldn't run. She'd call the guards to punish me after they dispose of Sally's body. If I took Helen out first, Sally would take flight and run. She'd be more worried about saving her ass than alerting the guards. With any luck, I'd have enough time to get the keys, free myself, and snatch up Sally before she alerted the watchmen.

So, I niggled Helen. I wanted to ruffle her feathers. Once she grabbed the bars, I'd make my move. With my angelic talents, I was speedier than the average creature, even a druid. Well, at least in theory. I made sure I stood back far enough. If I kept the distance between us, she might feel brave enough to step up to the bars, in my reach. Thus I began baiting her.

"Helen, rumor has it that Val dumped you. How did he put it?" I tapped my finger on my throbbing lip. "Oh, I remember. He referred to you as entertainment," I snickered as my eyes took on a hunted look.

"You realize the only reason he spent one minute with you was for me? During all that time he was whispering sweet nothings into your ear, he was getting information for *me*." I paused, hoping to kick-up some dirt. "I think he's more into younger women. You're starting to show your age. I hear Botox works well." I laughed, driving the taunt into the center of her black heart, as if it were my dagger. I was quite enthralled, watching the steam roll off my sister's back.

"Careful what you say, angel! The little imp is still alive," she hissed. Right then and there, I began to seethe. I almost blew my plan. If I let her goad me, then I'd lost the fight and my daughter's life.

I smiled sweetly. "I think if you were going to kill her, you would've by now."

"What makes you think we haven't?" Helen's eyes turned icy.

"Because I'm still standing here, alive." I hit the target right on the mark. I could see it in Helen's burning eyes. "You don't have any power in this family, Helen. Both you and Sally are puppets on a string. I bet you can't wipe your ass without permission," I mocked. "I may be locked up and could possibly lose my life, but at least I'd be free. Bet you can't say the same."

It worked! Helen had fallen right into my hands, figuratively speaking. The next chain of events toppled like a domino effect. I went into Zop mode. Just like I'd hoped, the blonde stepped up to the bars. Without delay, I heaved my dagger, end over end, and stopped with a renowned thud, piercing her heart. With a look of disbelief, the blonde collapsed to her knees. I dashed to her side before she'd hit the floor, snatching the key off her belt. Swiftly, I jammed the key into the keyhole, and with a click, the door gave way. I was out of the cell, eyeballing Sally as her fat legs ran down the dank corridor, just as I'd expected.

Unexpectedly, I was halted in my tracks by the gentle grasp of a hand. Startled, my eyes fell upon Helen lying in a puddle of her own blood. It was only a matter of minutes before death took its claim. "Wait, Stevie!" the malevolence in her voice had vanished.

I kneeled beside her withering body. Her face had drained of color. She spoke with difficulty. "Yes," I whispered.

"I just want to know," she swallowed, "how do you do it?"

"How do I do what?" My eyes were drawn to a thin line of blood that trailed down her delicate chin.

"How do you get two men to fall in love with you at the same time?" Her eyes were waning. "Aidan and Val are in love with you. I don't know how you have captured both their hearts when I can't even hold one." In the next breath, the life in Helen's eyes smothered as her body went limp.

Suddenly I was overwhelmed with guilt. If we had been in another life, another world, we might've been close like *real* sisters. In this *life*, we were mortal enemies by default. Yet my heart ached for her loss. I'd have to sort this out later. Right now, I had to catch Sally. Swiftly, I grabbed the hilt of my dagger still lodged in Helen's chest. I turned my one good eye away and pulled the blade out. I cringed feeling the bloody knife slide from her limp body. She was dead, but it didn't make me feel any better. I'd never enjoyed taking the life of another.

I sprinted down the dark corridor, not sure of which way to go. I stretched my ears for any sounds. Right away, echoes of feet tromping were in the near distance. The footfalls were heavy, and the runner's breathing appeared stressed, panting. It had to be my mistrusted friend, Sally. I darted up the stairs, following the dust trail. When I spotted my dear old chum, I didn't hesitate. I charged, tackling her from behind. We both went spiraling down the flight of stairs. With each blow, my body felt a new pain. By the time we crashed at the bottom, my agony had past and fire had taken its place.

Dragging Sally to her feet, I seized control, holding her hostage by my knife pressed against her throat. Through clenched teeth, I demanded, "Take me to *your* husband, now, and don't tell me you don't know where he's at," I threatened, pressing the cold steel tighter.

"Okay, okay! Don't hurt me. It's that way." She raised her hand, pointing.

Then, she started this nervous rambling. "I didn't want to betray you. They made me lie. Aidan and I were never married. He hardly knows I exist."

After all these years, I was finally getting answers to the questions that haunted me. "Who put you up to framing me?" I hissed, still keeping the knife pressed against her throat.

"It was Dr. Van Dunn and Helen. Aidan had no idea of his sister's scheming. Van forced me to join their crusade. He said since I failed the Family's expectations, I had no other choice. It was that or death." I got the feeling Sally was trying to excuse her misdeeds.

"Shut up," I snapped. "Who helped you that day at the cottage?"

"It was Van," she rambled, flinching from the prick of the blade. "He was the one who drugged you."

"What happened to Aidan?"

"When Aidan returned to the castle, he walked into an ambush, ordered by his Uncle Van. I lied about him taking part in your abduction. That's all I know! I swear!"

"Cough it up, Sally!" I pressed tighter. "Who killed my mother and her boyfriends?"

"Alright! Alright!" Sally squawked, her eyes wide with fear. "It was Helen who killed your mother. She blamed Sara for her mother's death. When she overheard your conversation about the angel dust with Aidan, she followed him to your house that night. When the two of you left, Helen found the angel dust on the ground by Aidan's car. He must've dropped it when he shifted. Helen took the dust and well, you get what happened next."

"As for the boyfriends, by Van's orders, Zak killed the owner of the grocery store. I can't remember his name."

"Charlie! Charlie was his name," I growled.

"Sorry! My mind is a bit cloudy on some details." Sally dragged in a sharp breath and continued. "It was explained to me that since Zak was dead, Nim, Zak's brother, who was also a man in black, finished off Francis."

"Why did the MIB take their life? They weren't a threat to the Family."

"The Family concerned themselves with Sara marrying the grocery store owner, that she might skip out on the contract. I understand Charles had a nice nest egg set aside. He also planned to make Sara the beneficiary of his life insurance policy. It was well over a million. Sadly, for Sara, Charles never made it to his private attorney's office that morning. He was murdered in his front yard.

Now it all made sense to me. I pushed further, "Did Sara know what Charlie was doing?"

Sally paused as if she was deciding whether or not to tell me, then she spilled the beans. "To my understanding, Sara refused to marry him without the policy." Why would I be shocked? Sara was very resourceful. Of course, she'd marry Charlie and take his riches. I felt like I didn't even know my own mother.

My teeth gritted, furiously. It all made sense now. "*Go* on! Finish!"

"The last one, Francis, he was a liability. He was a loose cannon and was wanted for armed robbery in Texas."

"What?" I gagged on the word.

"Francis was a small-time thug, though a bit ambitious. He knew about Sara's arrangement with the Family. After he and your mother gambled their entire fortune away, Francis set out to blackmail Van for more money or else he'd go public and expose the Family's dark secrets. He was good at snooping."

I cringed inwardly. Francis was creepy, but I had no idea of the level he'd stoop too.

Sally furthered her story, "Francis had to be dealt with. The Family had planned on killing Sara anyhow, so they decided to take out the boyfriend first."

"How did the Family find evidence against me?"

Sally gave way to an awkward sigh. "You should know the answer to that. They used magick on the prosecutor, the judge, your lawyer, and even the kitchen sink. Don't you know by now our family has every sort of reach possible?"

"They're not *my* family," I clarified.

"Like it or not, they are! Your father and mine are brothers. We're cousins."

I gasped, "You're *lying*."

"I wouldn't dare attempt that now, not with a knife pointing at my throat."

"Your father's still alive?"

"I don't know. My parents severed their ties with me. Unlike your father, mine felt the Family's beliefs were unconquerable as a god. As it seems, I'm not the only family member extricated. My father, Thaddeus, had a falling out with your dad, his brother Jon, over his marriage to Sara, an outsider. Consequently, Jon was cast out, never to return. Because of your father's status, the Family hid Lilith's pregnancy from him." Sally gave pause. I sensed her struggle, "As for Sara, she knew about Lilith's condition."

"How did my mother know?" I couldn't wrap my head around this tall tale.

"Aidan's uncle had the pleasure of confiding in Sara," Sally confessed. "Van had taken an interest to her. To encourage Sara's assistance, he offered her a generous incentive to keep the pregnancy out of earshot from Jon. Van, of course, didn't reveal the real truth of his endeavor. He had other plans for Jon and Sara.

"Let me guess… *me!*"

"Yes. Van is quite diabolical."

"What happened to Helen's mom?"

"As the story unfolds, Lilith had no idea of Van's involvement. She had her own selfish agenda. Lilith chose not to reveal her pregnancy to Jon. Rather, she hastily sought out a back-alley abortion clinic, but the Family stepped in before she had the procedure done."

"What insidious scheme did the Family have in store for Lilith?"

"For the remaining term of her pregnancy, the Family held her as a prisoner in a small room, keeping her under lock and key. They were on a suicide watch."

All I could say was, "Wow!"

"The Family has its issues," Sally relented with a wicked grin.

I snorted, though I didn't comment.

Sally went on with more of the story. "When she gave birth, the Family took the infant away from Lilith and gave the baby to Van and his wife to raise. They adopted Helen like they had adopted Aidan. In the end, Lilith ran away with some man she'd met at a bar.

Now I understood Helen's contempt toward my parents and me. The pain of guilt really began to hit me hard. I wished I'd known. I continued to listen.

"Later, Lilith was found face down, drifting in the bayou, dead. I don't know if it was by the hands of the Family or the stranger she ran away with. No one is sharing that information with me. Anyhow, Helen blamed your mom for the death of her mother, and she despised you because your dad loved you."

"Your story certainly puts a new light on things. I had no idea."

"I think things could've been different between the two of you if she had known the full story."

"Why didn't you tell her the truth? She might've been able to move past her pain. Maybe she would've had a better life." This family seemed stricken with one horrible problem after another. No wonder Dad left.

"The Family had forbidden anyone to tell Helen. They are masters of holding truths. Secrets amidst secrets."

"You call them family? I call them the devil! Helen may have been just as depraved, but she deserved the truth."

"I guess like all families, we have our issues too. Take me, for example. I'm an embarrassment to the Family, a disgrace."

I felt sorry for Sally and Helen. Yet I couldn't help either one. Helen was dead, and Sally needed professional help. Right now, I had my own crisis, getting Aidan and my child free from this hellhole. "Enough," I ordered crossly. "Who has my child?"

"Dr. Van had taken her to a foster family up North," Sally clacked. "He didn't give any names."

"Stop!" I tightened the knife, gritting my teeth. "I mean *now*?"

"Ouch!" Sally sputtered. "The... the child's in the... the sacred chamber. The members are having a ceremony tonight. Something about midnight and the full moon."

"Oh, mother of god!" My panic soared. Dawn in the sacred chamber meant one thing. Those monsters planned to extract her essence. Helen wasn't lying after all. With no time to lose, I had to find Aidan. I shoved Sally forward to hurry her fat legs. "Take me to find Aidan!" I thrust her forward once more. "Let's go!" I rushed, hell-bent on time. My daughter's life depended on me, and anyone else could meet their maker if they got in my way.

Darkness had fallen on the walls of the castle. It was a wonder we were able to find our way through the corridors. I pulled my collar over my mouth and nose. The dust was thick and smelled of a graveyard, musty and stale.

I prayed Sally didn't have guards waiting to attack. In my condition, I doubted I could fight off anyone, even a grandmother for that matter. I needed to reach Aidan fast. With any luck, he might be in better shape than me. It would take the two of us to free Dawn. His healing touch certainly would be helpful.

Around the corner and down another flight of stairs, we finally reached his cell. I noticed a torch and plucked it off the wall. I turned to Sally. "Hand me your lighter."

Her brows wrinkled. "What?"

"Are you that stupid? The smell of cigarettes reeks from you! Smokers have lighters. Hand the freaking thing to me!" I held out my hand, losing patience.

Sally regretfully sighed, slapping the red lighter into my palm. I flicked the lighter and a small flame popped up. I smiled into her face as if it was Christmas. Hurriedly, I lit the torch. Seconds later, a blaze ignited, shedding a generous light down the corridor.

"Take this torch," I instructed. "Hold it up high where the light will shine." I had to set some ground rules. "If you even look like you're going to do something foolish, I will end your life. Do I make myself clear?"

She nodded. "I won't run." Sally's voice reminded me of a child, small and timid. Without another word, I handed the torch to her. The flame spread its glorious light into the cell. I could see well enough now. I yanked the key out of my pocket and unlocked the iron door. The door squeaked loudly as I tugged. When my eyes landed on Aidan, my heart sank. He lay limp on the floor, unconscious. I ran to him, lifting his head into my lap, his eyes slowly opened as though he was drugged or by the looks of him, beaten to a bloody pulp. "Stevie," he muttered hoarsely.

"It's me," I whispered, holding back tears. "I'm going to get you out of here." A faint smile toyed with the corners of his mouth. I smiled back, but nothing inside me felt the glee of a smile. I scanned over Aidan's pummeled body and staggered from shock. No argument, Van was a heartless *bastard*. He'd left his nephew rotting in this dungeon. When I thought my hatred for the Family couldn't get any worse, I realized I was utterly wrong.

"How did you find me?" Aidan croaked.

"I'll explain later," I replied, fumbling with the key as my hands trembled. "Hold your breath that this key works." I forced a smile at Aidan as I slipped the key into the padlock of the left cuff. I held my breath. If the key didn't match, we were as good as dead, including my child. The key had to work! The thin metal key slid down into the slot, fitting like a glove. "So far, so good," I whispered to Aidan. Then carefully, I turned the key. The lock clicked and the cuff opened, falling to the dirty floor with a loud clang. I glimpsed up at Aidan, he'd given way to a sigh of relief. I joined him with a smile.

With no more time to waste, I hurried along, unlocking the other restrains. The clanging of iron echoed off the walls. The sound made me happy. It was music to my ears.

"Here! Let me help you." I slid my arm under Aidan's arm and hoisted him to his feet. This Aidan wasn't the man I remembered, strong and unstoppable. This person was weak and unsteady, his drawn face needled with pain.

When we tried to take a step, Aidan stumbled, falling back into my arms. Before I knew what had happened, he'd gathered me into his embrace, squeezing me tight. Taken off guard, I hesitated, unsure of my feelings for him or if I could trust him. Then again, he was wasting away in this cold cell, embarking upon death. I relented and returned the embrace. We stood in silence, locked in each other's arms. Just like old times, he whispered against my hair. "I've missed you." A prick of memory-lane tugged heavily at my heart. At this point, I didn't want to visit my archive of emotions. I started to pull away but lingered when I gazed into his deep blues. I lent him a tight smile, still urging him. "We have to go *now*. They have Dawn in that god-forsaken chamber. Can you walk?"

"I think so," Aidan nodded.

"Good! We have to hurry."

He looked over at Sally and flashed a scornful look. "What's she doing here?"

"Sally's my prisoner. She's going to help us escape. Otherwise, I'm gonna slit her throat myself." I smiled up at him as if I were talking about having brunch.

Aidan half-laughed, teasing, "You do me proud, babe," his eyes twinkled, reminding me of the past. My heart skipped a beat. Damn! He still had that effect on me. I'd figure that one out later when I could think more clearly.

On the edge of spitefulness, my attention sidled to Sally. "Here, help *your* husband. I'll take the lead," I thought I'd let Sally sweat a bit more under Aidan's careful eye.

His brows furrowed, "Husband?"

I wallowed my eyes. "I'll explain later."

"Yeah, later." Suspicion hid behind his glint as he glared at Sally.

"Let's go! Sally, which way is the chamber?"

Her eyes grew wide. She began fidgeting, acting strange, even for her.

"What? Spit it out," I demanded, not hiding the asinine in my voice.

Her shoulders slumped, voice quavering. "The location of the hallowed sanctum is unknown to me! Women aren't permitted."

I dropped my arm from Aidan and stomped forward, leaning into

589

Sally's face, sparks of fire ignited from my eyes. "Why didn't you *tell me* this earlier?"

"I was afraid you'd kill me," she cried.

"*What the hell*, Sally," I berated her. "We could've been looking for that devil's den all this *time*." My voice ascended to a murderous falsetto.

"You're crazy," Sally yammered. "I never know what's going to set you off!"

"My child is on the brink of being murdered!" I shook my white-knuckled fist in her pale face. "How else do you expect me to act?" Sally had struck my last nerve. I gritted my teeth as I raised my dagger to her throat. Just when I was about to take justice into my own hands, Aidan placed his firm hand over mine.

"Wait! I know the way." Our eyes locked as I stepped back, dropping the dagger to my side. Though anger still boiled my blood. "Let's get going!"

I turned a cold eye to Sally. I'd deal with her later.

Quickly we moved through the shadowy corridors, around corner after corner, following Aidan to the chamber that he'd sworn on his life was the shortcut.

I felt grateful for small favors. The torch had been a beacon, spreading its generous light down the narrow passage. Down the slippery slope and with one slip, we could've fallen to our death. Once we reached ground level, my lungs expanded. We were far from being out of the woods of danger; hence, our journey had just begun.

After what seemed an eternity, we came to an abrupt halt at the end of our path. Alarmed, I swiped the torch from Sally's grasp, holding it up next to the barrier. I ran my fingers across the dust and cobwebs that clung to the stone. Ready to spit nails, I spun on my heels, teeth gritting at Aidan. "I thought you said this was a short cut? Where's the freaking entrance," I thundered.

"Wait a minute." He stepped up under the light next to me. He squatted down and brushed his hands over the wall. I watched in silence as his finger trailed over the stone. He stopped, surging to his feet, facing me, "This is a door! The chamber's just on the other side of this stone." One corner of his lip suggested a smile.

I on the other hand failed to see this as a triumph moment. "You got any brainstorm ideas on how we're supposed to get *past* that *freaking* rock?" I rested my hands on my hips, ready to fire bullets.

"Hmm, dynamite maybe?" He rubbed his stubble, seeming too calm. "Unless it's protected by a Fort Knox spell, there's no breaking it."

I lit into him as if he was my last supper. "You mean to tell me that you didn't give that little tidbit any consideration?" I fumed. "What's wrong with you?" I wanted to shove him off his feet. Instead, I did what any insane gal would do, I started pacing in a small circle, rambling like a person off Prozac. "I should've left both of you in that damn cell and did this myself!"

"No need for your cavalier babble." Acid formed off Aidan's tongue.

I stopped in my tracks, face strained. "Screw you! Move out of my way." I pushed him back. I needed space. "Since neither one of you can help, I guess it's all left up to me. Stay out of my way!"

Aidan threw his hands up. "Get over yourself," he huffed, joining Sally's side. I didn't understand. What was wrong with him? His child was in danger. He should be over here helping me! By choice, he stood to the side, a bystander at best. I shot him a fiery glare.

I couldn't deal with him right now. I had to set aside my irritation and focus solely on that damn door. My powers had worked once before. They'd work again… *I hoped.*

I made my way up to the barrier. By the looks of it, it had to be more than a foot thick. I released a sharp breath and placed my hands flat against the massive rock. The stone thrummed as though it was melding to me. I instantly gasped, jerking my hands to my chest. My heart rate was soaring.

Once more, I steadied my feet, drawing in a deep breath, placing my hands back on the stone. This time the vibration didn't startle me. I embraced it as I closed my eyes, reaching deep to the core, where my essence rested. I heaved the inner strength like a tornado sucking up everything in its deadly path. I commanded my powers.

Without warning, my essence surged to the surface, and fire shot forward, spewing everywhere.

When the explosion quieted, my eyes fell on Aidan and Sally. They were crouched behind a rock, unscathed. As for the door, it was still intact. I gawked at the stone door.

For a moment, I eyeballed the two huddled together in each other's arms. If they were an item, it meant nothing to me. What got under my skin was that he wasn't offering his skills to help bust this door down. Aidan had more druid magick in his pinky than I had in my whole body. What was *his* problem? "Where are your druid abilities? I need your help here!"

Aidan charged to his feet. His face harsh and cold. "I might be a druid, but I'm not superman. My forte is of another. Not explosives." His defiance made me incensed.

"Fine! I'll move this damn rock myself." I turned my back to him, facing the door.

I took in another deep breath and exhaled, interweaving all my energy to the center of my core. I placed my hands upon the door once more and closed my eyes. Visions flashed through my mind, visions of all my pain from the past, the loss of my father, the death of my mother, and her involvement in my father's death. I recalled the men in black, Helen, Sally, Van, and even Aidan, who played a large part in destroying my life. But it was not until I homed in on my child and her imminent danger that my essence inside me began to rise. My heart started racing like a locomotive train. I sensed the force of fire that boiled within me that it might erupt to the heavens. I didn't care as long as that damn door blew off its hinges.

With no warning, the ground started to rumble. In the next breath, things got hairy. The ground began shaking as if we were in an earthquake. Boulders fell from the ceiling, smashing violently to the ground, shattering around us. I ignored the avalanche as I strained to keep my hands flat on the door. I was not letting go, even if a slab of stone toppled me.

Once the ground settled, my eyes raked over the dust-filled dungeon, and a smile traced the line of my lips. Victory! A delighted taste as my heart lurched with joy. The gap was only a small space, but it was wide enough for us to squeeze through.

Depleted of energy, I crumpled to the ground. On all fours, I raked in the fetid air. Aidan limped to my side, gathering his arm around my waist to assist me. Instantly, I felt repulsed. I jerked free of his hand. I hissed through gritted teeth, "Don't touch me!" I couldn't even look him in the eyes.

"I see some things never change." The sardonic tone in his voice felt different to me. I couldn't put my finger on it and frankly, I didn't care. I had other problems that were much more pressing.

Not without effort, I tugged on my wobbly legs and stood erect. Still weak, I leaned against the wall for support. "That's where you're wrong, DuPont." I panted. "Everything has changed, *especially* me."

He glared at me as if he wanted to strangle me.

Time was running out. We had to get out of here. An argument would only delay finding Dawn. I believed in picking your battles wisely. This battle was one I'd pass on.

Without another word, I sidestepped Aidan and made my way to the small space in the stone until I'd caught a glimpse of Sally. She'd remained frozen, wide-eyed, and shivering with fear. I gawked at her. "Let's go!" I urged. I supposed it wasn't enough that I had to deal with Aidan's ill manners, now Sally had gone zombie on me. My eyes narrowed. "What's wrong now," I huffed, heatedly.

"I can't!" Her eyes welled up.

"What do you mean you can't?" I stepped up to her, puzzled by her fear-stricken face.

"There's no way I can fit through that tiny crack." She pointed to it. "I can stay here and stall anyone who comes my way. I won't betray you. I promise! I've done enough harm for this Family to last a lifetime."

It would be easy to think that Sally had been more of a victim than a participant. After all, the Family had a way of bringing out the worst in folks. Perhaps Sally deserved a second chance... a second try that Helen didn't have the luxury of getting because of my deadly hand. I knew my guilt would be riding on my shoulder for the rest of my life, and I guess I'd accepted my fate the moment my dagger left my hand.

"Look! I can't deny I don't harbor ill feelings toward you." I sighed. "Despite my position, I'm not leaving you to your death. If they find you, they won't spare your life."

"No!" Sally shook her head stepping back. "Go without me. I'll only hold you back. Save your child and then come back for me. If you can't make it back, then leave me here. I've made my bed. I'd rather face death than live with myself." Guilt riddled her face. "I'm sure you can understand that."

I was no stranger to self-blame. Stunned, I stared back at her. Was Sally feeling remorse? I wanted to believe her, yet, I knew far too well, her talents… cunningness and manipulation. Yet, considering the injustice she'd endeavored from the Family, it was not in me to turn my back on her either. I guess that was the human part of me.

"You're coming with us, cuz. We'll sort our differences out later. You're going to fit through that rock even if I have to downsize you."

Aidan stifled a laugh.

"All right! I'll try." Sally didn't sound so sure of herself. Maybe when we get back home, she and I could work on our relationship. Since our fathers were brothers that made her family, regardless of her past deeds. Dad always said family sticks together through thick and thin. That was a good enough reason for me to take Sally in.

Aidan went first and I stayed back, letting Sally go second. It didn't take a rocket scientist to understand that Sally couldn't fit through that tight space without assistance. Following the plan, Aidan took Sally's arm, and I got the wonderful pleasure of thrusting her rump.

The task was challenging. It took several tries, but we finally forced Sally through the tight opening. I reckoned after this, she'd have some serious bruises.

Once we were all clear of the door, not letting another minute slide, the three of us hauled ass, rushing down another dark path. Aidan in the front veered to the right and down another flight of stairs. I followed second, and Sally brought up the rear.

As we impinged upon a new passage, a faint light flickered in the distance. A familiar dripping of water bounced off the stone. Suddenly, I realized where we were. Yet how could that be possible? Aidan's castle had vanished.

I picked up the pace, joining Aidan's side. I tugged his sleeve, not wanting to alert any guards. Voices easily vibrated down these dusty corridors. A mute could hear us. "DuPont," I called to him. "What is this place?" I kept my voice low.

An impish grin stretched across his face. "Don't you know?"

I tossed him an icy snarl. "Can't you just answer the question?"

"What fun is that?"

"Taunting me is fun?"

"Quite," he merely answered.

"I want to know what I'm walking into. Can you please cooperate?"

"I presume you'll find out soon enough," he haughtily replied as he pushed past me.

I didn't bother with trying to worm an answer out of him. He'd never tell me.

Sally's soft giggles wafted over my shoulder. It was more than irritating. Somehow, I managed to ignore her ridicule. Getting into a squabble with either one didn't interest me. The only thing that mattered to me was finding my child.

∼

We seemed to have worked our way farther down into the bowels of this godforsaken place. I'd put my trust in Aidan to lead us to the sacred chamber. I hoped I hadn't made a misjudgment.

When we drew upon the soft light, we came to a shrieking halt. There in the vast chamber, standing before my eyes, were thirteen men in black robes, their faces obscured.

At that very minute, it was as clear to me as a cloudless sky. That all this time I'd been at Aidan's castle. An overwhelming sense came over me as if I'd stepped back in time. Everything had remained exactly as I remembered. The throne sat high on its platform in its grandiose stature, only with a different occupant this time.

Strange, I thought, as if his presence held some enchantment over me. My head began to spin, my blood surged, churning and churning. I'd never met this creature, though an introduction was not necessary. I got the impression that he was aware of my presence as well.

Seated upon the throne in all his wicked glory, I uttered his name, *"Mustafa!"* We were connected. I could smell his acerbic blood coursing through his veins.

I slipped a sideways glance at Aidan. I assumed by the starkness in his eyes, he was no stranger to this creature. I wondered how well acquainted they were.

For a second, I stared in silence, breathless of the creature's beauty. His brilliance was blinding. I squinted, cuffing my hand over my eyes to block the glare. The immortal was majestic in such a way that he appeared elusive. He reminded me of the angels in the fresco paintings high above on the ceiling of Aidan's formal dining room. The similarities were staggering. I stalled, gaping at his omnipotence. The creature had massive gold wings, that when stretched apart, were at least twenty feet wide. His black locks flowed to his broad shoulders. Armor draped his body in bold colors of red and glimmering gold. I wondered how a creature who possessed such magnificence could be so abominable.

Compelled, I eased out from the safety of the shadows and into the light of which may be my very death. With eerie pricking the back of my neck, the dark robes parted, just like in my past dreams. I edged forward until my eyes fell upon a small table.

Suddenly my worst fear clenched my chest as my eyes landed on a toddler bound in shackles. Holy mother of god! *The sacrifice!* The young child began to whimper. "Dawn!" I cried to her. The terror in her tiny face mirrored mine.

Without thinking, I dashed to her side, but with no avail. Given no warning, my body was shoved back into the air and violently slammed to the cold stone floor. Pain shot through my body. Rather than allowing the agony to consume me, I used it as fuel. In one sweep, I sprung to my feet ready to fight. "I know who you are!" I bellowed at the godlike creature. I held my clenched fist to my side as I secretly tried to summon my essence. Despite my effort, I sensed nothing within my core. I didn't understand. It was as if I were empty. I touched my bare neck. Damn! I needed my necklace.

"Yes. Our blood is the same. We are connected, my hybrid daughter." Apart from his radiance, I knew the angel's heart reeked of iniquity.

I hid the urge to cringe. Instead, I stepped forward, forcing my voice out from my gut. I refused to let him see me quaking in my boots. Hell, if I'd give him the satisfaction. Shoulders straightened, I responded with renewed strength. "I might share your DNA, but I am *not* your daughter, Mustafa!" My green eyes shot shards at the dark angel.

Suddenly, his sick laughter echoed among the sea of black robes.

I pushed past the urge to go commando on his evil ass as I slowly inched closer to my child. With one quick glimpse, my heart sank at her sight.

The toddler had Aidan's black hair, but she had my freckles. By my calculations, Dawn couldn't have been older than three years old. Despite her condition, she was beautiful. I bit down on my lip to keep from losing it. I smiled into her sweet face. She smiled back, but her eyes were *tormented*. My heart was breaking in two. I had to *save* her! I didn't care if I lost my life doing so.

"Ah!" The dark angel reigned in my attention. I snapped my head up in his direction. I paused, remaining cautious as I kept Dawn in the corner of my eye. He spoke out. "You are more like me than you know." His voice was musical, yet cold. My finger twitched for my dagger as I kept my eyes centered on the dark angel. I crept closer to Dawn, hoping I'd go unnoticed. "She is quite lovely." The creature paused. "How wonderful you have decided to join us in our celebration."

"Yes, sorry to pop in uninvited." I tried not to sneer. Still, I never was one to hide my true feelings.

"You are most welcome, my daughter." I flinched at his reference to me. I'd never claim him as my father, on second thought just maybe it might appease him.

"Since you speak of me as your blood, perhaps you will permit one request?"

"Only one?" the dark angel smiled. "You are quite bold asking such. I have yet to receive a thank-you for my help in freeing you from prison." The dark angel sat back on his throne, his eyes raked over me with disappointment.

"What are you talking about?" I stared at him confused.

"Do you honestly think the human system would've let you go free with three murders against your name?"

I didn't answer.

The creature sneered, full of arrogance. "Of course not! It was I who set you free, and due to such, I'm afraid that you have run out of favors, dear one."

"Then let me offer you something you can't refuse." I inched closer. Only a few more feet to go, and I'd be by Dawn's side. "If you accept me as your daughter, then you must accept this child as your grand-daughter. Can you not take mercy upon her and allow me to take her place? My life for hers. Let my child go free, and I will stand by your side in your crusade to conquer the world!"

Yet, the second I saw his bitter regard, my bargain had fallen upon muted ears.

As I stared into the depth of pure evil, I realized his part in this contrivance. He had been the anonymity who masterminded my father's death. It may have been by my mother's hand that carried out the insidious act, but it was his doings that set it into motion. It was he who brought it to the forefront. It was he who played God, destroying my life and now possibly my firstborn. For that, I had never loathed a living being more than him.

The enlightened beast eyed me with great caution as he sat with an ostentatious smirk. He was in control, and he didn't hide his obvious enjoyment either. "Yes. How righteous of you to offer yourself." One could easily fall prey to his hypnotic voice. Strangely enchanting, yet it sickened me, for it was methodical. "Therefore, you must realize my answer." His eyes grew taut and deadly.

My breath caught in my throat. The dark angel had denied my plea. He wanted me gone. Perhaps my thorn in his side was a bit too much, though I didn't give a rat's ass if I inconvenienced him or not. He wouldn't get rid of me that easily.

I went into action, letting my Zophasemin instinct take charge. I drew my dagger, aiming for the beast's cold black heart. As the knife left my palm, sailing through the air at a remarkable speed and headed right for my target, I rolled on the floor in a somersault. In a fraction of a second, I'd landed by my daughter's side like a cat on all fours. Not wasting a precious moment, I began unfastening the restraints. I rushed with trembling hands, fearing I would fail. *Where is Aidan!* I frantically wondered. I needed goddamn backup!

Before I could gather my daughter in my arms, my body was thrust into the air, thirty feet high, dangling in suspension like a trapeze artist, only free of wires. I glimpsed below, realizing if I fell, it would be my death. Frozen, I couldn't move. I was helpless and worse, useless. Mounting fear shredded my insides. "Mustafa, please," I cried out. Instead of his mercy, something glimmered in the corner of my eyes. I slowly lifted my eyes, and to my horror my knife hovered, pointing its deadly blade at eye level. Panic seized me and tears streamed down my cheeks. I'd whispered a prayer right before I hurled curses at the dark angel. A fool I had become for making such a hasty move, and now I may have cost my child her life. I cursed again.

Mustafa rose to his feet. "You have made a grave mistake testing me, my daughter. You cannot defeat me. I am wise, far beyond your years. That move, Essence, cost your child's life!" His depraved voice sliced through my heart.

"No! Mustafa, wait! Can you not see I am terrified of you? I acted hastily. I know that now. Please forgive me. I only want to protect my child. Haven't you ever wanted to protect someone dear to you?"

"You have been with the humans far too long my young foolish daughter. Mystical creatures like us do not waste emotions on needless things. We accept our destiny and embrace it." His voice came across as foreign and something far from natural.

"Human or not, I know you have a heart. Can you not have mercy on this innocent child and let her live?"

"There is a greater cause we must confront, than save a child's life."

"In my book, there is nothing grander than the life of an innocent child." I desperately needed to make him understand.

The dark angel gave me a sideways glance. "How so, my human daughter?"

"I may not have had the pleasure of spending time with my daughter, yet it doesn't waver my feelings. I love her with all my heart. I'd be willing to sacrifice my life, my magickal abilities if you would let her live."

"You'd give your entire existence up for your child's life in return?"

I didn't hesitate for an instant. "Yes! A million times, *yes*. Anything. Take me! I will bow down at your feet. You will become my God if that is what you wish. Just relinquish the child to Aidan, and I will leave with you right now. Whatever you want, I will do. Just spare her life. You have my loyalty!" My heart was pounding against my chest.

The dark angel pondered a moment. "For a hybrid, you do know how to appease one's greed." He drew in a long breath. "As grand as your offer may be, it is still not as grand as your daughter's life force."

"Then if not for the benefits, do the right thing and let this child go with her life still intact. You know you are wrong for doing this!" Horror seeped into my bones. It was clear to me that he'd made up his mind, he wasn't relenting.

In a desperate attempt, I searched for Aidan, hoping he would be advancing on the dark angel. As I caught sight of him, my last hope plummeted to the ground. He had been taken down by the guardsmen. His body lay lifeless on the floor. He appeared dead as blood seeped from his forehead. Realization struck. I'd been left alone to face Mustafa.

Despair gushed through my veins.

I turned my gaze upon my child's sweet, but tortured face. Even still, she managed a smile under a pool of tears. I smiled back as my spirit longed for her. This couldn't be happening! Not *my* child! Is there a God who would have mercy upon me and spare my baby? Never have I asked for anything but this! "*Please...* save my daughter!" I begged of this from a God I didn't know.

Unexpectedly the toddler began softly singing a lullaby, one I remembered as a child that my father used to sing to me. In a soft, gentle melody, she began singing.

Through choked tears, I began singing with her. As my voice intertwined with hers, our eyes locked. I struggled to loosen the magickal grip, but it was pointless. My mind flooded with desperation, yearning to scoop her up into my arms, promising her I would love and protect her always. I wanted to whisper in her ear, reassuring her that everything was going to be all right. Yet, I knew it wasn't.

My plea fell on muted ears. The dark angel wouldn't allow such a privilege, and my prayers went unanswered. In the next breath, while forced to dangle in the air, I eyed that monster stripping my child's essence from her. Within seconds, Dawn's tiny body went limp, softly closing her sweet eyes as if she had fallen asleep. So peacefully, her body stilled. I knew she was gone forever, and I, an all-powerful, genetically engineered angel was powerless in saving my own daughter. I'd failed. I lost her before I ever had a chance.

Tears blinded my vision as I cried out in raw anguish. The chamber echoed from my bloodcurdling screams.

Then an inner strength took hold. I reigned in my stricken heart and turned it into savage fury. Deadly calm fell over me as my eyes met Mustafa's. In the pools of my menacing greens, a reflection of my threat gleamed. "Wherever you hide I will find you. I *will* get justice for the death of my daughter. You mark my word, Dark One."

As if my threat fell on mute ears, he paid me no mind as his body quivered. I knew what had transpired... the full moon, the gathering, the ensue of my daughter's essence. The dark angel had stolen her life force for his own selfish gain.

Ironic, I thought. The very protection Aidan and I used to save our own lives cost the life of our firstborn. At that moment, I had a new goal in life. As I held my blazing glare at Mustafa, I hoped he realized it too.

With no warning, I heard a familiar voice shouting in the Zophasemin language. *Val!* Still jutting in the air, I twisted in the direction of his voice, and my eyes fell upon his golden glitter. Through my raspy voice, I called his name. "Val!"

He returned a look of longing, and I watched as he went into skilled action. Fighting broke out. Fireballs whizzed past me, men in armor swinging swords and the violent clashing of steel ringing in my ears. My eyes followed as the Zop leader and his fighters took the black robes by leaps and bounds.

I turned my attention back to the dark angel. His eyes appeared glossy and his lids were droopy. For the first time, I could see his effusion illuminate. That sick son of a bitch was drunk on my daughter's life force. Worse, he took delight knowing I knew by the amusement in his face.

Then he spoke in a hurried voice. "I must leave now. It was so nice of you to drop by. We shall meet again, my daughter." A triumphant grin had spread across his hardened face right before he vanished out of sight. The murderous Zophasemin dissolved, leaving his followers to their doom.

Along with his disappearance, came his release. All at once, I began spiraling to the ground, falling to my death. I braced myself for the impact until I landed into a cushion of sturdy arms. When my gaze lifted, my eyes landed on Val's face. I whispered, misty-eyed, "I couldn't save her!" A deep pain struck my heart like a cold dead frost.

When our eyes locked, I threw my arms around him and hugged him tightly, weeping into his shoulder.

"You tried! You did your best!" Tenderly Val consoled me. "I got you. It's over. It's over," he repeated as he cradled me in his arms. Through the heart-wrenching tears, I pulled myself away and quickly ran to Dawn's side.

"Dawn! Oh, dear god, Dawn," I sobbed. With my trembling hands, I began tugging at the restraints, trying to rip them apart. Once she was free, I gathered her into my arms, rocking her back and forth, singing the song she and I sang before her last breath. Her body still felt warm as if she was merely sleeping. I glanced up and I saw Aidan standing behind me, silently watching.

I heard Val shout to his soldiers in his Zop tongue, giving orders. I was thankful for him taking charge. Val instructed one of his men to gather everyone up and prepare to leave. "We are getting the hell out of this fucking dungeon," he announced to his soldiers. Then he whispered in my ear. "Honey, we have to get to safety. Let me help you." He nodded over at one of his Zop soldiers, standing beside him. "Allow one of my men to take Dawn's body." Val gently placed his hand on my shoulder. The Zop stepped forward, yet I didn't yield.

"I can't trust *your* men!" My voice was laden with mistrust.

"Yes, miss, you can," the Zop spoke in a gentle voice. "I'll take care of your loved one. I promise."

"No! Get away from me," I screeched like a madwoman. "Can't I have a moment with my daughter?" I drew Dawn closer to my chest. "Aidan," I called out. "You can heal her! You have to heal her!"

Aidan's mouth popped open and shut. His tongue appeared stuck.

Through the haze of my frenzy, I heard Val's voice of reason, "Sweetie, no one can bring her back. I'm sorry."

"I'm not letting her go! Leave me be," I demanded, choking over tears.

Val squatted down next to me. His hand tenderly stroked my back. "We have to leave. Let me help you."

I didn't move. All I wanted to do was hold my daughter, but logic told me that I had lost my mind. I knew if I stayed in this dungeon, I'd lose myself completely. So, I yielded, "Okay." Reluctantly, I gave Dawn's body to the soldier.

As I rose to my feet, I caught a glimpse of Aidan. He stood motionless, aloof as the Zop carried our child away. Suddenly, I felt a sting of confusion and something else... *envy*. How blessed Aidan had been to have spent time with our child. At least one of us had been there for her.

Disrupted from my thoughts, Val nudged my arm, bringing me back to our impending situation. "We need to go," he urged tenderly.

"Where are we?" I knew we were in the dungeon of Aidan's castle. The castle possessed magick within its walls. That explained how it had vanished.

"We are in Limbus," Val said.

"Where?" my mind was cloudy with grief, I couldn't think.

Then Aidan interjected. "It's the fifth dimension, parallel to earth. There are twelve dimensions in the galaxy. This place is off-limits to humans. Only magickal creatures are permitted to enter this realm."

I nodded as a reply. Conversation with Aidan right now would be like sandpaper skirting across raw blisters. It baffled me how cold and unattached he'd seemed over the death our daughter. re was no display of any emotion from him. For that reason, I'd prefer to keep my distance.

I turned to Val. "How do we leave this place?"

"Have you ever watched Oz," Val smiled.

"Are we going up in an air balloon?" I didn't care if we were going on a magic carpet ride as long as we were getting the hell out of this dungeon.

Val gathered me into his arms. "Something like that." He flashed a reassuring grin.

"Wait!" I bellowed. "Where's Sally?" I scanned over the limp bodies spread about, blood veiling the cobbled-stone floor. When my eyes fell upon my cousin, I saw the fright in her face. I fretted that Sally might've been in shock. She stood half-hidden behind one of the stone pillars. Tears were streaming down her cheeks as her body heaved. I pushed off Val and made my way to her side, stepping over a sea of blood-stained bodies.

When I reached her side, I grasped my arms around her neck, drawing her into my arms, soothing her. Through all the stabbing pain of loss, I hoped she and I could become friends. I broke our embrace and looked into her tear-filled eyes. "We have to go! C'mon." I reached for her hand, but her feet stayed planted. I turned, facing her.

"You're taking me with you?" She sounded surprised.

"Yeah! I'm not leaving you here."

"But I don't deserve your mercy. This is all my fault. Your child…" She struggled with the words. I understood her pain far too well. I staggered over the fact that I was still standing erect. I reckoned I'd have my meltdown when I was alone.

"Sally, we all have contributed to this. It's not just your fault. I played a part in this as well. I don't blame you any more than I blame myself. You're a victim of this family as I am." I paused. "Now come on." I grabbed her hand, and this time she followed.

When we returned to Val and the others, I climbed into Val's arms once again and nodded for us to go. Immediately, I sought out the Zop carrying Dawn, but he was absent. "Wait," I cried. "Where is Dawn?" I panicked.

Val's eyes softened, brushing a strand of hair from my face. "The Zop went ahead. I promise he will take good care of her."

I nodded. My throat was so tight with pain, I couldn't speak.

Val took the wheel, giving directions. Aidan, due to his injuries couldn't orb on his own. Val gave orders for him to ride on the back of one of the soldiers, and another Zop had gathered Sally in his grasp.

Val had me in his arms. I locked my hands around his neck, and as I held tightly, I buried my face into his shoulder, bursting into tears. No one could hear me other than Val. While I sobbed, he gently held me close, whispering consoling words and kissing me.

REGRET ME NOT

*L*ightning flashed across the bruised sky, and thunder grumbled, announcing its presence. Rain fell. I stared numbly out the window in the kitchen, sipping coffee. It was early morning, the day of the funeral. The house was quiet. Since I had trouble sleeping, I decided to go ahead and get dressed for the day.

Thankfully, Jeffery and Dom took care of all the arrangements. Jeffery insisted on a jazz funeral. Aidan seemed aloof as usual, not taking an interest in our daughter. The liquor cabinet seemed to be his main concern these days. My mind was in no shape to make the simplest decision, even tying a shoelace. I left the decision in the hands of my trusted friends.

Later that morning at the ceremony, I was left speechless. Folks showed up in their best Sunday duds, ready for high-stepping to the jaunty tunes. The brass band took the lead, playing the typical jazz that New Orleans was renowned for, a tradition that went way back.

Much like Ms. Noel's funeral, leading the procession was the black buggy, trimmed in gold, pulled by two white stallions. The driver sat tall in his seat on top of the buggy, dressed in a tailored suit, wearing a top hat and white gloves.

Despite the constant downpour, our family followed behind the musicians, and the second line of folks soon collected, bringing up the rear from St. Charles Avenue to the backstreets. All marching to the lively tunes, carving a path to the grave site. It felt as though the whole city had joined us on this dreary day and time of mourning.

~

We stood under an umbrella, trying to shield ourselves from the storm. Against the pounding downpour, the preacher spoke loudly, giving his sermon as Dawn's small coffin lowered into the ground. I stared at the pink coffin as if I were in a trance. It was her favorite color, Sally shared.

My mind was riddled with shame. I didn't have a right to call myself a mother. What kind of mother didn't know her own daughter's favorite color? Me! I hated myself. Dawn's death was my fault. My stomach knotted.

At the site, Aidan stood at my left and Jeffery on my right. Dom was on Jeff's right. With me in the middle, we all huddled as we wept over our loss. A child's death was something a parent should never have to endure ever!

I spotted Val hanging back at the cemetery's entrance with several of his men. Sally didn't feel comfortable standing with us, so she stayed behind with Val.

I had recognized several members of Jeffery's family from Ms. Noel's funeral. The rest of the folks attending, their faces were unknown to me. I noted the strangers from the neighborhood, the Garden District came bearing flowers. It was nice seeing so many faces attending the services. I appreciated everyone's support.

This week had been one of the worst times of my life. In fact, it'd been nothing but downhill from that point on. When we first returned home from the castle, it was a bittersweet homecoming. Jeffery and Dom both couldn't tear themselves apart from Aidan. Tears were shared between the three.

Then with the announcement of Dawn's death, more tears came. I stood back and let the guys have their reuniting and time of mourning. A special bond had formed between those three, long before I came into the picture. Jeffery and Dom had been Aidan's family for many years. They needed their moment alone.

As reasonable and understanding I could be with the guys, I had never felt more alone. I was grieving over Dawn too. I yearned for comfort, someone to talk to, someone to hold me and tell me everything was going to be all right, even though I knew it wasn't.

It wasn't like I was shut-out or ignored by the guys, rather the opposite. Dom and Jeffery had been very accommodating, but it wasn't what I needed. My mind kept drifting to Val. I craved for his touch, his love. I was sure that my feelings for Aidan had changed. The intense connection we once shared was gone. It was Val that filled my heart, and the guilt burned like frostbite.

Since we'd been back, Val has been keeping his distance. I guess with Aidan alive and living with us, *only temporarily*, Val probably thought Aidan and I were rekindling our love. If the truth be told, it was the furthest thing *from* the truth. Nothing was the same.

As I stood there half listening to the preacher, I felt like I was a ticking time bomb ready to implode at any minute. Regardless of my much-needed meltdown, somehow, I managed to remain silent.

Aidan squeezed my hand, the first act of kindness I'd received from him since our return. Startled, I lifted my head and glanced into his face. He responded with a thin-lined smile. His eyes were dull and bloodshot, not the vibrate blues that I remembered. Aidan had been hitting the bottle pretty hard. I reckoned he had his own way of grieving. So for now, I'd let him.

The unspoken words between Aidan and I had put us both on edge. When I brought him to the house after that terrible encounter with Mustafa, he'd insisted that I stay with him. I declined his offer and every night from that point on, I had to continually refuse his invite. I was sure my rejection was the onset for his cold-shoulder toward me. I just couldn't make myself, and my excuses were running thin. Sooner or later, I was going to have to tell him.

Our relationship had changed. Aidan was different, the way he moved. Even his speech pattern appeared off. Then again, the death of a child changed anyone. Even though we both were suffering, I couldn't be there for him in the way he expected, especially when my heart was somewhere else. I desired Val. What good did that do me? He wasn't here beside me, and by the distance he kept, I assumed he wanted it that way.

It was just as well. I had unfinished business with Aidan, questions about his involvement with my incarceration. I especially wanted to know how he stole Dawn from the Family and managed to hide her during the period of her short life. For now, I'd give him space. I thought he needed time to heal, as I did. When our grief had subsided, then I would confront Aidan.

As for Val, I'd have to put him on the backburner until I had resolved my untied issues. I had to find Mustafa and end his life. Val could come with me or he could remain behind.

Either way, Mustafa *must* die.

Jarred from my thoughts, the preacher had asked everyone to bow their heads for the last prayer. I chose not to partake. At this point, if God could forsake my child and allow such cruelty to exist in this world, I figured what I had to say wouldn't be suitable at a funeral and among good folks.

In the final good-byes, each person threw a white rose on the small coffin. I found myself unable to move. The line moved forward, exiting the grave site, but I stayed still. Rain poured down in sheets, saturating me as I stood without the umbrella's protection. I didn't care. I watched the yard keepers shovel the first dirt onto my child's tiny coffin. Soon she'd be totally entombed, and only the gravestone would be all that was left, marking her once existence.

Aidan nudged my arm, and I pulled away. "You're going to drown standing out here," he barked over the roaring rain. I didn't reply. I just looked at him blankly, then back at the increasing dirt that toppled the tiny coffin. Aidan attempted once more. "Sweetheart, come on!"

My head snapped back up at him as my eyes narrowed. I spoke as a person on the brink of insanity. "Don't call me that!"

Aidan's eyes looked confused as he asked, "What do you mean? I call you that name all the time." His hand extended to me. I didn't move.

"You haven't ever called me sweetheart." I shook my head. It didn't matter right now anyhow. "Please," I went back, watching the keepers.

"Pardon me?" His dark brows knitted.

I turned my eyes back to him. "Please let me have this moment alone." I dismissed Aidan and focused my gaze on the shoveling. Without looking up I said, "I've never had the opportunity to sing to her or do one damn thing with her. So… do you mind leaving?" It was my last chance. "Can you give me that much?" As a tear escaped, anger tore through my spirit. It wasn't fair. Aidan had the opportunity to be with our daughter. I had only seconds, and not very pleasant ones. Every time I closed my eyes, I saw her tormented face as she lay helplessly.

I saw the confusion in Aidan's eyes. Thankfully, he backed off. "Sure, whatever you need." He stepped away. His jaw twitched.

Then I heard Jeffery say, "Boo, do you want me to stay behind with you? I can go find a spot to sit and give you whatever time you need." His voice was soft and kind.

"No. I'm okay. Go with Aidan. He needs you... but thanks," I said as my voice sounded flat and dull to my ears. It reflected how I felt... empty inside.

My eye caught a glimpse of Val talking to Dom and Jeffery. Whatever they were discussing, it didn't last long. Val turned from them and went in another direction.

I turned my attention back to the dirt and the coffin. A rush of panic flooded my mind. I needed to be closer to Dawn. I had to see her just one last time. At this point, I'd lost my mind. I stepped up to the edge of the grave and crumbled to my knees. One of the keepers called out to me in a flash of fear. Everything after that seemed tunneled.

Water had started to collect, and I watched in horror. I screamed at the keepers, "Take her out! It's filling up with water." My face twisted with sheer fright. I couldn't abandon her again. I had to *save* Dawn, my frail mind reasoned. This time no one was going to stop me from saving her. As my legs went over the dugout, tears, and rain blinded me. I was aware my behavior was insane, but I had snapped.

Drenched to the bone and shivering, I slipped down into the ditch. The water was freezing, but my only thoughts were to get Dawn out of that trap. Just when my hands clasped the small coffin, I felt warm arms encircling me, lifting me out of the mud and icy water. When I looked up, it was Val bringing me back to sanity.

When our eyes locked, I touched his worried face. Right then, I no longer doubted his love for me. He leaned in and kissed me softly as he held me tight in his arms. I surrendered, collapsing, nestling my rain-beaten face into the niche of his warm embrace, and sobbed. I trusted him with my life. I felt... what was that strange word? *Safe.*

～

I'd waken with a startled breath. As the former day crept back into my mind, I recognized the familiar scent and soft bed. Val had taken me to his pad. Relief washed over me. Going back to my house gave me a dreadful sense that I wasn't ready to confront. Sooner or later, I had to go back. For now, I only wanted to be with Val just for a little while. I heard light footsteps and glanced up. I couldn't help but smile.

"Hello, sleeping beauty!" Val grinned as he came into the dim room and sat on the edge of the bed next to me. "I thought you might like some soup or something to eat." His soft eyes glanced over me. I noticed he had put one of his T-shirts on me and got rid of the drenched black dress I'd worn earlier. The T-shirt felt soft against my skin, and it smelled of citrus, like Val.

For a minute, we shared a glance. As if the world stood still, frozen in time, just the two of us only existed. Then Val made a move. As he came to me, gently placing his weight on top of me, shifting on his elbows. I had knocked the blanket off, leaving only the thin material of his T-shirt covering me. I wanted *him*, and by the sensual look in his eyes, he wanted me too. Gently he kissed me, and I hungrily kissed him back. His smooth hands moved under my shirt to my bare skin. I shivered from his touch, and I began tugging at his shirt. In one sweep, he had his off, and mine followed in a puddle on the floor next to his. His pants came next, and we both relished in each other's bareness. The only frail piece of clothing left was a lacy pair of panties and his boxers.

His hands moved over my skin, and I raked his back as I pressed against him greedily. Soon we were immersed in each other. His hands began to explore places I had no idea existed. My mind went wild under his singeing caresses. I opened myself to this man... my desire, my heart, and, yes, my love. I should've known. It was always Val who possessed my heart.

Just when we were about to take our affections to the next level, a profound knock resonated at the door. At first, the taps were calm, but as seconds passed, the knocking began to pound angrily. Val cursed under his breath as he started to rise from the bed. I tugged his arm, pulling him back to me. "No! They'll go away. Don't answer the door!" I practically pleaded, panting slightly.

"Don't worry. I won't be long." Val assured me in a husky voice as he kissed me on the lips before he sprang from the bed and threw on his pants.

He rushed from my sight. Quietly, I lay there with the sheets drawn over my breast and listened as he threw the door wide open. To my disappointment, alarm hit me like an iceberg. "Dammit," I hissed under my breath. "I can't believe he followed me!" Aidan had nerve coming here. By the sound of it, if I didn't get in there, those two might end up in a brawl of the century. *Crap!* I snatched up Val's T-shirt and threw it on as I'd made a dive toward the igniting commotion.

I wasn't surprised, catching both men towering over each other. I felt like an ant to their enormous size. I hesitated for a moment. I didn't know how to stop a guy fight. I ran my fingers through my hair, starting to panic. I didn't need this sort of trouble right now!

"Look! Stevie isn't your possession. She's free to decide for herself. If she wants to go with you, I won't stop her but it will be a cold day in hell before I let you barge into my home and force Stevie against her will." Val stood in a war stance, facing off against Aidan. In return, Aidan sneered as he glimpsed at the small apartment. I suppose it wasn't exactly on the cover of *Homes & Gardens*. What a snob, I thought.

"She's not exactly in her right frame of mind. Contrary to her best interest, you were going to sleep with her regardless?" Aidan's dark blues looked fierce.

Holy mother of god!

"Oh, that's rich! The pot's calling the kettle black," Val fired back. By now, both men were toe-to-toe.

"What kettle is that?" Aidan stood his ground.

Oh, lord! I had to block those two before they created mass destruction. "Boys, wait!" I jumped between the two snarling men, shoving them apart. Considering their monolithic frames, I could've been crushed. Thankfully, they both stepped back. "No one is fighting tonight," I clarified, and in the same breath, I glanced up at Val. I'd already hated myself for what I was going to do next. I exhaled a sigh. "I have to go back. I'm sorry." Regret hid behind my smile, not for desiring Val, but for having to leave. There was so much I wanted to say to him. Setting aside my breaking heart, I'd have to do this talk another time.

"You don't have to leave on his account." The inflection of Val's baritone voice was a strong clue about how he felt about Aidan. As I observed the two and their heated stance, it came to mind that Val once dated Helen. I questioned whether I wasn't the only girl causing tension between the two.

Suddenly, a swirl of dread clenched my gut. I'd almost forgotten. I haven't told Aidan or Val about Helen's death. I shuttered thinking of that day when I'd reveal my dark secret. I sensed neither one would take her death well, an ending by my hand that I was not proud to claim. I feared that once the truth came to light, both men would hate me forever. I wouldn't blame them, but for now, I'd delay my secret. Perhaps another time.

"I have to get back to Dom and Jeffery." I'd hoped he understood that I wasn't returning home for Aidan's sake. "Do you have my… um… clothes?" Val paused, staring back at me with a nettled face. I knew he was full of questions and ire all at the same time. I expected it. I had the same feelings too.

"Your clothes are folded up over the chair in the bedroom," he said, running his hand through his tossed hair.

"Okay, thanks!" I reached around Val's waist and gave him a tight hug. I knew he didn't want me to go. His arms were too possessive as he clung to me briefly. I wished I could've given him more reassurance. Truth be told, with everything surrounding my life, what did I have to give? I loved him, but was it enough?

On the other side of the fence, loving Val didn't help my problem with Aidan. With all things considered, my priorities had to be set in order. First, I had to settle my differences with Aidan.

I had a debt to pay. I'd intended to hunt Mustafa down and kill him. I might be digging my own grave, but in my opinion, I didn't see another way out. I wanted Mustafa dead. I reckoned that was the human side of me.

JALOUX

*T*he ride home resembled an eternity. We were in my
Mustang, and Aidan was taking his aggression out on my
car. I decided the pouty child needed to be called out, so I spoke up.
"Care to share?" I was snide, but he deserved worse.

"I'm not in a talkative mood right now, if you don't mind?" He
clenched his teeth as he grinded the gears.

"Suit yourself, but you're going to strip the gears if you keep
jerking the stick that way," I said in a devil-may-care tone.

"If I damage your car, I'll buy you another."

"Whatever!" I slipped down in the seat and leaned my head back.
Let him blow off some steam. If I were in his shoes, I'd feel betrayed
too. Aidan and I definitely needed to talk. Considering his mood now,
I'd approach him tomorrow. Not only did I have questions for him, I
needed to set him straight.

Finally, we'd reached the mansion. I'd planned on ducking in my
room, staying under the radar of anyone's notice. If I had to endure
another guest expressing their condolences one more time, it might
send me into orbit. I needed to empty my brain. I had one of Dom's
sleeping pills that Jeffery slipped me earlier today. All I craved was a
little solitude and blissful sleep. Judging by Aidan's tight jaw, I imagined our conversation wouldn't be a stroll in the park. But tonight, I
needed rest.

~

Once Aidan and I entered the front door, a mishmash of chatter drifted from the back of the house. It sounded like the guests had congregated in the kitchen and family room.

Strange how I felt disconnected. All these good people attending my daughter's funeral, and I didn't know anyone. I supposed my social skills were inept.

Since everyone's attention was distracted, I thought I had a clear shot to my bedroom. Impolite or not, I wasn't in the mood for sharing my grief with strangers.

Besides Dom and Jeffery, the only family member I had was Sally, and I wasn't sure how I felt about that. Aidan had a minion of relatives, and yet no one came. What a crappy family. On the other hand, if they were like Van, it was best they kept their distance.

I started to make a beeline for the stairs, but I was abruptly halted by a firm hand. My eyes snapped up. Two very dark blues were glaring back at me. Immediately, I tried to free myself. "You're hurting me," I hissed, keeping my voice low. I didn't feel like putting on a sideshow for our guests.

"You're not going anywhere until you explain yourself." His voice came off hard and threatening.

I inhaled a haggard breath. "Aidan, let's not do this tonight. I'm tired."

"You can sleep later. Start explaining," he demanded like I was his property. Strange, his behavior reminded me of Sam. How ironic.

My brow arched. "An explanation for what?"

"You can start with why you were with Valor."

My whole body stiffened. Dammit! He had to do this with a full house of strangers? "Did I not say I'm tired?" I glared back at him as equally. Still his iron grip didn't loosen, and by the petulance in his blues, I saw he didn't have any plans of letting this subject rest tonight. "You can't wait until morning?"

"Nope. I. Want. Answers. Now!" Aidan's face snarled into rage.

I took another pointed sigh. It looked like sleep for me would be stalled. "Fire away," I demanded as he still held me captive.

"I asked you a question. I want an answer!"

I knew the time would come when I had to tell him. "Val is my friend… a very close and dear friend."

"You were naked in his bed. I think that pushes past the line of friendship." His dark gaze held mine.

"Well, there you have it. Can I go now?" I held a bland stare.

"You're such a deceiving bitch," Aidan growled.

"I'll take bitch, but *deceiving*?"

"Our bed was still warm when you jumped in that Zop's bed. Who else have you been sleeping with?" Aidan's face started to blister.

And with no more energy than I possessed, I'd wished he'd knock me out. Then I could at least deal with him in the morning. "I suppose, if you include the men at the lovely Haven Hospital while I was drugged to oblivion, I don't know, maybe another twenty." My voice sounded hollow.

Aidan scoffed as he abruptly released his grip on my arm. "What happened to you," his voice was wounding. "You're not the same girl I fell in love with back in Tangi."

"You're right. I'm not." I looked him straight in the eyes with no apologies. It was true. The old Stevie had died the day they captured her. I lost my life, my freedom, and worst of all, my child. The old Stevie didn't exist any longer!

I spat out my last words before I turned for the stairs. "That young girl you once knew died that day at the cottage where you left her wide open to the predators of your family. Good night." I held my voice at an even tone. Then I twirled on my heels headed to my bedroom, leaving Aidan standing alone.

Just to ease my frayed nerves, I locked my door. It wouldn't keep Aidan out, but it made me feel a little safer.

As my eyes washed over the bedroom, it suddenly felt too big for just me. I wanted to be with Val, still tucked in his bed with *him*. I hugged my waist trying to rein in the emptiness that threatened. Maybe when the house quieted, I'd sneak out and head back to Val's place. On second thought, I might be the last person he wanted to see right now. I did leave with Aidan.

To add to the mix of troubles, Aidan's outburst tonight by acting like a jilted lover, Val may never believe my true feelings. The thought of Aidan touching me made my skin crawl. He was so different now, or maybe I was fooled into believing Aidan was good. I shook my head, frustrated, confused, and tired. I sighed and slumped my heavy shoulders.

I crossed over to my bed and flopped down. I leaned down, unbuckled the straps on my heels and kicked them off. I sat there for a moment, raking in the solitude. Aidan and I had a lot to discuss. We shared a child together, a deceased child. It was time for Aidan and me to clear the air. I supposed I should do this in the morning, be done with it, and maybe the healing process could commence.

Too tired to undress, I just slept in my dress. Besides, it smelled of Val.

∽

The sun popped up early, shining its stream of light right in my face. I began to stir, and before I cleared my head of sleep, all my sorrow and pain came flooding back. I stilled for a minute, dreading this day. I wanted to escape to a remote island where no one could find me. Living in bliss sounded so tempting.

I looked down, and I had forgotten I'd slept in my clothes. The black dress clung to my body, only a bit more wrinkled.

Suddenly the dress felt stifling and itchy. I had to get it off my skin. I reached to pull the zipper down, but it had jammed. With my patience depleted, I ripped it off, tearing the delicate material to shreds. As it fell to the floor in a puddle, it reminded me of last night with Val. I picked up the torn garment and buried my face into the cloth. I drew in its fragrance. Val's delicious citrus scent still lingered, along with an earthy smell, and then something else... *the grave site.* I dropped the dress as though it had burned my hands. Tears started to fall. I wiped the moisture from my eyes and started for the shower until I caught a glimpse of a shadow in the corner, sitting in my chair by the window. I snapped my head around, and my mouth dropped. It dawned on me that my body was fully exposed. Last night I'd been in such a rush I'd left behind my undergarments. I just threw on the dress and fled out the door with Aidan hot on my trail. Instantly, I tried covering myself, but I only had two hands. Flushed and vulnerable, I spoke up in a piqued voice. "How did you get in *my* room? I'd locked my door!"

His wolf-like eyes raked over me very slowly. By the time he reached my face, my cheeks were on fire. It reminded me of a time, long ago. A time I wanted to forget. He finally rose to his feet and stepped into the dim light. He spoke in a deep throaty voice, "My, don't you look eatable this morning." Aidan smiled, but it didn't touch his eyes.

I had no intention of dignifying that with an answer. I stood there, glowering at my intruder.

Aidan sauntered around me, slowly, circling me with apparent menace in his blues. "Well, well, cat got your tongue?" His voice spewed of venom as he continued to strut, encroaching upon me as a predator. Then abruptly he halted, standing to my back. I listened over my shoulder, careful not to breathe. One thing Aidan hadn't considered, since his absence, I'd had combat training. He took a strand of my hair into his hand and inhaled a deep whiff. "You cut your hair. I like it long," he scoffed against my ear. Goose bumps rolled down my neck as I turned to face him. I saw how pleased he was by the possessive glint in his eyes. I held my gaze equal to his. The sign of fear revealed weakness, I did my best to hide it.

"Leave my room, *now!*" I demanded, teeth clenched.

"I'm sorry, sweetheart, but you can't get rid of me that easily." His lips stretched over stained teeth into a seedy smile. When did Aidan have tarnished teeth? I asked myself internally. "Don't forget, it is my money that bought you this fine house and all the exquisite accessories that come with it. Therefore, I'll leave when I'm good and fucking ready." He shoved me down to the cold floor, forcing himself on top of me. While his huge body held me trapped, he spread my legs apart. With one hand, he unfastened his pants as the other handheld me against my will. He'd been drinking. I could smell the whiskey on his breath.

"Aidan, no! Please," I begged.

"Did you say *no* to your boyfriend, Valor?" His eyes were bloodshot, and his words were slightly slurred.

"Get off me! You're drunk," I screamed.

Out of the blue I heard a big clang. Aidan went limp. His head was blocking my view. I strained to the side. Once my eyes landed on the obscured silhouette hovering, my heart jump started. Jeffery came with a heavy cast-iron skillet to my aid. A huge relief washed over me, but then strangely, instead of assisting me from the restrain of Aidan's limp body, Jeffery leaned over, rushing his words.

"Wake up, Stevie! Wake the mofo up! Trouble is brewing!"

My brows knitted in confusion, then I sat straight up in bed, gasping. My eyes raked over the room and the corner from where Aidan sat. I exhaled. The chair was empty. Oh, dear lord! Another nightmare! My forehead was beaded with cold sweat. When I threw the covers off, I realized that I was wearing the same black dress from yesterday. My instinct was to rip it off my body, but I sensed I had more urgent matters to handle than the dream. That *vivid* dream. I quickly jumped up, peeling the garment off. I threw on my sweats and rushed downstairs. Jeffery came to me in that dream. Something bad was up! I felt its chill down to the bone.

When I reached the kitchen, everyone, including Sally, was sitting at the table. Dom had made his usual breakfast.

Immediately all eyes fell upon me. I thought, how *odd*. Still it didn't appear any different than any other morning.

Then I glanced at Aidan. He sat there with a smirk plastered across his face. Jeffery fidgeted in his seat. Sally sat quietly. She was never silent unless she was frightened. I caught Dom fiddling with his food. Strangely, he didn't take any bites. In fact, no one was eating. Everyone's mood felt tense. Something was off. I spotted an empty bottle of bourbon on the counter. Bingo! I slide my gaze back at Aidan. His eyes were heavy-lidded and red. The man was shitfaced. Alcohol and bloodthirsty rage were a deadly combination.

I was dealing with a very volatile problem. Strange how Aidan was behaving. He appeared removed from our daughter's death, but he was livid over my relationship with Val. I sensed his jealousy had nothing to do with his love for me. The opposite of what I once believed. Aidan viewed me as his possession.

I had my trusted knife tucked in the back of my sweats. Not to toot my own horn, but with stern practice, I'd gotten pretty good with my aim.

On the other hand, Aidan was even faster. With his druid magick, I didn't have a chance. I thought if I soothed the drunk, everyone could get away safely. I exhaled a tart breath. It would've been so much easier if Jeffery had whopped Aidan over the head with that cast-iron skillet back in my dream. Aidan would be sleeping it off or knocked out, and we'd be safe.

Then I heard steps from behind. I slowly turned. I had no idea who o expect coming at this point. I braced myself. Since that day at the cottage, I was a bit jumpy of surprises.

When my eyes landed on Val, a sense of relief washed through my mind. He was standing in the kitchen door, eyeballing our situation. His body was stiff, face harsh.

I suddenly realized the profundity of our problem. Why else did Val come? As happy as I was to see the Zop leader, I still wished he'd stayed home or anywhere but here. I feared his presence might acerbate Aidan's hostility.

I decided there was no time like the future to jump in. "What's going on this morning?" I kept my voice light as I glanced around at everyone. When I got back around to Aidan's face, cold eyes snipped at me.

I hoped to divert the attention on me. I would stall Aidan while Val got everyone out before any real harm was done. I was grateful for the dream. Interesting. Old Jeff may have some of his aunt's gifts after all. Thanks to him, I was alerted to a highly ignitable situation that could go bad in a split second, and I quickly needed to handle Mr. Drunk-Ass.

Val stood quiet as his eyes combed over everyone, assessing the potential problem. I avoided eye contact with him. I didn't want to make the unpredictable problem worse.

"Stevie, how nice it is that you decided to join us this gracious morning." Aidan's words were slightly slurred, just like in the dream. "Do you know the servants are quite loyal to you?

Aidan stated a rhetorical question. He wasn't searching for a reply. I held my tongue, something that didn't come easy for me.

"My servant betrayed me, calling your lover boy to come protect you from the big bad wolf." Aidan sneered at Val. The Zop remained marble-like, keeping his eyes on point.

I wasn't as controlled. Referring to a family member as a servant didn't fly with me. Despite Aidan's dangerous nature. "Whoa! No one in this house is a servant. If you want something as little as toilet paper, you better learn how to fetch it yourself. No one is waiting on your pampered ass!"

"Don't tell me what I can or cannot do," Aidan sibilated, "I gifted you an exquisite lifestyle. Therefore, if I dare to reference to someone as a servant or *whore*, I believe I've purchased the right." I glimpsed over at Val. His jaw was flexing. The tension was like a toxic gas, lighting a simple match would blow everything to the heavens.

I let out a down-reaching sigh as I raked my fingers through my uncombed hair. "Aidan, let's not do this," I asked. "Why don't you get some rest. You look tired. When you wake up, I think you'll see this from a different perspective."

"A different perspective?" Aidan roared as he charged to his feet in a fit of rage, knocking the table across the room and sending all the spattered food and dishes crashing. I caught Val in the corner of my eye. Swiftly, he'd stepped directly in front of me, shielding me. My heart did a little pitter-patter for my hero, but still, I was a big girl. I could handle the madman and his temper tantrums.

Everyone else had scattered in different directions. From what I could tell, no one had gotten hurt except for a minor cut or two. Val remained steady, under Aidan's blaze. There was no love lost between the two men. In hindsight, I feared the outcome if they went to blows. "That's right, Zop. Step between us." Aidan reminded me of a lion defending his territory.

My stomach knotted. It was me that put my family in this dangerous position, letting Aidan stay in this house. Now it was up to me to get us out of this turbulence.

I went into action.

Distracting Val wasn't my intentions, but I had to touch him. He gave me strength in so many ways. I tugged softly on his belt loop and leaned my forehead gently against the center of his back for a brief minute before I pulled away. I had to fight my own battles. If Val got hurt in this whirlwind that I'd created, I would never forgive myself. Defusing Aidan's unpredictable temper was like treading through a mine field, any step could cost lives. I inhaled a deep breath, then I cautiously slid out from behind Val's protection. Now I was an open target. I caught a sideways glimpse at Val standing in his warrior stance. Alarm lodged in my throat. I needed to think fast. "Aidan, this is between you and me. Let's clear everyone out, and we can talk," I forced a smile.

"Oh, come on! It's all in the family." He threw out his arms wide as if he was embracing the city. Reasoning with a drunk was insane, but I saw no other recourse. I learned that early in life with mom.

I swallowed hard, and I engaged, needles pricking my neck.

"They're not part of this. Why should we bring them into our dispari-ty?" From the corner of my eye, I caught Val ushering everyone out. A breath of relief eased into my lungs.

"Stop," Aidan shrieked. The room stilled. He turned his icy glare on me. "Maybe they need to hear about the whore you have become."

His words stung more than I wanted to confess. Though letting Aidan anger me would be giving him what he wanted. The way I saw it, I had two choices. Either I appealed to his softer side or knock him the fuck out. While cold cocking him was a huge stretch and an appealing idea, I had to keep it real.

I began to negotiate.

"Look. You're right about being angry." My voice softened. "You've been very generous to me, to Jeffery and Dom too." I cajoled. "Aidan, this isn't you. Let's sit down over a cup of coffee and talk through our differences. You don't want to hurt anyone." I hoped the sober-minded Aidan would overcome the drunk, perilous Aidan.

"Don't I?" he amused. "Don't get self-righteous with me," he leered. "How much pain can you be suffering when our child's body hasn't grown cold before you are in *his* bed?" Aidan cut his venomous eyes at Val.

"Aidan!" I took a step closer. "Don't do this to yourself." I choked back tears. "Please," I begged. This hostile Aidan standing before me was a stranger to me. The swagger, the pride, the confidence had all perished. Nothing made sense to me, and yet everything did.

"Please what? Please turn the other cheek while you share your bed with everyone, *but* me," he wailed.

My jaw dropped. All this time it wasn't about our daughter's death, rather it was about me not sleeping with *him*. Anger, fear, and regret gyrated through my mind. Still, I had to swallow my pride. Aidan's highly volatile temperament had to be contained. My heart kicked up several notches thinking of all the possibilities this situation could go down. "I get why you're upset. Let's get everyone out. Then just you and I pop a squat and talk."

"What's there to talk about? You turned your back on me with him!"

"It's not like that, and you know it!"

"No, I don't know! I thought we loved each other! When did you stop?" His words didn't feel sincere to me as if he were an alien.

621

My stomach tightened. "I thought you betrayed me! When Sally came to the cottage that day, she played this elaborate scheme that the two of you were married. She was very convincing." Aidan glanced over at Sally as she quailed under his stare. "I believed her!"

"You'd believe this lying bitch over me?"

"That day at the cottage, I first thought she had lost her mind, but then… "

"Stop!" He waved his hand to hush me, "This is foolishness. Your cousin had been acting on her own accord."

"Sally wasn't alone," my voice rose. "She was standing in front of me while my captor seized me from behind, stabbing me with some unknown drug."

"Did Sally reveal her accomplice?"

"No. I didn't see my captor's face." Cynicism laced my voice.

"What? You don't believe her?" Aidan snapped, eyes piercing.

"In the beginning, I was led to believe it was you," I said. "Then Sally claimed it was your uncle Van."

"Ah! There you have it. It was my uncle."

"You're right," I rolled my eyes. "How stupid of me," I forced a tight smile.

Though I held my tongue, I sensed something wasn't right. Having said that while my captor's face remained anonymous, I caught a good look at my adductor's hand. The hideous ring with the eye. Despite Sally's claims, the hand I saw belonged to a *young* man, a hand I was *very* familiar with. I might've been hazy about a lot of things that day, but one thing I was certain of… the hand of my captor looked identical to *Aidan's hand*. All the same, I didn't plan to share my suspicions with him, not until I had proof. In the meantime, my reservations about Sally, Van, *and* Aidan continued.

"You said you were drugged?" Aidan asked, drawing me back from my thoughts.

"Yes," I answered.

"I'm sorry for your misfortunes," Aidan mused as though he possessed a secret joke.

"Thank you." I eyed him dubiously.

He laughed to himself.

"Excuse me," I asked as my brows furrowed.

"Don't you think if I wanted your family and associates dead, that you'd be dead as well? You must know, I am quite an accomplished druid?" His arrogance beseeched him.

"I see that now." I slightly shifted the subject. "Where did you go?"

"Pardon me?"

"You abandoned me at the cottage. I found that *lousy* newspaper!" My voice cracked.

"Come again?" He shook his head as if he'd forgotten.

"The newspaper! My mother's death! She was poisoned! Remember?"

Val's feet shifted. Glimpsing in the corner of my eye, I saw anger rising off his shoulders. I shivered at how this scenario could pan out if I weren't careful.

"Oh, yes. I recall," he coughed. Funny, such a human behavior for an immortal. "I left to see if there was any truth to the story," Aidan drawled. "I was trying to prevent you unnecessary grief."

"If you're trying to protect me, then why didn't you take the publication with you rather than leaving it in plain sight?"

"When I realized I'd forgotten the paper, it was too late to turn back," he smiled, but it wasn't the warm fuzzy kind. Everything about him seemed to clash, his demeanor, his story, or maybe my eyes were opening for the first time?

I walked over to where the table had been thrown, now sitting on its side. I went to lift the heavy wood, but Aidan had taken it from me and sat it upright. He placed a chair beside me and took one for himself. We both settled at the table, seated across from one another. Dom returned, handing Aidan a cup of fresh brewed coffee and left the steaming pot on the table.

Val remained on alert, taking a stool at the island. Jeffery joined Val while Sally scurried upstairs. Dom dallied around as though he was busy cleaning the kitchen.

Apart from Sally, they all stayed, as if they were wary of Aidan's state of mind and leaving my side to have me face him alone. Obviously, I sensed the risk too. I hid my trembling hands under the table, hoping it went unnoticed.

"Why did you not return to the cottage?" I held my voice even.

"I returned, only too late. They had already taken you."

His tale had holes. Everything that Aidan did was precise, down to scratching his ass. He didn't make mistakes, and he sure as hell didn't *forget*.

I clutched myself with great caution. "Did you try to find me?"

He shifted in his seat. "No. I didn't," he admitted too easily.

I bit back a snap. His admittance stung. "Did you not worry about my whereabouts?"

"Yes, of course. I sought my uncle out. He informed me of your condition."

"Condition! You knew I was pregnant?"

"Yes. How could I have not known? We had unprotected sex."

"Oh, yeah, that's right. We didn't." I remembered during the infusion, we couldn't use protection. Moving forward with further questions, I pushed. "Why would you give your uncle the time of day after he...?"

"Don't be so hard on the old man. He's a bit ambitious."

"He wanted me on a silver platter, and you think I'm being too hard? Nice!" Apparently, his uncle meant more to him than I once thought. And I was the rag that got tossed in the dumpster, I reckoned. "What did your uncle say?"

"He explained to me that he'd arranged for you to stay at a resort in Switzerland." It was as if Aidan was reciting a well-rehearsed play.

"You believed him, just like that?"

"Of course. Our child was the Family's destiny."

I leaned in closer. "While I was pregnant with *your* child, they discarded me like a pesky rat in the alley. Have you ever heard of Haven?"

"No, as a matter of fact, I haven't."

"You should. The staff are such a delight." A wave of disgust welled up in my throat.

"I presumed you were safe and happy."

"That's rich!"

"How bad could it have been?" His blues raked over me. "You look pretty healthy to me."

I nearly went for his throat, but the glint in Val's eyes halted me. Instead, I bit out, "How perceptive of you, Aidan."

"Contrary to your belief, I do understand your resistance. I know our family can be harsh. Our traditions seem extreme to outsiders."

"More like evil."

Aidan paused, his blues darkened. "You don't understand. Our child, the firstborn, had to be conceived on *All Hallows' Eve* in order for her to receive the purest source." Aidan shoved his coffee to the side. "Since you and I infused our powers, our daughter was the next in line. One way or another, we needed the essence. We had been planning this for centuries. The Family had invested far too much to accept defeat."

I sat back, blinking shock. There I had it. Was there anything these vile people wouldn't sink to? "Were you in on this plan to take my child's life?"

"No. Certainly not! I had the misunderstanding that she would replace you with a suitable mate."

"If that were true, how did Mustafa end up with Dawn?"

Aidan shrugged, staring at me openly. "I'm not sure. When I was captured, I lost contact of the child and any outside contact."

"I see." I bit back curses that choked my breath.

He leaned his head to the side catching my gaze. "Unfortunately, the end did not justify the means."

"So, you believe it was a setup? The Family locked you away so they could hand my child over to Mustafa for him to take her essence?"

Aidan reached to clasp my hand, but I jerked away. I shuttered over the thought of him touching me.

"I can't be certain." He leaned back into his chair relaxing. Remorse remained vacant in his eyes.

"Could Van have set this up?" Sally swore it was Van who helped her. I recalled seeing a young man's hand. Yet I remember how Van hungered for my essence." It seemed the most logic explanation and the most illogical. "By the way, where is your loving uncle?"

"I haven't been in touch with him in some time." I caught a slight grimace in the corner of his lip. Something wasn't adding up. I remembered how Van clung to Aidan's shirt-tail.

Moving on to my next question. "So, is it true? There's some weird cosmic force between us?"

Aidan paused for a minute, locking his dark blues onto me. "Yes. It's true." Briefly he glanced over at Val, then back to me. His eyes were harsh. "You're as much a part of me as I am you. Sorry, toots, looks like you're stuck with me."

My voice became steely calm. "That's where you are wrong. I have a choice. I will never choose you. How could I? I blame you for Dawn's death!"

"Some things are beyond our control. Even our daughter's fate."

I flinched from his words.

"How much time did you have with Dawn," I asked. "A year?" I stared into his empty blues. "How did you find her?"

"Find her? I've never lost Dawn."

Jolted by his answer, I just sat there speechless.

"The Family informed me of her caretakers."

"You knew for nearly two years where she lived, and you never bothered seeing her?"

"I did visit her once on her last birthday." Aidan sat there with a blank stare as though he was bored. It was as if I was looking at a stranger.

Suddenly I remembered the video. "I saw the video. Helen showed me a brief take of you helping Dawn blowout her candles," I sneered. "I'm guessing that was all for show."

"Hmm... Helen must've stolen the clip."

Funny how he had an answer for everything. I moved on to the next obvious question. "Do you know Mustafa?"

"I am aware of the angel. I'm afraid I've never had the pleasure of getting to know him."

I shook my head. How could it be a pleasure meeting this deviled angel when he murdered our child? I blurted out, "I don't believe Mustafa acted alone," I paused, staring at the black-hearted bastard's impassive face. "If you didn't help him, then tell me who did?"

"I told you once! Must I spell it out for you? I don't know." A flash of anger wavered in his glint.

"I deserve answers," I refuted.

"Life doesn't always give us what we deserve, toots."

"No kidding! Dawn is dead, and I believe you had a hand in it."

Aidan slightly rose from his seat as his face turned crimson red. I spotted Val planting his feet on the floor as if he were ready to spring into action. "I'll tell you this," he snarled, "Listen carefully. I do not intend to say this again. *I* am not guilty of Dawn's death or throwing you into a mental hospital. End this charade of interrogation." By his riposte, I sensed he was on the brink of exploding.

"Okay, I believe you," my breath notched. "Sorry."

Aidan settled back down in his seat, gnarling.

For a moment, quiet wafted into the air.

Aidan broke the tense silence, counterstriking. "Your father is the blame for this mishap."

"*My* father?"

Suddenly a dark brow arched. "You don't know."

"Know what?" What did he mean?

"You are utterly in the dark," he mused.

A wry tingle began to spread over my body. I feared whatever was next.

"You don't know about your mother?"

"I'm not following you."

"I see that Sara kept you in the dark."

"Do you know something about my mother that I am not aware of?"

"Sweetheart, I'm only beginning to get to the good stuff."

"Then spit it out." I drummed my fingers over the table, holding my stare.

"Mustafa and your mom had an affair. He was the one who helped provide the enchanted car for her."

It was like the bottom had fallen out, and I was falling. "Are you kidding?"

"I hate to be the bearer of bad news, but no. It's the truth."

"How did my mother get involved with him?"

"If you must know," he exhaled, "In the beginning, Mustafa was assigned to watch over your parents. As the romance between Mustafa and Sara progressed into full bloom, he shirked his duties and lusted after your lovely mother. Unable to stop herself, she fell in love with him, and they ended up... "

Abruptly I interrupted. "Spare me the details. I'm not *that* naïve. Why are you telling me this?" *I now wore* just one more knife to twist in my side.

"I'm saying you may or may *not* have any of your druid father's DNA."

"Shut up! You never mentioned three years ago anything about conception between,"—I swallowed hard—"that *monster* and my mother!"

"You seem to be missing the point!"

627

I glared up at him, "Then fucking enlighten me."

"There is more than one way to skin a cat," he paused for his meaning to sink in... or was it to taunt me? Aidan went on to explain. "Celestial birth isn't like human birth. First of all, it's unnatural. Angels were not created to procreate. That's why the giants of old were so damn vicious."

"That's supposed to make me feel better?"

"Let me clarify, please."

I nodded, holding my tongue any further.

"I didn't lie about the genetic alterations. The Family's scientist, through alien advancement, were able to create something solid, unlike the giants of old. I did not lie about Sara suffering from an alien disease onset by the pregnancy." Aidan drawled. "However, I may have evaded a few details."

"Are you saying that Sara and Mustafa are... " I couldn't say it.

"Oh, they had an affair. Don't worry. You were still a test-tube baby," he grinned, jerking my string. "You were not conceived as the Nephilim. The half angel-half human creatures were impossible to control. The Family wanted a super strength being who's... *manageable*."

"Manageable," I scoffed.

"Our scientist used your father's DNA in order for Sara to carry you to trimester. Once the risk of losing the fetus had waned, our scientist altered your father's DNA. They replaced those cells with a special strand of DNA, enabling cell tissue to metastasize. In fact, the damage your mother suffered came from the *super-cell* regeneration. Coupled with the angel's DNA didn't help either." Aidan paused, dragging in a harsh breath like a longtime smoker. "There are only traces of your father's DNA. That is why you *reek* of human."

"I'd rather smell like my father than stink of alcohol and greed." My eyes tightened. "It sickens me to think how far your family will go to get what they want. Both my parents are dead because of your family's supreme self-preference."

"Sweetheart," his cadence in his voice spewed with arrogance. "Great achievement is usually born of great sacrifice and is never the result of selfishness."

"That's original. You got that quote from Napoleon Hill."

"Touché! I'm impressed. You are smarter than the average hybrid."

"Thanks!" *Not!*

"However, as irreconcilable our difference may be, it was your parents who came to *my* family."

"I don't care," I shouted. "Lives are lost because of your pernicious ambition. You and your Illuminist family have to be stopped."

Aidan's brow shot up, surprised.

"What?" I lashed out. "You didn't think I'd figured out your secret society?"

"Actually, I am quite impressed."

"You forget too easily. My father was one of the thirteen bloodlines."

"True, but Jon forfeited his position. The Illuminati do not take kindly to apostates."

"I remember you once carried the same beliefs as my father."

"And I remember you once shared my bed."

A short laugh escaped my lips. "I guess I saw the error of my ways."

"I can protect you."

"I'm sorry?" My brows furrowed.

"I. Can. Protect. You," he repeated, sharply.

I blinked, staring at him as I saw his irony. "Like the way you protected Dawn?"

He stilled, a vein throbbed at his temple. "Dawn's fate was out of my hands. Sad things happen, and one must move on."

"And you call this moving on?" I waved my hand at his liquor and empty glass.

"Yes, quite frankly I do." His supremacy epitomized the true mark of the Illuminati. "We're about to be in a shit-storm."

A curt laugh escaped my lips. "I think I've been in a shit storm for some time now."

"You have no clue to what is coming."

"Oh, yes I do! We've just begun."

He smiled like he'd discovered the cure for cancer. "This system, as we know it, is coming to a screeching halt. The great tribulations will devour this world." Without warning, his eyes hardened. I recalled that look in Sam's eyes. "The end… is approaching, and it will destroy any living creature in its wake."

"Why should I believe you?"

"You don't have to trust my word. You already sense it. I see it in your eyes."

"Okay, I'll give you that. Explain to me how this will go down."

"First, the religions will go. Then the governments will collapse, starvation and disease will spread throughout the world," Aidan sighed. "If you don't join the Family, then you might as well swallow poison. You're as good as dead anyway. Suffering will be *boundless*." His sharp eyes were disturbing, yet calm. There was something in his movement, his voice, that made me certain he was speaking the truth.

All at once, Aidan did a one eighty flip, flashing a lustful sneer and raking his eyes over me. I was losing my patience with all his mood swings. *Dr. Jekyll and Mr. Hyde much?*

He leaned in and whispered, "Join me and I'll show you what a real man does to a sweet morsel like yourself." He carefully drew back, sitting straight in his chair, eyeing my response.

Bile threatened as his scent of liquor and cigarettes repulsed me. Cigarettes! *When did Aidan start smoking?*

Suddenly, Aidan's interested had shifted to riling Val. He didn't know the Zop leader as well as I did. Val would never fall for such lame bullshit. *I* on the other hand didn't have that kind of moxie.

That was when I erupted. In one swift move, I grasped my dagger, aiming it straight for Aidan's throat. But Val grabbed my hand in midair, snaking his other hand around my waist. When our eyes locked, I calmed, nodding for him to take the knife. I snarled at Aidan as his face gleamed with loathing.

I'd reached my limit. My lungs were closing, the air was stifling. I shared a sideways glance with Val, willing him to get me out of here. Getting my subtle hint, he swept me into his arms and we disappeared.

Considering how my presence irritated Aidan, I figured, out of sight, out of mind. The situation became too volatile for me to remain. Once I was gone, and no longer an eyesore for Aidan, he'd sleep off the booze. Although just for back up, I hoped Jeffery made good with that cast-iron skillet, just in case.

NEW WORLD ORDER

*W*e landed in the back alleyway a few doors down. In the background, a cat hissed, and a couple of dogs were barking. The smell of rotted food drifted in the air.

Once my feet were planted, I'd made a run for the nearest dumpster. My dinner from last night was coming up, and I couldn't stop it. After I'd finished puking my guts up, I realized Val had been beside me, holding my hair back. Could this guy get any better? I tossed a weak smile at him as I indelicately wiped my mouth. For a minute silence rested between us as we shared a moment, gazing in each other's eyes.

"Let's do something fun!" The gold specks in his eyes glistened.

I bit my bottom lip. "I don't know," I shrugged.

"I think it would do you good."

I chewed on my lip, weighing whether or not I should leave the boys and Sally alone with Aidan. "Oh, why not! What do you have in mind?"

"Let's go to a good old-fashioned bayou cookout. Some human friends of mine are throwing it tonight. It'll get you out of the house and away from *him*."

"*Him* meaning Aidan."

"Yup!"

"Okay, but I don't have anything to wear."

Val's eyes swept over me.

"I don't want to wear sweats." I tugged on my top.

"No problem, I'll take you shopping."

"That's sweet, but I can call Jeffery and he... "

Val stopped me in midsentence. "No! I don't want to risk Aidan coming in Jeffery's place, and *my* pad's out." Val thought for a minute as he kicked a rock. "Aidan acts like he owns you."

"You saw that too." I shook my head. "I don't know what I ever saw in him."

Val raked his fingers through his hair. "Men like that think women are property."

"I agree," I paused briefly. "Have you had many encounters with Aidan when you were dating his sister?"

Val released a deep sigh. "Some," he answered curtly, brow arched. "I wouldn't exactly say Helen and I dated. It was more of a mutual enjoyment."

"Why do you say that?"

"She wasn't the relationship kind of gal, too unpredictable." Val leaned against the picket fence, hands stuffed in his pockets.

"How did you come to dislike Aidan so much?" Some things were better left alone, but I was more curious than nine cats.

The corner of Val's lip tightened. "Let's go somewhere a little more suited for private conversation." Val glimpsed over his shoulder.

"Lead the way, chief!"

In a single swift motion, Val had me pressed against his body, wrapping his arms around me like a warm blanket. Erratically my heart began to pound. It was obvious how he affected me. The glint in his eyes revealed he knew it too, and a faint smile painted my face. Val and I had feelings for each other. It was apparent.

It was different with Val. Aidan and Val were as different as night and day. A relationship with Aidan had been doomed from the very start. I was so young and inexperienced. How could I have possibly known what I wanted? Setting aside all things, he was the father of my child, a child I was denied. Would I ever feel closure with Aidan? Could I walk away without looking back? These were questions I couldn't answer, and I wasn't sure I'd ever be able to.

My mind felt muddled, like a fog in the early morning. Right now, all I wanted was to be with Val. With him, everything seemed simple and easy. The dreadful memories of old seemed further in the distance when I was with him.

"You ready to fly?" Val jarred my thoughts. My gaze captured his bright face. A dazzling white smile that I could drink forever.

"Ready as I'll ever be," I smiled back.

$\sim$

Wow! I raked over the surroundings. We had landed somewhere in the midst of the bayou. I stood on a short dock leading up to a boathouse. In its rustic state, it was charming. It was nothing more than a bare, wood-framed cabin that looked like it had never been touched with paint.

In the background, birds were chirping as the sound of water trickled slowly downstream, insects were humming and dragonflies fluttered about, hovering on the surface of the murky water. The smell of wet soil and fish hovered in the water and the cluster of trees. In its rawness, it was breathtaking.

"Welcome to my humble abode." Val smiled, proudly.

"Yeah, it's pretty humble all right." Even through my climbing panic, I couldn't peel my eyes away as I peered about in every direction, Spanish moss hanging from the low branches, cypress trees, majestic, with a broad buttressed base and green foliage clinging to its massive trunk.

"It'll grow on you," Val promised.

"Are there alligators?" I felt my lips go cold.

"Silly girl, it's the bayou! Of course there are gators!"

"Holy mother of god! This is the *best* you can do?" My brows knitted, affright.

"Oh, come on! Where's your adventure? Don't worry! Gators aren't out."

"That's a relief." I wrapped my arms around my waist, trying to hold back my need to scream bloody hell.

"But when twilight falls, it might be best if you didn't venture too far from the cabin. They like to roam at night."

"Holy shit! Take me home! I mean it! I hate gators!" I rested my hands on my hips, glaring at Val. It didn't help ease my nerves any when he roared with laughter. *Men were such difficult creatures... or*

633

should I say Zops.

I just shook my head and stalked past him, entering the dim cabin. Val followed behind me with a trail of laughter.

"I'll open up the windows. There's usually a great breeze that flows through." He turned around with a huge grin and froze when he saw the look of terror plastered to my face. "What's wrong now?" His brows scrunched.

"Have I mentioned how much I hate snakes too?"

He cuffed his hand over his mouth. Obviously he was stifling a laugh. "No, I don't believe you have." Humor in his tone was as deep as his voice.

My face soured like a double dose of lemons. "Well, I don't like snakes either!"

Val crossed the floor in only one stride and gathered me into his arms. "Freckles, nothing is going to happen to you here. What you see is the life of the bayou, a mystical place of great wonder. That's why so many of our kind are drawn to this place."

"Just for the record, I'm not the usual Zop." Suddenly the light banter between Val and me changed as the memories flashed through my mind of the conversation with Aidan. I shivered, worrying. "Do you think Jeffery and Dom are safe? Sally too?" I chewed the inside of my cheek.

"I think they're perfectly fine. Maybe Aidan will take a liking to Sally again?"

"Aidan and Sally were a couple?"

"You didn't know?"

"I reckon not." I dragged in a fretful breath. "They both denied hooking up." In spite of their claims, I had suspicions that neither one was entirely truthful. "How long have they been messing around?"

"It's been on again and off again for years."

"Did you see them together?"

"Yeah, from time to time. I'd crossed their paths now and again when Helen and I were together."

"Really! Were they serious?"

"Not from what I could tell." Val opened a window, then made his way back to me. "Or at least Aidan wasn't committed. He had another girl stringing along besides Sally. Why? Do you know something that I don't?" His brow arched.

I shook my head. "Probably not. It's just Aidan's and Sally's story seems off. You know, he says, she says." I shrugged. "It's not important now."

"Aidan only tells what he feels is necessary." Val's words were smothered in bitterness.

I felt unsure about the next question, but I couldn't stop myself. "Did you ever see Aidan and Sally together in Tangi?"

"No, it was here in New Orleans. They have a huge plantation on the outskirts of town." Val seemed to know more about Aidan than I did. It struck me wrong too.

"*They* as in together?"

"Yes. As in plural, couple, pair…"

"I get it! I get it!" I held my palm out. In my next breath, I asked, "So, *they* have the floating castle?"

"No. This one is permanent. It's an old plantation just on the outskirt of the city."

"Plantation? On land?"

"He didn't tell you?" Val sounded as surprised as I was.

"No, he didn't." Clearly I was left in the dark about a lot of things.

"Don't beat yourself up over it. Aidan is a master of deception."

I sensed something more between Val and Aidan. Funny how history repeated itself. Sam came to mind. "Why do I get the feeling that there's something you're not telling me?"

Suddenly, Val's face tensed. "Let's go sit outside on the porch and get comfortable." He touched the small of my back, ushering me to the deck.

"Sure," I smiled. While I seemed at ease on the surface, my mind was reeling on the inside. What other inconceivable trouble must I face before the sun sets today, I fretted.

I was happy to get out of the cabin and into the river air. The smell of musk and dirty socks triggered my sensitive stomach. The cabin definitely had the traits of a *guy's pad*.

After we both settled down in a couple of chairs in a corner of the deck, Val rested his elbows on his knees, leaning forward. When my eyes lifted, I saw uneasiness in his expression.

I took his hand into mine. "What's wrong," I asked.

"I've known Aidan from way back."

"Oh!" I stiffened.

"I never told you this, but I have a sister."

Taken aback, "You have a sibling?"

"*Had*, depending on how you look at it." Val's jaw twitched.

"You said *had* as if in the past?"

"Yes. My sister's been missing for a while now."

"Oh, my!"

"Helen and my sister were friends." A pain hit. Hearing her name whirled me back to the dark secret I'd been keeping about Helen's death. I knew eventually I'd have to tell him, but for now, I pushed it down and focused on Val as he explained. "Aidan dated my sister, Sienna."

"I'm confused. I thought he was dating Sally?"

"He was dating both. Neither girl knew."

"What a dog!"

"You got that right!" Val bit back a snarl. "Anyway, despite his wondering eye, there was talk of marriage. He'd even went as far as giving my sister an engagement ring. The marriage never happened. Instead, Sienna disappeared, and Aidan ducked out of the country for months until you moved to Tangi. That's when he resurfaced."

"Do you think my coming to Tangi had anything to do with your sister's disappearance?"

"Not directly."

"I don't understand."

It seemed Val was warring with his inter-self. Then he just said it, "I think there's a triangle between Aidan, you *and* Sienna's vanishing."

My brow perked. "Do you think I'm responsible?"

"No! Hell no! What I *do* think, is that Sienna found out about the prior arrangement between the families, the blood contract binding Aidan and you to marriage. I think my sister confronted Aidan and the argument went sour."

My eyes orbed, surprised. "How did you learn about the blood contract?"

"When you revealed your past to me, it had solidified what I have been already suspecting. Things have a way getting back to me." He smiled, but it didn't match his wounded eyes.

"Rumors, huh?"

"Yeah," Val snorted a curt laugh and shrugged. "Even the angels gossip."

I smiled. "Small world, huh?"

"Yeah, very." Then the cadence in his deep voice became dour. "I never told you this," he breathed. "But, I knew you were framed. I tried finding you, but you went off the grid."

My mouth dropped. "That first night in your bar, you knew who I was?"

"Yes."

"Why are you now just telling me this?"

"I actually wasn't sure of my hunch until your essence rattled the floor in my bar. Afterwards, I knew without a doubt you were the souped-up Zop." He dropped his eyes from mine, staring out at the river.

"Why are you sharing this with me now?"

"I think you have a right to know," his brows furrowed, deeply. "I hate secrets." His eyes latched hold of mine. I looked away, feeling like the worst person ever. The secret I held was much darker and I was sure he'd hate me when I told him. I bit my bottom lip, quickly changing the subject. "Did you hear what Aidan said about my genetic code? I don't have *any* trace of human."

"I heard."

"This is good news. I'm not a hybrid. I'm a full blooded Zop!"

Val rooted his fingers through his disheveled curls. "I have to be honest with you."

"Okay." I didn't breathe.

"I understand how the Illuminati played God, creating you in a lab. They used human DNA in the beginning, then they replaced it with a replica super-cell substance that they designed to boost your abilities. Making *you* a very powerful young angel."

"Wow," I stated as my mouth hung open.

He tossed a lopsided grin. "I did some snooping."

"Yeah, I guess so," I paused, mulling over the enlightened facts he'd landed in my lap. Then my heart lurched. "Since I no longer have human DNA, wouldn't that make me a pure Zop?"

"Not necessarily. You are still an impure according to my kind."

I wanted to gnaw off my arm, grrr! "You explained to me that I am an outcast, consequences of my human traits!"

"Yes and no. There's more to it. Only those who have been blessed

637

with divine creation are pure and natural. I'm sorry, Freckles. That's our law." Val squeezed my knee, showing empathy.

I didn't need his pity. Acceptance was what I needed. All my life I'd been disconnected, an outsider. Now that I'd found a kinship with creatures like myself, I still was marked as an outcast. I sighed with frustration. "I hate being alone."

Val gathered my chin in his hand, drawing my eyes to his level, "You're not alone." He smiled, brightly. "I'm here with you, aren't I?"

"Yes, but for how long?" I let myself sink into his golden eyes.

"I can't answer that," Val barely whispered.

This was a battle I couldn't win. "Okay, enough about me. Tell me more about your sister. You said she disappeared?"

"Yeah," swiftly Val's face dropped as he sighed, "As it went down, Aidan wouldn't let my sister out of his sight. It was like she was his possession."

"I find it odd that Aidan never mentioned your sister." I paused, sitting straight in my chair. "Now it makes perfect sense. You didn't want to help me because of... "

Val interrupted. "You got it."

"Why am I not surprised."

Val's upper lip twisted.

"I can't wrap my head around all this devilry. Will Aidan and the Illuminati ever stop destroying lives?"

"Good question." Val shook his head.

"Is there anything I can do to help in your search for your sister?" My heart went out to him.

"I don't know where else to look." Pain colored his face. "I've turned every rock there is, but I keep coming up empty handed."

Chills crept over the back of my neck as I recalled how Aidan eliminated Sam's body. Even though the death of Sam was justified, I prayed that Aidan hadn't gone to that same measure with Val's sister. Tears welled. "You can't give up!"

"I know." There was anger behind Val's glint. An anger I often saw in myself.

"Were you close?"

"Yes, very. She was my little sister, and I failed her."

"How?"

"I tried warning her about Aidan. She wouldn't hear it. My sister idolized him. I should've forced her to listen to me."

I squeezed his hand, leaning toward him. "There was nothing you could've done. This isn't your fault."

"I should've locked her up and thrown the key away or…" Val pressed his lips tight.

"And, she would've hated you for it."

"But she'd be alive." Val's eyes filled with sorrow.

"You can't be certain she's gone now. You have to know that!"

"I guess so," Val nodded, inhaling a somber breath. "The unknowing is worse than her death."

"I know." I was familiar with that feeling far too well.

"I have to ask," he started, his eyes, intense, "Are you still carrying a torch for *him*?"

Taken off guard, I paused, glimpsing over-way at the river. The buzz of insects were in harmony with the flow of the stream. I listened for a moment. As strange as it seemed though, I wasn't a woodsy kinda girl, but the strum of the bayou seemed to ease my mind. I sighed, looking Val in the face. I answered as honestly as I could, but even then, my heart acted upon its own accord. "I won't lie. I have mixed feelings. He was my first, and we did share a child together, even though there wasn't much sharing." Then I whispered. "You must know you are the one. It's you I dream about, who I desire, not *Aidan*."

"How can I relax knowing there is unfinished business between you two? I saw it in your eyes today." Val searched deep into my eyes.

"After today, I think that business is resolved. He's not the same person." My hand lifted to his stubbled chin. His features were breathtaking, like an angel. Our eyes locked. "Let's enjoy our time together now."

"For now." Val's eyes crinkled as he leaned in and kissed me. It was sweet, yet, compared to last time, the spark seemed absent. Considering everything we'd been through today, it was no wonder. I stayed in a constant confusion.

Val drew back with a possessive glint. "You can't go back to him. He's dangerous and cannot be trusted."

"I don't plan to," I inhaled, "My eyes are wide open now."

"I'm glad to hear that." He smiled, but it didn't reach his eyes. "You know, we have to stop them."

"I agree, but they're indestructible."

A mischievous grin stained Val's face. "Funny you should say that," his eyes twinkled. "We are on the brink of war."

I choked on my breath. "Oh my god! Aidan was not joking."

"As much as I hate to admit it, part of what Aidan said is true. It's the part about the Illuminati taking over that I disagree with. That's why our side is gathering forces."

Trepidation curled around my spine. "Our side! Zop?"

"Not just the *Zophasemin* but the entire galaxy. Spiritual forces are gathering as we speak."

"Whoa! We might be facing extermination."

"It won't come to that. We plan to fight back!" The conviction in Val's tone screamed volumes.

"Oh, dear lord!"

"If the Illuminati succeeds, we are doomed. You think Hitler was bad, stick around. The Illuminati is the *mother* of all monstrosities." Determination rode strongly in his face.

"I'm afraid!" I was inspired looking at Val and his intensity, but at the same breath, I was utterly terrified.

"You and me both." He brushed his thumb across my cheek.

"What will come of Jeffery and Dom? Innocent people?" I sat there blinking, unable to process this nightmare. Aidan's warning of the world ending, Val speaking of war, it was really happening. I snapped my head up, catching Val's eyes, "Do you think we stand a chance?"

"I don't know." Wary lines etched across Val's face. "The Illuminati's enforcement is infinite, endorsed with supernatural forces far more powerful and far more advanced than we have ever encountered."

"But you're angels! You have special powers." I stared at Val with disbelief.

"Yes, we have abilities, not like the Family's."

"I can help," I rushed. "The Illuminati created me for war. My genetic design is twofold. You said yourself I was powerful." It just hit me like a ton of bricks falling from the sky. *I* was a weapon.

Val raised my hand to his lips and gently kissed my palm. I blinked back.

"Absolutely, not! You are nowhere near ready for something of this magnitude."

"I might be the answer to your prayers." I damn near screamed.

"Don't you think they have created others like you?"

"If there are others like me then that's even more reason why you need me," I countered.

"It's not only genetically engineered angels in this war, Freckles."

"I already know about the fey," I explained.

"I'm not talking about the Seelie or Unseelie."

"Who, then?" I dared to ask.

"The Illuminati has harvested the DNA of the giants. They're bringing back the Nephilim as we speak. I know you've heard of area 51?"

"I have, but I thought the Nephilim were irrepressible?"

"True. They were impossible to control in the past. However, the Family found a way to bypass that problem. They discovered a way to create mass armies of genetically altered giants. They are contained at area 51. It is the best unkept secret the government has ever had. These altered giants are trained assassins, invincible, and with the flip of a switch, they can eradicate an entire species. Ever heard of genocide?" Val's words were filled with hard truth.

"Yes." I began to feel my skin growing pale. I thought surely I'd faint.

"If we don't fight back that's what we are facing, but the Illuminati are not the only enemies that we are dealing with." Val's jaw tightened. "Sweetie, I'm sorry to bring his name up."

My brows dipped down into a v as my heart hammered at my chest. "No," I softly whispered.

But Val didn't listen. "Mustafa took your daughter's life force in order to preserve his own life. He no longer is an ally of the Family. They plan to kill him. Therefore he's been gathering his own army as well. I felt you should know what you're up against."

I jumped up, knocking my chair over. "Stop, Val!" I held up my hands in protest. "I can't hear anymore." I stalked past him to the far side of the deck and held my head over to vomit. I couldn't bear thinking about that murderous angel. I was sickened with fright for my family and even Val. With my brain about to implode, I wiped my mouth with my sleeve. It wasn't long before I heard the shuffle of soft footfalls, it was Val coming up behind me. Instantaneously, his arms snaked around my waist. I turned around and buried my face into his consoling chest. He towered over my small frame, and I molded easily to his body. I felt safe in his arms.

"Val," I softly spoke.

"Yes," he replied, tenderly.

"You are so special to me and I can't imagine not having you in my life." I spoke just above a whisper. He was my rock and I adored him for that.

His golden eyes twinkled as he answered, "I know." Then he bent to kiss me on my forehead, and I smiled. Though he didn't speak his heart, it wasn't necessary. I knew he cared about me. He had been by my side through everything. I trusted him with my life and maybe my heart too.

It seemed we stayed embraced in each other's arms for a long while. Then Val interjected, gazing into my eyes. "He can't stay with you. If he hurts you, I'll kill him." I didn't' doubt that Val would carry his threat out without hesitance or regret.

I trembled over the thought of those two brawling. "I'll handle it."

Val groaned. "I'd rather you let me take care of your rodent infestation." An impish grin stretched the corners of his lips.

"No! I rather you not," I sternly declined. "I really don't think Aidan will hurt me. Besides, if you got hurt, it'd kill me." Laughter filled my eardrums as I felt the rise and fall of Val's chest as he roared.

"Stop it!" I slugged him in the arm, then I rolled my eyes. "Of course you are more than capable of defending yourself. It's just," I hesitated. "Aidan's diabolical, and… " I couldn't finish what I needed to say.

Val gently took my chin into his grasp. "I can hold my own, Freckles." His eyes glittered as he smiled. His deep voice was reassuring. I loved when he spoke in his native tongue.

I needed to know the answer right then and there. Then I asked in our Zop language, "You think I'm pretty awesome, don't you?" I smiled into his bright face.

He laughed, and then he hugged me tight. "I do. I really do." I shook my head and giggled to myself. The damnedest thing… this man had me, and he knew it too. Oh, well. It could be a lot worse.

THE BAYOU

*V*al made sure the coast was clear at my house before we popped in.

It was a huge relief to discover that Aidan had clocked out from the liquor he'd ingested, sleeping most of the day. The house had settled, nothing compared to earlier today.

I had the opportunity to grab a quick bath and throw on some decent clothes for the barbecue. Even Val used my shower and changed clothing.

I found a note on the counter in the kitchen from Dom. He had taken Sally to dinner and planned to go shopping afterward. Jeffery stayed home, spending the evening alone.

When I could no longer bear to look at his pouty face, I invited him to come along. Although before I'd finished my sentence, he'd grabbed his picnic basket full of goodies as if he'd read my mind.

Off we went, the three of us in the Mustang, Val volunteered to be the designated driver. We could've ridden on his shirt-tail in a matter of seconds, but I didn't feel comfortable materializing in front of unacquainted people. Couple with Val's uncertainty of who was coming, we thought the human means of travel would be the wisest. It was a nice change, and glimpsing at Jeffery, I think he appreciated the grounded ride. I spotted him dabbing his forehead with a napkin after we'd decided on our means of transportation.

As it turned out, I think Val enjoyed the ride the most, leaving tire tracks in our wake, coiling corners, nearly tilting the car on two wheels a couple of times.

Poor Jeffery got stuck in the backseat with his long legs bunched up to his neck. I reckoned by the dire expression on his face, he didn't care much for the ride either. After a short distance down the road and the speediness of Val's playful driving, Jeffery's face paled. I smiled to myself. Obviously, my good friend wasn't a thrill seeker, or at least a race car thriller. I loved my Jeffery, either way.

Passed the out-skirts of the city, we ventured down an unmarked dirt-road, headed to the invite. I could hear the river only a few feet away in the distance, on the other side of the tree line. The water ebbing downstream and its strange spoor of fish and mud wafted into the air. For a second, I thought I'd seen a pair of red eyes crest the surface of the water. I shivered, drawing my knees to my chest. I slid a sideways glance at Val. "How bad are the gators in this swamp?" Dread stiffened the hairs on my neck.

A curt snicker floated over the purr of the car as Val held his laugh back. "We're at the basin, low ground. If a little old gator comes after you, you'll have plenty of time to shimmy up a tree." The gold specks in his eyes sparkled with humor.

"Funny guy," I growled as my eyes shot daggers at him.

"Chile," Jeffery chimed from the backseat, "If a gator comes for *me*, *gurrrlfriend*, I'm pushin' you in front!" He pursed his lips. "Ain't no gator gettin' none of this!" His hands rolled over his body, fluidly.

"Jeffery, where's the love, bro," I teased. Both Val and I laughed. Jeffery pouted.

When we turned off the road onto a dirt drive toward what I presumed must be the place, I caught sight of a small frame house nestled back amidst the mossed trees. There were telltale signs that the house once had been white. Now, the paint had chipped away, giving the weather-worn house a sense of eeriness.

I picked up on a soft hum of cicadas in the background that seemed to flow with the river stream behind the house.

As I drew in my surroundings, I came to appreciate the rawness of this place. There was life here. From human to critter, they all depended on the bayou for existence.

Val parked the car in a clearing by the side of the house. Before I place my hand on the door handle, Val was opening my door and extending his hand. I thought how sweet. I smiled in his face, accepting his offer.

As I eased out of the car I stopped, my smile fading. My eyes fell upon several long-haired, bandana wearing, tattooed, scruffy-looking men, chugging down long-neck beers. Though I was put off, the men appeared to be in good spirits, laughing, gathered around a home-made cinderblock barbeque pit.

Gray smoke curled from the grill's blaze, and a sweet aroma drifted our way. Whatever they were cooking, it smelled delicious.

Mirroring my same concerns, Jeffery spoke up. "I think I might best sit in this nice car." He hugged his basket close to his chest. "Them folks ain't the sort to take kindly to me or my exquisite caviar. As lovely as I am, I gotta sneakin' suspicion, they'd prefer eatin' me rather than the fish eggs." Jeffery's lips tightened, carefully eye-balling our new acquaintances.

Val teased. "They don't bite, bro, but they might take those nasty eggs and use 'em for baiting gators." Then he winked at me.

Jeffery almost shrieked. "I say *hell* to the *nah!* No ugly mofo beast is gonna touch my Beluga Caviar! It was near impossible to get these lovely black eggs. They're sorta off the market, if you get what I mean," he yammered on. "Don't think I won't hurt a bitch! Uh-hmm, I ain't playin'." He snapped his fingers and bounced his head in a rhythmic motion.

Val burst into laughter. I stifled mine, just a little. Then I had to say my worries too. "Jeff does have a point. These folks seem a bit sketchy." They reminded me of the folks at *The Devil's Den*." I counted ten people, seven men and three women. I spotted bikes parked on the other side of the dirt drive. By the jackets that clung to their chest, it was safe to assume these locals belonged to a biker's gang, a type you didn't want to cross or meet in a dark alley. Rough folks in this neck of the bayou had a particular skill of bad. Not even a genetically engi-neered angel wanted to cross *these* Louisianans.

I glared at Val, full of sarcasm. "Gee, I feel overdressed." Val's eyes combed over me from head to toe, amusement glued to his face.

I guess if my raggedy jeans and scuffed-up boots might be over the top for *his* friends, my friend here, Jeffery, was really going to make an impression, looking like a James Cagney black and white movie wearing a scarf tucked into his smoking jacket.

Val chuckled. "You and Jeff will fit in just fine. C'mon. They're not so bad once you get to know them." Val smiled at me and glanced down at Jeffery coiled in the backseat. "Come on, bro! You can hold your own. Besides, I'll protect you. I give you my word." Val reached his arm out to help Jeff climb out of the tight back seat. I think Jeffery liked Val's assistance by the sparkle in his eyes. Then he complained. "I like tight situations, but that backseat ain't one of 'em. Uh-hmm, it sure ain't!" Jeffery pursed his lips as he held on a moment too long to Val's arm.

Val and I couldn't help laughing at that comment. Like I said, I love my Jeffery.

Soon we heard shouts coming from the circle of men. One of the bikers bellowed at Val in an offbeat French. "Qu'est-ce que tu fou la?" (What the hell you doing here?)

Val yelled back. "Comme d'hab'!" (Same shit, different day.) I just stared at him in awe. I had no idea Val spoke French. Sometimes you think you know someone, and then you get a surprise slapped in the face.

The tall biker stepped out from among the others and greeted Val with a hardy bro hug. You know, the hug where men grasp each other's hand and lean in, pounding each other's back 'till it stings like an old-fashioned beating.

The biker appeared easy on the eyes in a rough, down and dirty way. A good way, if you get my drift. His hair was coal black, a little long, and its curls laid nicely around his ears. His eyes gleamed like dark chocolate, matching his bronze tan. He had defined arms with a strange tattoo starting from his biceps up to his neck, resembling scrolls or a vine. It reminded me of ancient scrolls or symbols like runes. It was enthralling and intimidating at the same time. He was a big man, standing as tall and broad as Val. Starting with his boots to his sleeveless black tee and bandana, he fit the profile of a true biker, and that little shade across his chiseled chin made him appear quite tantalizing.

Once I reached Val's side, the biker's deep-brown eyes hitched with mine, though when he spoke, it wasn't directed at me. His odd behavior threw me off a bit. Looking straight at me, he spoke in a deep husky voice in partial French. He cursed. "*Merde!* (Oh, shit!) I see you finally caught a decent *fille*! *Non* one of those *grosse puffiest*? *Oui?*" (Skanky Sluts)

"True. Watch this one. She's a spitfire." Val winked at me. Then Val's friend gave me his undivided attention by taking my hand and kissing it gently. "Enchanté!" A glint in his deep browns told me he was trouble. Quite a ladies' man.

I replied back, "Evening!" I half smiled.

He didn't' reply back but with only a slight smirk in his expression. Then he turned his full attention on Val and skipped right over Jeffery. "Did you come to *c'est la fete*?" (Party)

"Mon un copain," (My buddy) "I sure did and brought friends too! This is my *copine*, (girlfriend) Stevie, and our good *ami*, (friend) Jeffery. Guys! Meet Nick Bourdain." Val politely introduced us.

"Bonjour, everyone! Welcome!" Then the friend leaned in to Val and whispered, "Tacopine est raiment bonne!" (Your girlfriend is hot!) The Cajun smiled as he elbowed Val in the ribs. My *boyfriend* just smiled, glancing over his shoulder at me. Little did they know I knew a little French myself?

Val, with a glint in his eyes, said to his tall, dark, and handsome *ami*, "Watch out. She doesn't play."

"What? Will *elle m'a poignard`e dans le dos?*" (Will she knife me in the back) The biker mocked Val's warning.

"Nope, *mon ami. Copine* will do it to your face, and she hits her target every time," Val smiled, proudly.

"Hmm, *dat petite one?*" Surprise seeped into the biker's voice, but his eyes displayed an admiration. I played along, acting as if I hadn't a clue to what they were discussing. In school, I'd taken several courses of French and during the summer, I'd go down to the library and check out tutorial tapes, teaching myself. I caught on pretty fast too. I smiled inwardly. This should be interesting.

"Come, let's all have a good time! Yes? *C'est `a boire qu'il nous faut!*" (Something to drink is what we need!) "I have a head start. *Un peu saoul!*" (A bit drunk!)

"Guess I better catch up, eh?" Val patted his friend on the back as we approached the small cluster of people.

Everyone stood around the warm fire as the introductions circled around with broken French and English. Jeffery started to relax after everyone welcomed him with open arms. That's what I loved about this strange place. With all its diversity and weirdness, folks here seemed to be open to everyone, no stiff shirts around the working class. Despite the bayou's constant threat, I found myself loving this extraordinary state. It felt like home.

After a while, everyone kicked back and enjoyed in the light-hearted natter. I settled down, leaning against one of the old trucks that was mostly rust and flat tires. It had to have been as old as the house. Circling the line of the vehicle, weeds had grown past the thread bared tires, and vines had taken home, creeping over the cab and bed.

Val disappeared to the bathroom, called the backwater, and I was left alone. Jeffery was handing out his expensive caviar and crackers. I never cared for the nasty stuff.

When I looked up, the Cajun was strutting his way to me. Although the biker seemed sober by his steady feet, he must've chugged down a couple of cases of beer tonight. I watched him down one whole bottle in one gulp, and without hesitation, he opened another. Apparently, he was accustomed to drinking. There was something about a man who could hold his liquor. I watched as he approached.

"Finally, she is alone." His French accent appeared deeper than earlier. I suspect it might've had something to do with the alcohol.

"Yeah, these days that's a rarity." I tossed a slight tug of a smile at the biker.

"You are too beautiful to hang with such trash. You should get with me. I could teach you a thing or two. Yes?" The Cajun leaned against the truck, invading my personal space, breathing his beer breath in my face. "If you like, I could, *chéri* take the *crème de at frambroise?*" (Cream off your raspberry?) "Or maybe *je peux t'embrasser?*" (I kiss you?)

It didn't take me speaking French to understand that this dude was coming on to me while his friend had his back turned.

"You're a pig," I hissed.

The Cajun arched his eyebrow. "*Oui,* a pig you might enjoy!" He flashed a pearly smile.

"Throw in another log. I think we're not through barbequing," I replied in short.

The Cajun paused, searching deeply into my eyes. "Je suis raiment de`sole`!" (I'm truly sorry.) I was only having some fun with you. Nick likes to tease. Yes?"

"I see that, and Nick likes referring to himself in third person as well," I snorted.

"So are you some kind of good girl saving yourself?" His grin felt naughty.

"I don't see how that's any of your business."

"Bebè, you are wound up too tight."

"And you are an expert?" I smirked.

"I can tell. It's deep in your *âme*" (Soul).

I laughed, "I have no soul." My face reflected coldness.

His eyes searched deep into mine. "Qu'est-ce que tu foul'a?" (What the hell you doing here?)

I kept a straight face. "My mother moved me here." Why was he asking me all these questions?

"Smart woman, your mom. She come to the right place. Yes?"

"No," I said, irritated.

"No? Why?" His brows knitted.

"She died."

"Oh, I'm terribly sorry. You are so young to lose your mother."

"Thank you." I didn't want to share my problems with this guy. I looked away, spotting Jeffery chatting with one of the biker girls. I changed the subject quickly. "Are any of these ladies your date?"

"Maybe? The night is still young." A little arrogance flashed in his eyes.

"So what? You say 'Woman, come hither!'" I mimicked his accent, lowering my voice.

His eyes glittered. "*Oui*, something like that."

"You see a girl you want, you just take her even if she has a man?"

"*Oui!* Old Nick has his way with the ladies," he brazenly teased.

"Well, saint Nick, not *this* lady," I flashed a smug grin. I had it with his unconcealed arrogance. I pushed off from the truck and started to pass him, then he grabbed my arm, and through his throaty voice, he whispered, "If you were mine, I'd never let you out of my sight."

"*So says the Cajun womanizer.* You are so full of shit," I called him out on his absurdity. When I looked into his eyes, there was laughter and something else. A challenge? Just what I needed, another man in my life. I jerked my arm free, snarled at the Cajun, and without another word, I walked away.

Moments later when Val returned to my side from the call of nature,

649

I nearly bit his head off as I lit into him, "Your friend is a horny bastard!"

Val burst into guffaws, and everyone else followed. Obviously, Nick's reputation served him well. As I stood there gawking at Val, I mumbled, "Te de vier!" (Dickhead) What else could I've said after he laughed in my face? I wasn't sure I liked Val around these friends. He was different.

Later, after we'd eaten smoked pig, (no not the Cajun) with side dishes of roasted potatoes and corn on the cob, we all gathered around the fire. Some sat in lawn chairs, others sat on the ground. Val made a spot for himself beside Jeffery on a large tree stump. I joined them by crawling into Val's lap. There was a slight chill in the air, blowing off the river. Snuggling up to Val, embraced in his arms and sitting close to the fire, soothed my chill. I laid my head against his shoulder, resting my eyes. The day had been a tough one, and the effects of the day was starting to wear on me.

It seemed the food and drink were taking its toll as quiet began to settle over the circle of friends. Everyone seemed to drift off into their private thoughts.

When I opened my eyes, I spotted Nick eye-balling me. It took me by surprise and made me very uncomfortable. Earlier, I thought his flirting was annoying but harmless. Now I was beginning to wonder if his interest was teetering on weird? I glimpsed at Val, and as we shared a familiar glance, I leaned over and kissed him for what seemed like forever. Then I heard his friend bellow out! "I didn't think *ange* kiss?" (angels' kiss) He taunted.

"There's lots of things a Zop can do, which I won't say in mix company," Val threw back at his friend.

"Such a gentleman. A real woman wants hot passion. Throw her down and make love to her as though it's the last. Passion, my friend, passion!"

"Don't worry, Saint Nick. I have this handled," Val called back.

"*Frere!* (*Brother*) What do you know? *Il `ecoute pas personne parce qu'il est!*" (He doesn't listen to anyone because he's in love.)

The gang began laughing. I rolled my eyes. I glanced at Jeffery, and he had his basket of goodies clung to his chest, hugging it tightly. Maybe we should leave.

"Val, let's go!"

"Are you sure?" He looked surprised.

"Yeah. I'm feeling a bit uneasy."

"Okay." Val dragged in a deep sigh.

I slipped off him and realized, I needed to use the bathroom first. That trip back down this long bumpy road would be torture if I didn't go. "Hey, is there a bathroom I could use, and please, don't you dare point to that damn swamp," I warned.

I could see the humor in Val's glint. "Yup, go around to the back part of the house. Just go in. No one's in there."

"Okay, I'll be back." I turned to Jeff. "Come with me, please."

"I'm already with you, honey. I think I need to tinkle too, and I ain't taking no risk going out by the bayou where some big alligator might think I'm dangling my thang as bait. Oh no, he can't get this!" Jeffery was up and on his way to the back of the house nearly five paces ahead of me. I think it was fair to say Jeffery hated gators worse than me. Even still, I couldn't help laughing, and at the same time, I was grossed out by the picture painted in my brain.

When we reached the back porch, the backlight was shining brightly and only the screen door closed. We stepped up to the wooden porch, our footfall thumped against the planks. I noted a couple of rocking chairs in the corner and a couple of potted plants of bright-red geranium sitting on the other side of the chairs.

Wasting no time, Jeffery made a nosedive straight for the bathroom, first. I suppose with his wiggling and holding his knees together like a five year old, he couldn't wait another minute. I stepped into the kitchen, the screen squeaking in my ear, and stood just inside, waiting. I figured by the age of the house, there was only one bathroom.

While I was picking on my nails with growing impatience for Jeffery to finish, out of nowhere, I heard a woman's voice from the back, calling, "I'm comin'! Just hold on to your knickers," she called out in a heavy French pitch. I stiffened. I could've sworn Val said no one was here.

In my next breath, an elderly lady, small frame, limped into the kitchen. "What you need, child?" Her voice was choppy like most aging.

I began to stammer. "I'm-I'm so-so *sorry*. We were told the house was empty. My friend and I need to borrow your bathroom, if you would be so kind, ma'am."

"Why didn't you say so? Come in!" She spread her lips into a tooth-less grin. I smiled back.

The elderly lady went to the stove where a kettle was steaming. I spotted two white cups in saucers laid out on the counter. I sensed she was expecting me for tea. The lady turned the burner off and started to pour herself a cup. She glimpsed up at me, "Would you care for some tea?" I noticed she had stunning blue eyes. They were such an odd color. I first thought she might be blind, they were so pale, but she seemed to know her way around too well to be sightless.

"Sure, thank you." I didn't know why I said yes. I wasn't in the mood for conversation, yet I was drawn to her.

"Here, come have a seat. Your friend will be in there for a while. He's not use to spicy foods." She set a white cup and saucer full of piping tea on the table and waved for me to sit. "By the way, I'm Mable." She took her seat at the table.

"Hello, Mable. I'm Stevie." I smiled, thinking how much I dreaded using the bathroom after Jeffery. I eased out an oh-well sigh and seated myself next to the lady of the house.

For a minute I sat silent, sipping tea. The taste was a little bitter but familiar. "What kind of tea is this," I asked, curious.

"Oolong."

"It's nice." I held my cup up, the corners of my mouth slightly tugged.

"Thank you." She placed her tea down into its saucer and cleared her throat. "The man you come with tonight, is he your boyfriend," she inquired.

"Sorta. We haven't made it official."

"Do you know why?" Her eyes were sober.

"Uh… we're taking it slow."

"Oh, I see."

I smiled, feeling awkward, sipping my tea.

"He is *immonde*?" (not of this world)

I damn near spewed my drink, choking. "Excuse me," I coughed.

"I see him from time to time." She took a short breath as though she was a little winded, "His feet may touch dirt, but he is far from earthly. He belongs to another realm, as you are *amarrer* to another." (Tied) She lifted her cup to her lips and slurped the golden liquid.

"I'm sorry?" Play dumb, deny, deny, I coaxed myself.

"You are locked into a bond that is unbreakable, are you not?" The elderly woman's mouth knitted tightly.

Chills began to creep down my spine. "I'm bound to many." I didn't mean to sound snide, but she caught me off guard.

Then our conversation really got weird. "The company you keep are without *âme*." (soul) Her eyes were too piercing. "Se prennent pour le centre da min de (Think they're the center of the universe). Those bankers," the odd lady whispered, leaning in, "maybe *they* are."

It was as if she was in my head. "I'm not following you." I played as if I was nescient to her meaning.

"There are consequences when you toy with black magick."

I blinked, lost for words.

"Let me see your cup," the lady soothed me into obeying.

Without a word, I slid my cup and saucer over to her. She snatched up the set, placing the saucer on top of the cup, holding it tightly together. Then she flipped the set over and separated the two dishes. She held the cup, peering inside at the wet leaves. She studied it for several minutes.

I watched, frozen.

Unannounced, the lady's face soured, lines deepened over her face. She glimpsed up at me. "There is pain. You have lost. A child?" she stared up at me, asking.

"Yes," I simply answered. I swallowed the knot rising in my throat. I didn't want to fall apart.

The lady continued. "I see trouble... a *joker*. This one is full of trickery. He is wearing some sort of jewelry that marks him."

I gasped, needles pricking my neck. I sat there silent.

"He is an imposter. Beware!" She holds the cup closer. "There is going to be great change to your life and those you hold close to your heart." Her face lifted with excitement. "Ah! This is good!" I was fretful of her definition of *good*. "There is *faire l'amour*!" (Love) You will find a lost love, your true love." She glanced up into my face and smiled.

I frowned.

"*Non, non!* He will be your *amour ne dépendant de rien*." (true love) She went on. "He is dark, but his heart will change. You like this! No?"

"I'm happy with someone now."

"I don't think so." She shook her head. "Believe half of what you see and trust nothing."

"Come again?" Suddenly my blood iced. Aidan once told me a similar riddle.

"Nothing is what it seems. The one you are with is not the one."

"I know my heart," I disputed.

"Maybe, maybe not," she shrugged. "You are young."

I crossed my arms, tired of this conversation. Where is Jeffery? Did he fall? I stared at the lady as she eyed me carefully through her strange colored eyes.

"I see someone from your past will emerge." She tilted the cup to the side for me to view. "See this line?"

I nodded.

"This line shows that a dark-haired, blued-eyed man from your past will become your *protecteur*." Her face puzzled. "Though I can't see his face." She studied the tea leaves closer, face tensed. "Something is blocking my view. He is hazy."

I rolled my eyes. I couldn't help it. "I don't need protecting."

"*No?*" Mable nodded at my feet. "Check your boots and pants too."

I reached in both boots and found nothing. I dug in the back of my pants. Nothing! *Enculè de at mère!* (Motherf...!) I took a sharp breath. "Excusez-moi. I need to have a word with someone." I said through clenched teeth as I leaped from my chair heading out the door.

"Oh," the lady called out to me. "Will you give someone a message for me?"

I stopped and turned back, facing her. "Sure." I held my hand on the screen door, tapping my foot.

"Please tell my *petit-fils* (grandson) he needs to paint my house. I like white," the elderly lady smiled.

"*Ce qui est le nom de votre petit-fils?*" (What is your grandson's name)

"*Nicholas.*" She spoke one word.

"You mean Nick? Right outside *here*?" I pointed.

"*Oui!*" She nodded her head.

I went straight to the source. Peering around, I didn't see Val anywhere. It didn't matter. I had a knife to pick with his *ami.* (friend) It wasn't hard finding Nick. He was the drunk in the lawn chair next to the fire. I walked straight up to him without even considering the girl he was speaking to and placed my hands on each arm of his chair. Then I leaned down low into his shit-face, "You took my knives! I

654

want them back *now*. You thief," I demanded. His eyes were heavy-lidded.

"What are you talking about?" He slurred with a smile on the edge of his lips.

"You thieving bastard! Give me my knives," I bellowed.

"Didn't your *mère* (mother) teach you manners?"

Now he pissed me off. "Don't talk about my *mère* when *ta mère elle a accouché dans une poubelle!*" (your mother gave birth in a trash can)

Before I took my next breath, my feet went airborne, and I had been thrown over the Cajun's shoulder like a potato sack, and with each determined stride he brazenly took, I became angrier. He had no idea who he was messing with. Damn, where was *Val*? My eyes combed over the heads of folks, trying to spot the Zop.

Then abruptly, I was released on my derrière, leaving me to look up into two very heated black eyes. Before I could make my complaint known, the Cajun snatched me up on my feet. His hands were possessive, resting on my hips. Our faces were so close I could smell the liquor on his breath. "Just because you are a *une belle fille* (pretty girl) does not give you the right to say such defiling things about my *mère!*"

My hands were pressed against his chest, captive by his iron grip.

Of course, I never backed down as I fired back. "You took my knives," I howled.

"Where did you learn Cajun French?" He appeared enamored yet pissed.

"Does it matter," I spat.

The Cajun paused for a second. "Val is right. You are trouble." The corner of his lip turned up.

"Yeah? You think this is bad wait till I warm up, then I'm a riot."

"*Chéri*, you talk too much. I'm going to kiss you. *Aucun entretien.*" (No talk) His black eyes gleamed with determination.

"Like hell if you are," I protested, wiggling from his grasp. Then the Frenchman made his move. Our lips locked, and I couldn't get free, or maybe I didn't try hard enough. It all was sort of fuzzy to me.

Before I knew what was happening, his mouth covered mine. His kiss was urgent and exploratory. Parting my lips, I found myself grasping his hair and bringing him down to meet my height for more of his luscious kisses. His arms slipped around my waist, lifting me off the ground. I remembered dangling my feet as he dove deeper, punishing me with his angry lips. I was shocked at my own eager response.

Then abruptly we broke apart. Both of us were heaving. I wiped the remains of his kisses off my swollen lips, and without thinking, I slapped him. "Don't ever touch me again," I hissed. Then I remembered my promise. "Oh, by the way. Your grandmother wanted me to give you a message," I paused, trying to catch my breath. "She wants her house painted white." Then I stomped past the Cajun, leaving him alone, rubbing his jaw with a dumbfounded look splattered across his face. Maybe it was the slap. I might have rattled his pea-sized brain. God! I *hated* that Cajun.

WHAT'S A GIRL GONNA DO?

On the trip back, we all were quiet and drawn to our own thoughts. I kept telling myself, it was the combination of beer, strange food, and I'm-just-running-out-of-excuses kinda night. Man, did I feel a heavy dose of guilt, kissing that Cajun. Why did I let him do that? I didn't even like him.

Then my mind flashed to that lady and our peculiar conversation. Chills covered my body. I slipped a sideways glance at Val. I sighed, knowing that the lady, Mable, was right about Val. The thought of his origin made me feel oceans apart from him. Even still, I believed if we worked hard at it, we had a chance. So why did I have this sinking feeling?

First things first. I needed to face Aidan. This wasn't going to be easy. I'd rather have my arms amputated than approach him and his blazing temper. Considering everything that had transpired, my imprisonment, Mom's death, the death of Dawn, feelings changing, for his sake and mine, we needed to let go of each other. We might be bound as one, but we didn't have to share the same living quarters or even the same life.

Next, Val. I wasn't sure how he'd handle it when I ask him to let me face Aidan by myself, and last but not least, I needed to tell him about the Cajun. I hoped he wouldn't be too disappointed in me. It wasn't necessary. I'd carried the weight of shame on my shoulders for the both of us.

Finally, after I settled with both Aidan and Val, I intended to hunt down Mustafa and *kill* him. Once that bastard paid for taking Dawn's life then I might be able to maintain some resemblance of a normal life.

When we reached home, I woke up Jeffery. It boggled me how he could fall asleep crunched up in the backseat, snoring.

Watching Jeffery drag himself into the house, it occurred to me that we all needed a good night's rest. I couldn't wait to feel the comfort of my soft bed and the soothing purr of Snowball.

As I entered through the gate, Val softly tapped my arm and motioned for me to stay back with him. I gathered he'd sensed a shift between us by the v in his brows. I climbed the steps leading to the front porch and flopped down on the top step, one of my favorite spots to perch. When I sat there, I felt like I was on top of the world, over-looking the neighborhood.

A cool breeze scented the air with crepe myrtle. I instinctively drew in a deep breath, savoring the sweet perfume. I loved living in the Garden District. In my wildest dreams, I'd never imagined I would've ended up in this exquisite place. I smiled to myself, gazing down the street.

Val came and joined me. His long legs stretched out as he sighed, tiredly.

I rested my chin in my hands, elbows propped on my knees.

Val casually etched his arm around my waist, drawing me closer. "What's wrong," he asked wearily.

I took in a piercing breath. This wasn't going to be easy. "Val, you know how much you mean to me?"

"Absolutely, Freckles." The corner of his lips stretched.

I hid my eyes under my lashes. I couldn't look at him. "I don't know exactly how to tell you this. So I'll just say it. Your friend, Nick, *kissed* me."

A handful of seconds passed before he spoke. "Did you kiss him back?" Val's voice was even, no indication of how he was taking this.

"Not at first." I felt my pulse in my throat going off the charts.

"Sounds like you kissed him back." Surprise flushed his face.

"I don't know what came over me." My eyes welled up with moisture. I still evaded his eyes.

"Did he come on to you first?" His arm fell from me as he drew away, folding his arms.

"Yes, but it's my fault," I blurted out, hastily. He'd stolen my knives! I confronted him."

"Ah hell! Don't tell me you insulted his mama?" Val's face winced as if he'd eaten a spoiled lemon.

"Yeah, I did." Quiet washed over us. Unable to bear the hard silence, I rushed to my defense. "Neither one of us planned it. It just happened. He was drunk and I'd had a few beers." I waited for Val to say something, but he didn't utter a word. "I'm sorry. It's been eating away at me all night." My eyes lifted to his face, pleading.

"Did it go any further?" I couldn't believe he'd ask that.

"Are you kidding me? I don't even like the guy."

"But you kissed him?"

"I know." I wanted to die. "That's what is so mind blowing!"

He sighed. "I'm glad you told me. It's okay." Val shrugged.

"It's just *okay*?" My eyes blinked with incredulity. "If you had kissed another girl, I would've been livid."

"You're not me," Val pointed out.

"Are you upset with Nick?" although, it sounded like his discord was fixed on me. Some kinda bro code, I reckoned. The girl always took the blame.

"Nope. He's a man. You're a beautiful woman. Nick goes after what he wants."

"And you're okay if he goes after *your* girlfriend?" I wanted a reaction out of him. Anything but this lukewarm bullshit.

"Nick can't steal something that is not mine, Freckles."

I sat there, gaping. "I'm confused?"

"Do any of us actually belong to anyone?" He shrugged.

"Now you're talking in circles!" I shook my head, baffled.

"Why do you think I'm not making sense?" he half laughed.

"Because you fight for what's yours!" I spoke with conviction.

"One thing you're forgetting, we are not bound like a human marriage. I have no right nor claim to you."

"What is that supposed to mean?"

"I mean, if you choose another, I will have no choice but to let you go."

"Then why are you so resolved about Aidan leaving?"

"Because he's a loose cannon, and I don't want you hurt."

"So your feelings for me plays no part in your dislike for Aidan?"

"No, it doesn't."

"You've got to be kidding?" Now I was really confused.

"Look! I'm not saying I don't care. It's just humans are different than my kind. You're not human, but you have lived like one all your life. You are accustomed to *their* behavior. In the Zop culture, we're not possessive. My kind doesn't waste energy on attachments and jealousy. Emotions are treacherous and will destroy a nation. We prefer uncomplicated lives." He shrugged. "Simply, we're not wired like humans."

"I'm not human, and I'm *wired* that way. I think it's called a choice."

"Your emotions stem from your upbringing. You should be happy I'm not the jealous type, kicking every man's ass for glancing at you." Val smiled while reaching for my hand.

"Sorry," I pulled away. My face pinched, "I want passion and love and possessiveness and all that crazy emotional stuff."

"Sorry, Freckles. That's not me. Don't get me wrong, I want you… a lot. However you look at it, I have to set aside my feelings and think about my kind. I'm in a high-ranking position. I have to maintain and keep my perspective in check. There's no future for us. My kind would never accept you."

"I thought we were going to work through this! Tonight you referred to me as *your copine!*" (girlfriend)

"True. I'm sorry if I have misled you. I was trying not to shame you among the others," his eyes were somber.

"Shame me!" I scoffed. "Why would I feel ashamed?"

"Humans are preoccupied with labels. I didn't want anyone to think you were… " Good thing he didn't finish that last word. My eyes were fired up.

"Most of your friends were too hammered to care." I looked away, then I turned back, facing him. "I thought we were good."

"You can't possibly think we are okay when there is unresolved dissension between us?"

"I thought we had something special." I blinked, unbelieving my ears.

"Special won't help us when the Zop society refuses to accept you."

I clenched my teeth, eyes narrowed. "I don't need acceptance from a bunch of radical angels! I thought you loved me!"

"Freckles, you know how much you mean to me. Despite my feelings, we have to take everything into consideration, and with the war brewing… "

"Don't use this war as an excuse!"

"I'm not," Val snapped.

"Tell me this. If you don't feel jealousy, then why would you not touch me as long as I had feelings for Aidan?"

"I don't want a woman whose heart belongs to another man."

"So now that my heart is free from the clenches of the-great-white Aidan, it's okay if *your* friends play grab ass with me as long as I keep *my* heart in check?"

"Now you're behaving ridiculous."

"Oh! Then I must be *your* entertainment," I bit out the words as if they tasted like gasoline.

"You're *not* my entertainment," Val's lips tightened. "I do care about you. As for a relationship, we'd only be spinning our wheels."

"If we can't have a relationship, then what future do we have?"

"A future is relative," he flashed a strained smile. "Let's take this day by day. Enjoy each other while we can." Val reached to draw me into his arms, but I wasn't having it.

"Stop!" I pushed his hands away. "If we have no future, then we have no present. According to the *impure* race, it's all or nothing, no settling." I'd made my decision, and I was cemented to it.

"Freckles, my hands are tied. You have to know that our antinomy breaks my heart too."

"Does it?" I raked in a wincing breath. "Do you know what I like about being human?"

"No, but I have a sneaky feeling you're going to tell me."

"I have the freedom to choose who I want to spend my life with, and no species, race, or even an angel can tell me otherwise. Good night!"

I left Val sitting there with his freaking mouth gaping.

"I'm done with men. Period," I mumbled to myself as I shut the door behind me.

~

Nearly four in the morning, I couldn't close my eyes. After staring at the ceiling and nowhere near drifting to sleep, I decided to go make myself some hot cocoa. I had just sat down at the island and took a sip when I heard the stairs creaking. I didn't even need to look up to know who was coming. The footsteps gave it away, heavy and short. Sally peeked her head around the corner into the kitchen, and asked meekly, "Do you mind some company?" She smiled, unsure of herself.

We hadn't exactly been best of friends. I get her hesitance, but I had softened. Setting aside my grievances, I'd begun to see her in another light. She was as much a victim as I was. "Sure." I smiled openly. I leaned over and pulled out the stool next to me. "Would you like some hot cocoa?"

"Oh, that does sound good!" She started to rise.

"No, stay put. I'll get it for you." In a short moment, I returned with a hot cup and set it down beside her.

"Thanks!" She lifted the cup to her lips and carefully sipped, then she exhaled. "You couldn't sleep either?"

"Yep," I answered curtly sipping my drink.

"Me either." She band her fingers around the warm cup.

"Are you okay?" I saw concern in her eyes. I might like this girl after all.

"I'm doing much better. Especially after you opened your home to me. I want to thank you for your generosity. I don't deserve... "

I stopped her in midsentence. "Don't! We both were victims." I forced a painful smile. The memories were agonizing, back in that cottage, I would never forget, not even in death. Nonetheless, it helped knowing that she was remorseful. It was time to put it to rest and move on.

"Thank you. I mean that." She became a little misty eyed.

"I know you do, and you're welcome." I took another sip of my cocoa. "How's Aidan doing? Any better?"

"He's sulking." Apprehension came to mind as I watched her fidget with her hair. Then I realized why.

"Have you been sleeping with him?" It was apparent, I saw it in her deep brown eyes.

Sally looked down at her cup, and she glanced back at me, embarrassment streaked her face. "He needed someone to comfort him. You were... " Her words became stifled.

662

"I sort of knew it." I leaned over and squeezed her hand. "Hey, I'm glad he has you. Really!" I smiled.

"You're not mad?" Her eyes had the look of startle.

"No, not at all. Aidan and I are finished." My lips tugged at the corners, yet not quite a smile.

"Yeah. I'm not sure how long we'll last. He is a bit of a queen, always demanding."

"Well, don't let him boss you around. Stand up to him when he tries."

Silence was shared between us for a moment while we sipped our drinks.

"While it's been nice staying here, we can't keep accepting your hospitality. We're leaving in the morning. Aidan thinks it's best if he returns to his mansion on the outskirts of town. It once was a plantation over a hundred years ago. It's been in his family from the beginning."

"That sounds nice." I didn't tell her I knew about the mansion.

"He invited me to come with him. If it's okay with you, I'd like to go."

"Sally, you're an adult. If you want to be with him, then you should. In fact, you both have my blessing."

"Thanks." She lulled briefly, thinking. "I may not be the brightest, though, I can't help myself. I love him." She hid her eyes behind her lashes. "Unfortunately falling in love isn't necessarily a good thing," she huffed, downhearted. "His love for me is not reciprocated. He's not over you yet."

I flinched. "No, he's angry at me. Give him time. He'll come to see what a great gal you are." I rubbed her upper arm, trying to sooth her. Although, deep down, I feared Sally might be right. "You'll be fine, and if you need a listening ear, I'm only a phone call away." I smiled, but underneath, I sensed trouble.

"Well," her brows furrowed, and a look of a jilted lover spurned her face, "Aidan has been making comments about you that give me pause."

"What has he been saying?" I'd smelt mayhem.

She opened and clenched her mouth as if the words were fighting against her.

I watched under a careful eye as my suspicion spiked.

"Aidan spoke about," she swallowed hard, "some kind of supernatural infusion binding you two together." Sally fidgeted with her cup. "The alcohol was talking." She glimpsed up at me, eyes sadden, and forcing a smile. "He wasn't making any sense. Anyway, he was bragging about how he had no intentions of freeing you.

"What do you mean?" My breath froze in my chest.

"He claims to have possession of an incantation that can break some spell that binds you two together." She tipped her shoulder. "I'm not sure exactly what his intentions are but it worries me."

The shock felt like a child on Christmas getting a pony, but then the parent for some unknown reason decided to take it away. I was mortified. "He can break the infusion," I whispered, dazed. "Is *he* awake?"

"Uh-huh, he's taking a shower."

"Sally, I'm sorry, but I have to speak to him *now.*" I leapt from my chair and rushed to the stairs.

"Wait! He's not dressed!" she shouted to my backside. I didn't respond, I had urgent business to settle.

Leaving Sally in my wake, I darted upstairs and coiled the corner to his bedroom. I didn't bother knocking. I marched right into his room as if I owned the place, which *I* did.

It was perfect timing. Aidan had stepped out of the bathroom as I entered. His head snapped up at me, surprise colored his face. I reckoned he was expecting Sally. Good! Catching him off guard might work in my favor. Before he could wipe the startled look off his face, I laid into him, firing questions. "What the hell," I began to vociferate loudly, "You have the incantation to break our bondage, and yet, you refuse to use it?" My combative eyes narrowed at him as he didn't shy away with his nudity, all full Monty.

"You are correct. Nor shall I ever. It is our protection."

"Bullshit," I caterwauled. "The truth is you don't want to let me go!"

"Believe what you wish. There's a great deal more at stake here than a little thing such as our bondage." His voice seethe of satire.

"What possibly can be lording over us that can be worse," I countered.

A flash of humor glinted in his blues. "If we break the connection, it can put a target on *your* back. Do you want that?"

"The Illuminati?"

"Of course."

"Who else?"

Aidan fluidly covered himself with a towel as water dripped from his wavy black curls. A little tinge struck and the image of us together that night long ago at the cottage haunted my mind. My cheeks flushed.

"Otherworldly sorts." He didn't elaborate.

"I appreciate your thoughtfulness, but it's time that we cut the cord. Bottom line, I *want* my freedom!" I stood with my arms folded at an impasse.

"Sorry, toots. It's not going to happen."

"Aidan, don't you want to move on? You'd be free to have any woman you want!" I'd hoped reasoning with his selfish side might soften him.

"Sweetheart, I have my freedom. It's you who is held hostage."

"Really? If I am a hostage then so are you!" I bit back, not backing down.

There was a sparkle to his glint. "I am never a slave to anyone. You, matter-of-fact, will be mine for eternity."

"Why do you hate me? It's not like you want me." Then I revealed his secret, "I know about you and Sally hooking up."

The corner of his lip twitched. "Men will be men, Ms. Collins." His voice was as hard and frosty as a frozen pond.

"What did I ever see in you?"

"I gave you a fantasy," Aidan amused. "Just like most girls, you love make-believe."

"I never asked for a fantasy. I never asked to be sold. I never asked for *anything* from you or your family, the Illuminati. Whatever your people call yourselves." I clenched my teeth, fuming with anger.

He sneered. "That makes two of us. I never wanted this either. I suppose we both have *suffered*."

I gasped. "I'm glad you're leaving my house! The sooner, the better," I bellowed.

"I couldn't agree more." His voice was cold and unmovable.

I whipped on my feet, heading for the door but stopped as I rested my hand on the knob. I turned facing his glare. I had one more thing I needed to clear up. I carefully pronounced each word to make sure he understood my full intentions. "I *will* find a way to break free from this bondage. I *will* never be your prisoner!" I pivoted on my heels, leaving, but halted as laughter wafted over my shoulder.

The cadence in his tone chilled my bones. It came to mind a time when I once loved his laughter, but this... this was far more sinister, a stranger I did not know. Nor wanted to.

"You won't break it." He called to my back. "A little thing you haven't considered is that we both have to agree, and I will *never* in a thousand years relent."

"You're a monster!" I shouted, feeling the full brunt of his words.

"Oh, is that all," he mocked as if he was bursting to tell his secret. "Tell me, do you feel anything at night while alone in bed?" Aidan stormed a crossed the room. In a blink, he was in my face before I had time to react. His tobacco-stained teeth gnashing from rage.

I held my stare equally, though, I wanted to flee. Rather instead, I planted my feet, firm. I refused to let him intimidate me. "Say that again?"

"Can you feel me inside you?" His voice was low, deep, and throaty.

"What the hell are you talking about?" I stared back at him, confused.

"Do you feel me thrusting inside you?" His blues took on a sultry gaze, though demented. He leaned in whispering in my ear vulgarities, things he wanted to do to me. His sexual taste made my skin crawl.

"Shut-up!" I stepped back. The last thing I wanted was to be up in his crawl space.

"When I'm sharing my bed with another, you should feel every inch of me." His breath became labored as if he was becoming aroused. "You will spread your legs for me while I do things to you that will make your dead father roll over in his grave."

"*You're* disgusting!" I fired back, sick at my stomach. This was not the man I once loved. It was like he came back from the dead as a vicious vampire. He had no soul.

"Am I?" His face filled with amusement as he leaned in, forcing me against the wall.

My stomach lurched, and I thought I might lose my entire insides. His crassness broke boundaries.

Then it hit me. "You knew I was with Val that day you nearly busted his door down?" I held my hand to my lips, gasping.

"You're a smart girl." His eyes glistened with loathing, but strangely, they didn't fire up.

"And Sally?"

"What about her?" His face remained cold.

Oh dear lord! "Tell me you're not using her to hurt me?"

Silence hovered. I got my answer without a single word.

"She deserves better," I spat.

"Does she?" his voice was catty.

"I think she does!"

"Sally can leave anytime," he practically cooed. "*You*, sweetheart, do not have that luxury."

I bit my lip, holding back the curses I wanted to hurl at him. "Do you really think holding me to this binding spell is going to make things better between us?"

"I don't care about *better*," he chewed on that last word. "I lost that hope when you didn't wait for me."

"Don't put this blame on me! You listened to your depraved uncle rather than trying to find me."

"My uncle has his flaws, but I trust his word."

How could one person change so much in a few years? I stared at him as if I didn't recognize him. He once hated Van. What had happened to him? "You trust your uncle!" I scoffed. "This is the same man that had blackmailed you and wanted to take my Essence. How can you ever trust this man?"

"I apologize for his careless judgment. Needless to say, my uncle and I have come to terms with our differences. I have come to respect his wisdom."

"That's rich! First, you've lived three hundred years and Van has lived merely sixty. Not even a fraction of your life and yet you find solace in his wisdom. I think you've been drinking the Kool-Aid. You honor a man that deserves to die," I gritted through my teeth.

He reached to touch my face but stopped. With no warning, he gave way to a curt gasp. By the reflection in his orbed blues, I saw my eyes glowing. Odd, I thought. Why would he become alarmed over the exact ability I'd inherited from him? He was fully aware that our abilities had emerged.

"Why do you act as if you've never seen eyes fire up?"

"I've... I've never seen such a thing." Fear racked his brain.

I glared at him in disbelief. Maybe when he was held captive in that dungeon, they wiped his memories of his abilities. Anything was possible with this Family. "You don't remember?"

"Remember what?" he looked at me oddly.

"Never mind but then, I realized how blessed he'd been, and here he was belly-aching over stupid crap. It struck a chord with me. "You had the pleasure of spending time with Dawn. Do you know how much *I* hate you for that?"

"I suppose we can agree on one thing, then."

There was no question, we couldn't keep going like this. I took in a sharp breath, calming myself. "Do you really want to continue torturing each other?"

He stood there smirking. "Who is doing the torturing? I have exactly what I want... *your freedom*." He broke out in a wide smile, but it wasn't an earnest one. It was the smile of a psychopath after a kill.

I stood there as if an ice bucket of water had been poured over me. Shock, stun, rage and pain coursed through me like a lightning bolt. The Aidan I once knew and loved no longer existed, if he ever had.

"Yeah, we'll see about that." Leaving it as that, I twirled on my heels and left his room, slamming the door behind me.

I paused momentarily outside his door, glimpsing at my hands. They were shaking, my whole body quivered. Suddenly my stomach began to roil. Sickness hit, and I darted for the bathroom.

THE UNPAINTED HOUSE

A week had past and the house had quiet. It seemed that everyone returned back to their old routines. Finally, I'd found a little peace of mind.

Since our break up, there hasn't been any word from Val. It was like he'd fallen off the face of the earth. I didn't call him or visit his bar either. We were over, and I wanted my space. Aidan stayed clear of me too.

I did hear from Sally and things were going well according to her. She seemed happy with Aidan. Despite my reservations, I wished her happiness.

For me, I decided to comply with an old woman's request. I had nothing better to do. I went down to the local supply store and bought ten gallons of paint and supplies. The list was endless, paint brushes, scraper, everything one would need to paint an old house. It'd be a nice project to keep my mind from wandering. So after I loaded down my Mustang, off I went to the countryside.

I didn't get why the Cajun hadn't taken care of his *grand mères'* house. I assumed he stayed in a drunken stupor a tad too much. How hard would it be to paint a house?

Once I reached the location, I parked and got out. The place was quiet and felt different during the day. Its eeriness didn't seem that bad. I went to the door to let the lady of the house know what I was doing. The door was closed, and all the lights were out. I knocked several times. Still, it was quiet like as a mouse. After no one came to the door, I assumed no one was home. Maybe she was out making groceries, as folks say around here. The locals had their unique style of lingo.

I decided to go ahead and paint. I didn't think the Cajun's grandmother would mind if I helped. I started pulling out the gallons of white paint, the best that money could buy. I laid out all my tools. Then I went to the garage and got the tall ladder. After everything was in order, I climbed to the top and started scraping. I finished one side of the house, and I started painting the cool white over the bare wood.

It was a sultry day. The heat in this neck of the woods could be brutal. Heavy clothes were absolutely out of the question. Instead, I found my tattered blue jean cutoffs pushed to the back of my closet. I assumed that the fashion guru, Jeffery, had a hand in hiding my favorite shorts. I slipped on a simple white T-shirt. I didn't bother with a bra, it was too hot. Anyway, what did I care? No one was going to see me. I tied my tee in a knot, hugging my boobs, and I wore a baseball cap to avoid paint in my shoulder-length hair.

I left my car radio on and sang to the hip-hop tunes as I painted, starting from the top and working my way down. This felt great. I missed labored work and helping someone out too. I was happy, the first time in a long while.

I had no idea how much time had passed. I had started early. I was enjoying the solitude, listening to the catchy tunes on my favorite radio station, Q93, when I heard a motorcycle rolling up the dirt drive. When I looked up, my heart dropped, and so did my chin. *Damn! What was he doing here?*

I stopped what I was doing and froze. I didn't bother coming down off the ladder. The unexpected visitor had a strange look on his face as he pulled up and got off his bike. He strutted up to the ladder and cupped his hand over his eyes and hollered, "What the hell do you think you're doing?" He spoke in his heavy Cajun voice.

"Well, I'm giving an old woman her wishes. You got a problem with that, take it up with her," I said nonchalantly. I went back to stroking the paint brush.

"You talk to my *grand-mère*, yes?"

"Yeah! You might not remember because you were shitfaced the other night. She asked me to give you a message. She wanted her house painted white. I figured I didn't have anything else to do..." I kept painting.

"And you thought you'd do the old woman a favor. Yes?"

"Yep." I dipped my brush in the bucket and swiped it across the bare wood.

The Cajun scratched his messy hair while it gleamed almost blue in the sunlight. He was just as handsome as I'd recalled, dark tan, broad shoulders, tall, sexy accent too. *Stop it!* I warned myself. This guy was awful. "Hmm, do you have any more brushes? I can help," he offered.

I looked surprised. "What, no party to go to?" I smirked.

"If you are going to start with me, you will not like what I do to you, *chéri!*" he smiled, but it wasn't a kind one. Nice teeth though.

I stopped and looked down at him. "Cajun, you don't scare me. I got this, and I still want my damn knives back."

"You don't say?"

"I do very much say." I mocked his accent.

He walked over and grabbed a scraper and started below me at the bottom around the windowsill. I'd forgotten he was below me until he interrupted my humming to the catchy tune on the radio. "So what did my grandmother say to you?"

"It's personal, if you don't mind."

"Did you have a nice chat?"

"Yeah. She even fixed me tea."

"Did your friend speak to her?"

"No. Nature called him to the bathroom."

"And you didn't find this strange." The Cajun's voice lined with suspicion.

"No, other than she said Jeffery would be in the bathroom a while." Now that I thought about it, she did seem to know things. "Your grandmother reminded me of someone I once knew."

"You don't say?"

I stopped abruptly and twisted around, looking down at the Cajun. "Why the drill? I had a conversation with a sweet little old lady. Maybe you should talk to her a little more often. She shouldn't have to ask a complete stranger to get her grandson to paint her house. You should take better care of her than getting drunk and partying all the time. Don't you have any... "

All at once I slipped from the ladder, screaming the whole way down. Just my luck, I landed in the Cajun's arms. That damn fool knocked me off the ladder! As soon as I landed in his arms, I squirmed out of his grip. I broke free and landed on my ass in the dirt, which I seemed to do a lot lately. He reached out, offering his hand, and I swatted at his lousy gesture as I gathered myself to my own damn feet.

"What the hell!" I looked at the ground on the other side of the ladder, and the paint had tumbled to the ground and splattered everywhere. "Look what you did! Now you went and spilt paint! Besides the fact that you could've broken my neck," I yammered at him.

"I could think of other ways to break your neck, if you like for me to show you?"

"Va te faire foutre!" (Fuck off) I stormed.

"*Excusez moi?* You could not have possibly spoken to my *grand-mère.*"

"Oh sweet! You think I'm lying?" I met his glare evenly.

"*Non!*" He smiled eerily.

"Then what?" I rolled my eyes as I folded my arms around my chest.

"*Mon grand-mère* is dead."

"What?" My breath caught in my throat. "Oh my god! I'm so sorry. Where will you be holding the funeral?"

He held an odd twinkle in his eyes. "You must have the gift too like my grand-*mère.*"

"What are you talking about?" he knew I was like Val. Then again, he was pretty lit that night. He might not remember.

"She's been gone for years now. I think you saw her ghost."

"Oh my! Then her death wasn't recent?" I glanced back at the house and pointed. "But she offered me tea!"

"Oui," his eyes sparkled with amusement. "She was gifted too."

"Gift? I've never heard it called that. It's more like a hurricane that never stops." I shook my head. "I'm sorry for overstepping my bounds. I just wanted to help." I sighed. Man, did I feel stupid. Then I remembered Ms. Noel's ghost. Maybe it's an angel thing. Come to think about it, she did mention running into Val from time to time.

"*Non, non!* You did good. Very sweet. Never thought you would be such a sweet…"

I shot green daggers at the Cajun. Too bad they weren't my real

672

knives. Rather instead, I scoffed, snapping back, "Thanks for the vote of confidence." I paused. "So the lady of the house that I spoke to the other night wasn't real?" I was still shaken.

"Oh, *chéri*, she was real. Just not human."

"Have you ever seen her ghost?" I asked.

"*Non*. Only those with the gift have the privilege."

"What do you mean 'gift'?"

"Things such as speaking to the dead, healing, traiteur… those with magick."

"Oh." I averted my eyes to the cluster of trees swaying to the breeze.

"So you come today to carry out an old woman's wish? Yes?"

"Yes." I still stared at the stand of trees.

"Hmm… do you dress this way when you paint?" The Cajun's mien pivoted into a lustful drool. "If so, I'd like to come more often. I like what you wear. Do you always look so, how do you say in English, scanty?" His wolf-like eyes crept over my body. Instinctively, I wanted to cover myself. *Crap! Men are pigs!* "Of course, if you were mine, I'd only want you to dress like this for my eyes only. *Non* for anyone else." His eyes kept roaming.

I frowned. "I wasn't expecting company. It's hot. I'm working."

"I saw that… and your ass hanging out of your shorts too. I like!" My face flushed from his wolfish smirk.

"I don't like the way you're eyeballing me. Stop it," I demanded.

"It is a compliment. I meant no harm."

Avoiding his ogling, I quickly changed the subject. "You have my knives?"

"Those knives mean a lot to you. Yes?"

"Yeah, I keep them for souvenirs from the last three men I killed." I lashed a wicked smile. His black eyes twinkled.

"Ah, now you tease old Nick. *Tsk-tsk.*" He wagged his finger at me.

I looked the Cajun in the face. "No, Nick, I never joke about killing. I have a nervous tic. Whenever a man gets fresh with me, he ends up with a knife thrust in his heart," I said with no glint of humor.

"*Peut-être* (Maybe) I shouldn't give back your knives." He threatened without any apprehension.

"So you admit you took them?" I pushed.

"*Non!* I only admit to having possession." He smiled like a rotten thief.

"You care to wager over those knives?" I was feeling the onset of a challenge.

"Why are these knives so important to you?" his eyes dug into me, studying me.

"They're special, and they belong to me." I placed my hands on my hips regarding him snootily. "Are we on?"

"Special, huh. I like the sound of that. What is your *parié*?" (wager)

"Whoever hits the target three out of four gets the knives. Deal?"

"Oh! You think you can beat Old Nick, *petite-fille*?" (little girl)

"I already have." I flashed a confident smile. I could see he liked a challenge.

The tall, dark Cajun drew a small circle, making a target with the white paint on the trunk of an old cypress tree several paces away. I watched, thinking there was no way the mortal could throw a bull's-eye at that distance and hit his mark on that tiny target. I gloated to myself. He thought he had the advantage. I'd appease his ego... for a while. I smiled inwardly. This should be fun.

When he returned to my side, he said, "Ladies first. Yes!"

"Nope. I think you should go first. Show me how a real man does it." Sarcasm rolled off my tongue.

"Your *petit copain* (boyfriend) didn't tell me you were a *séductrice.*" (temptress) He flashed a white wicked smile.

"Val is not my *copain.*"

"*Non?*"

"Nope. Thanks to that damn kiss the other night, we are officially over," I sighed.

"Ah, *chéri*, I am truly sorry. I shall talk to him and tell him it was all me and my drunk ass."

"Oh! You think I meant your kiss? Sorry, I was referring to someone else's," I said very coldly. Then I heard chuckles flowing from the Cajun's mouth.

"You are one *salope frigide!*" (frigid bitch)

"I love it when you talk dirty," I mocked. The look he gave me might've scared most, but I wasn't the norm. "Are you going to throw or do you need to be coddled?"

"I see why your *petit copain* left you standing at the altar."

"We didn't make it that far. And FYI, I left him. Sorry to disappoint," I smiled with venom.

He shook his head. "Bebè, you didn't disappoint *moi*! I couldn't care less."

"Then shut up and throw the knife," I ordered. Old Nick looked very irritated at me as he flipped the knife in his hand, expertly. I watched how he handled it, and I was impressed. I stood and watched him throw all four knives. Each one landed in the bull's-eye zone, but none was in the dead center.

Now it was my turn. He went and pulled the knives out of the tree and returned the knives to me with a full-on gloat. I laughed to myself as he handed them to me. I thought I might play with him a little bit first. I stepped up to the mark.

"Eh, if you need a little closer," the Cajun interrupted, "I'll allow it, since you are a *fille*."

I smiled. "That's so sweet of you!" Then my smile dropped, and I got real. "No chance, *bucko*." I firmly put my hand against his chest and shoved him out of the way. "I'm going to show you how the real pros do this." I struck a nerve as the Cajun snarled at me in silence, but there was a glint of praise in his eyes.

I started thumbing with the knife clumsily. I dropped it a couple of times. I'd switched hands as though I wasn't sure which one to use. Then I swung the knife, nearly nicking the Cajun. Luckily, he was quick on his feet. A rush of curses filled the air as I stifled a laugh. It was fun toying with this arrogant douche bag. That was what he got for laughing at me earlier, but what did he know? After all, I was a genetically engineered angel. I had the upper hand. Several, in fact. I almost felt bad taking advantage of the Cajun.

Almost.

Then within a soft breath, I barely took aim and threw the remaining three knives at the same time. My beautiful knives whizzed through the air fast and precise, hitting the tree at the same time, blade to blade clanked, dead center on the bull's-eye. Perfecto!

Suddenly silence fell as the ringing of steel plagued my ears. My *non ami* almost turned blue as his laughs jammed in his throat. Then I turned to him with my gloat and announced, "You have no idea what you're dealing with!" I left him gaping as I went and plucked my knives out of the tree and found the other one on the ground off to the left, only a couple of feet past the tree. I sure did miss my little shiny friends. I walked right past the Cajun without another word, got into my car, and peeled out of the drive, throwing small beads of rocks onto his Harley as I floored the gas. Bullets of curses hailed into the trail of dust that followed behind me. I laughed the whole way home.

I didn't bother taking back any of the paint and supplies. I figured he should paint his own *grand-mère*'s house so she could rest in peace. He owed her that much. What an awful person. Funny! The ghost of the house, his *grand-mère*, claimed I'd meet a dark man who'd become my protector. Well, I could scratch him off the list of possible candidates. He couldn't even take care of his grandmother's house. I was done with men.

BABYLON'S FALLEN

*T*he bottom fell out about 6:00 p.m. right after dinner. The beginning of the night started out great. After we'd finished eating, I insisted on doing the dishes to give Dom and Jeffery a break. Well, mostly Dom. Jeffery usually directed more than lifted a finger, much less a dish. Rather instead, he often bragged about how a celebrity like himself should never have dishpan hands. Like I'd said often, I love my Jeffery.

As the evening unfolded, the guys had just taken a seat in the family room, sipping their wine, when Jeffery flipped on the television. Dom wanted to watch the news, and Jeffery wanted to watch the latest episode of *Housewives of Atlanta*. He was dancing to one of the House-wives' catchy tunes. Jeffery kept repeating, *Gone with the Wind*. I laughed, rolling my eyes as I finished up rinsing the last dish.

Right then, I realized I belonged here with those two. They completed me. Dom kept me grounded, and Jeffery kept me in stitches. After the long journey of Dad's death, Mom's death and finally, Dawn's short life, I'd come to understand that life is precious. No one had a guarantee there would be a tomorrow. If I died tonight, I had absolute certainty that my life was complete and most of all happy.

Then I took a bottomless breath. If I were so satisfied, why did I miss having a special man to hold me at night, to share my life with?

After leaving Val on the porch alone, he hadn't bothered reaching out to me. Aidan finally left for his mansion. A blessing, I sure wouldn't forget. Of course, I'd never be completely free of him unless he agreed to break the spell. Wow, a magickal divorce. How ironic? I scoffed to myself. Hell would freeze over before Aidan Bane DuPont would set me free.

Out of the blue, the doorbell rang. My head popped up. Who could that be? We weren't expecting company.

I dried my hands with the dish towel and tossed it aside. I rushed to the front door. Without checking through the peep-hole, I swung the door open, and my heart sunk. There standing on my front porch was the last person I'd expected to greet... Nicholas Bourdain.

I frowned.

Disappointment painted my face red. I was hoping for Val. What a sap I was, thinking he'd changed his mind.

The Cajun interrupted my thoughts. "Don't worry! I didn't come for another kiss. I'm here on business. Val sent me. Ask me in," he woofed. "I don't want to discuss this in front of your neighbors."

"What? You can't say please?" I stood there, gripping the door. The Cajun folded his arms and glared at me.

My eyes raked over him but stopped at his muddy boots. "Take your shoes off and don't sit on my furniture. Your clothes are filthy." I snarled my nose at him. "You need a bath too!"

Amusement teased his eyes.

"If you like to bathe me, I'd happily comply, *chéri*." He flashed his pearly whites.

I rolled my eyes. "Not a chance. Bye!" I went to slam the door in his face, but he quickly stepped inside the door and pushed past me. "Wait a damn minute, Frenchman!" I stormed after him.

By this time, Dom and Jeffery had come to inspect the commotion. The Cajun ignored me and started speaking to Dom in perfect French.

"Val m'a envoyé. Nous devons partir maintenant! Ils viennent après la jeune fille. " (Val sent me. We have to leave now! They're coming after the girl.)

Both Dom and Jeffery shared glances.

"Holy cow! It's happening." I looked at Dom and Jeffery, fear spread to each of us. "The Illuminati are seizing the world!" Then I turned my attention to the Cajun. "Where is Val?"

"He's with his kind. They're gathering forces now."

"I want you to take me there," I demanded.

"*Non!* If you go anywhere near the Zop, they will kill you."

"How do you know about the Zop?"

"I know plenty. Get moving! We have to go!" The Cajun urged, barking orders. I stood there, staring at him for a brief second.

"Okay, you win!" I dropped my arms and grabbed my keys and headed out the door.

The Cajun grabbed my upper arm and jerked me around, facing him. "Those keys are no use to you!" he warned. "You have to leave your vehicles behind. They might have detectors that can trace our location."

My head was spinning, I couldn't think. "Who am I riding with," I blurted.

The Cajun smiled. "Don't worry. I handle my bike like I handle my women." There was an intrinsic glint in his eyes.

"Disgusting pig," I mumbled under my breath. As I stalked past him, I heard his laugh trail behind me as I slammed the door, leaving him inside.

Standing on the front porch, I paused. My mind was reeling with terror for my family, and I was angry at Val for sending that French pig in his place. How could he dismiss me at a time such as this? Then again, we were no longer together. Still, I wanted to be in the mix of this battle. If anyone had reason enough, it should be me, but I was treated like a defenseless girl, even worse... an outcast. I felt betrayed by Val.

When I stepped out onto the front porch, I'd glanced down at the street spotting Nick's gang on their bikes parked against the curb. I took note of one nice looking Harley, black and silver chrome, empty seated with the key left in its ignition. Suddenly, a spark lit under my ass, and I flew into action. I had to move fast. I took two steps at a time down the long steps, swinging the gate open and running past the bikers until I reached the Harley. Swiftly, I straddled the bike and kick-started the engine. The gentle sound and rumble of the motor between my legs gave me a little flicker of excitement. "Sweet," I mumbled to myself. The current of daringness surged through me like a quick flash of memories before death. I eased off the throttle giving the bike more gas.

Before I knew it, I was speeding off. Quickly, I hugged the corner, and as I turned, straightening the wheels, I let it rip, accelerating this sweet ride into a thundering bolt of lightning down the street. *I gotta get me one of these!* I smiled to myself.

I knew time wasn't on my side. I had to get to Val before any of these clowns caught up with me. I'd worry about Frenchie when he caught up. Right now, everything came second. First and foremost, I needed to speak with Val.

By the time I reached Val's place, I had figured every cop in the parish would be hot on my trail. Weaving in and out of traffic at a high speed, even I was amazed that I hadn't crashed. Although it was a delightful thought destroying the Cajun's bike might push the guy over the ledge.

I parked directly in front of Val's bar in plain view. As much as I hated greeting an angry biker, I hated it even more if the bike ended up stolen. I clenched the key in my hand as I ran past the bar.

My next thought, I knew exactly where Val would be. The Zop race was huge. The only place that could accommodate a fraction of the Zop nation would be Val's gym. I was positive he'd be there, though I feared I might be too late and even worse, meeting an early death by a supremacist Zop. I'd darted past the stairwells and burst through the double doors.

Immediately, I was seized by two Zop-guards. They were giant size, and I fretted they might rip me in two with one jerk. Instinct kicked in, and I screamed for my life. Through the haze of terror, I spotted Val on top of a table with his full attention on his warriors. When he heard my bellow, his head snapped up in my direction.

Silence blew in like a frigid storm, and Val's brows dipped into an angry snare. He ordered the guards, "Bring the girl here! Do not harm her." He spoke with great strength and leadership. The Zop soldiers obeyed. As they made their way, the crowd parted, allowing the two guards and me to pass. When we reached Val, the two guards dropped me roughly at his feet. He bent down close to my face, his expression was hard. "This better be good!" A vein in his neck was pulsing, swelling dangerously.

It threw me off momentarily, realizing that Val's anger was directed at me. Despite his vile mood, I had to push past that. I had something to say and I was determined to say it. "I might be an impure, but I can fight better than any Zop standing in this gym." I stood straight, shoulders back, eyes daring anyone to try me.

"You're over your head," Val belted above the crowd. "Stay where you belong, with the humans. Nick will protect you."

I scoffed. "You think a human can protect me?"

Val growled under his breath as he leaped down off the table. I knew this look. In five—oops, no—three seconds, my feet went airborne and the rest, well, you know.

Once we burst through the doors outside, I had to face another audience. The Cajun and his gang were all hanging directly in front of Val's bar. I noticed Jeffery and Dom were with the gang too. I felt relieved they were safe.

Val dropped me right in front of Nick. *Oh, great!* I thought.

Deliver me to thy enemy!

Val threw his finger in my face and bit back the strident words he wanted to say, instead he restrained himself, though, his face remained deeply flushed.

"Look! I told Nick to help you. The Illuminati has a price on your head. This isn't a game. It's war. Do you understand?"

"Yes! I do. That's why I'm here. I want to fight too!"

"No! This war calls for heavenly creatures. You may have the making of a Zop, but you are earthbound. In order to fight this war, we have to transform into our celestial bodies, not this human body you see."

"I don't understand?" My brows creased with incertitude.

Val ran his fingers through his hair and let out an exasperated sigh. "I don't have time to explain." Then he cupped my face in his hands. "You have to trust me. I'm looking out for you." Val stopped for a second as though he was getting choked up. "This war is a spiritual battle. I have to go back to my natural state. A spirit form." He hesitated. "I'm not coming back, Freckles. For the last time, allow me to gaze upon your beautiful face." Tears streamed down my face as Val gently wiped my cheeks with his thumb.

"I can't believe this is happening!"

"It's our reality."

"You're leaving me behind!" I strangled the thought of never seeing him again.

"Freckles, I do love you. The other night I want you to know that I didn't set out to hurt you. I said what I said in hopes that you might move on. I thought if you hated me, it might be easier. War is at hand, and I didn't know how to explain the magnitude of what we are facing." Val's eyes filled with sorrow. "If… if not for this war, I'd give up everything for you. Unfortunately, I can't, and we can't be together, ever!"

"Why do you have to fight? Let the Illuminati have whatever it is they want," I asked earnestly.

"No. I can't do that. Don't you see? They'll come after you. I have to stop this invasion."

"You're only one Zop. You can't stop them single handedly."

"You're right, but what other choice do we have? It's more than just you and me involved here. Our whole galaxy faces annihilation. Don't you see? I can't turn away. I have a responsibility."

"I don't want to face life without you."

"Freckles, you have to move on in life. Make a new life. Fall in love. It's not destined for us to be together. Destiny has someone else for you." His golden eyes sparkled.

"No way! I'm done with you rotten men!" I crossed my arms.

Val chortled. "Somehow I think you will find some poor bastard who will love you bigger than life itself."

"It won't be you." I choked on the words. Val took my chin in his hand, and he bent down. "You'll see me in your dreams." Val's eyes searched deeply into mine. All I could do was nod. Then he kissed me gently.

When my eyes opened, he was gone, and I collapsed to the ground, blinded by tears. I knew our relationship had ended, but I guess a part of me didn't believe it until now, and it sucked!

Nick, without saying a word, gathered me into his arms and sat me on his bike. He whispered softly, "Just hang on. I won't let you fall." Strangely, his voice was comforting to me.

Distraught and checked out, I didn't pay attention nor cared where Nick and his gang were taking me. Once we stopped, my mind was swooned over Val's last words and the horror of my whole world crumbling that I didn't bother looking up to see where we had settled.

Through my haze, I was lay across a warm bed and a soft shawl covered my body. I recalled the Cajun ordering me to drink some clear liquid. I sniffed the liquid and knew instantly what it was... moonshine. Ms. Noel kept a stock of glass jars filled of this stuff. I tilted my head back and swallowed, choking and gasping from the burn, though it didn't last long before the effects set in. Soon I was drifting off to sleep as my mind became numb like the rest of me... my heart and my conscientiousness. Soon, the darkness devoured the light. I didn't remember another thing until I woke up the next morning.

The birds seemed happy as they chirped, bouncing from limb to limb, tree to tree. It was like any other day, or at least the creatures of the bayou seemed to believe so. I kicked the shawl off and climbed out of bed, making my way throughout the house. The small rooms were dim, no lights on, just a faint light coming from the windows.

I entered the kitchen and went to the center of the room, tugging on a long chain attached to the ceiling lamp. As my eyes adjusted to light, I gasped with surprise. We were back at Nick's grandmother's home. The house was aged and still had its original plank-board flooring. No special perks, but cozy enough. A faint breeze blew in from the bayou. I walked to the back screen door and listened for a moment to the motion of the water and the sounds of nature.

Suddenly, breakfast came to mind. I needed to feel useful. First, I checked out the fridge, I spotted a gallon of milk, butter, jam and bacon. Next I checked out the cabinet, I counted, flour, salt, baking powder and Crisco oil. Great for biscuits! I heard chickens cackling out back. I found an old basket and went for the chicken coop. It had been a while ago since I'd had the privilege of gathering eggs, but I still remembered how. Before Dad died, I had been the egg whisperer. I used to think it was the funniest thing how this big white-looking ball could pop out of a chicken's tiny rump. Sorta gross when I thought about it now. I laughed to myself.

When I returned, I'd collected a brimming basket of two dozen eggs. I spotted an old apron and slipped it on and tied a bow in the back. By the small print of flowers and its tattered ends, I assumed it belonged to Nick's grandmother. Out of respect, I asked her if she didn't mind. I didn't want to offend the lady of the house.

In no time flat, I began fumbling through the cabinets. I spied a roller and an old cutter that came in handy. I vigorously rolled out the dough and cut each individual biscuit and placed them on a flat pan. I'd preheated the oven to three hundred fifty degrees Fahrenheit and stuck the pan inside to cook for twenty minutes.

Once the biscuits turned a golden brown, I snatched up a couple of potholders and pulled the piping-hot tray of bread from the oven. The sweet aroma of fresh bread spread throughout the whole house. Nick came waltzing into the kitchen. I glanced up but quickly went back to cooking.

"Oh! I didn't know you can cook. It smells good." Nick sounded surprised.

I cocked a brow and replied, "There are many things of which you do not know that *I* am quite capable of doing."

"I can see. You are the first rich girl I know who can make biscuits from flour."

"I doubt you have ever been around a rich girl."

"True. I have no use for spoiled brats, kicking their feet when they can't get their ice cream."

"I see we are going to be such *great* friends," I teased with spite. Little did he know I wasn't *one of those girls*.

"Please be respectful. This is my *grand-mère*'s kitchen."

"I am fully aware of your grandmother. After all, I've met her. A nice lady." I went right along with preparing breakfast without looking at the annoying Cajun.

"*Oui*. I remember," he said right as he went out the screen door.

I just looked up and smiled. Then I went back to pulling the plates out of the cabinet.

I placed five plates on the table. We each got scrambled eggs, bacon, biscuits, and gravy. I lucked out finding blackberry jam stored in the pantry and homemade butter in the small fridge. There was enough coffee for everyone to have a large cup. Thank *goodness*.

When the Cajun returned, he had the strangest tint to his face. Taking his seat at the table, he glimpsed at the extra plate and back at me. A puzzled glint toyed with his deep brown eyes. "There are only four of us. Are you expecting company?" he asked in his heavy French tone.

I didn't know how to say this to the Cajun or how he'd feel, so I replied curtly. "It's for *Mable*... your grandmother."

"*Mon grand-mère?* Are you joking," Nick laughed, surprised.

I laid a butter-knife with the butter down on the table then I looked the Cajun in the eye, sternly. "I don't joke about the dead. If you must know, the plate is a token of appreciation to your *grand-mère*. Out of respect, I'm letting her know that the kitchen belongs to her."

The Cajun sat there for a minute and held my stare. His eyes were intense. I was pretty sure he'd thought I had lost my mind. Then this Cajun had a way of taking me off guard. "My *grand-mère* spoke about you. She saw you in a vision. She warned me of your coming and for me to be nice." He chuckled. "Obviously, I do not *do* everything my *grand-mère* asks." He waved his butter knife aimlessly. "I know she told you some*thing*. I'll find out what she confided in you. You mark my word!" He flashed an arrogant smile.

Our conversation ceased when Dom and Jeffery entered the kitchen. Dom's eyes appled as his eyes swiped over the spread of food set out on the table. "Ah, Stevie, I would've gotten up and helped you with breakfast," Dom offered.

"I didn't mind. I enjoy cooking," It reminded me of a time when I was a kid. "Guys, come sit." I took my chair. "I thought you might like some extra sleep." I smiled trying to make light of our unforeseen future.

The Cajun greeted the guys with a curt nod. His mouth was too full to speak.

"Well, it's a lovely breakfast, if I do say," Jeffery complimented my cooking which was out of character of my dear friend. "Does anyone know when we can return home?" Jeffery bounced his glance around the table at everyone. Yet no one uttered a word.

"Jeff," I interjected. "We may never be able to go back. Time will only tell."

"What!" Jeffery squealed louder than an opera singer off key.

"I suppose we are best to prepare for the worst and hope for the best," Dom added.

"I think the bottom is about to fall out from under us," I went on and added, "As far as we know, we are refugees running for our lives. Everything we own, our home and money, is most likely gone. Though, at this point, we can only speculate."

My eyes stopped on Jeffery. Frozen, his eyes were bugged out of his head and his mouth was gaping wide enough for fly catching. The poor guy's face went pale. "*But-but,*" he stammered. "I belong to the little old, fat ladies society club! How am I gonna face those old biddies with no money?"

I couldn't laugh. This poor man appeared as if he might be having a stroke. "Jeff, sweetie, those ladies' are just as poor as you are now."

"Oh lord have mercy on my ratchet soul!" He fanned himself with his hand. "Jesus come take me away," he bawled.

Unable to stifle a laugh, I broke into chortles. "Jeffery," I snorted. "Bro, you might want to look the word *ratchet* up."

Everyone joined in laughter.

Jeffery's face twisted almost into a completely different dimension. He reminded me of a 3D movie. "I don't know what is so funny," he fluttered. "After losing a billion lovely dollars, it makes my soul and every other part of my delicious body retch! Y'all need to get over yourselves, you is in the same poor boat as me!" Jeffery stuck his lips out snapping his fingers and bobbing his head.

I swear, someone needed to monitor that skinny man's TV viewing. He could be more dramatic than any of those housewives on Bravo.

I glimpsed over at the Cajun. He sat there quiet for a minute with a gloating face. "See, that is the very reason I am not wealthy. Take me for example, the whole world can go to hell in a hand basket, and I will still eat and have a roof over my head. And why? Because I did not allow myself to become lazy and fat, all dependent on money. I'm smart like that." Nick tapped his temple with his butter knife as a smirk painted his face. Apart from his exaggerated self-opinion and uncivilized nature, the man possessed quite a come-hither charm excluding that he needed a bath.

Before I could stop myself, the words flowed from my mouth, "Yes Cajun, we all know what you do best. Getting shitfaced and forcing your affections upon innocent girls." I grinned, right when I shoved a large bite of eggs in my mouth.

A flash of ire toyed in the Cajun's dark eyes. "I've never heard any girl complain of my... er, affections. Yes?" Nick took a huge bite of his eggs, mocking me. I glared at him for a moment. Then I decided there no point in slinging dirt this morning, so I turned the conversation back to earlier. "I'm hoping Mable will appear to me again. Maybe she can tell me something about the uprising."

"If our government turns on us, people are going to get desperate," the Cajun added his two cents.

"Who is Mable," Jeff interrupted. He was always the last to know.

The Cajun answered, "She's my dead *grand-mère*. Her ghost appeared to Stevie the other night."

Jeffery's mouth dropped opened. "Gurrrl! Not right here in this very kitchen when I was... ?"

"Yep. Right where you sit, Jeff." I smiled innocently, batting my lashes.

"Just a whole bunch of weird follows you, gurrrlfriend." Jeffery's lips pursed.

"You can say that again. I'd take boring any day over this *celte saloperie!*" (peace of crap) I glared at the Cajun.

"Stevie! Not at the table, especially when we are guest." Dom scolded me. Then he turned to Nick. "Pardon! She is not herself, I'm afraid."

The Cajun slapped a couple of pieces of bacon on a dry biscuit, then he blurted out to Dom, "Il fait frais. Je l'ai vue plus mauvaise." (It is cool. I have seen her worse.)

The small kitchen filled with cackles from everyone but me. I failed to see the humor. I withdrew my napkin from my lap to my plate and scooted myself from the table and politely made my way out the screen door. I needed some swamp air.

When I came around to the front of the old house, I noticed all my paint supplies were cleaned and placed nicely in a toolbox. I spotted empty buckets in the dumpster. Then I turned my gaze toward the house. Surprise swirled around me as my eyes combed over the freshly painted house. "Well, color me stunned! The Cajun followed through with his grandmother's wishes after all." I spoke to myself as my eyes brushed over the fresh paint.

Then it came to me why we were here and the dire predicament we were facing. I sat in one of the rockers and closed my eyes. The heat against my skin was soothing.

I think I drifted off to sleep. When I opened my eyes, the sun had climbed to mid sky. Unaware, I heard crunching grass. I didn't bother looking up. With the big guy's heavy footing, I knew instantly. "Cajun, you're going to need to learn how to walk lighter. A deaf mute can hear you coming," I spoke flatly, not looking up.

"Don't worry about me, *fille stupide*. (stupid girl) I can handle myself when I have to. You should worry about yourself. You keep up this nasty attitude, and I might have to change it for you." The Cajun sat beside me on a turned-over bucket.

I scoffed. "You have no idea who you're dealing with, do you?" I held my face to the warm sun with my eyes shut.

"I could easily describe you," he gave a deep grunted laugh— "but if my grandmother is listening, I'd rather she not hear the words I wish to say."

I smirked. "I didn't mean your opinion of me. I couldn't give a rat's ass what you think. I meant… what I am."

"I think you are much like Val. *Non! De quell que manière que.* (However, you have some special gift.) *Non* woman can throw those daggers as far as you. Impossible!" His deep eyes sparkled with wonder.

I smiled with a wicked grin. I thought, *should I warn him or show him?* I pushed myself to my feet. "I think action speaks louder than words." I reached for the sheath strapped over my shoulder and grabbed my knives. The Cajun didn't waste time going stiff. "Although tempting, I'm not throwing my knives at you." I tossed a sideways smile.

"I never trust a woman with a knife who hates as you do."

I smiled brightly. "I think you're catching on! Now watch," I said. Then I summoned the voltaic magick within me. I opened my hand, willing one of the knives to ascend. With ease, it lifted, hovering at eye level.

Nick's eyes orbed followed by a string of curse words, then swiftly, I released the knife straight for the tree, sailing past the Cajun, missing his ear by a fraction. I laughed to myself watching the Cajun jump. His face paled then quickly blazed. I think he wanted to strangle me. At any cost, I found myself doubled over, chuckling in hysterics while tears streamed down my face.

I couldn't remember the last time I'd had a good laugh. Then a noise interrupted the fun. My head snapped up as quickly as the humor vanished. Someone unexpected was approaching. Both the Cajun and I stood silently, listening to the tires rolling over gravel. The trees blocked the view, but I didn't need to see. I knew the newcomer. It was *Aidan.* He'd found me. That goddamn binding spell was a GPS. As long as we held that spellbound hex between us, I'd never be free of his reach. Dammit to hell!

"Do you know this intruder," Nick asked with caution filling his voice.

"Yes," I said flatly.

"Friend or foe?"

No matter how hard I tried to pull away, my eyes stayed glued to the oncoming visitor. "Maybe both," I whispered.

"I have us protected." The Cajun lifted his shirt, showing a 44 Auto Mag pistol.

I glanced down at the steel and scoffed. "Oh, you are so out of your league here, Cajun. Put your damn gun back into your pants and try not to blow off the parts you treasure most," I advised. "In fact, get in the house. Keep out of sight. Let me handle him," I ordered, keeping my eyes on the approaching car.

Moments later, a bright yellow jeep cleared the stand of trees. "I have a bad feeling about this," I mumbled to Nick. "Don't do anything stupid. This guy isn't human."

"Don't worry about me. Like I said, I can handle myself."

I didn't bother to answer. I sauntered over to meet Aidan, halfway. I played it cool. "Hey! How's it going?" I smiled with my hand cupped over my eyes, blocking the sunlight.

"It's going well. I hope you didn't mind, but I took the liberty to bring some of your things. You know, clothes, toothbrush."

"Thanks!" Aidan placed the bags by my feet. "How did you get into my house?" I stayed back a few feet in case he made a move. My radar sensors were on high alert.

"Oh, I had a key," he shrugged slyly while pulling it off his key-ring. "Here!" he handed it to me. "I won't be needing it any longer." He flashed his deviled grin. Strange though, I'd seen that same grin a million times, but this one, I sensed differently.

"You are very thoughtful." I kept my voice even. "How did you find me?" As if I didn't know.

He lazily kicked at the ground for a second, then he lifted his blues back at me. "The connection." Briefly he smiled. He looked away at the small white frame house for a moment then focused back at me. "I heard that Val returned to his natural state. I'm sorry about your breakup... "

"You knew this?" I stared him in the eye as suspicion oozed over me like thick-cold blood.

Aidan's attention switched to the Cajun. His eyes took on a hunted look. Strange how his eyes used to spark like fire whenever he became hostile. Nick stood back watching, a few paces behind me. Crap! I told him to keep out of sight. "Is he your *new* boyfriend?" Rivalry steamed off Aidan's tight shoulders. I looked back and sneered in silence at the Cajun, hoping he'd take the hint.

I turned back to Aidan and relented, "Not hardly." My snugness was apparent in my voice. Aidan laughed, but it didn't reach his eyes. I needed to stall him as long as possible, so I averted the subject. Last thing I needed was a dead Cajun.

"How's Sally?"

"She's well. She wanted me to tell you, hello!"

"Tell her I said, hi." A moment of silence dropped between us. Then I asked, "What do you know about the uprising? Do I have anything to worry about?" My heart yammered in my ears.

"There's nothing to concern your pretty little head over. I have your back. After all, you will always be my girl. I still care about you." His voice didn't sound sincere, rather feigned.

"Aidan, if you really care, then do the ceremony. It's not fair to Sally." In a soft, soothing voice, I reasoned, "You need to be free too!" I tried to appeal to his tender side.

"Maybe." He simply answered with no sign of emotion. He kept eyeing Nick though, and just my luck, the Cajun kept growling in a low tone, taunting Aidan. Crap! That damn Frenchman's head might end up on a platter yet, either by Aidan or *me*.

Aidan leaned in and hugged me tightly. I was taken off my feet. I didn't expect a hug, and when he kissed me, it felt unnatural and foreign. I didn't return his forwardness. It turned my stomach. When he finally released me, his eyes were smothering. Apparently, my lack of interest didn't suit his highness.

When I pulled away from his luring blues, my eyes dropped to his hand. With no warning, everything went into a tailspin. I strangled on empty words. My lips felt cold and dry. A vision wheeled in my mind to that day, to that spine-chilling day when my life ceased, and there it laid before my eyes. There was no denying it nor going back. That identical ring, the ring with that disgusting eye symbol worn on the very *same* hand, and the very *same* finger. Instantly, I wanted to vomit.

My mind had taken me back to the past. It was happening all over again… the exact cologne, the same terrifying dread clawing to get out, only the face was no longer hidden. Certainty shuddered through me. With complete utter acuity, I knew that Aidan was the *faceless* boy! It was *he* who betrayed me, who framed me for murders I didn't commit. It was as if he'd locked me up himself and thrown the key away. Like a plane crashing into the deep blue sea, cold and bitter, I saw past his lies. Sally and Aidan were together in this all along. *The newspaper!* He had left that damn paper for me to find. His plan was to arouse panic in me in order for my essence to become blocked, making me vulnerable for the taking. I'd been such a fool. Of course it was *him*. Who else could've done a more thorough job?

I glared up at him, and pure panic penetrated my blood. I turned to Nick and screamed, "*Run!*" Then I stretched my arm to the wind, commanding my knives. They obeyed as the flash of steel torpedoed my target. Nick hit the ground as my blades whizzed past. The deadly blades stopped in suspension, only an inch from Aidan's throat, corralling him against a tree. My eyes flamed, and right at the moment, I was certain I was in absolute, complete control.

"It was you who framed me! *You* and Sally," I spoke calm yet my voice carried a certainty of danger. When my eyes leveled with his, I saw the raw fear in his deep blues. This was the beginning of the end.

My tribulations.

691

ABOUT THE AUTHOR

 Jo Wilde lives on a small farm in Waskom, Texas, right on the border of Louisiana, with her husband and their three children. She is a stay at home mom and is earning her BA in English.

Growing up, Jo lived in a time when women were to be seen rather than heard. This notion didn't sit well with her. She often found herself in a pickle, speaking her mind, attending outrageous concerts, hanging out with the cool kids, and pushing the limits of what society deemed as acceptable. Now that she's settled down and has a family of her own, she saves her inner rebel for her books. Jo loves writing stories about strong, spunky female-roles that don't take any bull and makes no excuses. She is best known for her young adult book, The CROSSING. And she promises there are more coming soon!

To learn more about Jo Wilde and discover more Next Chapter authors, visit our website at www.nextchapter.pub.

The Angel Series Collection - Books 1-3
ISBN: 978-4-82417-373-7
Paperback Edition

Published by
Next Chapter
2-5-6 SANNO
SANNO BRIDGE
143-0023 Ota-Ku, Tokyo
+818035793528

31st May 2023

Milton Keynes UK
Ingram Content Group UK Ltd.
UKHW041907240823
427419UK00003B/149